FLANNERY O'CONNOR was born in Savannah, Georgia, on March 25, 1925, and was raised as a devout Roman Catholic in Milledgeville, Georgia. Upon graduation from the Graduate Program of the Women's College of Georgia, O'Connor attended the writing program at the State University of Iowa, receiving her MFA in 1947. Among the strongest influences on O'Connor's work were the writings of William Faulkner and Nathanael West, from whom she derived her conception of the grotesque in literature. Following the publication of numerous short stories in literary journals, O'Connor's first novel, *WISE BLOOD*, was published in 1952. Suffering from a hereditary rheumatic ailment, she spent the next twelve years writing at the family farm in Milledgeville under the care of her mother, Regina, and the strictest medical supervision. *A GOOD MAN IS HARD TO FIND*, a collection of short stories, was published in 1955, and another novel, *THE VIOLENT BEAR IT AWAY*, appeared in 1960. Though seriously ill, O'Connor made an extensive series of lecture tours, received an honorary degree from Smith College in 1963, and that same year, won first prize in the annual O'Henry short story awards (as she had previously done in 1956). After her death on August 3, 1964, another collection of short stories, *EVERYTHING THAT RISES MUST CONVERGE*, was published (1965), as well as a volume of unpublished lectures and essays and various critical articles, *MYSTERY AND MANNERS* (1969).

SIGNET CLASSICS for Your Library

(0451)

☐ **EMMA by Jane Austen.** Afterword by Graham Hough. (515242—$1.95)

☐ **MANSFIELD PARK by Jane Austen.** Afterword by Marvin Mudrick. (517520—$3.50)

☐ **NORTHANGER ABBEY by Jane Austen.** Afterword by Elizabeth Hardwick. (518349—$2.50)*

☐ **PERSUASION by Jane Austen.** Afterword by Marvin Murdick. (517156—$2.95)

☐ **PRIDE AND PREJUDICE by Jane Austen.** Afterword by Joann Morse. (516621—$1.50)

☐ **SENSE AND SENSIBILITY by Jane Austen.** Afterword by Caroline G. Mercer. (518268—$2.25)*

☐ **JANE EYRE by Charlotte Brontë.** Afterword by Arthur Ziegler. (518845—$1.95)*

☐ **WUTHERING HEIGHTS by Emily Brontë.** Foreword by Goeffrey Moore. (516508—$1.75)

☐ **FRANKENSTEIN or THE MODERN PROMETHEUS by Mary Shelley.** Afterword by Harold Bloom. (511328—$1.50)

☐ **THE AWAKENING and SELECTED SHORT STORIES by Kate Chopin.** Edited by Barbara Solomon. (517490—$2.95)

☐ **ADAM BEDE by George Eliot.** Foreword by F. R. Leavis. (518489—$3.50)*

☐ **DANIEL DERONDA by George Eliot.** Introduction by Irving Howe. (512049—$3.50)

☐ **MIDDLEMARCH by George Eliot.** Afterword by Frank Kermode. (517504—$4.95)

☐ **THE MILL ON THE FLOSS by George Eliot.** Afterword by Morton Berman. (515439—$3.50)

☐ **SILAS MARNER by George Eliot.** Afterword by Walter Allen. (516788—$1.75)

*Prices slightly higher in Canada

THREE BY
Flannery O'Connor

WISE BLOOD

THE VIOLENT BEAR IT AWAY

EVERYTHING THAT RISES MUST CONVERGE

A SIGNET CLASSIC

NEW AMERICAN LIBRARY

Contents

Introduction to
Three by Flannery O'Connor

I

Wise Blood was first published in 1952. The author was twenty-seven years old, and she had struggled with this novel for at least five of these. She had begun to write it in the early spring of 1947, possibly even a few months before, while she was still a graduate student in the Writers' Workshop at the State University of Iowa, and a version of the first chapter was included, under the title, "Train," as the last of six stories comprising her thesis as a candidate for a Master's degree in Fine Arts.

Flannery O'Connor had appeared in Iowa City in September of 1945, fresh from Milledgeville, Georgia, bearing a fifteen-pound muskrat coat and a talent of proportionate weight, balanced by a steely will, not only to brave the Iowa snows far from her native mild southern air, but to endure the long, cold process of pushing that talent to its outermost limits. Paul Engle, director of the Workshop, agreed to accept her, on the basis of submitted examples of work that was already "imaginative, tough, alive," and "filled with insight about human weakness, hard and compassionate," as he later described it. She took a cooler view of her abilities at that time, remarking years afterward that if she had known how bad her early stories were, she would have stopped writing altogether. An exaggeration, I think, but she knew that if she was to write at all she wanted to write, as she said, "as well as I can, or a little better." Now she turned all her energies and intelligence to this end.

Her fellow aspirants found her affable and friendly, and she seems to have enjoyed the social life among them, chiefly shared meals and conversation on shared interests, more than she had the undergraduate galas at Georgia State College for Women, in Milledgeville, where she was so far from being the stereotypical dancing *belle* that she must have felt that there was scant room for her particular charms—an altogether unflirtatious manner and a shy taciturnity, lit up by a mordant wit and a bright, if slightly malicious, smile. She never forgot why she was there, however, and she seems to have wasted little of her time, always knowing when to retire to the lonely business at hand, the long struggle to make the language do her bidding in the effective conveyance of a sense of reality she was to serve all her days.

Her teachers were impressed with her gifts and her serious application to their development; and even professional recognition of a modest kind was not long in coming. In 1946, she sold a story, "The Geranium," written for her thesis, to *Accent* magazine. Significantly, the story deals with themes that would recur throughout her work in years to come: displacement, homelessness and homesickness. The last story she wrote, "Judgement Day," is in a sense a rewriting, a strengthening and perfecting of this early one, and it measures the distance she had traveled, both in character and as an artist, during her short life.

As well as learning all she could about writing from her teachers there, Flannery enriched her stay at Iowa by close reading of authors to whom she had never been exposed at college, where the curriculum provided a general standard background knowledge of English literature, and where, moreover, she had majored—for the last time ever—in Sociology. She remarks in a letter that when she left home she had never heard of Faulkner, Kafka, or Joyce, much less read them. Here at the university, directed by the references of both her teachers and her fellow students, she read them all, and a great deal else besides: the Catholic novelists Mauriac, Bernanos, Bloy, Greene, Waugh; among the southern writers, Faulkner, Allen Tate, and Caroline Gordon, R. P. Warren, Eudora Welty, Katherine Anne Porter, and Peter Taylor; of the great Russians, not so much Tolstoy but Dostoevsky, Turgenev, Chekhov, and, most importantly of all, Gogol, a kindred spirit, from whom she learned how effectively underlying religious themes could be treated with grotesquely comic characters. She mentions, too, that she learned something from Hawthorne (to whom she would later refer increasingly), Flaubert, and Balzac. She read much of Henry James, from "a sense of High Duty and because when I read James I feel that something is happening to me, in slow motion but happening nevertheless." She thereafter meant that something should happen to her own readers, not necessarily in slow motion, but she had begun to recognize that good fiction must be experienced—even undergone—and not merely perused. She became a great admirer of Joseph Conrad, as well; she read almost all his works, and he remained a presence throughout her writing life. From him she took a definition of her fictional aims, when he wrote of his own:

My task, which I am trying to achieve, is, by the power of the written word, to make you hear, to make you feel—it is, before all, to make you *see*. That—and no more, and it is everything. If I succeed, you shall find there, according to your deserts, encouragement, consolation, fear, charm, all you demand—and, perhaps, also that glimpse of truth for which you have forgotten to ask.

All this reading was naturally electrifying both to her will and to her imagination. She comments in one of her letters that writers are most often set going not so much by life as by something they have read. Before she went to graduate school, the first work to attract her attention to such effect was, not surprisingly, the *Humorous Tales* of Edgar Allan Poe. Although she was later to describe this as "an influence I would rather not think about," she never disclaimed it, and we can see in his cast of characters figures who lingered in her deepest memory and didn't have to be thought about in order to affect her imagination and be turned to her later, more profound, purposes.

There is, however, considerable evidence to suggest that when she came to begin her first novel, she had been much affected—possibly even set going—by another writer and his work. The writer was the poet T.S. Eliot, and the work that seems to have moved her so powerfully was *The Waste Land*. As published, *Wise Blood* is 232 pages long, but the author's papers, collected at Georgia College in Milledgeville, contain about two thousand pages of discarded manuscript sheets, false starts, "dead ends taken," as she called such unused material. This mass gives evidence not only of her early floundering, and the patience and care she was willing to take to satisfy her own demands on herself, but how many ideas and how many specific references she drew from her reading of Eliot's poem, and how great its impact on her. There are other influences to be discerned in these fragments, influences most often shrugged off in the course of this early struggle to hammer out her own style and mode of dealing with character, but on the evidence there is good reason to think that as Gogol is believed to have planned his unfinished trilogy on Dante's *Divine Comedy*, with the journey of Chichikov in *Dead Souls* as a Russian *Inferno*, O'Connor at first intended to base her novel and the encounters of her then bewildered hero on those of the speaker in The *Waste Land*. She nowhere mentions Eliot as an influence, but twelve of his books in her personal library attest to his early and continuing presence in her mind, and not only the discarded manuscript portions but passage traces remaining in the novel itself, in at least one of the stories, "A Stroke of Good Fortune" (drawn from a discarded chapter of the embryonic *Wise Blood*), and even as late as *The Violent Bear It Away*, would seem to prove it beyond much doubt. This should come as no surprise, for in Eliot she found no alien philosophy, or vision, or sense of life, but another writer "with Christian concerns," as she described herself to be, one who, like herself, openly avowed them and embodied them in his work.

From the outset, however, Flannery O'Connor had, as Allen Tate told her, the instinct of every good writer—to write about what she knew. Even while she was still somewhat mirroring the poet, she would go about her storytelling in accordance with this instinct, creating southern figures whom her imagination could bring to concrete life, and who spoke a vividly colloquial language she could handle superbly. The setting in which she placed them, however, was as much a waste land as the one Eliot had envisioned. This scene in the novel was from the beginning, and remained, the fragmented and mobile modern world, on the heels of a devastating and disruptive war, in which there had been as many spiritual casualties as any other kind, as many wandering refugees and "displaced persons" created, and as great a shift in values and mores. Her counterpart of Eliot's sordid London was the debased city of Taulkinham, inhabited by rootless individuals, sleazy, hostile, self-seeking, untrustworthy, cut off from each other and from every source of spiritual, intellectual, or emotional nutriment. The figure she planned to set against this ground was a young country boy, dragged by the army from his home in Eastrod, Tennessee, in a part of the country that still retained what the author called elsewhere "a distinctly Old Testament flavor," and sent halfway around the globe to fight in some corner of the Second World War; then returned, wounded in body and soul, to a broken-down society, his family and home gone and his bearings hopelessly lost. The action was to encompass his journey to "the city," and to recount his travail in this new post-war urban moral wilderness, where he still hoped to find the equivalent of his lost community. Characteristically, she had outlined no precise course of this conflict for her hero, except that he was at first to contend against, and then succumb to, "modern" ideas and mores, in their various embodiments. The eventual resolution of the situation was still a mystery even to her, except that Hazel would ultimately reject these, but how and in what terms she had no idea, and planned to find out only in the course of the writing itself, once the character had a *persona* of his own, and a will which he would follow wherever it led until he found his lost Eastrod. Even then, she knew exactly where she believed his true home to be, but she had no idea how she was to bring him there.

Gifted as she was, this projected novel was a daunting challenge, how great probably even she was not at once aware. Certainly she had to struggle long and hard before her early mistakes became apparent to her and she was able to recast her character and her story into the form in which we finally see them. She knew her gift for creating grotesque figures with grotesque ideas, in grotesque situations, and in the beginning she planned to contrast these to the then relative innocence and good will of her protagonist. She invented a stream of weird types, all of them talkative, and the confusion grew. In time, she realized that she had to clear the air and either eliminate some of her characters or replace them with people whose actions, as well as their talk, could carry her story forward.

In 1947, she had not only earned her Master's degree at Iowa, she had also won a publisher's prize for a first novel, on the basis of the first six chapters of *Wise Blood* (still untitled). She stayed in Iowa City an additional year, as a part-time teaching assistant, and continued to work on her book and enlarge her reading. It was probably during this extra year that she realized that the substructure she was relying on from Eliot was not the right one for the novel, and took the first steps toward a major change in her approach to solving the dramatic problems. This conjecture can be made because, although the Hazel depicted in "The Train" (as it reappeared in *The Sewanee Review* in 1948) is certainly the Hazel of his early incarnation (including the name "Wickers"), the Hazel of "The Peeler," designated the fourth chapter and already written and accepted by the *Partisan Review* by June of the same year, is almost unrecognizable as the friendly and pathetic boy on the train. He has by now pretty much assumed the final, unforgettable personality we know from the finished novel, and his companions in Taulkinham have been narrowed down and altered to those with whom he deals in the final version. The first chapter was later rewritten to conform to this change.

Evidently, by the time she reached Yaddo, the writer's colony near Saratoga Springs, New York, where she went by invitation after she left Iowa City, she had already begun to remove her story from her first general plan, reconceive the characters, and rebuild the whole in an entirely new way, retaining only the urban wasteland setting.

She had probably not been entirely comfortable with Eliot's mythic points of reference, or with the figure of Tiresias in the background. These came from lately acquired knowledge, not from things she "knew" except as abstracts. She seemed to find her own proper, native ground when she re-character-ized her hero and re-based him firmly on someone she *did* know and understand and believe in: the biblical, historical figure of St. Paul, fulminating enemy of Christ, who was waylaid on the road to Damascus and briefly blinded before becoming a passionate apostle. Just so is Hazel stopped in his Essex, in preparation for his own witness.

A few faint images from *The Waste Land* are still to be recognized in the final version of *Wise Blood*. The figure in Eliot's line, "There is always another walking beside you," becomes for O'Connor, "the wild ragged figure who moves from tree to tree in the back of Hazel's mind." The shadow which, in Eliot, "strides behind you by day and rises up to meet you in the evening," is enlarged upon in her description of Hazel's shadow as "now behind him and now before him and now and then broken up by other people's shadows, but when it was by itself, stretching out behind him, it was a thin, nervous shadow walking backwards." Like Hazel him-self.

By the time she had completed the novel, however, she had wisely abandoned most explicit references to the poem, ex-cept for one unmistakable echo, when her antic anti-hero, Enoch, says of the shrunken mummy whose embalmed re-mains represent all that unspirited mortal man can hope to become after death, "He was once as tall as you or me." In Eliot, this refers to the reduction by drowning of the formerly handsome and tall Phoenician sailor. In O'Connor, it seems to hint at a previous and higher definition of man and his destiny than the post-Christian world, and Hazel's "modern" nihilist philosophy, would allow. The dry and shriveled figure is exactly what Hazel would reduce man to; it is his "new Jesus," as Enoch has intuited, and as Hazel himself recog-nizes, with a revulsion that signifies a bad conscience despite his furious, even murderous, defense of his new belief in what he can "see" for himself.

Even so, she never lost her sense of the power of Eliot's mix of the gross and the transcendent, the sublime vision growing out of, and imposed as a measure on, the vulgarities, visual and audible, of human spiritual and sensible reality in present-day life. She knew, however—without benefit of theory, but with the instincts and judgment of a born artist —that her own story was not being told right, and she had no intention of letting it go until it was. Feeling her way along, bullying herself, in the end she brought it off. This was accomplished by an instinctive but thoughtful process of elimination of redundant characters and situations; by selecting only those people and events that carried meaning and felt life; by cutting away everything that she thought might further obscure a mysterious subject; by relocating much of the conflict of the hero to his own interior will, or wills, and then *showing* what he wills, simplifying what he says and does, with almost no reflective authorial comment or clarification by any character expressing the author's point of view.

Most importantly of all, Hazel himself was remolded from a character in the process of formation, a confused lamb among wolves, into a temperamental zealot who has already made up his mind to reject everything that has formed him in the past—not only his belief in Christ and his sense of objective sin, but the nameless, unplaced guilt instilled in him by his iron-lined mother with her primitively harsh religion, and by his grandfather, a circuit-riding preacher who had for years "ridden over three counties with Jesus hidden in his head like a stinger." The rebellious young man is determined to lay these ghosts forever and join his contemporaries in the "free" world of the present. The tender and timid Hazel Wickers, alias Weaver, of the earlier versions now stalks onto the scene as the rude and contemptuous Hazel *Motes* (the new name suggesting his spiritual blindness) who encounters Mrs. Hitchcock in the Pullman, and at once attacks her with a sneering observation that redefines him at a stroke: "I reckon you think you been redeemed." The first line of essential motion is here drawn, and Hazel comes to life as he never had in the chapters she so rightly discarded. The image of a baffled searcher was in any case less suited to the direct and hard-driving style she was developing, which better conveyed certainty, however wrong-headed, than well-meaning confusion.

Her descriptive means changed as much as her characterizations. Note this description from the published *Wise Blood*:

The train was racing through tree tops that fell away at intervals and showed the sun standing, very red, on the edge of the farthest woods. Nearer, the plowed fields curved and faded and the few hogs nosing in the furrows looked like large spotted stones.

If we can find hardly a trace of the early rather sentimental Hazel in his new incarnation, it is equally hard to find anything of *this* O'Connor in her treatment of the same scene, only a year or two earlier, in "The Train": "Now the train was greyflying past instants of trees and quick spaces of field and a motionless sky that sped darkening away in the opposite direction." Goodbye and good riddance to both.

The people with whom Hazel comes in contact in the city are for the most part utterly indifferent to his new convictions and his preachments on the subject when he founds his automobile-based Church of Truth Without Jesus Christ Crucified. But this is not because they are Christians. Even those who profess to be are frauds and scoundrels. The novel in its final form is sparsely populated, but every character is clearly conceived and acidly drawn, and each has an active and essential part to play in the working out of Hazel's illumination and destiny. Most of all, however, it is Hazel's own part to assert throughout his dangerous freedom and independence of will and, even as a penitent, to arrogate to himself alone, without benefit of counsel from any more benign authority, the right to indict himself, try himself, convict himself, sentence himself, and carry out the terrible sentence. Ill-tutored, misguided, but passionately sincere, he meets a fate that is severely logical in the light of his nature and the circumstances, historical and personal, that have produced him.

"*Wise Blood*," said Flannery O'Connor, "is a very hopeful book." This may not be at once apparent to the reader accustomed to more conventionally happy endings, but indeed it is—in her terms. Whether or not one accepts those terms, it is necessary at least to understand them, if the reader is to apprehend the author's deepest intentions in this novel, and in all her fiction.

When the book appeared in print, there was an initial rush to oversimplify, given the provenance of the writer, and the southern aspects of her characters. Commentators tended, in the light of their own prejudices and preconceptions, to see her as another chronicler of southern grotesqueries or, more often, to use a term she loathed: another "Southern Gothic" writer, an eccentric writing about eccentrics. Southerners disliked it for what they saw as mockery of themselves and of Protestantism, and in her own locale it was regarded as a shockingly immoral book. It was anything but immoral, of course. Nor was it meant to reflect ill on the South or southerners, least of all on their religion. The particular scene was intended to reflect the general one, the *hic et ubique* in the mid-twentieth century United States. Northerners, too, including critics, though professing themselves not to be surprised by anything that happened in the South, found it too strong for their blood, and they, too, almost uniformly misunderstood it.

With such a reception, it was no wonder that the book had no wide circulation, except perhaps among other writers, many of whom greatly admired it, and recognized the emergence of a strong and original talent. Robert Lowell had met her at Yaddo, and had come to admire her both as a person and as a writer. He gave her his full approbation for this first book. It was not long before John Crowe Ransom had offered her a Kenyon Fellowship to facilitate her future work; and personal letters of commendation from many others armored her against the general disapproval and incomprehension. The novelist Caroline Gordon, who had seen the manuscript just before publication, and made instructive technical suggestions quickly acted upon by the author, was most enthusiastic. She sent the book to J.F. Powers, mentioning that in her opinion only Kafka had previously succeeded in achieving some of O'Connor's effects. He wrote back to add his praise to the book, but mused, "Kafka? No, Kafka was much too young and tender to play in that league." The league was of course major, and a beanball in any one of her play-off games was likely to prove fatal, as her subsequent work was to demonstrate.

II

Flannery O'Connor was not arrogant, and she took the early hostile criticism to *Wise Blood* seriously and thoughtfully, even though she still had no intention of changing her concerns and seriously comic general mode of treating them. She acknowledged the difficulties she had posed in the first book, however, and proposed to eliminate some of these by greater humanization of her characters. As she wrote to Caroline Gordon, "My first book was about freaks, but from now on I'm going to write about folks."

This resolution may have been prompted, too, by the new circumstances in which she found herself, for she had in the meantime suffered a severe personal reversal. Since leaving Yaddo, in early 1949, she had been contentedly living in the country near Ridgefield, Connecticut, with Robert Fitzgerald and his family. There she had spent a year and a half working on her book, and she had barely brought it to a conclusion, around Christmas of 1950, and was preparing to do final polishing, when she was stopped in her way and nearly killed by the auto-immune disease that was to alter her existence once and for all. When she was fifteen, she had lost her father to lupus erythematosus and, although the disease was not then thought to be hereditary, nor to carry any hereditary predisposition, she herself had developed it in a most serious form, at the age of twenty-five. She survived the first onslaught, but it was now clear that she could not, as she had hoped and planned, continue to live in the north. She was forced to return permanently to Milledgeville, to a severely restricted life, in the care of her mother, and near enough to Atlanta to be in constant touch with the doctor who had managed to save her. "Permanently" meant, she must have thought, for the roughly three years she probably expected to go on living, since her father had survived only that long after his first attack, and the disease was still without a cure.

However that was to be, she intended to use those years. When she learned what was really wrong with her health, she settled in at Andalusia, the farm near town, to which she and her mother had moved because it was better suited to her care; bought herself a pair of peacocks for amusement and aesthetic satisfaction, and began to write stories for an eventual collection. Under the pressures of her situation, her gifts flowered. Her writing grew in power and took on an extraordinary finish. Exactly three years later, she had completed a group of nine stunning short stories. These were to establish beyond question her right to be regarded as one of the preeminent talents of her time. There was little or no equivocation in the reception of this book by the critics. The stories were almost universally praised, although understanding did not entirely keep pace and many people mistakenly read them as only cruel and hard, and still found her characters to be more like "freaks" than "folks" anyone might wish to be identified with. In any event, there was no doubt that these stories were likely to be not so much read as experienced, and experienced with pain, at that. Liked or not, readily understood or not, however, they were obviously first-rate, and her reputation was firmly established.

At the same time, her sense of her personal situation was a little eased, as well, in that the lupus had in her case responded to the cortisone treatment developed since her father's death, and her prospects for a longer life and continued productivity were much improved. She had accommodated herself to life on the farm, and recognized this place, and even the limitations on her freedom, as ideal for her work. In this atmosphere of renewed hope, she began a new novel, or, as she said, "something that may become a novel." It was eventually to become *The Violent Bear It Away*.

Her physical ordeal was by no means over, however (it was never to be), and now it was even further complicated by the fact that the steroid medication that alone was keeping her alive was at the same time causing grave necrosis— deterioration of the bones—beginning in the hips, and she was forced to take to crutches in order to walk at all. There was no way out of this checkmate, so she adapted herself to it, as she had to her relative isolation, with a willed acceptance grounded in her ever-deepening faith, and the sardonic humor that was so much a part of her personality and her mind. She had begun to realize that her forced return to the South had not signaled the end of her writing life, but rather what she could regard as a benevolent redirection of her course that would greatly enrich it. She began to see that she had been constrained to come back exactly where she belonged, as the particular artist she was.

The new stories reflected this. They had no literary sources to set her going. These were no longer necessary. The newspapers would suffice. She was surrounded on all sides with material for her fiction; and the stories had grown out of things she saw and heard about her, sensory experience, however slight, broadened by imaginative experience and invention, and immensely deepened by her penetration to the level of allegorical and anagogical understanding which made them seem to her worth writing. This region, Baldwin County, Georgia, was for her what John Crowe Ransom called "the world's body," and gave her the personae and the material of what she called her "romance" fiction, in which the life of the soul, whether for good or for ill, is sacramentally lived in the manners and actions (the thoughts, words, and deeds) of the characters, in concrete settings and situations in a particular place and time, and cannot be separated from these but must be seen through them.

The South, still "Christ-haunted, if no longer Christ-centered," where manners were still distinctive, and individuality ran strong, provided for her a scene with which she had a life-long familiarity, and which in itself had contributed to the formation of her imagination. The stories henceforth, although no more regional than *Everyman*, were to be firmly planted in the red earth of Middle Georgia, and peopled with figures she had looked upon and listened to all her days, if only from the distance of her own sheltered and genteel, Roman Catholic, background. Her imagination was now further fed by a stream of country folk who "came to the back door" of the farmhouse, and she listened to and observed them carefully, spinning off wild and wonderful inventions from what she saw and heard, as she understood it in the light of what she knew and believed. Her ear was constantly refreshed by the rich language that flowed around her, to be used by her with consummate artistry and to hilarious effect. She had always been funny—her conversation and her letters were a delight to her friends—and the fiction, although more often than not dreadful in the surface resolution of her stories, was also extremely funny. She enjoyed her own jokes and felt a little embarrassed by the fact that she couldn't read most of her stories aloud without laughing so hard that she would have to pause before she could go on. This is not to say that she was deriding her absurd and perverse figures or mocking them by the death sentences she eventually meted out to so many. Her concern for the people she wrote about was at bottom of the utmost seriousness, and sprang from a kind of tough-minded respect for them and their dignity as human beings, and a hope for them born of austere and uncondescending charity. "If charity were a stick," she once wrote to a friend, "I could imagine myself laying about me with it." In more than one instance, she would defend one of her characters against the too-harsh judgment of readers who found some of them far more odious than she did.

In 1955, a few months before the appearance of the story collection in April of 1956, *New World Writing* published a draft of the first chapter of the novel she continued to hope to write, and occasionally to struggle with. This chapter appeared under the title, "You Can't Be Any Poorer Than Dead." By this time no one was surprised by what the title portended. Now, since it seemed that she was to live longer than she had perhaps expected to, she turned to this project with a will, and again, by the sweat of her brow and a labor of five long years, she prevailed over the most difficult and seemingly intractable material.

The Violent Bear It Away, which appeared in 1960, further enhanced her reputation, both for better and for worse. The people who appreciated what she was doing, and how well she was doing it, found it masterly, a finer book by far than *Wise Blood*. Those who had hated the stories, hated the new novel equally. It was just as complex and demanding as *Wise Blood*, but it was neither as funny nor as grotesque. It was, if anything, even more violent and unsettling in its denouement, and its religious challenge was more open.

As had been the case with the first novel, one of the chief characters, old Mason Tarwater (who, although he dies on the first page, is a tremendous presence throughout the book) was seen mistakenly by some critics and readers as plain crazy. The author, however, privately confirmed him as in her view basically in the right, and declared herself to be behind him one hundred percent.

The living protagonist, Francis Marion Tarwater, aged fourteen, is an unconvinced and strayed prophet, not only called to this uncomfortable vocation by destiny, but "trained" in it by his explosive great-uncle Mason, who has devoted himself to prophecy and moonshining and the education of the heir apparent on a remote farm in a clearing near a settlement called Powderhead, until his sudden death at the breakfast table. Having failed to carry out his first assignment, the proper burial of the old man in a grave marked by a cross, young Tarwater sets off, ostensibly to demonstrate his refusal to carry out the second, as well. This was to be the baptism of his little cousin, Bishop, the idiot son of Tarwater's uncle in the city, George Rayber, a fanatical rationalist, teacher of psychology, who believes that he has escaped the powerful old man and his perfervid Christian teachings, and wishes likewise to "save" his nephew. Accompanied and coached by an unseen new friend, a comic but sinister voice in his ear and mind, hideously embodied only in the final pages of the novel, Tarwater opposes and challenges his uncle and would-be mentor on every level of his being. Although the fierce boy accepts none of the schoolteacher's rationalism and psychology, neither does he accept his own previous formation and calling, whether in general or in the particular charge his dead great-uncle has laid upon him. If the old man suggests a red-clay John the Baptizer, an uncompromising voice bellowing in the wilderness, the boy seems reminiscent of a sulky Jonah, stubbornly refusing to follow his vocation until he is forced to a final choice.

Tarwater's own inner battle against belief and acceptance, and his simultaneous attraction to both, provides a dramatic subplot to his conflict with Rayber, and these two wars, with their stunning outcome, comprise the action of the novel. The underlying premise of the whole, however, is the author's belief, reflected in the old man, that baptism in Christ is a matter of life and death. Of the fearsome events in this novel, she wrote, "I don't set out to be more drastic, but this happens automatically. If I write a novel in which the central action is a baptism, I know that for the larger percentage of my readers, baptism is a meaningless rite; therefore I have to embue this action with an awe and terror which will suggest its awful mystery. I have to distort the look of the thing in order to represent as I see them both the mystery and the fact."

Apart from four notes sounded by a thrush among the pines (again resonant of *The Waste Land*) at the beginning and end of the book, purely literary sources, or traces, even unconscious ones, in this novel or in the way it is built and written, are not apparent. Flannery O'Connor is never more uniquely herself than here. Her weaknesses—a lack of perfect familiarity with the terminology of the secular sociologists, psychologists, and rationalists she often casts as adversary figures, and an evident weighting of the scales against them all—are present in the character of Rayber (who combines all three categories). But her peculiar strengths—her ability to convey real religious conviction, and the equal force of an individual's inner impulse to refuse and oppose it, and her dramatization of such conflict—are evident throughout, as are the wild humor and withering irony that characterize all her work, and the ambiguity which lends it much of its fascination. The novel is finely constructed. Architecture, joinery, and details of language and dialogue are superb. There is hardly a misplaced or unneeded word. Portraiture is memorable, and her painterly descriptions of the settings for the action mysteriously suggest a battleground for supernatural combat in which all of nature, as well, is taking part as witness. The world of the spirit and the world of matter, the invisible and the visible, she forcefully suggests, are inseparable.

Much has been said concerning Flannery O'Connor's own unwavering religious commitment. No one doubts it now, and it seems strange to remember that for some time it went unrecognized, if not taken for its opposite, even by her fellow Catholics. It had not been until 1957 that she made any public statement, at least in print, on the subject. For Granville Hicks' symposium, *The Living Novel*, she wrote a piece she called "The Fiction Writer and His Country," in the course of which she plainly stated her motivating convictions. Even in this article, however, she did not declare that what she called her "Christian orthodoxy" was specifically Catholic. No doubt she thought that to do so would only confound the confusion, since so few people (including many Catholics) fully or clearly understood much that such a statement implied. Certainly she had no wish to be regarded as polemical, as indeed she was not. Her sympathy for sincere

Protestants, and even for vividly subjective Christians, is manifest in her work, although she shows herself to be intolerant of distortions. She said only that such orthodoxy meant for her that "the meaning of life is centered in our Redemption by Christ," adding that what she saw in the world she saw in relation to that.

She knew, however, that her vocation as a writer was defined by her limitations. She knew that she must do what her talent allowed her to do best. With her particular gifts, what she was best able to reflect in her stories was "the broken condition of mankind and the devil by which we are possessed," reflections which in themselves implied the need of such redemption, whether in everyday life or at the moment of death. As to why such extreme measures as hers were necessary, she went on to say that

> The novelist with Christian concerns will find in modern life distortions which are repugnant to him, and his problem will be to make these appear as distortions to an audience which is used to seeing them as natural; and he may well be forced to take ever more violent means to get his vision across to this hostile audience. When you can assume that your audience holds the same beliefs you do, you can relax and use more normal means of talking to it; when you have to assume that it does not, then you have to make your vision apparent by shock—to the hard of hearing you shout, and for the almost-blind you draw large and startling figures.

This clarification was duly noted, and some retrospective understanding of the fiction ensued. She was even then, however, hardly recognized as a Catholic writer, although most reviewers had begun to mention the statistical fact. For one thing, the outward signs were missing. Only one of the stories has a Catholic protagonist, or any liturgical content or setting whatever.

What she called the Catholic sacramental view of life—that the sensible, material world and all of "real" human life was in itself sacramental, the visible container of the invisible—was no longer a familiar one in secularized culture, or even in the fragmented Christian world, of today. It was, though, a view that was absolutely central to her own thinking, and it was entirely compatible to her conception of the function of the artist as being to show—to "make them see"—the invisible world within the visible one that by now almost entirely absorbed the interest of most of western mankind.

She believed that, in Marianne Moore's words, art must be "lit with piercing glances into the life of things/It must acknowledge the spiritual forces which have made it." This belief she continued to implement, and in her own art to imply, if only by its absence, a lost vision or sense of wholeness, in the individual and in the community of mankind. Flannery O'Connor's mind was deeply Catholic, but her fiction was no more parochial than it was regional.

III

She had hoped to write a third novel, arduous as the process was for her. Only one chapter, or "beginning section" was completed. No one knows what she had in mind for this novel, if indeed she herself knew exactly. It was not her way to plan a story, long or short. Characters were developed who then took on a life of their own, and very often what they did in the course of the action came, as she said, as a discovery even to her. It is not unreasonable, however, to speculate that here she may have considered taking on the immense difficulties of dealing with a conversion more conventional than the bloody rebirths of Hazel Motes and Tarwater. The protagonist, Walter Tilman, is discovered by his mother to have been reading a book containing a flaming letter from St. Jerome to Heliodorus, Bishop of Altinum, both Fourth-century patristic figures of great importance.

This unexpected development suggests at least one possibility. In the last year of her life, Flannery O'Connor had written to one of her friends, "I've been writing for eighteen years and I've reached the point where I can't do again what I know I can do well, and the larger things I need to do now, I doubt my capacity for doing." We have no way of knowing what she considered these larger things to be, but it is surely possible that one of them may have been an attempt to handle, by whatever explosive means she could invent, the restoration of an American southerner, from a culture estranged for centuries from traditional Catholic Christianity, to the ancient faith that had united Christendom for even more centuries, and to which she herself so strongly adhered. Here certainly would have been a more formidable challenge than any she had faced before.

However that may be, there is nothing else new in the situation outlined by the characters she sketched in the material intended to open the unfinished novel. The scene is a farm or country place, bounded by the signature "line of dark trees," and the actors are almost all members of the same family—in this case, as in so many of the stories, an emotional desert. One difference is that this family contains a full complement: an afflicted father, a perpetually furious mother, and two semi-petrified offspring.

The family in an O'Connor story is more often than not incomplete: one or more parent is dead or gone, children or the young do battle with widowed mothers or fathers, or with uncles, great-uncles or grandparents; the old chafe under lives lived with hostile or indifferent children. The trouble does not seem to lie with the incompleteness of the family, although in some instances the presence of a second parent, or actual parents, would surely have had its effect, although not necessarily for the better (*viz*, Mr. and Mrs. Pitts in "A View of the Woods"). The trouble lies in the pride, egotism and plain cussedness of the individuals. Original sin, as she called it, in all its forms. The inscape of the characters themselves is the "territory held largely by the devil," in which she occupied herself with showing "the action of grace." If she stuck with family relationships and situations as a ground, it was because she wrote of obscure, "unimportant," people, and some kind of family community is where most of us live, and where even our cosmic dramas are enacted and our souls won or lost.

This choice of subject continued to hold true in the stories gathered together after her death and published under her own title, *Everything That Rises Must Converge*, a line she had taken from her reading of the French Jesuit paleontologist and visionary theologian, Teilhard de Chardin. Some of these stories had been written in the interim between the appearance of her first collection and the publication of *The Violent Bear It Away*. "Greenleaf" dates back to 1956, "A View of the Woods" to 1957, and "The Enduring Chill" to 1958. The writing of these appears to have been a respite she likened to a vacation in the mountains that she occasionally gave herself as a rest from the rigors of novel-writing. The composition of the remaining six stories followed the final relief of completing the novel, and all were written in the four years that remained to her. There was nothing like the rush of creativity that occurred during the three years in which she had written the first collection of nine stories, although her production continued to be steady (about one a year until the final burst of speed), and all the new ones were splendid examples of her mature power as a writer.

The title story of *Everything That Rises Must Converge* concerns a mother and son, both flawed, but in very different ways, squabbling their way downtown on a bus, en route to an encounter with death. A new element for O'Connor is introduced in her treatment, for the first time, of a current social issue: the evolving relations between blacks and whites, and the violence that sometimes attended it. Blacks in her fiction heretofore have been most often commentators, slyly or wryly mocking in their comments to white characters on actions they mostly observe peripherally. Sometimes they have taken on a mythic quality—Buford, in *The Violent Bear It Away*, for example; Astor, in "The Displaced Person," and especially the lawn ornament representing black suffering in "The Artificial Nigger." They have been at times mischievous, even guilty, like Sulk, in "The Displaced Person," but by and large, they have been observed by O'Connor entirely from the outside. As she said, she didn't feel herself able to get inside their heads, and she forebore to equip them with thoughts she had imagined for them. In "Everything That Rises Must Converge," written in 1961, when the civil rights movement was in full swing and desegregation in the South an actual fact, and blacks had begun to externalize those thoughts and feelings of anger they had repressed so long, she finally saw fit to write a story in which a black would take a key, and very active, role. In the light of what she does, we can be in no doubt of the black woman's sentiments.

The mother and son on the bus believe that they hold very different attitudes toward the new dispensation. The mother, a silly but kindly, hard-working and gaily self-sacrificing widow, is nevertheless unreconstructed in her views on racial matters: "They should rise, yes, but on their own side of the fence." She is no more nor less than a product of her culture and, in particular, of her generation, and she will never be able to change, but she is in fact a much purer soul than her surly son. Julian "realizes that he is much too intelligent ever to be a success." He believes himself to be enlightened, liberal and realistic; actually he cares nothing for the blacks themselves, and his apparently respectful friendliness toward them is chiefly a means of tormenting his mother. He is a typical O'Connor weakling, hopelessly but restively dependent on his mother (and secretly he shares her outlived romantic values), but his cruelty to her is even more gratuitous than that of most such sons we encounter in the stories. Among other fantasies, he daydreams of "giving her a stroke" by bringing home a "beautiful, suspiciously Negroid woman" and confronting her with his engagement.

The convergence of the old white culture and the rising blacks is suggested by the identical new hats the two women are wearing. This delights the son, until he sees that his mother's discomfiture has dissolved into amusement. The black woman is accompanied by her own small son, who falls into an instant and joyous flirtation with the white mother. The two innocents plainly relish their unself-conscious rapport, until the huge and bellicose black mother recalls the child with the significant command, "Quit yo' foolishness before I knock the living Jesus out of you."

When the young man and his mother reach their stop, which turns out to be that of the black pair as well, the incorrigibly naïve old lady prepares to do something "as natural to her as breathing"—give the child a nickel. Her son realizes that this will be an affront (although she would have done the same thing had the child been white), and tries to stop her. She is determined, though, and while she can only find a penny in her bag, she offers it to the delighted child. The encounter becomes a confrontation, and ends in tragedy, with the blindly malevolent young man left at the portal of the "world of guilt and sorrow," facing a self-revelation that will either make or break him.

Large social issues as such were never the stuff of Flannery O'Connor's work, and even here her concern is with the personal effects of a social situation, and the encounter with devastating self-knowledge, together with larger realities, in the individual. It is interesting to note that O'Connor seems more willing to excuse the fatuous old lady than she is the son. The author pointedly implies that, for all her unrecognized sins, she is on her way "home" (which for O'Connor is always the cloudless kingdom of God), and that, like a child herself, she has called for a long-remembered black nurse to come and take her there, where they can live together in peace and love. In the wars between the generations, which she recounts in so many stories, O'Connor is not particularly on the side of the young, despite the maddening foibles, and even evils, of the old; she deals out justice with an even hand.

"Greenleaf" was written some five years earlier, and it was one of the author's most widely honored stories in its day. Still set in the insular world of a southern country home and farm, as yet threatened only by the upward mobility of a low-class white dairyman and his family, "Greenleaf" revolved around a figure not unfamiliar in O'Connor's work: a self-satisfied but sorely pressed middle-aged widow struggling to keep order on her "place" amid an assortment of human elements who seem bent on destroying all her earthbound accomplishments and hopes. In Mrs. May's case, these include two irresponsible sons who torture her, and the family of Mr. Greenleaf, her shiftless and devious dairyman. Countering her own spoiled heirs are the two sons of Greenleaf, who are as peaceful, hard-working and effective as hers are quarrelsome and unproductive. Countering the stiff-backed and materialistic owner is Mrs. Greenleaf, a vast and slovenly "mystic" who occupies her time with what she calls prayer healing.

This repulsive figure is quixotically allotted a more important part to play in what follows than the grotesquely comic one she at first suggests, for she, too, is a prophetess of sorts, and foretells the coming climax in a prayer howled during one of her sessions. "You have to take virtue where you find it," Flannery O'Connor might have said, and meant it.

A nonhuman element of threat has now appeared in the form of a scrub bull belonging to the Greenleaf sons, which has been allowed to run loose on Mrs. May's farm, endangering her milk herd and destroying her rest by his nocturnal vigils under her bedroom window, where he chews noisily on her shrubbery. This figure for the pursuing Christ seems almost to revert to Greek mythology and the earthly visits of Zeus to mortals he desires. But when the bull is described as "crowned" with a hedge-wreath ripped loose and encircling his horns, suggesting a crown of thorns, his interest in Mrs. May takes on a deeper aspect, and it appears that the presence of a waiting Christ is figured not as "Christ the Tiger," but as a scrawny bull standing under her window, "chewing calmly like an uncouth country suitor."

At the same time, on the surface level of the story, he is simply a troublesome stray bull, and Mrs. May is determined to get rid of him. Her outrage is compounded when she learns who owns him, and finds that the father is therefore reluctant to carry out her orders to kill the animal. She gets her way, and he is destroyed, but not before he, approaching her "like a wild, tormented lover," has had his way with her, as well. The story is in O'Connor's best vein, one she had perfected: grimly comic, but mysterious and terrifying at the same time.

In "A View of the Woods," written in 1957, she broke new ground again, this time metaphysical ground. Effective as the story is, however, there is a curiously unresolved impression left by the ending, exceeding the ambiguity that almost always characterizes her endings. Judging from letters about it, she intended, for the first and only time, to pronounce damnation on one of her characters, and this was in itself a rather daring move. Damnation is hard to come by, according to the doctrine she embraced. It must be chosen deliberately, freely, and with full knowledge that the choice is a grave sin. It is not the same as "doom," which refers to natural death, and which is everyone's lot, although it may be invited out of season. Mr. Fortune is certainly a terrible old man, vain, cruel, avaricious, and a worshiper of false gods, but he is also ignorant, almost too ignorant to merit the distinction she would grant him. It is interesting to note what to Flannery O'Connor's mind constitutes the damnable, given the number of murders she had seen as pardonable under certain hopeful conditions. Mr. Fortune's sins—deliberate cruelty to his helpless family ("fools," he contemptuously calls them); the despoiling of nature—*are* grave, but the worst of all is the corruption he would work on his nine-year-old granddaughter. It is perhaps for this crime, (the "scandalizing of little ones" anathematized in the New Testament) that she condemns him finally in this unsettling story.

Both "The Enduring Chill" and "The Comforts of Home" treat of selfish grown-up sons with annoying mothers, although the scenes and the problems differ considerably. Asbury Fox is a failed "artist," wretched, mean-spirited and, by his own fault, extremely ill. He blames all his troubles on his mother, whom he has tried to escape altogether by taking his imaginary talents north. He has come home only to die, as he thinks, but he is in for an even worse surprise. For his sins, he is finally delivered into his mother's hands for good, by inexorable truth, the spirit of which he sees descending upon him when his situation is explained to him in simple medical terms. Thomas, in "The Comforts of Home," is just the opposite. A contented and successful historian, safe among his books, he wants *his* mother entirely to himself, for the sake of the comfortable life she provides for him. He can bear with her vagaries, even her immoderate charity, until, overflowing with a love he alone cannot absorb, she brings home a psychopathic girl, a witless "nymphomaniac" and "congenital" liar, irresponsibly destructive and self-destructive. It is a foolish act on the natural level; she cannot help the girl, but neither can she bear to abandon her to the jail cell that certainly awaits her if she is turned out. Thomas, whose moderate charity cannot survive if it must cost him his comfort, is helplessly furious and, when he is unable to persuade his mother to be "sensible," stoops to a low subterfuge that brings his life crashing down around his head. As always, O'Connor's sympathies lie with the "fool of God," in this case the mother whose "daredevil" charity is not perfunctory but deeply involving, leading her to forego the affections of a son she dotes on. Despite her apparent lack of wisdom, her face puts her son in mind of a sibyl, but it doesn't seem to occur to him that she speaks for the sacred.

The story was written in 1959 and published in 1960. After it appeared, she wrote to John Hawkes that it contained "a very interesting devil that might appeal to (him)." That devil appears in the person of the son's hated dead father, who now so effectively misguides the son that we are not surprised to hear her call him literally a devil. There is at least one devil in almost every story, one who is forced to "call his name," as she put it, or at least show his hand. Again to John Hawkes, with whom she carried on some argumentative correspondence on the subject of the demonic, she wrote, "I want to be certain that the Devil gets identified as the Devil and not simply taken for this or that psychological tendency . . ."

She always resisted facile psychological explanations of her characters and their motives for action. On the subject of Thomas's father, whom he has loathed in his lifetime, she wanted it clearly understood that Freud cannot explain the mystery of the situation, of Thomas's personality, or of the dead father's hatred of the mother. She wrote to a friend about the story, "But do we have to see Oedipus in every man who doesn't like his father? The old man's animosity is directed at the mother because she's his opposite as far as virtue goes . . ." Thomas loves his mother but he loves his comforts above all. It is to *these* that he is wedded, and proves a jealous husband.

In "The Lame Shall Enter First," O'Connor went back to discarded early versions of *The Violent Bear It Away*, which had contained a rough young customer called Rufus Florida Johnson. She was fond of him, and although she had revised the novel and excluded him from it, she had not forgotten this demon. Now she brought him out in a story which is in some ways an echo of the novel. This time, the sociologist is Sheppard, a City Recreational Director, a widower with a small boy, not an idiot but too dull to feed his father's pride. The child, Norton, is sick with grief for his dead mother, having been told by his agnostic father that she is gone forever, simply does not exist, and that he must stop his unnatural mourning and get on with the "unselfish" life his father wants him to lead. Sheppard's interest is concentrated on a delinquent he has met at the reformatory where he helps out between Little League games. Johnson is a backwoods boy with a monstrous club foot and a high I.Q., brought up by his grandfather whose religious theories have finally sent him off "to the hills with a remnant." He is proud of his criminality; he is good at it and has no interest in reforming. He is, though, homeless and hungry, and when Sheppard invites him to come and live with him and his son, he sullenly accepts. To rehabilitate such a boy would be no less than a feast for Sheppard's pride. There is a battle between Sheppard and Johnson, carried on over a period of weeks, which becomes a test of strength between opposing wits, wills, endurance, and basic beliefs. Like Rayber in the novel, the beleaguered do-gooder comes to hate his charge. Johnson, although certainly diabolic, is like one of those biblical devils who recognize Christ, and his particular odium for his benefactor grows from outrage that Sheppard supposes he can save him by his own efforts. "God, kid," he asks Norton, "how do you stand it? He thinks he's Jesus Christ."

Norton has been comforted by Johnson's assurance that his mother is indeed alive and in heaven, if she believed in Jesus and wasn't a whore. The child is overjoyed, and spends his days looking for her in the sky, through the telescope Sheppard has bought to develop Johnson's knowledge. Although he likes to read and devours the encyclopedia, Johnson is more interested in dangerous games with the police: vandalizing houses. When he allows himself to be caught, it is for the purpose of humiliating Sheppard, who finally gives up, bleakly recognizing his limitations and his failure. But he has another surprise coming, one that will completely open his eyes to his real poverty, and leave him far more destitute than Johnson ever was.

"Revelation" was the last story Flannery O'Connor wrote under the illusion that her life would continue on a fairly even keel. It was completed in 1963, and a few revisions were made in January of 1964. It was then sent to the *Sewanee Review*, which published it in the Spring issue. When the proofs came back in February, she was in the hospital being prepared for surgery. Any operation is inadvisable for a lupus patient, but this one could not be avoided. Every precaution was taken, but the lupus was reactivated in a severe form. She was now in the last year of her life, and as she had not felt really well during the preceding fall while she was working on "Revelation," she may have understood this intuitively. In any event, in these last three stories she was to write in that final year there appear features that may be seen as summings-up of all she had been trying to do in her work. There is a metaphor for the vision behind her work as a whole; there is a telling image of herself as an artist and the effect she hoped her works would have on readers; and finally, a portrait of strength of character, and of faith, hope, and love, against all odds and in the face of death itself.

Most of "Revelation" takes place in a doctor's office. Here an assortment of wonderfully drawn characters from every social stratum, defined most of all by what they say, await their turns. The central figure is a country *pharisienne*, a monument of complacency and self-congratulation, who observes and categorizes the others according to a system of her own that reflects all too sharply the social stratification more widely accepted than most of us would like to think. Ruby Turpin, accompanying her husband who has been kicked in the shin by a cow, indirectly communicates her low opinion of everyone there except a "stylish lady" waiting with her sick and very ugly daughter. The daughter, a churlish "book-worm," almost insistently named Mary Grace, is pigeon-holed by Mrs. Turpin with the words, "You must be in college, I see you reading a book there."

The book the girl is reading is called *Human Development*, but it cannot distract her enough from the stream of obtusely self-satisfied commentary and self-praise she is being forced to listen to, and the state of mind it all implies. Driven finally into an uncontrollable rage, the girl breaks the outward calm of the scene by throwing her book straight at Mrs. Turpin's head and leaping for her throat. As she is being restrained and sedated, she delivers an order to the now speechless tormentor: "Go back to hell where you came from, you old wart hog."

Although Mrs. Turpin cannot imagine why such a message should be addressed to *her*, she knows that it is, recognizes the power of authenticity in it, and it continues to haunt her even when she and her husband have gone home to rest and recover from their shock. Later in the afternoon, she sets off to "scoot down" with a hose her hogs in the "pig parlor," and there, like what O'Connor called a "female Jacob shouting at the Lord over a hogpen," she has it out with Him. The blessing she extracts is a vision that grandly sums up, in an unforgettable metaphor, the whole point of O'Connor's fiction: the proper, sensible, and complacent members of society, their specious virtues being burned away, are shown bringing up the rear of the great horde of preposterous humanity making its way heavenward into the starry skies.

What image could better express what Flannery O'Connor has tried to show us in her stories, long and short? And what did she herself do but "throw the book" at us all? There is nothing self-congratulatory in her portrait of Mary Grace, who is one of the ugliest creatures she ever invented. But even this fact reminds us that her stories were at times and by some as much dispraised for their "ugliness" as they were praised for their power.

Both "Parker's Back" and "Judgement Day" were written when she was more or less *in extremis*. She kept the notebook in which she was working on the former under her pillow in the hospital where doctors were making a final effort to save her life. When she went home for a last short stay, the doctor told her that she was not to work, but that it would be all right for her to write a little fiction—a misimpression that gave her some dry amusement. Three weeks later, she was dead at the age of thirty-nine.

"Parker's Back" was the last story she wrote, although it precedes "Judgement Day" in the order of the collection. O.E. Parker, the baffled ex-sailor, whose unrecognized spiritual urge for beauty and order is expressed by the tattoos he compulsively acquires, is a new kind of figure for O'Connor, and in the short story becomes one of her most memorable vehicles for totally unanticipated religious experience.

Parker is shown at the outset as in thrall to a homely and arid young woman, Sarah Ruth, the waspish daughter of a "straight-gospel preacher," away "spreading it in Florida." The sailor cannot understand the attraction, but marries this spiritually prickly maiden, chiefly because he "can't get her any other way," but also because he feels his familiar instinctive compulsion, which has characterized his whole life. In his youth, the one thing that has stirred him to his depths, and brought into play his *will*, is the sight of a tattooed man in a carnival, who seems to him to suggest a world of beauty he has never before imagined. He at once begins his emulation, but his efforts do not turn out so happily: when he studies his "overall look," he finds that the effect was "not one intricate arabesque of colors but of something haphazard and botched"—an image for his whole life and acquired experience so far.

When he learns that he can in no way please his shrewish wife, he decides to get one more picture punctured into his skin, this time a religious subject that he feels cannot fail to win her over, even though she has let him know that she dislikes his tattoos as much or more than she disapproves of the rest of him. From an assortment—"The Good Shepherd, The Smiling Jesus, Forbid Them Not, Jesus the Physician's Friend, and some other less reassuring versions," he chooses from the sample book one that has stopped him by the stare of "all-demanding eyes": a Byzantine head of Christ, Pantocrator—All-mighty. There is no place left for the design on Parker except his back, and although he will be able to see it himself only with the aid of "double-mirrors," he knows that this is the one he wants.

The work is undertaken by an "artist," who is himself decorated with a miniature but perfect owl (symbolizing wisdom) on the top of his bald head. At Parker's demand, he reproduces the design exactly as it was in the book, in mosaic style, composed of tiny blocks of color which eventually form a whole. Here indeed is an image of the artist in general, who imprints with a careful structure important designs upon our minds (even if only on the backs of our minds), which will ultimately have their effect on us and our understanding, if we take the trouble to look at them. Even if we don't, they are still there, affecting us unconsciously. In particular, it is an image of Flannery O'Connor as the artist she was, for the image she imprinted on us all by her work is that of Christ, All-mighty and Judge, with all-demanding eyes which "will be obeyed."

As "Parker's Back" was in some ways culled from the ruined hopes for a novel (in the fragments of which another but very different tattooed man appears), "Judgement Day," the penultimate story written, also had its roots in the past. O'Connor had never relinquished her early story, "The Geranium," although it had been published. It had never satisfied her, except for the protagonist and his situation in itself: an old Georgia country man, exiled through his own prideful mistake in judgment to a narrow apartment in New York City, where he must live miserably in an alien environment with a duty-proud daughter and her hostile husband. In the earlier story, old Dudley is a passive and hopeless figure; and even in his loneliness, he brusquely rejects the overtures of a kind young black who treats him with friendliness but as an equal, something he is too inflexible and foolish to accept. He takes to his chair and will no longer leave the apartment, finding his only consolation in the sight of a sickly geranium on a window-ledge across the air shaft from his room. One morning he sees that the geranium has fallen and is lying on the sidewalk in its cracked pot, six floors below. The owner of the plant rudely refuses Dudley's suggestion that it be retrieved, telling him to go down and get it himself if he likes. Dudley tries, but cannot bring himself to leave the room, lest he run into the black who has "caught" him pretending to fire a hunting gun on the stairs, and before whom he feels a permanent humiliation. His nasty neighbor across the air shaft then invites him to stop looking at his window anyway, and Dudley is left alone with his pride and sorrow.

Apparently troubled for years by the inconclusiveness of the story, complete as it was in purely dramatic terms, O'Connor made a third attempt to rewrite it. One of the scenes in the last version is drawn from the abandoned third novel, to be used in a story she thought she had time to complete.

The mature style of "Judgement Day" is richer than in either of the earlier versions, but the greater change lies in another realm: Tanner's personality and his attitude toward his predicament, and the action his spirit leads him to take in dealing with it. This is a radical departure from the first flaccid sufferer, a permanent prisoner of his pride. Tanner is a more humble but much more powerful and courageous old man, ready to reverse his early sinful mistake—coming north to avoid working for the newly-rich black man who has just bought the field in which Tanner and his old black friend, Coleman Parrum, have built a shack and are living. Tanner now knows exactly what he wants, which is to get back to Georgia, dead or alive, and he takes heroic steps to accomplish this end, even after he has suffered a stroke.

Again the current social scene of the sixties and the new open hostility of many blacks, is taken into account, and this time it is the friendly overture of the white man that is contemptuously repulsed by the black actor who lives on the same floor. Tanner had hoped they might go fishing together, but his approach is so anachronistically tactless that his effort to make some human contact is foredoomed, even dangerous. This failure makes him all the more eager to get home to his former housemate and real friend. He now knows that he would be willing to work for the new black land-owner or anyone else, in order to stay where he knows he belongs. He has renounced his former pride and he humbly sets out for home, toward what seems for him a beatific vision: the sight of the face of the stationmaster in his green eyeshade (a vaguely Jungian image), and the wrinkled face of Coleman, bending over him—or even over his coffin—in the cold early morning air of home. Tottering off, fortified by a psalm, he meets his fate, but gains his destination, with all that it implies in Flannery O'Connor's imagery.

His aggressive grappling with the difficulties he has created for himself suggests the development in the author's sense of how all difficulties ought to be met. Adversity in her own life, endured and countered with faith and energy, had strengthened her, clarified her thinking, and steadied as well as focused her hope. She seems to have preferred to leave as implicit recommendation his active courage, humility, and sureness of vision in exile, rather than the pitiable despair and paralysis of Dudley. Perhaps, too, she simply wanted to get the poor old man out of New York, "no kind of place," where she had left him so long ago.

Nothing I have said in these pages can suggest the richness and craftsmanship of the works in these three books you are about to read. The only way to find out all that is in a good story—its artistry and its multi-layered meanings—is to read it, which is to say, experience it. I would ask only that you keep in mind some of the references I have proposed to you, in order to deepen your understanding of what underlies the marvelous surface of Flannery O'Connor's tales. When you have understood them well, you will find more happy endings than you might otherwise have recognized. To begin with, I would remind you of what she said in her own introduction to the second edition of *Wise Blood*: that the book had been written with zest and was meant to be read that way. This is equally true of the rest.

—SALLY FITZGERALD

WISE BLOOD

Wise Blood has reached the age of ten and is still alive. My critical powers are just sufficient to determine this, and I am gratified to be able to say it. The book was written with zest and, if possible, it should be read that way. It is a comic novel about a Christian *malgré lui*, and as such, very serious, for all comic novels that are any good must be about matters of life and death. *Wise Blood* was written by an author congenitally innocent of theory, but one with certain preoccupations. That belief in Christ is to some a matter of life and death has been a stumbling block for readers who would prefer to think it a matter of no great consequence. For them Hazel Motes' integrity lies in his trying with such vigor to get rid of the ragged figure who moves from tree to tree in the back of his mind. For the author Hazel's integrity lies in his not being able to. Does one's integrity ever lie in what he is not able to do? I think that usually it does, for free will does not mean one will, but many wills conflicting in one man. Freedom cannot be conceived simply. It is a mystery and one which a novel, even a comic novel, can only be asked to deepen.

1962

Chapter 1

Hazel Motes sat at a forward angle on the green plush train seat, looking one minute at the window as if he might want to jump out of it, and the next down the aisle at the other end of the car. The train was racing through tree tops that fell away at intervals and showed the sun standing, very red, on the edge of the farthest woods. Nearer, the plowed fields curved and faded and the few hogs nosing in the furrows looked like large spotted stones. Mrs. Wally Bee Hitchcock, who was facing Motes in the section, said that she thought the early evening like this was the prettiest time of day and she asked him if he didn't think so too. She was a fat woman with pink collars and cuffs and pear-shaped legs that slanted off the train seat and didn't reach the floor.

He looked at her a second and, without answering, leaned forward and stared down the length of the car again. She turned to see what was back there but all she saw was a child peering around one of the sections and, farther up at the end of the car, the porter opening the closet where the sheets were kept.

"I guess you're going home," she said, turning back to him again. He didn't look, to her, much over twenty, but he had a stiff black broad-brimmed hat on his lap, a hat that an elderly country preacher would wear. His suit was a glaring blue and the price tag was still stapled on the sleeve of it.

He didn't answer her or move his eyes from whatever he was looking at. The sack at his feet was an army duffel bag and she decided that he had been in the army and had been released and that now he was going home. She wanted to get close enough to see what the suit had cost him but she found herself squinting instead at his eyes, trying almost to look into them. They were the color of pecan shells and set in deep sockets. The outline of a skull under his skin was plain and insistent.

She felt irked and wrenched her attention loose and squinted at the price tag. The suit had cost him $11.98. She felt that that placed him and looked at his face again

3

as if she were fortified against it now. He had a nose like a shrike's bill and a long vertical crease on either side of his mouth; his hair looked as if it had been permanently flattened under the heavy hat, but his eyes were what held her attention longest. Their settings were so deep that they seemed, to her, almost like passages leading somewhere and she leaned halfway across the space that separated the two seats, trying to see into them. He turned toward the window suddenly and then almost as quickly turned back again to where his stare had been fixed.

What he was looking at was the porter. When he had first got on the train, the porter had been standing between the two cars—a thick-figured man with a round yellow bald head. Haze had stopped and the porter's eyes had turned toward him and away, indicating which car he was to go into. When he didn't go, the porter said, "To the left," irritably, "to the left," and Haze had moved on.

"Well," Mrs. Hitchcock said, "there's no place like home."

He gave her a glance and saw the flat of her face, reddish under a cap of fox-colored hair. She had got on two stops back. He had never seen her before that. "I got to go see the porter," he said. He got up and went toward the end of the car where the porter had begun making up a berth. He stopped beside him and leaned on a seat arm, but the porter didn't look at him. He was pulling a wall of the section farther out.

"How long does it take you to make one up?"

"Seven minutes," the porter said, not looking at him.

Haze sat down on the seat arm. He said, "I'm from Eastrod."

"That isn't on this line," the porter said. "You on the wrong train."

"Going to the city," Haze said. "I said I was raised in Eastrod."

The porter didn't say anything.

"Eastrod," Haze said, louder.

The porter jerked the shade down. "You want your berth made up now, or what you standing there for?" he asked.

"Eastrod," Haze said. "Near Melsy."

The porter wrenched one side of the seat flat. "I'm from Chicago," he said. He wrenched the other side down. When he bent over, the back of his neck came out in three bulges.

"Yeah, I bet you are," Haze said with a leer.

"Your feet in the middle of the aisle. Somebody going to want to get by you," the porter said, turning suddenly and brushing past.

Haze got up and hung there a few seconds. He looked as if he were held by a rope caught in the middle of his back and attached to the train ceiling. He watched the porter move in a fine controlled lurch down the aisle and disappear at the other end of the car. He knew him to be a Parrum nigger from Eastrod. He went back to his section and folded into a slouched position and settled one foot on a pipe that ran under the window. Eastrod filled his head and then went out beyond and filled the space that stretched from the train across the empty darkening fields. He saw the two houses and the rust-colored road and the few Negro shacks and the one barn and the stall with the red and white CCC snuff ad peeling across the side of it.

"Are you going home?" Mrs. Hitchcock asked.

He looked at her sourly and gripped the black hat by the brim. "No, I ain't," he said in a sharp high nasal Tennessee voice.

Mrs. Hitchcock said neither was she. She told him she had been a Miss Weatherman before she married and that she was going to Florida to visit her married daughter, Sarah Lucile. She said it seemed like she had never had time to take a trip that far off. The way things happened, one thing after another, it seemed like time went by so fast you couldn't tell if you were young or old.

He thought he could tell her she was old if she asked him. He stopped listening to her after a while. The porter passed back up the aisle and didn't look at him. Mrs. Hitchcock lost her train of talk. "I guess you're on your way to visit somebody?" she asked.

"Going to Taulkinham," he said and ground himself into the seat and looked at the window. "Don't know nobody there, but I'm going to do some things.

"I'm going to do some things I never have done before," he said and gave her a sidelong glance and curled his mouth slightly.

She said she knew an Albert Sparks from Taulkinham. She said he was her sister-in-law's brother-in-law and that he . . .

"I ain't from Taulkinham," he said. "I said I'm going there, that's all." Mrs. Hitchcock began to talk again but he cut her short and said, "That porter was raised in the same place where I was raised but he says he's from Chicago."

Mrs. Hitchcock said she knew a man who lived in Chi . . .

"You might as well go one place as another," he said. "That's all I know."

Mrs. Hitchcock said well that time flies. She said she hadn't seen her sister's children in five years and she didn't know if she'd know them if she saw them. There were three of them, Roy, Bubber, and John Wesley. John Wesley was six years old and he had written her a letter, dear Mammadoll. They called her Mammadoll and her husband Papadoll . . .

"I reckon you think you been redeemed," he said.

Mrs. Hitchcock snatched at her collar.

"I reckon you think you been redeemed," he repeated.

She blushed. After a second she said yes, life was an inspiration and then she said she was hungry and asked him if he didn't want to go into the diner. He put on the fierce black hat and followed her out of the car.

The dining car was full and people were waiting to get in it. He and Mrs. Hitchcock stood in line for a half-hour, rocking in the narrow passageway and every few minutes flattening themselves against the side to let a trickle of people through. Mrs. Hitchcock talked to the woman on the side of her. Hazel Motes looked at the wall. Mrs. Hitchcock told the woman about her sister's husband who was with the City Water Works in Toolafalls, Alabama, and the lady told about a cousin who had cancer of the throat. Finally they got almost up to the entrance of the diner and could see inside it. There was a steward beckoning people to places and handing out menus. He was a white man with greased black hair and a greased black look to his suit. He moved like a crow, darting from table to table. He motioned for two people and the line moved up so that Haze and Mrs. Hitchcock and the lady she was talking to were ready to go next. In a minute two more people left. The steward beckoned and Mrs. Hitchcock and the woman walked in and Haze followed them. The man stopped him and said, "Only two," and pushed him back to the doorway.

Haze's face turned an ugly red. He tried to get behind the next person and then he tried to get through the line to go back to the car he had come from but there were too many people bunched in the opening. He had to stand there while everyone around looked at him. No one left for a while. Finally a woman at the far end of the car got up and the steward jerked his hand. Haze hesitated and saw the hand jerk again. He lurched up the aisle, falling against two tables on the way and getting his hand wet in somebody's coffee. The steward placed him with three youngish women dressed like parrots.

Their hands were resting on the table, red-speared at

the tips. He sat down and wiped his hand on the tablecloth.
He didn't take off his hat. The women had finished eating
and were smoking cigarettes. They stopped talking when
he sat down. He pointed to the first thing on the menu and
the steward, standing over him, said, "Write it down, sonny,"
and winked at one of the women; she made a noise in
her nose. He wrote it down and the steward went away
with it. He sat and looked in front of him, glum and intense,
at the neck of the woman across from him. At intervals
her hand holding the cigarette would pass the spot on her
neck; it would go out of his sight and then it would pass
again, going back down to the table; in a second a straight
line of smoke would blow in his face. After it had blown
at him three or four times, he looked at her. She had a
bold game-hen expression and small eyes pointed directly
on him.

"If you've been redeemed," he said, "I wouldn't want
to be." Then he turned his head to the window. He saw
his pale reflection with the dark empty space outside coming
through it. A boxcar roared past, chopping the empty space
in two, and one of the women laughed.

"Do you think I believe in Jesus?" he said, leaning toward
her and speaking almost as if he were breathless. "Well
I wouldn't even if He existed. Even if He was on this
train."

"Who said you had to?" she asked in a poisonous Eastern
voice.

He drew back.

The waiter brought his dinner. He began eating slowly
at first, then faster as the women concentrated on watching
the muscles that stood out on his jaw when he chewed.
He was eating something spotted with eggs and livers. He
finished that and drank his coffee and then pulled his money
out. The steward saw him but he wouldn't come total the
bill. Every time he passed the table, he would wink at
the women and stare at Haze. Mrs. Hitchcock and the
lady had already finished and gone. Finally the man came
and added up the bill. Haze shoved the money at him and
then pushed past him out of the car.

For a while he stood between two train cars where there
was fresh air of a sort and made a cigarette. Then the porter
passed between the two cars. "Hey you, Parrum," he called.

The porter didn't stop.

Haze followed him into the car. All the berths were
made up. The man in the station in Melsy had sold him
a berth because he said he would have to sit up all night
in the coaches; he had sold him an upper one. Haze went

to it and pulled his sack down and went into the men's room and got ready for the night. He was too full and he wanted to hurry and get in the berth and lie down. He thought he would lie there and look out the window and watch how the country went by a train at night. A sign said to get the porter to let you into the uppers. He stuck his sack up into his berth and then went to look for the porter. He didn't find him at one end of the car and he started back to the other. Going around the corner he ran into something heavy and pink; it gasped and muttered, "Clumsy!" It was Mrs. Hitchcock in a pink wrapper, with her hair in knots around her head. She looked at him with her eyes squinted nearly shut. The knobs framed her face like dark toadstools. She tried to get past him and he tried to let her but they were both moving the same way each time. Her face became purplish except for little white marks over it that didn't heat up. She drew herself stiff and stopped and said, "What is the matter with you?" He slipped past her and dashed down the aisle and ran into the porter so that the porter fell down.

"You got to let me into the berth, Parrum," he said.

The porter picked himself up and went lurching down the aisle and after a minute he came lurching back again, stone-faced, with the ladder. Haze stood watching him while he put the ladder up; then he started up it. Halfway up, he turned and said, "I remember you. Your father was a nigger named Cash Parrum. You can't go back there neither, nor anybody else, not if they wanted to."

"I'm from Chicago," the porter said in an irritated voice. "My name is not Parrum."

"Cash is dead," Haze said. "He got the cholera from a pig."

The porter's mouth jerked down and he said, "My father was a railroad man."

Haze laughed. The porter jerked the ladder off suddenly with a wrench of his arm that sent the boy clutching at the blanket into the berth. He lay on his stomach for a few minutes and didn't move. After a while he turned and found the light and looked around him. There was no window. He was closed up in the thing except for a little space over the curtain. The top of the berth was low and curved over. He lay down and noticed that the curved top looked as if it were not quite closed; it looked as if it were closing. He lay there for a while, not moving. There was something in his throat like a sponge with an egg taste; he didn't want to turn over for fear it would move. He wanted the light off. He reached up without turning and felt for the button and snapped it and the darkness sank down on him and then faded a little with light from the aisle that came in through the foot of space not closed. He wanted it all dark, he didn't want it diluted. He heard the porter's footsteps coming down the aisle, soft into the rug, coming steadily down, brushing against the green curtains and fading up the other way out of hearing. Then after a while when he was almost asleep, he thought he heard them again coming back. His curtains stirred and the footsteps faded.

In his half-sleep he thought where he was lying was like a coffin. The first coffin he had seen with someone in it was his grandfather's. They had left it propped open with a stick of kindling the night it had sat in the house with the old man in it, and Haze had watched from a distance, thinking: he ain't going to let them shut it on him; when the time comes, his elbow is going to shoot into the crack. His grandfather had been a circuit preacher, a waspish old man who had ridden over three counties with Jesus hidden in his head like a stinger. When it was time to bury him, they shut the top of his box down and he didn't make a move.

Haze had had two younger brothers; one died in infancy and was put in a small box. The other fell in front of a mowing machine when he was seven. His box was about half the size of an ordinary one, and when they shut it, Haze ran and opened it up again. They said it was because he was heartbroken to part with his brother, but it was not; it was because he had thought, what if he had been in it and they had shut it on him.

He was asleep now and he dreamed he was at his father's burying again. He saw him humped over on his hands and knees in his coffin, being carried that way to the graveyard. "If I keep my can in the air," he heard the old man say, "nobody can shut nothing on me," but when they got his box to the hole, they let it drop down with a thud and his father flattened out like anybody else. The train jolted and stirred him half awake again and he thought, there must have been twenty-five people in Eastrod then, three Motes. Now there were no more Motes, no more Ashfields, no more Blasengames, Feys, Jacksons . . . or Parrums—even niggers wouldn't have it. Turning in the road, he saw in the dark the store boarded and the barn leaning and the smaller house half carted away, the porch gone and no floor in the hall.

It had not been that way when he was eighteen years old and had left it. Then there had been ten people there and he had not noticed that it had got smaller from his father's time. He had left it when he was eighteen years old because the army had called him. He had thought at first he would shoot his foot and not go. He was going to be a preacher like his grandfather and a preacher can always do without a foot. A preacher's power is in his neck and tongue and arm. His grandfather had traveled three counties in a Ford automobile. Every fourth Saturday he had driven into Eastrod as if he were just in time to save them all from Hell, and he was shouting before he had the car door open. People gathered around his Ford because he seemed to dare them to. He would climb up on the nose of it and preach from there and sometimes he would climb onto the top of it and shout down at them. They were like stones! he would shout. But Jesus had died to redeem them! Jesus was so soul-hungry that He had died, one death for all, but He would have died every soul's death for one! Did they understand that? Did they understand that for each stone soul, He would have died ten million deaths, had His arms and legs stretched on the cross and nailed ten million times for one of them? (The old man would point to his grandson, Haze. He had a particular disrespect for him because his own face was repeated almost exactly in the child's and seemed to mock him.) Did they know that even for that boy there, for that mean sinful unthinking boy standing there with his dirty hands clenching and unclenching at his sides, Jesus would die ten million deaths before He would let him lose his soul? He would chase him over the waters of sin! Did they doubt Jesus could walk on the waters of sin? That boy had been redeemed and Jesus wasn't going to leave him ever. Jesus would never let him forget he was redeemed. What did the sinner think there was to be gained? Jesus would have him in the end!

The boy didn't need to hear it. There was already a deep black wordless conviction in him that the way to avoid Jesus was to avoid sin. He knew by the time he was twelve years old that he was going to be a preacher. Later he saw Jesus move from tree to tree in the back of his mind, a wild ragged figure motioning him to turn around and come off into the dark where he was not sure of his footing, where he might be walking on the water and not know it and then suddenly know it and drown. Where he wanted to stay was in Eastrod with his two eyes open, and his hands always handling the familiar thing, his feet on the known track, and his tongue not too loose. When he was eighteen and the army called him, he saw the war as a trick to lead him into temptation, and he would have shot his foot except that he trusted himself to get back in a few months, uncorrupted. He had a strong confidence in his power to resist evil; it was something he had inherited, like his face, from his grandfather. He thought that if the government wasn't through with him in four months, he would leave anyway. He had thought, then when he was eighteen years old, that he would give them exactly four months of his time. He was gone four years; he didn't get back, even for a visit.

The only things from Eastrod he took into the army with him were a black Bible and a pair of silver-rimmed spectacles that had belonged to his mother. He had gone to a country school where he had learned to read and write but that it was wiser not to; the Bible was the only book he read. He didn't read it often but when he did he wore his mother's glasses. They tired his eyes so that after a short time he was always obliged to stop. He meant to tell anyone in the army who invited him to sin that he was from Eastrod, Tennessee, and that he meant to get back there and stay back there, that he was going to be a preacher of the gospel and that he wasn't going to have his soul damned by the government or by any foreign place it sent him to.

After a few weeks in the camp, when he had some friends —they were not actually friends but he had to live with them—he was offered the chance he had been waiting for; the invitation. He took his mother's glasses out of his pocket and put them on. Then he told them he wouldn't go with them for a million dollars and a feather bed to lie on; he said he was from Eastrod, Tennessee, and that he was not going to have his soul damned by the government or any foreign place they . . . but his voice cracked and he didn't finish. He only stared at them, trying to steel his face. His friends told him that nobody was interested in his goddam soul unless it was the priest and he managed to answer that no priest taking orders from no pope was going to tamper with his soul. They told him he didn't have any soul and left for their brothel.

He took a long time to believe them because he wanted to believe them. All he wanted was to believe them and get rid of it once and for all, and he saw the opportunity here to get rid of it without corruption, to be converted to nothing instead of to evil. The army sent him halfway around the world and forgot him. He was wounded and they remembered him long enough to take the shrapnel out of his chest—they said they took it out but they never showed it to him and he felt it still in there, rusted, and poisoning him—and then they sent him to another desert and forgot him again. He had all the time he could want to study his soul in and assure himself that it was not there. When he was thoroughly convinced, he saw that this was something that he had always known. The misery he had was a longing for home; it had nothing to do with Jesus. When the army finally let him go, he was pleased to think that he was still uncorrupted. All he wanted was to get back to Eastrod, Tennessee. The black Bible and his mother's glasses were still in the bottom of his duffel bag. He didn't read any book now but he kept the Bible because it had come from home. He kept the glasses in case his vision should ever become dim.

When the army had released him two days before in a city about three hundred miles north of where he wanted to be, he had gone immediately to the railroad station there and bought a ticket to Melsy, the nearest railroad stop to Eastrod. Then since he had to wait four hours for the train, he went into a dark dry-goods store near the station. It was a thin cardboard-smelling store that got darker as it got deeper. He went deep into it and was sold a blue suit and a dark hat. He had his army suit put in a paper sack and he stuffed it into a trashbox on the corner. Once outside in the light, the new suit turned glare-blue and the lines of the hat seemed to stiffen fiercely.

He was in Melsy at five o'clock in the afternoon and he caught a ride on a cotton-seed truck that took him more than half the distance to Eastrod. He walked the rest of the way and got there at nine o'clock at night, when it had just got dark. The house was as dark as the night and open to it and though he saw that the fence around it had partly fallen and that weeds were growing through the porch floor, he didn't realize all at once that it was only a shell, that there was nothing here but the skeleton of a house. He twisted an envelope and struck a match to it and went through all the empty rooms, upstairs and down. When the envelope burnt out, he lit another one and went through them all again. That night he slept on the floor in the kitchen, and a board fell on his head out of the roof and cut his face.

There was nothing left in the house but the chifforobe in the kitchen. His mother had always slept in the kitchen and had her walnut chifforobe in there. She had given thirty dollars for it and hadn't bought herself anything else big again. Whoever had got everything else, had left that. He opened all the drawers. There were two lengths of wrapping cord in the top one and nothing in the others. He was surprised nobody had come and stolen a chifforobe like that. He took the wrapping cord and tied it around the legs and through the floor boards and - left a piece of paper in each of the drawers: THIS SHIFFER-ROBE BE-LONGS TO HAZEL MOTES. DO NOT STEAL IT OR YOU WILL BE HUNTED DOWN AND KILLED.

He thought about the chifforobe in his half-sleep and decided his mother would rest easier in her grave, knowing it was guarded. If she came looking any time at night, she would see. He wondered if she walked at night and came there ever. She would come with that look on her face, unrested and looking; the same look he had seen through the crack of her coffin. He had seen her face through the crack when they were shutting the top on her. He was sixteen then. He had seen the shadow that came down over her face and pulled her mouth down as if she wasn't any more satisfied dead than alive, as if she were going to spring up and shove the lid back and fly out and satisfy herself: but they shut it. She might have been going to fly out of there, she might have been going to spring. He saw her in his sleep, terrible, like a huge bat, dart from the closing, fly out of there, but it was falling dark on top of her, closing down all the time. From inside he saw it closing, coming closer closer down and cutting off the light and the room. He opened his eyes and saw it closing and he sprang up between the crack and wedged his head and shoulders through it and hung there, dizzy, with the dim light of the train slowly showing the rug below. He hung there over the top of the berth curtain and saw the porter at the other end of the car, a white shape in the darkness, standing there watching him and not moving.

"I'm sick!" he called. "I can't be closed up in this thing. Get me out!"

The porter stood watching him and didn't move.

"Jesus," Haze said, "Jesus."

The porter didn't move. "Jesus been a long time gone," he said in a sour triumphant voice.

Chapter 2

He didn't get to the city until six the next evening. That morning he had got off the train at a junction stop to get some air and while he had been looking the other way, the train had slid off. He had run after it but his hat had blown away and he had had to run in the other direction to save the hat. Fortunately, he had carried his duffel bag out with him lest someone should steal something out of it. He had to wait six hours at the junction stop until the right train came.

When he got to Taulkinham, as soon as he stepped off the train, he began to see signs and lights. PEANUTS, WESTERN UNION, AJAX, TAXI, HOTEL, CANDY. Most of them were electric and moved up and down or blinked frantically. He walked very slowly, carrying his duffel bag by the neck. His head turned to one side and then the other, first toward one sign and then another. He walked the length of the station and then he walked back as if he might be going to get on the train again. His face was stern and determined under the heavy hat. No one observing him would have known that he had no place to go. He walked up and down the crowded waiting room two or three times, but he did not want to sit on the benches there. He wanted a private place to go to.

Finally he pushed open a door at one end of the station where a plain black and white sign said, MEN'S TOILET. WHITE. He went into a narrow room lined on one side with wash-basins and on the other with a row of wooden stalls. The walls of this room had once been a bright cheerful yellow but now they were more nearly green and were decorated with handwriting and with various detailed drawings of the parts of the body of both men and women. Some of the stalls had doors on them and on one of the doors, written with what must have been a crayon, was the large word, WELCOME, followed by three exclamation points and something that looked like a snake. Haze entered this one.

He had been sitting in the narrow box for some time, studying the inscriptions on the sides and door, before he

14

noticed one that was to the left over the toilet paper. It was written in a drunken-looking hand. It said,

Mrs. Leora Watts!
60 Buckley Road
The friendliest bed in town!
Brother.

After a while he took a pencil out of his pocket and wrote down the address on the back of an envelope.

Outside he got in a yellow taxi and told the driver where he wanted to go. The driver was a small man with a big leather cap on his head and the tip of a cigar coming out from the center of his mouth. They had driven a few blocks before Haze noticed him squinting at him through the rear-view mirror. "You ain't no friend of hers, are you?" the driver asked.

"I never saw her before," Haze said.

"Where'd you hear about her? She don't usually have no preachers for company." He did not disturb the position of the cigar when he spoke; he was able to speak on either side of it.

"I ain't any preacher," Haze said, frowning. "I only seen her name in the toilet."

"You look like a preacher," the driver said. "That hat looks like a preacher's hat."

"It ain't," Haze said, and leaned forward and gripped the back of the front seat. "It's just a hat."

They stopped in front of a small one-story house between a filling station and a vacant lot. Haze got out and paid his fare through the window.

"It ain't only the hat," the driver said. "It's a look in your face somewheres."

"Listen," Haze said, tilting the hat over one eye, "I'm not a preacher."

"I understand," the driver said. "It ain't anybody perfect on this green earth of God's, preachers nor nobody else. And you can tell people better how terrible sin is if you know from your own personal experience."

Haze put his head in at the window, knocking the hat accidentally straight again. He seemed to have knocked his face straight too for it became completely expressionless. "Listen," he said, "get this: I don't believe in anything."

The driver took the stump of cigar out of his mouth. "Not in nothing at all?" he asked, leaving his mouth open after the question.

"I don't have to say it but once to nobody," Haze said.

The driver closed his mouth and after a second he returned the piece of cigar to it. "That's the trouble with you preachers," he said. "You've all got too good to believe in anything," and he drove off with a look of disgust and righteousness.

Haze turned and looked at the house he was going into. It was little more than a shack but there was a warm glow in one front window. He went up on the front porch and put his eye to a convenient crack in the shade, and found himself looking directly at a large white knee. After some time he moved away from the crack and tried the front door. It was not locked and he went into a small dark hall with a door on either side of it. The door to the left was cracked and let out a narrow shaft of light. He moved into the light and looked through the crack.

Mrs. Watts was sitting alone in a white iron bed, cutting her toenails with a large pair of scissors. She was a big woman with very yellow hair and white skin that glistened with a greasy preparation. She had on a pink nightgown that would better have fit a smaller figure.

Haze made a noise with the doorknob and she looked up and observed him standing behind the crack. She had a bold steady penetrating stare. After a minute, she turned it away from him and began cutting her toenails again.

He went in and stood looking around him. There was nothing much in the room but the bed and a bureau and a rocking chair full of dirty clothes. He went to the bureau and fingered a nail file and then an empty jelly glass while he looked into the yellowish mirror and watched Mrs. Watts, slightly distorted, grinning at him. His senses were stirred to the limit. He turned quickly and went to her bed and sat down on the far corner of it. He drew a long draught of air through one side of his nose and began to run his hand carefully along the sheet.

The pink tip of Mrs. Watts's tongue appeared and moistened her lower lip. She seemed just as glad to see him as if he had been an old friend but she didn't say anything.

He picked up her foot, which was heavy but not cold, and moved it about an inch to one side, and kept his hand on it.

Mrs. Watts's mouth split in a wide full grin that showed her teeth. They were small and pointed and speckled with green and there was a wide space between each one. She reached out and gripped Haze's arm just above the elbow. "You huntin' something?" she drawled.

If she had not had him so firmly by the arm, he might have leaped out the window. Involuntarily his lips formed the words, "Yes, mam," but no sound came through them.

"Something on your mind?" Mrs. Watts asked, pulling his rigid figure a little closer.

"Listen," he said, keeping his voice tightly under control, "I come for the usual business."

Mrs. Watts's mouth became more round, as if she were perplexed at this waste of words. "Make yourself at home," she said simply.

They stared at each other for almost a minute and neither moved. Then he said in a voice that was higher than his usual voice, "What I mean to have you know is: I'm no goddam preacher."

Mrs. Watts eyed him steadily with only a slight smirk. Then she put her other hand under his face and tickled it in a motherly way. "That's okay, son," she said. "Momma don't mind if you ain't a preacher."

Chapter 3

His second night in Taulkinham, Hazel Motes walked along down town close to the store fronts but not looking in them. The black sky was underpinned with long silver streaks that looked like scaffolding and depth on depth behind it were thousands of stars that all seemed to be moving very slowly as if they were about some vast construction work that involved the whole order of the universe and would take all time to complete. No one was paying any attention to the sky. The stores in Taulkinham stayed open on Thursday nights so that people could have an extra opportunity to see what was for sale. Haze's shadow was now behind him and now before him and now and then broken up by other people's shadows, but when it was by itself, stretching behind him, it was a thin nervous shadow walking backwards. His neck was thrust forward as if he were trying to smell something that was always being drawn away. The glary light from the store windows made his blue suit look purple.

After a while he stopped where a lean-faced man had a card table set up in front of a department store and was demonstrating a potato peeler. The man had on a small canvas hat and a shirt patterned with bunches of upside-down pheasants and quail and bronze turkeys. He was pitching his voice under the street noises so that it reached every ear distinctly as if in a private conversation. A few people gathered around. There were two buckets on the card table, one empty and the other full of potatoes. Between the two buckets there was a pyramid of green cardboard boxes and, on top of the stack, one peeler was open for demonstration. The man stood in front of this altar, pointing over it at various people. "How about you?" he said, pointing at a damp-haired pimpled boy. "You ain't gonna let one of these go by?" He stuck a brown potato in one side of the open machine. The machine was a square tin box with a red handle, and as he turned the handle, the potato went into the box and then in a second, backed out the other side, white. "You ain't gonna let one of these go by!" he said.

The boy guffawed and looked at the other people gathered around. He had yellow hair and a fox-shaped face.

"What's yer name?" the peeler man asked.

"Name Enoch Emery," the boy said and snuffled.

"Boy with a pretty name like that ought to have one of these," the man said, rolling his eyes, trying to warm up the others. Nobody laughed but the boy. Then a man standing across from Hazel Motes laughed, not a pleasant laugh but one that had a sharp edge. He was a tall cadaverous man with a black suit and a black hat on. He had on dark glasses and his cheeks were streaked with lines that looked as if they had been painted on and had faded. They gave him the expression of a grinning mandrill. As soon as he laughed, he began to move forward in a deliberate way, jiggling a tin cup in one hand and tapping a white cane in front of him with the other. Just behind him there came a child, handing out leaflets. She had on a black dress and a black knitted cap pulled down low on her forehead; there was a fringe of brown hair sticking out from it on either side; she had a long face and a short sharp nose. The man selling peelers was irritated when he saw the people looking at this pair instead of him. "How about you, you there," he said, pointing at Haze. "You'll never be able to get a bargain like this in any store."

Haze was looking at the blind man and the child. "Hey!" Enoch Emery said, reaching across a woman and punching his arm. "He's talking to you! He's talking to you!" Enoch had to punch him again before he looked at the peeler man.

"Whyn't you take one of these home to yer wife?" the peeler man was saying.

"Don't have one," Haze muttered, looking back at the blind man again.

"Well, you got a dear old mother, ain't you?"

"No."

"Well pshaw," the man said, with his hand cupped to the people, "he needs one theseyer just to keep him company."

Enoch Emery thought that was so funny that he doubled over and slapped his knee, but Hazel Motes didn't look as if he had heard it yet. "I'm going to give away a half a dozen peeled potatoes to the first person purchasing one theseyer machines," the man said. "Who's gonna step up first? Only a dollar and a half for a machine'd cost you three dollars in any store!" Enoch Emery began fumbling in his pockets. "You'll thank the day you ever stopped here," the man said, "you'll never forget it. Ever' one of you people purchasing one theseyer machines'll never forget it!"

The blind man was moving forward slowly, saying in a kind of garbled mutter, "Help a blind preacher. If you won't repent, give up a nickel. I can use it as good as you. Help a blind unemployed preacher. Wouldn't you rather have me beg than preach? Come on and give a nickel if you won't repent."

There were not many people gathered around but the ones who were began to move off. When the machine-seller saw this, he leaned, glaring over the card table. "Hey you!" he yelled at the blind man. "What you think you doing? Who you think you are, running people off from here?" The blind man didn't pay any attention to him. He kept on rattling the cup and the child kept on handing out the pamphlets. He passed Enoch Emery and came on toward Haze, hitting the white cane out at an angle from his leg. Haze leaned forward and saw that the lines on his face were not painted on; they were scars.

"What the hell you think you doing?" the man selling peelers yelled. "I got these people together, how you think you can horn in?"

The child held one of the pamphlets out to Haze and he grabbed it. The words on the outside of it said, "Jesus Calls You."

"I'd like to know who the hell you think you are!" the man with the peelers was yelling. The child went back to where he was and handed him a tract. He looked at it for an instant with his lip curled and then he charged around the card table, upsetting the bucket of potatoes. "These damn Jesus fanatics," he yelled, glaring around, trying to find the blind man. New people gathered, hoping to see a disturbance. "These goddam Communist foreigners!" the peeler man screamed. "I got this crowd together!" He stopped, realizing there was a crowd.

"Listen folks," he said, "one at a time, there's plenty to go around, just don't push, a half a dozen peeled potatoes to the first person stepping up to buy." He got back behind the card table quietly and started holding up the peeler boxes. "Step on·up, plenty to go around," he said, "no need to crowd."

Haze didn't open his tract. He looked at the outside of it and then he tore it across. He ·put the two pieces together and tore them across again. He kept re-stacking the pieces and tearing them again until he had a little handful of confetti. He turned his hand over and let the shredded leaflet sprinkle to the ground. Then he looked up and saw the blind man's child not three feet away, watching him. Her mouth was open and her eyes glittered on him like two chips of green bottle glass. She had a white gunny sack hung over her shoulder. Haze scowled and began rubbing his sticky hands on his pants.

"I seen you," she said. Then she moved quickly over to where the blind man was standing now, beside the card table, and turned her head and looked at Haze from there. Most of the people had moved off.

The peeler man leaned over the card table and said, "Hey!" to the blind man. "I reckon that showed you. Trying to horn in."

"Lookerhere," Enoch Emery said, "I ain't got but a dollar sixteen cent but I . . ."

"Yah," the man said, "I reckon that'll show you you can't muscle in on me. Sold eight peelers, sold . . ."

"Give me one of them," the blind man's child said, pointing to the peelers.

"Hanh," he said.

She was untying a handkerchief. She untied two fifty-cent pieces out of the knotted corner of it. "Give me one of them," she said, holding out the money.

The man eyed it with his mouth hiked to one side. "A buck fifty, sister," he said.

She pulled her hand in quickly and all at once glared at Hazel Motes as if he had made a noise at her. The blind man was moving on. She stood a second glaring at Haze, and then she turned and followed the blind man. Haze started.

"Listen," Enoch Emery said, "I ain't got but a dollar sixteen cent and I want me one of them . . ."

"You can keep it," the man said, taking the bucket off the card table. "This ain't no cut-rate joint."

Haze could see the blind man moving down the street some distance away. He stood staring after him, jerking his hands in and out of his pockets as if he were trying to move forward and backward at the same time. Then suddenly he thrust two dollars at the man selling peelers and snatched a box off the card table and started running down the street. In a second Enoch Emery was panting at his elbow. "My, I reckon you got a heap of money," Enoch Emery said.

Haze saw the child catch up with the blind man and take him by the elbow. They were about a block ahead of him. He slowed down some and saw Enoch Emery there. Enoch had on a yellowish white suit and a pinkish white shirt and his tie was the color of green peas. He was smiling. He looked like a friendly hound dog with light mange. "How long you been here?" he inquired.

"Two days," Haze muttered.

"I been here two months," Enoch said. "I work for the city. Where you work?"

"Not working," Haze said.

"That's too bad," Enoch said. "I work for the city." He skipped a step to get in line with Haze, then he said, "I'm eighteen year old and I ain't been here but two months and I already work for the city."

"That's fine," Haze said. He pulled his hat down farther on the side Enoch Emery was on and walked very fast. The blind man up ahead began to make mock bows to the right and left.

"I didn't ketch your name good," Enoch said.

Haze said his name.

"You look like you might be follerin' them hicks," Enoch remarked. "You go in for a lot of Jesus business?"

"No," Haze said.

"No, me neither, not much," Enoch agreed. "I went to thisyer Rodemill Boys' Bible Academy for four weeks. Thisyer woman that traded me from my daddy she sent me. She was a Welfare woman. Jesus, four weeks and I thought I was going to be sanctified crazy."

Haze walked to the end of the block and Enoch stayed at his elbow, panting and talking. When Haze started across the street, Enoch yelled, "Don't you see theter light! That means you got to wait!" A cop blew a whistle and a car blasted its horn and stopped short. Haze went on across, keeping his eyes on the blind man in the middle of the block. The policeman kept on blowing his whistle. He crossed the street to where Haze was and stopped him. He had a thin face and oval-shaped yellow eyes.

"You know what that little thing hanging up there is for?" he asked, pointing to the traffic light over the intersection.

"I didn't see it," Haze said.

The policeman looked at him without saying anything. A few people stopped. He rolled his eyes at them. "Maybe you thought the red ones was for white folks and the green ones for niggers," he said.

"Yeah I thought that," Haze said. "Take your hand off me."

The policeman took his hand off and put it on his hip. He backed one step away and said, "You tell all your friends about these lights. Red is to stop, green is to go—men and women, white folks and niggers, all go on the same light. You tell all your friends so when they come to town, they'll know." The people laughed.

"I'll look after him," Enoch Emery said, pushing in

by the policeman. "He ain't been here but only two days. I'll look after him."

"How long you been here?" the cop asked.

"I was born and raised here," Enoch said. "This is my ol' home town. I'll take care of him for you. Hey wait!" he yelled at Haze. "Wait on me!" He pushed out of the crowd and caught up with him. "I reckon I saved you that time," he said.

"I'm obliged," Haze said.

"It wasn't nothing," Enoch said. "Whyn't we go in Walgreen's and get us a soda? Ain't no night clubs open this early."

"I don't like drug stores," Haze said. "Good-by."

"That's all right," Enoch said. "I reckon I'll go along and keep you company for a while." He looked up ahead at the blind man and the child and said, "I sho wouldn't want to get messed up with no hicks this time of night, particularly the Jesus kind. I done had enough of them myself. Thisyer Welfare woman that traded me from my daddy didn't do nothing but pray. Me and daddy we moved around with a sawmill where we worked and it set up outside Boonville one summer and here come thisyer woman." He caught hold of Haze's coat. "Only objection I got to Taulkinham is there's too many people on the streets," he said confidentially. "Look like all they want to do is knock you down—well here she come and I reckon she took a fancy to me. I was twelve year old and I could sing some hymns good I learnt off a nigger. So here she comes taking a fancy to me and traded me off my daddy and took me to Boonville to live with her. She had a brick house but it was Jesus all day long." A little man lost in a pair of faded overalls jostled him. "Whyn't you look wher you going?" Enoch growled.

The little man stopped and raised his arm in a vicious gesture and a nasty-dog look came on his face. "Who you tellin' what?" he snarled.

"You see," Enoch said, jumping to catch up with Haze, "all they want to do is knock you down. I ain't never been to such a unfriendly place before. Even with that woman. I stayed with her for two months in that house of hers," he went on, "and then come fall she sent me to the Rodemill Boys' Bible Academy and I thought that sho was going to be some relief. This woman was hard to get along with—she wasn't old, I reckon she was forty year old—but she sho was ugly. She had theseyer brown glasses and her hair was so thin it looked like ham gravy trickling over her skull. I thought it was going to be some certain relief to get to theter Academy. I had run away oncet on her and she got me back and come to find out she had papers on me and she could send me to the penitentiary if I didn't stay with her so I sho was glad to get to theter Academy. You ever been to a academy?"

Haze didn't seem to hear the question.

"Well, it won't no relief," Enoch said. "Good Jesus, it won't no relief. I run away from there after four weeks and durn if she didn't get me back and brought me to that house of hers again. I got out though." He waited a minute. "You want to know how?"

After a second he said, "I scared hell out of that woman, that's how. I studied on it and studied on it. I even prayed. I said, 'Jesus, show me the way to get out of here without killing thisyer woman and getting sent to the penitentiary,' and durn if He didn't. I got up one morning at just daylight and I went in her room without my pants on and pulled the sheet off her and giver a heart attact. Then I went back to my daddy and we ain't seen hide of her since.

"Your jaw just crawls," he observed, watching the side of Haze's face. "You don't never laugh. I wouldn't be surprised if you wasn't a real wealthy man." *Irony*

Haze turned down a side street. The blind man and the girl were on the corner a block ahead. "Well, I reckon we going to ketch up with them after all," Enoch said. "You know many people here?"

"No," Haze said.

"You ain't gonna know none neither. This is one more hard place to make friends in. I been here two months and I don't know nobody. Look like all they want to do is knock you down. I reckon you got a right heap of money," he said. "I ain't got none. Had, I'd sho know what to do with it." The blind man and his child stopped on the corner and turned up the left side of the street. "We ketchin' up," he said. "I bet we'll be at some meeting singing hymns with her and her daddy if we don't watch out."

Up in the next block there was a large building with columns and a dome. The blind man and the girl were going toward it. There was a car parked in every space around the building and on the other side of the street and up and down the streets near it. "That ain't no picture show," Enoch said. The blind man and the girl turned up the steps to the building. The steps went all the way across the front, and on either side there were stone lions sitting on pedestals. "Ain't no church," Enoch said. Haze stopped at the steps. He looked as if he were trying to settle his face into an expression. He pulled the black hat forward at a sharp angle and started toward the two, who had sat down in the corner by one of the lions. He came up to where the blind man was without saying anything and stood leaning forward in front of him as if he were trying to see through the black glasses. The child stared at him.

The blind man's mouth thinned slightly. "I can smell the sin on your breath," he said.

Haze drew back.

"What'd you follow me for?"

"I never followed you," Haze said.

"She said you were following," the blind man said, jerking his thumb in the direction of the child.

"I ain't followed you," Haze said. He felt the peeler box in his hand and looked at the girl. Her black knitted cap made a straight line across her forehead. She grinned suddenly and then quickly drew her expression back together as if she smelled something bad. "I ain't followed you no-where," Haze said. "I followed her." He stuck the peeler out at her.

At first she looked as if she were going to grab it, but she didn't. "I don't want that thing," she said. "What you think I want with that thing? Take it. It ain't mine. I don't want it!"

"You take it," the blind man said. "You put it in your sack and shut up before I hit you."

Haze thrust the peeler at her again.

"I won't have it," she muttered.

"You take it like I told you," the blind man said. "He never followed you."

She took it and shoved it in the sack where the tracts were. "It ain't mine," she said. "I got it but it ain't mine."

"I followed her to say I ain't beholden for none of her fast eye like she gave me back there," Haze said, looking at the blind man.

"What you mean?" she shouted. "I never looked at you with no fast eye. I only watched you tearing up that tract. He tore it up in little pieces," she said, pushing the blind man's shoulder. "He tore it up and sprinkled it all over the ground like salt and wiped his hands on his pants."

"He followed me," the blind man said. "Nobody would follow you. I can hear the urge for Jesus in his voice."

"Jesus," Haze muttered. "My Jesus." He sat down by the girl's leg and set his hand on the step next to her foot. She had on sneakers and black cotton stockings.

"Listen at him cursing," she said in a low tone. "He never followed you, Papa."

The blind man gave his edgy laugh. "Listen boy," he said, "you can't run away from Jesus. Jesus is a fact."

"I know a whole heap about Jesus," Enoch said. "I attended thisyer Rodemill Boys' Bible Academy that a woman sent me to. If it's anything you want to know about Jesus, just ast me." He had got up on the lion's back and he was sitting there sideways, cross-legged. *Folly of learning*

"I come a long way," Haze said, "since I would believe anything. I come halfway around the world."

"Me too," Enoch Emery said.

"You ain't come so far that you could keep from following me," the blind man said. He reached out suddenly and his hands covered Haze's face. For a second Haze didn't move or make any sound. Then he knocked the hands off.

"Quit it," he said in a faint voice. "You don't know anything about me."

"My daddy looks just like Jesus," Enoch remarked from the lion's back. "His hair hangs to his shoulders. Only difference is he's got a scar acrost his chin. I ain't never seen who my mother is."

"Some preacher has left his mark on you," the blind man said with a kind of snicker. "Did you follow for me to take it off or give you another one?"

"Listen here, there's nothing for your pain but Jesus," the child said suddenly. She tapped Haze on the shoulder. He sat there with his black hat tilted forward over his face. "Listen," she said in a louder voice, "this here man and woman killed this little baby. It was her own child but it was ugly and she never give it any love. This child had Jesus and this woman didn't have nothing but good looks and a man she was living in sin with. She sent the child away and it come back and she sent it away again and it come back again and ever' time she sent it away, it come back to where her and this man was living in sin. They strangled it with a silk stocking and hung it up in the chimney. It didn't give her any peace after that, though. Everything she looked at was that child. Jesus made it beautiful to haunt her. She couldn't lie with that man without she saw it, staring through the chimney at her, shining through the brick in the middle of the night."

"My Jesus," Haze muttered.

"She didn't have nothing but good looks," she said in the loud fast voice. "That ain't enough. No sirree."

"I hear them scraping their feet inside there," the blind man said. "Get out the tracts, they're fixing to come out."

"It ain't enough," she repeated.

"What we gonna do?" Enoch asked. "What's inside theter building?"

"A program letting out," the blind man said. "My congregation."

The child took the tracts out of the gunny sack and gave him two bunches of them, tied with a string. "You and the other boy go over on that side and give out," he said to her. "Me and the one that followed me'll stay over here."

"He don't have no business touching them," she said. "He don't want to do anything but shred them up."

"Go like I told you," the blind man said.

She stood there a second, scowling. Then she said, "You come on if you're coming," to Enoch Emery and Enoch jumped off the lion and followed her over to the other side.

Haze ducked down a step but the blind man's hand shot out and clamped him around the arm. He said in a fast whisper, "Repent! Go to the head of the stairs and renounce your sins and distribute these tracts to the people!" and he thrust a stack of pamphlets into Haze's hand.

Haze jerked his arm away but he only pulled the blind man nearer. "Listen," he said, "I'm as clean as you are."

"Fornication and blasphemy and what else?" the blind man said.

"They ain't nothing but words," Haze said. "If I was in sin I was in it before I ever committed any. There's no change come in me." He was trying to pry the fingers off from around his arm but the blind man kept wrapping them tighter. "I don't believe in sin," Haze said, "take your hand off me."

"Jesus loves you," the blind man said in a flat mocking voice, "Jesus loves you, Jesus loves you . . ."

"Nothing matters but that Jesus don't exist," Haze said, pulling his arm free.

"Go to the head of the stairs and distribute these tracts and . . ."

"I'll take them up there and throw them over into the bushes!" Haze shouted. "You be watching and see can you see."

"I can see more than you!" the blind man yelled, laughing. "You got eyes and see not, ears and hear not, but you'll have to see some time."

"You be watching if you can see!" Haze said, and started running up the steps. A crowd of people were already coming out the auditorium doors and some were halfway down the steps. He pushed through them with his elbows out like sharp wings and when he got to the top, a new surge of them pushed him back almost to where he had started up. He fought through them again until somebody shouted, "Make room for this idiot!" and people got out of his way. He rushed to the top and pushed his way over to the side and stood there, glaring and panting.

"I never followed him," he said aloud. "I wouldn't follow a blind fool like that. My Jesus." He stood against the building, holding the stack of leaflets by the string. A fat man stopped near him to light a cigar and Haze pushed his shoulder. "Look down yonder," he said. "See that blind man down there? He's giving out tracts and begging. Jesus. You ought to see him and he's got this here ugly child dressed up in woman's clothes, giving them out too. My Jesus."

"There's always fanatics," the fat man said, moving on.

"My Jesus," Haze said. He leaned forward near an old woman with blue hair and a collar of red wooden beads. "You better get on the other side, lady," he said. "There's a fool down there giving out tracts." The crowd behind the old woman pushed her on, but she looked at him for an instant with two bright flea eyes. He started toward her through the people but she was already too far away and he pushed back to where he had been standing against the wall. "Sweet Jesus Christ Crucified," he said, "I want to tell you people something. Maybe you think you're not clean because you don't believe. Well you are clean, let me tell you that. Every one of you people are clean and let me tell you why if you think it's because of Jesus Christ Crucified you're wrong. I don't say he wasn't crucified but I say it wasn't for you. Listenhere, I'm a preacher myself and I preach the truth." The crowd was moving fast. It was like a large spread raveling and the separate threads disappeared down the dark streets. "Don't I know what exists and what don't?" he cried. "Don't I have eyes in my head? Am I a blind man? Listenhere," he called, "I'm going to preach a new church—the church of truth without Jesus Christ Crucified. It won't cost you nothing to join my church. It's not started yet but it's going to be." The few people who were left glanced at him once or twice. There were tracts scattered below over the sidewalk and out on the street. The blind man was sitting on the bottom step. Enoch Emery was on the other side, standing on the lion's head, trying to balance himself, and the child was standing near him, watching Haze. "I don't need Jesus," Haze said. "What do I need with Jesus? I got Leora Watts."

He went down the stairs quietly to where the blind man was and stopped. He stood there a second and the blind man laughed. Haze moved away, and started across the street. He was on the other side before the voice pierced after him. He turned and saw the blind man standing in the middle of the street, shouting, "Hawks, Hawks, my name is Asa Hawks when you try to follow me again!" A car had to swerve to the side to keep from hitting him. "Repent!" he shouted and laughed and ran forward a little way, pretending he was going to come after Haze and grab him.

Haze drew his head down nearer his hunched shoulders and went on quickly. He didn't look back until he heard other footsteps coming behind him.

"Now that we got shut of them," Enoch Emery panted, "whyn't we go somewher and have us some fun?"

"Listen," Haze said roughly, "I got business of my own. I seen all of you I want." He began walking very fast.

Enoch kept skipping steps to keep up. "I been here two months," he said, "and I don't know nobody. People ain't friendly here. I got me a room and there ain't never nobody in it but me. My daddy said I had to come. I wouldn't never have come but he made me. I think I seen you sommers before. You ain't from Stockwell, are you?"

"No."

"Melsy?"

"No."

"Sawmill set up there oncet," Enoch said. "Look like you had a kind of familer face."

They walked on without saying anything until they got on the main street again. It was almost deserted. "Goodby," Haze said.

"I'm going thisaway too," Enoch said in a sullen voice. On the left there was a movie house where the electric bill was being changed. "We hadn't got tied up with them hicks we could have gone to a show," he muttered. He strode along at Haze's elbow, talking in a half mumble, half whine. Once he caught at his sleeve to slow him down and Haze jerked it away. "My daddy made me come," he said in a cracked voice. Haze looked at him and saw he was crying, his face seamed and wet and a purple-pink color. "I ain't but eighteen year old," he cried, "an' he made me come and I don't know nobody, nobody here'll have nothing to do with nobody else. They ain't friendly. He done gone off with a woman and made me come but she ain't going to stay for long, he'll beat hell out of her before she gets herself stuck to a chair. You the first familer face I seen in two months. I seen you sommers before. I know I seen you sommers before."

Haze looked straight ahead with his face set and Enoch kept up the half mumble, half blubber. They passed a church and a hotel and an antique shop and turned up Mrs. Watts's street.

"If you want you a woman you don't have to be follering nothing looked like that kid you give a peeler to," Enoch said. "I heard about where there's a house where we could have us some fun. I could pay you back next week."

"Look," Haze said, "I'm going where I'm going—two doors from here. I got a woman. I got a woman, see? And that's where I'm going—to visit her. I don't need to go with you."

"I could pay you back next week," Enoch said. "I work at the city zoo. I guard a gate and I get paid ever' week."

"Get away from me," Haze said.

"People ain't friendly here. You ain't from here but you ain't friendly neither."

Haze didn't answer him. He went on with his neck drawn close to his shoulder blades as if he were cold.

"You don't know nobody neither," Enoch said. "You ain't got no woman nor nothing to do. I knew when I first seen you you didn't have nobody nor nothing but Jesus. I seen you and I knew it."

"This is where I'm going in at," Haze said, and he turned up the walk without looking back at Enoch.

Enoch stopped. "Yeah," he cried, "oh yeah," and he ran his sleeve under his nose to stop the snivel. "Yeah," he cried, "go on where you goin' but lookerhere." He slapped at his pocket and ran up and caught Haze's sleeve and rattled the peeler box at him. "She give me this. She give it to me and there ain't nothing you can do about it. She told me where they lived and ast me to visit them and bring you—not you bring me, me bring you—and it was you follerin' them." His eyes glinted through his tears and his face stretched in an evil crooked grin. "You act like you think you got wiser blood than anybody else," he said, "but you ain't! I'm the one has it. Not you. *Me.*"

Haze didn't say anything. He stood there for an instant, small in the middle of the steps, and then he raised his arm and hurled the stack of tracts he had been carrying. It hit Enoch in the chest and knocked his mouth open. He stood looking, with his mouth hanging open, at where it had hit his front, and then he turned and tore off down the street; and Haze went into the house.

Since the night before was the first time he had slept with any woman, he had not been very successful with Mrs.

Watts. When he finished, he was like something washed ashore on her, and she had made obscene comments about him, which he remembered off and on during the day. He was uneasy in the thought of going to her again. He didn't know what she would say when he opened the door and she saw him there.

When he opened the door and she saw him there, she said, "Ha ha."

The black hat sat on his head squarely. He came in with it on and when it knocked the electric light bulb that hung down from the middle of the ceiling, he took it off. Mrs. Watts was in bed, applying a grease to her face. She rested her chin on her hand and watched him. He began to move around the room, examining this and that. His throat got dryer and his heart began to grip him like a little ape clutching the bars of its cage. He sat down on the edge of her bed, with his hat in his hand.

Mrs. Watts's grin was as curved and sharp as the blade of a sickle. It was plain that she was so well-adjusted that she didn't have to think any more. Her eyes took everything in whole, like quicksand. "That Jesus-seeing hat!" she said. She sat up and pulled her nightgown from under her and took it off. She reached for his hat and put it on her head and sat with her hands on her hips, walling her eyes in a comical way. Haze stared for a minute, then he made three quick noises that were laughs. He jumped for the electric light cord and took off his clothes in the dark.

Once when he was small, his father took him to a carnival that stopped in Melsy. There was one tent that cost more money a little off to one side. A dried-up man with a horn voice was barking it. He didn't say what was inside. He said it was so SINsational that it would cost any man that wanted to see it thirty-five cents, and it was so EXclusive, only fifteen could get in at a time. His father sent him to a tent where two monkeys danced, and then he made for it, moving close to the walls of things like he moved. Haze left the monkeys and followed him, but he didn't have thirty-five cents. He asked the barker what was inside.

"Beat it," the man said. "There ain't no pop and there ain't no monkeys."

"I already seen them," he said.

"That's fine," the man said, "beat it."

"I got fifteen cents," he said. "Whyn't you lemme in and I could see half of it?" It's something about a privy, he was thinking. It's some men in a privy. Then he thought, maybe it's a man and a woman in a privy. She wouldn't want me in there. "I got fifteen cents," he said.

"It's more than half over," the man said, fanning with his straw hat. "You run along."

"That'll be fifteen cents worth then," Haze said.

"Scram," the man said.

"Is it a nigger?" Haze asked. "Are they doing something to a nigger?"

The man leaned off his platform and his dried-up face drew into a glare. "Where'd you get that idear?" he said.

"I don't know," Haze said.

"How old are you?" the man asked.

"Twelve," Haze said. He was ten.

"Gimme that fifteen cents," the man said, "and get in there."

He slid the money on the platform and scrambled to get in before it was over. He went through the flap of the tent and inside there was another tent and he went through that. All he could see were the backs of the men. He climbed up on a bench and looked over their heads. They were looking down into a lowered place where something white was lying, squirming a little, in a box lined with black cloth. For a second he thought it was a skinned animal and then he saw it was a woman. She was fat and she had a face like an ordinary woman except there was a mole on the corner of her lip, that moved when she grinned, and one on her side.

"Had one of them•ther built into ever' casket," his father, up toward the front, said, "be a heap ready to go sooner."

Haze recognized the voice without looking. He slid down off the bench and scrambled out of the tent. He crawled out under the side of the outside one because he didn't want to pass the barker. He got in the back of a truck and sat down in the far corner of it. The carnival was making a tin roar outside.

His mother was standing by the washpot in the yard, looking at him, when he got home. She wore black all the time and her dresses were longer than other women's. She was standing there straight, looking at him. He moved behind a tree and got out of her view, but in a few minutes, he could feel her watching him through the tree. He saw the lowered place and the casket again and a thin woman in the casket who was too long for it. Her head stuck up at one end and her knees were raised to make her fit. She had a cross-shaped face and hair pulled close to her head. He stood flat against the tree, waiting. She left the washpot and came toward him with a stick. She said, "What you seen?

"What you seen?" she said.

"What you seen," she said, using the same tone of voice all the time. She hit him across the legs with the stick, but he was like part of the tree. "Jesus died to redeem you," she said.

"I never ast him," he muttered.

She didn't hit him again but she stood looking at him, shut-mouthed, and he forgot the guilt of the tent for the nameless unplaced guilt that was in him. In a minute she threw the stick away from her and went back to the washpot, still shut-mouthed.

The next day he took his shoes in secret out into the woods. He didn't wear them except for revivals and in the winter. He took them out of the box and filled the bottoms of them with stones and small rocks and then he put them on. He laced them up tight and walked in them through the woods for what he knew to be a mile, until he came to a creek, and then he sat down and took them off and eased his feet in the wet sand. He thought, that ought to satisfy Him. Nothing happened. If a stone had fallen he would have taken it as a sign. After a while he drew his feet out of the sand and let them dry, and then he put the shoes on again with the rocks still in them and he walked a half-mile back before he took them off.

Chapter 4

He got out of Mrs. Watts's bed early in the morning before
any light came in the room. When he woke up, her arm
was flung across him. He leaned up and lifted it off and
eased it down by her side, but he didn't look at her. There
was only one thought in his mind: he was going to buy
a car. The thought was full grown in his head when he
woke up, and he didn't think of anything else. He had never
thought before of buying a car; he had never even wanted
one before. He had driven one only a little in his life and
he didn't have any license. He had only fifty dollars but
he thought he could buy a car for that. He got stealthily
out the bed, without disturbing Mrs. Watts, and put his
clothes on silently. By six-thirty, he was down town, looking
for used-car lots.

Used-car lots were scattered among the blocks of old
buildings that separated the business section from the railroad
yards. He wandered around in a few of them before they
were open. He could tell from the outside of the lot if
it would have a fifty-dollar car in it. When they began to
be open for business, he went through them quickly, paying
no attention to anyone who tried to show him the stock.
His black hat sat on his head with a careful, placed expression
and his face had a fragile look as if it might have been
broken and stuck together again, or like a gun no one knows
is loaded.

It was a wet glary day. The sky was like a piece of
thin polished silver with a dark sour-looking sun in one
corner of it. By ten o'clock he had canvassed all the better
lots and was nearing the railroad yards. Even here, the
lots were full of cars that cost more than fifty dollars. Finally
he came to one between two deserted warehouses. A sign
over the entrance said: SLADE'S FOR THE LATEST.

There was a gravel road going down the middle of
the lot and over to one side near the front, a tin shack with
the word, OFFICE, painted on the door. The rest of the lot
was full of old cars and broken machinery. A white boy
was sitting on a gasoline can in front of the office. He
had the look of being there to keep people out. He wore
a black raincoat and his face was partly hidden under a

leather cap. There was a cigarette hanging out of one corner of his mouth and the ash on it was about an inch long.

Haze started off toward the back of the lot where he saw a particular car. "Hey!" the boy yelled. "You don't just walk in here like that. I'll show you what I got to show," but Haze didn't pay any attention to him. He went on toward the back of the lot where he saw the car. The boy came huffing behind him, cursing. The car he saw was on the last row of cars. It was a high rat-colored machine with large thin wheels and bulging headlights. When he got up to it, he saw that one door was tied on with a rope and that it had an oval window in the back. This was the car he was going to buy.

"Lemme see Slade," he said.

"What you want to see him for?" the boy asked in a testy voice. He had a wide mouth and when he talked he used one side only of it.

"I want to see him about this car," Haze said.

"I'm him," the boy said. His face under the cap was like a thin picked eagle's. He sat down on the running board of a car across the gravel road and kept on cursing.

Haze walked around the car. Then he looked through the window at the inside of it. Inside it was a dull greenish dust-color. The back seat was missing but it had a two-by-four stretched across the seat frame to sit on. There were dark green fringed window shades on the two side-back windows. He looked through the two front windows and he saw the boy sitting on the running board of the car across the gravel road. He had one trouser leg hitched up and he was scratching his ankle that stuck up out of a pulp of yellow sock. He cursed far down in his throat as if he were trying to get up phlegm. The two window glasses made him a yellow color and distorted his shape. Haze moved quickly from the far side of the car and came around in front. "How much is it?" he asked.

"Jesus on the cross," the boy said. "Christ nailed."

"How much is it?" Haze growled, paling a little.

"How much do you think it's worth?" the boy said. "Give us a estimit."

"It ain't worth what it would take to cart it off. I wouldn't have it."

The boy gave all his attention to his ankle where there was a scab. Haze looked up and saw a man coming from between two cars over on the boy's side. As he came closer, he saw that the man looked exactly like the boy except that he was two heads taller and he had on a sweat-stained brown felt hat. He was coming up behind the boy, between a row of cars. When he got just behind him, he stopped and waited a second. Then he said in a sort of controlled roar, "Get your butt off that running board!"

The boy snarled and disappeared, scrambling between two cars.

The man stood looking at Haze. "What you want?" he asked.

"This car here," Haze said.

"Seventy-fi' dollars," the man said.

On either side of the lot there were two old buildings, reddish with black empty windows, and behind there was another without any windows. "I'm obliged," Haze said, and he started back toward the office.

When he got to the entrance, he glanced back and saw the man about four feet behind him. "We might argue it some," he said.

Haze followed him back to where the car was.

"You won't find a car like that ever' day," the man said. He sat down on the running board that the boy had been sitting on. Haze didn't see the boy but he was there, sitting up on the hood of a car two cars over. He was sitting huddled up as if he were freezing but his face had a sour composed look. "All new tires," the man said.

"They were new when it was built," Haze said.

"They was better cars built a few years ago," the man said. "They don't make no more good cars."

"What you want for it?" Haze asked again.

The man stared off, thinking. After a while he said, "I might could let you have it for sixty-fi'."

Haze leaned against the car and started to roll a cigarette but he couldn't get it rolled. He kept spilling the tobacco and then the papers.

"Well, what you want to pay for it?" the man asked. "I wouldn't trade me a Chrysler for a Essex like that. That car yonder ain't been built by a bunch of niggers."

"All the niggers are living in Detroit now, putting cars together," he said, making conversation. "I was up there a while myself and I seen. I come home."

"I wouldn't pay over thirty dollars for it," Haze said.

"They got one nigger up there," the man said, "is almost as light as you or me." He took off his hat and ran his finger around the sweat band inside it. He had a little bit of carrot-colored hair.

"We'll drive it around," the man said, "or would you like to get under and look up it?"

"No," Haze said.

The man gave him a half look. "You pay when you leave," he said easily. "You don't find what you looking for in one there's others for the same price obliged to have it." Two cars over the boy began to curse again. It was like a hacking cough. Haze turned suddenly and kicked his foot into the front tire. "I done tole you them tires won't bust," the man said.

"How much?" Haze said.

"I might could make it fifty dollar," the man offered.

Before Haze bought the car, the man put some gas in it and drove him around a few blocks to prove it would run. The boy sat hunched up in the back on the two-by-four, cursing. "Something's wrong with him howcome he curses so much," the man said. "Just don't listen at him." The car rode with a high growling noise. The man put on the brakes to show how well they worked and the boy was thrown off the two-by-four at their heads. "Goddam you," the man roared, "quit jumping at us thataway. Keep your butt on the board." The boy didn't say anything. He didn't even curse. Haze looked back and he was sitting huddled up in the black raincoat with the black leather cap pulled down almost to his eyes. The only thing different was that the ash had been knocked off his cigarette.

He bought the car for forty dollars and then he paid the man extra for five gallons of gasoline. The man had the boy go in the office and bring out a five-gallon can of gas to fill up the tank with. The boy came cursing and lugging the yellow gas can, bent over almost double. "Give it here," Haze said, "I'll do it myself." He was in a terrible hurry to get away in the car. The boy jerked the can away from him and straightened up. It was only half full but he held it over the tank until five gallons would have spilled out slowly. All the time he kept saying, "Sweet Jesus, sweet Jesus, sweet Jesus."

"Why don't he shut up?" Haze said suddenly. "What's he keep talking like that for?"

"I don't never know what ails him," the man said and shrugged.

When the car was ready the man and the boy stood by to watch him drive it off. He didn't want anybody watching him because he hadn't driven a car in four or five years. The man and the boy didn't say anything while he tried to start it. They only stood there, looking in at him. "I wanted this car mostly to be a house for me," he said to the man. "I ain't got any place to be."

"You ain't took the brake off yet," the man said.

He took off the brake and the car shot backward because

the man had left it in reverse. In a second he got it going forward and he drove off crookedly, past the man and the boy still standing there watching. He kept going forward, thinking nothing and sweating. For a long time he stayed on the street he was on. He had a hard time holding the car in the road. He went past railroad yards for about a half-mile and then warehouses. When he tried to slow the car down, it stopped altogether and then he had to start it again. He went past long blocks of gray houses and then blocks of better, yellow houses. It began to drizzle rain and he turned on the windshield wipers; they made a great clatter like two idiots clapping in church. He went past blocks of white houses, each sitting with an ugly dog face on a square of grass. Finally he went over a viaduct and found the highway.

He began going very fast.

The highway was ragged with filling stations and trailer camps and roadhouses. After a while there were stretches where red gulleys dropped off on either side of the road and behind them there were patches of field buttoned together with 666 posts. The sky leaked over all of it and then it began to leak into the car. The head of a string of pigs appeared snout-up over the ditch and he had to screech to a stop and watch the rear of the last pig disappear shaking into the ditch on the other side. He started the car again and went on. He had the feeling that everything he saw was a broken-off piece of some giant blank thing that he had forgotten had happened to him. A black pick-up truck turned off a side road in front of him. On the back of it an iron bed and a chair and table were tied, and on top of them, a crate of barred-rock chickens. The truck went very slowly, with a rumbling sound, and in the middle of the road. Haze started pounding his horn and he had hit it three times before he realized it didn't make any sound. The crate was stuffed so full of wet barred-rock chickens that the ones facing him had their heads outside the bars. The truck didn't go any faster and he was forced to drive slowly. The fields stretched sodden on either side until they hit the scrub pines.

The road turned and went down hill and a high embankment appeared on one side with pines standing on it, facing a gray boulder that jutted out of the opposite gulley wall. White letters on the boulder said, WOE TO THE BLASPHEMER AND WHOREMONGER! WILL HELL SWALLOW YOU UP? The pick-up truck slowed even more as if it were reading the sign and Haze pounded his empty horn. He beat on it and beat on it but it didn't make any sound.

The pick-up truck went on, bumping the glum barred-rock chickens over the edge of the next hill. Haze's car was stopped and his eyes were turned toward the two words at the bottom of the sign. They said in smaller letters, "Jesus Saves."

He sat looking at the sign and he didn't hear the horn. An oil truck as long as a railroad car was behind him. In a second a red square face was at his car window. It watched the back of his neck and hat for a minute and then a hand came in and sat on his shoulder. "What you doing parked in the middle of the road?" the truck driver asked.

Haze turned his fragile placid-looking face toward him. "Take your hand off me," he said. "I'm reading the sign."

The driver's expression and his hand stayed exactly the way they were, as if he didn't hear very well.

"There's no person a whoremonger, who wasn't something worse first," Haze said. "That's not the sin, nor blasphemy. The sin came before them."

The truck driver's face remained exactly the same.

"Jesus is a trick on niggers," Haze said.

The driver put both his hands on the window and gripped it. He looked as if he intended to pick up the car. "Will you get your goddam outhouse off the middle of the road?" he said.

"I don't have to run from anything because I don't believe in anything," Haze said. He and the driver looked at each other for about a minute. Haze's look was the more distant; another plan was forming in his mind. "Which direction is the zoo in?" he asked.

"Back around the other way," the driver said. "Did you exscape from there?"

"I got to see a boy that works in it," Haze said. He started the car up and left the driver standing there, in front of the letters painted on the boulder.

Chapter 5

That morning Enoch Emery knew when he woke up that today the person he could show it to was going to come. He knew by his blood. He had wise blood like his daddy.

At two o'clock that afternoon, he greeted the second-shift gate guard. "You ain't but only fifteen minutes late," he said irritably. "But I stayed. I could of went on but I stayed." He wore a green uniform with yellow piping on the neck and sleeves and a yellow stripe down the outside of each leg. The second-shift guard, a boy with a jutting shale-textured face and a toothpick in his mouth, wore the same. The gate they were standing by was made of iron bars and the concrete arch that held it was fashioned to look like two trees; branches curved to form the top of it where twisted letters said, CITY FOREST PARK. The second-shift guard leaned against one of the trunks and began prodding between his teeth with the pick.

"Ever' day," Enoch complained; "look like ever' day I lose fifteen good minutes standing here waiting for you."

Every day when he got off duty, he went into the park, and every day when he went in, he did the same things. He went first to the swimming pool. He was afraid of the water but he liked to sit up on the bank above it if there were any women in the pool, and watch them. There was one woman who came every Monday who wore a bathing suit that was split on each hip. At first he thought she didn't know it, and instead of watching openly on the bank, he had crawled into some bushes, snickering to himself, and had watched from there. There had been no one else in the pool—the crowds didn't come until four o'clock—to tell her about the splits and she had splashed around in the water and then lain up on the edge of the pool asleep for almost an hour, all the time without suspecting there was somebody in the bushes looking at her. Then on another day when he stayed a little later, he saw three women, all with their suits split, the pool full of people, and nobody paying them any mind. That was how the city was—always surprising him. He visited a whore when he felt like it but he was always being shocked by the looseness he saw in the open. He crawled into the bushes out of

40

a sense of propriety. Very often the women would pull the suit straps down off their shoulders and lie stretched out.

The park was the heart of the city. He had come to the city and—with a knowing in his blood—he had established himself at the heart of it. Every day he looked at the heart of it; every day; and he was so stunned and awed and overwhelmed that just to think about it made him sweat. There was something, in the center of the park, that he had discovered. It was a mystery, although it was right there in a glass case for everybody to see and there was a typewritten card over it telling all about it. But there was something the card couldn't say and what it couldn't say was inside him, a terrible knowledge without any words to it, a terrible knowledge like a big nerve growing inside him. He could not show the mystery to just anybody; but he had to show it to somebody. Who he had to show it to was a special person. This person could not be from the city but he didn't know why. He knew he would know him when he saw him and he knew that he would have to see him soon or the nerve inside him would grow so big that he would be forced to steal a car or rob a bank or jump out of a dark alley onto a woman. His blood all morning had been saying the person would come today.

He left the second-shift guard and approached the pool from a discreet footpath that led behind the ladies' end of the bath house to a small clearing where the entire pool could be seen at once. There was nobody in it—the water was bottle-green and motionless—but he saw, coming up the other side and heading for the bath house, the woman with the two little boys. She came every other day or so and brought the two children. She would go in the water with them and swim down the pool and then she would lie up on the side in the sun. She had a stained white bathing suit that fit her like a sack, and Enoch had watched her with pleasure on several occasions. He moved from the clearing up a slope to some abelia bushes. There was a nice tunnel under them and he crawled into it until he came to a slightly wider place where he was accustomed to sit. He settled himself and adjusted the abelia so that he could see through it properly. His face was always very red in the bushes. Anyone who parted the abelia sprigs at just that place, would think he saw a devil and would fall down the slope and into the pool. The woman and the two little boys entered the bath house.

Enoch never went immediately to the dark secret center of the park. That was the peak of the afternoon. The other things he did built up to it. When he left the bushes, he would go to the FROSTY BOTTLE, a hotdog stand in the shape of an Orange Crush with frost painted in blue around the top of it. Here he would have a chocolate malted milk-shake and would make some suggestive remarks to the waitress, whom he believed to be secretly in love with him. After that he would go to see the animals. They were in a long set of steel cages like Alcatraz Penitentiary in the movies. The cages were electrically heated in the winter and air-conditioned in the summer and there were six men hired to wait on the animals and feed them T-bone steaks. The animals didn't do anything but lie around. Enoch watched them every day, full of awe and hate. Then he went *there.*

The two little boys ran out of the bath house and dived into the water, and simultaneously a grating noise issued from the driveway on the other side of the pool. Enoch's head pierced out of the bushes. He saw a high rat-colored car passing, which sounded as if its motor were dragging out the back. The car passed and he could hear it rattle around the turn in the drive and on away. He listened care-fully, trying to hear if it would stop. The noise receded and then gradually grew louder. The car passed again. Enoch saw this time that there was only one person in it, a man. The sound of it died away again and then grew louder. The car came around a third time and stopped almost directly opposite Enoch across the pool. The man in the car looked out the window and down the grass slope to the water where the two little boys were splashing and screaming. Enoch's head was as far out of the bushes as it would come and he was squinting. The door by the man was tied on with a rope. The man got out the other door and walked in front of the car and came halfway down the slope to the pool. He stood there a minute as if he were looking for somebody and then he sat down stiffly on the grass. He had on a blue suit and a black hat. He sat with his knees drawn up. "Well, I'll be dog," Enoch said. "Well, I'll be dog."

He began crawling out of the bushes immediately, his heart moving so fast it was like one of those motorcycles at fairs that the fellow drives around the walls of a pit. He even remembered the man's name—Mr. Hazel Motes. In a second he appeared on all fours at the end of the abelia and looked across the pool. The blue figure was still sitting there in the same position. He had the look of being held there, as if by an invisible hand, as if, if the hand lifted up, the figure would spring across the pool in one leap without the expression on his face changing once.

The woman came out of the bath house and went to the diving board. She spread her arms out and began to bounce, making a big flapping sound with the board. Then suddenly she swirled backward and disappeared below the water. Mr. Hazel Motes's head turned very slowly, following her down the pool.

Enoch got up and went down the path behind the bath house. He came stealthily out on the other side and started walking toward Haze. He stayed on the top of the slope, moving softly in the grass just off the sidewalk, and making no noise. When he was directly behind him, he sat down on the edge of the sidewalk. If his arms had been ten feet long, he could have put his hands on Haze's shoulders. He studied him quietly.

The woman was climbing out of the pool, chinning herself up on the side. First her face appeared, long and cadaverous, with a bandage-like bathing cap coming down almost to her eyes, and sharp teeth protruding from her mouth. Then she rose on her hands until a large foot and leg came up from behind her and another on the other side and she was out, squatting there, panting. She stood up loosely and shook herself, and stamped in the water dripping off her. She was facing them and she grinned. Enoch could see part of Hazel Motes's face watching the woman. It didn't grin in return but it kept on watching her as she padded over to a spot of sun almost directly under where they were sitting. Enoch had to move a little closer to see.

The woman sat down in the spot of sun and took off her bathing cap. Her hair was short and matted and all colors, from deep rust to a greenish yellow. She shook her head and then she looked up at Hazel Motes again, grinning through her pointed teeth. She stretched herself out in the spot of sun, raising her knees and settling her backbone down against the concrete. The two little boys, at the other end of the water, were knocking each other's heads against the side of the pool. She settled herself until she was flat against the concrete and then she reached up and pulled the bathing suit straps off her shoulders.

"King Jesus!" Enoch whispered and before he could get his eyes off the woman, Hazel Motes had sprung up and was almost to his car. The woman was sitting straight up with the suit half off her in front, and Enoch was looking both ways at once.

He wrenched his attention loose from the woman and

darted after Hazel Motes. "Wait on me!" he shouted and waved his arms in front of the car which was already rattling and starting to go. Hazel Motes cut off the motor. His face behind the windshield was sour and frog-like; it looked as if it had a shout closed up in it; it looked like one of those closet doors in gangster pictures where someone is tied to a chair behind it with a towel in his mouth.

"Well," Enoch said, "I declare if it ain't Hazel Motes. How are you, Hazel?"

"The guard said I'd find you at the swimming pool," Hazel Motes said. "He said you hid in the bushes and watched the swimming."

Enoch blushed. "I allus have admired swimming," he said. Then he stuck his head farther through the window. "You were looking for me?" he exclaimed.

"That blind man," Haze said, "that blind man named Hawks—did his child tell you where they lived?"

Enoch didn't seem to hear. "You came out here special to see me?" he said.

"Asa Hawks. His child gave you the peeler. Did she tell you where they lived?"

Enoch eased his head out of the car. He opened the door and climbed in beside Haze. For a minute he only looked at him, wetting his lips. Then he whispered, "I got to show you something."

"I'm looking for those people," Haze said. "I got to see that man. Did she tell you where they lived?"

"I got to show you this thing," Enoch said. "I got to show it to you, here, this afternoon. I got to." He gripped Hazel Motes's arm and Haze shook him off.

"Did she tell you where they live?" he said again.

Enoch kept wetting his lips. They were pale except for his fever blister, which was purple. "Cert'nly," he said. "Ain't she invited me to come to see her and bring my mouth organ? I got to show you this thing, then I'll tell you."

"What thing?" Haze muttered.

"This thing I got to show you," Enoch said. "Drive straight on ahead and I'll tell you where to stop."

"I don't want to see anything of yours," Haze Motes said. "I want that address."

Enoch didn't look at Hazel Motes. He looked out the window. "I won't be able to remember it unless you come," he said. In a minute the car started. Enoch's blood was beating fast. He knew he had to go to the FROSTY BOTTLE and the zoo before there, and he foresaw a terrible struggle with Hazel Motes. He would have to get him there, even if he had to hit him over the head with a rock and carry him on his back up to it.

Enoch's brain was divided into two parts. The part in communication with his blood did the figuring but it never said anything in words. The other part was stocked up with all kinds of words and phrases. While the first part was figuring how to get Hazel Motes through the FROSTY BOTTLE and the zoo, the second inquired, "Where'd you get thisyer fine car? You ought to paint you some signs on the outside it, like 'Step-in, baby'—I seen one with that on it, then I seen another, said . . ."

Hazel Motes's face might have been cut out of the side of a rock.

"My daddy once owned a yeller Ford automobile he won on a ticket," Enoch murmured. "It had a roll-top and two aerials and a squirrel tail all come with it. He swapped it off. Stop here! Stop here!" he yelled—they were passing the FROSTY BOTTLE.

"Where is it?" Hazel Motes said as soon as they were inside. They were in a dark room with a counter across the back of it and brown stools like toad stools in front of the counter. On the wall facing the door there was a large advertisement for ice cream, showing a cow dressed up like a housewife.

"It ain't here," Enoch said. "We have to stop here on the way and get something to eat. What you want?"

"Nothing," Haze said. He stood stiffly in the middle of the room with his hands in his pockets.

"Well, sit down," Enoch said. "I have to have a little drink."

Something stirred behind the counter and a woman with bobbed hair like a man's got up from a chair where she had been reading the newspaper, and came forward. She looked sourly at Enoch. She had on a once-white uniform clotted with brown stains. "What you want?" she said in a loud voice, leaning close to his ear. She had a man's face and big muscled arms.

"I want a chocolate malted milkshake, baby girl," Enoch said softly. "I want a lot of ice cream in it."

She turned fiercely from him and glared at Haze.

"He says he don't want nothing but to sit down and look at you for a while," Enoch said. "He ain't hungry but for just to see you."

Haze looked woodenly at the woman and she turned her back on him and began mixing the milkshake. He sat down on the last stool in the row and started cracking his knuckles.

Enoch watched him carefully. "I reckon you done changed some," he said after a few minutes.

Haze got up. "Give me those people's address. Right now," he said.

It came to Enoch in an instant—the police. His face was suddenly suffused with secret knowledge. "I reckon you ain't as uppity as you was last night," he said. "I reckon maybe," he said, "you ain't got so much cause now as you had then." Stole theter automobile, he thought.

Hazel Motes sat back down.

"Howcome you jumped up so fast down yonder by the pool?" Enoch asked. The woman turned around to him with the malted milk in her hand. "Of course," he said evilly, "I wouldn't have had no truck with a ugly dish like that neither."

The woman thumped the malted milk on the counter in front of him. "Fifteen cents," she roared.

"You're worth more than that, baby girl," Enoch said. He snickered and began gassing his malted milk through the straw.

The woman strode over to where Haze was. "What you come in here with a son of a bitch like that for?" she shouted. "A nice quiet boy like you to come in here with a son of a bitch. You ought to mind the company you keep." Her name was Maude and she drank whisky all day from a fruit jar under the counter. "Jesus," she said, wiping her hand under her nose. She sat down in a straight chair in front of Haze but facing Enoch, and folded her arms across her chest. "Ever' day," she said to Haze, looking at Enoch, "ever' day that son of a bitch comes in here."

Enoch was thinking about the animals. They had to go next to see the animals. He hated them; just thinking about them made his face turn a chocolate purple color as if the malted milk were rising in his head.

"You're a nice boy," she said. "I can see, you got a clean nose, well keep it clean, don't go messin' with a son a bitch like that yonder. I always know a clean boy when I see one." She was shouting at Enoch, but Enoch watched Hazel Motes. It was as if something inside Hazel Motes was winding up, although he didn't move on the outside. He only looked pressed down in that blue suit, as if inside it, the thing winding was getting tighter and tighter. Enoch's blood told him to hurry. He raced the milkshake up the straw.

"Yes sir," she said, "there ain't anything sweeter than a clean boy. God for my witness. And I know a clean one when I see him and I know a son a bitch when I see him and there's a heap of difference and that pus-marked bastard zlurping through that straw is a goddamned son a bitch and you a clean boy had better mind how you keep him company. I know a clean boy when I see one."

Enoch screeched in the bottom of his glass. He fished fifteen cents from his pocket and laid it on the counter and got up. But Hazel Motes was already up; he was leaning over the counter toward the woman. She didn't see him right away because she was looking at Enoch. He leaned on his hands over the counter until his face was just a foot from hers. She turned around and stared at him.

"Come on," Enoch started, "we don't have no time to be sassing around with her. I got to show you this right away, I got . . ."

"I AM clean," Haze said.

It was not until he said it again that Enoch caught the words.

"I AM clean," he said again, without any expression on his face or in his voice, just looking at the woman as if he were looking at a wall. "If Jesus existed, I wouldn't be clean," he said.

She stared at him, startled and then outraged. "What do you think I care!" she yelled. "Why should I give a goddam what you are!"

"Come on," Enoch whined, "come on or I won't tell you where them people live." He caught Haze's arm and pulled him back from the counter and toward the door.

"You bastard!" the woman screamed, "what do you think I care about any of you filthy boys?"

Hazel Motes pushed the door open quickly and went out. He got back in his car and Enoch climbed in behind him. "Okay," Enoch said, "drive straight on ahead down this road."

"What you want for telling me?" Haze said. "I'm not staying here. I have to go. I can't stay here any longer."

Enoch shuddered. He began wetting his lips. "I got to show it to you," he said hoarsely. "I can't show it to nobody but you. I had a sign it was you when I seen you drive up at the pool. I knew all morning somebody was going to come and then when I saw you at the pool, I had thisyer sign."

"I don't care about your signs," Haze said.

"I go to see it ever' day," Enoch said. "I go ever' day but I ain't ever been able to take nobody else with me. I had to wait on the sign. I'll tell you them people's address just as soon as you see it. You got to see it," he said. "When you see it, something's going to happen."

"Nothing's going to happen," Haze said.

He started the car again and Enoch sat forward on the seat. "Them animals," he muttered. "We got to walk by them first. It won't take long for that. It won't take a minute." He saw the animals waiting evil-eyed for him, ready to throw him off time. He thought, what if the police were screaming out here now with sirens and squad cars and they got Hazel Motes just before he showed it to him.

"I got to see those people," Haze said.

"Stop here! Stop here!" Enoch yelled.

There was a long shining row of steel cages over to the left and behind the bars, black shapes were sitting or pacing. "Get out," Enoch said. "This won't take one second."

Haze got out. Then he stopped. "I got to see those people," he said.

"Okay, okay, come on," Enoch whined.

"I don't believe you know the address."

"I do! I do!" Enoch cried. "It begins with a three, now come on!" He pulled Haze toward the cages. Two black bears sat in the first one, facing each other like two matrons having tea, their faces polite and self-absorbed. "They don't do nothing but sit there all day and stink," Enoch said. "A man comes and washes them cages out ever' morning with a hose and it stinks just as much as if he'd left it." He went past two more cages of bears, not looking at them, and then he stopped at the next cage where there were two yellow-eyed wolves nosing around the edges of the concrete. "Hyenas," he said. "I ain't got no use for hyenas." He leaned closer and spit into the cage, hitting one of the wolves on the leg. It shuttled to the side, giving him a slanted evil look. For a second he forgot Hazel Motes. Then he looked back quickly to make sure he was still there. He was right behind him. He was not looking at the animals. Thinking about them police, Enoch thought. He said, "Come on, we don't have time to look at all theseyer monkeys that come next." Usually he stopped at every cage and made an obscene comment aloud to himself, but today the animals were only a form he had to get through. He hurried past the cages of monkeys, looking back two or three times to make sure Hazel Motes was behind him. At the last of the monkey cages, he stopped as if he couldn't help himself.

"Look at that ape," he said, glaring. The animal had its back to him, gray except for a small pink seat. "If I had a ass like that," he said prudishly, "I'd sit on it. I wouldn't be exposing it to all these people come to this park. Come on, we don't have to look at theseyer birds that come next." He ran past the cages of birds and then he was at the end of the zoo. "Now we don't need the car," he said, going on ahead, "we'll go right down that hill yonder through them trees." Haze had stopped at the last cage for birds. "Oh Jesus," Enoch groaned. He stood and waved his arms wildly and shouted, "Come on!" but Haze didn't move from where he was looking into the cage.

Enoch ran back to him and grabbed him by the arm but Haze pushed him off and kept on looking in the cage. It was empty. Enoch stared. "It's empty!" he shouted. "What you have to look in that ole empty cage for? You come on!" He stood there, sweating and purple. "It's empty!" he shouted. And then he saw it wasn't empty. Over in one corner on the floor of the cage, there was an eye. The eye was in the middle of something that looked like a piece of mop sitting on an old rag. He squinted close to the wire and saw that the piece of mop was an owl with one eye open. It was looking directly at Hazel Motes. "That ain't nothing but a ole hoot owl," he moaned. "You seen them things before."

"I AM clean," Haze said to the eye. He said it just the way he said it to the woman in the FROSTY BOTTLE. The eye shut softly and the owl turned its face to the wall.

He's done murdered somebody, Enoch thought. "Oh sweet Jesus, come on!" he wailed. "I got to show you this right now." He pulled him away but a few feet from the cage, Haze stopped again, looking at something in the distance. Enoch's eyesight was very poor. He squinted and made out a figure far down the road behind them. There were two smaller figures jumping on either side of it.

Hazel Motes turned back to him suddenly and said, "Where's this thing? Let's see it right now and get it over with. Come on."

"Ain't that where I been trying to take you?" Enoch said. He felt the perspiration drying on him and stinging and his skin was pin-pointed, even in his scalp. "We got to cross this road and go down this hill. We got to go on foot," he said.

"Why?" Haze muttered.

"I don't know," Enoch said. He knew something was going to happen to him. His blood stopped beating. All the time it had been beating like drum noises and now it had stopped. They started down the hill. It was a steep hill, full of trees painted white from the ground up four feet. They looked as if they had on ankle-socks. He gripped

Hazel Motes's arm. "It gets damp as you go down," he said, looking around vaguely. Hazel Motes shook him off. In a second, Enoch gripped his arm again and stopped him. He pointed down through the trees. "Muvseevum," he said. The strange word made him shiver. That was the first time he had ever said it aloud. A piece of gray building was showing where he pointed. It grew larger as they went down the hill, then as they came to the end of the wood and stepped out on the gravel driveway, it seemed to shrink suddenly. It was round and soot-colored. There were columns at the front of it and in between each column there was an eyeless stone woman holding a pot on her head. A concrete band was over the columns and the letters, M V S E V M, were cut into it. Enoch was afraid to pronounce the word again.

"We got to go up the steps and through the front door," he whispered. There were ten steps up to the porch. The door was wide and black. Enoch pushed it in cautiously and inserted his head in the crack. In a minute he brought it out again and said, "All right, go on in and walk easy. I don't want to wake up theter ole guard. He ain't very friendly with me." They went into a dark hall. It was heavy with the odor of linoleum and creosote and another odor behind these two. The third one was an undersmell and Enoch couldn't name it as anything he had ever smelled before. There was nothing in the hall but two urns and an old man asleep in a straight chair against the wall. He had on the same kind of uniform as Enoch and he looked like a dried-up spider stuck there. Enoch looked at Hazel Motes to see if he was smelling the undersmell. He looked as if he were. Enoch's blood began to beat again, urging him forward. He gripped Haze's arm and tiptoed through the hall to another black door at the end of it. He cracked it a little and inserted his head in the crack. Then in a second he drew it out and crooked his finger in a gesture for Haze to follow him. They went into another hall, like the last one, but running crosswise. "It's in that first door yonder," Enoch said in a small voice. They went into a dark room full of glass cases. The glass cases covered the walls and there were three coffin-like ones in the middle of the floor. The ones on the walls were full of birds tilted on varnished sticks and looking down with dried piquant expressions.

"Come on," Enoch whispered. He went past the two cases in the middle of the floor and toward the third one. He went to the farthest end of it and stopped. He stood looking down with his neck thrust forward and his hands clutched together; Hazel Motes moved up beside him.

The two of them stood there, Enoch rigid and Hazel Motes bent slightly forward. There were three bowls and a row of blunt weapons and a man in the case. It was the man Enoch was looking at. He was about three feet long. He was naked and a dried yellow color and his eyes were drawn almost shut as if a giant block of steel were falling down on top of him.

"See theter notice," Enoch said in a church whisper, pointing to a typewritten card at the man's foot, "it says he was once as tall as you or me. Some A-rabs did it to him in six months." He turned his head cautiously to see Hazel Motes.

All he could tell was that Hazel Motes's eyes were on the shrunken man. He was bent forward so that his face was reflected on the glass top of the case. The reflection was pale and the eyes were like two clean bullet holes. Enoch waited, rigid. He heard footsteps in the hall. Oh Jesus Jesus, he prayed, let him hurry up and do whatever he's going to do! The woman with the two little boys came in the door. She had one by each hand, and she was grinning. Hazel Motes had not raised his eyes once from the shrunken man. The woman came toward them. She stopped on the other side of the case and looked down into it and the reflection of her face appeared grinning on the glass, over Hazel Motes's.

She snickered and put two fingers in front of her teeth. The little boys' faces were like pans set on either side to catch the grins that overflowed from her. When Haze saw her face on the glass, his neck jerked back and he made a noise. It might have come from the man inside the case. In a second Enoch knew it had. "Wait!" he screamed, and tore out of the room after Hazel Motes.

He overtook him halfway up the hill. He caught him by the arm and swung him around and then he stood there, suddenly weak and light as a balloon, and stared. Hazel Motes grabbed him by the shoulders and shook him. "What is that address!" he shouted. "Give me that address!"

Even if Enoch had been sure what the address was, he couldn't have thought of it then. He could not even stand up. As soon as Hazel Motes let him go, he fell backward and landed against one of the white-socked trees. He rolled over and lay stretched out on the ground, with an exalted look on his face. He thought he was floating. A long way off he saw the blue figure spring and pick up a rock, and he saw the wild face turn, and the rock hurtle toward him; he shut his eyes tight and the rock hit him on the forehead.

When he came to again, Hazel Motes was gone. He lay there a minute. He put his fingers to his forehead and then held them in front of his eyes. They were streaked with red. He turned his head and saw a drop of blood on the ground and as he looked at it, he thought it widened like a little spring. He sat straight up, frozen-skinned, and put his finger in it, and very faintly he could hear his blood beating, his secret blood, in the center of the city.

Then he knew that whatever was expected of him was only just beginning.

Chapter 6

That evening Haze drove his car around the streets until he found the blind man and the child again. They were standing on a corner, waiting for the light to change. He drove the Essex at some distance behind them for about four blocks up the main street and then turned it after them down a side street. He followed them on into a dark section past the railroad yards and watched them go up on the porch of a box-like two-story house. When the blind man opened the door a shaft of light fell on him and Haze craned his neck to see him better. The child turned her head, slowly, as if it worked on a screw, and watched his car pass. His face was so close to the glass that it looked like a paper face pasted there. He noted the number of the house and a sign on it that said, ROOMS FOR RENT.

Then he drove back down town and parked the Essex in front of a movie house where he could catch the drain of people coming out from the picture show. The lights around the marquee were so bright that the moon, moving overhead with a small procession of clouds behind it, looked pale and insignificant. Haze got out of the Essex and climbed up on the nose of it.

A thin little man with a long upper lip was at the glass ticket box, buying tickets for three portly women who were behind him. "Gotta get these girls some refreshments too," he said to the woman in the ticket box. "Can't have 'em starve right before my eyes."

"Ain't he a card?" one of the women hollered. "He keeps me in stitches!"

Three boys in red satin lumberjackets came out of the foyer. Haze raised his arms. "Where has the blood you think you been redeemed by touched you?" he cried.

The women all turned around at once and stared at him.

"A wise guy," the little thin man said, and glared as if someone were about to insult him.

The three boys moved up, pushing each other's shoulders.

Haze waited a second and then he cried again. "Where has the blood you think you been redeemed by touched you?"

53

"Rabble rouser," the little man said. "One thing I can't stand it's a rabble rouser."

"What church you belong to, you boy there?" Haze asked, pointing at the tallest boy in the red satin lumberjacket.

The boy giggled.

"You then," he said impatiently, pointing at the next one. "What church you belong to?"

"Church of Christ," the boy said in a falsetto to hide the truth.

"Church of Christ!" Haze repeated. "Well, I preach the Church Without Christ. I'm member and preacher to that church where the blind don't see and the lame don't walk and what's dead stays that way. Ask me about that church and I'll tell you it's the church that the blood of Jesus don't foul with redemption."

"He's a preacher," one of the women said. "Let's go."

"Listen, you people, I'm going to take the truth with me wherever I go," Haze called. "I'm going to preach it to whoever'll listen at whatever place. I'm going to preach there was no Fall because there was nothing to fall from and no Redemption because there was no Fall and no Judgment because there wasn't the first two. Nothing matters but that Jesus was a liar."

The little man herded his girls into the picture show quickly and the three boys left but more people came out and he began over and said the same thing again. They left and some more came and he said it a third time. Then they left and no one else came out; there was no one there but the woman in the glass box. She had been glaring at him all the time but he had not noticed her. She wore glasses with rhinestones in the bows and she had white hair stacked in sausages around her head. She stuck her mouth to a hole in the glass and shouted, "Listen, if you don't have a church to do it in, you don't have to do it in front of this show."

"My church is the Church Without Christ, lady," he said. "If there's no Christ, there's no reason to have a set place to do it in."

"Listen," she said, "if you don't get from in front of this show, I'll call the police."

"There's plenty of shows," he said and got down and got back in the Essex and drove off. That night he preached in front of three other picture shows before he went to Mrs. Watts.

In the morning he drove back to the house where the blind man and the child had gone in the night before. It was yellow clapboard, the second one in a block of them, all alike. He went up to the front door and rang the bell.

After a few minutes a woman with a mop opened it. He said he wanted to rent a room.

"What you do?" she asked. She was a tall bony woman, resembling the mop she carried upside-down.

He said he was a preacher.

The woman looked at him thoroughly and then she looked behind him at his car. "What church?" she asked.

He said the Church Without Christ.

"Protestant?" she asked suspiciously, "or something foreign?"

He said no mam, it was Protestant.

After a minute she said, "Well, you can look at it," and he followed her into a white plastered hall and up some steps at the side of it. She opened a door into a back room that was a little larger than his car, with a cot and a chest of drawers and a table and straight chair in it. There were two nails on the wall to hang clothes on. "Three dollars a week in advance," she said. There was one window and another door opposite the door they had come in by. Haze opened the extra door, expecting it to be a closet. It opened out onto a drop of about thirty feet and looked down into a narrow bare back yard where the garbage was collected. There was a plank nailed across the door frame at knee level to keep anyone from falling out. "A man named Hawks lives here, don't he?" Haze asked quickly.

"Downstairs in the front room," she said, "him and his child." She was looking down into the drop too. "It used to be a fire-escape there," she said, "but I don't know what happened to it."

He paid her three dollars and took possession of the room, and as soon as she was out of the way, he went down the stairs and knocked on the Hawkses' door.

The blind man's child opened it a crack and stood looking at him. She seemed at once to have to balance her face so that her expression would be the same on both sides. "It's that boy, Papa," she said in a low tone. "The one that keeps following me." She held the door close to her head so he couldn't see in past her. The blind man came to the door but he didn't open it any wider. His look was not the same as it had been two nights before; it was sour and unfriendly, and he didn't speak, he only stood there.

Haze had got what he had to say in mind before he left his room. "I live here," he said. "I thought if your girl wanted to give me so much eye, I might return her some of it." He wasn't looking at the girl; he was staring at the black glasses and the curious scars that started somewhere behind them and ran down the blind man's cheeks.

"What I give you the other night," she said, "was a

looker indignation for what I seen you do. It was you give me the eye. You should have seen him, Papa," she said, "looked me up and down."

"I've started my own church," Haze said. "The Church Without Christ. I preach on the street."

"You can't let me alone, can you?" Hawks said. His voice was flat, nothing like it had been the other time. "I didn't ask you to come here and I ain't asking you to hang around," he said.

Haze had expected a secret welcome. He waited, trying to think of something to say. "What kind of a preacher are you?" he heard himself murmur, "not to see if you can save my soul?" The blind man pushed the door shut in his face. Haze stood there a second facing the blank door, and then he ran his sleeve across his mouth and went out.

Inside, Hawks took off his dark glasses and, from a hole in the window shade, watched him get in his car and drive off. The eye he put to the hole was slightly rounder and smaller than his other one, but it was obvious he could see out of both of them. The child watched from a lower crack. "Howcome you don't like him, Papa?" she asked, "—because he's after me?"

"If he was after you, that would be enough to make me welcome him," he said.

"I like his eyes," she observed. "They don't look like they see what he's looking at but they keep on looking."

Their room was the same size as Haze's but there were two cots and an oil cooking stove and a wash basin in it and a trunk that they used for a table. Hawks sat down on one of the cots and put a cigarette in his mouth. "Goddam Jesus-hog," he muttered.

"Well, look what you used to be," she said. "Look what you tried to do. You got over it and so will he."

"I don't want him hanging around," he said. "He makes me nervous."

"Listen here," she said, sitting down on the cot with him, "you help me to get him and then you go away and do what you please and I can live with him."

"He don't even know you exist," Hawks said.

"Even if he don't," she said, "that's all right. That's howcome I can get him easy. I want him and you ought to help and then you could go on off like you want to."

He lay down on the cot and finished the cigarette; his face was thoughtful and evil. Once while he was lying there, he laughed and then his expression constricted again. "Well, that might be fine," he said after a while. "That might be the oil on Aaron's beard."

"Listen here," she said, "it would be the nuts! I'm just crazy about him. I never seen a boy that I liked the looks of any better. Don't run him off. Tell him how you blinded yourself for Jesus and show him that clipping you got."

"Yeah, the clipping," he said.

Haze had gone out in his car to think and he had decided that he would seduce Hawks's child. He thought that when the blind preacher saw his daughter ruined, he would realize that he was in earnest when he said he preached The Church Without Christ. Besides this reason, there was another: he didn't want to go back to Mrs. Watts. The night before, after he was asleep, she had got up and cut the top of his hat out in an obscene shape. He felt that he should have a woman, not for the sake of the pleasure in her, but to prove that he didn't believe in sin since he practiced what was called it; but he had had enough of her. He wanted someone he could teach something to and he took it for granted that the blind man's child, since she was so homely, would also be innocent.

Before he went back to his room, he went to a dry-goods store to buy a new hat. He wanted one that was completely opposite to the old one. This time he was sold a white panama with a red and green and yellow band around it. The man said they were really the thing and particularly if he was going to Florida.

"I ain't going to Florida," he said. "This hat is opposite from the one I used to have is all."

"You can use it anywheres," the man said; "it's new."

"I know that," Haze said. He went outside and took the red and green and yellow band off it and thumped out the crease in the top and turned down the brim. When he put it on, it looked just as fierce as the other one had.

He didn't go back to the Hawkses' door until late in the afternoon, when he thought that they would be eating their supper. It opened almost at once and the child's head appeared in the crack. He pushed the door out of her hand and went in without looking at her directly. Hawks was sitting at the trunk. The remains of his supper were in front of him but he wasn't eating. He had barely got the black glasses on in time.

"If Jesus cured blind men, howcome you don't get Him to cure you?" Haze asked. He had prepared this sentence in his room.

"He blinded Paul," Hawks said.

Haze sat down on the edge of one of the cots. He looked around him and then back at Hawks. He crossed and uncrossed his knees and then he crossed them again. "Where'd you get them scars?" he asked.

The fake blind man leaned forward and smiled. "You still have a chance to save yourself if you repent," he said. "I can't save you but you can save yourself."

"That's what I've already done," Haze said. "Without the repenting. I preach how I done it every night on the . . ."

"Look at this," Hawks said. He took a yellow newspaper clipping from his pocket and handed it to him, and his mouth twisted out of the smile. "This is how I got the scars," he muttered. The child made a sign to him from the door to smile and not look sour. As he waited for Haze to finish reading, the smile slowly returned.

The headline on the clipping said, EVANGELIST PROMISES TO BLIND SELF. The rest of it said that Asa Hawks, an evangelist of the Free Church of Christ, had promised to blind himself to justify his belief that Christ Jesus had redeemed him. It said he would do it at a revival on Saturday night at eight o'clock, the fourth of October. The date on it was more than ten years before. Over the headline was a picture of Hawks, a scarless, straight-mouthed man of about thirty, with one eye a little smaller and rounder than the other. The mouth had a look that might have been either holy or calculating, but there was a wildness in the eyes that suggested terror.

Haze sat staring at the clipping after he had read it. He read it three times. He took his hat off and put it on again and got up and stood looking around the room as if he were trying to remember where the door was.

"He did it with lime," the child said, "and there was hundreds converted. Anybody that blinded himself for justification ought to be able to save you—or even somebody of his blood," she added, inspired.

"Nobody with a good car needs to be justified," Haze murmured. He scowled at her and hurried out the door, but as soon as it was shut behind him, he remembered something. He turned around and opened it and handed her a piece of paper, folded up several times into a small pellet shape; then he hurried out to his car.

Hawks took the note away from her and opened it up. It said, BABE, I NEVER SAW ANYBODY THAT LOOKED AS GOOD AS YOU BEFORE IS WHY I CAME HERE. She read it over his arm, coloring pleasantly.

"Now you got the written proof for it, Papa," she said.

"That bastard got away with my clipping," Hawks muttered.

"Well you got another clipping, ain't you?" she asked, with a little smirk.

"Shut your mouth," he said and flung himself down on

the cot. The other clipping was one that said, EVANGE-LIST'S NERVE FAILS.

"I can get it for you," she offered, standing close to the door so that she could run if she disturbed him too much, but he had turned toward the wall as if he were going to sleep.

Ten years ago at a revival he had intended to blind himself and two hundred people or more were there, waiting for him to do it. He had preached for an hour on the blindness of Paul, working himself up until he saw himself struck blind by a Divine flash of lightning and, with courage enough then, he had thrust his hands into the bucket of wet lime and streaked them down his face; but he hadn't been able to let any of it get into his eyes. He had been possessed of as many devils as were necessary to do it, but at that instant, they disappeared, and he saw himself standing there as he was. He fancied Jesus, Who had expelled them, was standing there too, beckoning to him; and he had fled out of the tent into the alley and disappeared.

"Okay, Pa," she said, "I'll go out for a while and leave you in peace."

Haze had driven his car immediately to the nearest garage where a man with black bangs and a short expressionless face had come out to wait on him. He told the man he wanted the horn made to blow and the leaks taken out of the gas tank, the starter made to work smoother and the windshield wipers tightened.

The man lifted the hood and glanced inside and then shut it again. Then he walked around the car, stopping to lean on it here and there, and thumping it in one place and another. Haze asked him how long it would take to put it in the best order.

"It can't be done," the man said.

"This is a good car," Haze said. "I knew when I first saw it that it was the car for me, and since I've had it, I've had a place to be that I can always get away in."

"Was you going some place in this?" the man asked.

"To another garage," Haze said, and he got in the Essex and drove off. At the other garage he went to, there was a man who said he could put the car in the best shape over-night, because it was such a good car to begin with, so well put together and with such good materials in it, and because, he added, he was the best mechanic in town, working in the best-equipped shop. Haze left it with him, certain that it was in honest hands.

you know what?, A bastard shall not enter the kingdom of heaven!" she said.

Chapter 7

The next afternoon when he got his car back, he drove it out into the country to see how well it worked on the open road. The sky was just a little lighter blue than his suit, clear and even, with only one cloud in it, a large blinding white one with curls and a beard. He had gone about a mile out of town when he heard a throat cleared behind him. He slowed down and turned his head and saw Hawks's child getting up off the floor onto the two-by-four that stretched across the seat frame. "I been here all the time," she said, "and you never known it." She had a bunch of dandelions in her hair and a wide red mouth on her pale face.

"What do you want to hide in my car for?" he said angrily. "I got business before me. I don't have time for foolishness." Then he checked his ugly tone and stretched his mouth a little, remembering that he was going to seduce her. "Yeah sure," he said, "glad to see you."

She swung one thin black-stockinged leg over the back of the front seat and then let the rest of herself over. "Did you mean 'good to look at' in that note, or only 'good'?" she asked.

"The both," he said stiffly.

"My name is Sabbath," she said. "Sabbath Lily Hawks. My mother named me that just after I was born because I was born on the Sabbath and then she turned over in her bed and died and I never seen her."

"Unh," Haze said. His jaw tightened and he entrenched himself behind it and drove on. He had not wanted any company. His sense of pleasure in the car and in the afternoon was gone.

"Him and her wasn't married," she continued, "and that makes me a bastard, but I can't help it. It was what he done to me and not what I done to myself."

"A bastard?" he murmured. He couldn't see how a preacher who had blinded himself for Jesus could have a bastard. He turned his head and looked at her with interest for the first time.

She nodded and the corners of her mouth turned up. "A real bastard," she said, catching his elbow, "and do you know what? A bastard shall not enter the kingdom of heaven!" she said.

Haze was driving his car toward the ditch while he stared at her. "How could you be . . . ," he started and saw the red embankment in front of him and pulled the car back on the road.

"Do you read the papers?" she asked.

"No," he said.

"Well, there's this woman in it named Mary Brittle that tells .you what to do when you don't know. I wrote her a letter and ast her what I was to do."

"How could you be a bastard when he blinded him . . . ," he started again.

"I says, 'Dear Mary, I am a bastard and a bastard shall not enter the kingdom of heaven as we all know, but I have this personality that makes boys follow me. Do you think I should neck or not? I shall not enter the kingdom of heaven anyway so I don't see what difference it makes.' "

"Listen here," Haze said, "if he blinded himself how . . ."

"Then she answered my letter in the paper. She said, 'Dear Sabbath, Light necking is acceptable, but I think your real problem is one of adjustment to the modern world. Perhaps you ought to re-examine your religious values to see if they meet your needs in Life. A religious experience can be a beautiful addition to living if you put it in the proper prespective and do not let it warf you. Read some books on Ethical Culture.' "

"You couldn't be a bastard," Haze said, getting very pale. "You must be mixed up. Your daddy blinded himself."

"Then I wrote her another letter," she said, scratching his ankle with the toe of her sneaker, and smiling. "I says, 'Dear Mary, What I really want to know is should I go the whole hog or not? That's my real problem. I'm adjusted okay to the modern world.' "

"Your daddy blinded himself," Haze repeated.

"He wasn't always as good as he is now," she said. "She never answered my second letter."

"You mean in his youth he didn't believe but he came to?" he asked. "Is that what you mean or ain't it?" and he kicked her foot roughly away from his.

"That's right," she said. Then she drew herself up a little. "Quit that feeling my leg with yours," she said.

The blinding white cloud was a little ahead of them, moving to the left. "Why don't you turn down that dirt road?" she asked. The highway forked off onto a clay road and he turned onto it. It was hilly and shady and the country showed to advantage on either side. One side was dense honeysuckle and the other was open and slanted down to a telescoped view of the city. The white cloud was directly in front of them.

"How did he come to believe?" Haze asked. "What changed him into a preacher for Jesus?"

"I do like a dirt road," she said, "particularly when it's hilly like this one here. Why don't we get out and sit under a tree where we could get better acquainted?"

After a few hundred feet Haze stopped the car and they got out. "Was he a very evil-seeming man before he came to believe," he asked, "or just part way evil-seeming?"

"All the way evil," she said, going under the barbed wire fence on the side of the road. Once under it she sat down and began to take off her shoes and stockings. "How I like to walk in a field is barefooted," she said with gusto.

"Listenhere," Haze muttered, "I got to be going back to town. I don't have time to walk in any field," but he went under the fence and on the other side he said, "I suppose before he came to believe he didn't believe at all."

"Let's us go over that hill yonder and sit under the trees," she said.

They climbed the hill and went down the other side of it, she a little ahead of Haze. He saw that sitting under a tree with her might help him to seduce her, but he was in no hurry to get on with it, considering her innocence. He felt it was too hard a job to be done in an afternoon. She sat down under a large pine and patted the ground close beside her for him to sit on, but he sat about five feet away from her on a rock. He rested his chin on his knees and looked straight ahead.

"I can save you," she said. "I got a church in my heart where Jesus is King."

He leaned in her direction, glaring. "I believe in a new kind of jesus," he said, "one that can't waste his blood redeeming people with it, because he's all man and ain't got any God in him. My church is the Church Without Christ!"

She moved up closer to him. "Can a bastard be saved in it?" she asked.

"There's no such thing as a bastard in the Church Without Christ," he said. "Everything is all one. A bastard wouldn't be any different from anybody else."

"That's good," she said.

He looked at her irritably, for something in his mind was already contradicting him and saying that a bastard couldn't, that there was only one truth—that Jesus was a liar—and that her case was hopeless. She pulled open her collar and lay down on the ground full length. "Ain't my feet white, though?" she asked raising them slightly.

Haze didn't look at her feet. The thing in his mind said that the truth didn't contradict itself and that a bastard couldn't be saved in the Church Without Christ. He decided he would forget it, that it was not important.

"There was this child once," she said, turning over on her stomach, "that nobody cared if it lived or died. Its kin sent it around from one to another of them and finally to its grandmother who was a very evil woman and she couldn't stand to have it around because the least good thing made her break out in these welps. She would get all itching and swoll. Even her eyes would itch her and swell up and there wasn't nothing she could do but run up and down the road, shaking her hands and cursing and it was twicet as bad when this child was there so she kept the child locked up in a chicken crate. It seen its granny in hell-fire, swoll and burning, and it told her everything it seen and she got so swoll until finally she went to the well and wrapped the well rope around her neck and let down the bucket and broke her neck.

"Would you guess me to be fifteen years old?" she asked.

"There wouldn't be any sense to the word, bastard, in the Church Without Christ," Haze said.

"Why don't you lie down and rest yourself?" she inquired.

Haze moved a few feet away and lay down. He put his hat over his face and folded his arms across his chest. She lifted herself up on her hands and knees and crawled over to him and gazed at the top of his hat. Then she lifted if off like a lid and peered into his eyes. They stared straight upward. "It don't make any difference to me," she said softly, "how much you like me."

He trained his eyes into her neck. Gradually she lowered her head until the tips of their noses almost touched but still he didn't look at her. "I see you," she said in a playful voice.

"Git away!" he said, jumping violently.

She scrambled up and ran around behind the tree. Haze put his hat back on and stood up, shaken. He wanted to get back in the Essex. He realized suddenly that it was parked on a country road, unlocked, and that the first person passing would drive off in it.

"I see you," a voice said from behind the tree.

He walked off quickly in the opposite direction toward the car. The jubilant expression on the face that looked from around the tree, flattened.

He got in his car and went through the motions of starting it but it only made a noise like water lost somewhere in the pipes. A panic took him and he began to pound the starter. There were two instruments on the dashboard with needles that pointed dizzily in first one direction and then another, but they worked on a private system, independent of the whole car. He couldn't tell if it was out of gas or not. Sabbath Hawks came running up to the fence. She got down on the ground and rolled under the barbed wire and then stood at the window of the car, looking in at him. He turned his head at her fiercely and said, "What did you do to my car?" Then he got out and started walking down the road, without waiting for her to answer. After a second, she followed him, keeping her distance.

Where the highway had forked off onto the dirt road, there had been a store with a gas pump in front of it. It was about a half-mile back; Haze kept up a steady fast pace until he reached it. It had a deserted look, but after a few minutes a man appeared from out of the woods behind it, and Haze told him what he wanted. While the man got out his pick-up truck to drive them back to the Essex, Sabbath Hawks arrived and went over to a cage about six feet high that was at the side of the shack. Haze had not noticed it until she came up. He saw that there was something alive in it, and went near enough to read a sign that said, TWO DEADLY ENEMIES. HAVE A LOOK FREE.

There was a black bear about four feet long and very thin, resting on the floor of the cage; his back was spotted with bird lime that had been shot down on him by a small chicken hawk that was sitting on a perch in the upper part of the same apartment. Most of the hawk's tail was gone; the bear had only one eye.

"Come on here if you don't want to get left," Haze said roughly, grabbing her by the arm. The man had his truck ready and the three of them drove back in it to the Essex. On the way Haze told him about the Church Without Christ; he explained its principles and said there was no such thing as a bastard in it. The man didn't comment. When they got out at the Essex, he put a can of gas in the tank and Haze got in and tried to start it but nothing happened. The man opened up the hood and studied the inside for a while. He was a one-armed man with two sandy-colored teeth and eyes that were slate-blue and thoughtful. He had not spoken more than two words yet. He looked for a long time under the hood while Haze stood by, but he didn't touch anything. After a while he shut it and blew his nose.

"What's wrong in there?" Haze asked in an agitated voice. "It's a good car, ain't it?"

The man didn't answer him. He sat down on the ground and eased under the Essex. He wore hightop shoes and gray socks. He stayed under the car a long time. Haze got down on his hands and knees and looked under to see what he was doing but he wasn't doing anything. He was just lying there, looking up, as if he were contemplating; his good arm was folded on his chest. After a while, he eased himself out and wiped his face and neck with a piece of flannel rag he had in his pocket.

"Listenhere," Haze said, "that's a good car. You just give me a push, that's all. That car'll get me anywhere I want to go."

The man didn't say anything but he got back in the truck and Haze and Sabbath Hawks got in the Essex and he pushed them. After a few hundred yards the Essex began to belch and gasp and jiggle. Haze stuck his head out the window and motioned for the truck to come alongside. "Ha!" he said. "I told you, didn't I? This car'll get me anywhere I want to go. It may stop here and there but it won't stop permanent. What do I owe you?"

"Nothing," the man said, "not a thing."

"But the gas," Haze said, "how much for the gas?"

"Nothing," the man said with the same level look. "Not a thing."

"All right, I thank you," Haze said and drove on. "I don't need no favors from him," he said.

"It's a grand auto," Sabbath Hawks said. "It goes as smooth as honey."

"It ain't been built by a bunch of foreigners or niggers or one-arm men," Haze said. "It was built by people with their eyes open that knew where they were at."

When they came to the end of the dirt road and were facing the paved one, the pick-up truck pulled alongside again and while the two cars paused side by side, Haze and the slate-eyed man looked at each other out of their two windows. "I told you this car would get me anywhere I wanted to go," Haze said sourly.

"Some things," the man said, " 'll get some folks somewheres," and he turned the truck up the highway.

Haze drove on. The blinding white cloud had turned into a bird with long thin wings and was disappearing in the opposite direction.

Chapter 8

Enoch Emery knew now that his life would never be the same again, because the thing that was going to happen to him had started to happen. He had always known that something was going to happen but he hadn't known what. If he had been much given to thought, he might have thought that now was the time for him to justify his daddy's blood, but he didn't think in broad sweeps like that, he thought what he would do next. Sometimes he didn't think, he only wondered; then before long he would find himself doing this or that, like a bird finds itself building a nest when it hasn't actually been planning to.

What was going to happen to him had started to happen when he showed what was in the glass case to Haze Motes. That was a mystery beyond his understanding, but he knew that what was going to be expected of him was something awful. His blood was more sensitive than any other part of him; it wrote doom all through him, except possibly in his brain, and the result was that his tongue, which edged out every few minutes to test his fever blister, knew more than he did.

The first thing that he found himself doing that was not normal was saving his pay. He was saving all of it, except what his landlady came to collect every week and what he had to use to buy something to eat with. Then to his surprise, he found he wasn't eating very much and he was saving that money too. He had a fondness for supermarkets; it was his custom to spend an hour or so in one every afternoon after he left the city park, browsing around among the canned goods and reading the cereal stories. Lately he had been compelled to pick up a few things here and there that would not be bulky in his pockets, and he wondered if this could be the reason he was saving so much money on food. It could have been, but he had the suspicion that saving the money was connected with some larger thing. He had always been given to stealing but he had never saved before.

At the same time, he began cleaning up his room. It was a little green room, or it had once been green, in the attic of an elderly rooming house. There was a mummified look and feel to this residence, but Enoch had never thought before of brightening the part (corresponding to the head) that he lived in. Then he simply found himself doing it.

First, he removed the rug from the floor and hung it out the window. This was a mistake because when he went to pull it back in, there were only a few long strings left with a carpet tack caught in one of them. He imagined that it must have been a very old rug and he decided to handle the rest of the furniture with more care. He washed the bed frame with soap and water and found that under the second layer of dirt, it was pure gold, and this affected him so strongly that he washed the chair. It was a low round chair that bulged around the legs so that it seemed to be in the act of squatting. The gold began to appear with the first touch of water but it disappeared with the second and with a little more, the chair sat down as if this were the end of long years of inner struggle. Enoch didn't know if it was for him or against him. He had a nasty impulse to kick it to pieces, but he let it stay there, exactly in the position it had sat down in, because for the time anyway, he was not a foolhardy boy who took chances on the meanings of things. For the time, he knew that what he didn't know was what mattered.

The only other piece of furniture in the room was a washstand. This was built in three parts and stood on bird legs six inches high. The legs had clawed feet that were each one gripped around a small cannon ball. The lowest part was a tabernacle-like cabinet which was meant to contain a slop-jar. Enoch didn't own a slop-jar but he had a certain reverence for the purpose of things and since he didn't have the right thing to put in it, he left it empty. Directly over this place for the treasure, there was a gray marble slab and coming up from behind it was a wooden trellis-work of hearts, scrolls and flowers, extending into a hunched eagle wing on either side, and containing in the middle, just at the level of Enoch's face when he stood in front of it, a small oval mirror. The wooden frame continued again over the mirror and ended in a crowned, horned headpiece, showing that the artist had not lost faith in his work.

As far as Enoch was concerned, this piece had always been the center of the room and the one that most connected him with what he didn't know. More than once after a big supper, he had dreamed of unlocking the cabinet and getting in it and then proceeding to certain rites and mysteries that he had a very vague idea about in the morning. In his cleaning up, his mind was on the washstand from the first, but as was usual with him, he began with the least important thing and worked around and in toward the center where the meaning was. So before he tackled the washstand, he took care of the pictures in the room.

These were three, one belonging to his landlady (who was almost totally blind but moved about by an acute sense of smell) and two of his own. Hers was a brown portrait of a moose standing in a small lake. The look of superiority on this animal's face was so insufferable to Enoch that, if he hadn't been afraid of him, he would have done something about it a long time ago. As it was, he couldn't do anything in his room but what the smug face was watching, not shocked because nothing better could be expected and not amused because nothing was funny. If he had looked all over for one, he couldn't have found a roommate that irritated him more. He kept up a constant stream of inner comment, uncomplimentary to the moose, though when he said anything aloud, he was more guarded. The moose was in a heavy brown frame with leaf designs on it and this added to his weight and his self-satisfied look. Enoch knew the time had come when something had to be done; he didn't know what was going to happen in his room, but when it happened, he didn't want to have the feeling that the moose was running it. The answer came to him fully prepared: he realized with a sudden intuition that taking the frame off him would be equal to taking the clothes off him (although he didn't have on any) and he was right because when he had done it, the animal looked so reduced that Enoch could only snicker and look at him out the corner of his eye.

After this success he turned his attention to the other two pictures. They were over calendars and had been sent him by the Hilltop Funeral Home and the American Rubber Tire Company. One showed a small boy in a pair of blue Doctor Denton sleepers, kneeling at his bed, saying, "And bless daddy," while the moon looked in at the window. This was Enoch's favorite painting and it hung directly over his bed. The other pictured a lady wearing a rubber tire and it hung directly across from the moose on the opposite wall. He left it where it was, pretty certain that the moose only pretended not to see it. Immediately after he finished with the pictures, he went out and bought chintz curtains, a bottle of gilt, and a paint brush with all the money he had saved.

This was a disappointment to him because he had hoped that the money would be for some new clothes for him, and here he saw it going into a set of drapes. He didn't know what the gilt was for until he got home with it; when he got home with it, he sat down in front of the slop-jar cabinet in the washstand, unlocked it, and painted the inside of it with the gilt. Then he realized that the cabinet was to be used FOR something.

Enoch never nagged his blood to tell him a thing until it was ready. He wasn't the kind of a boy who grabs at any possibility and runs off, proposing this or that preposterous thing. In a large matter like this, he was always willing to wait for a certainty, and he waited for this one, certain at least that he would know in a few days. Then for about a week his blood was in secret conference with itself every day, only stopping now and then to shout some order at him.

On the following Monday, he was certain when he woke up that today was the day he was going to know on. His blood was rushing around like a woman who cleans up the house after the company has come, and he was surly and rebellious. When he realized that today was the day, he decided not to get up. He didn't want to justify his daddy's blood, he didn't want to be always having to do something that something else wanted him to do, that he didn't know what it was and that was always dangerous.

Naturally, his blood was not going to put up with any attitude like this. He was at the zoo by nine-thirty, only a half-hour later than he was supposed to be. All morning his mind was not on the gate he was supposed to guard but was chasing around after his blood, like a boy with a mop and a bucket, beating something here and sloshing down something there, without a second's rest. As soon as the second-shift guard came, Enoch headed toward town.

Town was the last place he wanted to be because anything could happen there. All the time his mind had been chasing around it had been thinking how as soon as he got off duty he was going to sneak off home and go to bed.

By the time he got into the center of the business district he was exhausted and he had to lean against Walgreen's window and cool off. Sweat crept down his back and provoked him to itch so that in just a few minutes he appeared to be working his way across the glass by his muscles, against a background of alarm clocks, toilet waters, candies, sanitary pads, fountain pens, and pocket flashlights, displayed in all colors to twice his height. He appeared to be working his way to a rumbling noise which came from the center of a small alcove that formed the entrance to the drug store. Here was a yellow and blue, glass and steel machine, belching popcorn into a cauldron of butter and salt. Enoch approached, already with his purse out, sorting his money. His purse was a long gray leather pouch, tied at the top with a drawstring. It was one he had stolen from his daddy and he treasured it because it was the only thing he owned now that his daddy had touched (besides himself). He sorted out two nickels and handed them to a pasty boy in a white apron who was there to serve the machine. The boy felt around in its vitals and filled a white paper bag with the corn, not taking his eye off Enoch's purse the while. On any other day Enoch would have tried to make friends with him but today he was too preoccupied even to see him. He took the bag and began stuffing the pouch back where it had come from. The youth's eye followed to the very edge of the pocket. "That thang looks like a hawg bladder," he observed enviously.

"I got to go now," Enoch murmured and hurried into the drug store. Inside, he walked abstractedly to the back of the store, and then up to the front again by the other aisle as if he wanted any person who might be looking for him to see he was there. He paused in front of the soda fountain to see if he would sit down and have something to eat. The fountain counter was pink and green marble linoleum and behind it there was a red-headed waitress in a lime-colored uniform and a pink apron. She had green eyes set in pink and they resembled a picture behind her of a Lime-Cherry Surprise, a special that day for ten cents. She confronted Enoch while he studied the information over her head. After a minute she laid her chest on the counter and surrounded it by her folded arms, to wait. Enoch couldn't decide which of several concoctions was the one for him to have until she ended it by moving one arm under the counter and bringing out a Lime-Cherry Surprise. "It's okay," she said, "I fixed it this morning after breakfast."

"Something's going to happen to me today," Enoch said.

"I told you it was okay," she said. "I fixed it today."

"I seen it this morning when I woke up," he said, with the look of a visionary.

"God," she said, and jerked it from under his face. She turned around and began slapping things together; in a second she slammed another—exactly like it, but fresh—in front of him.

"I got to go now," Enoch said, and hurried out. An eye caught at his pocket as he passed the popcorn machine but he didn't stop. I don't want to do it, he was saying to himself. Whatever it is, I don't want to do it. I'm going home. It'll be something I don't want to do. It'll be something

I ain't got no business doing. And he thought of how he had had to spend all his money on drapes and gilt when he could have bought him a shirt and a phosphorescent tie. It'll be something against the law, he said. It's always something against the law. I ain't going to do it, he said, and stopped. He had stopped in front of a movie house where there was a large illustration of a monster stuffing a young woman into an incinerator.

I ain't going in no picture show like that, he said, giving it a nervous look. I'm going home. I ain't going to wait around in no picture show. I ain't got the money to buy a ticket, he said, taking out his purse again. I ain't even going to count thisyer change.

It ain't but forty-three cent here, he said, that ain't enough. A sign said the price of a ticket for adults was forty-five cents, balcony, thirty-five. I ain't going to sit in no balcony, he said, buying a thirty-five cent ticket.

I ain't going in, he said.

Two doors flew open and he found himself moving down a long red foyer and then up a darker tunnel and then up a higher, still darker tunnel. In a few minutes he was up in a high part of the maw, feeling around, like Jonah, for a seat. I ain't going to look at it, he said furiously. He didn't like any picture shows but colored musical ones.

The first picture was about a scientist named The Eye who performed operations by remote control. You would wake up in the morning and find a slit in your chest or head or stomach and something you couldn't do without would be gone. Enoch pulled his hat down very low and drew his knees up in front of his face; only his eyes looked at the screen. That picture lasted an hour.

The second picture was about life at Devil's Island Penitentiary. After a while, Enoch had to grip the two arms of his seat to keep himself from falling over the rail in front of him.

The third picture was called, "Lonnie Comes Home Again." It was about a baboon named Lonnie who rescued attractive children from a burning orphanage. Enoch kept hoping Lonnie would get burned up but he didn't appear to get even hot. In the end a nice-looking girl gave him a medal. It was more than Enoch could stand. He made a dive for the aisle, fell down the two higher tunnels, and raced out the red foyer and into the street. He collapsed as soon as the air hit him.

When he recovered himself, he was sitting against the wall of the picture show building and he was not thinking any more about escaping his duty. It was night and he had the feeling that the knowledge he couldn't avoid was almost on him. His resignation was perfect. He leaned against the wall for about twenty minutes and then he got up and began to walk down the street as if he were led by a silent melody or by one of those whistles that only dogs hear. At the end of two blocks he stopped, his attention directed across the street. There, facing him under a street light, was a high rat-colored car and up on the nose of it, a dark figure with a fierce white hat on. The figure's arms were working up and down and he had thin, gesticulating hands, almost as pale as the hat. "Hazel Motes!" Enoch breathed, and his heart began to slam from side to side like a wild bell clapper.

There were a few people standing on the sidewalk near the car. Enoch didn't know that Hazel Motes had started the Church Without Christ and was preaching it every night on the street; he hadn't seen him since that day at the park when he had showed him the shriveled man in the glass case.

"If you had been redeemed," Hazel Motes was shouting, "you would care about redemption but you don't. Look inside yourselves and see if you hadn't rather it wasn't if it was. There's no peace for the redeemed," he shouted, "and I preach peace, I preach the Church Without Christ, the church peaceful and satisfied!"

Two or three people who had stopped near the car started walking off the other way. "Leave!" Hazel Motes cried. "Go ahead and leave! The truth don't matter to you. Listen," he said, pointing his finger at the rest of them, "the truth don't matter to you. If Jesus had redeemed you, what difference would it make to you? You wouldn't do nothing about it. Your faces wouldn't move, neither this way nor that, and if it was three crosses there and Him hung on the middle one, that one wouldn't mean no more to you and me than the other two. Listen here. What you need is something to take the place of Jesus, something that would speak plain. The Church Without Christ don't have a Jesus but it needs one! It needs a new jesus! It needs one that's all man, without blood to waste, and it needs one that don't look like any other man so you'll look at him. Give me such a jesus, you people. Give me such a new jesus and you'll see how far the Church Without Christ can go!"

One of the people watching walked off so there were only two left. Enoch was standing in the middle of the street, paralyzed.

"Show me where this new jesus is," Hazel Motes cried, "and I'll set him up in the Church Without Christ and then you'll see the truth. Then you'll know once and for all that you haven't been redeemed. Give me this new jesus, somebody, so we'll all be saved by the sight of him!"

Enoch began shouting without a sound. He shouted that way for a full minute while Hazel Motes went on.

"Look at me!" Hazel Motes cried, with a tare in his throat, "and you look at a peaceful man! Peaceful because my blood has set me free. Take counsel from your blood and come into the Church Without Christ and maybe somebody will bring us a new jesus and we'll all be saved by the sight of him!"

An unintelligible sound spluttered out of Enoch. He tried to bellow, but his blood held him back. He whispered, "Listenhere, I got him! I mean I can get him! You know! Him! Him I shown you to. You seen him yourself!"

His blood reminded him that the last time he had seen Haze Motes was when Haze Motes had hit him over the head with a rock. And he didn't even know yet how he would steal it out of the glass case. The only thing he knew was that he had a place in his room prepared to keep it in until Haze was ready to take it. His blood suggested he just let it come as a surprise to Haze Motes. He began to back away. He backed across the street and over a piece of sidewalk and out into the other street and a taxi had to stop short to keep from hitting him. The driver put his head out the window and asked him how he got around so well when God had made him by putting two backs together instead of a back and a front.

Enoch was too preoccupied to think about it. "I got to go now," he murmured, and hurried off.

Chapter 9

Hawks kept his door bolted and whenever Haze knocked on it, which he did two or three times a day, the ex-evangelist sent his child out to him and bolted the door again behind her. It infuriated him to have Haze lurking in the house, thinking up some excuse to get in and look at his face; and he was often drunk and didn't want to be discovered that way.

Haze couldn't understand why the preacher didn't welcome him and act like a preacher should when he sees what he believes is a lost soul. He kept trying to get into the room again; the window he could have reached was kept locked and the shade pulled down. He wanted to see, if he could, *behind* the black glasses.

Every time he went to the door, the girl came out and the bolt shut inside; then he couldn't get rid of her. She followed him out to his car and climbed in and spoiled his rides or she followed him up to his room and sat. He abandoned the notion of seducing her and tried to protect himself. He hadn't been in the house a week before she appeared in his room one night after he had gone to bed. She was holding a candle burning in a jelly glass and wore, hanging onto her thin shoulders, a woman's nightgown that dragged on the floor behind her. Haze didn't wake up until she was almost up to his bed, and when he did, he sprang from under his cover into the middle of the room.

"What you want?" he said.

She didn't say anything and her grin widened in the candle light. He stood glowering at her for an instant and then he picked up the straight chair and raised it as if he were going to bring it down on her. She lingered only a fraction of a second. His door didn't bolt so he propped the chair under the knob before he went back to bed.

"Listen," she said when she got back to their room, "nothing works. He would have hit me with a chair."

"I'm leaving out of here in a couple of days," Hawks said, "you better make it work if you want to eat after I'm gone." He was drunk but he meant it.

Nothing was working the way Haze had expected it to. He had spent every evening preaching, but the membership of the Church Without Christ was still only one person: himself. He had wanted to have a large following quickly to impress the blind man with his powers, but no one had followed him. There had been a sort of follower but that had been a mistake. That had been a boy about sixteen years old who had wanted someone to go to a whorehouse with him because he had never been to one before. He knew where the place was but he didn't want to go without a person of experience, and when he heard Haze, he hung around until he stopped preaching and then asked him to go. But it was all a mistake because after they had gone and got out again and Haze had asked him to be a member of the Church Without Christ, or more than that, a disciple, an apostle, the boy said he was sorry but he couldn't be a member of that church because he was a Lapsed Catholic. He said that what they had just done was a mortal sin, and that should they die unrepentant of it they would suffer eternal punishment and never see God. Haze had not enjoyed the whorehouse anywhere near as much as the boy had and he had wasted half his evening. He shouted that there was no such thing as sin or judgment, but the boy only shook his head and asked him if he would like to go again the next night.

If Haze had believed in praying, he would have prayed for a disciple, but as it was all he could do was worry about it a lot. Then two nights after the boy, the disciple appeared.

That night he preached outside of four different picture shows and every time he looked up, he saw the same big face smiling at him. The man was plumpish, and he had curly blond hair that was cut with showy sideburns. He wore a black suit with a silver stripe in it and a wide-brimmed white hat pushed onto the back of his head, and he had on tight-fitting black pointed shoes and no socks. He looked like an ex-preacher turned cowboy, or an ex-cowboy turned mortician. He was not handsome but under his smile, there was an honest look that fitted into his face like a set of false teeth.

Every time Haze looked at him, the man winked.

At the last picture show he preached in front of, there were three people listening to him besides the man. "Do you people care anything about the truth?" he asked. "The only way to the truth is through blasphemy, but do you care? Are you going to pay any attention to what I've been saying or are you just going to walk off like everybody else?"

There were two men and a woman with a cat-faced baby sprawled over her shoulder. She had been looking at Haze as if he were in a booth at the fair. "Well, come on," she said, "he's finished. We got to be going." She turned away and the two men fell in behind her.

"Go ahead and go," Haze said, "but remember that the truth don't lurk around every street corner."

The man who had been following reached up quickly and pulled Haze's pantsleg and gave him a wink. "Come on back heah, you folks," he said. "I want to tell you all about *me*."

The woman turned around again and he smiled at her as if he had been struck all along with her good looks. She had a square red face and her hair was freshly set. "I wisht I had my gittarr here," the man said, " 'cause I just somehow can say sweet things to music bettern plain. And when you talk about Jesus you need a little music, don't you, friends?" He looked at the two men as if he were appealing to the good judgment that was impressed on their faces. They had on brown felt hats and black town suits, and they looked like older and younger brother. "Listen, friends," the disciple said confidentially, "two months ago before I met the Prophet here, you wouldn't know me for the same man. I didn't have a friend in the world. Do you know what it's like not to have a friend in the world?"

"It ain't no worsen havinum that would put a knife in your back when you wasn't looking," the older man said, barely parting his lips.

"Friend, you said a mouthful when you said that," the man said. "If we had time, I would have you repeat that just so ever'body could hear it like I did." The picture show was over and more people were coming up. "Friends," the man said, "I know you're all interested in the Prophet here," pointing to Haze on the nose of the car, "and if you'll just give me time I'm going to tell you what him and his idears've done for me. Don't crowd because I'm willing to stay here all night and tell you if it takes that long."

Haze stood where he was, motionless, with his head slightly forward, as if he weren't sure that he was hearing.

"Friends," the man said, "lemme innerduce myself. My name is Onnie Jay Holy and I'm telling it to you so you can check up and see I don't tell you any lie. I'm a preacher and I don't mind who knows it but I wouldn't have you believe nothing you can't feel in your own hearts. You people coming up on the edge push right on up in here where you can hear good," he said. "I'm not selling a thing, I'm giving something away!" A considerable number of people had stopped.

"Friends," he said, "two months ago you wouldn't know me for the same man. I didn't have a friend in the world. Do you know what it's like not to have a friend in the world?"

A loud voice said, "It ain't no worsen havinum that would put . . ."

"Why, friends," Onnie Jay Holy said, "not to have a friend in the world is just about the most miserable and lonesome thing that can happen to a man or woman! And that's the way it was with me. I was ready to hang myself or to despair completely. Not even my own dear old mother loved me, and it wasn't because I wasn't sweet inside, it was because I never known how to make the natural sweetness inside me show. Every person that comes onto this earth," he said, stretching out his arms, "is born sweet and full of love. A little child loves ever'body, friends, and its nature is sweetness—until something happens. Something happens, friends, I don't need to tell people like you that can think for theirselves. As that little child gets bigger, its sweetness don't show so much, cares and troubles come to perplext it, and all its sweetness is driven inside it. Then it gets miserable and lonesome and sick, friends. It says, 'Where is all my sweetness gone? where are all the friends that loved me?' and all the time, that little beat-up rose of its sweetness is inside, not a petal dropped, and on the outside is just a mean lonesomeness. It may want to take its own life or yours or mine, or to despair completely, friends." He said it in a sad nasal voice but he was smiling all the time so that they could tell he had been through what he was talking about and come out on top. "That was the way it was with me, friends. I know what of I speak," he said, and folded his hands in front of him. "But all the time that I was ready to hang myself or to despair completely, I was sweet inside, like ever'body else, and I only needed something to bring it out. I only needed a little help, friends.

"Then I met this Prophet here," he said, pointing at Haze on the nose of the car. "That was two months ago, folks, that I heard how he was out to help me, how he was preaching the Church of Christ Without Christ, the church that was going to get a new jesus to help me bring my sweet nature into the open where ever'body could enjoy it. That was two months ago, friends, and now you wouldn't know me for the same man. I love ever'one of you people and I want you to listen to him and me and join our church, the Holy Church of Christ Without Christ, the new church with the new jesus, and then you'll all be helped like me!"

Haze leaned forward. "This man is not true," he said. "I never saw him before tonight. I wasn't preaching this church two months ago and the name of it ain't the Holy Church of Christ Without Christ!"

The man ignored this and so did the people. There were ten or twelve gathered around. "Friends," Onnie Jay Holy said, "I'm mighty glad you're seeing me now instead of two months ago because then I couldn't have testified to this new church and this Prophet here. If I had my gittarr with me I could say all this better but I'll just have to do the best I can by myself." He had a winning smile and it was evident that he didn't think he was any better than anybody else even though he was.

"Now I just want to give you folks a few reasons why you can trust this church," he said. "In the first place, friends, you can rely on it that it's nothing foreign connected with it. You don't have to believe nothing you don't understand and approve of. If you don't understand it, it ain't true, and that's all there is to it. No jokers in the deck, friends."

Haze leaned forward. "Blasphemy is the way to the truth," he said, "and there's no other way whether you understand it or not!"

"Now, friends," Onnie Jay said, "I want to tell you a second reason why you can absolutely trust this church—it's based on the Bible. Yes sir! It's based on your own personal interpitation of the Bible, friends. You can sit at home and interpit your own Bible however you feel in your heart it ought to be interpited. That's right," he said, "just the way Jesus would have done it. Gee, I wisht I had my gittarr here," he complained.

"This man is a liar," Haze said. "I never saw him before tonight. I never . . ."

"That ought to be enough reasons, friends," Onnie Jay Holy said, "but I'm going to tell you one more, just to show I can. This church is up-to-date! When you're in this church you can know that there's nothing or nobody ahead of you, nobody knows nothing you don't know, all the cards are on the table, friends, and that's a fack!"

Haze's face under the white hat began to take on a look of fierceness. Just as he was about to open his mouth again, Onnie Jay Holy pointed in astonishment to the baby in the blue bonnet who was sprawled limp over the woman's shoulder. "Why yonder is a little babe," he said, "a little bundle of helpless sweetness. Why, I know you people aren't going to let that little thing grow up and have all his sweetness pushed inside him when it could be on the outside to win friends and make him loved. That's why I want ever' one of you people to join the Holy Church of Christ Without Christ. It'll cost you each a dollar but what is a dollar? A few dimes! Not too much to pay to unlock that little rose of sweetness inside you!"

"Listen!" Haze shouted. "It don't cost you any money to know the truth! You can't know it for money!"

"You hear what the Prophet says, friends," Onnie Jay Holy said, "a dollar is not too much to pay. No amount of money is too much to learn the truth! Now I want each of you people that are going to take advantage of this church to sign on this little pad I have in my pocket here and give me your dollar personally and let me shake your hand!"

Haze slid down from the nose of his car and got in it and slammed his foot on the starter.

"Hey wait! Wait!" Onnie Jay Holy shouted, "I ain't got any of these friends' names yet!"

The Essex had a tendency to develop a tic by nightfall. It would go forward about six inches and then back about four; it did that now a succession of times rapidly; otherwise Haze would have shot off in it and been gone. He had to grip the steering wheel with both hands to keep from being thrown either out the windshield or into the back. It stopped this after a few seconds and slid about twenty feet and then began it again.

Onnie Jay Holy's face showed a great strain; he put his hand to the side of it as if the only way he could keep his smile on was to hold it. "I got to go now, friends," he said quickly, "but I'll be at this same spot tomorrow night. I got to go catch the Prophet now," and he ran off just as the Essex began to slide again. He wouldn't have caught it, except that it stopped before it had gone ten feet farther. He jumped on the running board and got the door open and plumped in, panting, beside Haze. "Friend," he said, "we just lost ten dollars. What you in such a hurry for?" His face showed that he was in some kind of genuine pain even though he looked at Haze with a smile that revealed all his upper teeth and the tops of his lowers.

Haze turned his head and looked at him long enough to see the smile before it was thrown forward at the windshield. After that the Essex began running smoothly. Onnie Jay took out a lavender handkerchief and held it in front of his mouth for some time. When he removed it, the smile was back on his face. "Friend," he said, "you and me have to get together on this thing. I said when I first heard you open your mouth, 'Why, yonder is a great man with great idears.' "

Haze didn't turn his head.

Onnie Jay took in a long breath. "Why, do you know who you put me in mind of when I first saw you?" he asked. After a minute of waiting, he said in a soft voice, "Jesus Christ and Abraham Lincoln, friend."

Haze's face was suddenly swamped with outrage. All the expression on it was obliterated. "You ain't true," he said in a barely audible voice.

"Friend, how can you say that?" Onnie Jay said. "Why I was on the radio for three years with a program that give real religious experiences to the whole family. Didn't you ever listen to it—called Soulsease, a quarter hour of Mood, Melody, and Mentality? I'm a real preacher, friend."

Haze stopped the Essex. "You get out," he said.

"Why friend!" Onnie Jay said. "You ought not to say such a thing! That's the absolute truth that I'm a preacher and a radio star."

"Get out," Haze said, reaching across and opening the door for him.

"I never thought you would treat a friend thisaway," Onnie Jay said. "All I wanted to ast you about was this new jesus."

"Get out," Haze said, and began to push him toward the door. He pushed him to the edge of the seat and gave him a shove and Onnie Jay fell out the door and into the road.

"I never thought a friend would treat me thisaway," he complained. Haze kicked his leg off the running board and shut the door again. He put his foot on the starter but nothing happened except a noise somewhere underneath him that sounded like a person gargling without water. Onnie Jay got up off the pavement and stood at the window. "If you would just tell me where this new jesus is you was mentioning," he began.

Haze put his foot on the starter a succession of times but nothing happened.

"Pull out the choke," Onnie Jay advised, getting up on the running board.

"There's no choke on it," Haze snarled.

"Maybe it's flooded," Onnie Jay said. "While we're waiting, you and me can talk about the Holy Church of Christ Without Christ."

"My church is the Church Without Christ," Haze said. "I've seen all of you I want to."

"It don't make any difference how many Christs you

add to the name if you don't add none to the meaning, friend," Onnie Jay said in a hurt tone. "You ought to listen to me because I'm not just an amateur. I'm an artist-type. If you want to get anywheres in religion, you got to keep it sweet. You got good idears but what you need is an artist-type to work with you."

Haze rammed his foot on the gas and then on the starter and then on the starter and then on the gas. Nothing happened. The street was practically deserted. "Me and you could get behind it and push it over to the curb," Onnie Jay suggested.

"I ain't asked for your help," Haze said.

"You know, friend, I certainly would like to see this new jesus," Onnie Jay said. "I never heard a idear before that had more in it than that one. All it would need is a little promotion."

Haze tried to start the car by forcing his weight forward on the steering wheel, but that didn't work. He got out and got behind it and began to push it over to the curb. Onnie Jay got behind with him and added his weight. "I kind of have had that idear about a new jesus myself," he remarked. "I seen how a new one would be more up-to-date.

"Where you keeping him, friend?" he asked. "Is he somebody you see ever' day? I certainly would like to meet him and hear some of his idears."

They pushed the car into a parking space. There was no way to lock it and Haze was afraid that if he left it out all night so far away from where he lived someone would be able to steal it. There was nothing for him to do but sleep in it. He got in the back and began to pull down the fringed shades. Onnie Jay had his head in the front, however. "You needn't to be afraid that if I seen this new jesus I would cut you out of anything," he said. "Why friend, it would just mean a lot to me for the good of my spirit."

Haze moved the two-by-four off the seat frame to make more room to fix up his pallet. He kept a pillow and an army blanket back there and he had a sterno stove and a coffee pot up on the shelf under the back oval window. "Friend, I would even be glad to pay you a little something to see him," Onnie Jay suggested.

"Listen here," Haze said, "you get away from here. I've seen all of you I want to. There's no such thing as any new jesus. That ain't anything but a way to say something."

The smile more or less slithered off Onnie Jay's face. "What you mean by that?" he asked.

"That there's no such thing or person," Haze said. "It

wasn't nothing but a way to say a thing." He put his hand on the door handle and began to close it in spite of Onnie Jay's head. "No such thing exists!" he shouted.

"That's the trouble with you innerleckchuls," Onnie Jay muttered, "you don't never have nothing to show for what you're saying."

"Get your head out my car door, Holy," Haze said.

"My name is Hoover Shoats," the man with his head in the door growled. "I known when I first seen you that you wasn't nothing but a crackpot."

Haze opened the door enough to be able to slam it. Hoover Shoats got his head out the way but not his thumb. A howl arose that would have rended almost any heart. Haze opened the door and released the thumb and then slammed the door again. He pulled down the front shades and lay down in the back of the car on the army blanket. Outside he could hear Hoover Shoats jumping around on the pavement and howling. When the howls died down, Haze heard a few steps up to the car and then an impassioned, breathless voice say through the tin, "You watch out, friend. I'm going to run you out of business. I can get my own new jesus and I can get Prophets for peanuts, you hear? Do you hear me, friend?" the hoarse voice said.

Haze didn't answer.

"Yeah and I'll be out there doing my own preaching tomorrow night. What you need is a little competition," the voice said. "Do you hear me, friend?"

Haze got up and leaned over the front seat and banged his hand down on the horn of the Essex. It made a sound like a goat's laugh cut off with a buzz saw. Hoover Shoats jumped back as if a charge of electricity had gone through him. "All right, friend," he said, standing about fifteen feet away, trembling, "you just wait, you ain't heard the last of me yet," and he turned and went off down the quiet street.

Haze stayed in his car about an hour and had a bad experience in it: he dreamed he was not dead but only buried. He was not waiting on the Judgment because there was no Judgment, he was waiting on nothing. Various eyes looked through the back oval window at his situation, some with considerable reverence, like the boy from the zoo, and some only to see what they could see. There were three women with paper sacks who looked at him critically as if he were something—a piece of fish—they might buy, but they passed on after a minute. A man in a canvas hat looked in and put his thumb to his nose and wiggled his fingers. Then a woman with two little boys on either side of her stopped and looked in, grinning. After a second, she pushed the boys out of view and indicated that she would climb in and keep him company for a while, but she couldn't get through the glass and finally she went off. All this time Haze was bent on getting out but since there was no use to try, he didn't make any move one way or the other. He kept expecting Hawks to appear at the oval window with a wrench, but the blind man didn't come.

Finally he shook off the dream and woke up. He thought it should be morning but it was only midnight. He pulled himself over into the front of the car and eased his foot on the starter and the Essex rolled off quietly as if nothing were the matter with it. He drove back to the house and let himself in but instead of going upstairs to his room, he stood in the hall, looking at the blind man's door. He went over to it and put his ear to the keyhole and heard the sound of snoring; he turned the knob gently but the door didn't move.

For the first time, the idea of picking the lock occurred to him. He felt in his pockets for an instrument and came on a small piece of wire that he sometimes used for a toothpick. There was only a dim light in the hall but it was enough for him to work by and he knelt down at the keyhole and inserted the wire into it carefully, trying not to make a noise.

After a while when he had tried the wire five or six different ways, there was a slight click in the lock. He stood up, trembling, and opened the door. His breath came short and his heart was palpitating as if he had run all the way here from a great distance. He stood just inside the room until his eyes got accustomed to the darkness and then he moved slowly over to the iron bed and stood there. Hawks was lying across it. His head was hanging over the edge. Haze squatted down by him and struck a match close to his face and he opened his eyes. The two sets of eyes looked at each other as long as the match lasted; Haze's expression seemed to open onto a deeper blankness and reflect something and then close again.

"Now you can get out," Hawks said in a short thick voice, "now you can leave me alone," and he made a jab at the face over him without touching it. It moved back, expressionless under the white hat, and was gone in a second.

Chapter 10

The next night, Haze parked the Essex in front of the Odeon Theater and climbed up on it and began to preach. "Let me tell you what I and this church stand for!" he called from the nose of the car. "Stop one minute to listen to the truth because you may never hear it again." He stood there with his neck thrust forward, moving one arm upward in a vague arc. Two women and a boy stopped.

"I preach there are all kinds of truth, your truth and somebody else's, but behind all of them, there's only one truth and that is that there's no truth," he called. "No truth behind all truths is what I and this church preach! Where you come from is gone, where you thought you were going to never was there, and where you are is no good unless you can get away from it. Where is there a place for you to be? No place.

"Nothing outside you can give you any place," he said. "You needn't to look at the sky because it's not going to open up and show no place behind it. You needn't to search for any hole in the ground to look through into somewhere else. You can't go neither forwards nor backwards into your daddy's time nor your children's if you have them. In yourself right now is all the place you've got. If there was any Fall, look there, if there was any Redemption, look there, and if you expect any Judgment, look there, because they all three will have to be in your time and your body and where in your time and your body can they be?

"Where in your time and your body has Jesus redeemed you?" he cried. "Show me where because I don't see the place. If there was a place where Jesus had redeemed you that would be the place for you to be, but which of you can find it?"

Another trickle of people came out of the Odeon and two stopped to look at him. "Who is that that says it's your conscience?" he cried, looking around with a constricted face as if he could smell the particular person who thought that. "Your conscience is a trick," he said, "it don't exist though you may think it does, and if you think it does, you had best get it out in the open and hunt it down and kill it, because it's no more than your face in the mirror is or your shadow behind you."

He was preaching with such concentration that he didn't notice a high rat-colored car that had been driven around the block three times already, while the two men in it hunted a place to park. He didn't see it when it pulled in two cars over from him in a space that another car had just pulled out of, and he didn't see Hoover Shoats and a man in a glare-blue suit and white hat get out of it, but after a few seconds, his head turned that way and he saw the man in the glare-blue suit and white hat up on the nose of it. He was so struck with how gaunt and thin he looked in the illusion that he stopped preaching. He had never pictured himself that way before. The man he saw was hollow-chested and carried his neck thrust forward and his arms down by his side; he stood there as if he were waiting for some signal he was afraid he might not catch.

Hoover Shoats was walking about on the sidewalk, striking a few chords on his guitar. "Friends," he called, "I want to innerduce you to the True Prophet here and I want you all to listen to his words because I think they're going to make you happy like they've made me!" If Haze had noticed Hoover he might have been impressed by how happy he looked, but his attention was fixed on the man on the nose of the car. He slid down from his own car and moved up closer, never taking his eyes from the bleak figure. Hoover Shoats raised his hand with two fingers pointed and the man suddenly cried out in a high nasal singsong voice. "The unredeemed are redeeming theirselves and the new jesus is at hand! Watch for this miracle! Help yourself to salvation in the Holy Church of Christ Without Christ!" He called it over again in exactly the same tone of voice, but faster. Then he began to cough. He had a loud consumptive cough that started somewhere deep in him and finished with a long wheeze. He expectorated a white fluid at the end of it.

Haze was standing next to a fat woman who after a minute turned her head and stared at him and then turned it again and stared at the True Prophet. Finally she touched his elbow with hers and grinned at him. "Him and you twins?" she asked.

"If you don't hunt it down and kill it, it'll hunt you down and kill you," Haze answered.

"Huh? Who?" she said.

He turned away and she stared at him as he got back

in his car and drove off. Then she touched the elbow of a man on the other side of her. "He's nuts," she said. "I never seen no twins that hunted each other down."

When he got back to his room, Sabbath Hawks was in his bed. She was pushed over into one corner of it, sitting with one arm drawn around her knees and one hand holding onto the sheet as if she meant to hang on by it. Her face was sullen and apprehensive. Haze sat down on the bed but he barely glanced at her. "I don't care if you hit me with the table," she said. "I'm not going. There's no place for me to go. He's run off on me and it was you run him off. I was watching last night and I seen you come in and hold that match to his face. I thought anybody would have seen what he was before that without having to strike no match. He's just a crook. He ain't even a big crook, just a little one, and when he gets tired of that, he begs on the street."

Haze leaned down and began untying his shoes. They were old army shoes that he had painted black to get the government off. He untied them and eased his feet out and sat there looking down, while she watched him cautiously.

"Are you going to hit me or not?" she asked. "If you are, go ahead and do it right now because I'm not going. I ain't got any place to go." He didn't look as if he were going to hit anything; he looked as if he were going to sit there until he died. "Listen," she said, with a quick change of tone, "from the minute I set eyes on you I said to myself, that's what I got to have, just give me some of him! I said look at those pee-can eyes and go crazy, girl! That innocent look don't hide a thing, he's just pure filthy right down to the guts, like me. The only difference is I like being that way and he don't. Yes sir!" she said. "I like being that way, and I can teach you how to like it. Don't you want to learn how to like it?"

He turned his head slightly and just over his shoulder he saw a pinched homely little face with bright green eyes and a grin. "Yeah," he said with no change in his stony expression, "I want to." He stood up and took off his coat and his trousers and his drawers and put them on the straight chair. Then he turned off the light and sat down on the cot again and pulled off his socks. His feet were big and white and damp to the floor and he sat there, looking at the two white shapes they made.

"Come on! Make haste," she said, knocking his back with her knee.

He unbuttoned his shirt and took it off and wiped his

face with it and dropped it on the floor. Then he slid his legs under the cover by her and sat there as if he were waiting to remember one more thing.

She was breathing very quickly. "Take off your hat, king of the beasts," she said gruffly and her hand came up behind his head and snatched the hat off and sent it flying across the room in the dark.

Chapter 11

The next morning toward noon a person in a long black raincoat, with a lightish hat pulled down low on his face and the brim of it turned down to meet the turned-up collar of the raincoat, was moving rapidly along certain back streets, close to the walls of the buildings. He was carrying something about the size of a baby, wrapped up in newspapers, and he carried a dark umbrella too, as the sky was an unpredictable surly gray like the back of an old goat. He had on a pair of dark glasses and a black beard which a keen observer would have said was not a natural growth but was pinned onto his hat on either side with safety pins. As he walked along, the umbrella kept slipping from under his arm and getting tangled in his feet, as if it meant to keep him from going anywhere.

He had not gone half a block before large putty-colored drops began to splatter on the pavement and there was an ugly growl in the sky behind him. He began to run, clutching the bundle in one arm and the umbrella in the other. In a second, the storm overtook him and he ducked between two show-windows into the blue and white tiled entrance of a drug store. He lowered his dark glasses a little. The pale eyes that looked over the rims belonged to Enoch Emery. Enoch was on his way to Hazel Motes's room.

He had never been to Hazel Motes's place before but the instinct that was guiding him was very sure of itself. What was in the bundle was what he had shown Hazel at the museum. He had stolen it the day before.

He had darkened his face and hands with brown shoe polish so that if he were seen in the act, he would be taken for a colored person; then he had sneaked into the museum while the guard was asleep and had broken the glass case with a wrench he'd borrowed from his landlady; then, shaking and sweating, he had lifted the shriveled man out and thrust him in a paper sack, and had crept out again past the guard, who was still asleep. He realized as soon as he got out of the museum that since no one had seen him to think he was a colored boy, he would be suspected immediately and would have to disguise himself. That was why he had on the black beard and dark glasses.

When he'd got back to his room, he had taken the new jesus out of the sack and, hardly daring to look at him, had laid him in the gilted cabinet; then he had sat down on the edge of his bed to wait. He was waiting for something to happen, he didn't know what. He knew something was going to happen and his entire system was waiting on it. He thought it was going to be one of the supreme moments in his life but apart from that, he didn't have the vaguest notion what it might be. He pictured himself, after it was over, as an entirely new man, with an even better personality than he had now. He sat there for about fifteen minutes and nothing happened.

He sat there for about five more.

Then he realized that he had to make the first move. He got up and tiptoed to the cabinet and squatted down at the door of it; in a second he opened it a crack and looked in. After a while, very slowly, he broadened the crack and inserted his head into the tabernacle.

Some time passed.

From directly behind him, only the soles of his shoes and the seat of his trousers were visible. The room was absolutely silent; there was no sound even from the street; the Universe might have been shut off; not a flea jumped. Then without any warning, a loud liquid noise burst from the cabinet and there was the thump of bone cracked once against a piece of wood. Enoch staggered backward, clutching his head and his face. He sat on the floor for a few minutes with a shocked expression on his whole figure. At the first instant, he had thought it was the shriveled man who had sneezed, but after a second, he perceived the condition of his own nose. He wiped it off with his sleeve and then he sat there on the floor for some time longer. His expression had showed that a deep unpleasant knowledge was breaking on him slowly. After a while he had kicked the ark door shut in the new jesus' face, and then he had got up and begun to eat a candy bar very rapidly. He had eaten it as if he had something against it.

The next morning he had not got up until ten o'clock—it was his day off—and he had not set out until nearly noon to look for Hazel Motes. He remembered the address Sabbath Hawks had given him and that was where his instinct was leading him. He was very sullen and disgruntled at having to spend his day off in such a way as this, and in bad weather, but he wanted to get rid of the new jesus so that if the police had to catch anybody for the robbery, they could catch Hazel Motes instead of him. He couldn't understand at all why he had let himself risk his skin for a dead shriveled-up part-nigger dwarf that had never done anything but get himself embalmed and then lain stinking in a museum the rest of his life. It was far beyond his understanding. He was very sullen. So far as he was now concerned, one jesus was as bad as another.

He had borrowed his landlady's umbrella and he discovered as he stood in the entrance of the drug store, trying to open it, that it was at least as old as she was. When he finally got it hoisted, he pushed his dark glasses back on his eyes and re-entered the downpour.

The umbrella was one his landlady had stopped using fifteen years before (which was the only reason she had lent it to him) and as soon as the rain touched the top of it, it came down with a shriek and stabbed him in the back of the neck. He ran a few feet with it over his head and then backed into another store entrance and removed it. Then to get it up again, he had to place the tip of it on the ground and ram it open with his foot. He ran out again, holding his hand up near the spokes to keep them open and this allowed the handle, which was carved to represent the head of a fox terrier, to jab him every few seconds in the stomach. He proceeded for another quarter of a block this way before the back half of the silk stood up off the spokes and allowed the storm to sweep down his collar. Then he ducked under the marquee of a movie house. It was Saturday and there were a lot of children standing more or less in a line in front of the ticket box.

Enoch was not very fond of children but children always seemed to like to look at him. The line turned and twenty or thirty eyes began to observe him with a steady interest. The umbrella had assumed an ugly position, half up and half down, and the half that was up was about to come down and spill more water under his collar. When this happened the children laughed and jumped up and down. Enoch glared at them and turned his back and lowered his dark glasses. He found himself facing a life-size four-color picture of a gorilla. Over the gorilla's head, written in red letters was, "GONGA! Giant Jungle Monarch and a Great Star! HERE IN PERSON! ! !" At the level of the gorilla's knee, there was more that said, "Gonga will appear in person in front of this theater at 12 A.M. *TODAY!* A free pass to the first ten brave enough to step up and shake his hand!"

Enoch was usually thinking of something else at the moment that Fate began drawing back her leg to kick him. When he was four years old, his father had brought him home a tin box from the penitentiary. It was orange and had a picture of some peanut brittle on the outside of it and green letters that said, A NUTTY SURPRISE! When Enoch had opened it, a coiled piece of steel had sprung out at him and broken off the ends of his two front teeth. His life was full of so many happenings like that that it would seem he should have been more sensitive to his times of danger. He stood there and read the poster twice through carefully. To his mind, an opportunity to insult a successful ape came from the hand of Providence. He suddenly regained all his reverence for the new jesus. He saw that he was going to be rewarded after all and have the supreme moment he had expected.

He turned around and asked the nearest child what time it was. The child said it was twelve-ten and that Gonga was already ten minutes late. Another child said that maybe the rain had delayed him. Another said, no not the rain, his director was taking a plane from Hollywood. Enoch gritted his teeth. The first child said that if he wanted to shake the star's hand, he would have to get in line like the rest of them and wait his turn. Enoch got in line. A child asked him how old he was. Another observed that he had funny-looking teeth. He ignored all this as best he could and began to straighten out the umbrella.

In a few minutes a black truck turned around the corner and came slowly up the street in the heavy rain. Enoch pushed the umbrella under his arm and began to squint through his dark glasses. As the truck approached, a phonograph inside it began to play "Tarara Boom Di Aye," but the music was almost drowned out by the rain. There was a large illustration of a blonde on the outside of the truck, advertising some picture other than the gorilla's.

The children held their line carefully as the truck stopped in front of the movie house. The back door of it was constructed like a paddy wagon, with a grate, but the ape was not at it. Two men in raincoats got out of the cab part, cursing, and ran around to the back and opened the door. One of them stuck his head in and said, "Okay, make it snappy, willya?" The other jerked his thumb at the children and said, "Get back willya, willya get back?"

A voice on the record inside the truck said, "Here's Gonga, folks, Roaring Gonga and a Great Star! Give Gonga a big hand, folks!" The voice was barely a mumble in the rain.

The man who was waiting by the door of the truck stuck his head in again. "Okay willya get out?" he said.

There was a faint thump somewhere inside the van. After a second a dark furry arm emerged just enough for the rain to touch it and then drew back inside.

"Goddam," the man who was under the marquee said; he took off his raincoat and threw it to the man by the door, who threw it into the wagon. After two or three minutes more, the gorilla appeared at the door, with the raincoat buttoned up to his chin and the collar turned up. There was an iron chain hanging from around his neck; the man grabbed it and pulled him down and the two of them bounded under the marquee together. A motherly-looking woman was in the glass ticket box, getting the passes ready for the first ten children brave enough to step up and shake hands.

The gorilla ignored the children entirely and followed the man over to the other side of the entrance where there was a small platform raised about a foot off the ground. He stepped up on it and turned facing the children and began to growl. His growls were not so much loud as poisonous; they appeared to issue from a black heart. Enoch was terrified and if he had not been surrounded by the children, he would have run away.

"Who'll step up first?" the man said. "Come on come on, who'll step up first? A free pass to the first kid stepping up."

There was no movement from the group of children. The man glared at them. "What's the matter with you kids?" he barked. "You yellow? He won't hurt you as long as I got him by this chain." He tightened his grip on the chain and jangled it at them to show he was holding it securely.

After a minute a little girl separated herself from the group. She had long wood-shaving curls and a fierce triangular face. She moved up to within four feet of the star.

"Okay okay," the man said, rattling the chain, "make it snappy."

The ape reached out and gave her hand a quick shake. By this time there was another little girl ready and then two boys. The line re-formed and began to move up.

The gorilla kept his hand extended and turned his head away with a bored look at the rain. Enoch had got over his fear and was trying frantically to think of an obscene remark that would be suitable to insult him with. Usually he didn't have any trouble with this kind of composition but nothing came to him now. His brain, both parts, was completely empty. He couldn't think even of the insulting phrases he used every day.

There were only two children in front of him by now. The first one shook hands and stepped aside. Enoch's heart was beating violently. The child in front of him finished and stepped aside and left him facing the ape, who took his hand with an automatic motion.

It was the first hand that had been extended to Enoch since he had come to the city. It was warm and soft.

For a second he only stood there, clasping it. Then he began to stammer. "My name is Enoch Emery," he mumbled. "I attended the Rodemill Boys' Bible Academy. I work at the city zoo. I seen two of your pictures. I'm only eighteen year old but I already work for the city. My daddy made me com . . ." and his voice cracked.

The star leaned slightly forward and a change came in his eyes: an ugly pair of human ones moved closer and squinted at Enoch from behind the celluloid pair. "You go to hell," a surly voice inside the ape-suit said, low but distinctly, and the hand was jerked away.

Enoch's humiliation was so sharp and painful that he turned around three times before he realized which direction he wanted to go in. Then he ran off into the rain as fast as he could.

By the time he reached Sabbath Hawks's house, he was soaked through and so was his bundle. He held it in a fierce grip but all he wanted was to get rid of it and never see it again. Haze's landlady was out on the porch, looking distrustfully into the storm. He found out from her where Haze's room was and went up to it. The door was ajar and he stuck his head in the crack. Haze was lying on his cot, with a washrag over his eyes; the exposed part of his face was ashen and set in a grimace, as if he were in some permanent pain. Sabbath Hawks was sitting at the table by the window, studying herself in a pocket mirror. Enoch scratched on the wall and she looked up. She put the mirror down and tiptoed out into the hall and shut the door behind her.

"My man is sick today and sleeping," she said, "because he didn't sleep none last night. What you want?"

"This is for him, it ain't for you," Enoch said, handing her the wet bundle. "A friend of his give it to me to give to him. I don't know what's in it."

"I'll take care of it," she said. "You needn't to worry none."

Enoch had an urgent need to insult somebody immediately; it was the only thing that could give his feelings even a temporary relief. "I never known he would have nothing to do with you," he remarked, giving her one of his special looks.

"He couldn't leave off following me," she said. "Sometimes it's thataway with them. You don't know what's in this package?"

"Lay-overs to catch meddlers," he said. "You just give it to him and he'll know what it is and you can tell him I'm glad to get shut of it." He started down the stairs and halfway he turned and gave her another special look. "I see why he has to put theter washrag over his eyes," he said.

"You keep your beeswax in your ears," she said. "Nobody asked you." When she heard the front door slam behind him, she turned the bundle over and began to examine it. There was no telling from the outside what was in it; it was too hard to be clothes and too soft to be a machine. She tore a hole in the paper at one end and saw what looked like five dried peas in a row but the hall was too dark for her to see clearly what they were. She decided to take the package to the bathroom, where there was a good light, and open it up before she gave it to Haze. If he was so sick as he said he was, he wouldn't want to be bothered with any bundle.

Early that morning he had claimed to have a terrible pain in his chest. He had begun to cough during the night—a hard hollow cough that sounded as if he were making it up as he went along. She was certain he was only trying to drive her off by letting her think he had a catching disease.

He's not really sick, she said to herself going down the hall, he just ain't used to me yet. She went in and sat down on the edge of a large green claw-footed tub and ripped the string off the package. "But he'll get used to me," she muttered. She pulled off the wet paper and let it fall on the floor; then she sat with a stunned look, staring at what was in her lap.

Two days out of the glass case had not improved the new jesus' condition. One side of his face had been partly mashed in and on the other side, his eyelid had split and a pale dust was seeping out of it. For a while her face had an empty look, as if she didn't know what she thought about him or didn't think anything. She might have sat there for ten minutes, without a thought, held by whatever it was that was familiar about him. She had never known anyone who looked like him before, but there was something in him of everyone she had ever known, as if they had all been rolled into one person and killed and shrunk and dried.

She held him up and began to examine him and after a minute her hands grew accustomed to the feel of his skin. Some of his hair had come undone and she brushed it back where it belonged, holding him in the crook of her arm and looking down into his squinched face. His mouth had been knocked a little to one side so that there was just a trace of a grin covering his terrified look. She began to rock him a little in her arm and a slight reflection of the same grin appeared on her own face. "Well I declare," she murmured, "you're right cute, ain't you?"

His head fitted exactly into the hollow of her shoulder. "Who's your momma and daddy?" she asked.

An answer came into her mind at once and she let out a short little bark and sat grinning, with a pleased expression in her eyes. "Well, let's go give him a jolt," she said after a while.

Haze had already been jolted awake when the front door slammed behind Enoch Emery. He had sat up and seeing she was not in the room, he had jumped up and begun to put on his clothes. He had one thought in mind and it had come to him, like his decision to buy a car, out of his sleep and without any indication of it beforehand: he was going to move immediately to some other city and preach the Church Without Christ where they had never heard of it. He would get another room there and another woman and make a new start with nothing on his mind. The entire possibility of this came from the advantage of having a car—of having something that moved fast, in privacy, to the place you wanted to be. He looked out the window at the Essex. It sat high and square in the pouring rain. He didn't notice the rain, only the car; if asked he would not have been able to say that it was raining. He was charged with energy and he left the window and finished putting on his clothes. Earlier that morning, when he had waked up for the first time, he had felt as if he were about to be caught by a complete consumption in his chest; it had seemed to be growing hollow all night and yawning underneath him, and he had kept hearing his coughs as if they came from a distance. After a while he had been sucked down into a strengthless sleep, but he had waked up with this plan, and with the energy to carry it out right away.

He snatched his duffel bag from under the table and began plunging his extra belongings into it. He didn't have much and a quarter of what he had was already in. His hand managed the packing so that it never touched the Bible that had sat like a rock in the bottom of the bag for the last few years, but as he rooted out a place for his second shoes, his fingers clutched around a small oblong object and he pulled it out. It was the case with his mother's glasses in it. He had forgotten that he had a pair of glasses. He put them on and the wall that he was facing moved up closer and wavered. There was a small white-framed mirror hung on the back of the door and he made his way to it and looked at himself. His blurred face was dark with excitement and the lines in it were deep and crooked. The little silver-rimmed glasses gave him a look of deflected sharpness, as if they were hiding some dishonest plan that would show in his naked eyes. His fingers began to snap nervously and he forgot what he had been going to do. He saw his mother's face in his, looking at the face in the mirror. He moved back quickly and raised his hand to take off the glasses but the door opened and two more faces floated into his line of vision; one of them said, "Call me Momma now."

The smaller dark one, just under the other, only squinted as if it were trying to identify an old friend who was going to kill it.

Haze stood motionless with one hand still on the bow of the glasses and the other arrested in the air at the level of his chest; his head was thrust forward as if he had to use his whole face to see with. He was about four feet from them but they seemed just under his eyes.

"Ask your daddy yonder where he was running off to—sick as he is?" Sabbath said. "Ask him isn't he going to take you and me with him?"

The hand that had been arrested in the air moved forward and plucked at the squinting face but without touching it; it reached again, slowly, and plucked at nothing and then it lunged and snatched the shriveled body and threw it against the wall. The head popped and the trash inside sprayed out in a little cloud of dust.

"You've broken him!" Sabbath shouted, "and he was mine!"

Haze snatched the skin off the floor. He opened the outside door where the landlady thought there had once been a fire-escape, and flung out what he had in his hand. The rain blew in his face and he jumped back and stood, with a cautious look, as if he were bracing himself for a blow.

"You didn't have to throw him out," she yelled. "I might have fixed him!"

He moved up closer and hung out the door, staring into the gray blur around him. The rain fell on his hat with loud splatters as if it were falling on tin.

"I knew when I first seen you you were mean and evil," a furious voice behind him said. "I seen you wouldn't let nobody have nothing. I seen you were mean enough to slam a baby against a wall. I seen you wouldn't never have no fun or let anybody else because you didn't want nothing but Jesus!"

He turned and raised his arm in a vicious gesture, almost

losing his balance in the door. Drops of rain water were splattered over the front of the glasses and on his red face and here and there they hung sparkling from the brim of his hat. "I don't want nothing but the truth!" he shouted, "and what you see is the truth and I've seen it!"

"Preacher talk," she said. "Where were you going to run off to?"

"I've seen the only truth there is!" he shouted.

"Where were you going to run off to?"

"To some other city," he said in a loud hoarse voice, "to preach the truth. The Church Without Christ! And I got a car to get there in, I got . . ." but he was stopped by a cough. It was not much of a cough—it sounded like a little yell for help at the bottom of a canyon—but the color and the expression drained out of his face until it was as straight and blank as the rain falling down behind him.

"And when were you going?" she asked.

"After I get some more sleep," he said, and pulled off the glasses and threw them out the door.

"You ain't going to get none," she said.

Chapter 12

In spite of himself, Enoch couldn't get over the expectation that the new jesus was going to do something for him in return for his services. This was the virtue of Hope, which was made up, in Enoch, of two parts suspicion and one part lust. It operated on him all the rest of the day after he left Sabbath Hawks. He had only a vague idea how he wanted to be rewarded, but he was not a boy without ambition: he wanted to become something. He wanted to better his condition until it was the best. He wanted to be THE young man of the future, like the ones in the insurance ads. He wanted, some day, to see a line of people waiting to shake his hand.

All afternoon, he fidgeted and fooled in his room, biting his nails and shredding what was left of the silk off the landlady's umbrella. Finally he denuded it entirely and broke off the spokes. What was left was a black stick with a sharp steel point at one end and a dog's head at the other. It might have been an instrument for some specialized kind of torture that had gone out of fashion. Enoch walked up and down his room with it under his arm and realized that it would distinguish him on the sidewalk.

About seven o'clock in the evening, he put on his coat and took the stick and headed for a little restaurant two blocks away. He had the sense that he was setting off to get some honor, but he was very nervous, as if he were afraid he might have to snatch it instead of receive it.

He never set out for anything without eating first. The restaurant was called the Paris Diner; it was a tunnel about six feet wide, located between a shoe shine parlor and a dry-cleaning establishment. Enoch slid in and climbed up on the far stool at the counter and said he would have a bowl of split-pea soup and a chocolate malted milkshake.

The waitress was a tall woman with a big yellow dental plate and the same color hair done up in a black hairnet. One hand never left her hip; she filled orders with the other one. Although Enoch came in every night, she had never learned to like him.

Instead of filling his order, she began to fry bacon; there

was only one other customer in the place and he had finished his meal and was reading a newspaper; there was no one to eat the bacon but her. Enoch reached over the counter and prodded her hip with his stick. "Listenhere," he said, "I got to go. I'm in a hurry."

"Go then," she said. Her jaw began to work and she stared into the skillet with a fixed attention.

"Lemme just have a piece of theter cake yonder," he said, pointing to a half of pink and yellow cake on a round glass stand. "I think I got something to do. I got to be going. Set it up there next to him," he said, indicating the customer reading the newspaper. He slid over the stools and began reading the outside sheet of the man's paper.

The man lowered the paper and looked at him. Enoch smiled. The man raised the paper again. "Could I borrow some part of your paper that you ain't studying?" Enoch asked. The man lowered it again and stared at him; he had muddy unflinching eyes. He leafed deliberately through the paper and shook out the sheet with the comic strips and handed it to Enoch. It was Enoch's favorite part. He read it every evening like an office. While he ate the cake that the waitress had torpedoed down the counter at him, he read and felt himself surge with kindness and courage and strength.

When he finished one side, he turned the sheet over and began to scan the advertisements for movies that filled the other side. His eye went over three columns without stopping; then it came to a box that advertised Gonga, Giant Jungle Monarch, and listed the theaters he would visit on his tour and the hours he would be at each one. In thirty minutes he would arrive at the Victory on 57th Street and that would be his last appearance in the city.

If anyone had watched Enoch read this, he would have seen a certain transformation in his countenance. It still shone with the inspiration he had absorbed from the comic strips, but something else had come over it: a look of awakening.

The waitress happened to turn around to see if he hadn't gone. "What's the matter with you?" she said. "Did you swallow a seed?"

"I know what I want," Enoch murmured.

"I know what I want too," she said with a dark look.

Enoch felt for his stick and laid his change on the counter. "I got to be going."

"Don't let me keep you," she said.

"You may not see me again," he said, "—the way I am."

"Any way I don't see you will be all right with me," she said.

Enoch left. It was a pleasant damp evening. The puddles on the sidewalk shone and the store windows were steamy and bright with junk. He disappeared down a side street and made his way rapidly along the darker passages of the city, pausing only once or twice at the end of an alley to dart a glance in each direction before he ran on. The Victory was a small theater, suited to the needs of the family, in one of the closer subdivisions; he passed through a succession of lighted areas and then on through more alleys and back streets until he came to the business section that surrounded it. Then he slowed up. He saw it about a block away, glittering in its darker setting. He didn't cross the street to the side it was on but kept on the far side, moving forward with his squint fixed on the glary spot. He stopped when he was directly across from it and hid himself in a narrow stair cavity that divided a building.

The truck that carried Gonga was parked across the street and the star was standing under the marquee, shaking hands with an elderly woman. She moved aside and a gentleman in a polo shirt stepped up and shook hands vigorously, like a sportsman. He was followed by a boy of about three who wore a tall Western hat that nearly covered his face; he had to be pushed ahead by the line. Enoch watched for some time, his face working with envy. The small boy was followed by a lady in shorts, she by an old man who tried to draw extra attention to himself by dancing up instead of walking in a dignified way. Enoch suddenly darted across the street and slipped noiselessly into the open back door of the truck.

The handshaking went on until the feature picture was ready to begin. Then the star got back in the van and the people filed into the theater. The driver and the man who was master of ceremonies climbed in the cab part and the truck rumbled off. It crossed the city rapidly and continued on the highway, going very fast.

There came from the van certain thumping noises, not those of the normal gorilla, but they were drowned out by the drone of the motor and the steady sound of wheels against the road. The night was pale and quiet, with nothing to stir it but an occasional complaint from a hoot owl and the distant muted jarring of a freight train. The truck sped on until it slowed for a crossing, and as the van rattled over the tracks, a figure slipped from the door and almost fell, and then limped hurriedly off toward the woods.

Once in the darkness of a pine thicket, he laid down a pointed stick he had been clutching and something bulky and loose that he had been carrying under his arm, and began to undress. He folded each garment neatly after he had taken it off and then stacked it on top of the last thing he had removed. When all his clothes were in the pile, he took up the stick and began making a hole in the ground with it.

The darkness of the pine grove was broken by paler moonlit spots that moved over him now and again and showed him to be Enoch. His natural appearance was marred by a gash that ran from the corner of his lip to his collarbone and by a lump under his eye that gave him a dulled insensitive look. Nothing could have been more deceptive for he was burning with the intensest kind of happiness.

He dug rapidly until he had made a trench about a foot long and a foot deep. Then he placed the stack of clothes in it and stood aside to rest a second. Burying his clothes was not a symbol to him of burying his former self; he only knew he wouldn't need them any more. As soon as he got his breath, he pushed the displaced dirt over the hole and stamped it down with his foot. He discovered while he did this that he still had his shoes on, and when he finished, he removed them and threw them from him. Then he picked up the loose bulky object and shook it vigorously.

In the uncertain light, one of his lean white legs could be seen to disappear and then the other, one arm and then the other: a black heavier shaggier figure replaced his. For an instant, it had two heads, one light and one dark, but after a second, it pulled the dark back head over the other and corrected this. It busied itself with certain hidden fastenings and what appeared to be minor adjustments of its hide.

For a time after this, it stood very still and didn't do anything. Then it began to growl and beat its chest; it jumped up and down and flung its arms and thrust its head forward. The growls were thin and uncertain at first but they grew louder after a second. They became low and poisonous, louder again, low and poisonous again; they stopped altogether. The figure extended its hand, clutched nothing, and shook its arm vigorously; it withdrew the arm, extended it again, clutched nothing, and shook. It repeated this four or five times. Then it picked up the pointed stick and placed it at a cocky angle under its arm and left the woods for the highway. No gorilla in existence, whether in the jungles of Africa or California, or in New York City in the finest apartment in the world, was happier at that moment than this one, whose god had finally rewarded it.

A man and woman sitting close together on a rock just off the highway were looking across an open stretch of valley at a view of the city in the distance and they didn't see the shaggy figure approaching. The smokestacks and square tops of buildings made a black uneven wall against the lighter sky and here and there a steeple cut a sharp wedge out of a cloud. The young man turned his neck just in time to see the gorilla standing a few feet away, hideous and black, with its hand extended. He eased his arm from around the woman and disappeared silently into the woods. She, as soon as she turned her eyes, fled screaming down the highway. The gorilla stood as though surprised and presently its arm fell to its side. It sat down on the rock where they had been sitting and stared over the valley at the uneven skyline of the city.

Chapter 13

On his second night out, working with his hired Prophet and the Holy Church of Christ Without Christ, Hoover Shoats made fifteen dollars and thirty-five cents clear. The Prophet got three dollars an evening for his services and the use of his car. His name was Solace Layfield; he had consumption and a wife and six children and being a Prophet was as much work as he wanted to do. It never occurred to him that it might be a dangerous job. The second night out, he failed to observe a high rat-colored car parked about a half-block away and a white face inside it, watching him with the kind of intensity that means something is going to happen no matter what is done to keep it from happening.

The face watched him for almost an hour while he performed on the nose of his car every time Hoover Shoats raised his hand with two fingers pointed. When the last showing of the movie was over and there were no more people to attract, Hoover paid him and the two of them got in his car and drove off. They drove about ten blocks to where Hoover lived; the car stopped and Hoover jumped out, calling, "See you tomorrow night, friend"; then he went inside a dark doorway and Solace Layfield drove on. A half-block behind him the other rat-colored car was following steadily. The driver was Hazel Motes.

Both cars increased their speed and in a few minutes they were heading rapidly toward the outskirts of town. The first car cut off onto a lonesome road where the trees were hung over with moss and the only light came like stiff antennae from the two cars. Haze gradually shortened the distance between them and then, grinding his motor suddenly, he shot ahead and rammed the back end of the other car. Both cars came to a stop.

Haze backed the Essex a little way down the road, while the other Prophet got out of his car and stood squinting in the glare from Haze's lights. After a second, he came up to the window of the Essex and looked in. There was no sound but from crickets and tree frogs. "What you want?"

he said in a nervous voice. Haze didn't answer, he only looked at him, and in a second the man's jaw slackened and he seemed to perceive the resemblance in their clothes and possibly in their faces. "What you want?" he said in a higher voice. "I ain't done nothing to you."

Haze ground the motor of the Essex again and shot forward. This time he rammed the other car at such an angle that it rolled to the side of the road and over into the ditch.

The man got up off the ground where he had been thrown and ran back to the window of the Essex. He stood about four feet away, looking in.

"What you keep a thing like that on the road for?" Haze said.

"It ain't nothing wrong with that car," the man said. "Howcome you knockt it in the ditch?"

"Take off that hat," Haze said.

"Listenere," the man said, beginning to cough, "what you want? Quit just looking at me. Say what you want."

"You ain't true," Haze said. "What do you get up on top of a car and say you don't believe in what you do believe in for?"

"Whatsit to you?" the man wheezed. "Whatsit to you what I do?"

"What do you do it for?" Haze said. "That's what I asked you."

"A man has to look out for hisself," the other Prophet said.

"You ain't true," Haze said. "You believe in Jesus."

"Whatsit to you?" the man said. "What you knockt my car off the road for?"

"Take off that hat and that suit," Haze said.

"Listenere," the man said, "I ain't trying to mock you. He bought me thisyer suit. I thrown my othern away."

Haze reached out and brushed the man's white hat off. "And take off that suit," he said.

The man began to sidle off, out into the middle of the road.

"Take off that suit," Haze shouted and started the car forward after him. Solace began to lope down the road, taking off his coat as he went. "Take it all off," Haze yelled, with his face close to the windshield.

The Prophet began to run in earnest. He tore off his shirt and unbuckled his belt and ran out of the trousers. He 'began grabbing for his feet as if he would take off his shoes too, but before he could get at them, the Essex knocked him flat and ran over him. Haze drove about twenty feet and stopped the car and then began to back it. He backed it over the body and then stopped and got out. The Essex stood half over the other Prophet as if it were pleased to guard what it had finally brought down. The man didn't look so much like Haze, lying on the ground on his face without his hat or suit on. A lot of blood was coming out of him and forming a puddle around his head. He was motionless all but for one finger that moved up and down in front of his face as if he were marking time with it. Haze poked his toe in his side and he wheezed for a second and then was quiet. "Two things I can't stand," Haze said, "—a man that ain't true and one that mocks what is. You shouldn't ever have tampered with me if you didn't want what you got."

The man was trying to say something but he was only wheezing. Haze squatted down by his face to listen. "Give my mother a lot of trouble," he said through a kind of bubbling in his throat. "Never giver no rest. Stole theter car. Never told the truth to my daddy or give Henry what, never give him . . ."

"You shut up," Haze said, leaning his head closer to hear the confession.

"Told where his still was and got five dollars for it," the man gasped.

"You shut up now," Haze said.

"Jesus . . ." the man said.

"Shut up like I told you to now," Haze said.

"Jesus hep me," the man wheezed.

Haze gave him a hard slap on the back and he was quiet. He leaned down to hear if he was going to say anything else but he wasn't breathing any more. Haze turned around and examined the front of the Essex to see if there had been any damage done to it. The bumper had a few splurts of blood on it but that was all. Before he turned around and drove back to town, he wiped them off with a rag.

Early the next morning he got out of the back of the car and drove to a filling station to get the Essex filled up and checked for his trip. He hadn't gone back to his room but had spent the night parked in an alley, not sleeping but thinking about the life he was going to begin, preaching the Church Without Christ in the new city.

At the filling station a sleepy-looking white boy came out to wait on him and he said he wanted the tank filled up, the oil and water checked, and the tires tested for air, that he was going on a long trip. The boy asked him where he was going and he told him to another city. The boy asked him if he was going that far in this car here and he said yes he was. He tapped the boy on the front of his shirt. He said nobody with a good car needed to worry about anything, and he asked the boy if he understood that. The boy said yes he did, that that was his opinion too. Haze introduced himself and said that he was a preacher for the Church Without Christ and that he preached every night on the nose of this very car here. He explained that he was going to another city to preach. The boy filled up the gas tank and checked the water and oil and tested the tires, and while he was working, Haze followed him around, telling him what it was right to believe. He said it was not right to believe anything you couldn't see or hold in your hands or test with your teeth. He said he had only a few days ago believed in blasphemy as the way to salvation, but that you couldn't even believe in that because then you were believing in something to blaspheme. As for the Jesus who was reported to have been born at Bethlehem and crucified on Calvary for man's sins, Haze said, He was too foul a notion for a sane person to carry in his head, and he picked up the boy's water bucket and bammed it on the concrete pavement to emphasize what he was saying. He began to curse and blaspheme Jesus in a quiet intense way but with such conviction that the boy paused from his work to listen. When he had finished checking the Essex, he said that there was a leak in the gas tank and two in the radiator and that the rear tire would probably last twenty miles if he went slow.

"Listen," Haze said, "this car is just beginning its life. A lightning bolt couldn't stop it!"

"It ain't any use to put water in it," the boy said, "because it won't hold it."

"You put it in just the same," Haze said, and he stood there and watched while the boy put it in. Then he got a road map from him and drove off, leaving little bead-chains of water and oil and gas on the road.

He drove very fast out onto the highway, but once he had gone a few miles, he had the sense that he was not gaining ground. Shacks and filling stations and road camps and 666 signs passed him, and deserted barns with CCC snuff ads peeling across them, even a sign that said, "Jesus Died for YOU," which he saw and deliberately did not read. He had the sense that the road was really slipping back under him. He had known all along that there was no more country but he didn't know that there was not another city.

He had not gone five miles on the highway before he

heard a siren behind him. He looked around and saw a black patrol car coming up. It drove alongside him and the patrolman in it motioned for him to pull over to the edge of the road. The patrolman had a red pleasant face and eyes the color of clear fresh ice.

"I wasn't speeding," Haze said.

"No," the patrolman agreed, "you wasn't."

"I was on the right side of the road."

"Yes you was, that's right," the cop said.

"What you want with me?"

"I just don't like your face," the patrolman said. "Where's your license?"

"I don't like your face either," Haze said, "and I don't have a license."

"Well," the patrolman said in a kindly voice, "I don't reckon *you* need one."

"Well I ain't got one if I do," Haze said.

"Listen," the patrolman said, taking another tone, "would you mind driving your car up to the top of the next hill? I want you to see the view from up there, puttiest view you ever did see."

Haze shrugged but he started the car up. He didn't mind fighting the patrolman if that was what he wanted. He drove to the top of the hill, with the patrol car following close behind him. "Now you turn it facing the embankment," the patrolman called. "You'll be able to see better thataway." Haze turned it facing the embankment. "Now maybe you better had get out," the cop said. "I think you could see better if you was out."

Haze got out and glanced at the view. The embankment dropped down for about thirty feet, sheer washed-out red clay, into a partly burnt pasture where there was one scrub cow lying near a puddle. Over in the middle distance there was a one-room shack with a buzzard standing hunch-shouldered on the roof.

The patrolman got behind the Essex and pushed it over the embankment and the cow stumbled up and galloped across the field and into the woods; the buzzard flapped off to a tree at the edge of the clearing. The car landed on its top, with the three wheels that stayed on, spinning. The motor bounced out and rolled some distance away and various odd pieces scattered this way and that.

"Them that don't have a car, don't need a license," the patrolman said, dusting his hands on his pants.

Haze stood for a few minutes, looking over at the scene. His face seemed to reflect the entire distance across the clearing and on beyond, the entire distance that extended from his eyes to the blank gray sky that went on, depth after depth, into space. His knees bent under him and he sat down on the edge of the embankment with his feet hanging over.

The patrolman stood staring at him. "Could I give you a lift to where you was going?" he asked.

After a minute he came a little closer and said, "Where was you going?"

He leaned on down with his hands on his knees and said in an anxious voice, "Was you going anywheres?"

"No," Haze said.

The patrolman squatted down and put his hand on Haze's shoulder. "You hadn't planned to go anywheres?" he asked anxiously.

Haze shook his head. His face didn't change and he didn't turn it toward the patrolman. It seemed to be concentrated on space.

The patrolman got up and went back to his car and stood at the door of it, staring at the back of Haze's hat and shoulder. Then he said, "Well, I'll be seeing you," and got in and drove off.

After a while Haze got up and started walking back to town. It took him three hours to get inside the city again. He stopped at a supply store and bought a tin bucket and a sack of quicklime and then he went on to where he lived, carrying these. When he reached the house, he stopped outside on the sidewalk and opened the sack of lime and poured the bucket half full of it. Then he went to a water spigot by the front steps and filled up the rest of the bucket with water and started up the steps. His landlady was sitting on the porch, rocking a cat. "What you going to do with that, Mr. Motes?" she asked.

"Blind myself," he said and went on in the house.

The landlady sat there for a while longer. She was not a woman who felt more violence in one word than in another; she took every word at its face value but all the faces were the same. Still, instead of blinding herself, if she had felt that bad, she would have killed herself and she wondered why anybody wouldn't do that. She would simply have put her head in an oven or maybe have given herself too many painless sleeping pills and that would have been that. Perhaps Mr. Motes was only being ugly, for what possible reason could a person have for wanting to destroy their sight? A woman like her, who was so clear-sighted, could never stand to be blind. If she had to be blind she would rather be dead. It occurred to her suddenly that when she was dead she would be blind too.

She stared in front of her intensely, facing this for the first time. She recalled the phrase, "eternal death," that preachers used, but she cleared it out of her mind immediately, with no more change of expression than the cat. She was not religious or morbid, for which every day she thanked her stars. She would credit a person who had that streak with anything, though, and Mr. Motes had it or he wouldn't be a preacher. He might put lime in his eyes and she wouldn't doubt it a bit, because they were all, if the truth was only known, a little bit off in their heads. What possible reason could a sane person have for wanting to not enjoy himself any more?

She certainly couldn't say.

Chapter 14

But she kept it in mind because after he had done it, he continued to live in her house and every day the sight of him presented her with the question. She first told him he couldn't stay because he wouldn't wear dark glasses and she didn't like to look at the mess he had made in his eye sockets. At least she didn't think she did. If she didn't keep her mind going on something else when he was near her, she would find herself leaning forward, staring into his face as if she expected to see something she hadn't seen before. This irritated her with him and gave her the sense that he was cheating her in some secret way. He sat on her porch a good part of every afternoon, but sitting out there with him was like sitting by yourself; he didn't talk except when it suited him. You asked him a question in the morning and he might answer it in the afternoon, or he might never. He offered to pay her extra to let him keep his room because he knew his way in and out, and she decided to let him stay, at least until she found out how she was being cheated.

He got money from the government every month for something the war had done to his insides and so he was not obliged to work. The landlady had always been impressed with the ability to pay. When she found a stream of wealth, she followed it to its source and before long, it was not distinguishable from her own. She felt that the money she paid out in taxes returned to all the worthless pockets in the world, that the government not only sent it to foreign niggers and a-rabs, but wasted it at home on blind fools and on every idiot who could sign his name on a card. She felt justified in getting any of it back that she could. She felt justified in getting anything at all back that she could, money or anything else, as if she had once owned the earth and been dispossessed of it. She couldn't look at anything steadily without wanting it, and what provoked her most was the thought that there might be something valuable hidden near her, something she couldn't see.

To her, the blind man had the look of seeing something. His face had a peculiar pushing look, as if it were going forward after something it could just distinguish in the distance. Even when he was sitting motionless in a chair, his face had the look of straining toward something. But she knew he was totally blind. She had satisfied herself of that as soon as he took off the rag he used for a while as a bandage. She had got one long good look and it had been enough to tell her he had done what he'd said he was going to do. The other boarders, after he had taken off the rag, would pass him slowly in the hall, tiptoeing, and looking as long as they could, but now they didn't pay any attention to him; some of the new ones didn't know he had done it himself. The Hawks girl had spread it over the house as soon as it happened. She had watched him do it and then she had run to every room, yelling what he had done, and all the boarders had come running. That girl was a harpy if one ever lived, the landlady felt. She had hung around pestering him for a few days and then she had gone on off; she said she hadn't counted on no honest-to-Jesus blind man and she was homesick for her papa; he had deserted her, gone off on a banana boat. The landlady hoped he was at the bottom of the salt sea; he had been a month behind in his rent. In two weeks, of course, she was back, ready to start pestering him again. She had the disposition of a yellow jacket and you could hear her a block away, shouting and screaming at him, and him never opening his mouth.

The landlady conducted an orderly house and she told him so. She told him that when the girl lived with him, he would have to pay double; she said there were things she didn't mind and things she did. She left him to draw his own conclusions about what she meant by that, but she waited, with her arms folded, until he had drawn them. He didn't say anything, he only counted out three more dollars and handed them to her. "That girl, Mr. Motes," she said, "is only after your money."

"If that was what she wanted she could have it," he said. "I'd pay her to stay away."

The thought that her tax money would go to support such trash was more than the landlady could bear. "Don't do that," she said quickly. "She's got no right to it." The next day she called the Welfare people and made arrangements to have the girl sent to a detention home; she was eligible.

She was curious to know how much he got every month from the government and with that set of eyes removed, she felt at liberty to find out. She steamed open the government envelope as soon as she found it in the mailbox the next time; in a few days she felt obliged to raise his rent. He had made arrangements with her to give him his meals and as the price of food went up, she was obliged to raise his board also; but she didn't get rid of the feeling that she was being cheated. Why had he destroyed his eyes and saved himself unless he had some plan, unless he saw something that he couldn't get without being blind to everything else? She meant to find out everything she could about him.

"Where were your people from, Mr. Motes?" she asked him one afternoon when they were sitting on the porch. "I don't suppose they're alive?"

She supposed she might suppose what she pleased; he didn't disturb his doing nothing to answer her. "None of my people's alive either," she said. "All Mr. Flood's people's alive but him." She was a Mrs. Flood. "They all come here when they want a hand-out," she said, "but Mr. Flood had money. He died in the crack-up of an airplane."

After a while he said, "My people are all dead."

"Mr. Flood," she said, "died in the crack-up of an airplane."

She began to enjoy sitting on the porch with him, but she could never tell if he knew she was there or not. Even when he answered her, she couldn't tell if he knew it was she. She herself. Mrs. Flood, the landlady. Not just anybody. They would sit, he only sit, and she sit rocking, for half an afternoon and not two words seemed to pass between them, though she might talk at length. If she didn't talk and keep her mind going, she would find herself sitting forward in her chair, looking at him with her mouth not closed. Anyone who saw her from the sidewalk would think she was being courted by a corpse.

She observed his habits carefully. He didn't eat much or seem to mind anything she gave him. If she had been blind, she would have sat by the radio all day, eating cake and ice cream, and soaking her feet. He ate anything and never knew the difference. He kept getting thinner and his cough deepened and he developed a limp. During the first cold months, he took the virus, but he walked out every day in spite of that. He walked about half of each day. He got up early in the morning and walked in his room—she could hear him below in hers, up and down, up and down—and then he went out and walked before breakfast and after breakfast, he went out again and walked until midday. He knew the four or five blocks around the house and he didn't go any farther than those. He could have kept on one for all she saw. He could have stayed in his room, in one spot, moving his feet up and down. He could have been dead and get all he got out of life but the exercise. He might as well be one of them monks, she thought, he might as well be in a monkery. She didn't understand it. She didn't like the thought that something was being put over her head. She liked the clear light of day. She liked to see things.

She could not make up her mind what would be inside his head and what out. She thought of her own head as a switchbox where she controlled from; but with him, she could only imagine the outside in, the whole black world in his head and his head bigger than the world, his head big enough to include the sky and planets and whatever was or had been or would be. How would he know if time was going backwards or forwards or if he was going with it? She imagined it was like you were walking in a tunnel and all you could see was a pin point of light. She had to imagine the pin point of light; she couldn't think of it at all without that. She saw it as some kind of a star, like the star on Christmas cards. She saw him going backwards to Bethlehem and she had to laugh.

She thought it would be a good thing if he had something to do with his hands, something to bring him out of himself and get him in connection with the real world again. She was certain he was out of connection with it; she was not certain at times that he even knew she existed. She suggested he get himself a guitar and learn to strum it; she had a picture of them sitting on the porch in the evening and him strumming it. She had bought two rubber plants to make where they sat more private from the street, and she thought that the sound of him strumming it from behind the rubber plant would take away the dead look he had. She suggested it but he never answered the suggestion.

After he paid his room and board every month, he had a good third of the government check left but that she could see, he never spent any money. He didn't use tobacco or drink whisky; there was nothing for him to do with all that money but lose it, since there was only himself. She thought of benefits that might accrue to his widow should he leave one. She had seen money drop out of his pocket and him not bother to reach down and feel for it. One day when she was cleaning his room, she found four dollar bills and some change in his trash can. He came in about that time from one of his walks. "Mr. Motes," she said, "here's a dollar bill and some change in this waste basket. You know where your waste basket is. How did you make that mistake?"

"It was left over," he said. "I didn't need it."

She dropped onto his straight chair. "Do you throw it away every month?" she asked after a time.

"Only when it's left over," he said.

"The poor and needy," she muttered. "The poor and needy. Don't you ever think about the poor and needy? If you don't want that money somebody else might."

"You can have it," he said.

"Mr. Motes," she said coldly, "I'm not charity yet!" She realized now that he was a mad man and that he ought to be under the control of a sensible person.

The landlady was past her middle years and her plate was too large but she had long race-horse legs and a nose that had been called Grecian by one boarder. She wore her hair clustered like grapes on her brow and over each ear and in the middle behind, but none of these advantages were any use to her in attracting his attention. She saw that the only way was to be interested in what he was interested in. "Mr. Motes," she said one afternoon when they were sitting on the porch, "why don't you preach any more? Being blind wouldn't be a hinderance. People would like to go see a blind preacher. It would be something different." She was used to going on without an answer. "You could get you one of those seeing dogs," she said, "and he and you could get up a good crowd. People'll always go to see a dog.

"For myself," she continued, "I don't have that streak. I believe that what's right today is wrong tomorrow and that the time to enjoy yourself is now so long as you let others do the same. I'm as good, Mr. Motes," she said, "not believing in Jesus as a many a one that does."

"You're better," he said, leaning forward suddenly. "If you believed in Jesus, you wouldn't be so good."

He had never paid her a compliment before! "Why Mr. Motes," she said, "I expect you're a fine preacher! You certainly ought to start it again. It would give you something to do. As it is, you don't have anything to do but walk. Why don't you start preaching again?"

"I can't preach any more," he muttered.

"Why?"

"I don't have time," he said, and got up and walked off the porch as if she had reminded him of some urgent business. He walked as if his feet hurt him but he had to go on.

Some time later she discovered why he limped. She was cleaning his room and happened to knock over his extra pair of shoes. She picked them up and looked into them as if she thought she might find something hidden there. The bottoms of them were lined with gravel and broken glass and pieces of small stone. She spilled this out and sifted it through her fingers, looking for a glitter that might mean something valuable, but she saw that what she had in her hand was trash that anybody could pick up in the alley. She stood for some time, holding the shoes, and finally she put them back under the cot. In a few days she examined them again and they were lined with fresh rocks. Who's he doing this for? she asked herself. What's he getting out of doing it? Every now and then she would have an intimation of something hidden near her but out of her reach. "Mr. Motes," she said that day, when he was in her kitchen eating his dinner, "what do you walk on rocks for?"

"To pay," he said in a harsh voice.

"Pay for what?"

"It don't make any difference for what," he said. "I'm paying."

"But what have you got to show that you're paying for?" she persisted.

"Mind your business," he said rudely. "You can't see."

The landlady continued to chew very slowly. "Do you think, Mr. Motes," she said hoarsely, "that when you're dead, you're blind?"

"I hope so," he said after a minute.

"Why?" she asked, staring at him.

After a while he said, "If there's no bottom in your eyes, they hold more."

The landlady stared for a long time, seeing nothing at all.

She began to fasten all her attention on him, to the neglect of other things. She began to follow him in his walks, meeting him accidentally and accompanying him. He didn't seem to know she was there, except occasionally when he would slap at his face as if her voice bothered him, like the singing of a mosquito. He had a deep wheezing cough and she began to badger him about his health. "There's no one," she would say, "to look after you but me, Mr. Motes. No one that has your interest at heart but me. Nobody would care if I didn't." She began to make him tasty dishes and carry them to his room. He would eat what she brought, immediately, with a wry face, and hand back the plate without thanking her, as if all his attention were directed elsewhere and this was an interruption he had to suffer. One morning he told her abruptly that he was going to get his food somewhere else, and named the place, a

diner around the corner, run by a foreigner. "And you'll
rue the day!" she said. "You'll pick up an infection. No
sane person eats there. A dark and filthy place. Encrusted!
It's you that can't see, Mr. Motes.

"Crazy fool," she muttered when he had walked off.
"Wait till winter comes. Where will you eat when winter
comes, when the first wind blows the virus into you?"

She didn't have to wait long. He caught influenza before
winter and for a while he was too weak to walk out and
she had the satisfaction of bringing his meals to his room.
She came earlier than usual one morning and found him
asleep, breathing heavily. The old shirt he wore to sleep
in was open down the front and showed three strands of
barbed wire, wrapped around his chest. She retreated backwards to the door and then she dropped the tray. "Mr.
Motes," she said in a thick voice, "what do you do these
things for? It's not natural."

He pulled himself up.

"What's that wire around you for? It's not natural,"
she repeated.

After a second he began to button the shirt. "It's natural,"
he said.

"Well, it's not normal. It's like one of them gory stories,
it's something that people have quit doing—like boiling
in oil or being a saint or walling up cats," she said. "There's
no reason for it. People have quit doing it."

"They ain't quit doing it as long as I'm doing it," he
said.

"People have quit doing it," she repeated. "What do
you do it for?"

"I'm not clean," he said.

She stood staring at him, unmindful of the broken dishes
at her feet. "I know it," she said after a minute, "you
got blood on that night shirt and on the bed. You ought
to get you a washwoman . . ."

"That's not the kind of clean," he said.

"There's only one kind of clean, Mr. Motes," she muttered.
She looked down and observed the dishes he had made
her break and the mess she would have to get up and she
left for the hall closet and returned in a minute with the
dust pan and broom. "It's easier to bleed than sweat,
Mr. Motes," she said in the voice of High Sarcasm. "You
must believe in Jesus or you wouldn't do these foolish
things. You must have been lying to me when you named
your fine church. I wouldn't be surprised if you weren't
some kind of a agent of the pope or got some connection
with something funny."

"I ain't treatin' with you," he said and lay back down, coughing.

"You got nobody to take care of you but me," she reminded him.

Her first plan had been to marry him and then have him committed to the state institution for the insane, but gradually her plan had become to marry him and keep him. Watching his face had become a habit with her; she wanted to penetrate the darkness behind it and see for herself what was there. She had the sense that she had tarried long enough and that she must get him now while he was weak, or not at all. He was so weak from the influenza that he tottered when he walked; winter had already begun and the wind slashed at the house from every angle, making a sound like sharp knives swirling in the air.

"Nobody in their right mind would like to be out on a day like this," she said, putting her head suddenly into his room in the middle of the morning on one of the coldest days of the year. "Do you hear that wind, Mr. Motes? It's fortunate for you that you have this warm place to be and someone to take care of you." She made her voice more than usually soft. "Every blind and sick man is not so fortunate," she said, "as to have somebody that cares about him." She came in and sat down on the straight chair that was just at the door. She sat on the edge of it, leaning forward with her legs apart and her hands braced on her knees. "Let me tell you, Mr. Motes," she said, "few men are as fortunate as you but I can't keep climbing these stairs. It wears me out. I've been thinking what we could do about it."

He had been lying motionless on the bed but he sat up suddenly as if he were listening, almost as if he had been alarmed by the tone of her voice. "I know you wouldn't want to give up your room here," she said, and waited for the effect of this. He turned his face toward her; she could tell she had his attention. "I know you like it here and wouldn't want to leave and you're a sick man and need somebody to take care of you as well as being blind," she said and found herself breathless and her heart beginning to flutter. He reached to the foot of the bed and felt for his clothes that were rolled up there. He began to put them on hurriedly over his night shirt. "I been thinking how we could arrange it so you would have a home and somebody to take care of you and I wouldn't have to climb these stairs, what you dressing for today, Mr. Motes? You don't want to go out in this weather.

"I been thinking," she went on, watching him as he

went on with what he was doing, "and I see there's only one thing for you and me to do. Get married. I wouldn't do it under any ordinary condition but I would do it for a blind man and a sick one. If we don't help each other, Mr. Motes, there's nobody to help us," she said. "Nobody. The world is a empty place."

The suit that had been glare-blue when it was bought was a softer shade now. The panama hat was wheat-colored. He kept it on the floor by his shoes when he was not wearing it. He reached for it and put it on and then he began to put on his shoes that were still lined with rocks.

"Nobody ought to be without a place of their own to be," she said, "and I'm willing to give you a home here with me, a place where you can always stay, Mr. Motes, and never worry yourself about."

His cane was on the floor near where his shoes had been. He felt for it and then stood up and began to walk slowly toward her. "I got a place for you in my heart, Mr. Motes," she said and felt it shaking like a bird cage; she didn't know whether he was coming toward her to embrace her or not. He passed her, expressionless, out the door and into the hall. "Mr. Motes!" she said, turning sharply in the chair, "I can't allow you to stay here under no other circumstances. I can't climb these stairs. I don't want a thing," she said, "but to help you. You don't have anybody to look after you but me. Nobody to care if you live or die but me! No other place to be but mine!"

He was feeling for the first step with his cane.

"Or were you planning to find you another rooming house?" she asked in a voice getting higher. "Maybe you were planning to go to some other city!"

"That's not where I'm going," he said. "There's no other house nor no other city."

"There's nothing, Mr. Motes," she said, "and time goes forward, it don't go backward and unless you take what's offered you, you'll find yourself out in the cold pitch black and just how far do you think you'll get?"

He felt for each step with his cane before he put his foot on it. When he reached the bottom, she called down to him. "You needn't to return to a place you don't value, Mr. Motes. The door won't be open to you. You can come back and get your belongings and then go on to wherever you think you're going." She stood at the top of the stairs for a long time. "He'll be back," she muttered. "Let the wind cut into him a little."

That night a driving icy rain came up and lying in her

bed, awake at midnight, Mrs. Flood, the landlady, began to weep. She wanted to run out into the rain and cold and hunt him and find him huddled in some half-sheltered place and bring him back and say, Mr. Motes, Mr. Motes, you can stay here forever, or the two of us will go where you're going, the two of us will go. She had had a hard life, without pain and without pleasure, and she thought that now that she was coming to the last part of it, she deserved a friend. If she was going to be blind when she was dead, who better to guide her than a blind man? Who better to lead the blind than the blind, who knew what it was like?

As soon as it was daylight, she went out in the rain and searched the five or six blocks he knew and went from door to door, asking for him, but no one had seen him. She came back and called the police and described him and asked for him to be picked up and brought back to her to pay his rent. She waited all day for them to bring him in the squad car, or for him to come back of his own accord, but he didn't come. The rain and wind continued and she thought he was probably drowned in some alley by now. She paced up and down in her room, walking faster and faster, thinking of his eyes without any bottom in them and of the blindness of death.

Two days later, two young policemen cruising in a squad car found him lying in a drainage ditch near an abandoned construction project. The driver drew the squad car up to the edge of the ditch and looked into it for some time. "Ain't we been looking for a blind one?" he asked.

The other consulted a pad. "Blind and got on a blue suit and ain't paid his rent," he said.

"Yonder he is," the first one said, and pointed into the ditch. The other moved up closer and looked out of the window too.

"His suit ain't blue," he said.

"Yes it is blue," the first one said. "Quit pushing up so close to me. Get out and I'll show you it's blue." They got out and walked around the car and squatted down on the edge of the ditch. They both had on tall new boots and new policemen's clothes; they both had yellow hair with sideburns, and they were both fat, but one was much fatter than the other.

"It might have uster been blue," the fatter one admitted.

"You reckon he's daid?" the first one asked.

"Ast him," the other said.

"No, he ain't daid. He's moving."

"Maybe he's just unconscious," the fatter one said,

taking out his new billy. They watched him for a few seconds. His hand was moving along the edge of the ditch as if it were hunting something to grip. He asked them in a hoarse whisper where he was and if it was day or night.

"It's day," the thinner one said, looking at the sky. "We got to take you back to pay your rent."

"I want to go on where I'm going," the blind man said.

"You got to pay your rent first," the policeman said. "Ever' bit of it!"

The other, perceiving that he was conscious, hit him over the head with his new billy. "We don't want to have no trouble with him," he said. "You take his feet."

He died in the squad car but they didn't notice and took him on to the landlady's. She had them put him on her bed and when she had pushed them out the door, she locked it behind them and drew up a straight chair and sat down close to his face where she could talk to him. "Well, Mr. Motes," she said, "I see you've come home!"

His face was stern and tranquil. "I knew you'd come back," she said. "And I've been waiting for you. And you needn't to pay any more rent but have it free here, any way you like, upstairs or down. Just however you want it and with me to wait on you, or if you want to go on somewhere, we'll both go."

She had never observed his face more composed and she grabbed his hand and held it to her heart. It was resistless and dry. The outline of a skull was plain under his skin and the deep burned eye sockets seemed to lead into the dark tunnel where he had disappeared. She leaned closer and closer to his face, looking deep into them, trying to see how she had been cheated or what had cheated her, but she couldn't see anything. She shut her eyes and saw the pin point of light but so far away that she could not hold it steady in her mind. She felt as if she were blocked at the entrance of something. She sat staring with her eyes shut, into his eyes, and felt as if she had finally got to the beginning of something she couldn't begin, and she saw him moving farther and farther away, farther and farther into the darkness until he was the pin point of light.

THE VIOLENT
BEAR IT AWAY

"FROM THE DAYS OF JOHN THE BAPTIST UNTIL NOW, THE KINDGOM OF HEAVEN SUFFERETH VIOLENCE, AND THE VIOLENT BEAR IT AWAY."

Matthew 11:12

Part 1

Chapter 1

Francis Marion Tarwater's uncle had been dead for only half a day when the boy got too drunk to finish digging his grave and a Negro named Buford Munson, who had come to get a jug filled, had to finish it and drag the body from the breakfast table where it was still sitting and bury it in a decent and Christian way, with the sign of its Saviour at the head of the grave and enough dirt on top to keep the dogs from digging it up. Buford had come along about noon and when he left at sundown, the boy, Tarwater, had never returned from the still.

The old man had been Tarwater's great-uncle, or said he was, and they had always lived together so far as the child knew. His uncle had said he was seventy years of age at the time he had rescued and undertaken to bring him up; he was eighty-four when he died. Tarwater figured this made his own age fourteen. His uncle had taught him Figures, Reading, Writing, and History beginning with Adam expelled from the Garden and going on down through the presidents to Herbert Hoover and on in speculation toward the Second Coming and the Day of Judgment. Besides giving him a good education, he had rescued him from his only other connection, old Tarwater's nephew, a schoolteacher who had no child of his own at the time and wanted this one of his dead sister's to raise according to his own ideas.

The old man was in a position to know what his ideas were. He had lived for three months in the nephew's house on what he had thought at the time was Charity but what he said he had found out was not Charity or anything like it. All the time he had lived there, the nephew had secretly been making a study of him. The nephew, who had taken him in under the name of Charity, had at the same time been creeping into his soul by the back door, asking him questions that meant more than one thing, planting traps around the house and watching him fall into them, and finally coming up with a written study of him for a schoolteacher magazine. The stench of his behavior had reached heaven and the Lord Himself had rescued the old man.

He had sent him a rage of vision, had told him to fly with the orphan boy to the farthest part of the backwoods and raise him up to justify his Redemption. The Lord had assured him a long life and he had snatched the baby from under the schoolteacher's nose and taken him to live in the clearing, Powderhead, that he had a title to for his lifetime.

The old man, who said he was a prophet, had raised the boy to expect the Lord's call himself and to be prepared for the day he would hear it. He had schooled him in the evils that befall prophets; in those that come from the world, which are trifling, and those that come from the Lord and burn the prophet clean; for he himself had been burned clean and burned clean again. He had learned by fire.

He had been called in his early youth and had set out for the city to proclaim the destruction awaiting a world that had abandoned its Saviour. He proclaimed from the midst of his fury that the world would see the sun burst in blood and fire and while he raged and waited, it rose every morning, calm and contained in itself, as if not only the world, but the Lord Himself had failed to hear the prophet's message. It rose and set, rose and set on a world that turned from green to white and green to white and green to white again. It rose and set and he despaired of the Lord's listening. Then one morning he saw to his joy a finger of fire coming out of it and before he could turn, before he could shout, the finger had touched him and the destruction he had been waiting for had fallen in his own brain and his own body. His blood had been burned dry and not the blood of the world.

Having learned much by his own mistakes, he was in a position to instruct Tarwater—when the boy chose to listen—in the hard facts of serving the Lord. The boy, who had ideas of his own, listened with an impatient conviction that he would not make any mistakes himself when the time came and the Lord called him.

That was not the last time the Lord had corrected the old man with fire, but it had not happened since he had taken Tarwater from the schoolteacher. That time his rage of vision had been clear. He had known what he was saving the boy from and it was saving and not destruction he was seeking. He had learned enough to hate the destruction that had to come and not all that was going to be destroyed.

Rayber, the schoolteacher, had shortly discovered where they were and had come out to the clearing to get the baby back. He had had to leave his car on the dirt road and walk a mile through the woods on a path that appeared and disappeared before he came to the corn patch with the gaunt two-story shack standing in the middle of it. The old man had been fond of recalling for Tarwater the red sweating bitten face of his nephew bobbing up and down through the corn and behind it the pink flowered hat of a welfare-woman he had brought along with him. The corn was planted up to four feet from the porch that year and as the nephew came out of it, the old man appeared in the door with his shotgun and shouted that he would shoot any foot that touched his step and the two stood facing each other while the welfare-woman bristled out of the corn, ruffled like a peahen upset on the nest. The old man said if it hadn't been for the welfare-woman, his nephew wouldn't have taken a step. Both their faces were scratched and bleeding from thorn bushes and a switch of blackberry bush hung from the sleeve of the welfare-woman's blouse.

She had only to let out her breath slowly as if she were releasing the last patience on earth and the nephew lifted his foot and planted it on the step and the old man shot him in the leg. He recalled for the boy's benefit the nephew's expression of outraged righteousness, a look that had so infuriated him that he had raised the gun slightly higher and shot him again, this time taking a wedge out of his right ear. The second shot flushed the righteousness off his face and left it blank and white, revealing that there was nothing underneath it, revealing, the old man sometimes admitted, his own failure as well, for he had tried and failed, long ago, to rescue the nephew. He had kidnapped him when the child was seven and had taken him to the backwoods and baptized him and instructed him in the facts of his Redemption, but the instruction had lasted only for a few years; in time the child had set himself a different course. There were moments when the thought that he might have helped the nephew on to his new course himself became so heavy in the old man that he would stop telling the story to Tarwater, stop and stare in front of him as if he were looking into a pit which had opened up before his feet.

At such times he would wander into the woods and leave Tarwater alone in the clearing, occasionally for days, while he thrashed out his peace with the Lord, and when he returned, bedraggled and hungry, he would look the way the boy thought a prophet ought to look. He would look as if he had been wrestling a wildcat, as if his head were still full of the visions he had seen in its eyes, wheels of light and strange beasts with giant wings of fire and four heads turned to the four points of the universe. These were the times that Tarwater knew that when he was called, he would say, "Here I am, Lord, ready!" At other times when there was no fire in his uncle's eye and he spoke only of the sweat and stink of the cross, of being born again to die, and of spending eternity eating the bread of life, the boy would let his mind wander off to other subjects.

The old man's thought did not always move at the same rate of speed through every point in his story. Sometimes, as if he did not want to think of it, he would speed over the part where he shot the nephew and race on, telling how the two of them, the nephew and the welfare-woman (whose very name was comical—Bernice Bishop) had scuttled off, making a disappearing rattle in the corn, and how the welfare-woman had screamed, "Why didn't you tell me? You knew he was crazy!" and how when they came out of the corn on the other side, he had noted from the upstairs window where he had run that she had her arm around the nephew and was holding him up while he hopped into the woods. Later he learned that he had married her though she was twice his age and he could only possibly get one child out of her. She had never let him come back again.

And the Lord, the old man said, had preserved the one child he had got out of her from being corrupted by such parents. He had preserved him in the only possible way: the child was dim-witted. The old man would pause here and let the weight of this mystery sink in on Tarwater. He had made, since he learned of that child's existence, several trips into town to try to kidnap him so that he could baptize him, but each time he had come back unsuccessful. The schoolteacher was on his guard and the old man was too fat and stiff now to make an agile kidnapper.

"If by the time I die," he had said to Tarwater, "I haven't got him baptized, it'll be up to you. It'll be the first mission the Lord sends you."

The boy doubted very much that his first mission would be to baptize a dim-witted child. "Oh no it won't be," he said. "He don't mean for me to finish up your leavings. He has other things in mind for me." And he thought of Moses who struck water from a rock, of Joshua who made the sun stand still, of Daniel who stared down lions in the pit.

"It's no part of your job to think for the Lord," his great-uncle said. "Judgment may rack your bones."

The morning the old man died, he came down and cooked the breakfast as usual and died before he got the first spoonful to his mouth. The downstairs of their house was all kitchen, large and dark, with a wood stove at one end of it and a board table drawn up to the stove. Sacks of feed and mash were stacked in the corners and scrapmetal, woodshavings, old rope, ladders, and other tinder were wherever he or Tarwater had let them fall. They had slept in the kitchen until a bobcat sprang in the window one night and frightened his uncle into carrying the bed upstairs where there were two empty rooms. The old man prophesied at the time that the stairsteps would take ten years off his life. At the moment of his death, he sat down to his breakfast and lifted his knife in one square red hand halfway to his mouth, and then with a look of complete astonishment, he lowered it until the hand rested on the edge of the plate and tilted it up off the table.

He was a bull-like old man with a short head set directly into his shoulders and silver protruding eyes that looked like two fish straining to get out of a net of red threads. He had on a putty-colored hat with the brim turned up all around and over his undershirt a grey coat that had once been black. Tarwater, sitting across the table from him, saw red ropes appear in his face and a tremor pass over him. It was like the tremor of a quake that had begun at his heart and run outward and was just reaching the surface. His mouth twisted down sharply on one side and he remained exactly as he was, perfectly balanced, his back a good six inches from the chair back and his stomach caught just under the edge of the table. His eyes, dead silver, were focussed on the boy across from him.

Tarwater felt the tremor transfer itself and run lightly over him. He knew the old man was dead without touching him and he continued to sit across the table from the corpse, finishing his breakfast in a kind of sullen embarrassment as if he were in the presence of a new personality and couldn't think of anything to say. Finally he said in a querulous tone, "Just hold your horses. I already told you I would do it right." The voice sounded like a stranger's voice, as if the death had changed him instead of his great-uncle.

He got up and took his plate out the back door and set

it down on the bottom step and two long-legged black game roosters tore across the yard and finished what was on it. He sat down on a long pine box on the back porch and his hands began absently to unravel a length of rope while his long face stared ahead beyond the clearing over the woods that ran in grey and purple folds until they touched the light blue fortress line of trees set against the empty morning sky.

Powderhead was not simply off the dirt road but off the wagon track and footpath, and the nearest neighbors, colored not white, still had to walk through the woods, pushing plum branches out of their way to get to it. Once there had been two houses; now there was only the one house with the dead owner inside and the living owner outside on the porch, waiting to bury him. The boy knew he would have to bury the old man before anything would begin. It was as if there would have to be dirt over him before he would be thoroughly dead. The thought seemed to give him respite from something that pressed on him.

A few weeks before, the old man had started an acre of corn to the left and had run it beyond the fenceline almost up to the house on one side. The two strands of barbed-wire ran through the middle of the patch. A line of fog, hump-shaped, was creeping toward it like a white hound dog ready to crouch under and crawl across the yard.

"I'm going to move that fence," Tarwater said. "I ain't going to have any fence I own in the middle of a patch." The voice was loud and strange and disagreeable. Inside his head it continued: you ain't the owner. The schoolteacher owns it.

I own it, Tarwater said, because I'm here and can't nobody get me off. If any schoolteacher comes to claim the property, I'll kill him.

The Lord may send you off, he thought. There was a complete stillness over everything and the boy felt his heart begin to swell. He held his breath as if he were about to hear a voice from on high. After a few moments he heard a hen scratching beneath him under the porch. He ran his arm fiercely under his nose and gradually his face paled again.

He had on a faded pair of overalls and a grey hat pulled down over his ears like a cap. He followed his uncle's custom of never taking off his hat except in bed. He had always followed his uncle's customs up to this date but: if I want to move that fence before I bury him, it wouldn't be a soul to hinder me, he thought; no voice will be uplifted. Bury him first and get it over with, the loud stranger's disagreeable voice said. He got up and went to look for the shovel.

The pine box he had been sitting on was his uncle's coffin but he didn't intend to use it. The old man was too heavy for a thin boy to hoist over the side of a box and though old Tarwater had built it himself a few years before, he had said that if it wasn't feasible to get him into it when the time came, then just to put him in the hole as he was, only to be sure the hole was deep. He wanted it ten foot, he said, not just eight. He had worked on the box a long time and when he finished it, he had scratched on the lid, MASON TARWATER, WITH GOD, and had climbed into it where it stood on the back porch, and had lain there some time, nothing showing but his stomach which rose over the top like over-leavened bread. The boy had stood at the side of the box, studying him. "This is the end of us all," the old man said with satisfaction, his gravel voice hearty in the coffin.

"It's too much of you for the box," Tarwater said. "I'll have to sit on the lid to press you down or wait until you rot a little."

"Don't wait," old Tarwater had said. "Listen. If it ain't feasible to use the box when the time comes, if you can't lift it or whatever, just get me in the hole but I want it deep. I want it ten foot, not just eight, ten. You can roll me to it if nothing else. I'll roll. Get two boards and set them down the steps and start me rolling and dig where I stop and don't let me roll over into it until it's deep enough. Prop me with some bricks so I won't roll into it and don't let the dogs nudge me over the edge before it's finished. You better pen up the dogs," he said.

"What if you die in bed?" the boy asked. "How'm I going to get you down the stairs?"

"I ain't going to die in bed," the old man said. "As soon as I hear the summons, I'm going to run downstairs. I'll get as close to the door as I can. If I should get stuck up there, you'll have to roll me down the stairs, that's all."

"My Lord," the child said.

The old man sat up in the box and brought his fist down on the edge of it. "Listen," he said. "I never asked much of you. I taken you and raised you and saved you from that ass in town and now all I'm asking in return is when I die to get me in the ground where the dead belong and set up a cross over me to show I'm there. That's all in the world I'm asking you to do. I ain't even asking you to go for the niggers and try to get me in the plot with my daddy. I could ask you that but I ain't. I'm doing everything to make it easy for you. All I'm asking you is to get me in the ground and set up a cross."

"I'll be doing good if I get you in the ground," Tarwater said. "I'll be too wore out to set up any cross. I ain't bothering with trifles."

"Trifles!" his uncle hissed. "You'll learn what a trifle is on the day those crosses are gathered! Burying the dead right may be the only honor you ever do yourself. I brought you out here to raise you a Christian, and more than a Christian, a prophet!" he hollered, "and the burden of it will be on you!"

"If I don't have the strength to do it," the child said, watching him with a careful detachment, "I'll notify my uncle in town and he can come out and take care of you. The schoolteacher," he drawled, observing that the pockmarks in his uncle's face had already turned pale against the purple. "He'll tend to you."

The threads that restrained the old man's eyes thickened. He gripped both sides of the coffin and pushed forward as if he were going to drive it off the porch. "He'd burn me," he said hoarsely. "He'd have me cremated in an oven and scatter my ashes. 'Uncle,' he said to me, 'you're a type that's almost extinct!' He'd be willing to pay the undertaker to burn me to be able to scatter my ashes," he said. "He don't believe in the Resurrection. He don't believe in the Last Day. He don't believe in the bread of life . . ."

"The dead don't bother with particulars," the boy interrupted.

The old man grabbed the front of his overalls and pulled him up against the side of the box and glared into his pale face. "The world was made for the dead. Think of all the dead there are," he said, and then as if he had conceived the answer for all the insolence in the world, he said, "There's a million times more dead than living and the dead are dead a million times longer than the living are alive," and he released him with a laugh.

The boy had shown only by a slight quiver that he was shaken by this, and after a minute he had said, "The schoolteacher is my uncle. The only blood connection with good sense I'll have and a living man and if I wanted to go to him, I'd go; now."

The old man looked at him silently for what seemed a full minute. Then he slammed his hands flat on the sides of the box and roared, "Whom the plague beckons, to the plague! Whom the sword to the sword! Whom fire to fire!" And the child trembled visibly.

"I saved you to be free, your own self!" he had shouted,

"and not a piece of information inside his head! If you were living with him, you'd be information right now, you'd be inside his head, and what's furthermore," he said, "you'd be going to school."

The boy grimaced. The old man had always impressed on him his good fortune in not being sent to school. The Lord had seen fit to guarantee the purity of his up-bringing, to preserve him from contamination, to preserve him as His elect servant, trained by a prophet for prophesy. While other children his age were herded together in a room to cut out paper pumpkins under the direction of a woman, he was left free for the pursuit of wisdom, the companions of his spirit Abel and Enoch and Noah and Job, Abraham and Moses, King David and Solomon, and all the prophets, from Elijah who escaped death, to John whose severed head struck terror from a dish. The boy knew that escaping school was the surest sign of his election.

The truant officer had come only once. The Lord had told the old man to expect it and what to do and old Tarwater had instructed the boy in his part against the day when, as the devil's emissary, the officer would appear. When the time came and they saw him cutting across the field, they were ready. The child got behind the house and the old man sat on the steps and waited. When the officer, a thin bald-headed man with red galluses, stepped out of the field onto the packed dirt of the yard, he greeted old Tarwater warily and commenced his business as if he had not come for it. He sat down on the steps and spoke of poor weather and poor health. Finally, gazing out over the field, he said, "You got a boy, don't you, that ought to be in school?"

"A fine boy," the old man said, "and I wouldn't stand in his way if anybody thought they could teach him. You boy!" he called. The boy didn't come at once. "Oh you boy!" the old man shouted.

In a few minutes Tarwater appeared from around the side of the house. His eyes were open but not well-focused. His head rolled uncontrollably on his slack shoulders and his tongue lolled in his open mouth.

"He ain't bright," the old man said, "but he's a mighty good boy. He knows to come when you call him."

"Yes," the truant officer said, "well yes, but it might be best to leave him in peace."

"I don't know, he might take to schooling," the old man said. "He ain't had a fit for going on two months."

"I speck he better stay at home," the officer said. "I wouldn't want to put a strain on him," and he commenced to speak of other things. Shortly he took his leave and the two of them watched with satisfaction as the diminishing figure moved back across the field and the red galluses were finally lost to view.

If the schoolteacher had got hold of him, right now he would have been in school, one among many, indistinguishable from the herd, and in the schoolteacher's head, he would be laid out in parts and numbers. "That's where he wanted me," the old man said, "and he thought once he had me in that schoolteacher magazine, I would be as good as in his head." The schoolteacher's house had had little in it but books and papers. The old man had not known when he went there to live that every living thing that passed through the nephew's eyes into his head was turned by his brain into a book or a paper or a chart. The schoolteacher had appeared to have a great interest in his being a prophet, chosen by the Lord, and had asked numerous questions, the answers to which he had sometimes scratched down on a pad, his little eyes lighting every now and then as if in some discovery.

The old man had fancied he was making progress in convincing the nephew again of his Redemption, for he at least listened though he did not *say* he believed. He seemed to delight to talk about the things that interested his uncle. He questioned him at length about his early life, which old Tarwater had practically forgotten. The old man had thought this interest in his forebears would bear fruit, but what it bore, what it bore, stench and shame, were dead words. What it bore was a dry and seedless fruit, incapable even of rotting, dead from the beginning. From time to time, the old man would spit out of his mouth, like gobbets of poison, some of the idiotic sentences from the schoolteacher's piece. Wrath had burned them on his memory, word for word. "His fixation of being called by the Lord had its origin in insecurity. He needed the assurance of a call, and so he called himself."

"Called myself!" the old man would hiss, "called myself!" This so enraged him that half the time he could do nothing but repeat it. "Called myself. I called myself. I, Mason Tarwater, called myself! Called myself to be beaten and tied up. Called myself to be spit on and snickered at. Called myself to be struck down in my pride. Called myself to be torn by the Lord's eye. Listen boy," he would say and grab the child by the straps of his overalls and shake him slowly, "even the mercy of the Lord burns." He would let go the straps and allow the boy to fall back into the thorn bed of that thought, while he continued to hiss and groan.

"Where he wanted me was inside that schoolteacher magazine. He thought once he got me in there, I'd be as good as inside his head and done for and that would be that, that would be the end of it. Well, that wasn't the end of it! Here I sit. And there you sit. In freedom. Not inside anybody's head!" and his voice would run away from him as if it were the freest part of his free self and were straining ahead of his heavy body to be off. Something of his great-uncle's glee would take hold of Tarwater at that point and he would feel that he had escaped some mysterious prison. He even felt he could smell his freedom, pine-scented, coming out of the woods, until the old man would continue, "You were born into bondage and baptized into freedom, into the death of the Lord, into the death of the Lord Jesus Christ."

Then the child would feel a sullenness creeping over him, a slow warm rising resentment that this freedom had to be connected with Jesus and that Jesus had to be the Lord.

"Jesus is the bread of life," the old man said.

The boy, disconcerted, would look off into the distance over the dark blue treeline where the world stretched out, hidden and at its ease. In the darkest, most private part of his soul, hanging upsidedown like a sleeping bat, was the certain, undeniable knowledge that he was not hungry for the bread of life. Had the bush flamed for Moses, the sun stood still for Joshua, the lions turned aside before Daniel only to prophesy the bread of life? Jesus? He felt a terrible disappointment in that conclusion, a dread that it was true. The old man said that as soon as he died, he would hasten to the banks of the Lake of Galilee to eat the loaves and fishes that the Lord had multiplied.

"Forever?" the horrified boy asked.

"Forever," the old man said.

The boy sensed that this was the heart of his great-uncle's madness, this hunger, and what he was secretly afraid of was that it might be passed down, might be hidden in the blood and might strike some day in him and then he would be torn by hunger like the old man, the bottom split out of his stomach so that nothing would heal or fill it but the bread of life.

He tried when possible to pass over these thoughts, to keep his vision located on an even level, to see no more than what was in front of his face and to let his eyes stop at the surface of that. It was as if he were afraid that if he let his eye rest for an instant longer than was needed to place something—a spade, a hoe, the mule's hind quarters before his plow, the red furrow under him—that the thing would suddenly stand before him, strange and terrifying, demanding that he name it and name it justly and be judged for the name he gave it. He did all he could to avoid this threatened intimacy of creation. When the Lord's call came, he wished it to be a voice from out of a clear and empty sky, the trumpet of the Lord God Almighty, untouched by any fleshly hand or breath. He expected to see wheels of fire in the eyes of unearthly beasts. He had expected this to happen as soon as his great-uncle died. He turned his mind off this quickly and went to get the shovel. The schoolteacher is a living man, he thought as he went, but he'd better not come out here and try to get me off this property because I'll kill him. Go to him and be damned, his uncle had said. I've saved you from him this far and if you go to him the minute I'm in the ground there's nothing I can do about it.

The shovel lay against the side of the hen house. "I'll never set my foot in the city again," the boy said to himself aloud. "I'll never go to him. Him nor nobody else will ever get me off this place.

He decided to dig the grave under the fig tree because the old man would be good for the figs. The ground was sandy on top and solid brick underneath and the shovel made a clanging sound when he struck it in the sand. Two hundred pounds of dead mountain to bury, he thought, and stood with one foot on the shovel, leaning forward, studying the white sky through the leaves of the tree. It would take all day to get a hole big enough out of this rock and the schoolteacher would burn him in a minute.

Tarwater had seen the schoolteacher once from a distance of about twenty feet and he had seen the dim-witted child closer up. The little boy somewhat resembled old Tarwater except for his eyes which were grey like the old man's but clear, as if the other side of them went down and down into two pools of light. It was plain to look at him that he did not have any sense. The old man had been so shocked by the likeness and the unlikeness that the time he and Tarwater had gone there, he had only stood in the door, staring at the little boy and rolling his tongue around outside his mouth as if he had no sense himself. That had been the first time he had seen the child and he could not forget him. "Married her and got one child out of her and that without sense," he would murmur. "The

Lord preserved him and now He means to see he's baptized."

"Well whyn't you get on with it then?" the boy asked, for he wanted something to happen, wanted to see the old man in action, wanted him to kidnap the child and have the schoolteacher have to come after him so that he could get a closer look at his other uncle. "What ails you?" he asked. "What makes you tarry so long? Why don't you make haste and steal him?"

"I take my directions from the Lord God," the old man said, "Who moves in His own time. I don't take them from you."

The white fog had eased through the yard and disappeared into the next bottom and the air was clear and blank. His mind continued to dwell on the schoolteacher's house. "Three months there," his great-uncle had said. "It shames me. Betrayed for three months in the house of my own kin and if when I'm dead you want to turn me over to my betrayer and see my body burned, go ahead! Go ahead, boy," he had shouted, sitting up splotch-faced in his box. "Go ahead and let him burn me but watch out for the Lord's lion after that. Remember the Lord's lion set in the path of the false prophet! I been leavened by the yeast he don't believe in," he had said, "and I won't be burned! And when I'm gone, you'll be better off in these woods by yourself with just as much light as the sun wants to let in than you'll be in the city with him."

He kept on digging but the grave did not get any deeper. "The dead are poor," he said in the voice of the stranger. You can't be any poorer than dead. He'll have to take what he gets. Nobody to bother me, he thought. Ever. No hand uplifted to hinder me from anything; except the Lord's and He ain't said anything. He ain't even noticed me yet.

A sand-colored hound beat its tail on the ground nearby and a few black chickens scratched in the raw clay he was turning up. The sun had slipped over the blue line of trees and circled by a haze of yellow was moving slowly across the sky. "Now I can do anything I want to," he said, softening the stranger's voice so that he could stand it. Could kill off all those chickens if I had a mind to, he thought, watching the worthless black game bantams that his uncle had been fond of keeping.

He favored a lot of foolishness, the stranger said. The truth is he was childish. Why, that schoolteacher never did him any harm. You take, all he did was to watch him and write down what he seen and heard and put it in a paper for schoolteachers to read. Now what was wrong in that? Why nothing. Who cares what a schoolteacher reads? And the old fool acted like he had been killed in his very soul. Well he wasn't so near dead as he thought he was. Lived on fourteen years and raised up a boy to bury him, suitable to his own taste.

As Tarwater slashed at the ground with the shovel, the stranger's voice took on a kind of restrained fury and he kept repeating, you got to bury him whole and completely by hand and that schoolteacher would burn him in a minute.

After he had dug for an hour or more, the grave was only a foot deep, not as deep yet as the corpse. He sat down on the edge of it for a while. The sun was like a furious white blister in the sky.

The dead are a heap more trouble than the living, the stranger said. That schoolteacher wouldn't consider for a minute that on the last day all the bodies marked by crosses will be gathered. In the rest of the world they do things different than what you been taught.

"I been there once," Tarwater muttered. "Nobody has to tell me."

His uncle two or three years before had gone to call on the lawyers to try to get the property unentailed so that it would skip the schoolteacher and go to Tarwater. Tarwater had sat at the lawyer's twelfth-story window and looked down into the pit of the street while his uncle transacted the business. On the way from the railroad station he had walked tall in the mass of moving metal and concrete speckled with the very small eyes of people. The glitter of his own eyes was shaded under the stiff roof-like brim of a new gray hat, balanced perfectly straight on his buttressing ears. Before coming he had read facts in the almanac and he knew that there were 75,000 people here who were seeing him for the first time. He wanted to stop and shake hands with each of them and say his name was F. M. Tarwater and that he was here only for the day to accompany his uncle on business at a lawyers. His head jerked backwards after each passing figure until they began to pass too thickly and he observed that their eyes didn't grab at you like the eyes of country people. Several people bumped into him and this contact that should have made an acquaintance for life, made nothing because the hulks shoved on with ducked heads and muttered apologies that he would have accepted if they had waited.

Then he had realized, almost without warning, that this place was evil—the ducked heads, the muttered words, the hastening away. He saw in a burst of light that these people were hastening away from the Lord God Almighty. It was to the city that the prophets came and he was here in the midst of it. He was here enjoying what should have repelled him. His lids narrowed with caution and he looked at his uncle who was rolling on ahead of him, no more concerned with it all than a bear in the woods. "What kind of prophet are you?" the boy hissed.

His uncle paid him no attention, did not stop.

"Call yourself a prophet!" he continued in a high rasping carrying voice.

His uncle stopped and turned. "I'm here on bidnis," he said mildly.

"You always said you were a prophet," Tarwater said. "Now I see what kind of prophet you are. Elijah would think a heap of you."

His uncle thrust his head forward and his eyes began to bulge. "I'm here on bidnis," he said. "If you been called by the Lord, then be about your own mission."

The boy paled slightly and his gaze shifted. "I ain't been called *yet*," he muttered. "It's you that's been called."

"And I know what times I'm called and what times I ain't," his uncle said and turned and paid him no more attention.

At the lawyer's window, he knelt down and let his face hang out upsidedown over the floating speckled street moving like a river of tin below and watched the glints on it from the sun which drifted pale in a pale sky, too far away to ignite anything. When he was called, on that day when he returned, he would set the city astir, he would return with fire in his eyes. You have to do something particular here to make them look at you, he thought. They ain't going to look at you just because you're here. He considered his uncle with renewed disgust. When I come for good, he said to himself, I'll do something to make every eye stick on me, and leaning forward, he saw his new hat drop down gently, lost and casual, dallied slightly by the breeze on its way to be smashed in the tin river below. He clutched at his bare head and fell back inside the room.

His uncle was in argument with the lawyer, both hitting the desk that separated them, bending their knees and hitting their fists at the same time. The lawyer, a tall dome-headed man with an eagle's nose, kept repeating in a restrained shriek, "But I didn't make the will. I didn't make the law," and his uncle's gravel voice grated, "I can't help it. My daddy wouldn't have seen a fool inherit his property. That's not how he intended it."

"My hat is gone," Tarwater said.

The lawyer threw himself backwards into his chair and screaked it toward Tarwater and saw him without interest from pale blue eyes and screaked it forward again and said to his uncle, "There's nothing I can do. You're wasting your time and mine. You might as well resign yourself to this will."

"Listen," old Tarwater said, "at one time I thought I was finished, old and sick and about to die and no money, nothing, and I accepted his hospitality because he was my closest blood connection and you could have called it his duty to take me, only I thought it was Charity, I thought . . ."

"I can't help what you thought or did or what your connection thought or did," the lawyer said and closed his eyes.

"My hat fell," Tarwater said.

"I'm only a lawyer," the lawyer said, letting his glance rove over the lines of clay-colored books of law that fortressed his office.

"A car is liable to have run over it by now."

"Listen," his uncle said, "all the time he was studying me for this paper. Taking secret tests on me, his own kin, crawling into my soul through the back door and then says to me, 'Uncle, you're a type that's almost extinct!' Almost extinct!" the old man piped, barely able to force a thread of sound from his throat. "You see how extinct I am!"

The lawyer closed his eyes again and smiled into one cheek.

"Other lawyers," the old man growled and they had left and visited three more, without stopping, and Tarwater had counted eleven men who might have had on his hat or might not. Finally when they came out of the fourth lawyer's office, they sat down on the window ledge of a bank building and his uncle felt in his pocket for some biscuits he had brought and handed one to Tarwater. The old man unbuttoned his coat and allowed his stomach to ease forward and rest on his lap while he ate. His face worked wrathfully; the skin between the pockmarks appeared to jump from one spot to another. Tarwater was very pale and his eyes glittered with a peculiar hollow depth. He had an old work kerchief tied around his head, knotted at the four corners. He didn't observe the passing people who observed him now. "Thank God we're finished and can go home," he muttered.

"We ain't finished here," the old man said and got up abruptly and started down the street.

"My Lord!" the boy groaned, jumping to catch up with him. "Can't we sit down for one minute? Ain't you got any sense? They all tell you the same thing. It's only one law and it's nothing you can do about it. I got sense enough to get that; why ain't you? What's the matter with you?"

The old man strode on with his head thrust forward as if he were smelling out an enemy.

"Where we going?" Tarwater asked after they had walked out of the business streets and were passing between rows of grey bulbous houses with sooty porches that overhung the sidewalks. "Listen," he said, hitting at his uncle's hip, "I never ast to come."

"You would have ast to come soon enough," the old man muttered. "Get your fill now."

"I never ast for no fill. I never ast to come at all. I'm here before I knew this here was here."

"Just remember," the old man said, "just remember that I told you to remember when you ast to come that you never liked it when you were here," and they kept on going, crossing one length of sidewalk after another, row after row of overhanging houses with half-open doors that let a little dried light fall on the stained passageways inside. Finally they came out into another section where the houses were clean and squat and almost identical and each had a square of grass in front of it. After a few blocks Tarwater dropped down on the sidewalk and said, "I ain't going no further. I don't even know where I'm going and I ain't going no further." His uncle didn't stop or look back. In a second he jumped up and followed him again in a panic lest he be left.

The old man kept straining forward as if his blood scent were leading him closer and closer to the place where his enemy was hiding. He suddenly turned up the short walk of a pale yellow brick house and moved rigidly to the white door, his heavy shoulders hunched as if he were going to crash through it. He struck the wood with his fist, ignoring a polished brass knocker. At that instant Tarwater realized that this was where the schoolteacher lived, and he stopped where he was and remained rigid, his eye on the door. He knew by some obscure instinct that the door was going to open and reveal his destiny. In his mind's eye, he saw the schoolteacher about to appear in it, lean and evil, waiting to engage whom the Lord would send to conquer him. The boy clamped his teeth together to keep them from chattering. The door opened.

A small pink-faced boy stood in it with his mouth hung in a silly smile. He had white hair and a knobby forehead. He wore steel-rimmed spectacles and had pale silver eyes like the old man's except that they were clear and empty. He was gnawing on a brown apple core.

The old man stared at him, his lips parting slowly until his mouth hung open. He looked as if he beheld an unspeakable mystery. The little boy made an unintelligible noise and pushed the door almost shut, hiding himself all but one spectacled eye.

Suddenly a tremendous indignation seized Tarwater. He eyed the small face peering from the crack. He searched his mind fiercely for the right word to hurl at it. Finally he said in a slow emphatic voice, "Before you was here, I was here."

The old man stared at him, his lips parting slowly until "He don't have good sense," he said. "Can't you see he don't have good sense? He don't know what you're talking about."

The boy grew more furious than ever. He swung around on his heel to leave.

"Wait," his uncle said and caught him. "Get behind that hedge yonder and hide yourself. I'm going in there and baptize him."

Tarwater's mouth was agape.

"Get behind there like I told you," he said and gave him a push toward the hedge. Then the old man braced himself. He turned and went back to the door. Just as he reached it, it was flung open and a lean young man with heavy black-rimmed spectacles stood in it, his head thrust forward, glaring at him.

Old Tarwater raised his fist. "The Lord Jesus Christ sent me to baptize that boy!" he shouted. "Stand aside. I mean to do it!"

Tarwater's head popped up from behind the hedge. Breathlessly he took the schoolteacher in—the narrow boney face slanting backwards from the jutting jaw, the hair that receded from the high forehead, the eyes encircled in glass. The white-haired child had caught hold of his father's leg and was hanging onto it. The schoolteacher pushed him back into the house. Then he stepped outside and slammed the door behind him and continued to glare at the old man as if he dared him to take a step.

"That boy cries out for his baptism," the old man said. "Precious in the sight of the Lord even an idiot!"

"Get off my property," the nephew said in a tight voice

as if he were keeping it calm by force. "If you don't, I'll have you put back in the asylum where you belong."

"You can't touch the servant of the Lord!" the old man hollered.

"You get away from here!" the nephew shouted, losing control of his voice. "Ask the Lord why He made him an idiot in the first place, uncle. Tell him I want to know why!"

The boy's heart was beating so fast he was afraid it was going to gallop out of his chest and disappear forever. He was head and shoulders out of the shrubbery.

"Yours not to ask!" the old man shouted. "Yours not to question the mind of the Lord God Almighty. Yours not to grind the Lord into your head and spit out a number!"

"Where's the boy?" the nephew asked, looking around suddenly as if he had just thought of it. "Where's the boy you were going to raise into a prophet to burn my eyes clean?" and he laughed.

Tarwater lowered his head into the bush again, instantly disliking the schoolteacher's laugh which seemed to reduce him to the least importance.

"His day is going to come," the old man said. "Either him or me is going to baptize that child. If not me in my day, him in his."

"You'll never lay a hand on him," the schoolteacher said. "You could slosh water on him for the rest of his life and he'd still be an idiot. Five years old for all eternity, useless forever. Listen," he said, and the boy heard his taut voice turn low with a kind of subdued intensity, a passion equal and opposite to the old man's, "he'll never be baptized—just as a matter of principle, nothing else. As a gesture of human dignity, he'll never be baptized."

"Time will discover the hand that baptizes him," the old man said.

"Time will discover it," the nephew said and opened the door behind him and stepped back inside and slammed it on himself.

The boy had risen from the shrubbery, his head swirling with excitement. He had never been back there again, never seen his cousin again, never seen the schoolteacher again, and he hoped to God, he told the stranger digging the grave along with him now, that he would never see him again though he had nothing against him himself and he would dislike to have to kill him but if he came out here, messing in what was none of his business except by law, then he would be obliged to.

Listen, the stranger said, what would he want to come

out here for—where there's nothing?

Tarwater didn't answer. He didn't search out the stranger's face but he knew by now that it was sharp and friendly and wise, shadowed under a stiff broad-brimmed panama hat that obscured the color of his eyes. He had lost his dislike for the thought of the voice. Only every now and then it sounded like a stranger's voice to him. He began to feel that he was only just now meeting himself, as if as long as his uncle had lived, he had been deprived of his own acquaintance. I ain't denying the old man was a good one, his new friend said, but like you said: you can't be any poorer than dead. They have to take what they can get. His soul is off this mortal earth now and his body is not going to feel the pinch, of fire or anything else.

"It was the last day he was thinking of," Tarwater murmured.

Well now, the stranger said, don't you think any cross you set up in the year 1952 would be rotted out by the year the Day of Judgment comes in? Rotted to as much dust as his ashes if you reduced him to ashes? And lemme ast you this: what's God going to do with sailors drowned at sea that the fish have et and the fish that et them et by other fish and they et by yet others? And what about people that get burned up naturally in house fires? Burnt up one way or another or lost in machines until they're pulp? And all those sojers blasted to nothing? What about all those that there's nothing left of to burn or bury?

If I burnt him, Tarwater said, it wouldn't be natural, it would be deliberate.

Oh I see, the stranger said. It ain't the Day of Judgment for him you're worried about. It's the Day of Judgment for you.

That's my bidnis, Tarwater said.

I ain't buttin into your bidnis, the stranger said. It don't mean a thing to me. You're left by yourself in this empty place. Forever by yourself in this empty place with just as much light at that dwarf sun wants to let in. You don't mean a thing to a soul as far as I can see.

"Redeemed," Tarwater muttered.

Do you smoke? the stranger asked.

Smoke if I want to and don't if I don't, Tarwater said. Bury if need be and don't if don't.

Go take a look at him and see if he's fell off his chair, his friend suggested.

Tarwater let the shovel drop in the grave and returned to the house. He opened the front door a crack and put his face to it. His uncle glared slightly to the side of him like a judge intent upon some terrible evidence. The boy shut the door quickly and went back to the grave, cold in spite of the sweat that stuck his shirt to his back. He began digging again.

The schoolteacher was too smart for him, that's all, the stranger said presently. You remember well enough how he said he kidnapped him when the schoolteacher was seven years of age. Gone to town and persuaded him out of his own backyard and brought him out here and baptized him. And what come of it? Nothing. The schoolteacher don't care now if he's baptized or if he ain't. It don't mean a thing to him one way or the other. Don't care if he's Redeemed or not neither. He only spent four days out here; you've spent fourteen years and now got to spend the rest of your life.

You see he was crazy all along, he continued. Wanted to make a prophet out of that schoolteacher too, but the schoolteacher was too smart for him. He got away.

He had somebody to come for him, Tarwater said. His daddy came and got him back. Nobody came and got me back.

The schoolteacher himself come after you, the stranger said, and got shot in the leg and the ear for his trouble.

I was not yet one year old, Tarwater said. A baby can't walk off and leave.

You ain't a baby now, his friend said.

The grave did not appear to get any deeper though he continued to dig. Look at the big prophet, the stranger jeered, and watched him from the shade of the speckled tree shadows. Lemme hear you prophesy something. The truth is the Lord ain't studying about you. You ain't entered His Head.

Tarwater turned around abruptly and worked from the other side and the voice continued from behind him. Anybody that's a prophet has got to have somebody to prophesy to. Unless you're just going to prophesy to yourself, he amended—or go baptize that dim-witted child, he added in a tone of high sarcasm.

The truth is, he said after a minute, the truth is that you're just as smart, if you ain't actually smarter, than the schoolteacher. Because he had somebody—his daddy and his mother—to tell him the old man was crazy, whereas you ain't had anybody and yet you've figured it out for yourself. Of course, it's taken you longer, but you've come to the right conclusion: you know he was a crazy man even when he wasn't in the asylum, even those last years.

Or if he wasn't actually crazy, he was the same thing in a different way: he didn't have but one thing on his mind. He was a one-notion man. Jesus. Jesus this and Jesus that. Ain't you in all your fourteen years of supporting his foolishness fed up and sick to the roof of your mouth with Jesus? My Lord and Saviour, the stranger sighed, I am if you ain't.

After a pause he continued. The way I see it, he said, you can do one of two things. One of them, not both. Nobody can do both of two things without straining themselves. You can do one thing or you can do the opposite.

Jesus or the devil, the boy said.

No no no, the stranger said, there ain't no such thing as a devil. I can tell you that from my own self-experience. I know that for a fact. It ain't Jesus or the devil. It's Jesus or *you*.

Jesus or me, Tarwater repeated. He put the shovel down for a rest and thought: he said the schoolteacher was glad to come. He said all he had to do was go out in the schoolteacher's back yard where he was playing and say, Let's you and me go to the country for a while—you have to be born again. The Lord Jesus Christ sent me to see to it. And the schoolteacher got up and took hold of his hand without a word and came with him and all the four days while he was out here he said the schoolteacher was hoping they wouldn't come for him.

Well that's all the sense a seven-year-old boy's got, the stranger said. You can't expect no more from a child. He learned better as soon as he got back to town; his daddy told him the old man was crazy and not to believe a word of what all he had learnt him.

There's not the way he told it, Tarwater said. He said that when the schoolteacher was seven years old, he had good sense but later it dried up. His daddy was an ass and not fit to raise him and his mother was a whore. She ran away from here when she was eighteen years old.

It took her that long? the stranger said in an incredulous tone. My, she was kind of an ass herself.

My great-uncle said he hated to admit it that his own sister was a whore but he had to say it to say the truth, the boy said.

Shaw, you know yourself that it give him great satisfaction to admit she was a whore, the stranger said. He was always admitting somebody was an ass or a whore. That's all a prophet is good for—to admit somebody else is an ass or a whore. And anyway, he asked slyly, what do you know about whores? Where have you ever run up on one of them?

Certainly I know what one of them is, the boy said.

The Bible is full of them. He knew what they were and to what they were liable to come, and just as Jezebel was discovered by dogs, an arm here and a foot there, so said his great-uncle, it had almost been with his own mother and grandmother. The two of them, along with his grandfather, had been killed in an automobile crash, leaving only the schoolteacher alive in that family, and Tarwater himself, for his mother (unmarried and shameless) had lived just long enough after the crash for him to be born. He had been born at the scene of the wreck.

The boy was very proud that he had been born in a wreck. He had always felt that it set his existence apart from the ordinary one and he had understood from it that the plans of God for him were special, even though nothing of consequence had happened to him so far. Often when he walked in the woods and came upon some bush a little removed from the rest, his breath would catch in his throat and he would stop and wait for the bush to burst into flame. It had not done it yet.

His uncle had never seemed to be aware of the importance of the way he had been born, only of how he had been born again. He would often ask him why he thought the Lord had rescued him out of the womb of a whore and let him see the light of day at all, and then why, having done it once, He had gone and done it again, allowing him to be baptized by his great-uncle into the death of Christ, and then having done it twice, gone on and done it a third time, allowing him to be rescued by his great-uncle from the schoolteacher and brought to the backwoods and given a chance to be brought up according to the truth. It was because, his uncle said, the Lord meant him to be trained for a prophet, even though he was a bastard, and to take his great-uncle's place when he died. The old man compared their situation to that of Elijah and Elisha.

All right, the stranger said, I suppose you know what one of them is. But there's a heap else you don't know. You go ahead and put your feet in his shoes. Elisha after Elijah like he said. But just lemme ast you this: where is the voice of the Lord? I haven't heard it. Who's called you this morning? Or any morning? Have you been told what to do? You ain't even heard the sound of natural

thunder this morning. There ain't a cloud in the sky.
The trouble with you, I see, he concluded, is that you
ain't got but just enough sense to believe every word
he told you.

The sun was directly overhead, apparently dead still,
holding its breath, waiting out the noontime. The grave
was about two feet deep. Ten foot now, remember, the
stranger said and laughed. Old men are selfish. You got
to expect the least of them. The least of everybody, he
added and let out a flat sigh that was like a gust of sand
raised and dropped suddenly by the wind.

Tarwater looked up and saw two figures cutting across
the field, a colored man and woman, each dangling an
empty vinegar jug by a finger. The woman, tall and Indianlike,
had on a green sun hat. She stooped under the fence without
pausing and came on across the yard toward the grave;
the man held the wire down and swung his leg over and
followed at her elbow. They kept their eyes on the hole
and stopped at the edge of it, looking down into the raw
ground with shocked satisfied expressions. The man, Buford,
had a crinkled face, darker than his hat. "Old man passed,"
he said.

The woman lifted her head and let out a slow sustained
wail, piercing and formal. She set her jug down on the
ground and crossed her arms and then lifted them in
the air and wailed again.

"Tell her to shut up that," Tarwater said. "I'm in
charge here now and I don't want no nigger-mourning."

"I seen his spirit for two nights," she said. "Seen him
two nights and he was unrested."

"He ain't been dead but since this morning," Tarwater
said. "If you all want your jugs filled, give them to me
and dig while I'm gone."

"He'd been predicting his passing for many years,"
Buford said. "She seen him in her dream several nights
and he wasn't rested. I known him well. I known him
very well indeed."

"Poor sweet sugar boy," the woman said to Tarwater,
"what you going to do here now by yourself in this
lonesome place?"

"Mind my bidnis," the boy said, jerking the jug out
of her hand. He started off so quickly that he almost fell.
He stalked across the back field toward the rim of trees
that surrounded the clearing.

The birds had gone into the deep woods to escape the
noon sun and one thrush, hidden some distance ahead

of him, called the same four notes again and again, stopping each time after them to make a silence. Tarwater began to walk faster, then he began to lope, and in a second he was running like something hunted, sliding down slopes waxed with pine needles and grasping the limbs of trees to pull himself, panting, up the slippery inclines. He crashed through a wall of honeysuckle and leapt across a sandy near-dry stream bed and fell down against the high clay bank that formed the back wall of a cove where the old man kept his extra liquor hidden. He hid it in a hollow of the bank, covered with a large stone. Tarwater began to fight at the stone to pull it away, while the stranger stood over his shoulder panting, He was crazy! He was crazy! That's the long and short of it, he was crazy!

Tarwater got the stone away and pulled out a black jug and sat down against the bank with it. Crazy! the stranger hissed, collapsing by his side.

The sun appeared, a furious white, edging its way secretly behind the tops of the trees that rose over the hiding place.

Any man, seventy years of age, to bring a baby out into the backwoods to raise him right! Suppose he had died when you were four years old instead of fourteen? Could you have toted mash to the still then and supported yourself? I never heard of no four-year-old running a still.

Never did I hear of that, he continued. You weren't anything to him but something that would grow big enough to bury him when the time came and now that he's dead, he's shut of you but you got two hundred and fifty pounds of him to put below the face of the earth. And don't think he wouldn't heat up like a coal stove to see you take a drop of liquor, he added. Though he had a weakness for it himself. When he couldn't stand the Lord one instant longer, he got drunk, prophet or no prophet. Hah. He might say it would hurt you but what he meant was you might get so much you wouldn't be in no fit condition to bury him. He said he brought you out here to raise you according to principle and that was the principle: that you should be fit when the time came to bury him so he would have a cross to mark where he was at.

A prophet with a still! He's the only prophet I ever heard of making liquor for a living.

After a minute he said in a softer tone as the boy took a long swallow from the black jug, well, a little won't interfere. Moderation never hurt no one.

A burning arm slid down Tarwater's throat as if the

devil were already reaching inside him to finger his soul. He squinted at the angry sun creeping behind the topmost fringe of trees.

Take it easy, his friend said. Do you remember them nigger gospel singers you saw one time, all drunk, all singing, all dancing around that black Ford automobile? Jesus, they wouldn't have been near so glad they were Redeemed if they hadn't had that liquor in them. I wouldn't pay too much attention to my Redemption if I was you. Some people take everything too hard.

Tarwater drank more slowly. He had been drunk only one time before and that time his uncle had beat him with a piece of crate for it, saying liquor would dissolve a child's gut, another of his lies because his gut had not dissolved.

It should be clear to you, his kind friend said, how all your life you been tricked by that old man. You could have been a city slicker for the last fourteen years. Instead, you been deprived of any company but his, you been living in a two-story barn in the middle of this earth's bald patch, following behind a mule and plow since you were seven. And how do you know the education he give you is true to the facts? Maybe he taught you a system of figures nobody else uses? How do you know that two added to two makes four? Four added to four makes eight? Maybe other people don't think so. How do you know if there was an Adam or if Jesus eased your situation any when He redeemed you? Or how do you know if He actually done it? Nothing but that old man's word and it ought to be obvious to you by now that he was crazy. And as for Judgment Day, the stranger said, every day is Judgment Day.

Ain't you old enough to have learnt that yet for yourself? Don't everything you do, everything you have ever done, work itself out right or wrong before your eye and usually before the sun has set? Have you ever got by with anything? No you ain't nor ever thought you would. You might as well drink all that liquor since you've already drunk so much. Once you pass the moderation mark you've passed it, and that gyration you feel working down from the top of your brain, he said, that's the Hand of God laying a blessing on you. He has given you your release. That old man was the stone before your door and the Lord has rolled it away. He ain't rolled it quite far enough, of course. You got to finish up yourself but He's done the main part. Praise Him.

Tarwater had ceased to have any feelings in his legs. He dozed for a while, his head hanging to the side and his mouth open and the liquor trickling slowly down the side of his overalls where the jug had overturned in his lap. Eventually there was only a drip at the neck of the bottle, forming and filling and dropping, silent and measured and sun-colored. The bright even sky began to fade, coarsening with clouds until every shadow had gone in. He woke with a wrench forward, his eyes focussing and unfocussing on something that looked like a burnt rag hanging close to his face.

Buford said, "This ain't no way for you to act. Old man don't deserve this. There's no rest until the dead is buried." He was squatting on his heels, one hand gripped around Tarwater's arm. "I gone yonder to the door and seen him sitting there at the table, not even laid out on a cooling board. He ought to be laid out and have some salt on his bosom if you mean to keep him overnight."

The boy's lids pinched together to hold the image steady and in a second he made out two small red blistered eyes.

"He deserves to lie in a grave that fits him," Buford said. "He was deep in this life, he was deep in Jesus' misery."

"Nigger," the child said, working his strange swollen tongue, "take your hand off me."

Buford lifted his hand. "He needs to be rested," he said.

"He'll be rested all right when I get through with him," Tarwater said vaguely. "Go on and lea' me to my bidnis."

"Nobody going to bother you," Buford said, standing up. He waited a minute, bent, looking down at the limp figure sprawled against the bank. The boy's head was tilted backwards over a root that jutted out of the clay wall. His mouth hung open and his turned-up hat cut a straight line across his forehead, just over his half-open unseeing eyes. His cheekbones protruded, narrow and thin like the arms of a cross, and the hollows under them had an ancient look as if the child's skeleton beneath were as old as the world. "Nobody going to bother you," the Negro muttered, pushing through the wall of honeysuckle without looking back. "That going to be your trouble."

Tarwater closed his eyes again.

Some night bird complaining close by woke him up. It was not a screeching noise, only an intermittent hump-hump as if the bird had to recall his grievance each time before he repeated it. Clouds were moving convulsively across a black sky and there was a pink unsteady moon that appeared to be jerked up a foot or so and then dropped and jerked up again. This was because, as he observed in an instant, the sky was lowering, coming down fast to smother him. The bird screeched and flew off in time and Tarwater lurched into the middle of the stream bed and crouched on his hands and knees. The moon was reflected like pale fire in the few spots of water in the sand. He sprang at the wall of honeysuckle and began to tear through it, confusing the sweet familiar odor with the weight coming down on him. When he stood up on the other side, the black ground swung slowly and threw him down again. A flare of pink lightning lit the woods and he saw the black shapes of trees pierce out of the ground all around him. The night bird began to hump again from a thicket where he had settled.

He got up and began to move in the direction of the clearing, feeling his way from tree to tree, the trunks very cold and dry to his touch. There was distant thunder and a continuous flicker of pale lightning firing one section of woods and then another. Finally he saw the shack, standing gaunt-black and tall in the middle of the clearing, with the pink moon trembling directly over it. His eyes glittered like open pits of light as he moved across the sand, dragging his crushed shadow behind him. He didn't turn his head to that side of the yard where he had started the grave. He stopped at the far back corner of the house and squatted down on the ground and looked underneath at the litter there, chicken crates and barrels and old rags and boxes. He had a small box of wooden matches in his pocket.

He crawled under and began to set small fires, building one from another, and working his way out at the front porch, leaving the fire behind him eating greedily at the dry tinder and the floor boards of the house. He crossed the front side of the yard and went through the rutted field without looking back until he reached the edge of the opposite woods. Then he glanced over his shoulder and saw that the pink moon had dropped through the roof of the shack and was bursting and he began to run, forced on through the woods by two bulging silver eyes that grew in immense astonishment in the center of the fire behind him. He could hear it moving up through the black night like a whirling chariot.

Toward midnight he came out on the highway and

caught a ride with a salesman who was a manufacturer's representative, selling copper flues throughout the Southeast, and who gave the silent boy what he said was the best advice he could give any young fellow setting out to find himself a place in the world. While they sped forward on the black untwisting highway, watched on either side by a dark wall of trees, the salesman said that it had been his personal experience that you couldn't sell a copper flue to a man you didn't love. He was a thin fellow with a narrow face that appeared to have been worn down to the sharpest possible depressions. He wore a broad-brimmed stiff grey hat of the kind. used by businessmen who would like to look like cowboys. He said love was the only policy that worked 95% of the time. He said when he went to sell a man a flue, he asked first about that man's wife's health and how his children were. He said he had a book that he kept the names of his customers' families in and what was wrong with them. A man's wife had cancer, he put her name down in the book and wrote *cancer* after it and inquired about her every time he went to that man's hardware store until she died; then he scratched out the word *cancer* and wrote *dead* there. "And I say thank God when they're dead," the salesman said; "that's one less to remember."

"You don't owe the dead anything," Tarwater said in a loud voice, speaking for almost the first time since he had got in the car.

"Nor they you," said the stranger. "And that's the way it ought to be in this world—nobody owing nobody nothing."

"Look," Tarwater said suddenly, sitting forward, his face close to the windshield, "we're headed in the wrong direction. We're going back where we came from. There's the fire again. There's the fire we left!"

Ahead of them in the sky there was a faint glow, steady, and not made by lightning. "That's the same fire we came from!" the boy said in a high voice.

"Boy, you must be nuts," the salesman said. "That's the city we're coming to. That's the glow from the city lights. I reckon this is your first trip anywhere."

"You're turned around," the child said; "it's the same fire."

The stranger twisted his rutted face sharply. "I've never been turned around in my life," he said. "And I didn't come from any fire. I come from Mobile. And I know where I'm going. What's the matter with you?"

Tarwater sat staring at the glow in front of him. "I

was asleep," he muttered. "I'm just now waking up."

"You should have been listening to me," the salesman said. "I been telling you things you ought to know."

was saying", he mumbled. "I si mean waking up."
"You should have ... rec...", the salesman
said. "I was telling you ... you wanted to know

Chapter 2

If the boy had actually trusted his new friend, Meeks, the copper flue salesman, he would have accepted Meeks' offer to take him directly to his uncle's door and let him out. Meeks had turned on the car light and told him to climb over onto the back seat and root around until he found the telephone book and when Tarwater had climbed back with it, he had showed him how to find his uncle's name in the book. Tarwater wrote the address and the telephone number down on the back of one of Meeks' cards. Meeks' telephone number was on the other side and he said any time Tarwater wanted to contact him for a little loan or any assistance, not to be afraid to use it. What Meeks had decided after about a half hour of the boy was that he was just enough off in the head and just ignorant enough to be a very hard worker, and he wanted a very ignorant energetic boy to work for him. But Tarwater was evasive. "I got to contact this uncle of mine, my only blood connection," he said.

Meeks could look at this boy and tell that he was running away from home, that he had left a mother and probably a sot-father and probably four or five brothers and sisters in a two-room shack set in a brush-swept bare-ground clearing just off the highway and that he was hightailing it for the big world, having first, from the way he reeked, fortified himself with stump liquor. He didn't for a minute believe he had any uncle at any such respectable address. He thought the boy had set his finger down on the name, Rayber, by chance and said, "That's him. A schoolteacher. My uncle."

"I'll take you right to his door," Meeks had said, fox-like. "We pass there going through town. We pass right by there."

"No," Tarwater said. He was sitting forward on the seat, looking out the window at a hill covered with old used-car bodies. In the indistinct darkness, they seemed to be drowning into the ground, to be about half-submerged already. The city hung in front of them on the side of the mountain as if it were a larger part of the same pile, not yet buried so deep. The fire had gone out of it and it appeared settled into its unbreakable parts.

The boy did not intend to go to the schoolteacher's until daylight and when he went he intended to make it plain that he had not come to be beholden or to be studied for a schoolteacher magazine. He began trying to remember the schoolteacher's face so that he could stare him down in his mind before he actually faced him. He felt that the more he could recall about him, the less advantage the new uncle would have over him. The face had not been one that held together in his mind, though he remembered the sloping jaw and the black-rimmed glasses. What he could not picture were the eyes behind the glasses. He had no memory of them and there was every kind of contradiction in the rubble of his great-uncle's descriptions. Sometimes the old man had said the nephew's eyes were black and sometimes brown. The boy kept trying to find eyes that fit mouth, nose that fit chin, but every time he thought he had a face put together, it fell apart and he had to begin on a new one. It was as if the schoolteacher, like the devil, could take on any look that suited him.

Meeks was telling him about the value of work. He said that it had been his personal experience that if you wanted to get ahead, you had to work. He said this was the law of life and it was no way to get around it because it was inscribed on the human heart like love thy neighbor. He said these two laws were the team that worked together to make the world go round and that any individual who wanted to be a success and win the pursuit of happiness, that was all he needed to know.

The boy was beginning to see a consistent image for the schoolteacher's eyes and was not listening to this advice. He saw them dark gray, shadowed with knowledge, and the knowledge moved like tree reflections in a pond where far below the surface shadows a snake may glide and disappear. He had made a habit of catching his great-uncle in contradictions about the schoolteacher's appearance.

"I forget what color eyes he's got," the old man would say, irked. "What difference does the color make when I know the look? I know what's behind it."

"What's behind it?"

"Nothing. He's full of nothing."

"He knows a heap," the boy said. "I don't reckon it's anything he don't know."

"He don't know it's anything he can't know," the

old man said. "That's his trouble. He thinks if it's something he can't know then somebody smarter than him can tell him about it and he can know it just the same. And if you were to go there, the first thing he would do would be to test your head and tell you what you were thinking and howcome you were thinking it and what you ought to be thinking instead. And before long you wouldn't belong to your self no more, you would belong to him."

The boy had no intention of allowing this to happen. He knew enough about the schoolteacher to be on his guard. He knew two complete histories, the history of the world, beginning with Adam, and the history of the schoolteacher, beginning with his mother, old Tarwater's own and only sister who had run away from Powderhead when she was eighteen years old and had become—the old man said he would mince no words, even with a child—a whore, until she had found a man by the name of Rayber who was willing to marry one. At least once a week, beginning at the beginning, the old man had reviewed this history through to the end.

His sister and this Rayber had brought two children into the world, one the schoolteacher and one a girl who had turned out to be Tarwater's mother and who, the old man said, had followed in the natural footsteps of her own mother, being already a whore by the time she was eighteen.

The old man had a great deal to say about Tarwater's conception, for the schoolteacher had told him that he himself had got his sister this first (and last) lover because he thought it would contribute to her *self-confidence*. The old man would say this, imitating the schoolteacher's voice and making it sillier than the boy felt it probably was. The old man was thrown into a fury of exasperation that there was not enough scorn in the world to cast upon this idiocy. Finally he would give up trying. The lover had shot himself after the accident, which was a relief to the schoolteacher for he wanted to bring up the baby himself.

The old man said that with the devil having such a heavy role in his beginning, it was little wonder that he should have an eye on the boy and keep him under close surveillance during his time on earth, in order that the soul he had helped call into being might serve him forever in hell. "You are the kind of boy," the old man said, "that the devil is always going to be offering to assist, to give you a smoke or a drink or a ride, and to ask you your bidnis. You had better mind how you

take up with strangers. And keep your bidnis to yourself."
It was to foil the devil's plans for him that the Lord had
seen to his upbringing.

"What line you going to get into?" Meeks asked.

The boy didn't appear to hear.

Whereas the schoolteacher had led his sister into evil,
with success, old Tarwater had made every attempt to
lead his own sister to repentance, without success. Through
one means or another, he had managed to keep up with
her after she ran away from Powderhead; but even after
she married, she would not listen to any word that had
to do with her salvation. He had twice been thrown out
of her house by her husband—each time with the assistance
of the police because the husband was a man of no force
—but the Lord had prompted him constantly to go back,
even in the face of going to jail. When he could not
get inside the house, he would stand outside it and shout
and then she would let him in lest he attract the attention
of the neighbors. The neighborhood children would gather
to listen to him and she would have to let him in.

It was not to be wondered at, the old man would say,
that the schoolteacher was no better than he was with
such a father as he had. The man, an insurance salesman,
wore a straw hat on the side of his head and smoked a
cigar and when you told him his soul was in danger, he
offered to sell you a policy against any contingency. He
said he was a prophet too, a prophet of life insurance,
for every right-thinking Christian, he said, knew that
it was his Christian duty to protect his family and provide
for them in the event of the unexpected. There was no
use treating with him, the old man said; his brain was
as slick as his eyeballs and the truth would no more soak
into it than rain would penetrate tin. The schoolteacher,
with Tarwater blood in him, at least had his father's strain
diluted. "Good blood flows in his veins," the old man said.
"And good blood knows the Lord and there ain't a thing
he can do about having it. There ain't a way in the world
he can get rid of it."

Meeks abruptly poked the boy in the side with his
elbow. He said if it was one thing a person needed to
learn it was to pay attention to older people than him
when they gave him good advice. He said he himself had
graduated from the School of Experience with an H.L.L.
degree. He asked the boy if he knew what was an H.L.L.
degree. Tarwater shook his head. Meeks said the H.L.L.
degree was the Hard Lesson from Life degree. He said it
was the quickest got and that it stayed learnt the longest.

The boy turned his head to the window.

One day the old man's sister had worked a perfidy on him. He had been in the habit of going on Wednesday afternoon because on that afternoon the husband played a golf game and he could find her alone. On this particular Wednesday, she did not open the door but he knew she was inside because he heard footsteps. He beat on the door a few times to warn her and when she wouldn't open it, he began to shout, for her and for all who would hear.

While he was telling this to Tarwater, he would jump up and begin to shout and prophesy there in the clearing the same way he had done it in front of her door. With no one to hear but the boy, he would flail his arms and roar, "Ignore the Lord Jesus as long as you can! Spit out the bread of life and sicken on honey. Whom work beckons, to work! Whom blood to blood! Whom lust to lust! Make haste, make haste. Fly faster and faster. Spin yourselves in a frenzy, the time is short! The Lord is preparing a prophet. The Lord is preparing a prophet with fire in his hand and eye and the prophet is moving toward the city with his warning. The prophet is coming with the Lord's message. 'Go warn the children of God,' saith the Lord, 'of the terrible speed of justice.' Who will be left? Who will be left when the Lord's mercy strikes?"

He might have been shouting to the silent woods that encircled them. While he was in his frenzy, the boy would take up the shotgun and hold it to his eye and sight along the barrel, but sometimes as his uncle grew more and more wild, he would lift his face from the gun for a moment with a look of uneasy alertness, as if while he had been inattentive, the old man's words had been dropping one by one into him and now, silent, hidden in his bloodstream, were moving secretly toward some goal of their own.

His uncle would prophesy until he exhausted himself and then he would fall with a thud on the sway-back step and sometimes it would be five or ten minutes before he could go on and relate how the sister had worked the perfidy on him.

Whenever he came to this part of the story, his breath would at once come short as if he were struggling to run up a hill. His face would get redder and his voice thinner and sometimes it would give out completely and he would sit there on the step, beating the porch floor with his fist while he moved his lips and no sound came out. Finally he would pipe, "They grabbed me. Two. From behind. The door behind. Two."

His sister had had two men and a doctor behind the door, listening, and the papers made out to commit him to the asylum if the doctor thought he was crazy. When he understood what was happening, he had raged through her house like a blinded bull, everything crashing behind him, and it had taken two of them and the doctor and two neighbors to get him down. The doctor had said he was not only crazy but dangerous and they had taken him to the asylum in a strait jacket.

"Ezekiel was in the pit for forty days," he would say, "but I was in it for four years," and he would stop at that point and warn Tarwater that the servants of the Lord Jesus could expect the worse. The boy could see that this was so. But no matter how little they had now, his uncle said, their reward in the end was the Lord Jesus Himself, the bread of life!

The boy would have a hideous vision of himself sitting forever with his great-uncle on a green bank, full and sick, staring at a broken fish and a multiplied loaf.

His uncle had been in the asylum four years because it had taken him four years to understand that the way for him to get out was to stop prophesying on the ward. It had taken him four years to discover what the boy felt he himself would have discovered in no time at all. But at least in the asylum the old man had learned caution and when he got out, he put everything he had learned to the service of his cause. He proceeded about the Lord's business like an experienced crook. He had given the sister up but he intended to help her boy. He planned to kidnap the child and keep him long enough to baptize him and instruct him in the facts of his Redemption and he mapped out his plan to the last detail and carried it out exactly.

Tarwater liked this part best because in spite of himself he had to admire his uncle's craft. The old man had persuaded Buford Munson to send his daughter in to get a job cooking for the sister and with the girl once in the house, he had been able to find out what he needed to know. He learned that there were two children now instead of one and that his sister sat in her nightgown all day drinking whiskey out of a medicine bottle. While Luella Munson washed and cooked and took care of the children, his sister lay on the bed sipping from the bottle and reading books that she had to buy fresh every night from the drugstore. But the principle reason the kidnapping had been so easy was because his great-uncle had had the full cooperation of the schoolteacher himself, a thin boy with a boney pale face and a pair of gold-rimmed spectacles that were always falling down his nose.

The two of them, the old man said, had liked each other from the first. The day he had gone to do the kidnapping, the husband was away on business and the sister, shut up in her room with the bottle, didn't even know the time of day. All the old man had done was to walk in and tell Luella Munson that his nephew was going off to spend a few days with him in the country and then he had gone out to the back yard and spoken to the schoolteacher who had been digging holes and lining them with broken glass.

He and the schoolteacher had taken the train as far as the junction and had walked the rest of the way to Powderhead. The old man had explained to him that he was not taking him on this trip for pleasure but because the Lord had sent him to do it, to see that he was born again and instructed in his Redemption. All these facts were new to the schoolteacher, for his parents had never taught him anything, old Tarwater said, except not to wet the bed.

In four days the old man taught him what was necessary to know and baptized him. He made him understand that his true father was the Lord and not the simpleton in town and that he would have to lead a secret life in Jesus until the day came when he would be able to bring the rest of his family around to repentance. He had made him understand that on the last day it would be his destiny to rise in glory in the Lord Jesus. Since this was the first time anybody had bothered to tell these facts to the schoolteacher, he could not hear too much of them, and as he had never seen woods before or been in a boat or caught a fish or walked on roads that were not paved, they did all those things too and, his uncle said, he even allowed him to plow. His sallow face had become bright in four days. At this point Tarwater would begin to weary of the story.

The schoolteacher had spent four days in the clearing because his mother had not missed him for three days and when Luella Munson had mentioned where he had gone, she had to wait another day before his father came home and she could send him after the child. She would not come herself, the old man said, for fear the wrath of God would strike her at Powderhead and she would not be able to get back to the city again. She had wired the schoolteacher's father and when the simpleton arrived at the clearing, the schoolteacher was in despair at having to leave. The light had left his eyes. He had gone but the old man insisted that he had been able to tell by the look on his face that he would never be the same boy again.

"If he didn't say he didn't want to go, you can't be sure he didn't," Tarwater would say contentiously.

"Then why did he try to come back?" the old man asked. "Answer me that. Why one week later did he run away and try to find his way back and got his picture in the paper when the state patrol found him in the woods? I ask you why. Tell me that if you know so much."

"Because here was less bad than there," Tarwater said. "Less bad don't mean good, it only means better-than."

"He tried to come back," his uncle said slowly, emphasizing each word, "to hear more about God his Father, more about Jesus Christ Who had died to redeem him and more of the Truth I could tell him."

"Well go on," Tarwater would say irritably, "get on with the rest of it." The story always had to be taken to completion. It was like a road that the boy had travelled on so often that half the time he didn't look where they were going, and when at certain points he would become aware where they were, he would be surprised to see that the old man had not got farther on with it. Sometimes his uncle would lag at one point as if he didn't want to face what was coming and then when he finally came to it, he would try to get past it in a rush. At such points, Tarwater plagued him for details. "Tell about when he came when he was fourteen years old and had already decided none of it was true and he give you all that sass."

"Bah," the old man would say. "He was living in confusion. I don't say it was his fault then. They told him I was a crazy man. But I'll tell you one thing: he never believed them neither. They kept him from believing me but I kept him from believing them and he never took on none of their ways though he took on worse ones. And when he got shut of the three of them in that crash, nobody was gladder than he was. Then he turned his mind to raising you. Said he was going to give you every advantage, every advantage." The old man snorted. "You have me to thank for saving you from those advantages."

The boy looked off into the distance as though he were staring blankly at his invisible advantages.

"When he got shut of the three of them in that crash, this was the first place he came. On the very day they were killed he came out here to tell me. Straight out here.

Yes sir," the old man said with the greatest satisfaction, "straight out here. He hadn't seen me in years but this is where he came. I was the one he came to. I was the one he wanted to see. Me. I had never left his mind. I had taken my seat in it."

"You skipped all that part about how he came when he was fourteen and give you all that sass," Tarwater said.

"It was sass he got from them," the old man said. "Just parrot-mouthing all they had ever said about how I was a crazy man. The truth was even if they told him not to believe what I had taught him, he couldn't forget it. He never could forget that there was a chance that that simpleton was not his only father. I planted the seed in him and it was there for good. Whether anybody liked it or not."

"It fell amongst cockles," Tarwater said. "Say the sass."

"It fell in deep," the old man said, "or else after that crash he wouldn't have come out here hunting me."

"He only wanted to see if you were still crazy," the boy offered.

"The day may come," his great-uncle said slowly, "when a pit opens up inside you and you know some things you never known before," and he would give him such a prescient piercing look that the child would turn his face away, scowling fiercely.

His great-uncle had gone to live with the schoolteacher and as soon as he had got there, he had baptized Tarwater, practically under the schoolteacher's nose and the schoolteacher had made a blasphemous joke of it. But the old man could never tell this straight through. He always had to back up and tell why he had gone to live with the schoolteacher in the first place. He had gone for three reasons. One, he said, because he knew the schoolteacher wanted him. He was the only person in the schoolteacher's life who had ever taken two steps out of his way in his behalf. And two, because his nephew was the proper person to bury him and he wanted to have it understood with him how he wanted it done. And three, because the old man meant to see that Tarwater was baptized.

"I know all that," the boy would say, "get on with the rest of it."

"After the three of them perished and the house was his, he cleared it out," old Tarwater said. "He moved every stick of furniture out of it except a table and a chair or two and a bed or two and the crib he bought for you. Taken down all the pictures and all the curtains and taken up all the rugs. Even burned up all his mother's and sister's

and the simpleton's clothes, didn't want a thing of theirs
around. It wasn't anything left but books and papers
that he had collected. Papers everywhere," the old man
said. "Every room looked like the inside of a bird's nest.
I came a few days after the crash and when he saw me
standing there, he was glad to see me. His eyes lit up.
He was glad to see me. 'Ha,' he said, 'my house is swept
and garnished and here are the seven other devils, all
rolled into one!' " The old man slapped his knee with
pleasure.

"It don't sound to me like . . ."

"No, he didn't say so," the uncle said, "but I ain't
an idiot."

"If he didn't say so you can't be sure."

"I'm as sure," his uncle said, "as I am that this here,"
and he held up his hand, every short thick finger stretched
rigid in front of Tarwater's face, "is my hand and not
yours." There was something final in this that always made
the boy's impudence subside.

"Well get on with it," he would say. "If you don't
make haste, you'll never get to where he blasphemed at."

"He was glad to see me," his uncle said. "He opened
the door with all that house full of paper-trash behind
him and there I stood and he was glad to see me. It
was all underneath his face."

"What did he say?" Tarwater asked.

"He looked at my satchel," the old man said, "and
he said, 'Uncle, you can't live with me. I know exactly
what you want but I'm going to raise this child my way.' "

These words of the schoolteacher's had always caused
a quick charge of excitement to race through Tarwater,
an almost sensuous satisfaction. "It might have sounded
to you like he was glad to see you," he said. "It don't
sound that way to me."

"He wasn't but twenty-four years old," the old man
said. "His expression hadn't even set on his face yet.
I could still see the seven-year-old boy that had gone
off with me, except that now he had a pair of black-rimmed
glasses and a nose big enough to hold them up. The
size of his eyes had shrunk because his face had grown
but it was the same face all right. You could see behind
it to what he really wanted to say. When he came out
here later to get you back after I had stolen you, it was
already set. It was as set then as the outside of a penitentiary
but not now when I'm telling you about. Then it wasn't
set and I could see he wanted me. Else why had he come

out to Powderhead to tell me they were all dead? I ask you that? He could have let me alone."

The boy couldn't answer.

"Anyway," the old man said, "what all he gone on and done proved he wanted me right then because he took me in. He looked at my satchel and I said, 'I'm on your charity,' and he said, 'I'm sorry, Uncle. You can't live with me and ruin another child's life. This one is going to be brought up to live in the real world. He's going to be brought up to expect exactly what he can do for himself. He's going to be his own saviour. He's going to be free!' " The old man turned his head to the side and spit. "Free," he said. "He was full of such-like phrases. But then I said it. I said what changed his mind."

The boy sighed at this. The old man considered it his master stroke. He had said, "I never come to live with you. I come to die!"

"And you should have seen his face," he said. "He looked like he'd been pushed all of a sudden from behind. He hadn't cared if the other three were wiped out but when he thought of me going, it was like he was losing somebody for the first time. He stood there staring at me." And once, only once, the old man had leaned forward and said to Tarwater, in a voice that could no longer contain the pleasure of its secret, "He loved me like a daddy and he was ashamed of it!"

The boy's face had remained unmoved. "Yes," he said, "and you had told him a bare-face lie. You never had no intention of dying."

"I was sixty-nine years of age," his uncle said. "I could have died the next day as well as not. No man knows the hour of his death. I didn't have my life in front of me. It was not a lie, it was only a speculation. I told him, I said, 'I may live two months or two days.' And I had on my clothes that I bought to be buried in—all new."

"Ain't it that same suit you got on now?" the boy asked indignantly, pointing to the threadbare knee. "Ain't it that one you got on yourself right now?"

"I may live two months or two days, I said to him," his uncle said.

Or ten years or twenty, Tarwater thought.

"Oh it was a shock to him," the old man said.

It might have been a shock, the boy thought, but he wasn't all that sorry about it. The schoolteacher had merely said, "So I'm to put you away, Uncle? All right, I'll put you away. I'll do it with pleasure. I'll put you away for good and all," but the old man insisted that his words were one thing and his actions and the look on his face another.

His great-uncle had not been in the nephew's house ten minutes before he had baptized Tarwater. They had gone into the room where the crib was with Tarwater in it and as the old man looked at him for the first time—a wizened grey-faced scrawny sleeping baby—the voice of the Lord had come to him and said: HERE IS THE PROPHET TO TAKE YOUR PLACE. BAPTIZE HIM.

That? the old man had asked, that wizened grey-faced . . . and then as he wondered how he could baptize him with the nephew standing there, the Lord had sent the paper boy to knock on the door and the schoolteacher had gone to answer it.

When he came back in a few minutes, his uncle was holding Tarwater in one hand and with the other he was pouring water over his head out of the bottle that had been on the table by the crib. He had pulled off the nipple and stuck it in his pocket. He was just finishing the words of baptism as the schoolteacher came back in the door and he had had to laugh when he looked up and saw his nephew's face. It looked hacked, the old man said. Not even angry at first, just hacked.

Old Tarwater had said, "He's been born again and there ain't a thing you can do about it," and then he had seen the rage rise in the nephew's face and had seen him try to conceal it.

"Time has passed you by, Uncle," the nephew said. "That can't even irritate me. That only makes me laugh," and he laughed, a short forced bark, but the old man said his face was mottled. "Just as well you did it now," he said. "If you had got me when I was seven days instead of seven years, you might not have ruined my life."

"If it's ruined," the old man said, "it wasn't me that ruined it."

"Oh yes it was," the nephew said, advancing across the room, his face very red. "You're too blind to see what you did to me. A child can't defend himself. Children are cursed with believing. You pushed me out of the real world and I stayed out of it until I didn't know which was which. You infected me with your idiot hopes, your foolish violence. I'm not always myself, I'm not al . . ." but he stopped. He wouldn't admit what the old man knew. "There's nothing wrong with me," he said. "I've straightened the tangle you made. Straightened it by pure will power. I've made myself straight."

"You see," the old man said, "he admitted himself the seed was still in him."

Old Tarwater had laid the baby back in the crib but the nephew took him out again, a peculiar smile, the old man said, stiffening on his face. "If one baptism is good, two will be better," he said and he had turned Tarwater over and poured what was left in the bottle over his bottom and said the words of baptism again. Old Tarwater had stood there, aghast at this blasphemy. "Now Jesus has a claim on both ends," the nephew said.

The old man had roared, "Blasphemy never changed a plan of the Lord's!"

"And the Lord hasn't changed any of mine either," said the nephew coolly and put the baby back.

"And what did I do?" Tarwater asked.

"You didn't do nothing," the old man said as if what he did or didn't do was of no consequence whatsoever.

"It was me that was the prophet," the boy said sullenly.

"You didn't even know what was going on," his uncle said.

"Oh yes I did," the child said. "I was laying there thinking."

His uncle would ignore this and go on. He had thought for a while that by living with the schoolteacher, he might convince him again of all that he had convinced him of when he had kidnapped him as a child and he had had hope of it up until the time when the schoolteacher showed him the study he had written of him for the magazine. Then the old man had realized at last that there was no hope of his doing anything for the schoolteacher. He had failed the schoolteacher's mother and he had failed the schoolteacher, and now there was nothing to do but try to save Tarwater from being brought up by a fool. In this he had not failed.

The boy felt that the schoolteacher could have made more of an effort to get him back. He had come out and got shot in the leg and the ear but if he had used his head, he might have avoided that and got him back at the same time. "Why didn't he bring the law out here and get me back?" he had asked.

"You want to know why?" his uncle said. "Well I'll tell you why. I'll tell you exactly why. It was because he found you a heap of trouble. He wanted it all in his head. You can't change a child's pants in your head."

The boy would think: but if the schoolteacher hadn't written that piece on him, we might all three be living in town right now.

When the old man had read the piece in the schoolteacher magazine, he had at first not recognized who it was the schoolteacher was writing about, who the type was that was almost extinct. He had sat down to read the piece, full of pride that his nephew had succeeded in having a composition printed in a magazine. He had handed it carelessly to his uncle and said he might want to glance over it and the old man had sat down at once at the kitchen table and commenced to read it. He recalled that the schoolteacher had kept passing by the kitchen door to witness how he was taking the piece.

About the middle of it, old Tarwater had begun to think that he was reading about someone he had once known or at least someone he had dreamed about, for the figure was strangely familiar. "This fixation of being called by the Lord had its origin in insecurity. He needed the assurance of a call and so he called himself," he read. The schoolteacher kept passing by the door, passing and repassing, and finally he came in and sat down quietly on the other side of the small white metal table. When the old man looked up, the schoolteacher smiled. It was a very slight smile, the slightest that would do for any occasion. The old man knew from the smile who it was he had been reading about.

For the length of a minute, he could not move. He felt he was tied hand and foot inside the schoolteacher's head, a space as bare and neat as the cell in the asylum, and was shrinking, drying up to fit it. His eyeballs swerved from side to side as if he were pinned in a strait jacket again. Jonah, Ezekiel, Daniel, he was at that moment all of them—the swallowed, the lowered, the enclosed.

The nephew, his smile still fixed, reached across the table and put his hand on the old man's wrist in a gesture of pity. "You've got to be born again, Uncle," he said, "by your own efforts, back to the real world where there's no saviour but yourself."

The old man's tongue lay in his mouth like a stone but his heart began to swell. His prophet's blood surged in him, surged to floodtide for a miraculous release, though his face remained shocked, expressionless. The nephew patted his huge clenched fist and got up and left the kitchen, bearing away his smile of triumph.

The next morning when he went to the crib to give the baby his bottle, he found nothing in it but the blue magazine with the old man's message scrawled on the back of it: THE PROPHET I RAISE UP OUT OF THIS BOY WILL BURN YOUR EYES CLEAN.

"It was me could act," the old man said, "not him. He could never take action. He could only get everything inside his head and grind it to nothing. But I acted. And because I acted, you sit here in freedom, you sit here a rich man, knowing the Truth, in the freedom of the Lord Jesus Christ."

The boy would move his thin shoulder blades irritably as if he were shifting the burden of Truth like a cross on his back. "He came out here and got shot to get me back," he said obstinately.

"If he had really wanted you back, he could have got you," the old man said. "He could have had the law out here after me or got me put back in the asylum. There was plenty he could have done, but what happened to him was that welfare-woman. She persuaded him to have one of his own and let you go, and he was easy persuaded. And that one," the old man would say, beginning to brood on the schoolteacher's child again, "that one—the Lord gave him one he couldn't corrupt." And then he would grip the boy's shoulder and put a fierce pressure on it. "And if I don't get him baptized, it'll be for you to do," he said. "I enjoin you to do it, boy."

Nothing irritated the boy so much as this. "I take my orders from the Lord," he would say in an ugly voice, trying to pry the fingers out of his shoulder. "Not from you."

"The Lord will give them to you," the old man said, gripping his shoulder tighter.

"He had to change that one's pants and he done it," Tarwater muttered.

"He had the welfare-woman to do it for him," his uncle said. "She had to be good for something, but you can bet she ain't still around there. Bernice Bishop!" he said as if he found this the most idiotic name in the language. "Bernice Bishop!"

The boy had sense enough to know that he had been betrayed by the schoolteacher and he did not mean to go to his house until daylight, when he could see behind and before him. "I ain't going there until daylight," he said suddenly to Meeks. "You needn't to stop there because I ain't getting out there."

Meeks leaned casually against the door of the car, driving with half his attention and giving the other half to Tarwater. "Son," he said, "I'm not going to be a preacher to you. I'm not going to tell you not to lie. I ain't going to tell you nothing impossible. All I'm going to tell you is this: don't lie when you don't have to. Else when you do have to, nobody'll believe you. You don't have to lie to me. I know exactly what you done." A shaft of light plunged through the car window and he looked to the side and saw the white face beside him, staring up with soot-colored eyes.

"How do you know?" the boy asked.

Meeks smiled with pleasure. "Because I done the same thing myself once," he said.

Tarwater caught hold of the sleeve of the salesman's coat and gave it a quick pull. "On the Day of Judgment," he said, "me and you will rise and say we done it!"

Meeks looked at him again with one eyebrow cocked at the same angle he wore his hat. "Will we?" he asked. Then he said, "What line you gonna get into, boy?"

"What line?"

"What you going to do? What kind of *work?*"

"I know everything but the machines," Tarwater said, sitting back again. "My great-uncle learnt me everything but first I have to find out how much of it is true." They were entering the dilapidated outskirts of the city where wooden buildings leaned together and an occasional dim light lit up a faded sign advertising some remedy or other.

"What line was your great-uncle in?" Meeks asked.

"He was a prophet," the boy said.

"Is that right?" Meeks asked and his shoulders jumped several times as if they were going to leap over his head. "Who'd he prophesy to?"

"To me," Tarwater said. "Nobody else would listen to him and there wasn't anybody else for me to listen to. He grabbed me away from this other uncle, my only blood connection now, so as to save me from running to doom."

"You were a captive audience," Meeks said. "And now you're coming to town to run to doom with the rest of us, huh?"

The boy didn't answer at once. Then he said in a guarded tone, "I ain't said what I'm going to do."

"You ain't sure about what all this great-uncle of yours told you, are you?" Meeks asked. "You figure he might have got aholt to some misinformation."

Tarwater looked away, out the window, at the brittle forms of the houses. He was holding both arms close to his sides as if he were cold. "I'll find out," he said.

"Well how now?" Meeks asked.

The dark city was unfolding on either side of them and they were approaching a low circle of light in the distance. "I mean to wait and see what happens," he said after a moment.

"And suppose nothing don't happen?" Meeks asked.

The circle of light became huge and they swung into the center of it and stopped. It was a gaping concrete mouth with two red gas pumps set in front of it and a small glass office toward the back. "I say suppose nothing don't happen?" Meeks repeated.

The boy looked at him darkly, remembering the silence after his great-uncle's death.

"Well?" Meeks said.

"Then I'll make it happen," he said. "I can act."

"Attaboy," Meeks said. He opened the car door and put his leg out while he continued to observe his rider. Then he said, "Wait a minute. I got to call my girl."

A man was asleep in a chair tilted against the outside wall of the glass office and Meeks went inside without waking him up. For a minute Tarwater only craned his neck out the window. Then he got out and went to the office door to watch Meeks use the machine. It sat, small and black, in the center of a cluttered desk which Meeks sat down on as if it had been his own. The room was lined with automobile tires and had a concrete and rubber smell. Meeks took the machine in two parts and held one part to his head while he circled with his finger on the other part. Then he sat waiting, swinging his foot, while the horn buzzed in his ear. After a minute an acid smile began to eat at the corners of his mouth and he said, drawing in his breath, "Heythere, Sugar, hyer you?" and Tarwater, from where he stood in the door, heard an actual woman's voice, like one coming from beyond the grave, say, "Why Sugar, is that reely you?" and Meeks said it was him in the same old flesh and made an appointment with her in ten minutes.

Tarwater stood awestruck in the doorway. Meeks put the telephone together and then he said in a sly voice, "Now why don't you call your uncle?" and watched the boy's face change, the eyes swerve suspiciously to the side and the flesh drop around the boney mouth.

"I'll speak with him soon enough," he muttered, but he kept looking at the black coiled machine, fascinated. "How do you use it?" he asked.

"You dial it like I did. Call your uncle," Meeks urged.

"No, that woman is waiting on you," Tarwater said.

"Let 'er wait," Meeks said. "That's what she knows how to do best."

The boy approached it, taking out the card he had written

the number on. He put his finger on the dial and began gingerly to turn it.

"Great God," Meeks said and took the receiver off the hook and put it in his hand and thrust his hand to his ear. He dialed the number for him and then pushed him down in the office chair to wait but Tarwater stood up again, slightly crouched, holding the buzzing horn to his head, while his heart began to kick viciously at his chest wall.

"It don't speak," he murmured.

"Give him time," Meeks said, "maybe he don't like to get up in the middle of the night."

The buzzing continued for a minute and then stopped abruptly. Tarwater stood speechless, holding the earpiece tight against his head, his face rigid as if he were afraid that the Lord might be about to speak to him over the machine. All at once he heard what sounded like heavy breathing in his ear.

"Ask for your party," Meeks prompted. "How do you expect to get your party if you don't ask for him?"

The boy remained exactly as he was, saying nothing.

"I told you to ask for your party," Meeks said irritably. "Ain't you got good sense?"

"I want to speak with my uncle," Tarwater whispered.

There was a silence over the telephone but it was not a silence that seemed to be empty. It was the kind where the breath is drawn in and held. Suddenly the boy realized that it was the schoolteacher's child on the other side of the machine. The white-haired, blunted face rose before him. He said in a furious shaking voice, "I want to speak with my uncle. Not you!"

The heavy breathing began again as if in answer. It was a kind of bubbling noise, the kind of noise someone would make who was struggling to breathe in water. In a second it faded away. The horn of the machine dropped out of Tarwater's hand. He stood there blankly as if he had received a revelation he could not yet decipher. He seemed to have been stunned by some deep internal blow that had not yet made its way to the surface of his mind.

Meeks picked up the earpiece and listened but there was no sound. He put it back on the hook and said, "Come on. I ain't got this kind of time." He gave the stupefied boy a shove and they left, driving off into the city again. Meeks told him to learn to work every machine he saw. The greatest invention of man, he said, was the wheel and he asked Tarwater if he had ever thought how things were before it was a wheel, but the boy didn't answer him. He didn't even appear to be listening. He sat slightly forward and from time to time his lips moved as if he were speaking silently with himself.

"Well, it was terrible," Meeks said sourly. He knew the boy didn't have any uncle at any such respectable address and to prove it, he turned down the street the uncle was supposed to live on and drove slowly past the small shapes of squat houses until he found the number, visible in phosphorescent letters on a small stick set on the edge of the grass plot. He stopped the car and said, "Okay, kiddo, that's it."

"That's what?" Tarwater mumbled.

"That's your uncle's house," Meeks said.

The boy grabbed the edge of the window with both hands and stared out at what appeared to be only a black shape crouched in a greater darkness a little distance away. "I told you I wasn't going there until daylight," he said angrily; "go on."

"You're going there right now," Meeks said. "Because I ain't getting stuck with you. You can't go with me where I'm going."

"I ain't getting out here," the boy said.

Meeks reached across him and opened the car door. "So long, son," he said, "if you get real hungry by next week, you can contack me from that card and we might make a deal."

The boy gave him one white-faced outraged look and flung himself from the car. He moved up the short concrete walk to the doorstep and sat down abruptly, absorbed into the darkness. Meeks pulled the car door shut. His face hung for a moment watching the barely visible outline of the boy's shape on the step. Then he drew back and drove on. He won't come to no good end, he said to himself.

Chapter 3

Tarwater sat in the corner of the doorstep, scowling in the dark as the car disappeared down the block. He did not look up at the sky but he was unpleasantly aware of the stars. They seemed to be holes in his skull through which some distant unmoving light was watching him. It was as if he were alone in the presence of an immense silent eye. He had an intense desire to make himself known to the schoolteacher at once, to tell him what he had done and why and to be congratulated by him. At the same time, his deep suspicion of the man continued to work in him. He tried to bring the schoolteacher's face again to mind, but all he could manage was the face of the seven-year-old boy the old man had kidnapped. He stared at it boldly, hardening himself for the encounter.

Then he rose and faced the heavy brass knocker on the door. He touched it and jerked his hand away, burnt by a metallic coldness. He looked quickly over his shoulder. The houses across the street formed a dark jagged wall. The quiet seemed palpable, waiting. It seemed almost to be waiting patiently, biding its time until it should reveal itself and demand to be named. He turned back to the cold knocker and grabbed it and shattered the silence as if it were a personal enemy. The noise filled his head. He was aware of nothing but the racket he was making.

He beat louder and louder, bamming at the same time with his free fist until he felt he was shaking the house. The empty street echoed with his blows. He stopped once to get his breath and then began again, kicking the door frenziedly with the blunt toe of his heavy work shoe. Nothing happened. Finally, he stopped and the implacable silence descended around him, immune to his fury. A mysterious dread filled him. His whole body felt hollow as if he had been lifted like Habakkuk by the hair of his head, borne swiftly through the night and set down in the place of his mission. He had a sudden foreboding that he was about to step into a trap laid for him by the old man. He half-turned to run.

At once the glass panels on either side of the door

filled with light. There was a click and the knob turned. Tarwater jerked his hands up automatically as if he were pointing an invisible gun and his uncle, who had opened the door, jumped back at the sight of him.

The image of the seven-year-old boy disappeared forever from Tarwater's mind. His uncle's face was so familiar to him that he might have seen it every day of his life. He steadied himself and shouted, "My great-uncle is dead and burnt, just like you would have burnt him yourself!"

The schoolteacher remained absolutely still as if he thought that by looking long enough his hallucination would disappear. He had been roused by the vibration in the house and had run, half-asleep, to the door. His face was like the face of a sleep-walker who wakes and sees some horror of his dreams take shape before him. After a moment he muttered, "Wait here, deaf," and turned and went quickly out of the hall. He was barefooted and in his pajamas. He came back almost at once, plugging something into his ear. He had thrust on the black-rimmed glasses and he was sticking a metal box into the waist-band of his pajamas. This was joined by a cord to the plug in his ear. For an instant the boy had the thought that his head ran by electricity. He caught Tarwater by the arm and pulled him into the hall under a lantern-shaped light that hung from the ceiling. The boy found himself scrutinized by two small drill-like eyes set in the depths of twin glass caverns. He drew away. Already he felt his privacy imperilled.

"My great-uncle is dead and burnt," he said again. "I was the only one there to do it and I done it. I done your work for you," and as he said the last, a perceptible trace of scorn crossed his face.

"Dead?" the schoolteacher said. "My uncle? The old man's dead?" he asked in a blank unbelieving tone. He caught Tarwater abruptly by the arms and stared into his face. In the depths of his eyes, the boy, shocked, saw an instant's stricken look, plain and awful. It vanished at once. The straight line of the schoolteacher's mouth began turning into a smile. "And how did he go—with his fist in the air?" he asked. "Did the Lord arrive for him in a chariot of fire?"

"He didn't have no warning," Tarwater said, suddenly breathless. "He was eating his breakfast and I never moved him from the table. I set him on fire where he was and the house with him."

The schoolteacher said nothing but the boy read in his look a doubt that this had happened, a suspicion that he dealt with an interesting liar.

"You can go there and see for yourself," Tarwater said. "He was too big to bury. I done it the quickest way."

His uncle's eyes had the look now of being trained on a fascinating problem. "How did you get here? How did you know this was where you belonged?" he asked.

The boy had expended all his energy announcing himself. He was suddenly blank and stunned and he remained stupidly silent. He had never been this tired before. He felt he was about to fall.

The schoolteacher waited, searching his face impatiently. Then his expression changed again. He tightened his grip on Tarwater's arm and his eyes turned, glowering, toward the front door, which was still open. "Is he out there?" he asked in a low enraged voice. "Is this one of his tricks? Is he out there waiting to sneak in a window and baptize Bishop while you're here baiting me? Is that his senile game this time?"

The boy blanched. In his mind's eye he saw the old man, a dark shape standing behind the corner of the house, restraining his wheezing breath while he waited impatiently for him to baptize the dim-witted child. He stared shocked at the schoolteacher's face. There was a wedge-shaped gash in his new uncle's ear. The sight of it brought old Tarwater so close that the boy thought he could hear him laugh. With a terrible clarity he saw that the schoolteacher was no more than a decoy the old man had set up to lure him to the city to do his unfinished business.

His eyes began to burn in his fierce fragile face. A new energy seized him. "He's dead," he said. "You can't be any deader than he is. He's reduced to ashes. He don't even have a cross set up over him. If it's anything left of him, the buzzards wouldn't have it and the bones the dogs'll carry off. That's how dead he is."

The schoolteacher winced, but almost at once he was smiling again. He held Tarwater's arms tightly and peered into his face as if he were beginning to see a solution, one that intrigued him with its symmetry and rightness. "It's a perfect irony," he murmured, "a perfect irony that you should have taken care of the matter in that way. He got what he deserved."

The boy's pride swelled. "I done the needful," he said.

"Everything he touched he warped," the schoolteacher said. "He lived a long and useless life and he did you a great injustice. It's a blessing he's dead at last. You could have had everything and you've had nothing. All that can be changed now. Now you belong to someone who can help you and understand you." His eyes were alight with pleasure. "It's not too late for me to make a man of you!"

The boy's face darkened. His expression hardened until it was a fortress wall to keep his thoughts from being exposed; but the schoolteacher did not notice any change. He gazed through the actual insignificant boy before him to an image of him that he held fully developed in his mind.

"You and I will make up for lost time," he said. "We'll get you started now in the right direction."

Tarwater was not looking at him. His neck had suddenly snapped forward and he was staring straight ahead over the schoolteacher's shoulder. He heard a faint familiar sound of heavy breathing. It was closer to him than the beating of his own heart. His eyes widened and an inner door in them opened in preparation for some inevitable vision.

The small white-haired boy shambled into the back of the hall and stood peering forward at the stranger. He had on the bottoms to a pair of blue pajamas drawn up as high as they would go, the string tied over his chest and then again, harness-like, around his neck to keep them on. His eyes were slightly sunken beneath his forehead and his cheekbones were lower than they should have been. He stood there, dim and ancient, like a child who had been a child for centuries.

Tarwater clenched his fists. He stood like one condemned, waiting at the spot of execution. Then the revelation came, silent, implacable, direct as a bullet. He did not look into the eyes of any fiery beast or see a burning bush. He only knew, with a certainty sunk in despair, that he was expected to baptize the child he saw and begin the life his great-uncle had prepared him for. He knew that he was called to be a prophet and that the ways of his prophecy would not be remarkable. His black pupils, glassy and still, reflected depth on depth his own stricken image of himself, trudging into the distance in the bleeding stinking mad shadow of Jesus, until at last he received his reward, a broken fish, a multiplied loaf. The Lord out of dust had created him, had made him blood and nerve and mind, had made him to bleed and weep and think, and set him in a world of loss and fire all to baptize one idiot child that He need not have created in the first place and to cry out a gospel just as foolish. He tried to shout, "NO!" but it was like trying to shout in his sleep. The sound was saturated in silence, lost.

His uncle put a hand on his shoulder and shook him slightly to penetrate his inattention. "Listen boy," he said, "getting out from under the old man is just like coming out of the darkness into the light. You're going to have a chance now for the first time in your life. A chance to develop into a useful man, a chance to use your talents, to do what you want to do and not what he wanted—whatever idiocy it was."

The boy's eyes were focussed beyond him, the pupils dilated. The schoolteacher turned his head to see what it was that was keeping him from being responsive. His own face tightened. The little boy was creeping forward, grinning.

"That's only Bishop," he said. "He's not all right. Don't mind him. All he can do is stare at you and he's very friendly. He stares at everything that way." His hand tightened on the boy's shoulder and his mouth stretched painfully. "All the things that I would do for him—if it were any use—I'll do for you," he said. "Now do you see why I'm so glad to have you here?"

The boy heard nothing he said. The muscles in his neck stood out like cables. The dim-witted child was not five feet from him and was coming every instant closer with his lop-sided smile. Suddenly he knew that the child *recognized* him, that the old man himself had primed him from on high that here was the forced servant of God come to see that he was born again. The little boy was sticking out his hand to touch him.

"Git!" Tarwater screamed. His arm shot out like a whip and knocked the hand away. The child let out a bellow startlingly loud. He clambered up his father's leg, pulling himself up by the schoolteacher's pajama coat until he was almost on his shoulder.

"All right, all right," the schoolteacher said, "there, there, shut up, it's all right, he didn't mean to hit you," and he righted the child on his back and tried to slide him off but the little boy hung on, thrusting his head against his father's neck and never taking his eyes off Tarwater.

The boy had a vision of the schoolteacher and his child as inseparably joined. The schoolteacher's face was red and pained. The child might have been a deformed part of himself that had been accidentally revealed.

"You'll get used to him," he said.

"No!" the boy shouted.

It was like a shout that had been waiting, straining to burst out. "I won't get used to him! I won't have anything to do with him!" He clenched his fist and lifted it. "I won't have anything to do with him!" he shouted and the words were clear and positive and defiant like a challenge hurled in the face of his silent adversary.

Part 2

Chapter 4

After four days of Tarwater, the schoolteacher's enthusiasm had passed. He would admit no more than that. It had passed the first day and had been succeeded by determination, and while he knew that determination was a less powerful tool, he thought that in this case, it was the one best fitted for the job. It had taken him barely half a day to find out that the old man had made a wreck of the boy and that what was called for was a monumental job of reconstruction. The first day enthusiasm had given him energy but ever since, determination had exhausted him.

Although it was only eight o'clock in the evening, he had put Bishop to bed and had told the boy that he could go to his room and read. He had bought him books, among other things still ignored. Tarwater had gone to his room and had closed the door, not saying whether he intended to read or not, and Rayber was in bed for the night, lying too exhausted to sleep, watching the late evening light fade through the hedge that grew in front of his window. He had left his hearing aid on so that if the boy tried to escape, he would hear and could go after him. For the last two days he had looked poised to leave, and not simply to leave but to be gone, silently and in the night when he would not be followed. This was the fourth night and the schoolteacher lay thinking, with a wry expression on his face, how it differed from the first.

The first night he had sat until daylight by the side of the bed where, still dressed, the boy had fallen. He had sat there, his eyes shining, like a man who sits before a treasure he is not yet convinced is real. His eyes had moved over and over the sprawled thin figure which had appeared lost in an exhaustion so profound that it seemed doubtful it would ever move again. As he followed the outline of the face, he had realized with an intense stab of joy that his nephew looked enough like him to be his son. The heavy work shoes, the worn overalls, the atrocious stained hat filled him with pain and pity. He thought of his poor sister. The only real pleasure she had had in her life was the time she had had the lover who had given her this child, the hollow-cheeked boy who had come from the country to study divinity but whose mind Rayber (a graduate student at the time) had seen at once was too good for that. He had befriended him, and helped him to discover himself and then to discover her. He had engineered their meeting purposely and then had observed to his delight how it prospered and how the relationship developed them both. If there had been no accident, he felt sure the boy would have become completely stable. As it was, after the calamity he had killed himself, a prey to morbid guilt. He had come to Rayber's apartment and had stood confronting him with the gun. He saw again the long brittle face as raw red as if a blast of fire had singed the skin off it and the eyes that had seemed burnt too. He had not felt they were entirely human eyes. They were the eyes of repentance and lacked all dignity. The boy had looked at him for what seemed an age but was perhaps only a second, then he had turned without a word and left and killed himself as soon as he reached his own room.

When Rayber had first opened the door in the middle of the night and had seen Tarwater's face—white, drawn by some unfathomable hunger and pride—he had remained for an instant frozen before what might have been a mirror thrust toward him in a nightmare. The face before him was his own, but the eyes were not his own. They were the student's eyes, singed with guilt. He had left the door hurriedly to get his glasses and his hearing aid.

As he sat that first night by the bed, he had recognized something rigid and recalcitrant about the boy even in repose. He lay with his teeth bared and the hat clenched in his fist like a weapon. Rayber's conscience smote him that all these years he had left him to his fate, that he had not gone back and saved him. His throat had tightened, his eyes had begun to ache. He had vowed to make it up to him now, to lavish on him everything he would have lavished on his own child if he had had one who would have known the difference.

The next morning while Tarwater was still asleep, he had rushed out and bought him a decent suit, a plaid shirt, socks, and a red leather cap. He wanted him to have new clothes to wake up to, new clothes to indicate a new life.

After four days they were still untouched in the box on a chair in the room. The boy had looked at them as if the suggestion he put them on were equal to asking that he appear naked.

It was apparent from everything he did and said exactly who had brought him up. At every turn an almost uncontrollable fury would rise in Rayber at the brand of independence the old man had wrought—not a constructive independence but one that was irrational, backwoods, and ignorant. After Rayber had rushed back with the clothes, he had gone to the bed and put his hand on the still sleeping boy's forehead and decided that he had a fever and should not get up. He had prepared a breakfast on a tray and brought it to the room. When he appeared in the door with it, Bishop at his side, Tarwater was sitting up in the bed, in the act of shaking out his hat and putting it on. Rayber had said, "Don't you want to hang up your hat and stay a while?" and had given him such a smile of welcome and good will as he thought had possibly never been turned on him before.

The boy, with no look of appreciation or even interest, had pulled the hat down farther on his head. His gaze had turned with a peculiar glare of recognition to Bishop. The child had on a black cowboy hat and he was gaping over the top of a trashbasket that he clasped to his stomach. He kept a rock in it. Rayber remembered that Bishop had caused the boy some disturbance the night before and he pushed him back with his free hand so that he could not get in. Then stepping into the room, he closed the door and locked it. Tarwater looked at the closed door darkly as if he continued to see the child through it, still clasping his trashbasket.

Rayber set the tray down across his knees and stood back scrutinizing him. The boy seemed barely aware that he was in the room. "That's your breakfast," his uncle said as if he might not be able to identify it. It was a bowl of dry cereal and a glass of milk. "I thought you'd better stay in bed today," he said. "You don't look too chipper." He pulled up a straight chair and sat down. "Now we can have a real talk," he said, his smile spreading. "It's high time we got to know each other."

No expression of approval or pleasure lightened the boy's face. He glanced at the breakfast but did not pick up the spoon. He began to look around the room. The walls were an insistent pink, the color chosen by Rayber's wife. He used it now for a store room. There were trunks in the corners with crates piled on top of them. On the mantel, besides medicine bottles and dead electric lightbulbs and some old match boxes, was a picture of her. The boy's attention paused there and the corner of his mouth twitched slightly as if in some kind of comic recognition. "The welfare woman," he said.

His uncle reddened. The tone he detected under this

was old Tarwater's exactly. Without warning, irritation mounted in him. The old man might suddenly have obtruded his presence between them. He felt the same familiar fantastic anger, out of all proportion to its cause, that his uncle had always been able to stir in him. With an effort, he forced it out of his way. "That's my wife," he said, "but she doesn't live with us anymore. This is her old room you're in."

The boy picked up the spoon. "My great-uncle said she wouldn't hang around long," he said and began to eat rapidly as if he had established enough independence by this remark to eat somebody else's food. It was apparent from his expression that he found the quality of it poor.

Rayber sat and watched him, saying to himself in an effort to calm his irritation: this child hasn't had a chance, remember he hasn't had a chance. "God only knows what the old fool has told you and taught you!" he said with a sudden explosive force. "God only knows!"

The boy stopped eating and looked at him sharply. Then after a second he said, "He ain't had no effect on me," and returned to his eating.

"He did you a terrible injustice," Rayber said, wishing to impress this on him as often as he could. "He kept you from having a normal life, from getting a decent education. He filled your head with God knows what rot!"

Tarwater continued to eat. Then with a stony deliberateness, he looked up and his gaze fastened on the gash in his uncle's ear. Somewhere in the depths of his eyes a glint appeared. "Shot yer, didn't he?" he said.

Rayber took a package of cigarets from his shirt pocket and lit one, his motions inordinately slow from the effort he was making to calm himself. He blew the smoke straight into the boy's face. Then he tilted back in the chair and gave him a long hard look. The cigaret hanging from the corner of his mouth trembled. "Yes, he shot me," he said.

The glint in the boy's eyes followed the wires of the hearing aid down to the metal box stuck in his belt. "What you wired for?" he drawled. "Does your head light up?"

Rayber's jaw snapped and then relaxed. After a moment, after extending his arm stiffly and knocking the ash off his cigaret onto the floor, he replied that his head did not light up. "This is a hearing aid," he said patiently. "After the old man shot me I began to lose my hearing. I didn't have a gun when I went to get you back. If I'd stayed he would have killed me and I wouldn't have done you any good dead."

The boy continued to study the machine. His uncle's

face might have been only an appendage to it. "You ain't done me no good neither," he remarked.

"Do you understand me?" Rayber persisted. "I didn't have a gun. He would have killed me. He was a mad man. The time when I can do you good is beginning now, and I want to help you. I want to make up for all these years."

For an instant the boy's eyes left the hearing aid and rested on his uncle's eyes. "Could have got you a gun and come back terreckly," he said.

Stricken by the distinct sound of betrayal in his voice, Rayber could not say a word. He looked at him helplessly. The boy returned to his eating.

Finally Rayber said, "Listen." He took hold of the fist with the spoon in it and held it. "I want you to understand. He was crazy and if he had killed me, you wouldn't have this place to come to now. I'm no fool. I don't believe in senseless sacrifice. A dead man is not going to do you any good, don't you know that? Now I can do something for you. Now I can make up for all the time we've lost. I can help correct what he's done to you, help you to correct it yourself." He kept hold of the fist all the while it was being drawn insistently back. "This is our problem together," he said, seeing himself so clearly in the face before him that he might have been beseeching his own image.

With a quick yank, Tarwater managed to free his hand. Then he gave the schoolteacher a long appraising look, tracing the line of his jaw, the two creases on either side of his mouth, the forehead extending into skull until it reached the pie-shaped hairline. He gazed briefly at the pained eyes behind his uncle's glasses, appearing to abandon a search for something that could not possibly be there. The glint in his eye fell on the metal box half-sticking out of Rayber's shirt. "Do you think in the box," he asked, "or do you think in your head?"

His uncle had wanted to tear the machine out of his ear and fling it against the wall. "It's because of you I can't hear!" he said, glaring at the impassive face. "It's because once I tried to help you!"

"You never helped me none."

"I can help you now," he said.

After a second he sank back in his chair. "Perhaps you're right," he said, letting his hands fall in a helpless gesture. "It was my mistake. I should have gone back and killed him or let him kill me. Instead I let something in you be killed."

The boy put down his milk glass. "Nothing in me has

been killed," he said in a positive voice, and then he added, "And you needn't to worry. I done your work for you. I tended to him. It was me put him away. I was drunk as a coot and I tended to him." He said it as if he were recalling the most vivid point in his history.

Rayber heard his own heart, magnified by the hearing aid, suddenly begin to pound like the works of a gigantic machine in his chest. The boy's delicate defiant face, his glowering eyes still shocked by some violent memory, brought back instantly to him the vision of himself when he was fourteen and had found his way to Powderhead to shout imprecations at the old man.

An insight came to him that he was not to question until the end. He understood that the boy was held in bondage by his great-uncle, that he suffered a terrible false guilt for burning and not burying him, and he saw that he was engaged in a desperate heroic struggle to free himself from the old man's ghostly grasp. He leaned forward and said in a voice so full of feeling that it was barely balanced, "Listen, listen Frankie," he said, "you're not alone any more. You have a friend. You have more than a friend now." He swallowed. "You have a father."

The boy turned very white. His eyes were blackened by the shadow of some unspeakable outrage. "I ain't ast for no father," he said and the sentence struck like a whip across his uncle's face. "I ain't ast for no father," he repeated. "I'm out of the womb of a whore. I was born in a wreck." He flung this forth as if he were declaring a royal birth. "And my name ain't Frankie. I go by Tarwater and . . ."

"Your mother was not a whore," the schoolteacher said angrily. "That's just some rot he's taught you. She was a good healthy American girl, just beginning to find herself when she was struck down. She was . . ."

"I ain't fixing to hang around here," the boy said, looking about him as if he might throw over the breakfast tray and jump out the window. "I only come to find out a few things and when I find them out, then I'm going."

"What did you come to find out?" the schoolteacher asked evenly. "I can help you. All I want to do is help you any way I can."

"I don't need noner yer help," the boy said, looking away.

His uncle felt something tightening around him like an invisible strait jacket. "How do you mean to find out if you don't have help?"

"I'll wait," he said, "and see what happens."

"And suppose," his uncle asked, "nothing happens?"

An odd smile, like some strange inverted sign of grief, came over the boy's face. "Then I'll make it happen," he said, "like I done before."

In four days nothing had happened and nothing had been made to happen. They had simply covered—the three of them—the entire city, walking, and all night Rayber rewalked the same territory backwards in his sleep. It would not have been so tiring if he had not had Bishop. The child dragged backwards on his hand, always attracted by something they had already passed. Every block or so he would squat down to pick up a stick or a piece of trash and have to be pulled up and along. Whereas Tarwater was always slightly in advance of them, pushing forward on the scent of something. In four days they had been to the art gallery and the movies, they had toured department stores, ridden escalators, visited the supermarkets, inspected the water works, the post office, the railroad yards and the city hall. Rayber had explained how the city was run and detailed the duties of a good citizen. He had talked as much as he had walked, and the boy for all the interest he showed might have been the one who was deaf. Silent, he viewed everything with the same noncommittal eye as if he found nothing here worth holding his attention but must keep moving, must keep searching for whatever it was that appeared just beyond his vision.

Once he had paused at a window where a small red car turned slowly on a revolving platform. Seizing on the display of interest, Rayber had said that perhaps when he was sixteen, he could have a car of his own. It might have been the old man who had replied that he could walk on his two feet for nothing without being beholden. Rayber had never, even when old Tarwater had lived under his roof, been so conscious of the old man's presence.

Once the boy had stopped suddenly in front of a tall building and had stood glaring up at it with a peculiar ravaged look of recognition. Puzzled, Rayber said, "You look as if you've been here before."

"I lost my hat there," he muttered.

"Your hat is on your head," Rayber said. He could not look at the object without irritation. He wished to God there were some way to get it off him.

"My first hat," the boy said. "It fell," and he had rushed on, away from the place as if he could not stand to be near it.

Only one other time had he shown a particular interest. He had stopped with a kind of lurch backwards in front of a large grimy garage-like structure with two yellow and blue painted windows in the front of it, and had stood there, precariously balanced as if he were arresting himself in the middle of a fall. Rayber recognized the place for some kind of pentecostal tabernacle. Over the door was a paper banner bearing the words, UNLESS YE BE BORN AGAIN YE SHALL NOT HAVE EVERLASTING LIFE. Beneath it a poster showed a man and woman and child holding hands. "Hear the Carmodys for Christ!" it said. "Thrill to the Music, Message, and Magic of this team!"

Rayber was well enough aware of the boy's trouble to understand the sinister pull such a place would have on his mind. "Does this interest you?" he asked drily. "Does it remind you of something in particular?"

Tarwater was very pale. "Horse manure," he whispered.

Rayber smiled. Then he laughed. "All such people have in life," he said, "is the conviction they'll rise again."

The boy steadied himself, his eyes still on the banner but as if he had reduced it to a small spot a great distance away.

"They won't rise again?" he said. The statement had the lilt of a question and Rayber realized with an intense thrill of pleasure that his opinion, for the first time, was being called for.

"No," he said simply, "they won't rise again." There was a profound finality in his tone. The grimy structure might have been the carcass of a beast he had just brought down. He put his hand experimentally on the boy's shoulder. It was suffered to remain there.

In a voice unsteady with the sudden return of enthusiasm he said, "That's why I want you to learn all you can. I want you to be educated so that you can take your place as an intelligent man in the world. This fall when you start school . . ."

The shoulder was roughly withdrawn and tne boy, throwing him one dark look, removed himself to the farthest edge of the sidewalk.

He wore his isolation like a mantle, wrapped it around himself as if it were a garment signifying the elect. Rayber had intended to keep notes on him and write up his most important observations but each night his energy had been too depleted to permit him to do any work. He had dropped off every night into a restless sleep, afraid that he would wake up and find the boy gone. He felt he had hastened his urge to leave by confronting him with the test. He had intended giving him the standard ones, intelligence and aptitude, and then going on to some he had perfected himself dealing with emotional factors. He had thought that in this way he could ferret to the center of the emotional infection. He had laid a simple aptitude test out on the kitchen table—the printed book and a few newly sharpened pencils. "This is a kind of game," he said. "Sit down and see what you can make of it. I'll help you begin."

The expression that came over the boy's face was very peculiar. His eyelids lowered just slightly; his mouth failed a smile by only a fraction; his look was compounded of fury and superiority. "Play with it yourself," he said. "I ain't taking no *test*," and he spit the word out as if it were not fit to pass between his lips.

Rayber sized up the situation. Then he said, "Maybe you don't really know how to read and write. Is that the trouble?"

The boy thrust his head forward. "I'm free," he hissed. "I'm outside your head. I ain't in it. I ain't in it and I ain't about to be."

His uncle laughed. "You don't know what freedom is," he said, "you don't . . ." but the boy turned and strode off.

It was no use. He could no more be reasoned with than a jackal. Nothing gave him pause—except Bishop, and Rayber knew that the reason Bishop gave him pause was because the child reminded him of the old man. Bishop looked like the old man grown backwards to the lowest form of innocence, and Rayber observed that the boy strictly avoided looking him in the eye. Wherever the child happened to be standing or sitting or walking seemed to be for Tarwater a dangerous hole in space that he must keep away from at all costs. Rayber was afraid that Bishop would drive him away with his friendliness. He was always creeping up to touch him and when the boy was aware of his being near, he would draw himself up like a snake ready to strike and hiss, "Git!" and Bishop would scurry off to watch him again from behind the nearest piece of furniture.

The schoolteacher understood this too. Every problem the boy had he had had himself and had conquered, or had for the most part conquered, for he had not conquered the problem of Bishop. He had only learned to live with it and had learned too that he could not live without it.

When he had got rid of his wife, he and the child had begun living together in a quiet automatic fashion like two bachelors whose habits were so smoothly connected that they no longer needed to take notice of each other. In the winter he sent him to a school for exceptional children and he had made great strides. He could wash himself, dress himself, feed himself, go to the toilet by himself and make peanut butter sandwiches though sometimes he put the bread inside. For the most part Rayber lived with him without being painfully aware of his presence but the moments would still come when, rushing from some inexplicable part of himself, he would experience a love for the child so outrageous that he would be left shocked and depressed for days, and trembling for his sanity. It was only a touch of the curse that lay in his blood.

His normal way of looking on Bishop was as an x signifying the general hideousness of fate. He did not believe that he himself was formed in the image and likeness of God but that Bishop was he had no doubt. The little boy was part of a simple equation that required no further solution, except at the moments when with little or no warning he would feel himself overwhelmed by the horrifying love. Anything he looked at too long could bring it on. Bishop did not have to be around. It could be a stick or a stone, the line of a shadow, the absurd old man's walk of a starling crossing the sidewalk. If, without thinking, he lent himself to it, he would feel suddenly a morbid surge of the love that terrified him—powerful enough to throw him to the ground in an act of idiot praise. It was completely irrational and abnormal.

He was not afraid of love in general. He knew the value of it and how it could be used. He had seen it transform in cases where nothing else had worked, such as with his poor sister. None of this had the least bearing on his situation. The love that would overcome him was of a different order entirely. It was not the kind that could be used for the child's improvement or his own. It was love without reason, love for something futureless, love that appeared to exist only to be itself, imperious and all demanding, the kind that would cause him to make a fool of himself in an instant. And it only began with Bishop. It began with Bishop and then like an avalanche covered everything his reason hated. He always felt with it a rush of longing to have the old man's eyes—insane, fish-colored, violent with their impossible vision of a world transfigured—turned on him once again. The longing was like an undertow in his blood dragging him backwards to what he knew to be madness.

The affliction was in the family. It lay hidden in the line of blood that touched them, flowing from some ancient source, some desert prophet or polesitter, until, its power unabated, it appeared in the old man and him and, he surmised, in the boy. Those it touched were condemned to fight it constantly or be ruled by it. The old man had been ruled by it. He, at the cost of a full life, staved it off. What the boy would do hung in the balance.

He had kept it from gaining control over him by what amounted to a rigid ascetic discipline. He did not look at anything too long, he denied his senses unnecessary satisfactions. He slept in a narrow iron bed, worked sitting in a straight-backed chair, ate frugally, spoke little, and cultivated the dullest for friends. At his high school he was the expert on testing. All his professional decisions were prefabricated and did not involve his participation. He was not deceived that this was a whole or a full life, he only knew that it was the way his life had to be lived if it were going to have any dignity at all. He knew that he was the stuff of which fanatics and madmen are made and that he had turned his destiny as if with his bare will. He kept himself upright on a very narrow line between madness and emptiness, and when the time came for him to lose his balance, he intended to lurch toward emptiness and fall on the side of his choice. He recognized that in silent ways he lived an heroic life. The boy would go either his way or old Tarwater's and he was determined to save him for the better course. Although Tarwater claimed to believe nothing the old man had taught him, Rayber could see clearly that there was still a backdrag of belief and fear in him keeping his responses locked.

By virtue of kinship and similarity and experience, Rayber was the person to save him, yet something in the boy's very look drained him, something in his very look, something starved in it, seemed to feed on him. With Tarwater's eyes on him, he felt subjected to a pressure that killed his energy before he had a chance to exert it. The eyes were the eyes of the crazy student father, the personality was the old man's, and somewhere between the two, Rayber's own image was struggling to survive and he was not able to reach it. After three days of walking, he was numb with fatigue and plagued with a sense of his own ineffectiveness. All day his sentences had not quite connected with his thought.

That night they had eaten at an Italian restaurant, dark and not crowded, and he had ordered ravioli for them because Bishop liked it. After each meal the boy removed a piece of paper and a stub of pencil from his pocket and wrote down a figure—his estimate of what the meal was worth. In time he would pay back the total sum, he had said, as he did not intend to be beholden. Rayber would have liked to see the figures and learn what his meals were valued at—the boy never asked the price. He was a finicky eater, pushing the food around on his plate before he ate it and putting each forkful in his mouth as if he suspected it was poisoned. He had pushed the ravioli about, his face drawn. He ate a little of it and then put the fork down.

"Don't you like that?" Rayber had asked. "You can have something else if you don't."

"It all come out the same slop bucket," the boy said.

"Bishop is eating his," Rayber said. Bishop had it smeared all over his face. Occasionally he would feed a spoonful into the sugar bowl or touch the tip of his tongue to the dish.

"That's what I said," Tarwater said, and his glance grazed the top of the child's head, "—a hog might like it."

The schoolteacher put his fork down.

Tarwater was glaring at the dark walls of the room. "He's like a hog," he said. "He eats like a hog and he don't think no more than a hog and when he dies, he'll rot like a hog. Me and you too," he said, looking back at the schoolteacher's mottled face, "will rot like hogs. The only difference between me and you and a hog is me and you can calculate, but there ain't any difference between him and one."

Rayber appeared to be gritting his teeth. Finally he said, "Just forget Bishop exists. You haven't been asked to have anything to do with him. He's just a mistake of nature. Try not even to be aware of him."

"He ain't my mistake," the boy muttered. "I ain't having a thing to do with him."

"Forget him," Rayber said in a short harsh voice.

The boy looked at him oddly as if he were beginning to perceive his secret affliction. What he saw or thought he saw seemed grimly to amuse him. "Let's leave out of here," he said, "and get to walking again."

"We are not going to walk tonight," Rayber said. "We are going home and go to bed." He said it with a firmness and finality he had not used before. The boy had only shrugged.

As Rayber lay watching the window darken, he felt that all his nerves were stretched through him like high tension wire. He began trying to relax one muscle at a time as the books recommended, beginning with those in the back of his neck. He emptied his mind of everything but the just visible pattern of the hedge against the screen. Still he was alert for any sound. Long after he lay in complete darkness, he was still alert, unrelaxed, ready to spring up at the least creak of a floor board in the hall. All at once he sat up, wide awake. A door opened and closed. He leapt up and ran across the hall into the opposite room. The boy was gone. He ran back to his own room and pulled his trousers on over his pajamas. Then grabbing his coat, he went out the house by way of the kitchen, barefooted, his jaw set.

Chapter 5

Keeping close to his side of the hedge, he crept through the dark damp grass toward the street. The night was close and very still. A light went on in a window of the next house and revealed, at the end of the hedge, the hat. It turned slightly and Rayber saw the sharp profile beneath it, the set thrust of a jaw very like his own. The boy was stopped still, most likely taking his bearings, deciding which direction to walk in.

He turned again and again. Rayber saw only the hat, intransigently ground upon his head, fierce-looking even in the dim light. It had the boy's own defiant quality, as if its shape had been formed over the years by his personality. It had been the first thing that Rayber had seen must go. It suddenly moved out of the light and vanished.

Rayber slipped through the hedge and followed, soundless on his bare feet. Nothing cast a shadow. He could barely make out the boy a quarter of a block in front of him, except when occasionally light from a window outlined him briefly. Since Rayber didn't know whether he thought he was leaving for good or only going for a walk on his own, he decided not to shout and stop him but to follow silently and observe. He turned off his hearing aid and pursued the dim figure as if in a dream. The boy walked even faster at night than in the day time and was always on the verge of vanishing.

Rayber felt the accelerated beat of his heart. He took a handkerchief out of his pocket and wiped his forehead and inside the neck of his pajama top. He walked over something sticky on the sidewalk and shifted hurriedly to the other side, cursing under his breath. Tarwater was heading toward town. Rayber thought it likely he was returning to see something that had secretly interested him. He might discover tonight what he would have found by testing if the boy had not been so pig-headed. He felt the insidious pleasure of revenge and checked it.

A patch of sky blanched, revealing for a moment the outlines of the housetops. Tarwater turned suddenly to the right. Rayber cursed himself før not stopping long enough to get his shoes. They had come into a neighborhood of large ramshackle boarding houses with porches that abutted the sidewalks. On some of them late sitters were rocking and watching the street. He felt eyes in the darkness move on him and he turned on the hearing aid again. On one porch a woman rose and leaned over the banister. She stood with her hands on her hips, looking him over, taking in his bare feet, the striped pajama coat under his seersucker suit. Irritated, he glanced back at her. The thrust of her neck indicated a conclusion formed. He buttoned his coat and hurried on.

The boy stopped on the next corner. His lean shadow made by a street light slanted to the side of him. The hat's shadow, like a knob at the top of it, turned to the right and then the left. He appeared to be considering his direction. Rayber's muscles felt suddenly weighted. He was not conscious of his fatigue until the pace slackened.

Tarwater turned to the left and Rayber began angrily to move again. They went down a street of dilapidated stores. When Rayber turned the next corner, the gaudy cave of a movie house yawned to the side of him. A knot of small boys stood in front of it. "Forgot yer shoes!" one of them chirruped. "Forgot yer shirt!"

He began a kind of limping lope.

The chorus followed him down the block. "Hi yo Silverwear, Tonto's lost his underwear! What in the heck do we care?"

He kept his eye wrathfully on Tarwater who was turning to the right. When he reached the corner and turned, he saw the boy stopped in the middle of the block, looking in a store window. He slipped into a narrow entrance a few yards farther on where a flight of steps led upward into darkness. Then he looked out.

Tarwater's face was strangely lit from the window he was standing before. Rayber watched curiously for a few moments. It looked to him like the face of someone starving who sees a meal he can't reach laid out before him. At last, something he *wants*, he thought, and determined that tomorrow he would return and buy it. Tarwater reached out and touched the glass and then drew his hand back slowly. He hung there as if he could not take his eyes off what it was he wanted. A pet shop, perhaps, Rayber thought. Maybe he wants a dog. A dog might make all the difference. Abruptly the boy broke away and moved on.

Rayber stepped out of the entrance and made for the window he had left. He stopped with a shock of disappointment. The place was only a bakery. The window was empty except for a loaf of bread pushed to the side that must have been overlooked when the shelf was cleaned for the night. He stared, puzzled, at the empty window for a second before he started after the boy again. Everything a false alarm, he thought with disgust. If he had eaten his dinner, he wouldn't be hungry. A man and woman strolling past looked with interest at his bare feet. He glared at them, then glanced to the side and saw his bloodless wired reflection in the glass of a shoe shop. The boy disappeared all at once into an alley. My God, Rayber thought, how long is this going on?

He turned into the alley, which was unpaved and so dark that he could not see Tarwater in it at all. He was certain that any minute he would cut his feet on broken glass. A garbage can materialized in his path. There was a noise like the collapse of a tin house and he found himself sitting up with his hand and one foot in something unidentifiable. He scrambled up and limped on, hearing his own curses like the voice of a stranger broadcast through his hearing aid. At the end of the alley, he saw the lean figure in the middle of the next block, and with a sudden fury he began to run.

The boy turned into another alley. Doggedly Rayber ran on. At the end of the second alley, the boy turned to the left. When Rayber reached the street, Tarwater was standing still in the middle of the next block. With a furtive look around him, he vanished, apparently into the building he had been facing. Rayber dashed forward. As he reached the place, singing burst flatly against his eardrums. Two blue and yellow windows glared at him in the darkness like the eyes of some Biblical beast. He stopped in front of the banner and read the mocking words, UNLESS YE BE BORN AGAIN. . . .

That the boy's corruption was this deep did not surprise him. What unstrung him was the thought that what Tarwater carried into the atrocious temple was his own imprisoned image. Enraged, he started around the building to locate a window he could look through and see the boy's face among the crowd. When he saw him, he would roar at him to come out. The windows near the front were all too high but toward the back, he found a lower one. He pushed through a straggly shrub beneath it and, his chin just above the ledge, looked into what appeared to be a small ante-room. A door on the other side of it opened onto a stage and there a man in a bright blue suit was standing in a spotlight, leading a hymn. Rayber could not see into the main body of the building where the people were. He was about to move away when the man brought the hymn to a close and began to speak.

"Friends," he said, "the time has come. The time we've all been waiting for this evening. Jesus said suffer the little children to come unto Him and forbid them not and maybe it was because He knew that it would be the little children that would call others to Him, maybe He knew, friends, maybe He hadda hunch."

Rayber listened angrily, too exhausted to move away once he had stopped.

"Friends," the preacher said, "Lucette has travelled the world over telling people about Jesus. She's been to India and China. She's spoken to all the rulers of the world. Jesus is wonderful, friends. He teaches us wisdom out of the mouths of babes!"

Another child exploited, Rayber thought furiously. It was the thought of a child's mind warped, of a child led away from reality, that always enraged him, bringing back to him his own childhood's seduction. Glaring at the spotlight, he saw the man there as a blur which he looked through, down the length of his life until what confronted him were the old man's fish-colored eyes. He saw himself taking the offered hand and innocently walking out of his own yard, innocently walking into six or seven years of unreality. Any other child would have thrown off the spell in a week. He could not have. He had analysed his case and closed it. Still, every now and then he would live over the five minutes it had taken his father to snatch him away from Powderhead. Through the blur of the man on the stage, as if he were looking into a transparent nightmare, he had the experience again. He and his uncle sat on the steps of the house at Powderhead watching his father emerge from the woods and sight them across the field. His uncle leaned forward, squinting, his hand cupped over his eyes, and he sat with his hands clenched between his knees, his heart threshing from side to side as his father moved closer and closer.

"Lucette travels with her mother and daddy and I want you to meet them because a mother and daddy have to be unselfish to share their only child with the world," the preacher said. "Here they are, friends—Mr. and Mrs. Carmody!"

While a man and woman moved into the light, Rayber had a clear vision of plowed ground, of the shaded red ridges that separated him from the lean figure approaching. He had let himself imagine that the field had an undertow that would drag his father backwards and suck him under, but he came on inexorably, only stopping every now and then to put a finger in his shoe and push out a clod of dirt.

"He's going to take me back with him," he said.

"Back with him where?" his uncle growled. "He ain't got any place to take you back to."

"He can't take me back with him?"

"Not where you were before."

"He can't take me back to town?"

"I never said nothing about town," his uncle said.

He saw vaguely that the man in the spotlight had sat down but that the woman was still standing. She became a blur and he saw his father again, getting closer and closer and he had one impulse to dart up and run through his uncle's house and tear out the back to the woods. He would have raced along the path, familiar to him then, and sliding and slipping over the waxy pine needles, he would have run down and down until he reached the thicket of bamboo and would have pushed through it and out onto the other side and would have fallen into the stream and lain there, panting and wheezing and safe where he had been born again, where his head had been thrust by his uncle into the water and brought up again into a new life. Sitting on the step, his leg muscles twitched as if they were ready for him to spring up but he remained absolutely still. He could see the line of his father's mouth, the line that had gone past the point of exasperation, past the point of loud wrath to a kind of stoked rage that would feed him for months.

While the woman evangelist, tall and raw-boned, was speaking of the hardships she had endured, he watched his father as he reached the edge of the yard and stepped onto the packed dirt, his face a slick pink from the exertion of crossing a field. He was drawing short hard breaths. For an instant he seemed about to reach forward and snatch him but he remained where he was. His pale eyes moved carefully over the rock-like figure watching him steadily from the steps, at the red hands knotted on the heavy thighs and then at the gun lying on the porch. He said, "His mother wants him back, Mason. I don't know why. For my part you could have him but you know how she is."

"A drunken whore," his uncle growled.

"Your sister, not mine," his father said, and then said, "All right boy, snap it up," and nodded curtly to him.

He explained in a high reedy voice the exact reason

he could not go back, "I've been born again."

"Great," his father said, "great." He took a step forward and grabbed his arm and yanked him to his feet. "Glad you got him fixed up, Mason," he said. "One bath more or less won't hurt the bugger."

He had had no chance to see his uncle's face. His father had already lept into the plowed field and was dragging him across the furrows while the pellets pierced the air over their heads. His shoulders, just under the window ledge, jumped. He shook his head to clear it.

"For ten years I was a missionary in China," the woman was saying, "for five years I was a missionary in Africa, and one year I was a missionary in Rome where minds are still chained in priestly darkness; but for the last six years, my husband and I have travelled the world over with our daughter. They have been years of trial and pain, years of hardship and suffering." She had on a long dramatic cape, one side of which was turned backward over her shoulder to reveal a red lining.

His father's face was suddenly very close to his own. "Back to the real world, boy," he was saying, "back to the real world. And that's me and not him, see? Me and not him," and he heard himself screaming, "It's him! Him! Him and not you! And I've been born again and there's not a thing you can do about it!"

"Christ in hell," his father said, "believe it if you want to. Who cares? You'll find out soon enough."

The woman's tone had changed. The sound of something grasping drew his attention again. "We have not had an easy time. We have been a hard-working team for Christ. People have not always been generous to us. Only here are the people really generous. I am from Texas and my husband is from Tennessee but we have travelled the world over. We know," she said in a deepened softened voice, "where the people are really generous."

Rayber forgot himself and listened. He felt a relief from his pain, recognizing that the woman was only after money. He could hear the beginning click of coins falling in a plate.

"Our little girl began to preach when she was six. We saw that she had a mission, that she had been called. We saw that we could not keep her to ourselves and so we have endured many hardships to give her to the world, to bring her to you tonight. To us," she said, "you are as important as the great rulers of the world!" Here she lifted the end of her cape and holding it out as a magician would make a low bow. After a moment she lifted her head, gazed in front of her as if at some grand vista, and disappeared from view. A little girl hobbled into the spotlight.

Rayber cringed. Simply by the sight of her he could tell that she was not a fraud, that she was only exploited. She was eleven or twelve with a small delicate face and a head of black hair that looked too thick and heavy for a frail child to support. A cape like her mother's was turned back over one shoulder and her skirt was short as if better to reveal the thin legs twisted from the knees. She held her arms over her head for a moment. "I want to tell you people the story of the world," she said in a loud high child's voice. "I want to tell you why Jesus came and what happened to Him. I want to tell you how He'll come again. I want to tell you to be ready. Most of all," she said, "I want to tell you to be ready so that on the last day you'll rise in the glory of the Lord."

Rayber's fury encompassed the parents, the preacher, all the idiots he could not see who were sitting in front of the child, parties to her degradation. She believed it, she was locked tight in it, chained hand and foot, exactly as he had been, exactly as only a child could be. He felt the taste of his own childhood pain laid again on his tongue like a bitter wafer.

"Do you know who Jesus is?" she cried. "Jesus is the word of God and Jesus is love. The Word of God is love and do you know what love is, you people? If you don't know what love is you won't know Jesus when He comes. You won't be ready. I want to tell you people the story of the world, how it never known when love come, so when love comes again, you'll be ready."

She moved back and forth across the stage, frowning as if she were trying to see the people through the fierce circle of light that followed her. "Listen to me, you people," she said, "God was angry with the world because it always wanted more. It wanted as much as God had and it didn't know what God had but it wanted it and more. It wanted God's own breath, it wanted His very Word and God said, 'I'll make my Word Jesus, I'll give them my Word for a king, I'll give them my very breath for theirs.'

"Listen you people," she said and flung her arms wide, "God told the world He was going to send it a king and the world waited. The world thought, a golden fleece will do for His bed. Silver and gold and peacock tails, a thousand suns in a peacock's tail will do for His sash. His mother will ride on a four-horned white beast and use the sunset for a cape. She'll trail it behind her over the ground and let the world pull it to pieces, a new one every evening."

To Rayber she was like one of those birds blinded to make it sing more sweetly. Her voice had the tone of a glass bell. His pity encompassed all exploited children—himself when he was a child, Tarwater exploited by the old man, this child exploited by parents, Bishop exploited by the very fact he was alive.

"The world said, 'How long, Lord, do we have to wait for this?' And the Lord said, 'My Word is coming, my Word is coming from the house of David, the king.' " She paused and turned her head to the side, away from the fierce light. Her dark gaze moved slowly until it rested on Rayber's head in the window. He stared back at her. Her eyes remained on his face for a moment. A deep shock went through him. He was certain that the child had looked directly into his heart and seen his pity. He felt that some mysterious connection was established between them.

" 'My Word is coming,' " she said, turning back to face the glare, " 'my Word is coming from the house of David, the king.' "

She began again in a dirge-like tone. "Jesus came on cold straw. Jesus was warmed by the breath of an ox. 'Who is this?' the world said, 'who is this blue-cold child and this woman, plain as the winter? Is this the Word of God, this blue-cold child? Is this His will, this plain winter-woman?'

"Listen you people!" she cried, "the world knew in its heart, the same as you know in your hearts and I know in my heart. The world said, 'Love cuts like the cold wind and the will of God is plain as the winter. Where is the summer will of God? Where are the green seasons of God's will? Where is the spring and summer of God's will?'

"They had to flee into Egypt," she said in a low voice and turned her head again and this time her eyes moved directly to Rayber's face in the window and he knew they sought it. He felt himself caught up in her look, held there before the judgment seat of her eyes.

"You and I know," she said turning again, "what the world hoped then. The world hoped old Herod would slay the right child, the world hoped old Herod wouldn't waste those children, but he wasted them. He didn't get the right one. Jesus grew up and raised the dead."

Rayber felt his spirit borne aloft. But not those dead!

he cried, not the innocent children, not you, not me when I was a child, not Bishop, not Frank! and he had a vision of himself moving like an avenging angel through the world, gathering up all the children that the Lord, not Herod, had slain.

"Jesus grew up and raised the dead," she cried, "and the world shouted, 'Leave the dead lie. The dead are dead and can stay that way. What do we want with the dead alive?' Oh you people!" she shouted, "they nailed Him to a cross and run a spear through His side and then they said, 'Now we can have some peace, now we can ease our minds.' And they hadn't but only said it when they wanted Him to come again. Their eyes were opened and they saw the glory they had killed.

"Listen world," she cried, flinging up her arms so that the cape flew out behind her, "Jesus is coming again! The mountains are going to lie down like hounds at His feet, the stars are going to perch on His shoulder and when He calls it, the sun is going to fall like a goose for His feast. Will you know the Lord Jesus then? The mountains will know Him and bound forward, the stars will light on His head, the sun will drop down at His feet, but will you know the Lord Jesus then?"

Rayber saw himself fleeing with the child to some enclosed garden where he would teach her the truth, where he would gather all the exploited children of the world and let the sunshine flood their minds.

"If you don't know Him now, you won't know Him then. Listen to me, world, listen to this warning. The Holy Word is in my mouth!

"The Holy Word is in my mouth!" she cried and turned her eyes again on his face in the window. This time there was a lowering concentration in her gaze. He had drawn her attention entirely away from the congregation.

Come away with me! he silently implored, and I'll teach you the truth, I'll save you, beautiful child!

Her eyes still fixed on him, she cried, "I've seen the Lord in a tree of fire! The Word of God is a burning Word to burn you clean!" She was moving in his direction, the people in front of her forgotten. Rayber's heart began to race. He felt some miraculous communication between them. The child alone in the world was meant to understand him. "Burns the whole world, man and child," she cried, her eye on him, "none can escape." She stopped a little distance from the end of the stage and stood silent, her whole attention directed across the small room to his face on the ledge. Her eyes were large and dark and fierce.

He felt that in the space between them, their spirits had broken the bonds of age and ignorance and were mingling in some unheard of knowledge of each other. He was transfixed by the child's silence. Suddenly she raised her arm and pointed toward his face. "Listen you people," she shrieked, "I see a damned soul before my eye! I see a dead man Jesus hasn't raised. His head is in the window but his ear is deaf to the Holy Word!"

Rayber's head, as if it had been struck by an invisible bolt, dropped from the ledge. He crouched on the ground, his furious spectacled eyes glittering behind the shrubbery. Inside she continued to shriek, "Are you deaf to the Lord's Word? The Word of God is a burning Word to burn you clean, burns man and child, man and child the same, you people! Be saved in the Lord's fire or perish in your own! Be saved in . . ."

He was groping fiercely about him, slapping at his coat pockets, his head, his chest, not able to find the switch that would cut off the voice. Then his hand touched the button and he snapped it. A silent dark relief enclosed him like shelter after a tormenting wind. For a while he sat limp behind the bush. Then the reason for his being here returned to him and he experienced a moment of loathing for the boy that earlier would have made him shudder. He wanted nothing but to get back home and sink into his own bed, whether the boy returned or not.

He got out of the shrubbery and started toward the front of the building. As he turned onto the sidewalk, the door of the tabernacle flew open and Tarwater flung himself out. Rayber stopped abruptly.

The boy stood confronting him, his face strangely mobile as if successive layers of shock were settling on it to form a new expression. After a moment he raised his arm in an uncertain gesture of greeting. The sight of Rayber seemed to afford him relief amounting to rescue.

Rayber's face had the wooden look it wore when his hearing aid was off. He did not see the boy's expression at all. His rage obliterated all but the general lines of his figure and he saw them moulded in an irreversible shape of defiance. He grabbed him roughly by the arm and started down the block with him. Both of them walked rapidly as if neither could leave the place fast enough. When they were well down the block, Rayber stopped and swung him around and glared into his face. Through his fury he could not discern that for the first time the boy's eyes were submissive. He snapped on his hearing aid and said fiercely, "I hope you enjoyed the show."

Tarwater's lips moved convulsively. Then he murmured, "I only gone to spit on it."

The schoolteacher continued to glare at him. "I'm not so sure of that."

The boy said nothing. He seemed to have suffered some shock inside the building that had permanently slowed his tongue.

Rayber turned and they walked away in silence. At any point along the way, he could have put his hand on the shoulder next to his and it would not have been withdrawn, but he made no gesture. His head was churning with old rages. The afternoon he had learned the full extent of Bishop's future had sprung to his mind. He saw himself rigidly facing the doctor, a man who had made him think of a bull, impassive, insensitive, his brain already on the next case. He had said, "You should be grateful his health is good. In addition to this, I've seen them born blind as well, some without arms and legs, and one with a heart outside."

He had lurched up, almost ready to strike the man. "How can I be grateful," he had hissed, "when one—just one—is born with a heart outside?"

"You'd better try," the doctor had said.

Tarwater walked slightly behind him and Rayber did not cast a glance back at him. His fury seemed to be stirring from buried depths that had lain quiet for years and to be working upward, closer and closer, toward the slender roots of his peace. When they reached the house he went in and straight to his bed without turning to look at the boy's white face which, drained but expectant, lingered a moment at the threshold of his door as if waiting for an invitation to enter.

Chapter 6

The next day, too late, he had the sense of opportunity missed. Tarwater's face had hardened again and the steely gleam in his eye was like the glint of a metal door sealed against an intruder. Rayber felt afflicted with a peculiar chilling clarity of mind in which he saw himself divided in two—a violent and a rational self. The violent self inclined him to see the boy as an enemy and he knew that nothing would hinder his progress with the case so much as giving in to such an inclination. He had waked up after a wild dream in which he chased Tarwater through an interminable alley that twisted suddenly back on itself and reversed the roles of pursuer and pursued. The boy had overtaken him, given him a thunderous blow on the head, and then disappeared. And with his disappearance there had come such an overwhelming feeling of release that Rayber had waked up with a pleasant anticipation that his guest would be gone. He was at once ashamed of the feeling. He settled on a rational, tiring plan for the day and by ten o'clock the three of them were on their way to the natural history museum. He intended to stretch the boy's mind by introducing him to his ancestor, the fish, and to all the great wastes of unexplored time.

They passed part of the territory they had walked over the night before but nothing was said about that trip. Except for the circles under Rayber's eyes, there was nothing about either of them to indicate it had been made. Bishop stumped along, squatting every now and then to pick up something off the sidewalk, while Tarwater, to avoid contamination with them, walked a good four feet to the other side and slightly in advance. I must have infinite patience, I must have infinite patience, Rayber kept repeating to himself.

The museum lay on the other side of the city park which they had not crossed before. As they approached it, the boy paled as if he were shocked to find a wood in the middle of the city. Once inside the park, he stopped and stood glaring about him at the huge trees whose ancient rustling branches intermingled overhead. Patches of light sifting through them spattered the concrete walks with sunshine. Rayber observed that something disturbed him. Then he realized that the place reminded him of Powderhead.

"Let's sit down," he said, wanting both to rest and to observe the boy's agitation. He sat down on a bench and stretched his legs in front of him. He suffered Bishop to climb into his lap. The child's shoelaces were untied and he tied them, for the moment ignoring the boy who was standing there, his face furiously impatient. When he finished tying the shoes, he continued to hold the child, sprawled and grinning, in his lap. The little boy's white head fitted under his chin. Above it Rayber looked at nothing in particular. Then he closed his eyes and in the isolating darkness, he forgot Tarwater's presence. Without warning his hated love gripped him and held him in a vise. He should have known better than to let the child onto his lap.

His forehead became beady with sweat; he looked as if he might have been nailed to the bench. He knew that if he could once conquer this pain, face it and with a supreme effort of his will refuse to feel it, he would be a free man. He held Bishop rigidly. Although the child started the pain, he also limited it, contained it. He had learned this one terrible afternoon when he had tried to drown him.

He had taken him to the beach, two hundred miles away, intending to effect the accident as quickly as possible and return bereaved. It had been a beautiful calm day in May. The beach, almost empty, had stretched down into the gradual swell of ocean. There was nothing to be seen but an expanse of sea and sky and sand and an occasional figure, stick-like, in the distance. He had taken him out on his shoulders and when he was chest deep in the water, had lifted him off, swung the delighted child high in the air and then plunged him swiftly below the surface on his back and held him there, not looking down at what he was doing but up, at an imperturbably witnessing sky, not quite blue, not quite white.

A fierce surging pressure had begun upward beneath his hands and grimly he had exerted more and more force downward. In a second, he felt he was trying to hold a giant under. Astonished, he let himself look. The face under the water was wrathfully contorted, twisted by some primeval rage to save itself. Automatically he released his pressure. Then when he realized what he had done, he pushed down again angrily with all his force until the struggle ceased under his hands. He stood sweating in the water, his own mouth as slack as the child's had been. The body, caught by an undertow, almost got away from him but he managed to come to himself and snatch it. Then as he looked at it, he had a moment of complete terror in which he envisioned his life without the child. He began to shout frantically. He plowed his way out of the water with the limp body. The beach which he had thought empty before had become peopled with strangers converging on him from all directions. A bald-headed man in red and blue Roman striped shorts began at once to administer artificial respiration. Three wailing women and a photographer appeared. The next day there had been a picture in the paper, showing the rescuer, striped bottom forward, working over the child. Rayber was beside him on his knees, watching with an agonized expression. The caption said, OVERJOYED FATHER SEES SON RE-VIVED.

The boy's voice broke in on him harshly. "All you got to do is nurse an idiot!"

The schoolteacher opened his eyes. They were bloodshot and vague. He might have been returning to consciousness after a blow on the head.

Tarwater was glaring to the side of him. "Come on if you're coming," he said, "and if you ain't, I'm going on about my bidnis."

Rayber didn't answer.

"So long," Tarwater said.

"And where would your business be?" Rayber asked sourly. "At another tabernacle?"

The boy reddened. He opened his mouth and said nothing.

"I nurse an idiot that you're afraid to look at," Rayber said. "Look him in the eye."

Tarwater shot a glance at the top of Bishop's head and left it there an instant like a finger on a candle flame. "I'd as soon be afraid to look at a dog," he said and turned his back. After a moment, as if he were continuing the same conversation, he muttered, "I'd as soon baptize a dog as him. It would be as much use."

"Who said anything about baptizing anybody?" Rayber said. "Is that one of your fixations? Have you taken that bug up from the old man?"

The boy whirled around and faced him. "I told you I only gone there to spit on it," he said tensely. "I ain't going to tell you again."

Rayber watched him without saying anything. He felt that his own sour words had helped him recover himself.

He pushed Bishop off and stood up. "Let's get going," he said. He had no intention of discussing it further, but as they moved on silently, he thought better of it.

"Listen Frank," he said, "I'll grant that you went to spit on it. I've never for a second doubted your intelligence. Everything you've done, your very presence here proves that you're above your background, that you've broken through the ceiling the old man set for you. After all, you escaped from Powderhead. You had the courage to attend to him the quickest way and then get out of there. And once out, you came directly to the right place."

The boy reached up and picked a leaf from a tree branch and bit it. A wry expression spread over his face. He rolled the leaf into a ball and threw it away. Rayber continued to speak, his voice detached, as if he had no particular interest in the matter, and his were merely the voice of truth, as impersonal as air.

"Say that you went to spit on it," he said, "the point is this: there's no need to spit on it. It's not worth spitting on. It's not that important. You've somehow enlarged the significance of it in your mind. The old man used to enrage me until I learned better. He wasn't worth my hate and he's not worth yours. He's only worth our pity." He wondered if the boy were capable of the steadiness of pity. "You want to avoid extremes. They are for violent people and you don't want . . ."—he broke off abruptly as Bishop let loose his hand and galloped away.

They had come out into the center of the park, a concrete circle with a fountain in the middle of it. Water rushed from the mouth of a stone lion's head into a shallow pool and the little boy was flying toward it, his arms flailing like a windmill. In a second he was over the side and in. "Too late, goddammit," Rayber muttered, "he's in." He glanced at Tarwater.

The boy stood arrested in the middle of a step. His eyes were on the child in the pool but they burned as if he beheld some terrible compelling vision. The sun shone brightly on Bishop's white head and the little boy stood there with a look of attention. Tarwater began to move toward him.

He seemed to be drawn toward the child in the water but to be pulling back, exerting an almost equal pressure away from what attracted him. Rayber watched, puzzled and suspicious, moving along with him but somewhat to the side. As he drew closer to the pool, the skin on the boy's face appeared to stretch tighter and tighter. Rayber had the sense that he was moving blindly, that where Bishop was he saw only a spot of light. He felt that something was being enacted before him and that if he could understand it, he would have the key to the boy's future. His muscles were tensed and he was prepared somehow to act. Suddenly his sense of danger was so great that he cried out. In an instant of illumination he understood. Tarwater was moving toward Bishop to baptize him. Already he had reached the edge of the pool. Rayber sprang and snatched the child out of the water and set him down, howling, on the concrete.

His heart was beating furiously. He felt that he had just saved the boy from committing some enormous indignity. He saw it all now. The old man *had* transferred his fixation to the boy, *had* left him with the notion that he must baptize Bishop or suffer some terrible consequence. Tarwater put his foot down on the marble edge of the pool. He leaned forward, his elbow on his knee, looking over the side at his broken reflection in the water. His lips moved as if he were speaking silently to the face forming in the pool. Rayber said nothing. He realized now the magnitude of the boy's affliction. He knew that there was no way to appeal to him with reason. There was no hope of discussing it sanely with him, for it was a compulsion. He saw no way of curing him except perhaps through some shock, some sudden concrete confrontation with the futility, the ridiculous absurdity of performing the empty rite.

He squatted down and began to take off Bishop's wet shoes. The child had stopped howling and was crying quietly, his face red and hideously distorted. Rayber turned his eyes away.

Tarwater was walking off. He was past the pool, his back strangely bent as if he were being driven away with a whip. He was moving off onto one of the narrow tree-shaded paths.

"Wait!" Rayber shouted. "We can't go to the museum now. We'll have to go home and change Bishop's shoes."

Tarwater could not have failed to hear but he kept on walking and in a second was lost to view.

Goddam backwoods imbecile, Rayber said under his breath. He stood looking at the path where the boy had disappeared. He felt no urge to go after him for he knew that he would be back, that he was held by Bishop. His feeling of oppression was caused now by the certain knowledge that there was no way to get rid of him. He would be with them until he had either accomplished what he came for, or until he was cured. The words the old man had scrawled on the back of the journal rose before him: THE PROPHET

I RAISE UP OUT OF THIS BOY WILL BURN YOUR EYES CLEAN. The sentence was like a challenge renewed. I will cure him, he said grimly. I will cure him or know the reason why.

Chapter 7

The Cherokee Lodge was a two-story converted warehouse, the lower part painted white and the upper green. One end sat on land and the other was set on stilts in a glassy little lake across which were dense woods, green and black farther toward the skyline, gray-blue. The long front side of the building, plastered with beer and cigaret signs, faced the highway, which ran about thirty feet away across a dirt road and beyond a narrow stretch of iron weed. Rayber had passed the place before but had never been tempted to stop.

He had selected it because it was only thirty miles from Powderhead and because it was cheap and he arrived there the next day with the two boys in time for them to take a walk and look around before they ate. The ride up had been oppressively silent, the boy sitting as usual on his side of the car like some foreign dignitary who would not admit speaking the language—the filthy hat, the stinking overalls, worn defiantly like a national costume.

Rayber had hit upon his plan in the night. It was to take him back to Powderhead and make him face what he had done. What he hoped was that if seeing and feeling the place again were a real shock, the boy's trauma might suddenly be revealed. His irrational fears and impulses would burst out and his uncle—sympathetic, knowing, uniquely able to understand—would be there to explain them to him. He had not said they were going to Powderhead. So far as the boy knew, this was to be a fishing trip. He thought that an afternoon of relaxation in a boat before the experiment would help ease the tension, his own as well as Tarwater's.

On the drive up, his thoughts had been interrupted once when he saw Bishop's face rise unorganized into the rearview mirror and then disappear as he attempted to crawl over the top of the front seat and climb into Tarwater's lap. The boy had turned and without looking at him had given the panting child a firm push onto the back seat again. One of Rayber's immediate goals was to make him understand that his urge to baptize the child was a kind of *sickness* and that a sign of returning health would be his ability to begin looking Bishop in the eye. Rayber felt that once he could look the child in the eye, he would have confidence in his ability to resist the morbid impulse to baptize him.

When they got out of the car, he watched the boy closely, trying to discover his first reaction to being in the country again. Tarwater stood for a moment, his head lifted sharply as if he detected some familiar odor moving from the pine forest across the lake. His long face, depending from the bulb-shaped hat, made Rayber think of a root jerked suddenly out of the ground and exposed to the light. The boy's eyes narrowed so that the lake must have been reduced to the width of a knife-blade in his sight. He looked at the water with a peculiar undisguised hostility. Rayber even thought that as his eye fell on it, he began to tremble. At least he was certain that his hands clenched. His glare steadied, then with his usual precipitous gait, he set off around the building without looking back.

Bishop climbed out of the car and thrust his face against his father's side. Absently Rayber put his hand on the little boy's ear and rubbed it gingerly, his fingers tingling as if they touched the sensitive scar of some old wound. Then he pushed the child aside, picked up the bag and started toward the screen door of the lodge. As he reached it, Tarwater came quickly around the side of the building with the distinct look to Rayber of being pursued. His feeling for the boy alternated drastically between compassion for his haunted look and fury at the way he was treated by him. Tarwater acted as if to see him at all required a special effort. Rayber opened the screen door and stepped inside, leaving the two boys to come in or not as they pleased.

The interior was dark. To the left he made out a reception desk with a heavy plain-looking woman behind it, leaning on her elbows. He set the bags down and gave her his name. He had the feeling that though her eyes were on him, they were looking behind him. He glanced around. Bishop was a few feet away, gaping at her.

"What's your name, Sugarpie?" she asked.

"His name is Bishop," Rayber said shortly. He was always irked when the child was stared at.

The woman tilted her head sympathetically. "I reckon you're taking him off to give his mother a little rest," she said, her eyes full of curiosity and compassion.

"I have him all the time," he said and added before he could stop himself, "his mother abandoned him."

"No!" she breathed. "Well," she said, "it takes all kinds of women. I couldn't leave a child like that."

You can't even take your eyes off him, he thought irritably and began to fill out the card. "Are the boats for rent?" he asked without looking up.

"Free for the guests," she said, "but anybody gets drowned, that's their lookout. How about him? Can he sit still in a boat?"

"Nothing ever happens to him," he murmured, finishing the card and turning it around to her.

She read it, then she glanced up and stared at Tarwater. He was standing a few feet behind Bishop, looking around him suspiciously, his hands in his pockets and his hat pulled down. She began to scowl. "That boy there—is yours too?" she asked, pointing the pen at him as if this were inconceivable.

Rayber realized that she must think he was someone hired for a guide. "Certainly, he's mine too," he said quickly and in a voice the boy could not fail to hear. He made it a point to impress on him that he was wanted, whether he cared to be wanted or not.

Tarwater lifted his head and returned the woman's stare. Then he took a stride forward and thrust his face at her. "What do you mean—is his?" he demanded.

"Is his," she said, drawing back. "You don't look it is all." Then she frowned as if, continuing to study him, she began to see a likeness.

"And I ain't it," he said. He snatched the card from her and read it. Rayber had written, "George F. Rayber, Frank and Bishop Rayber," and their address. The boy put the card down on the desk and picked up the pen, gripping it so hard that his fingers turned red at the tips. He crossed out the name *Frank* and underneath in an old man's meticulous hand he began to write something else.

Rayber looked at the woman helplessly and lifted his shoulders as if to say, "I have more than one problem," and shrug it off, but the gesture ended in a violent tremor. To his horror he felt the side of his mouth give a series of quick jerks. He had an instant's premonition that if he wished to save himself, he should leave at once, that the trip was doomed.

The woman handed him the key and, looking at him suspiciously, said, "Up the steps yonder and four doors down to the right. We don't have anybody to tote the bags."

He took the key and started up a rickety flight of steps to the left. Halfway up, he paused and said in a voice in which there was a remnant of authority, "Bring up that bag when you come, Frank."

The boy was finishing his essay on the card and gave no indication of hearing.

The woman's curious gaze followed Rayber up the stairs until he disappeared. She observed as his feet passed the level of her head that he had on one brown sock and one gray. His shoes were not run-down but he might have slept in his seersucker suit every night. He was in bad need of a haircut and his eyes had a peculiar look—like something human trapped in a switch box. Has come here to have a nervous breakdown, she said to herself. Then she turned her head. Her eyes rested on the two boys, who had not moved. And who wouldn't? she asked herself.

The afflicted child looked as if he must have dressed himself. He had on a black cowboy hat and a pair of short khaki pants that were too tight even for his narrow hips and a yellow t-shirt that had not been washed any time lately. Both his brown hightop shoes were untied. The upper part of him looked like an old man and the lower part like a child. The other, the mean-looking one, had picked up the desk card again and was reading over what he had written on it. He was so taken up with it that he did not see the little boy reaching out to touch him. The instant the child touched him, the country boy's shoulders leapt. He snatched his touched hand up and jammed it in his pocket. "Leave off!" he said in a high voice. "Git away and quit bothering me!"

"Mind how you talk to one of them there, you boy!" the woman hissed.

He looked at her as if it were the first time she had spoken to him. "Them there what?" he murmured.

"That there kind," she said, looking at him fiercely as if he had profaned the holy.

He looked back at the afflicted child and the woman was startled by the expression on his face. He seemed to see the little boy and nothing else, no air around him, no room, no nothing, as if his gaze had slipped and fallen into the center of the child's eyes and was still falling down and down and down. The little boy turned after a second and skipped off toward the steps and the country boy followed, so directly that he might have been attached to him by a tow-line. The child began to scramble up the steps on his hands and knees, kicking his feet up on each one. Then suddenly he flipped himself around and sat down squarely in the country boy's way and stuck his feet out in front of him, apparently wanting his shoes tied. The country boy stopped still. He hung over him like someone bewitched, his long arms bent uncertainly.

The woman watched fascinated. He ain't going to tie them, she said, not him.

He leaned over and began to tie them. Frowning furiously, he tied one and then the other and the child watched, completely absorbed in the operation. When the boy finished tying them, he straightened himself and said in a querulous voice, "Now git on and quit bothering me with them laces," and the child flipped over on his hands and feet and scrambled up the stairs, making a great din.

Confused by this kindness, the woman called, "Hey boy."

She had intended to say, "Whose boy are you?" but she said nothing, her mouth opening on a vanished sentence. His eyes as they turned and looked down at her were the color of the lake just before dark when the last daylight has faded and the moon has not risen yet, and for an instant she thought she saw something fleeing across the surface of them, a lost light that came from nowhere and vanished into nothing. For some moments they stared at each other without issue. Finally, convinced she had not seen it, she muttered, "Whatever devil's work you mean to do, don't do it here."

He continued to look down at her. "You can't just say NO," he said. "You got to do NO. You got to show it. You got to show you mean it by doing it. You got to show you're not going to do one thing by doing another. You got to make an end of it. One way or another."

"Don't you do nothing here," she said, wondering what he would do here.

"I never ast to come here," he said. "I never ast for that lake to be set down in front of me," and he turned and moved on up the stairs.

The woman looked in front of her for some time as if she were seeing her own thoughts before her like unintelligible handwriting on the wall. Then she looked down at the card on the counter and turned it over. "Francis Marion Tarwater," he had written. "Powderhead, Tennessee. NOT HIS SON."

Chapter 8

After they had had their lunch, the schoolteacher suggested they get a boat and fish awhile. Tarwater could tell that he was watching him again, his little eyes protected and precise behind his glasses. He had been watching him ever since he came but now he was watching in a different way: he was watching for something that he planned to make happen. The trip was designed to be a trap but the boy had no attention to spare for it. His mind was entirely occupied with saving himself from the larger grander trap that he felt set all about him. Ever since his first night in the city when he had seen once and for all that the schoolteacher was of no significance—nothing but a piece of bait, an insult to his intelligence—his mind had been engaged in a continual struggle with the silence that confronted him, that demanded he baptize the child and begin at once the life the old man had prepared him for.

It was a strange waiting silence. It seemed to lie all around him like an invisible country whose borders he was always on the edge of, always in danger of crossing. From time to time as they had walked in the city, he had looked to the side and seen his own form alongside him in a store window, transparent as a snakeskin. It moved beside him like some violent ghost who had already crossed over and was reproaching him from the other side. If he turned his head the opposite way, there would be the dim-witted boy, hanging onto the schoolteacher's coat, watching him. His mouth hung in a lopsided smile but there was a judging sternness about his forehead. The boy never looked lower than the top of his head except by accident for the silent country appeared to be reflected again in the center of his eyes. It stretched out there, limitless and clear.

Tarwater could have baptized him any one of a hundred times without so much as touching him. Each time the temptation came, he would feel that the silence was about to surround him and he was going to be lost in it forever. He would have fallen but for the wise voice that sustained him—the stranger who had kept him company while he dug his uncle's grave.

Sensations, his friend—no longer a stranger—said. Feelings. What you want is a sign, a real sign, suitable to a prophet. If you are a prophet, it's only right you should be treated like one. When Jonah dallied, he was cast three days in a belly of darkness and vomited up in the place of his mission. That was a sign; it wasn't no sensation.

It takes all my time to set you straight. Look at you, he said—going to that fancy-house of God, sitting there like an ape letting that girl-child bend your ear. What did you expect to see there? What did you expect to hear? The Lord speaks to prophets personally and He's never spoke to you, never lifted a finger, never dropped a gesture. And as for that strangeness in your gut, that comes from you, not the Lord. When you were a child you had worms. As likely as not you have them again.

The first day in the city he had become conscious of the strangeness in his stomach, a peculiar hunger. The city food only weakened him. He and his great-uncle had eaten well. If the old man had done nothing else for him, he had heaped his plate. Never a morning he had not a-wakened to the smell of fatback frying. The schoolteacher paid scarce attention to what he put inside him. For breakfast, he poured a bowl of shavings out of a cardboard box; in the middle of the day he made sandwiches out of lightbread; and at night he took them to a restaurant, a different one every night run by a different color of foreigner so that he would learn, he said, how other nationalities ate. The boy did not care how other nationalities ate. He had always left the restaurants hungry, conscious of an intrusion in his works. Since the breakfast he had finished sitting in the presence of his uncle's corpse, he had not been satisfied by food, and his hunger had become like an insistent silent force inside him, a silence inside akin to the silence outside, as if the grand trap left him barely an inch to move in, barely an inch in which to keep himself inviolate.

His friend was adamant that he refuse to entertain hunger as a sign. He pointed out that the prophets had been fed. Elijah had lain down under a juniper tree to die and had gone to sleep and an angel of the Lord had come and waked him and fed him a hearth-cake, had done it moreover twice and Elijah had risen and gone about his business, lasting on the two hearth-cakes forty days and nights. Prophets did not languish in hunger but were fed from the Lord's bounty and the signs given them were unmistakable. His friend suggested he demand an unmistakable sign, not a pang of hunger or a reflection of himself in a store window, but an unmistakable sign, clear and suitable—water bursting forth from a rock, for instance, fire sweeping down at his command and destroying some site he would point to, such as the tabernacle he had gone to spit on.

His fourth night in the city, after he had returned from listening to the child preach, he had sat up in the welfare-woman's bed and raising his folded hat as if he were threatening the silence, he had demanded an unmistakable sign of the Lord.

Now we'll see what class of prophet you are, his friend said. We'll see what the Lord has in mind for you.

The next day the schoolteacher had taken them into a park where trees were fenced together in a kind of island that cars were not allowed in. They had only but entered it when he felt a hush in his blood and a stillness in the atmosphere as if the air were being purged for the approach of revelation. He would have turned and run but the schoolteacher parked himself on a bench and pretended to go to sleep with the dimwit in his lap. The trees rustled thickly and the clearing rose to his mind's eye. He imagined the blackened spot in the center of it between the two chimneys, and saw rising from the ashes the burnt-out frames of his own and his uncle's bed. He opened his mouth to get air and the schoolteacher woke up and began asking questions.

He prided himself that from the first night he had answered his questions with the cunning of a Negro, giving no information, knowing nothing, and each time he was questioned, raising his uncle's fury until it was observable under his skin in patches of pink and white. A few of his ready answers and the schoolteacher was willing to move on.

They had walked deeper into the park and he began to feel again the approach of mystery. He would have turned and run in the opposite direction but it was all on him in an instant. The path widened and they were faced with an open space in the middle of the park, a concrete circle with a fountain in the center of it. Water rushed out of the mouth of a stone lion's head into a shallow pool below and as soon as the dim-witted boy saw the water, he gave a whoop and galloped off toward it, flapping his arms like something released from a cage.

Tarwater saw exactly where he was heading, knew exactly what he was going to do.

"Too late, goddamit," the schoolteacher muttered, "he's in."

The child stood grinning in the pool, lifting his feet slowly up and down as if he liked the feel of the wet seeping into his shoes. The sun, which had been tacking from cloud to cloud, emerged above the fountain. A blinding brightness fell on the lion's tangled marble head and gilded the stream of water rushing from his mouth. Then the light, falling more gently, rested like a hand on the child's white head. His face might have been a mirror where the sun had stopped to watch its reflection.

Tarwater started forward. He felt a distinct tension in the quiet. The old man might have been lurking near, holding his breath, waiting for the baptism. His friend was silent as if in the felt presence, he dared not raise his voice. At each step the boy exerted a force backward but he continued nevertheless to move toward the pool. He reached the rim of it and lifted his foot to swing it over the side. Just as his shoe touched the water, the schoolteacher bounded forward and snatched the dimwit out. The child split the silence with his bellow.

Slowly Tarwater's lifted foot came down on the edge of the pool and he leaned there, looking into the water where a wavering face seemed trying to form itself. Gradually it became distinct and still, gaunt and cross-shaped. He observed, deep in its eyes, a look of starvation. I wasn't going to baptize him, he said, flinging the silent words at the silent face. I'd drown him first.

Drown him then, the face appeared to say.

Tarwater stepped back, shocked. Scowling, he straightened himself and moved away. The sun had gone in and there were black caves in the tree branches. Bishop was lying on his back, roaring from a red distorted face, and the schoolteacher stood above him, staring at nothing in particular as if it were he who had received a revelation.

Well, that's your sign, his friend said—the sun coming out from under a cloud and falling on the head of a dimwit. Something that could happen fifty times a day without no one being the wiser. And it took that schoolteacher to save you and just in time. Left to yourself you would already have done it and been lost forever. Listen, he said, you have to quit confusing a madness with a mission. You can't spend your life fooling yourself this way. You have to take hold and put temptation behind you. If you baptize once, you'll be doing it the rest of your life. If it's an idiot this time, the next time it's liable to be a nigger. Save yourself while the hour of salvation is at hand.

But the boy was shaken. He scarcely heard the voice as he walked off deeper into the park and down a path he scarcely saw. When he finally took note of his surroundings, he was sitting on a bench, looking down at his feet where two pigeons were moving in drunken circles. On the other side of the bench was a man of a generally gray appearance who had been examining a hole in his shoe when Tarwater sat down but who stopped then and devoted himself to a close scrutiny of the boy. Finally he reached over and plucked Tarwater's sleeve. The boy looked up into two pale yellow-rimmed eyes.

"Be like me, young fellow," the stranger said, "don't let no jackasses tell you what to do." He was grinning wisely and his eyes held a malevolent promise of unwanted friendship. His voice sounded familiar but his appearance was as unpleasant as a stain.

The boy got up and left hastily. An interesting coincident, his friend observed, that he should say the same thing as I've been saying. You think there's a trap laid all about you by the Lord. There ain't any trap. There ain't anything except what you've laid for yourself. The Lord is not studying about you, don't know you exist, and wouldn't do a thing about it if He did. You're alone in the world, with only yourself to ask or thank or judge; with only yourself. And me. I'll never desert you.

The first sight that met his eyes when he got out of the car at the Cherokee Lodge was the little lake. It lay there, glass-like, still, reflecting a crown of trees and an infinite overarching sky. It looked so unused that it might only the moment before have been set down by four strapping angels for him to baptize the child in. A weakness working itself up from his knees reached his stomach and came upward and forced a tremor in his jaw. Steady, his friend said, everywhere you go you'll find water. It wasn't invented yesterday. But remember: water is made for more than one thing. Hasn't the time come? Don't you have to do something at last, one thing to prove you ain't going to do another? Hasn't your hour of dallying passed?

They ate their lunch in the dark other-end of the lobby where the woman who ran the place served meals. Tarwater ate voraciously. With an expression of intense concentration, he ate six buns filled with barbecue and drank three cans of beer. He might have been preparing himself for a long journey or for some action that would take all his strength. Rayber observed his sudden appetite for the poor food and decided that he was eating compulsively. He wondered if the beer might loosen his tongue, but in the boat he was as glum as ever. He sat hunched over, his hat pulled down, and scowled at the spot where his line disappeared in the water.

They had managed to get the boat away from the dock before Bishop came out of the lodge. The woman had drawn him to an icecooler and produced a green popsickle which she held up for him while she gazed fascinated into his mysterious face. They were in the middle of the lake before he came clattering down the dock, the woman running behind. She snatched him just in time to keep him from plunging over the edge.

Rayber made a frantic grabbing motion in the boat and cried out. Then he reddened and scowled. "Don't look," he said, "she'll take care of him. We need a break."

The boy gazed darkly where the accident had been prevented. The child was a black spot in the glare of his vision. The woman turned him around and started leading him back to the lodge. "It wouldn't have been no great loss if he had drowned," he observed.

Rayber had an instant's picture of himself, standing in the ocean, holding the child's limp body in his arms. With a kind of convulsive motion, he cleared his head of the image. Then he saw that Tarwater had observed his discomposure; he was looking at him with a distinct attention, a peculiar prescient look as if he were about to penetrate some secret.

"Nothing ever happens to that kind of child," Rayber said. "In a hundred years people may have learned enough to put them to sleep when they're born."

Something appeared to be working on the boy's face, struggling there, some war between agreement and outrage.

Rayber's blood burned beneath his skin. He tried to restrain the urge to confess. He leaned forward; his mouth opened and closed and then in a dry voice he said, "Once I tried to drown him," and grinned horribly at the boy.

Tarwater's lips parted as if only they had heard, but he said nothing.

"It was a failure of nerve," Rayber said. The glare on the water gave him the sensation of glancing at white fire each time he looked up or out where it was reflected on the water. He turned down the brim of his hat all the way around.

"You didn't have the guts," Tarwater said as if he would put it in a more accurate way. "He always told me you couldn't do nothing, couldn't act."

The schoolteacher leaned forward and said between his teeth, "I've resisted him. I've done that. What have you done? Maybe you attended to him the quickest way but it takes more than that to go against his will for good. Are you quite sure," he said, "are you quite sure you've overcome him? I doubt it. I think you're chained to him right now. I think you're not going to be free of him without my help. I think you've got problems that you're not capable of solving yourself."

The boy scowled and was silent.

The glare pierced Rayber's eyeballs fiercely. He did not think he could stand an afternoon of this. He felt recklessly compelled to pursue the subject. "How do you like being in the country again?" he growled. "Remind you of Powderhead?"

"I come to fish," the boy said disagreeably.

Goddam you, his uncle thought, all I'm trying to do is save you from being a freak. He was holding his line unbaited in the blinding water. He felt a madness on him to talk about the old man. "I remember the first time I ever saw him," he said. "I was six or seven. I was out in the yard playing and all of a sudden I felt something between me and the sun. Him. I looked up and there he was, those mad fish-colored eyes looking down at me. Do you know what he said to me—a seven year old child?" He tried to make his voice sound like the old man's. " 'Listen boy,' he said, 'the Lord Jesus Christ sent me to find you. You have to be born again.' " He laughed, glaring at the boy with his furious blistered-looking eyes. "The Lord Jesus Christ had my welfare so at heart that he sent a personal representative. Where was the calamity? The calamity was I believed him. For five or six years. I had nothing else but that. I waited on the Lord Jesus. I thought I'd been born again and that everything was going to be different or was different already because the Lord Jesus had a great interest in me."

Tarwater shifted on the seat. He seemed to listen as if behind a wall.

"It was the eyes that got me," Rayber said. "Children may be attracted to mad eyes. A grown person could have resisted. A child couldn't. Children are cursed with believing."

The boy recognized the sentence. "Some ain't," he said.

The schoolteacher smiled thinly. "And some who think they aren't are," he said, feeling that he was back in control. "It's not as easy as you think to throw it off. Do you know," he said, "that there's a part of your mind that works all the time, that you're not aware of yourself. Things go on in it. All sorts of things you don't know about."

Tarwater looked around him as if he were vainly searching for a way to get out of the boat and walk off.

"I think you're basically very bright," his uncle said. "I think you can understand the things that are said to you."

"I never came for no school lesson," the boy said rudely. "I come to fish. I ain't worried what my underhead is doing. I know what I think when I do it and when I get ready to do it, I don't talk no words. I do it." There was a dull anger in his voice. He was becoming aware of how much he had eaten. The food appeared to be sinking like a leaden column inside him and to be pushed back at the same time by the hunger it had intruded upon.

The schoolteacher watched him a moment and then said, "Well anyway, as far as the baptizing went, the old man could have spared himself. I was already baptized. My mother never overcame her upbringing and she had had it done. But the damage to me of having it done at the age of seven was tremendous. It made a lasting scar."

The boy looked up suddenly as if there had been a tug at his line. "Him back there," he said and jerked his head toward the lodge, "he ain't been baptized?"

"No," Rayber said. He looked at him narrowly. He thought that if he could get the right words in now, he might do some good, might give him a painless lesson. "I may not have the guts to drown him," he said, "but I have the guts to maintain my self-respect and not to perform futile rites over him. I have the guts not to become the prey of superstitions. He is what he is and there's nothing for him to be born into. My guts," he finished, "are in my head."

The boy only stared at him, his eyes filmed with a dull cast of nausea.

"The great dignity of man," his uncle said, "is his ability to say: I am born once and no more. What I can see and do for myself and my fellowman in this life is all of my portion and I'm content with it. It's enough to be a man." There was a light ring in his voice. He watched the boy closely to see if he had struck a chord.

Tarwater turned an expressionless face toward the rim of trees that made a paling around the lake. He appeared to stare into emptiness.

Rayber subsided again but he could stand it only a few minutes. He finished the cigaret and lit another. Then he decided to start off on a new tack and leave the morbid alone for a while. "I'll tell you what I've planned for us to do in a couple of weeks," he said in an almost affable tone. "We're going up for a plane ride. How about that?" He had been considering this, holding it in reserve, thinking it would be the greatest marvel he could produce, something that would surely stir the glum child out of himself.

There was no response. The boy's eyes looked glazed.

"Flying is the greatest engineering achievement of man," Rayber said in an irked voice. "Doesn't it stir your imagination even slightly? If it doesn't I'm afraid there's something wrong with you."

"I done flew," Tarwater said and suppressed a belch. He was entirely occupied with his nausea which he could feel minutely rising.

"How could you have flown?" his uncle asked angrily.

"Him and me give a dollar to go up in one at a fair once," he said. "The houses weren't nothing but matchboxes and the people were invisible—like germs. I wouldn't give you nothing for no airplane. A buzzard can fly."

The schoolteacher gripped both sides of the boat and pushed forward. "He's warped your whole life," he said hoarsely. "You're going to grow up to be a freak if you don't let yourself be helped. You still believe all that crap he taught you. You're eaten up with false guilt. I can read you like a book!" The words were out before he could stop them.

The boy did not even look at him. He leaned over the side of the boat and shuddered. The column, released, formed a sweetly sour circle on the water. A wave of dizziness came over him and then his head cleared. A ravenous emptiness raged in his stomach as if it had reestablished its rightful tenure. He washed his mouth out with a handful of the lake and then wiped his face on his sleeve.

Rayber trembled at his recklessness. He felt certain he had produced this by the word *guilt*. He put his hand on the boy's knee and said, "You'll feel better now."

Tarwater said nothing, glaring with his red-lidded wet eyes at the water as if he were glad he had polluted it.

"It's just as much relief," his uncle said, pressing his advantage, "to get something off your mind as off your stomach. When you tell somebody else your troubles, then they don't bother you so much, they don't get in your blood and make you sick. Somebody else shares the weight. God boy," he said, "you need help. You need to be saved right here and now from the old man and everything he stands for. And I'm the one who can save you." With his hat turned down all around he looked like a fanatical country preacher. His eyes glistened. "I know what your problem is," he said. "I know and I can help you. Something's eating you on the inside and I can tell you what it is."

The boy looked at him fiercely. "Why don't you shut your big mouth?" he said. "Why don't you pull that plug out of your ear and turn yourself off? I come to fish. I never came to have no traffic with you."

His uncle snapped the cigaret out of his fingers and it hit the water with a hiss. "Every day," he said coldly, "you remind me more of the old man. You're just like him. You have his future before you."

The boy put down his line. With rigid deliberate movements he lifted his right foot and pulled off his shoe, then his left foot and pulled off that shoe. Then he jerked the straps of his overalls off his shoulders and pulled them down, over his bottom and off. He had on a pair of long thin old man's drawers. He pulled his hat tight down on his head so that it would not possibly come off, then he threw himself out of the boat and swam away, smashing the glassy lake with his cupped fists as if he would like to make it sting and bleed.

My God! Rayber thought, I touched a nerve that time! He kept his eye on the hat in the receding spasm of water. The empty overalls lay at his feet. He grabbed them and felt in the pockets. He took out two stones, a nickel, a box of wooden matches and three nails. He had brought along the new suit and shirt and laid them out on a chair.

Tarwater reached the dock and climbed onto it, the drawers clinging to him, the hat still ground down on his forehead. He turned just in time to see his uncle thrust the bundled overalls below the surface of the water.

Rayber felt as if he had just run across a mined field. At once he was afraid he had made a mistake. The thin rigid figure on the dock did not move. It seemed no more than a wraith-like column of fragile white-hot rage, materialized for an instant, the makings of some pure unfathomable passion. The boy turned and started rapidly toward the lodge and Rayber decided it would be best to linger on the lake a while.

When he came in, he was startled to see Tarwater lying on the far cot in his new clothes and to see Bishop sitting on the other end of it, watching him as if he were mesmerized by the steel-like glint that came from the boy's eyes and was directed into his own. In the plaid shirt and new blue trousers, he looked like a changeling, half his old self and half his new, already half the boy he would be when he was rehabilitated.

Rayber's spirits rose cautiously. He was holding the shoes with the contents of the overall pockets in them. He set them down on the bed and said, "No hard feelings about the clothes, old man. That was just my round."

There was a strange suppressed excitement about the boy's whole figure, as if he had settled on an inevitable course of action. He did not get up, did not acknowledge the shoes, but he acknowledged his uncle's presence by shifting the glint in his eyes slightly, on him and then away. The schoolteacher might have been just enough present to be ignored. Then he looked back at Bishop, triumphantly, boldly, into the very center of his eyes.

Rayber stood puzzled in the doorway. "Who wants to go for a ride?" he asked.

Bishop jumped off the bed and was at his side in an instant. Tarwater started at the little boy's abrupt disappearance from his field of vision, but he did not get up or turn his face toward the schoolteacher in the door.

"Well, we'll leave Frank to his meditations," Rayber said and swung the child around by the shoulder and left with him, hastily. He wanted to escape before the boy changed his mind.

Chapter 9

The heat was not as intense on the road as it had been on the lake and he drove with a sense of refreshment he had not felt in the five days Tarwater had been with him. Once out of sight of the boy, he felt a pressure had been lifted from the atmosphere. He eliminated the oppressive presence from his thoughts and retained only those aspects of it that could be abstracted, clean, into the future person he envisioned.

The sky was a cloudless even blue and he drove without destination, though he meant before they returned to the lodge to stop and have the car filled for tomorrow's trip to Powderhead. Bishop was hanging out the window, his mouth open, letting the air dry his tongue. Automatically, Rayber reached over and locked the door and pulled him back in by his shirt. The child sat, solemnly taking his hat off his head and putting it on his feet, then taking it off his feet and putting it on his head. After he had done this a while, he climbed over the seat and disappeared into the back of the car.

Rayber continued to think of Tarwater's future, his thoughts rewarding except when every now and then the boy's actual face would lodge in the path of a plan. The sudden intrusion of the face made him think of his wife. He seldom thought of her anymore. She would not divorce him for fear she would be given custody of the child and she was now as far away as she could get, in Japan, in some welfare capacity. He was aware of his good fortune in getting rid of her. It was she who had prevented his going back and getting Tarwater away from the old man. She would have been glad enough to have had him if she had not seen him that day when they went to Powderhead to face the old man down. The baby had crawled into the door behind old Tarwater and had sat there, unblinking, as the old man raised his gun and shot Rayber in the leg and then in the ear. She had seen him; Rayber had not; but she would not forget the face. It was not simply that the child was dirty, thin, and gray; it was that its expression had no more changed when the gun went off than the old man's had. This had affected her deeply.

If there had not been something repellent in its face, she said, her maternal instinct would have made her rush forward and snatch it. She had even had that in mind before they arrived and she would have had the courage to do it in spite of the old man's gun; but the child's look had frozen her. It was the opposite of everything appealing. She could not express her exact revulsion, for her feeling was not logical. It had, she said, the look of an adult, not of a child, and of an adult with immovable insane convictions. Its face was like the face she had seen in some medieval paintings where the martyr's limbs are being sawed off and his expression says he is being deprived of nothing essential. She had had the sense, seeing the child in the door, that if it had known that at that moment all its future advantages were being stolen from it, its expression would not have altered a jot. The face for her had expressed the depth of human perversity, the deadly sin of rejecting defiantly one's own obvious good. He had thought all this was possibly her imagination but he understood now that it was not imagination but fact. She said she could not have lived with such a face; she would have been bound to destroy the arrogant look on it.

He reflected wryly that she had not been able to live with Bishop's face any better though there was no arrogance on it. The little boy had climbed up from the floor of the back seat and was hanging over breathing into his ear. By temperament and training she was ready to handle an exceptional child, but not one as exceptional as Bishop, not one bearing her own family name and the face of "that horrible old man." She had returned once in the last two years and demanded that he put Bishop in an institution because she said he could not adequately care for him—though it was plain from the look of him that he thrived like an air plant. His own behavior on that occasion was still a source of satisfaction to him. He had knocked her not quite halfway across the room.

He had known by that time that his own stability depended on the little boy's presence. He could control his terrifying love as long as it had its focus in Bishop, but if anything happened to the child, he would have to face it in itself. Then the whole world would become his idiot child. He had thought what he would have to do if anything happened to Bishop. He would have with one supreme effort to resist the recognition; with every nerve and muscle and thought, he would have to resist feeling anything at all, thinking anything at all. He would have to anesthetize his life. He shook his head to clear it of these unpleasant thoughts.

After it had cleared, they returned one by one. He felt a sinister pull on his consciousness, the familiar undertow of expectation, as if he were still a child waiting on Christ.

The car apparently of its own volition had turned onto a dirt road which without warning pierced his abstraction with its familiarity. He put on his brakes.

It was a narrow corrugated road sunk between deep red embankments. He looked about him angrily. He had not had the least intention of coming here today. His car was on the crest of a hill and the embankments on either side had the look of forming an entrance to a region he would enter at his peril. The road sloped down a quarter of a mile or so within his sight and then turned to disappear behind an edge of the wood. When he had been on this road the first time, he had ridden it backwards. A Negro with a mule and wagon had met him and his uncle at the junction and they had ridden, their feet dangling from the back of the wagon. He had leaned over most of the way, watching the mule's hoofprints in the dust as they rolled over them.

He decided finally that there would be wisdom in looking at the place today so that there would be no surprises for him when he returned tomorrow with the boy, but for some few moments, he did not move on. The road that lay in front of him he remembered as being four or five miles long. Then there was a stretch through the woods that would have to be walked and then the field to be crossed. He thought with distaste of crossing it twice, today and again tomorrow. He thought with distaste of crossing it at all. Then as if to stop his thinking, he put his foot down hard on the accelerator and took the road defiantly. Bishop jumped up and down, squealing and making unintelligible noises of delight.

The road grew narrower as it approached its end and presently he found himself going over what was no more than a rutted wagon path, his speed reduced to nothing. He stopped the car finally in a little clearing grown up in Johnson grass and blackberry bushes where what was left of the road touched the edge of the wood. Bishop jumped out and made for the blackberry bushes, attracted by the wasps that buzzed over them. Rayber leapt out and grabbed him just before he reached for one. Gingerly he picked the child a blackberry and handed it to him. The little boy studied it and then, with his fallen smile, returned it to him as if they were performing a ceremony. Rayber flung it away and turned to find the trail through the woods.

He took the child by the hand and pulled him along

on what he thought might shortly become a path. The forest rose about him, mysterious and alien. Descending to speak with the shade of my uncle, he thought irritably and wondered if the old man's charred bones would be lying in the ashes. At the thought he almost stopped but did not. Bishop could barely walk for gaping. He lifted his face to stare open-mouthed above him as if he were in some vast overwhelming edifice. His hat fell off and Rayber picked it up and clamped it on his head again and pulled him on. Somewhere below them out of the silence a bird sounded four crystal notes. The child stopped, his breath held.

Rayber knew suddenly that alone with Bishop he could not go to the bottom and cross the field. Tomorrow with the other boy, with his brain engaged, he would be able to make it. He remembered that somewhere along here there was a point where one could look out between two trees and see the clearing below. When he had first walked through the wood with his uncle, they had stopped at that place and his uncle had pointed down to where, far across the field, a sagging unpainted house stood in a bare hard-packed yard. "Yonder it is," he said, "and someday it'll be yours—these woods and that field and that fine house." He remembered that his heart had expanded unbelievably.

Suddenly he realized that the place *was* his. In the stress of having the boy return to him, he had never considered the property. He stopped, astounded by the fact that he owned all of this. His trees stood rising above him, majestic and aloof, as if they belonged to an order that had never budged from its first allegiance in the days of creation. His heart began to beat frenetically. Quickly he reduced the whole wood in probable board feet into a college education for the boy. His spirits lifted. He pulled the child along, intending to find the opening where the house could be seen. A few yards below, a sudden patch of sky indicated the spot. He let Bishop go and strode toward it.

The forked tree was familiar to him or seemed so. He put his hand on one trunk, leaned forward and looked out. His gaze moved quickly and unseeing across the field and stopped abruptly where the house had been. Two chimneys stood there, separated by a black space of rubble.

He stood expressionless, his heart strangely wrenched. If the bones were lying in the ashes he could not see them from this distance, but a vision of the old man, farther away in time, rose before him. He saw him standing on the edge of the yard, one hand lifted in an astounded greeting, while he stood a little way off in the field, his fists clenched, trying to shout, trying to make his adolescent fury come out in clear sensible words. He had only stood there shrilling, "You're crazy, you're crazy, you're a liar, you have a head full of crap, you belong in a nut house!" and then had turned and run, carrying away nothing but the registered change in the old man's expression, the sudden drop into some mysterious misery, which afterwards he had never been able to get out of his mind. He saw it as he stared at the two denuded chimneys.

He felt a pressure on his hand and glanced down, continuing to see the same expression and barely noting that it was Bishop he was looking at now. The child wanted to be lifted up to see. Absently he picked him up and held him in the fork of the tree and let him look out. The dull fence, the empty gray eyes seemed to Rayber to reflect the ravaged scene across the field. The little boy turned his head after a moment and gazed instead at him. A dreaded sense of loss came over him. He knew that he could not remain here an instant longer. He turned with the child and went quickly back through the woods the way he had come.

On the highway again, he drove gripping the wheel, his face tense, his mind turned on the problem of Tarwater as if his own and not only the boy's salvation depended on his solving it. He had ruined his plan by going to Powderhead too soon. He knew he could not go there again, that he would have to find another way. He went over the afternoon's experience in the boat. There, he thought, he had been on the right track. He had simply not gone far enough. He decided that he would put the whole thing verbally before the boy. He would not argue with him but only tell him, tell him in so many plain words that he had a compulsion and what it was. Whether he answered, whether he cooperated, he would have to listen. He could not escape knowing that there was someone who knew exactly what went on inside him and who understood it for the good reason that it was understandable. He would go the whole way this time and tell him everything. The boy should at least know that he had no secrets. Casually while they ate their supper, he would lift the compulsion from his mind, expose it to the light, and let him have a good look at it. What he did about it would be his own affair. All at once this seemed to him extremely simple, the way he should have proceeded in the first place. Only time simplifies, he thought.

He stopped for gas at a pink stucco filling station where pottery and whirligigs were sold. While the car was being filled, he got out and looked for something to take as a peace offering, for he wanted the encounter to be pleasant if possible. His eye roved over a shelf of false hands, imitation buck teeth, boxes of simulated dog dung to put on the rug, wooden plaques with cynical mottos burnt on them. Finally he saw a combination corkscrew-bottleopener that fit in the palm of the hand. He bought it and left.

When they returned to the room, the boy was still lying on the cot, his face set in a deadly calm as if his eyes had not moved since they left. Again Rayber had a vision of the face his wife must have seen and he experienced a moment's revulsion for the boy that made him tremble. Bishop climbed onto the bottom of the cot and Tarwater returned the child's gaze steadily. He seemed unaware that Rayber was in the room.

"I could eat a horse," the schoolteacher said. "Let's go down."

The boy turned his head and regarded him evenly, with no interest but with no hostility. "It's what you'll get," he said, "if you eat here."

Rayber, unamused, pulled out the corkscrew-bottleopener and dropped it negligently on his chest. "That might come in handy sometime," he said and turned and began to wash his hands at the basin.

In the mirror, he saw him pick it up gingerly and look at it. He pushed the corkscrew out of the circle and then meditatively pushed it back. He studied it back and front and held it in the palm of his hand where it fit like a half-dollar. Presently he said in a grudging voice, "I don't have no use for it but I thank you," and put it in his pocket.

He returned his attention to Bishop as if this were its natural place. He lifted himself on one elbow and fixed the child with a narrow look. "Git up, you," he said slowly. He might have been commanding a small animal he was successfully training. His voice was steady but experimental. The hostility in it seemed contained and directed toward some planned goal. The little boy was watching with complete fascination.

"Git up now, like I tol' you to," Tarwater repeated slowly.

The child obediently climbed down off the bed.

Rayber felt a twinge of ridiculous jealousy. He stood by, his brows working irritably as the boy moved out of the door without a word and Bishop followed him. After a moment he slung his towel into the basin and walked after them.

The lodge was shaking with the stamping of four couples dancing at the other end of the lobby where the woman who ran the place had a nickelodeon. The three of them sat down at the red tin table and Rayber turned off his hearing aid until the racket should stop. He sat glaring around him, disgruntled at this intrusion.

The dancers were about Tarwater's age but they might have belonged to a different species entirely. The girls could be distinguished from the boys only by their tight skirts and bare legs; their faces and heads were alike. They danced with a furious stern concentration. Bishop was entranced. He stood up in his chair, watching them, his head hanging forward as if any moment it might drop off. Tarwater, his eyes dark and distant, stared through them. They might have been insects buzzing across the surface of his vision.

When the music whined to a stop, they clambered back to their table and sprawled in their chairs. Rayber turned his hearing aid on and winced as Bishop's bellow blared into his head. The child was jumping up and down in his chair, roaring his disappointment. As soon as the dancers saw him, he stopped making the noise and stood still, devouring them with his gape. An angry silence fell over them. Their look was shocked and affronted as if they had been betrayed by a fault in creation, something that should have been corrected before they were allowed to see it. With pleasure Rayber could have dashed across the room and swung his lifted chair in their faces. They got up and pushed each other out sullenly, packed themselves in a topless automobile and roared off, sending an indignant spray of gravel against the side of the lodge. Rayber let out his breath as if it were sharp and might cut him. Then his eyes fell on Tarwater.

The boy was looking directly at him with an omniscient smile, faint but decided. It was a smile that Rayber had seen on his face before. It seemed to mock him from an ever-deepening inner knowledge that grew in indifference as it came nearer and nearer to a secret truth about him. Without warning its meaning pierced Rayber and he felt such a fury that for the moment all his strength left him. Go, he wanted to shout. Get your damn impudent face out of my sight! Go to hell! Go baptize the whole world!

The woman had been standing for some time at his side, waiting to take their order but she could have been invisible for all the notice he paid her. She began tapping the menu on a glass, then she slid it in front of his face. Without reading it, he said, "Three hamburger plates," and thrust it aside.

When she was gone, he said in a dry voice, "I want to lay some cards on the table." He sought the boy's eyes and steadied himself by the hated glint in them.

Tarwater looked at the table as if waiting for the cards to be laid on it.

"That means I want to talk straight to you," Rayber said, rigidly keeping the exasperation out of his voice. He strove to make his gaze, his tone, as indifferent as his listener's. "I have some things to say to you that you'll have to listen to. What you do about what I have to say is your own business. I have no further interest in telling you what to do. I only intend to put the facts before you." His voice was thin and brittle-sounding. He might have been reading from a paper. "I notice that you've begun to be able to look Bishop in the eye. That's good. It means you're making progress but you needn't think that because you can look him in the eye now, you've saved yourself from what's preying on you. You haven't. The old man still has you in his grip. Don't think he hasn't."

The boy continued to give him the same omniscient look. "It's you the seed fell in," he said. "It ain't a thing you can do about it. It fell on bad ground but it fell in deep. With me," he said proudly, "it fell on rock and the wind carried it away."

The schoolteacher grasped the table as if he were going to push it forward into the boy's chest. "Goddam you!" he said in a breathless harsh voice. "It fell in us both alike. The difference is that I know it's in me and I keep it under control. I weed it out but you're too blind to know it's in you. You don't even know what makes you do the things you do."

The boy looked at him angrily but he said nothing.

At least, Rayber thought, I've shocked that look off his face. He did not say anything for a few moments while he thought how to continue.

The woman returned with the three plates. She set them down slowly, giving herself time for observation. The man's face had a sweaty harassed look and so did the boy's. He threw her an ugly glance. The man began to eat at once as if he wanted to get it over with. The little boy took his bun apart and began to lick the mustard off it. The other boy looked at his as if it were probably bad meat and did not touch it. She left and watched indignantly for a few seconds from the kitchen door. The boy finally picked his hamburger up. He raised it half-way to his mouth and then put it down again. He picked it up and put it down twice without biting into it. Then he pulled his hat down and sat there, his arms folded. She had had enough and closed the door.

The schoolteacher leaned forward across the table, his eyes pin-pointed and very bright. "You can't eat," he said, "because something is eating you. And I intend to tell you what it is."

"Worms," the boy hissed as if his disgust could not be contained an instant longer.

"It takes guts to listen," Rayber said.

Tarwater leaned toward him with a kind of blaring attention. "You ain't got nothing to say to me that I don't have the guts to listen to," he said.

The schoolteacher sat back. "All right," he said, "then listen." He folded his arms and looked at him for an instant before he began. Then he started coldly. "The old man told you to baptize Bishop. You have that order lodged in your head like a boulder blocking your path."

The blood drained from the boy's face but his eyes did not swerve. They looked at Rayber furiously, the glint in them gone.

The schoolteacher spoke slowly, picking his words as if he were looking for the steadiest stones to step on across a rushing stream. "Until you get rid of this compulsion to baptize Bishop, you'll never make any progress toward being a normal person. I said in the boat you were going to be a freak. I shouldn't have said that. I only meant you had the choice. I want you to see the choice. I want you to make the choice and not simply be driven by a compulsion you don't understand. What we understand, we can control," he said. "You have to understand what it is that blocks you. I wonder if you're smart enough to take this in. It's not simple."

The boy's face seemed dry and old as if he had taken it in long ago, and now it was part of him like the current of death in his blood. The schoolteacher was touched by this muteness before the facts. His anger left him. The room was silent. A pink cast had fallen from the windows over the table. Tarwater looked away from his uncle at Bishop. The little boy's hair was pink and lighter than his face. He was sucking his spoon; his eyes were drowned in silence.

"I want to put two solutions before you," Rayber said. "What you do is up to you."

Tarwater looked at him again, with no mockery, no glint in his eye, but with no anticipation either, as if his course were irrevocably set.

"Baptism is only an empty act," the schoolteacher said. "If there's any way to be born again, it's a way that you accomplish yourself, an understanding about yourself that you reach after a long time, perhaps a long effort. It's nothing you get from above by spilling a little water and a few words. What you want to do is meaningless, so the easiest solution would be simply to do it. Right here now, with this glass of water. I would permit it in order to get it out of your mind. As far as I'm concerned, you may baptize him at once." He pushed his own glass of water across the table. His look was patient and ironical.

The boy's glance touched the top of the glass and then bounded off. His hand lying by the side of his plate twitched. He jammed it into his pocket and looked the other way, out the window. His whole aspect seemed shaken as if his integrity had been dangerously challenged.

The schoolteacher pulled back the glass of water. "I knew that would be too cheap for you," he said. "I knew you would refuse to do anything so unworthy of the courage you've already shown." He raised the glass and drank the rest of the water. Then he set it down on the table. He looked tired enough to collapse; his aspect was so weary that he might just have attained the top of a mountain he had been climbing for days.

After an interval he said, "The other way is not so simple. It's the way I've chosen for myself. It's the way you take as a result of being born again the natural way—through your own efforts. Your intelligence." His words had a disconnected sound. "The other way is simply to face it and fight it, to cut down the weed every time you see it appear. Do I have to tell you this? An intelligent boy like you?"

"You don't have to tell me nothing," Tarwater murmured.

"I don't have a compulsion to baptize him," Rayber said. "My own is more complicated, but the principle is the same. The way we have to fight it is the same."

"It ain't the same," Tarwater said. He turned toward his uncle. The glint had reappeared. "I can pull it up by the roots, once and for all. I can do something. I ain't like you. All you can do is think what you would have done if you had done it. Not me. I can do it. I can act." He was looking at his uncle now with a completely fresh contempt. "It's nothing about me like you," he said.

"There are certain laws that determine every man's conduct," the schoolteacher said. "You are no exception." He saw with perfect clarity that the only feeling he had for this boy was hate. He loathed the very sight of him.

"Wait and see," Tarwater said as if it needed only a short time to be proved.

"Experience is a terrible teacher," Rayber said.

The boy shrugged and got up. He walked off, across the room to the screen door where he stood looking out. At once Bishop climbed down off his chair and started after him, putting on his hat as he went. Tarwater stiffened when the child approached but he did not move and Rayber watched as the two of them stood there side by side, looking out the door—the two figures, hatted and somehow ancient, bound together by some necessity of nerve that excluded him. He was startled to see the boy put his hand on Bishop's neck just under his hat, open the door and guide him out of it. It occurred to him that what he meant by "doing something" was to make a slave of the child. Bishop would be at his command like a faithful dog. Instead of avoiding him, he planned to control him, to show who was master.

And I will not permit that, he said. If anyone controlled Bishop, it would be himself. He put his money on the table under the salt-shaker and went out after them.

The sky was a bright pink, casting such a weird light that every color was intensified. Each weed that grew out of the gravel looked like a live green nerve. The world might have been shedding its skin. The two were in front of him halfway down the dock, walking slowly, Tarwater's hand still resting just under Bishop's hat; but it seemed to Rayber that it was Bishop who was doing the leading, that the child had made the capture. He thought with a grim pleasure that sooner or later the boy's confidence in his own judgment would be brought low.

When they arrived at the end of the dock, they stood looking down into the water. Then to Rayber's chagrin, the boy lifted the child like a sack under the arms and lowered him over the edge of the dock into the boat that was tied there.

"I haven't given you permission to take Bishop out in the boat," Rayber said.

Tarwater may have heard or he may not; he did not answer. He sat down on the edge of the dock and for a few moments looked across the water at the opposite bank. Part of a red globe hung almost motionless in the far side of the lake as if it were the other end of the elongated sun cut through the middle by a swath of forest. Pink and salmon-colored clouds floated in the water at different depths. Suddenly Rayber wanted nothing so much as a half hour to himself, without sight of either of them. "But you may take him," he said, "if you'll be careful."

The boy didn't move. He was leaning forward, his thin

shoulders hunched, his hands gripped on the edge of the dock. He seemed poised there waiting to make a momentous move.

He dropped down into the boat with Bishop.

"You'll look after him?" Rayber asked.

Tarwater's face was like a very old mask, colorless and dry. "I'll tend to him," he said.

"Thanks," his uncle said. He experienced a short feeling of warmth for the boy. He strolled back down the dock to the lodge and when he reached the door, he turned and watched the boat move out into view on the lake. He raised his arm and waved but Tarwater showed no sign of seeing him and Bishop's back was turned. The small black-hatted figure sat like a passenger being borne by the surly oarsman across the lake to some mysterious destination.

Back in his room, Rayber lay on the cot trying to feel the release he had felt when he started out in the car in the afternoon. More than anything else, what he experienced in the boy's presence was the feeling of pressure and when it was taken off for a while, he realized how intolerable it was. He lay there thinking with distaste of the moment when the silent mutinous face would appear again in the door. He imagined the rest of the summer spent coping with the boy's cold intractability. He began to consider the possibility of his leaving of his own accord and after a moment he knew that this was actually what he wanted him to do. He no longer felt any challenge to rehabilitate him. All he wanted now was to get rid of him. He thought with horror of being stuck with him for good and began to consider ways that he might hasten his departure. He knew he would never leave as long as Bishop was around. The thought flew through his mind that he might put Bishop in an institution for a few weeks. He was shaken and turned his mind to other things. For a while he dozed and dreamed that he and Bishop were speeding away in the car, escaping safely from a lowering tornado-like cloud. He awoke to find the room growing dim.

He got up and went to the window. The boat with the two of them in it was near the middle of the lake, almost still. They were sitting there facing each other in the isolation of the water, Bishop small and squat, and Tarwater gaunt, lean, bent slightly forward, his whole attention concentrated on the opposite figure. They seemed to be held still in some magnetic field of attraction. The sky was an intense purple as if it were about to explode into darkness.

Rayber left the window and threw himself on the cot again but he was no longer sleepy. He had a peculiar sense of waiting, of marking time. He lay with his eyes closed as if listening to something he could hear only when his hearing aid was off. He had had this sense of waiting, kin in degree but not in kind, when he was a child and expected any moment that the city would blossom into an eternal Powderhead. Now he sensed that he waited for a cataclysm. He waited for all the world to be turned into a burnt spot between two chimneys.

All he would be was an observer. He waited with serenity. Life had never been good enough to him for him to wince at its destruction. He told himself that he was indifferent even to his own dissolution. It seemed to him that this indifference was the most that human dignity could achieve, and for the moment forgetting his lapses, forgetting even his narrow escape of the afternoon, he felt he had achieved it. To feel nothing was peace.

He watched idly as a round red moon rose into the lower corner of his window. It might have been the sun rising on the upsidedown half of the world. He came to a decision. When the boy came back he would say: Bishop and I are returning to town tonight. You may go with us under these conditions: not that you *begin* to cooperate, but that you cooperate, fully and completely, that you change your attitude, that you allow yourself to be tested, that you prepare yourself to enter school in the fall, and that you take that hat off your head right now and throw it out the window into the lake. If you can't meet these requirements, then Bishop and I are leaving by ourselves.

It had taken him five days to reach this state of clarity. He thought of his foolish emotions the night the boy had come, thought of himself sitting by the side of the bed, thinking that at last he had a son with a future. He saw himself again following the boy down back alleys to end finally at a detestable temple, saw the idiot figure of himself standing with his head in the window, listening to the mad child preach. It was unbelievable. Even the plan to take the boy back to Powderhead seemed ridiculous to him now and going to Powderhead this afternoon was the act of an insane person. His indecision, his uncertainty, his eagerness up to now appeared shameful and absurd to him. He felt that he had regained his senses after five days of madness. He could not wait for them to return so that he could deliver his ultimatum.

He closed his eyes and went over the scene in detail,

seeing the sullen face at bay, the haughty eyes forced to look down. His power would lie in the fact that he was indifferent now whether the boy stayed or went, or not indifferent for he positively wanted him to leave. He smiled at the thought that his indifference lacked that one perfection. Presently he dozed again, and again he and Bishop were fleeing in the car, the tornado just behind them.

When he awoke again, the moon travelling toward the middle of the window had lost its color. He sat up startled as if it were a face looking in on him, a pale messenger breathlessly arrived.

He got up and went to the window and leaned out. The sky was a hollow black and an empty road of moonlight crossed the lake. He leaned far out, his eyes narrowed, but he could see nothing. The stillness disturbed him. He turned the hearing aid on and at once his head buzzed with the steady drone of crickets and treefrogs. He searched for the boat in the darkness and could see nothing. He waited expectantly. Then an instant before the cataclysm, he grabbed the metal box of the hearing aid as if he were clawing his heart. The quiet was broken by an unmistakable bellow.

He did not move. He remained absolutely still, wooden, expressionless, as the machine picked up the sounds of some fierce sustained struggle in the distance. The bellow stopped and came again, then it began steadily, swelling. The machine made the sounds seem to come from inside him as if something in him were tearing itself free. He clenched his teeth. The muscles in his face contracted and revealed lines of pain beneath harder than bone. He set his jaw. No cry must escape him. The one thing he knew, the one thing he was certain of was that no cry must escape him.

The bellow rose and fell, then it blared out one last time, rising out of its own momentum as if it were escaping finally, after centuries of waiting, into silence. The beady night noises closed in again.

He remained standing woodenly at the window. He knew what had happened. What had happened ·was as plain to him as if he had been in the water with the boy and the two of them together had taken the child and held him under until he ceased to struggle.

He stared out over the empty still pond to the dark wood that surrounded it. The boy would be moving off through it to meet his appalling destiny. He knew with an instinct as sure as the dull mechanical beat of his heart that he had baptized the child even as he drowned him, that he was headed for everything the old man had prepared him for, that he moved off now through the black forest toward a violent encounter with his fate.

He stood there trying to remember something else before he moved away. It came to him finally as something so distant and vague in his mind that it might already have happened, a long time ago. It was that tomorrow they would drag the pond for Bishop.

He stood waiting for the raging pain, the intolerable hurt that was his due, to begin, so that he could ignore it, but he continued to feel nothing. He stood light-headed at the window and it was not until he realized there would be no pain that he collapsed.

Part 3

Chapter 10

The headlights revealed the boy at the side of the road, slightly crouched, his head turned expectantly, his eyes for an instant lit red like the eyes of rabbits and deer that streak across the highway at night in the path of speeding cars. His pantslegs were wet up to the knees as if he had been through a swamp. The driver, minute in the glassed cab, brought the looming truck to a halt and left the motor idling while he leaned across the empty seat and opened the door. The boy climbed in.

It was an auto-transit truck, huge and skeletal, carrying four automobiles packed in it like bullets. The driver, a wiry man with a nose sharply twisted down and heavy-lidded eyes, gave the rider a suspicious look and then shifted gears and the truck began to move again, rumbling fiercely. "You got to keep me awake or you don't ride, buddy," he said. "I ain't picking you up to do you a favor." His voice, from some other part of the country, curled at the end of each sentence.

Tarwater opened his mouth as if he expected words to come out of it but none came. He remained, staring at the man, his mouth half-open, his face white.

"I'm not kiddin', kid," the driver said.

The boy kept his elbows gripped into his sides to prevent his frame from shaking. "I only want to go as far as where this road joins 56," he said finally. There were queer ups and downs in his voice as if he were using it for the first time after some momentous failure. He appeared to listen to it himself, to be trying to hear beyond the quaver in it to some solid basis of sound.

"Start talking," the driver said.

The boy wet his lips. After a moment he said in a high voice, entirely out of control, "I never wasted my life talking. I always done something."

"What you done lately?" the man asked. "How come your pantslegs are wet?"

He looked down at his wet pantslegs and kept looking. They seemed to turn his mind entirely from what he had been going to say, to absorb his attention completely.

"Wake up, buddy," the driver said. "I say how come are your pantslegs wet?"

"Because I never took them off when I done it," he said. "I took off my shoes but I never taken off my pants."

"When you done what?"

"I'm going home," he said. "It's a place I get off at on 56 and then down that road a piece I take a dirt road. It's liable to be morning before I get there."

"How come your pantslegs are wet?" the driver persisted.

"I drowned a boy," Tarwater said.

"Just one?" the driver asked.

"Yes." He reached over and caught hold of the sleeve of the man's shirt. His lips worked a few seconds. They stopped and then started again as if the force of a thought were behind them but no words. He shut his mouth, then tried again but no sound came. Then all at once the sentence rushed out and was gone. "I baptized him."

"Huh?" the man said.

"It was an accident. I didn't mean to," he said breathlessly. Then in a calmer voice he said, "The words just come out of themselves but it don't mean nothing. You can't be born again."

"Make sense," the man said.

"I only meant to drown him," the boy said. "You're only born once. They were just some words that run out of my mouth and spilled in the water." He shook his head violently as if to scatter his thoughts. "There's nothing where I'm going but the stall," he began again, "because the house is burnt up but that's the way I want it. I don't want nothing of his. Now it's all mine."

"Of his whose?" the man muttered.

"Of my great-uncle's," the boy said. "I'm going back there. I ain't going to leave it again. I'm in full charge there. No voice will be uplifted. I shouldn't never have left it except I had to prove I wasn't no prophet and I've proved it." He paused and jerked the man's sleeve. "I proved it by drowning him. Even if I did baptize him that was only an accident. Now all I have to do is mind my own bidnis until I die. I don't have to baptize or prophesy."

The man only looked at him, shortly, and then back at the road.

"It's not going to be any destruction or any fire," the boy said. "There are them that can act and them that can't, and them that are hungry and them that ain't. That's all. I can act. And I ain't hungry." The words crowded out as if they were pushing each other forward. Then he was suddenly silent. He seemed to watch the darkness that the headlights pushed in front of them, always at the same distance. Sudden signs would spring up and vanish at the side of the road.

"That don't make sense but make up some more of it," the driver said. "I gotta stay awake. I ain't riding you just for a good time."

"I don't have no more to say," Tarwater said. His voice was thin, as if many more words would destroy it permanently. It seemed to break off after each sound had found its way out. "I'm hungry," he said.

"You just said you weren't hungry," the driver said.

"I ain't hungry for the bread of life," the boy said. "I'm hungry for something to eat here and now. I threw up my dinner and I didn't eat no supper."

The driver began to feel in his pocket. He pulled out half a bent sandwich wrapped in waxed paper. "You can have this," he said. "It don't have but one bite out of it. I didn't like it."

Tarwater took it and held it wrapped in his hand. He didn't open it.

"Okay, eat it!" the driver said in an exasperated voice. "What's the matter with you?"

"When I come to eat, I ain't hungry," Tarwater said. "It's like being empty is a thing in my stomach and it don't allow nothing else to come down in there. If I ate it, I would throw it up."

"Listen," the driver said, "I don't want you puking in here and if you got something catching, you get out right now."

"I'm not sick," the boy said. "I never been sick in my life except sometimes when I over ate myself. When I baptized him it wasn't nothing but words. Back home," he said, "I'll be in charge. I'll have to sleep in the stall until I get to where I can build me back a house. If I hadn't been a big fool I'd have taken him out and burned him up outside. I wouldn't have burned up the house along with him."

"Live and learn," the driver said.

"My other uncle knows everything," the boy said, "but that don't keep him from being a fool. He can't do nothing. All he can do is figure it out. He's got this wired head. There's an electric cord runs into his ear. He can read your mind. He knows you can't be born again. I know everything he knows, only I can do something about it. I did," he added.

"Can't you talk about something else?" the driver asked. "How many sisters you got at home?"

"I was born in a wreck," the boy said.

He took off his hat and rubbed his head. His hair was flat and thin, dark across his white forehead. He held the hat in his lap like a bowl and looked into it. He took out a box of wooden matches and a white card. "I put all this here in my hat when I drowned him," he said. "I was afraid my pockets would get wet." He held up the card close to his eyes and read it aloud. "T. Fawcett Meeks. Southern Copper Parts. Mobile, Birmingham, Atlanta." He stuck the card in the inside band of his hat and put the hat back on his head. He put the box of matches in his pocket.

The driver's head was beginning to roll. He shook it and said, "Talk, dammit."

The boy reached into his pocket and pulled out the combination corkscrew-bottleopener the schoolteacher had given him. "My uncle give me this," he said. "He ain't so bad. He knows a heap. I speck I'll be able to use this thing some time or other," and he looked at it lying compact in the center of his hand. "I speck it'll come in handy," he said, "to open something."

"Tell me a joke," the driver said.

The boy didn't look as if he knew any joke. He didn't look as if he knew what a joke was. "Do you know what the greatest invention of man is?" he asked finally.

"Naw," the driver said, "what?"

He didn't answer. He was staring ahead again into the darkness and seemed to have forgotten the question.

"What's the greatest invention of man?" the truck driver asked irritably.

The boy turned and looked at him without comprehension. There was a choking sound in his throat and then he said, "What?"

The driver glared at him. "What's the matter with you?"

"Nothing," the boy said. "I feel hungry but I ain't."

"You belong in the booby hatch," the driver muttered. "You ride through these states and you see they all belong in it. I won't see nobody sane again until I get back to Detroit."

For a few miles they rode in silence. The truck moved slower and slower. The driver's lids would fall as if they were weighted with lead and he would shake his head to open them. Almost at once they would close again. The truck began to veer. He shook his head once violently and pulled off the road onto a wide shoulder and leaned back and began to snore without once looking at Tarwater.

The boy sat quietly on his side of the cab. His eyes were open wide without the least look of sleep in them. They seemed not to be able to close but to be open forever on some sight that would never leave them. Presently they closed but his body did not relax. He sat rigidly upright, a still alert expression on his face as if under the closed lids an inner eye were watching, piercing out the truth in the distortion of his dream.

They were sitting facing each other in a boat suspended on a soft bottomless darkness only a little heavier than the black air around them, but the darkness was no hindrance to his sight. He saw through it as if it were day. He looked through the blackness and saw perfectly the light silent eyes of the child across from him. They had lost their diffuseness and were trained on him, fish-colored and fixed. By his side, standing like a guide in the boat, was his faithful friend, lean, shadow-like, who had counseled him in both country and city.

Make haste, he said. Time is like money and money is like blood and time turns blood to dust.

The boy looked up into his friend's eyes, bent upon him, and was startled to see that in the peculiar darkness, they were violet-colored, very close and intense, and fixed on him with a peculiar look of hunger and attraction. He turned his head away, unsettled by their attention.

No finaler act than this, his friend said. In dealing with the dead you have to act. There's no mere word sufficient to say NO.

Bishop took off his hat and threw it over the side where it floated right-side-up, black on the black surface of the lake. The boy turned his head, following the hat with his eyes, and saw suddenly that the bank loomed behind him, not twenty yards away, silent, like the brow of some leviathan lifted just above the surface of the water. He felt bodiless as if he were nothing but a head full of air, about to tackle all the dead.

Be a man, his friend counseled, be a man. It's only one dimwit you have to drown.

The boy edged the boat toward a dark clump of bushes and tied it. Then he removed his shoes, put the contents of his pockets into his hat and put the hat into one shoe, while all the time the gray eyes were fixed on him as if they were waiting serenely for a struggle already determined. The violet eyes, fixed on him also, waited with a barely concealed impatience.

This is no time to dwaddle, his mentor said. Once it's done, it's done forever.

The water slid out from the bank like a broad black tongue. He climbed out of the boat and stood still, feeling the mud between his toes and the wet clinging around his legs. The sky was dotted with fixed tranquil eyes like the spread tail of some celestial night bird. While he stood there gazing, for the moment lost, the child in the boat stood up, caught him around the neck and climbed onto his back. He clung there like a large crab to a twig and the startled boy felt himself sinking backwards into the water as if the whole bank were pulling him down.

Sitting upright and rigid in the cab of the truck, his muscles began to jerk, his arms flailed, his mouth opened to make way for cries that would not come. His pale face twitched and grimaced. He might have been Jonah clinging wildly to the whale's tongue.

The silence in the truck was corrugated with the snores of the driver, whose head rolled from side to side. The boy's jerking arms almost touched him once or twice as he struggled to extricate himself from a monstrous enclosing darkness. Occasionally a car would pass, illuminating for an instant his contorted face. He grappled with the air as if he had been flung like a fish on the shores of the dead without lungs to breathe there. The night finally began to fade. A plateau of red appeared in the eastern sky just above the treeline and a dun-colored light began to reveal the fields on either side. Suddenly in a high raw voice the defeated boy cried out the words of baptism, shuddered, and opened his eyes. He heard the sibilant oaths of his friend fading away on the darkness.

He sat trembling in the corner of the cab, exhausted, dizzy, holding his arms tight against his sides. The plateau had widened and was broken by the sun which rose through it majestically with a long red wingspread. With his eyes open, his face began to look less alert. Deliberately, forcefully, he closed the inner eye that had witnessed his dream.

In his hand he was clutching the truck driver's sandwich. His fingers had clenched it through. He loosened them and looked at it as if he had no idea what it was; then he put it in his pocket.

After a second he grabbed the driver's shoulder and shook him violently and the man woke up and grabbed the steering wheel convulsively as if the truck were moving at a high rate of speed. Then he perceived that it was not moving at all. He turned and glared at the boy. "What do you think you're doing in here? Where do you think you're going?" he asked in an enraged voice.

Tarwater's face was pale but determined. "I'm going home," he said. "I'm in charge there now."

"Well get out and go then," the driver said. "I don't ride nuts in the day time."

With dignity the boy opened the door and stepped down out of the cab. He stood, scowling but aloof, by the side of the road and waited until the gigantic monster had grated away and disappeared. The highway stretched in front of him, lean and gray, and he began to walk, putting his feet down hard on the ground. His legs and his will were good enough. He set his face toward the clearing. By sundown he would be there, by sundown he would be where he could begin to live his life as he had elected it, and where, for the rest of his days, he would make good his refusal.

Chapter 11

After he had walked about an hour, he took out the truck driver's pierced sandwich which he had stuck, still wrapped, in his pocket. He undid it and let the paper blow behind. The truck driver had bitten off one of the pointed ends. The boy put the unbitten end in his mouth but after a second he took it out again with faint teeth marks in it and put it back in his pocket. His stomach alone rejected it; his face looked violently hungry and disappointed.

The morning had opened up, clear and cloudless and brilliant. He walked on the embankment and did not look over his shoulder as cars came behind him and swiftly passed, but as each one disappeared on the narrowing strip of highway, he felt the distance between himself and his goal grow longer. The ground under him was strange to his feet, as if he were walking on the back of a giant beast which might any moment stretch a muscle and send him rolling into the ditch below. The sky was like a fence of light to keep it in. The glare forced him to lower his lids but on the other side of it, hidden from his daily sight but present to his inner eye that remained rigidly open, there stretched the clear gray borders of the country he had saved himself from crossing into.

He repeated every few yards, to force himself on faster, that he would soon be home, that there was only the rest of the day between him and the clearing. His throat and eyes burned with dryness and his bones felt brittle as if they belonged to a person older than himself and with much experience; and when he considered it—his experience—it was apparent to him that since his great-uncle's death, he had lived the lifetime of a man. It was as no boy that he returned. He returned tried in the fire of his refusal, with all the old man's fancies burnt out of him, with all the old man's madness smothered for good, so that there was never any chance it would break out in him. He had saved himself forever from the fate he had envisioned when, standing in the schoolteacher's hall and looking into the eyes of the dim-witted child, he had seen himself trudging off into the distance in the bleeding stinking mad shadow of Jesus, lost forever to his own inclinations.

The fact that he had actually baptized the child disturbed him only intermittently and each time he thought of it, he reviewed its accidental nature. It was an accident and nothing more. He considered only that the boy was drowned and that he had done it, and that in the order of things, a drowning was a more important act than a few words spilled in the water. He realized that in this small instance the schoolteacher had succeeded where he had failed. The schoolteacher had not baptized him. He recalled his words: "My guts are in my head." My guts are in my head too, the boy thought. Even if by some chance it had not been an accident, what was of no consequence in the first place was of no consequence in the second; and he had succeeded in drowning the child. He had not said NO, he had done it.

The sun, from being only a ball of glare, was becoming distinct like a large pearl, as if sun and moon had fused in a brilliant marriage. The boy's narrowed eyes made a black spot of it. When he was a child he had several times, experimentally, commanded the sun to stand still, and once for as long as he watched it—a few seconds—it had stood still, but when he turned his back, it had moved. Now he would have liked for it to get out of the sky altogether or to be veiled in a cloud. He turned his face enough to rid his vision of it and was aware again of the country which seemed to lie beyond the silence, or in it, stretching off into the distance around him.

Quickly he set his mind again on the clearing. He thought of the burnt spot in the center of it and he imagined with a careful deliberateness how he would pick up any burnt bone that he might find in the ashes of the house and sling it off into the nearest gulley. He envisioned the calm and detached person who would do this, who would clear out the rubble and build back the house. Beyond the glare, he was aware of another figure, a gaunt stranger, the ghost who had been born in the wreck and who had fancied himself destined at that moment to the torture of prophecy. It was apparent to the boy that this person, who paid him no attention, was mad.

As the sun burned brighter, he became more and more thirsty and his hunger and thirst combined in a pain that shot up and down him and across from shoulder to shoulder. He was about to sit down when ahead in a brush-swept space off the side of the road he saw a Negro's shack. A small colored boy stood in the yard, alone except for a razor-backed shoat. His eyes were already fixed on the boy coming down the road. As Tarwater came nearer he saw a cluster of colored children watching him from the shack door. There was a well to the side under a sugarberry tree and he quickened his pace.

"I want me some water," he said, approaching the forward boy. He took the sandwich from his pocket and handed it to him. The child, who was about the size and shape of Bishop, put it to his mouth with the same motion that he took it and never removed his eyes from the boy's face.

"Yonder hit," he said and pointed with the sandwich to the well.

Tarwater went to it and cranked the bucket up level with the rim. There was a dipper but he did not use it. He leaned over and put his face to the water and drank. He drank until he began to feel dizzy. Then he pulled off his hat and thrust his head into the water. As it touched the deeper parts of his face, a shock ran through him, as if he had never been touched by water before. He looked down into a gray clear pool, down and down to where two silent serene eyes were gazing at him. He tore his head away from the bucket and stumbled backwards while the blurred shack, then the hog, then the colored child, his eyes still fixed on him, came into focus. He slammed his hat down on his wet head and wiped his sleeve across his face and walked hastily away. The little Negroes watched him until he was off the place and had disappeared down the highway.

The vision stuck like a burr in his head and it took him more than a mile to realize he had not seen it. The water had strangely not assuaged his thirst. To take his mind off it, he reached in his pocket and pulled out the schoolteacher's present and began to admire it. It reminded him that he also had a nickel. The first store or filling station he came to, he would buy himself a drink and open it with the opener. The little instrument glittered in the center of his palm as if it promised to open great things for him. He began to realize that he had not adequately appreciated the schoolteacher while he had the opportunity. The lines of his uncle's face had already become less precise in his mind and he began to see again the eyes shadowed with knowledge that he had imagined before he went to the city. He returned the corkscrew-bottleopener to his pocket and held it there in his hand as if henceforth it would be his talisman.

Presently up ahead, he caught sight of the crossroads where 56 joined the highway he was on. The dirt road was not ten miles down from this point. There was a patched-together store and filling station on the far side of the crossroad. He hastened on in anticipation of the drink he was going to buy, his thirst growing by the second. Then as he came closer, he saw the large woman who stood in the door of the place. His thirst increased but his enthusiasm fled. She was leaning against the frame, her arms folded, and she filled almost the whole entrance. She was a black-eyed woman with a granite-like face and a tongue persistent to question. He and his great-uncle had traded at this place on occasion and when the woman was there, the old man had liked to linger and discourse, for he found her as pleasant as a shade tree. The boy had always stood by impatiently, kicking up the gravel, his face dark with boredom.

She spotted him across the highway and although she did not move or raise her hand, he could feel her eyes reeling him in. He crossed the highway and was drawn forward, scowling at a neutral space between her chin and shoulder. After he had arrived and stopped, she did not speak but only looked at him and he was obligated to direct a glance upward at her eyes. They were fixed on him with a black penetration. There was all knowledge in her stony face and the fold of her arms indicated a judgment fixed from the foundations of time. Huge wings might have been folded behind her without seeming strange.

"The niggers told me how you done," she said. "It shames the dead."

The boy pulled himself together to speak. He was conscious that no sass would do, that he was called upon by some force outside them both to answer for his freedom and make bold his acts. A tremor went through him. His soul plunged deep within itself to hear the voice of his mentor at its most profound depths. He opened his mouth to overwhelm the woman and to his horror what rushed from his lips, like the shriek of a bat, was an obscenity he had overheard once at a fair. Shocked, he saw the moment lost.

The woman did not move a muscle. Presently she said, "And now you come back. And who is going to hire out a boy who burns down houses?"

Still aghast at his failure, he said in a shaky voice, "I ain't ast nobody to hire me out."

"And shames the dead?"

"The dead are dead and stay that way," he said, gaining a little strength.

"And scorns the Resurrection and the Life?"

His thirst was like a rough hand clenched in his throat. "Sell me a purple drink," he said hoarsely.

The woman did not move.

He turned and went, his look as dark as hers. There were circles under his eyes and his skin seemed to have shrunk on the frame of his bones from dryness. The obscenity echoed sullenly in his head. The boy's mind was too fierce to brook impurities of such a nature. He was intolerant of unspiritual evils and with those of the flesh he had never truckled. He felt his victory sullied by the remark that had come from his mouth. He thought of turning and going back and flinging the right words at her but he had still not found them. He tried to think of what the schoolteacher would have said to her but no words of his uncle's would rise to his mind.

The sun was behind him now and his thirst had reached the point where it could not get worse. The inside of his throat felt as if it were coated with burning sand. He moved on doggedly. No cars were passing. He made up his mind that he would flag the next car that passed. He hungered now for companionship as much as food and water. He wanted to explain to someone what he had failed to explain to the woman and with the right words to wipe out the obscenity that had stained his thought.

He had gone almost two more miles when a car finally passed him and then slowed down and stopped. He had been trudging absently and had not waved it down but when he saw it stop, he began to run forward. By the time he reached it, the driver had leaned over and opened the door. It was a lavender and cream-colored car. The boy scrambled in without looking at the driver and closed the door and they drove on.

Then he turned and looked at the man and an unpleasant sensation that he could not place came over him. The person who had picked him up was a pale, lean, old-looking young man with deep hollows under his cheekbones. He had on a lavender shirt and a thin black suit and a panama hat. His lips were as white as the cigaret that hung limply from one side of his mouth. His eyes were the same color as his shirt and were ringed with heavy black lashes. A lock of yellow hair fell across his forehead from under his pushed-back hat. He was silent and Tarwater was silent. He drove at a leisurely rate and presently he turned in the seat and gave the boy a long personal look. "Live around here?" he asked.

"Not on this road," Tarwater said. His voice was cracked from dryness.

"Going somewheres?"

"To where I live," the boy croaked. "I'm in charge there now."

The man said nothing else for a few minutes. The window by the boy's side was cracked and patched with a piece of adhesive tape and the handle to lower it had been removed. There was a sweet stale odor in the car and there did not seem enough air to breathe freely. Tarwater could see a pale reflection of himself, eyeing him darkly from the window.

"Don't live on this road, huh?" the man said. "Where do your folks live?"

"No folks," Tarwater said. "It's only me. I take care of myself. Nobody tells me what to do."

"Don't huh?" the man said. "I see it's no flies on you."

"No," the boy said, "there's not."

There was something familiar to him in the look of the stranger but he could not place where he had seen him before. The man put his hand in the pocket of his shirt and brought out a silver case. He snapped it open and passed it over to Tarwater. "Smoke?" he said.

The boy had never smoked anything but rabbit tobacco and he did not want a cigaret. He only looked at them.

"Special," the man said, continuing to hold out the case. "You don't get one of this kind every day, but maybe you ain't had much experience smoking."

Tarwater took the cigaret and hung it in the corner of his mouth, exactly as the man's was hung. Out of another pocket, the man produced a silver lighter and flashed the flame over to him. The cigaret didn't light the first time but the second time he pulled in his breath, it lit and his lungs were unpleasantly filled with smoke. The smoke had a peculiar odor.

"Got no folks, huh?" the man said again. "What road do you live on?"

"It ain't even a road to it," the boy said. "I lived with my great-uncle but he's dead, burnt up, and now it's only me." He began to cough violently.

The man reached across the dashboard and opened the glove compartment. Inside, lying on its side, was a flat bottle of whiskey. "Help yourself," he said. "It'll kill that cough."

It was an old-looking stamped bottle without the paper front on it and with a bitten-off cork in the top. "I get that special too," the man said. "If there's flies on you, you can't drink it."

The boy grasped the bottle and began to pull at the cork,

and simultaneously there came into his head all his great-uncle's warnings about poisonous liquor, all his idiot restrictions about riding with strangers. The essence of all the old man's foolishness flooded his mind like a rising tide of irritation. He grasped the bottle the more firmly and pulled at the cork, which was too far in, with his fingers. He put the bottle between his knees and took the schoolteacher's corkscrew-bottleopener out of his pocket.

"Say, that's nifty," the man said.

The boy smiled. He pushed the corkscrew in the cork and pulled it out. Never a thought of the old man's but he would change it now. "This here thing will open anything," he said.

The stranger was driving slowly, watching him.

He lifted the bottle to his lips and took a long swallow. The liquid had a deep barely concealed bitterness that he had not expected and it appeared to be thicker than any whiskey he had ever had before. It burned his throat savagely and his thirst raged anew so that he was obliged to take another and fuller swallow. The second was worse than the first and he perceived that the stranger was watching him with what might be a leer.

"Don't like it, huh?" he said.

The boy felt a little dizzy but he thrust his face forward and said, "It's better than the Bread of Life!" and his eyes glittered.

He sat back and took the cork off the opener and put it back on the bottle and returned the bottle to the compartment. Already his motions seemed to be slowing down. It took him some time to get his hand back in his lap. The stranger said nothing and Tarwater turned his face to the window.

The liquor lay like a hot rock in the pit of his stomach, heating his whole body, and he felt himself pleasantly deprived of responsibility or of the need for any effort to justify his actions. His thoughts were heavy as if they had to struggle up through some dense medium to reach the surface of his mind. He was looking into thick unfenced woods. The car moved almost slow enough for him to count the outside trunks and he began to count them, one, one, one, until they began to merge and flow together. He leaned his head against the glass and his heavy lids closed.

After a few minutes the stranger reached over and pushed his shoulder but he did not stir. The man then began to drive faster. He drove about five miles, speeding, before he espied a turnoff into a dirt road. He took the turn and raced along for a mile or two and then pulled his car off the side of the road and drove down into a secluded declivity near the edge of the woods. He was breathing rapidly and sweating. He got out and ran around the car and opened the other door and Tarwater fell out of it like a loosely-filled sack. The man picked him up and carried him into the woods.

Nothing passed on the dirt road and the sun continued to move with a brilliant blandness on its way. The woods were silent except for an occasional trill or caw. The air itself might have been drugged. Now and then a large silent floating bird would glide into the treetops and after a moment rise again.

In about an hour, the stranger emerged alone and looked furtively about him. He was carrying the boy's hat for a souvenir and also the corkscrew-bottleopener. His delicate skin had acquired a faint pink tint as if he had refreshed himself on blood. He got quickly into his car and sped away.

When Tarwater woke up, the sun was directly overhead, very small and silver, sifting down light that seemed to spend itself before it reached him. He saw first his thin white legs stretching in front of him. He was propped up against a log that lay across a small open space between two very tall trees. His hands were loosely tied with a lavender handkerchief which his friend had thought of as an exchange for the hat. His clothes were neatly piled by his side. Only his shoes were on him. He perceived that his hat was gone.

The boy's mouth twisted open and to the side as if it were going to displace itself permanently. In a second it appeared to be only a gap that would never be a mouth again. His eyes looked small and seedlike as if while he was asleep, they had been lifted out, scorched, and dropped back into his head. His expression seemed to contract until it reached some point beyond rage or pain. Then a loud dry cry tore out of him and his mouth fell back into place.

He began to tear savagely at the lavender handkerchief until he had shredded it off. Then he got into his clothes so quickly that when he finished he had half of them on backwards and did not notice. He stood staring down at the spot where the displaced leaves showed him to have lain. His hand was already in his pocket bringing out the box of wooden matches. He kicked the leaves together and set them on fire. Then he tore off a pine branch and set it on fire and began to fire all the bushes around the spot until the fire was eating greedily at the evil ground,

burning every spot the stranger could have touched. When
it was a roaring blaze, he turned and ran, still holding the
pine torch and lighting bushes as he went.

He barely noticed when he ran out of the woods onto
the bare red road. It streaked beneath him like fire hardened
and only gradually as his breath choked him did he slow
down and begin to take his bearings. The sky, the woods
on either side, the ground beneath him, came to a halt
and the road assumed direction. It swung down between
high red embankments and then mounted a flat field plowed
to its edges on either side. Off in the distance a shack, sunk
a little on one side, seemed to be afloat on the red folds.
Down the hill the wooden bridge lay like the skeleton of
some prehistoric beast across the stream bed. It was the
road home, ground that had been familiar to him since
his infancy but now it looked like strange and alien country.

He stood clenching the blackened burnt-out pine bough.
Then after a moment he began to move forward again
slowly. He knew that he could not turn back now. He
knew that his destiny forced him on to a final revelation.
His scorched eyes no longer looked hollow or as if they
were meant only to guide him forward. They looked as
if, touched with a coal like the lips of the prophet, they
would never be used for ordinary sights again.

Chapter 12

The broad road began to narrow until it was no more than a rutted rain-washed gulley which disappeared finally into a blackberry thicket. The sun, red and mammoth, was about to touch the treeline. Tarwater paused an instant here. His glance passed over the ripening berries, turned sharply and pierced into the wood which lay dark and dense before him. He drew in his breath and held it a second before he plunged forward, blindly following the faint path that led down through the wood to the clearing. The air was laden with the odor of honeysuckle and the sharper scent of pine but he scarcely recognized what they were. His senses were stunned and his thought too seemed suspended. Somewhere deep in the wood a woodthrush called and as if the sound were a key turned in the boy's heart, his throat began to tighten.

A faint evening breeze had begun to stir. He stepped over a tree fallen across his path and plunged on. A thorn vine caught in his shirt and tore it but he didn't stop. Farther away the woodthrush called again. With the same four formal notes it trilled its grief against the silence. He was heading straight for a gap in the wood where, through a forked birch, the clearing could be seen below, down the long hill and across the field. Always when he and his great-uncle were returning from the road, they would stop there. It had given the old man the greatest satisfaction to look out over the field and in the distance see his house settled between its chimneys, his stall, his lot, his corn. He might have been Moses glimpsing the promised land.

As Tarwater approached the tree, his shoulders were set high and tense. He seemed to be preparing himself to sustain a blow. The tree, forked a few feet from the ground, loomed in his way. He stopped and with a hand on either trunk, he leaned forward through the fork and looked out at an expanse of crimson sky. His gaze, like a bird that flies through fire, faltered and dropped. Where it fell, two chimneys stood like grieving figures guarding the blackened ground between them. His face appeared to shrink as he looked.

He remained motionless except for his hands. They clenched and unclenched. What he saw was what he had expected to see, an empty clearing. The old man's body was no longer there. His dust would not be mingling with the dust of the place, would not be washed by the seeping rains into the field. The wind by now had taken his ashes, dropped them and scattered them and lifted them up again and carried each mote a different way around the curve of the world. The clearing was burned free of all that had ever oppressed him. No cross was there to say that this was ground that the Lord still held. What he looked out upon was the sign of a broken covenant. The place was forsaken and his own. As he looked, his dry lips parted. They seemed to· be forced open by a hunger too great to be contained inside him. He stood there open-mouthed, as if he had no further power to move.

He felt a breeze on his neck as light as a breath and he half-turned, sensing that someone stood behind him. A sibilant shifting of air dropped like a sigh into his ear. The boy turned white.

Go down and take it, his friend whispered. It's ours. We've won it. Ever since you first begun to dig the grave, I've stood by you, never left your side, and now we can take it over together, just you and me. You're not ever going to be alone again.

The boy shuddered convulsively. The presence was as pervasive as an odor, a warm sweet body of air encircling him, a violent shadow hanging around his shoulders.

He shook himself free fiercely and grabbed the matches from his pocket and tore off another pine bough. He held the bough under his arm and with a shaking hand struck a match and held it to the needles until he had a burning brand. He plunged this into the lower branches of the forked tree. The flames crackled up, snapping for the drier leaves and rushing into them until an arch of fire blazed upward. He walked backwards from the spot pushing the torch into all the bushes he was moving away from, until he had made a rising wall of fire between him and the grinning presence. He glared through the flames and his spirits rose as he saw that his adversary would soon be consumed in a roaring blaze. He turned and moved on with the burning brand tightly clenched in his fist.

The path twisted downward through reddened tree trunks that gradually grew darker as the sun sank out of sight. From time to time he plunged the torch into a bush or tree and left it blazing behind him. The wood became less dense. Suddenly it opened and he stood at its edge, looking out on the flat cornfield and far across to the two chimneys. Planes of purpling red above the treeline stretched back like stairsteps to reach the dusk. The corn the old man had left planted was up about a foot and moved in wavering lines of green across the field. It had been freshly plowed. The boy stood there, a small rigid, hatless figure, holding the blackened pine bough.

As he looked, his hunger constricted him anew. It appeared to be outside him, surrounding him, almost as if it were visible before him, something he could reach out for and not quite touch. He sensed a strangeness about the place as if there might already be an occupant. Beyond the two chimneys, his eyes moved over the stall, gray and weathered, and crossed the back field and stopped at the far black wall of woods. A deep-filled quiet pervaded everything. The encroaching dusk seemed to come softly in deference to some mystery that resided here. He stood, leaning slightly forward. He appeared to be permanently suspended there, unable to go forward or back. He became conscious of the very breath he drew. Even the air seemed to belong to another.

Then near the stall he saw a Negro mounted on a mule. The mule was not moving; the two might have been made out of rock. He started forward across the field boldly, raising his fist in a gesture that was half-greeting and half-threat, but after a second his hand opened. He waved and began to run. It was Buford. He would go home with him and eat.

Instantly at the thought of food, he stopped and his muscles contracted with nausea. He blanched with the shock of a terrible premonition. He stood there and felt a crater opening inside him, and stretching out before him, surrounding him, he saw the clear gray spaces of that country where he had vowed never to set foot. Mechanically he began to move forward. He came out on the hard ground of the yard a few feet from the fig tree, but his eyes took the far circuit to it, lingering above the stall and moving beyond it to the far treeline and back. He knew that the next sight to meet his eyes would be the half-dug gaping grave, almost at his feet.

The Negro was watching him steadily. He began to move forward on the mule. When the boy finally forced his eyes to move again, he saw the mule's hooves first and then Buford's feet hanging at its sides. Above, the brown crinkled face was looking down at him with a scorn that could penetrate any surface.

The grave, freshly mounded, lay between them. Tarwater

lowered his eyes to it. At its head, a dark rough cross was set starkly in the bare ground. The boy's hands opened stiffly as if he were dropping something he had been clutching all his life. His gaze rested finally on the ground where the wood entered the grave.

Buford said, "It's owing to me he's resting there. I buried him while you were laid out drunk. It's owing to me his corn has been plowed. It's owing to me the sign of his Saviour is over his head."

Nothing seemed alive about the boy but his eyes and they stared downward at the cross as if they followed below the surface of the earth to where its roots encircled all the dead.

The Negro sat watching his strange spent face and grew uneasy. The skin across it tightened as he watched and the eyes, lifting beyond the grave, appeared to see something coming in the distance. Buford turned his head. The darkening field behind him stretched downward toward the woods. When he looked back again, the boy's vision seemed to pierce the very air. The Negro trembled and felt suddenly a pressure on him too great to bear. He sensed it as a burning in the atmosphere. His nostrils twitched. He muttered something and turned the mule around and moved off, across the back field and down to the woods.

The boy remained standing there, his still eyes reflecting the field the Negro had crossed. It seemed to him no longer empty but peopled with a multitude. Everywhere, he saw dim figures seated on the slope and as he gazed he saw that from a single basket the throng was being fed. His eyes searched the crowd for a long time as if he could not find the one he was looking for. Then he saw him. The old man was lowering himself to the ground. When he was down and his bulk had settled, he leaned forward, his face turned toward the basket, impatiently following its progress toward him. The boy too leaned forward, aware at last of the object of his hunger, aware that it was the same as the old man's and that nothing on earth would fill him. His hunger was so great that he could have eaten all the loaves and fishes after they were multiplied.

He stood there, straining forward, but the scene faded in the gathering darkness. Night descended until there was nothing but a thin streak of red between it and the black line of earth but still he stood there. He felt his hunger no longer as a pain but as a tide. He felt it rising in himself through time and darkness, rising through the centuries, and he knew that it rose in a line of men whose lives were chosen to sustain it, who would wander in the world, strangers from that violent country where the silence is never broken except to shout the truth. He felt it building from the blood of Abel to his own, rising and engulfing him. It seemed in one instant to lift and turn him. He whirled toward the treeline. There, rising and spreading in the night, a red-gold tree of fire ascended as if it would consume the darkness in one tremendous burst of flame. The boy's breath went out to meet it. He knew that this was the fire that had encircled Daniel, that had raised Elijah from the earth, that had spoken to Moses and would in the instant speak to him. He threw himself to the ground and with his face against the dirt of the grave, he heard to command. GO WARN THE CHILDREN OF GOD OF THE TERRIBLE SPEED OF MERCY. The words were as silent as seeds opening one at a time in his blood.

When finally he raised himself, the burning bush had disappeared. A line of fire ate languidly at the treeline and here and there a thin crest of flame rose farther back in the woods where a dull red cloud of smoke had gathered. The boy stooped and picked up a handful of dirt off his great-uncle's grave and smeared it on his forehead. Then after a moment, without looking back he moved across the far field and off the way Buford had gone.

By midnight he had left the road and the burning woods behind him and had come out on the highway once more. The moon, riding low above the field beside him, appeared and disappeared, diamond-bright, between patches of darkness. Intermittently the boy's jagged shadow slanted across the road ahead of him as if it cleared a rough path toward his goal. His singed eyes, black in their deep sockets, seemed already to envision the fate that awaited him but he moved steadily on, his face set toward the dark city, where the children of God lay sleeping.

EVERYTHING
THAT RISES
MUST CONVERGE

Everything That Rises
Must Converge

Her doctor had told Julian's mother that she must lose twenty pounds on account of her blood pressure, so on Wednesday nights Julian had to take her downtown on the bus for a reducing class at the Y. The reducing class was designed for working girls over fifty, who weighed from 165 to 200 pounds. His mother was one of the slimmer ones, but she said ladies did not tell their age or weight. She would not ride the buses by herself at night since they had been integrated, and because the reducing class was one of her few pleasures, necessary for her health, and *free*, she said Julian could at least put himself out to take her, considering all she did for him. Julian did not like to consider all she did for him, but every Wednesday night he braced himself and took her.

She was almost ready to go, standing before the hall mirror, putting on her hat, while he, his hands behind him, appeared pinned to the door frame, waiting like Saint Sebastian for the arrows to begin piercing him. The hat was new and had cost her seven dollars and a half. She kept saying, "Maybe I shouldn't have paid that for it. No, I shouldn't have. I'll take it off and return it tomorrow. I shouldn't have bought it."

Julian raised his eyes to heaven. "Yes, you should have bought it," he said. "Put it on and let's go." It was a hideous hat. A purple velvet flap came down on one side of it and stood up on the other; the rest of it was green and looked like a cushion with the stuffing out. He decided it was less comical than jaunty and pathetic. Everything that gave her pleasure was small and depressed him.

She lifted the hat one more time and set it down slowly on top of her head. Two wings of gray hair protruded on either side of her florid face, but her eyes, sky-blue, were as innocent and untouched by experience as they must have been when she was ten. Were it not that she was a widow who had struggled fiercely to feed and clothe and put him through school and who was supporting him still, "until he got on his feet," she might have been a little girl that he had to take to town.

"It's all right, it's all right," he said. "Let's go." He opened the door himself and started down the walk to get her going. The sky was a dying violet and the houses stood out darkly against it, bulbous liver-colored monstrosities of a uniform ugliness though no two were alike. Since this had been a fashionable neighborhood forty years ago, his mother persisted in thinking they did well to have an apartment in it. Each house had a narrow collar of dirt around it in which sat, usually, a grubby child. Julian walked with his hands in his pockets, his head down and thrust forward and his eyes glazed with the determination to make himself completely numb during the time he would be sacrificed to her pleasure.

The door closed and he turned to find the dumpy figure, surmounted by the atrocious hat, coming toward him. "Well," she said, "you only live once and paying a little more for it, I at least won't meet myself coming and going."

"Some day I'll start making money," Julian said gloomily—he knew he never would—"and you can have one of those jokes whenever you take the fit." But first they would move. He visualized a place where the nearest neighbors would be three miles away on either side.

"I think you're doing fine," she said, drawing on her gloves. "You've only been out of school a year. Rome wasn't built in a day."

She was one of the few members of the Y reducing class who arrived in hat and gloves and who had a son who had been to college. "It takes time," she said, "and the world is in such a mess. This hat looked better on me than any of the others, though when she brought it out I said, 'Take that thing back. I wouldn't have it on my head,' and she said, 'Now wait till you see it on,' and when she put it on me, I said, 'We-ull,' and she said, 'If you ask me, that hat does something for you and you do something for the hat, and besides,' she said, 'with that hat, you won't meet yourself coming and going.'"

Julian thought he could have stood his lot better if she had been selfish, if she had been an old hag who drank and screamed at him. He walked along, saturated in depression, as if in the midst of his martyrdom he had lost his faith. Catching sight of his long, hopeless, irritated face, she stopped suddenly with a grief-stricken look, and pulled back on his arm. "Wait on me," she said. "I'm going back to the house and take this thing off and tomorrow I'm going to return it. I was out of my mind. I can pay the gas bill with that seven-fifty."

He caught her arm in a vicious grip. "You are not going to take it back," he said. "I like it."

"Well," she said, "I don't think I ought . . ."

"Shut up and enjoy it," he muttered, more depressed than ever.

"With the world in the mess it's in," she said, "it's a wonder we can enjoy anything. I tell you, the bottom rail is on the top."

Julian sighed.

"Of course," she said, "if you know who you are, you can go anywhere." She said this every time he took her to the reducing class. "Most of them in it are not our kind of people," she said, "but I can be gracious to anybody. I know who I am."

"They don't give a damn for your graciousness," Julian said savagely. "Knowing who you are is good for one generation only. You haven't the foggiest idea where you stand now or who you are."

She stopped and allowed her eyes to flash at him. "I most certainly do know who I am," she said, "and if you don't know who you are, I'm ashamed of you."

"Oh hell," Julian said.

"Your great-grandfather was a former governor of this state," she said. "Your grandfather was a prosperous landowner. Your grandmother was a Godhigh."

"Will you look around you," he said tensely, "and see where you are now?" and he swept his arm jerkily out to indicate the neighborhood, which the growing darkness at least made less dingy.

"You remain what you are," she said. "Your great-grandfather had a plantation and two hundred slaves."

"There are no more slaves," he said irritably.

"They were better off when they were," she said. He groaned to see that she was off on that topic. She rolled onto it every few days like a train on an open track. He knew every stop, every junction, every swamp along the way, and knew the exact point at which her conclusion would roll majestically into the station: "It's ridiculous. It's simply not realistic. They should rise, yes, but on their own side of the fence."

"Let's skip it," Julian said.

"The ones I feel sorry for," she said, "are the ones that are half white. They're tragic."

"Will you skip it?"

"Suppose we were half white. We would certainly have mixed feelings."

"I have mixed feelings now," he groaned.

"Well let's talk about something pleasant," she said. "I remember going to Grandpa's when I was a little girl. Then the house had double stairways that went up to what was really the second floor—all the cooking was done on the first. I used to like to stay down in the kitchen on account of the way the walls smelled. I would sit with my nose pressed against the plaster and take deep breaths. Actually the place belonged to the Godhighs but your grandfather Chestny paid the mortgage and saved it for them. They were in reduced circumstances," she said, "but reduced or not, they never forgot who they were."

"Doubtless that decayed mansion reminded them," Julian muttered. He never spoke of it without contempt or thought of it without longing. He had seen it once when he was a child before it had been sold. The double stairways had rotted and been torn down. Negroes were living in it. But it remained in his mind as his mother had known it. It appeared in his dreams regularly. He would stand on the wide porch, listening to the rustle of oak leaves, then wander through the high-ceilinged hall into the parlor that opened onto it and gaze at the worn rugs and faded draperies. It occurred to him that it was he, not she, who could have appreciated it. He preferred its threadbare elegance to anything he could name and it was because of it that all the neighborhoods they had lived in had been a torment to him—whereas she had hardly known the difference. She called her insensitivity "being adjustable."

"And I remember the old darky who was my nurse, Caroline. There was no better person in the world. I've always had a great respect for my colored friends," she said. "I'd do anything in the world for them and they'd . . ."

"Will you for God's sake get off that subject?" Julian said. When he got on a bus by himself, he made it a point to sit down beside a Negro, in reparation as it were for his mother's sins.

"You're mighty touchy tonight," she said. "Do you feel all right?"

"Yes I feel all right," he said. "Now lay off."

She pursed her lips. "Well, you certainly are in a vile humor," she observed. "I just won't speak to you at all."

They had reached the bus stop. There was no bus in sight and Julian, his hands still jammed in his pockets and his head thrust forward, scowled down the empty street. The frustration of having to wait on the bus as well as ride on it began to creep up his neck like a hot hand. The presence of his mother was borne in upon him as she gave a pained sigh. He looked at her bleakly. She was holding herself very erect under the preposterous hat, wearing it like a banner of her imaginary dignity. There was in him an evil urge to break her spirit. He suddenly unloosened his tie and pulled it off and put it in his pocket.

She stiffened. "Why must you look like *that* when you take me to town?" she said. "Why must you deliberately embarrass me?"

"If you'll never learn where you are," he said, "you can at least learn where I am."

"You look like a—thug," she said.

"Then I must be one," he murmured.

"I'll just go home," she said. "I will not bother you. If you can't do a little thing like that for me . . ."

Rolling his eyes upward, he put his tie back on. "Restored to my class," he muttered. He thrust his face toward her and hissed, "True culture is in the mind, the *mind*," he said, and tapped his head, "the mind."

"It's in the heart," she said, "and in how you do things and how you do things is because of who you *are*."

"Nobody in the damn bus cares who you are."

"I care who I am," she said icily.

The lighted bus appeared on top of the next hill and as it approached, they moved out into the street to meet it. He put his hand under her elbow and hoisted her up on the creaking step. She entered with a little smile, as if she were going into a drawing room where everyone had been waiting for her. While he put in the tokens, she sat down on one of the broad front seats for three which faced the aisle. A thin woman with protruding teeth and long yellow hair was sitting on the end of it. His mother moved up beside her and left room for Julian beside herself. He sat down and looked at the floor across the aisle where a pair of thin feet in red and white canvas sandals were planted.

His mother immediately began a general conversation meant to attract anyone who felt like talking. "Can it get any hotter?" she said and removed from her purse a folding fan, black with a Japanese scene on it, which she began to flutter before her.

"I reckon it might could," the woman with the protruding teeth said, "but I know for a fact my apartment couldn't get no hotter."

"It must get the afternoon sun," his mother said. She sat forward and looked up and down the bus. It was half filled.

Everybody was white. "I see we have the bus to ourselves," she said. Julian cringed.

"For a change," said the woman across the aisle, the owner of the red and white canvas sandals. "I come on one the other day and they were thick as fleas—up front and all through."

"The world is in a mess everywhere," his mother said. "I don't know how we've let it get in this fix."

"What gets my goat is all those boys from good families stealing automobile tires," the woman with the protruding teeth said. "I told my boy, I said you may not be rich but you been raised right and if I ever catch you in any such mess, they can send you on to the reformatory. Be exactly where you belong."

"Training tells," his mother said. "Is your boy in high school?"

"Ninth grade," the woman said.

"My son just finished college last year. He wants to write but he's selling typewriters until he gets started," his mother said.

The woman leaned forward and peered at Julian. He threw her such a malevolent look that she subsided against the seat. On the floor across the aisle there was an abandoned newspaper. He got up and got it and opened it out in front of him. His mother discreetly continued the conversation in a lower tone but the woman across the aisle said in a loud voice, "Well that's nice. Selling typewriters is close to writing. He can go right from one to the other."

"I tell him," his mother said, "that Rome wasn't built in a day."

Behind the newspaper Julian was withdrawing into the inner compartment of his mind where he spent most of his time. This was a kind of mental bubble in which he established himself when he could not bear to be a part of what was going on around him. From it he could see out and judge but in it he was safe from any kind of penetration from without. It was the only place where he felt free of the general idiocy of his fellows. His mother had never entered it but from it he could see her with absolute clarity.

The old lady was clever enough and he thought that if she had started from any of the right premises, more might have been expected of her. She lived according to the laws of her own fantasy world, outside of which he had never seen her set foot. The law of it was to sacrifice herself for him after she had first created the necessity to do so by making a mess of things. If he had permitted her sacrifices, it was only because her lack of foresight had made them necessary. All of her life had been a struggle to act like a Chestny without the Chestny goods, and to give him everything she thought a Chestny ought to have; but since, said she, it was fun to struggle, why complain? And when you had won, as she had won, what fun to look back on the hard times! He could not forgive her that she had enjoyed the struggle and that she thought *she* had won.

What she meant when she said she had won was that she had brought him up successfully and had sent him to college and that he had turned out so well—good looking (her teeth had gone unfilled so that his could be straightened), intelligent (he realized he was too intelligent to be a success), and with a future ahead of him (there was of course no future ahead of him). She excused his gloominess on the grounds that he was still growing up and his radical ideas on his lack of practical experience. She said he didn't yet know a thing about "life," that he hadn't even entered the real world—when already he was as disenchanted with it as a man of fifty.

The further irony of all this was that in spite of her, he had turned out so well. In spite of going to only a third-rate college, he had, on his own initiative, come out with a first-rate education; in spite of growing up dominated by a small mind, he had ended up with a large one; in spite of all her foolish views, he was free of prejudice and unafraid to face facts. Most miraculous of all, instead of being blinded by love for her as she was for him, he had cut himself emotionally free of her and could see her with complete objectivity. He was not dominated by his mother.

The bus stopped with a sudden jerk and shook him from his meditation. A woman from the back lurched forward with little steps and barely escaped falling in his newspaper as she righted herself. She got off and a large Negro got on. Julian kept his paper lowered to watch. It gave him a certain satisfaction to see injustice in daily operation. It confirmed his view that with a few exceptions there was no one worth knowing within a radius of three hundred miles. The Negro was well dressed and carried a briefcase. He looked around and then sat down on the other end of the seat where the woman with the red and white canvas sandals was sitting. He immediately unfolded a newspaper and obscured himself behind it. Julian's mother's elbow at once prodded insistently into his ribs. "Now you see why I won't ride on these buses by myself," she whispered.

The woman with the red and white canvas sandals had

risen at the same time the Negro sat down and had gone further back in the bus and taken the seat of the woman who
had got off. His mother leaned forward and cast her an ap-
proving look.

Julian rose, crossed the aisle, and sat down in the place of
the woman with the canvas sandals. From this position, he
looked serenely across at his mother. Her face had turned an
angry red. He stared at her, making his eyes the eyes of a
stranger. He felt his tension suddenly lift as if he had openly
declared war on her.

He would have liked to get in conversation with the Negro
and to talk with him about art or politics or any subject that
would be above the comprehension of those around them, but
the man remained entrenched behind his paper. He was either ignoring the change of seating or had never noticed it.
There was no way for Julian to convey his sympathy.

His mother kept her eyes fixed reproachfully on his face.
The woman with the protruding teeth was looking at him av-
idly as if he were a type of monster new to her.

"Do you have a light?" he asked the Negro.

Without looking away from his paper, the man reached in
his pocket and handed him a packet of matches.

"Thanks," Julian said. For a moment he held the matches
foolishly. A NO SMOKING sign looked down upon him from
over the door. This alone would not have deterred him; he had
no cigarettes. He had quit smoking some months before because he could not afford it. "Sorry," he muttered and
handed back the matches. The Negro lowered the paper and
gave him an annoyed look. He took the matches and raised
the paper again.

His mother continued to gaze at him but she did not take
advantage of his momentary discomfort. Her eyes retained
their battered look. Her face seemed to be unnaturally red, as
if her blood pressure had risen. Julian allowed no glimmer of
sympathy to show on his face. Having got the advantage, he
wanted desperately to keep it and carry it through. He would
have liked to teach her a lesson that would last her a while,
but there seemed no way to continue the point. The Negro
refused to come out from behind his paper.

Julian folded his arms and looked stolidly before him, facing her but as if he did not see her, as if he had ceased to
recognize her existence. He visualized a scene in which, the
bus having reached their stop, he would remain in his seat
and when she said, "Aren't you going to get off?" he would
look at her as at a stranger who had rashly addressed him.
The corner they got off on was usually deserted, but it was

well lighted and it would not hurt her to walk by herself the four blocks to the Y. He decided to wait until the time came and then decide whether or not he would let her get off by herself. He would have to be at the Y at ten to bring her back, but he could leave her wondering if he was going to show up. There was no reason for her to think she could always depend on him.

He retired again into the high-ceilinged room sparsely settled with large pieces of antique furniture. His soul expanded momentarily but then he became aware of his mother across from him and the vision shriveled. He studied her coldly. Her feet in little pumps dangled like a child's and did not quite reach the floor. She was training on him an exaggerated look of reproach. He felt completely detached from her. At that moment he could with pleasure have slapped her as he would have slapped a particularly obnoxious child in his charge.

He began to imagine various unlikely ways by which he could teach her a lesson. He might make friends with some distinguished Negro professor or lawyer and bring him home to spend the evening. He would be entirely justified but her blood pressure would rise to 300. He could not push her to the extent of making her have a stroke, and moreover, he had never been successful at making any Negro friends. He had tried to strike up an acquaintance on the bus with some of the better types, with ones that looked like professors or ministers or lawyers. One morning he had sat down next to a distinguished-looking dark brown man who had answered his questions with a sonorous solemnity but who had turned out to be an undertaker. Another day he had sat down beside a cigar-smoking Negro with a diamond ring on his finger, but after a few stilted pleasantries, the Negro had rung the buzzer and risen, slipping two lottery tickets into Julian's hand as he climbed over him to leave.

He imagined his mother lying desperately ill and his being able to secure only a Negro doctor for her. He toyed with that idea for a few minutes and then dropped it for a momentary vision of himself participating as a sympathizer in a sit-in demonstration. This was possible but he did not linger with it. Instead, he approached the ultimate horror. He brought home a beautiful suspiciously Negroid woman. Prepare yourself, he said. There is nothing you can do about it. This is the woman I've chosen. She's intelligent, dignified, even good, and she's suffered and she hasn't thought it *fun*. Now persecute us, go ahead and persecute us. Drive her out of here, but remember, you're driving me too. His eyes were narrowed and through the indignation he had generated, he saw his mother across the aisle, purple-faced, shrunken to the dwarf-like proportions of her moral nature, sitting like a mummy beneath the ridiculous banner of her hat.

He was tilted out of his fantasy again as the bus stopped. The door opened with a sucking hiss and out of the dark a large, gaily dressed, sullen-looking colored woman got on with a little boy. The child, who might have been four, had on a short plaid suit and a Tyrolean hat with a blue feather in it. Julian hoped that he would sit down beside him and that the woman would push in beside his mother. He could think of no better arrangement.

As she waited for her tokens, the woman was surveying the seating possibilities—he hoped with the idea of sitting where she was least wanted. There was something familiar-looking about her but Julian could not place what it was. She was a giant of a woman. Her face was set not only to meet opposition but to seek it out. The downward tilt of her large lower lip was like a warning sign: DON'T TAMPER WITH ME. Her bulging figure was encased in a green crepe dress and her feet overflowed in red shoes. She had on a hideous hat. A purple velvet flap came down on one side of it and stood up on the other; the rest of it was green and looked like a cushion with the stuffing out. She carried a mammoth red pocketbook that bulged throughout as if it were stuffed with rocks.

To Julian's disappointment, the little boy climbed up on the empty seat beside his mother. His mother lumped all children, black and white, into the common category, "cute," and she thought little Negroes were on the whole cuter than little white children. She smiled at the little boy as he climbed on the seat.

Meanwhile the woman was bearing down upon the empty seat beside Julian. To his annoyance, she squeezed herself into it. He saw his mother's face change as the woman settled herself next to him and he realized with satisfaction that this was more objectionable to her than it was to him. Her face seemed almost gray and there was a look of dull recognition in her eyes, as if suddenly she had sickened at some awful confrontation. Julian saw that it was because she and the woman had, in a sense, swapped sons. Though his mother would not realize the symbolic significance of this, she would feel it. His amusement showed plainly on his face.

The woman next to him muttered something unintelligible to herself. He was conscious of a kind of bristling next to him, a muted growling like that of an angry cat. He could not see anything but the red pocketbook upright on the bulging green thighs. He visualized the woman as she had stood waiting for her tokens—the ponderous figure, rising from the red shoes upward over the solid hips, the mammoth bosom, the haughty face, to the green and purple hat.

His eyes widened.

The vision of the two hats, identical, broke upon him with the radiance of a brilliant sunrise. His face was suddenly lit with joy. He could not believe that Fate had thrust upon his mother such a lesson. He gave a loud chuckle so that she would look at him and see that he saw. She turned her eyes on him slowly. The blue in them seemed to have turned a bruised purple. For a moment he had an uncomfortable sense of her innocence, but it lasted only a second before principle rescued him. Justice entitled him to laugh. His grin hardened until it said to her as plainly as if he were saying aloud: Your punishment exactly fits your pettiness. This should teach you a permanent lesson.

Her eyes shifted to the woman. She seemed unable to bear looking at him and to find the woman preferable. He became conscious again of the bristling presence at his side. The woman was rumbling like a volcano about to become active. His mother's mouth began to twitch slightly at one corner. With a sinking heart, he saw incipient signs of recovery on her face and realized that this was going to strike her suddenly as funny and was going to be no lesson at all. She kept her eyes on the woman and an amused smile came over her face as if the woman were a monkey that had stolen her hat. The little Negro was looking up at her with large fascinated eyes. He had been trying to attract her attention for some time.

"Carver!" the woman said suddenly. "Come heah!"

When he saw that the spotlight was on him at last, Carver drew his feet up and turned himself toward Julian's mother and giggled.

"Carver!" the woman said. "You heah me? Come heah!"

Carver slid down from the seat but remained squatting with his back against the base of it, his head turned slyly around toward Julian's mother, who was smiling at him. The woman reached a hand across the aisle and snatched him to her. He righted himself and hung backwards on her knees, grinning at Julian's mother. "Isn't he cute?" Julian's mother said to the woman with the protruding teeth.

"I reckon he is," the woman said without conviction.

The Negress yanked him upright but he eased out of her grip and shot across the aisle and scrambled, giggling wildly, onto the seat beside his love.

"I think he likes me," Julian's mother said, and smiled at the woman. It was the smile she used when she was being particularly gracious to an inferior. Julian saw everything lost. The lesson had rolled off her like rain on a roof.

The woman stood up and yanked the little boy off the seat as if she were snatching him from contagion. Julian could feel the rage in her at having no weapon like his mother's smile. She gave the child a sharp slap across his leg. He howled once and then thrust his head into her stomach and kicked his feet against her shins. "Be-have," she said vehemently.

The bus stopped and the Negro who had been reading the newspaper got off. The woman moved over and set the little boy down with a thump between herself and Julian. She held him firmly by the knee. In a moment he put his hands in front of his face and peeped at Julian's mother through his fingers.

"I see yoooooooo!" she said and put her hand in front of her face and peeped at him.

The woman slapped his hand down. "Quit yo' foolishness," she said, "before I knock the living Jesus out of you!"

Julian was thankful that the next stop was theirs. He reached up and pulled the cord. The woman reached up and pulled it at the same time. Oh my God, he thought. He had the terrible intuition that when they got off the bus together, his mother would open her purse and give the little boy a nickel. The gesture would be as natural to her as breathing. The bus stopped and the woman got up and lunged to the front, dragging the child, who wished to stay on, after her. Julian and his mother got up and followed. As they neared the door, Julian tried to relieve her of her pocketbook.

"No," she murmured, "I want to give the little boy a nickel."

"No!" Julian hissed. "No!"

She smiled down at the child and opened her bag. The bus door opened and the woman picked him up by the arm and descended with him, hanging at her hip. Once in the street she set him down and shook him.

Julian's mother had to close her purse while she got down the bus step but as soon as her feet were on the ground, she opened it again and began to rummage inside. "I can't find but a penny," she whispered, "but it looks like a new one."

"Don't do it!" Julian said fiercely between his teeth. There was a streetlight on the corner and she hurried to get under it so that she could better see into her pocketbook. The woman was heading off rapidly down the street with the child still hanging backward on her hand.

"Oh little boy!" Julian's mother called and took a few quick steps and caught up with them just beyond the lamppost. "Here's a bright new penny for you," and she held out the coin, which shone bronze in the dim light.

The huge woman turned and for a moment stood, her shoulders lifted and her face frozen with frustrated rage, and stared at Julian's mother. Then all at once she seemed to explode like a piece of machinery that had been given one ounce of pressure too much. Julian saw the black fist swing out with the red pocketbook. He shut his eyes and cringed as he heard the woman shout, "He don't take nobody's pennies!" When he opened his eyes, the woman was disappearing down the street with the little boy staring wide-eyed over her shoulder. Julian's mother was sitting on the sidewalk.

"I told you not to do that," Julian said angrily. "I told you not to do that!"

He stood over her for a minute, gritting his teeth. Her legs were stretched out in front of her and her hat was on her lap. He squatted down and looked her in the face. It was totally expressionless. "You got exactly what you deserved," he said. "Now get up."

He picked up her pocketbook and put what had fallen out back in it. He picked the hat up off her lap. The penny caught his eye on the sidewalk and he picked that up and let it drop before her eyes into the purse. Then he stood up and leaned over and held his hands out to pull her up. She remained immobile. He sighed. Rising above them on either side were black apartment buildings, marked with irregular rectangles of light. At the end of the block a man came out of a door and walked off in the opposite direction. "All right," he said, "suppose somebody happens by and wants to know why you're sitting on the sidewalk?"

She took the hand and, breathing hard, pulled heavily up on it and then stood for a moment, swaying slightly as if the spots of light in the darkness were circling around her. Her eyes, shadowed and confused, finally settled on his face. He did not try to conceal his irritation. "I hope this teaches you a lesson," he said. She leaned forward and her eyes raked his face. She seemed trying to determine his identity. Then, as if she found nothing familiar about him, she started off with a headlong movement in the wrong direction.

"Aren't you going on to the Y?" he asked.

"Home," she muttered.

"Well, are we walking?"

For answer she kept going. Julian followed along, his hands behind him. He saw no reason to let the lesson she had had go without backing it up with an explanation of its meaning. She might as well be made to understand what had happened to her. "Don't think that was just an uppity Negro woman," he said. "That was the whole colored race which will no longer take your condescending pennies. That was your black double. She can wear the same hat as you, and to be sure," he added gratuitously (because he thought it was funny), "it looked better on her than it did on you. What all this means," he said, "is that the old world is gone. The old manners are obsolete and your graciousness is not worth a damn." He thought bitterly of the house that had been lost for him. "You aren't who you think you are," he said.

She continued to plow ahead, paying no attention to him. Her hair had come undone on one side. She dropped her pocketbook and took no notice. He stopped and picked it up and handed it to her but she did not take it. *Coming unraveled*

"You needn't act as if the world had come to an end," he said, "because it hasn't. From now on you've got to live in a new world and face a few realities for a change. Buck up," he said, "it won't kill you."

She was breathing fast.

"Let's wait on the bus," he said.

"Home," she said thickly. *Heaven*

"I hate to see you behave like this," he said. "Just like a child. I should be able to expect more of you." He decided to stop where he was and make her stop and wait for a bus. "I'm not going any farther," he said, stopping. "We're going on the bus."

She continued to go on as if she had not heard him. He took a few steps and caught her arm and stopped her. He looked into her face and caught his breath. He was looking into a face he had never seen before. "Tell Grandpa to come get me," she said.

He stared, stricken.

"Tell Caroline to come get me," she said.

Stunned, he let her go and she lurched forward again, walking as if one leg were shorter than the other. A tide of darkness seemed to be sweeping her from him. "Mother!" he cried. "Darling, sweetheart, wait!" Crumpling, she fell to the pavement. He dashed forward and fell at her side, crying, "Mamma, Mamma!" He turned her over. Her face was fiercely distorted. One eye, large and staring, moved slightly to the left as if it had become unmoored. The other remained fixed on him, raked his face again, found nothing and closed.

"Wait here, wait here!" he cried and jumped up and began to run for help toward a cluster of lights he saw in the distance ahead of him. "Help, help!" he shouted, but his voice was thin, scarcely a thread of sound. The lights drifted farther away the faster he ran and his feet moved numbly as if they carried him nowhere. The tide of darkness seemed to sweep him back to her, postponing from moment to moment his entry into the world of guilt and sorrow.

Greenleaf

Mrs. May's bedroom window was low and faced on the east and the bull, silvered in the moonlight, stood under it, his head raised as if he listened—like some patient god come down to woo her—for a stir inside the room. The window was dark and the sound of her breathing too light to be carried outside. Clouds crossing the moon blackened him and in the dark he began to tear at the hedge. Presently they passed and he appeared again in the same spot, chewing steadily, with a hedge-wreath that he had ripped loose for himself caught in the tips of his horns. When the moon drifted into retirement again, there was nothing to mark his place but the sound of steady chewing. Then abruptly a pink glow filled the window. Bars of light slid across him as the venetian blind was slit. He took a step backward and lowered his head as if to show the wreath across his horns.

For almost a minute there was no sound from inside, then as he raised his crowned head again, a woman's voice, guttural as if addressed to a dog, said, "Get away from here, Sir!" and in a second muttered, "Some nigger's scrub bull."

The animal pawed the ground and Mrs. May, standing bent forward behind the blind, closed it quickly lest the light make him charge into the shrubbery. For a second she waited, still bent forward, her nightgown hanging loosely from her narrow shoulders. Green rubber curlers sprouted neatly over her forehead and her face beneath them was smooth as concrete with an egg-white paste that drew the wrinkles out while she slept.

She had been conscious in her sleep of a steady rhythmic chewing as if something were eating one wall of the house. She had been aware that whatever it was had been eating as long as she had had the place and had eaten everything from the beginning of her fence line up to the house and now was eating the house and calmly with the same steady rhythm would continue through the house, eating her and the boys, and then on, eating everything but the Greenleafs, on and on, eating everything until nothing was left but the Greenleafs on a little island all their own in the middle of what had been her place. When the munching reached her elbow, she jumped up and found herself, fully awake, standing in the middle of her room. She identified the sound at once: a cow was tearing at the shrubbery under her window. Mr. Greenleaf had left the lane gate open and she didn't doubt that the entire herd was on her lawn. She turned on the dim pink table lamp and then went to the window and slit the blind. The bull, gaunt and long-legged, was standing about four feet from her, chewing calmly like an uncouth country suitor.

For fifteen years, she thought as she squinted at him fiercely, she had been having shiftless people's hogs root up her oats, their mules wallow on her lawn, their scrub bulls breed her cows. If this one was not put up now, he would be over the fence, ruining her herd before morning—and Mr. Greenleaf was soundly sleeping a half mile down the road in the tenant house. There was no way to get him unless she dressed and got in her car and rode down there and woke him up. He would come but his expression, his whole figure, his every pause, would say: "Hit looks to me like one or both of them boys would not make their maw ride out in the middle of the night thisaway. If hit was my boys, they would have got thet bull up theirself."

The bull lowered his head and shook it and the wreath slipped down to the base of his horns where it looked like a menacing prickly crown. She had closed the blind then; in a few seconds she heard him move off heavily.

Mr. Greenleaf would say, "If hit was my boys they would never have allowed their maw to go after hired help in the middle of the night. They would have did it theirself."

Weighing it, she decided not to bother Mr. Greenleaf. She returned to bed thinking that if the Greenleaf boys had risen in the world it was because she had given their father employment when no one else would have him. She had had Mr. Greenleaf fifteen years but no one else would have had him five minutes. Just the way he approached an object was enough to tell anybody with eyes what kind of a worker he was. He walked with a high-shouldered creep and he never appeared to come directly forward. He walked on the perimeter of some invisible circle and if you wanted to look him in the face, you had to move and get in front of him. She had not fired him because she had always doubted she could do better. He was too shiftless to go out and look for another job; he didn't have the initiative to steal, and after she had told him three or four times to do a thing, he did it; but he never told her about a sick cow until it was too late to call the veterinarian and if her barn had caught on fire, he would have called his wife to see the flames before he began to put them out. And of the wife, she didn't even like to think. Beside the wife, Mr. Greenleaf was an aristocrat.

"If it had been my boys," he would have said, "they would have cut off their right arm before they would have allowed their maw to. . . ."

"If your boys had any pride, Mr. Greenleaf," she would like to say to him some day, "there are many things that they would not *allow* their mother to do."

The next morning as soon as Mr. Greenleaf came to the back door, she told him there was a stray bull on the place and that she wanted him penned up at once.

"Done already been here three days," he said, addressing his right foot which he held forward, turned slightly as if he were trying to look at the sole. He was standing at the bottom of the three back steps while she leaned out the kitchen door, a small woman with pale near-sighted eyes and grey hair that rose on top like the crest of some disturbed bird.

"Three days!" she said in the restrained screech that had become habitual with her.

Mr. Greenleaf, looking into the distance over the near pasture, removed a package of cigarets from his shirt pocket and let one fall into his hand. He put the package back and stood for a while looking at the cigaret. "I put him in the bull pen but he torn out of there," he said presently. "I didn't see him none after that." He bent over the cigaret and lit it and then turned his head briefly in her direction. The upper part of his face sloped gradually into the lower which was long and narrow, shaped like a rough chalice. He had deep-set fox-colored eyes shadowed under a grey felt hat that he wore slanted forward following the line of his nose. His build was insignificant.

"Mr. Greenleaf," she said, "get that bull up this morning before you do anything else. You know he'll ruin the breeding schedule. Get him up and keep him up and the next time there's a stray bull on this place, tell me at once. Do you understand?"

"Where you want him put at?" Mr. Greenleaf asked.

"I don't care where you put him," she said. "You are supposed to have some sense. Put him where he can't get out. Whose bull is he?"

For a moment Mr. Greenleaf seemed to hesitate between silence and speech. He studied the air to the left of him. "He must be somebody's bull," he said after a while.

"Yes, he must!" she said and shut the door with a precise little slam.

She went into the dining room where the two boys were eating breakfast and sat down on the edge of her chair at the head of the table. She never ate breakfast but she sat with them to see that they had what they wanted. "Honestly!" she said, and began to tell about the bull, aping Mr. Greenleaf saying, "It must be *somebody's* bull."

Wesley continued to read the newspaper folded beside his plate but Scofield interrupted his eating from time to time to look at her and laugh. The two boys never had the same reaction to anything. They were as different, she said, as night and day. The only thing they did have in common was that neither of them cared what happened to the place. Scofield was a business type and Wesley was an intellectual.

Wesley, the younger child, had had rheumatic fever when he was seven and Mrs. May thought that this was what had caused him to be an intellectual. Scofield, who had never had a day's sickness in his life, was an insurance salesman. She would not have minded his selling insurance if he had sold a nicer kind but he sold the kind that only Negroes buy. He was what Negroes call a "policy man." He said there was more money in nigger-insurance than any other kind, and before company, he was very loud about it. He would shout, "Mamma don't like to hear me say it but I'm the best nigger-insurance salesman in this county!"

Scofield was thirty-six and he had a broad pleasant smiling face but he was not married. "Yes," Mrs. May would say, "and if you sold decent insurance, some *nice* girl would be willing to marry you. What nice girl wants to marry a nigger-insurance man? You'll wake up some day and it'll be too late."

And at this Scofield would yodel and say, "Why Mamma, I'm not going to marry until you're dead and gone and then I'm going to marry me some nice fat farm girl that can take over this place!" And once he had added, "—some nice lady like Mrs. Greenleaf." When he had said this, Mrs. May had risen from her chair, her back stiff as a rake handle, and had gone to her room. There she had sat down on the edge of her bed for some time with her small face drawn. Finally she had whispered, "I work and slave, I struggle and sweat to keep this place for them and soon as I'm dead, they'll marry trash and bring it in here and ruin everything. They'll marry trash and ruin everything I've done," and she had made up her mind at that moment to change her will. The next day she had gone to her lawyer and had had the property entailed so that if they married, they could not leave it to their wives.

The idea that one of them might marry a woman even remotely like Mrs. Greenleaf was enough to make her ill. She had put up with Mr. Greenleaf for fifteen years, but the only way she had endured his wife had been by keeping entirely out of her sight. Mrs. Greenleaf was large and loose. The yard around her house looked like a dump and her five girls were always filthy; even the youngest one dipped snuff. Instead of making a garden or washing their clothes, her preoccupation was what she called "prayer healing."

Every day she cut all the morbid stories out of the newspaper—the accounts of women who had been raped and criminals who had escaped and children who had been burned and of train wrecks and plane crashes and the divorces of movie stars. She took these to the woods and dug a hole and buried them and then she fell on the ground over them and mumbled and groaned for an hour or so, moving her huge arms back and forth under her and out again and finally just lying down flat and, Mrs. May suspected, going to sleep in the dirt.

She had not found out about this until the Greenleafs had been with her a few months. One morning she had been out to inspect a field that she had wanted planted in rye but that had come up in clover because Mr. Greenleaf had used the wrong seeds in the grain drill. She was returning through a wooded path that separated two pastures, muttering to herself and hitting the ground methodically with a long stick she carried in case she saw a snake. "Mr. Greenleaf," she was saying in a low voice, "I cannot afford to pay for your mistakes. I am a poor woman and this place is all I have. I have two boys to educate. I cannot. . . ."

Out of nowhere a guttural agonized voice groaned, "Jesus! Jesus!" In a second it came again with a terrible urgency. "Jesus! Jesus!"

Mrs. May stopped still, one hand lifted to her throat. The sound was so piercing that she felt as if some violent unleashed force had broken out of the ground and was charging toward her. Her second thought was more reasonable: somebody had been hurt on the place and would sue her for everything she had. She had no insurance. She rushed forward and turning a bend in the path, she saw Mrs. Greenleaf sprawled on her hands and knees off the side of the road, her head down.

"Mrs. Greenleaf!" she shrilled, "what's happened?"

Mrs. Greenleaf raised her head. Her face was a patchwork

of dirt and tears and her small eyes, the color of two field peas, were red-rimmed and swollen, but her expression was as composed as a bulldog's. She swayed back and forth on her hands and knees and groaned, "Jesus, Jesus."

Mrs. May winced. She thought the word, Jesus, should be kept inside the church building like other words inside the bedroom. She was a good Christian woman with a large respect for religion, though she did not, of course, believe any of it was true. "What is the matter with you?" she asked sharply.

"You broken my healing," Mrs. Greenleaf said, waving her aside. "I can't talk to you until I finish."

Mrs. May stood, bent forward, her mouth open and her stick raised off the ground as if she were not sure what she wanted to strike with it.

"Oh Jesus, stab me in the heart!" Mrs. Greenleaf shrieked. "Jesus, stab me in the heart!" and she fell back flat in the dirt, a huge human mound, her legs and arms spread out as if she were trying to wrap them around the earth.

Mrs. May felt as furious and helpless as if she had been insulted by a child. "Jesus," she said, drawing herself back, "would be *ashamed* of you. He would tell you to get up from there this instant and go wash your children's clothes!" and she had turned and walked off as fast as she could.

Whenever she thought of how the Greenleaf boys had advanced in the world, she had only to think of Mrs. Greenleaf sprawled obscenely on the ground, and say to herself, "Well, no matter how far they *go*, they *came* from that."

She would like to have been able to put in her will that when she died, Wesley and Scofield were not to continue to employ Mr. Greenleaf. She was capable of handling Mr. Greenleaf; they were not. Mr. Greenleaf had pointed out to her once that her boys didn't know hay from silage. She had pointed out to him that they had other talents, that Scofield was a successful business man and Wesley a successful intellectual. Mr. Greenleaf did not comment, but he never lost an opportunity of letting her see, by his expression or some simple gesture, that he held the two of them in infinite contempt. As scrub-human as the Greenleafs were, he never hesitated to let her know that in any like circumstance in which his own boys might have been involved, they—O.T. and E.T. Greenleaf—would have acted to better advantage.

The Greenleaf boys were two or three years younger than the May boys. They were twins and you never knew when you spoke to one of them whether you were speaking to O.T. or E.T, and they never had the politeness to enlighten you.

They were long-legged and raw-boned and red-skinned, with bright grasping fox-colored eyes like their father's. Mr. Greenleaf's pride in them began with the fact that they were twins. He acted, Mrs. May said, as if this were something smart they had thought of themselves. They were energetic and hard-working and she would admit to anyone that they had come a long way—and that the Second World War was responsible for it.

They had both joined the service and, disguised in their uniforms, they could not be told from other people's children. You could tell, of course, when they opened their mouths but they did that seldom. The smartest thing they had done was to get sent overseas and there to marry French wives. They hadn't married French trash either. They had married nice girls who naturally couldn't tell that they murdered the king's English or that the Greenleafs were who they were.

Wesley's heart condition had not permitted him to serve his country but Scofield had been in the army for two years. He had not cared for it and at the end of his military service, he was only a Private First Class. The Greenleaf boys were both some kind of sergeants, and Mr. Greenleaf, in those days, had never lost an opportunity of referring to them by their rank. They had both managed to get wounded and now they both had pensions. Further, as soon as they were released from the army, they took advantage of all the benefits and went to the school of agriculture at the university—the tax-payers meanwhile supporting their French wives. The two of them were living now about two miles down the highway on a piece of land that the government had helped them to buy and in a brick duplex bungalow that the government had helped to build and pay for. If the war had made anyone, Mrs. May said, it had made the Greenleaf boys. They each had three little children apiece, who spoke Greenleaf English and French, and who, on account of their mother's background, would be sent to the convent school and brought up with manners. "And in twenty years," Mrs. May asked Scofield and Wesley, "do you know what those people will be?

"*Society*," she said blackly.

She had spent fifteen years coping with Mr. Greenleaf and, by now, handling him had become second nature with her. His disposition on any particular day was as much a factor in what she could and couldn't do as the weather was, and she had learned to read his face the way real country people read the sunrise and sunset.

She was a country woman only by persuasion. The late

Mr. May, a business man, had bought the place when land was down, and when he died it was all he had to leave her. The boys had not been happy to move to the country to a broken-down farm, but there was nothing else for her to do. She had the timber on the place cut and with the proceeds had set herself up in the dairy business after Mr. Greenleaf had answered her ad. "i seen yor add and i will come have 2 boys," was all his letter said, but he arrived the next day in a pieced-together truck, his wife and five daughters sitting on the floor in back, himself and the two boys in the cab.

Over the years they had been on her place, Mr. and Mrs. Greenleaf had aged hardly at all. They had no worries, no responsibilities. They lived like the lilies of the field, off the fat that she struggled to put into the land. When she was dead and gone from overwork and worry, the Greenleafs, healthy and thriving, would be just ready to begin draining Scofield and Wesley.

Wesley said the reason Mrs. Greenleaf had not aged was because she released all her emotions in prayer healing. "You ought to start praying, Sweetheart," he had said in the voice that, poor boy, he could not help making deliberately nasty.

Scofield only exasperated her beyond endurance but Wesley caused her real anxiety. He was thin and nervous and bald and being an intellectual was a terrible strain on his disposition. She doubted if he would marry until she died but she was certain that then the wrong woman would get him. Nice girls didn't like Scofield but Wesley didn't like nice girls. He didn't like anything. He drove twenty miles every day to the university where he taught and twenty miles back every night, but he said he hated the twenty-mile drive and he hated the second-rate university and he hated the morons who attended it. He hated the country and he hated the life he lived; he hated living with his mother and his idiot brother and he hated hearing about the damn dairy and the damn help and the damn broken machinery. But in spite of all he said, he never made any move to leave. He talked about Paris and Rome but he never went even to Atlanta.

"You'd go to those places and you'd get sick," Mrs. May would say. "Who in Paris is going to see that you get a salt-free diet? And do you think if you married one of those odd numbers you take out that *she* would cook a salt-free diet for you? No indeed, she would not!" When she took this line, Wesley would turn himself roughly around in his chair and ignore her. Once when she had kept it up too long, he had snarled, "Well, why don't you do something practical,

Woman? Why don't you pray for me like Mrs. Greenleaf would?"

"I don't like to hear you boys make jokes about religion," she had said. "If you would go to church, you would meet some nice girls."

But it was impossible to tell them anything. When she looked at the two of them now, sitting on either side of the table, neither one caring the least if a stray bull ruined her herd—which was their herd, their future—when she looked at the two of them, one hunched over a paper and the other teetering back in his chair, grinning at her like an idiot, she wanted to jump up and beat her fist on the table and shout, "You'll find out one of these days, you'll find out what *Reality* is when it's too late!"

"Mamma," Scofield said, "don't you get excited now but I'll tell you whose bull that is." He was looking at her wickedly. He let his chair drop forward and he got up. Then with his shoulders bent and his hands held up to cover his head, he tiptoed to the door. He backed into the hall and pulled the door almost to so that it hid all of him but his face. "You want to know, Sugarpie?" he asked.

Mrs. May sat looking at him coldly.

"That's O. T. and E. T.'s bull," he said. "I collected from their nigger yesterday and he told me they were missing it," and he showed her an exaggerated expanse of teeth and disappeared silently.

Wesley looked up and laughed.

Mrs. May turned her head forward again, her expression unaltered. "I am the only *adult* on this place," she said. She leaned across the table and pulled the paper from the side of his plate. "Do you see how it's going to be when I die and you boys have to handle him?" she began. "Do you see why he didn't know whose bull that was? Because it was theirs. Do you see what I have to put up with? Do you see that if I hadn't kept my foot on his neck all these years, you boys might be milking cows every morning at four o'clock?"

Wesley pulled the paper back toward his plate and staring at her full in the face, he murmured, "I wouldn't milk a cow to save your soul from hell."

"I know you wouldn't," she said in a brittle voice. She sat back and began rapidly turning her knife over at the side of her plate. "O. T. and E. T. are fine boys," she said. "They ought to have been my sons." The thought of this was so horrible that her vision of Wesley was blurred at once by a wall of tears. All she saw was his dark shape, rising quickly from the table. "And you two," she cried, "you two should have belonged to that woman!"

He was heading for the door.

"When I die," she said in a thin voice, "I don't know what's going to become of you."

"You're always yapping about when-you-die," he growled as he rushed out, "but you look pretty healthy to me."

For some time she sat where she was, looking straight ahead through the window across the room into a scene of indistinct greys and greens. She stretched her face and her neck muscles and drew in a long breath but the scene in front of her flowed together anyway into a watery grey mass. "They needn't think I'm going to die any time soon," she muttered, and some more defiant voice in her added: I'll die when I get good and ready.

She wiped her eyes with the table napkin and got up and went to the window and gazed at the scene in front of her. The cows were grazing on two pale green pastures across the road and behind them, fencing them in, was a black wall of trees with a sharp sawtooth edge that held off the indifferent sky. The pastures were enough to calm her. When she looked out any window in her house, she saw the reflection of her own character. Her city friends said she was the most remarkable woman they knew, to go, practically penniless and with no experience, out to a rundown farm and make a success of it. "Everything is against you," she would say, "the weather is against you and the dirt is against you and the help is against you. They're all in league against you. There's nothing for it but an iron hand!"

"Look at Mamma's iron hand!" Scofield would yell and grab her arm and hold it up so that her delicate blue-veined little hand would dangle from her wrist like the head of a broken lily. The company always laughed.

The sun, moving over the black and white grazing cows, was just a little brighter than the rest of the sky. Looking down, she saw a darker shape that might have been its shadow cast at an angle, moving among them. She uttered a sharp cry and turned and marched out of the house.

Mr. Greenleaf was in the trench silo, filling a wheelbarrow. She stood on the edge and looked down at him. "I told you to get up that bull. Now he's in with the milk herd."

"You can't do two thangs at oncet," Mr. Greenleaf remarked.

"I told you to do that first."

He wheeled the barrow out of the open end of the trench toward the barn and she followed close behind him. "And you needn't think, Mr. Greenleaf," she said, "that I don't know exactly whose bull that is or why you haven't been in any hurry to notify me he was here. I might as well feed O. T. and E. T.'s bull as long as I'm going to have him here ruining my herd."

Mr. Greenleaf paused with the wheelbarrow and looked behind him. "Is that them boys' bull?" he asked in an incredulous tone.

She did not say a word. She merely looked away with her mouth taut.

"They told me their bull was out but I never known that was him," he said.

"I want that bull put up now," she said, "and I'm going to drive over to O. T. and E. T.'s and tell them they'll have to come get him today. I ought to charge for the time he's been here—then it wouldn't happen again."

"They didn't pay but seventy-five dollars for him," Mr. Greenleaf offered.

"I wouldn't have had him as a gift," she said.

"They was just going to beef him," Mr. Greenleaf went on, "but he got loose and run his head into their pickup truck. He don't like cars and trucks. They had a time getting his horn out the fender and when they finally got him loose, he took off and they was too tired to run after him—but I never known that was him there."

"It wouldn't have paid you to know, Mr. Greenleaf," she said. "But you know now. Get a horse and get him."

In a half hour, from her front window she saw the bull, squirrel-colored, with jutting hips and long light horns, ambling down the dirt road that ran in front of the house. Mr. Greenleaf was behind him on the horse. "That's a Greenleaf bull if I ever saw one," she muttered. She went out on the porch and called, "Put him where he can't get out."

"He likes to bust loose," Mr. Greenleaf said, looking with approval at the bull's rump. "This gentleman is a sport."

"If those boys don't come for him, he's going to be a dead sport," she said. "I'm just warning you."

He heard her but he didn't answer.

"That's the awfullest looking bull I ever saw," she called but he was too far down the road to hear.

It was mid-morning when she turned into O. T. and E. T.'s driveway. The house, a new red-brick, low-to-the-ground building that looked like a warehouse with windows, was on top of a treeless hill. The sun was beating down directly on the white roof of it. It was the kind of house that everybody built now and nothing marked it as belonging to Greenleafs except three dogs, part hound and part spitz, that rushed out from behind it as soon as she stopped her car. She reminded herself that you could always tell the class of people by the class of dog, and honked her horn. While she sat waiting for someone to come, she continued to study the house. All the windows were down and she wondered if the government could have air-conditioned the thing. No one came and she honked again. Presently a door opened and several children appeared in it and stood looking at her, making no move to come forward. She recognized this as a true Greenleaf trait—they could hang in a door, looking at you for hours.

"Can't one of you children come here?" she called.

After a minute they all began to move forward, slowly. They had on overalls and were barefooted but they were not as dirty as she might have expected. There were two or three that looked distinctly like Greenleafs; the others not so much so. The smallest child was a girl with untidy black hair. They stopped about six feet from the automobile and stood looking at her.

"You're mighty pretty," Mrs. May said, addressing herself to the smallest girl.

There was no answer. They appeared to share one dispassionate expression between them.

"Where's your Mamma?" she asked.

There was no answer to this for some time. Then one of them said something in French. Mrs. May did not speak French.

"Where's your daddy?" she asked.

After a while, one of the boys said, "He ain't hyar neither."

"Ahhhh," Mrs. May said as if something had been proven. "Where's the colored man?"

She waited and decided no one was going to answer. "The cat has six little tongues," she said. "How would you like to come home with me and let me teach you how to talk?" She laughed and her laugh died on the silent air. She felt as if she were on trial for her life, facing a jury of Greenleafs. "I'll go down and see if I can find the colored man," she said.

"You can go if you want to," one of the boys said.

"Well, thank you," she murmured and drove off.

The barn was down the lane from the house. She had not seen it before but Mr. Greenleaf had described it in detail for it had been built according to the latest specifications. It was a milking parlor arrangement where the cows are milked from below. The milk ran in pipes from the machines to the milk house and was never carried in no bucket, Mr. Green-leaf said, by no human hand. "When you gonter get you one?" he had asked.

"Mr. Greenleaf," she had said, "I have to do for myself. I am not assisted hand and foot by the government. It would cost me $20,000 to install a milking parlor. I barely make ends meet as it is."

"My boys done it," Mr. Greenleaf had murmured, and then—"but all boys ain't alike."

"No indeed!" she had said. "I thank God for that!"

"I thank Gawd for ever-thang," Mr. Greenleaf had drawled.

You might as well, she had thought in the fierce silence that followed; you've never done anything for yourself.

She stopped by the side of the barn and honked but no one appeared. For several minutes she sat in the car, observing the various machines parked around, wondering how many of them were paid for. They had a forage harvester and a rotary hay baler. She had those too. She decided that since no one was here, she would get out and have a look at the milking parlor and see if they kept it clean.

She opened the milking room door and stuck her head in and for the first second she felt as if she were going to lose her breath. The spotless white concrete room was filled with sunlight that came from a row of windows head-high along both walls. The metal stanchions gleamed ferociously and she had to squint to be able to look at all. She drew her head out the room quickly and closed the door and leaned against it, frowning. The light outside was not so bright but she was conscious that the sun was directly on top of her head, like a silver bullet ready to drop into her brain.

A Negro carrying a yellow calf-feed bucket appeared from around the corner of the machine shed and came toward her. He was a light yellow boy dressed in the cast-off army clothes of the Greenleaf twins. He stopped at a respectable distance and set the bucket on the ground.

"Where's Mr. O. T. and Mr. E. T.?" she asked.

"Mist O. T. he in town, Mist E. T. he off yonder in the field," the Negro said, pointing first to the left and then to the right as if he were naming the position of two planets.

"Can you remember a message?" she asked, looking as if she thought this doubtful.

"I'll remember it if I don't forget it," he said with a touch of sullenness.

"Well, I'll write it down then," she said. She got in her car and took a stub of pencil from her pocket book and began to write on the back of an empty envelope. The Negro came and stood at the window. "I'm Mrs. May," she said as she wrote. "Their bull is on my place and I want him off *today*. You can tell them I'm furious about it."

"That bull lef here Sareday," the Negro said, "and none of us ain't seen him since. We ain't knowed where he was."

"Well, you know now," she said, "and you can tell Mr. O. T. and Mr. E. T. that if they don't come and get him today, I'm going to have their daddy shoot him the first thing in the morning. I can't have that bull ruining my herd." She handed him the note.

"If I knows Mist O. T. and Mist E. T.," he said, taking it, "they goin to say you go ahead on and shoot him. He done busted up one of our trucks already and we be glad to see the last of him."

She pulled her head back and gave him a look from slightly bleared eyes. "Do you expect me to take my time and my worker to shoot their bull?" she asked. "They don't want him so they just let him loose and expect somebody else to kill him? He's eating my oats and ruining my herd and I'm expected to shoot him too?"

"I speck you is," he said softly. "He done busted up . . ."

She gave him a very sharp look and said, "Well, I'm not surprised. That's just the way some people are," and after a second she asked, "Which is boss, Mr. O. T. or Mr. E. T.?" She had always suspected that they fought between themselves secretly.

"They never quarls," the boy said. "They like one man in two skins."

"Hmp. I expect you just never heard them quarrel."

"Nor nobody else heard them neither," he said, looking away as if this insolence were addressed to some one else.

"Well," she said, "I haven't put up with their father for fifteen years not to know a few things about Greenleafs."

The Negro looked at her suddenly with a gleam of recognition. "Is you my policy man's mother?" he asked.

"I don't know who your policy man is," she said sharply. "You give them that note and tell them if they don't come for that bull today, they'll be making their father shoot it tomorrow," and she drove off.

She stayed at home all afternoon waiting for the Greenleaf twins to come for the bull. They did not come. I might as well be working for them, she thought furiously. They are simply going to use me to the limit. At the supper table, she went over it again for the boys' benefit because she wanted them to see exactly what O. T. and E. T. would do. "They don't want that bull," she said, "—pass the butter—so they simply turn him loose and let somebody else worry about getting rid of him for them. How do you like that? I'm the victim. I've always been the victim."

"Pass the butter to the victim," Wesley said. He was in a worse humor than usual because he had had a flat tire on the way home from the university.

Scofield handed her the butter and said, "Why Mamma, ain't you ashamed to shoot an old bull that ain't done nothing but give you a little scrub strain in your herd? I declare," he said, "with the Mamma I got it's a wonder I turned out to be such a nice boy!"

"You ain't her boy, Son," Wesley said.

She eased back in her chair, her fingertips on the edge of the table.

"All I know is," Scofield said, "I done mighty well to be as nice as I am seeing what I come from."

When they teased her they spoke Greenleaf English but Wesley made his own particular tone come through it like a knife edge. "Well lemme tell you one thang, Brother," he said, leaning over the table, "that if you had half a mind you would already know."

"What's that, Brother?" Scofield asked, his broad face grinning into the thin constricted one across from him.

"That is," Wesley said, "that neither you nor me is her boy . . . ," but he stopped abruptly as she gave a kind of hoarse wheeze like an old horse lashed unexpectedly. She reared up and ran from the room.

"Oh, for God's sake," Wesley growled. "What did you start her off for?"

"I never started her off," Scofield said. "You started her off."

"Hah."

"She's not as young as she used to be and she can't take it."

"She can only give it out," Wesley said. "I'm the one that takes it."

His brother's pleasant face had changed so that an ugly family resemblance showed between them. "Nobody feels sorry for a lousy bastard like you," he said and grabbed across the table for the other's shirtfront.

From her room she heard a crash of dishes and she rushed back through the kitchen into the dining room. The hall door was open and Scofield was going out of it. Wesley was lying like a large bug on his back with the edge of the over-turned table cutting him across the middle and broken dishes scattered on top of him. She pulled the table off him and caught his arm to help him rise but he scrambled up and pushed her off with a furious charge of energy and flung himself out of the door after his brother.

She would have collapsed but a knock on the back door stiffened her and she swung around. Across the kitchen and back porch, she could see Mr. Greenleaf peering eagerly through the screenwire. All her resources returned in full strength as if she had only needed to be challenged by the devil himself to regain them. "I heard a thump," he called, "and I thought the plastering might have fell on you."

If he had been wanted someone would have had to go on a horse to find him. She crossed the kitchen and the porch and stood inside the screen and said, "No, nothing happened but the table turned over. One of the legs was weak," and without pausing, "the boys didn't come for the bull so tomorrow you'll have to shoot him."

The sky was crossed with thin red and purple bars and behind them the sun was moving down slowly as if it were descending a ladder. Mr. Greenleaf squatted down on the step, his back to her, the top of his hat on a level with her feet. "Tomorrow I'll drive him home for you," he said.

"Oh no, Mr. Greenleaf," she said in a mocking voice, "you drive him home tomorrow and next week he'll be back here. I know better than that." Then in a mournful tone, she said, "I'm surprised at O. T. and E. T. to treat me this way. I thought they'd have more gratitude. Those boys spent some mighty happy days on this place, didn't they, Mr. Greenleaf?"

Mr. Greenleaf didn't say anything.

"I think they did," she said. "I think they did. But they've forgotten all the nice little things I did for them now. If I recall, they wore my boys' old clothes and played with my boys' old toys and hunted with my boys' old guns. They swam in my pond and shot my birds and fished in my stream and I never forgot their birthday and Christmas seemed to roll around very often if I remember it right. And do they think of any of those things now?" she asked. "NOOOOO," she said.

For a few seconds she looked at the disappearing sun and Mr. Greenleaf examined the palms of his hands. Presently as if it had just occurred to her, she asked, "Do you know the real reason they didn't come for that bull?"

"Naw I don't," Mr. Greenleaf said in a surly voice.

"They didn't come because I'm a woman," she said. "You

can get away with anything when you're dealing with a woman. If there were a man running this place . . ."

Quick as a snake striking Mr. Greenleaf said, "You got two boys. They know you got two men on the place."

The sun had disappeared behind the tree line. She looked down at the dark crafty face, upturned now, and at the wary eyes, bright under the shadow of the hatbrim. She waited long enough for him to see that she was hurt and then she said, "Some people learn gratitude too late, Mr. Greenleaf, and some never learn it at all," and she turned and left him sitting on the steps.

Half the night in her sleep she heard a sound as if some large stone were grinding a hole on the outside wall of her brain. She was walking on the inside, over a succession of beautiful rolling hills, planting her stick in front of each step. She became aware after a time that the noise was the sun trying to burn through the tree line and she stopped to watch, safe in the knowledge that it couldn't, that it had to sink the way it always did outside of her property. When she first stopped it was a swollen red ball, but as she stood watching it began to narrow and pale until it looked like a bullet. Then suddenly it burst through the tree line and raced down the hill toward her. She woke up with her hand over her mouth and the same noise, diminished but distinct, in her ear. It was the bull munching under her window. Mr. Greenleaf had let him out.

She got up and made her way to the window in the dark and looked out through the slit blind, but the bull had moved away from the hedge and at first she didn't see him. Then she saw a heavy form some distance away, paused as if observing her. This is the last night I am going to put up with this, she said, and watched until the iron shadow moved away in the darkness.

The next morning she waited until exactly eleven o'clock. Then she got in her car and drove to the barn. Mr. Greenleaf was cleaning milk cans. He had seven of them standing up outside the milk room to get the sun. She had been telling him to do this for two weeks. "All right, Mr. Greenleaf," she said, "go get your gun. We're going to shoot that bull."

"I thought you wanted theseyer cans . . ."

"Go get your gun, Mr. Greenleaf," she said. Her voice and face were expressionless.

"That gentleman torn out of there last night," he murmured in a tone of regret and bent again to the can he had his arm in.

"Go get your gun, Mr. Greenleaf," she said in the same

triumphant toneless voice. "The bull is in the pasture with the
dry cows. I saw him from my upstairs window. I'm going to
drive you up to the field and you can run him into the empty
pasture and shoot him there."

He detached himself from the can slowly. "Ain't nobody
ever ast me to shoot my boys' own bull!" he said in a high
rasping voice. He removed a rag from his back pocket and
began to wipe his hands violently, then his nose.

She turned as if she had not heard this and said, "I'll wait
for you in the car. Go get your gun."

She sat in the car and watched him stalk off toward the
harness room where he kept a gun. After he had entered the
room, there was a crash as if he had kicked something out of
his way. Presently he emerged again with the gun, circled behind the car, opened the door violently and threw himself
onto the seat beside her. He held the gun between his knees
and looked straight ahead. He'd like to shoot me instead of
the bull, she thought, and turned her face away so that he
could not see her smile.

The morning was dry and clear. She drove through the
woods for a quarter of a mile and then out into the open
where there were fields on either side of the narrow road.
The exhilaration of carrying her point had sharpened her
senses. Birds were screaming everywhere, the grass was almost too bright to look at, the sky was an even piercing blue.
"Spring is here!" she said gaily. Mr. Greenleaf lifted one
muscle somewhere near his mouth as if he found this the
most asinine remark ever made. When she stopped at the second pasture gate, he flung himself out of the car door and
slammed it behind him. Then he opened the gate and she
drove through. He closed it and flung himself back in,
silently, and she drove around the rim of the pasture until she
spotted the bull, almost in the center of it, grazing peacefully
among the cows.

"The gentleman is waiting on you," she said and gave Mr.
Greenleaf's furious profile a sly look. "Run him into that next
pasture and when you get him in, I'll drive in behind you and
shut the gate myself."

He flung himself out again, this time deliberately leaving
the car door open so that she had to lean across the seat and
close it. She sat smiling as she watched him make his way
across the pasture toward the opposite gate. He seemed to
throw himself forward at each step and then pull back as if
he were calling on some power to witness that he was being
forced. "Well," she said aloud as if he were still in the car,
"it's your own boys who are making you do this, Mr. Green-

leaf." O. T. and E. T. were probably splitting their sides laughing at him now. She could hear their identical nasal voices saying, "Made Daddy shoot our bull for us. Daddy don't know no better than to think that's a fine bull he's shooting. Gonna kill Daddy to shoot that bull!"

"If those boys cared a thing about you, Mr. Greenleaf," she said, "they would have come for that bull. I'm surprised at them."

He was circling around to open the gate first. The bull, dark among the spotted cows, had not moved. He kept his head down, eating constantly. Mr. Greenleaf opened the gate and then began circling back to approach him from the rear. When he was about ten feet behind him, he flapped his arms at his sides. The bull lifted his head indolently and then lowered it again and continued to eat. Mr. Greenleaf stooped again and picked up something and threw it at him with a vicious swing. She decided it was a sharp rock for the bull leapt and then began to gallop until he disappeared over the rim of the hill. Mr. Greenleaf followed at his leisure.

"You needn't think you're going to lose him!" she cried and started the car straight across the pasture. She had to drive slowly over the terraces and when she reached the gate, Mr. Greenleaf and the bull were nowhere in sight. This pasture was smaller than the last, a green arena, encircled almost entirely by woods. She got out and closed the gate and stood looking for some sign of Mr. Greenleaf but he had disappeared completely. She knew at once that his plan was to lose the bull in the woods. Eventually, she would see him emerge somewhere from the circle of trees and come limping toward her and when he finally reached her, he would say, "If you can find that gentleman in them woods, you're better than me."

She was going to say, "Mr. Greenleaf, if I have to walk into those woods with you and stay all afternoon, we are going to find that bull and shoot him. You are going to shoot him if I have to pull the trigger for you." When he saw she meant business he would return and shoot the bull quickly himself.

She got back into the car and drove to the center of the pasture where he would not have so far to walk to reach her when he came out of the woods. At this moment she could picture him sitting on a stump, marking lines in the ground with a stick. She decided she would wait exactly ten minutes by her watch. Then she would begin to honk. She got out of the car and walked around a little and then sat down on the front bumper to wait and rest. She was very tired and she lay her head back against the hood and closed her eyes. She did not understand why she should be so tired when it was only mid-morning. Through her closed eyes, she could feel the sun, red-hot overhead. She opened her eyes slightly but the white light forced her to close them again.

For some time she lay back against the hood, wondering drowsily why she was so tired. With her eyes closed, she didn't think of time as divided into days and nights but into past and future. She decided she was tired because she had been working continuously for fifteen years. She decided she had every right to be tired, and to rest for a few minutes before she began working again. Before any kind of judgement seat, she would be able to say: I've worked, I have not wallowed. At this very instant while she was recalling a lifetime of work, Mr. Greenleaf was loitering in the woods and Mrs. Greenleaf was probably flat on the ground, asleep over her holeful of clippings. The woman had got worse over the years and Mrs. May believed that now she was actually demented. "I'm afraid your wife has let religion warp her," she said once tactfully to Mr. Greenleaf. "Everything in moderation, you know."

"She cured a man oncet that half his gut was eat out with worms," Mr. Greenleaf said, and she had turned away, half-sickened. Poor souls, she thought now, so simple. For a few seconds she dozed.

When she sat up and looked at her watch, more than ten minutes had passed. She had not heard any shot. A new thought occurred to her: suppose Mr. Greenleaf had aroused the bull chunking stones at him and the animal had turned on him and run him up against a tree and gored him? The irony of it deepened: O. T. and E. T. would then get a shyster lawyer and sue her. It would be the fitting end to her fifteen years with the Greenleafs. She thought of it almost with pleasure as if she had hit on the perfect ending for a story she was telling her friends. Then she dropped it, for Mr. Greenleaf had a gun with him and she had insurance.

She decided to honk. She got up and reached inside the car window and gave three sustained honks and two or three shorter ones to let him know she was getting impatient. Then she went back and sat down on the bumper again.

In a few minutes something emerged from the tree line, a black heavy shadow that tossed its head several times and then bounded forward. After a second she saw it was the bull. He was crossing the pasture toward her at a slow gallop, a gay almost rocking gait as if he were overjoyed to find her again. She looked beyond him to see if Mr. Greenleaf was coming out of the woods too but he was not. "Here he is, Mr. Greenleaf!" she called and looked on the other side of the pasture to see if he could be coming out there but he was not in sight. She looked back and saw that the bull, his head lowered, was racing toward her. She remained perfectly still, not in fright, but in a freezing unbelief. She stared at the violent black streak bounding toward her as if she had no sense of distance, as if she could not decide at once what his intention was, and the bull had buried his head in her lap, like a wild tormented lover, before her expression changed. One of his horns sank until it pierced her heart and the other curved around her side and held her in an unbreakable grip. She continued to stare straight ahead but the entire scene in front of her had changed—the tree line was a dark wound in a world that was nothing but sky—and she had the look of a person whose sight has been suddenly restored but who finds the light unbearable.

Mr. Greenleaf was running toward her from the side with his gun raised and she saw him coming though she was not looking in his direction. She saw him approaching on the outside of some invisible circle, the tree line gaping behind him and nothing under his feet. He shot the bull four times through the eye. She did not hear the shots but she felt the quake in the huge body as it sank, pulling her forward on its head, so that she seemed, when Mr. Greenleaf reached her, to be bent over whispering some last discovery into the animal's ear.

A View of the Woods

The week before, Mary Fortune and the old man had spent every morning watching the machine that lifted out dirt and threw it in a pile. The construction was going on by the new lakeside on one of the lots that the old man had sold to somebody who was going to put up a fishing club. He and Mary Fortune drove down there every morning about ten o'clock and he parked his car, a battered mulberry-colored Cadillac, on the embankment that overlooked the spot where the work was going on. The red corrugated lake eased up to within fifty feet of the construction and was bordered on the other side by a black line of woods which appeared at both ends of the view to walk across the water and continue along the edge of the fields.

He sat on the bumper and Mary Fortune straddled the hood and they watched, sometimes for hours, while the machine systematically ate a square red hole in what had once been a cow pasture. It happened to be the only pasture that Pitts had succeeded in getting the bitterweed off and when the old man had sold it, Pitts had nearly had a stroke; and as far as Mr. Fortune was concerned, he could have gone on and had it.

"Any fool that would let a cow pasture interfere with progress is not on my books," he had said to Mary Fortune several times from his seat on the bumper, but the child did not have eyes for anything but the machine. She sat on the hood, looking down into the red pit, watching the big disembodied gullet gorge itself on the clay, then, with the sound of a deep sustained nausea and a slow mechanical revulsion, turn and spit it up. Her pale eyes behind her spectacles followed the repeated motion of it again and again and her face —a small replica of the old man's—never lost its look of complete absorption.

No one was particularly glad that Mary Fortune looked like her grandfather except the old man himself. He thought it added greatly to her attractiveness. He thought she was the smartest and the prettiest child he had ever seen and he let the rest of them know that if, IF that was, he left anything to anybody, it would be Mary Fortune he left it to. She was now nine, short and broad like himself, with his very light blue eyes, his wide prominent forehead, his steady penetrating scowl and his rich florid complexion; but she was like him on the inside too. She had, to a singular degree, his intelligence, his strong will, and his push and drive. Though there was seventy years' difference in their ages, the spiritual distance between them was slight. She was the only member of the family he had any respect for.

He didn't have any use for her mother, his third or fourth daughter (he could never remember which), though she considered that she took care of him. She considered—being careful not to say it, only to look it—that she was the one putting up with him in his old age and that she was the one he should leave the place to. She had married an idiot named Pitts and had had seven children, all likewise idiots except the youngest, Mary Fortune, who was a throwback to him. Pitts was the kind who couldn't keep his hands on a nickel and Mr. Fortune had allowed them, ten years ago, to move onto his place and farm it. What Pitts made went to Pitts but the land belonged to Fortune and he was careful to keep the fact before them. When the well had gone dry, he had not allowed Pitts to have a deep well drilled but had insisted that they pipe their water from the spring. He did not intend to pay for a drilled well himself and he knew that if he let Pitts pay for it, whenever he had occasion to say to Pitts, "It's my land you're sitting on," Pitts would be able to say to him, "Well, it's my pump that's pumping the water you're drinking."

Being there ten years, the Pittses had got to feel as if they owned the place. The daughter had been born and raised on it but the old man considered that when she married Pitts she showed that she preferred Pitts to home; and when she came back, she came back like any other tenant, though he would not allow them to pay rent for the same reason he would not allow them to drill a well. Anyone over sixty years of age is in an uneasy position unless he controls the greater interest and every now and then he gave the Pittses a practical lesson by selling off a lot. Nothing infuriated Pitts more than to see him sell off a piece of the property to an outsider, because Pitts wanted to buy it himself.

Pitts was a thin, long-jawed, irascible, sullen, sulking individual and his wife was the duty-proud kind: It's my duty to stay here and take care of Papa. Who would do it if I didn't? I do it knowing full well I'll get no reward for it. I do it because it's my duty.

The old man was not taken in by this for a minute. He knew they were waiting impatiently for the day when they could put him in a hole eight feet deep and cover him up with dirt. Then, even if he did not leave the place to them, they figured they would be able to buy it. Secretly he had made his will and left everything in trust to Mary Fortune, naming his lawyer and not Pitts as executor. When he died Mary Fortune could make the rest of them jump; and he didn't doubt for a minute that she would be able to do it.

Ten years ago they had announced that they were going to name the new baby Mark Fortune Pitts, after him, if it were a boy, and he had not delayed in telling them that if they coupled his name with the name Pitts he would put them off the place. When the baby came, a girl, and he had seen that even at the age of one day she bore his unmistakable likeness, he had relented and suggested himself that they name her Mary Fortune, after his beloved mother, who had died seventy years ago, bringing him into the world.

The Fortune place was in the country on a clay road that left the paved road fifteen miles away and he would never have been able to sell off any lots if it had not been for progress, which had always been his ally. He was not one of these old people who fight improvement, who object to everything new and cringe at every change. He wanted to see a paved highway in front of his house with plenty of new-model cars on it, he wanted to see a supermarket store across the road from him, he wanted to see a gas station, a motel, a drive-in picture-show within easy distance. Progress had suddenly set all this in motion. The electric power company had built a dam on the river and flooded great areas of the surrounding country and the lake that resulted touched his land along a half-mile stretch. Every Tom, Dick and Harry, every dog and his brother, wanted a lot on the lake. There was talk of their getting a telephone line. There was talk of paving the road that ran in front of the Fortune place. There was talk of an eventual town. He thought this should be called Fortune, Georgia. He was a man of advanced vision, even if he was seventy-nine years old.

The machine that drew up the dirt had stopped the day before and today they were watching the hole being smoothed out by two huge yellow bulldozers. His property had amounted to eight hundred acres before he began selling lots. He had sold five twenty-acre lots on the back of the place and every time he sold one, Pitts's blood pressure had gone up twenty points. "The Pittses are the kind that would let a cow pasture interfere with the future," he said to Mary Fortune, "but not you and me." The fact that Mary Fortune was a Pitts too was something he ignored, in a gentlemanly fashion, as if it were an affliction the child was not responsible for. He liked to think of her as being thoroughly of his clay. He sat on the bumper and she sat on the hood with her bare feet on his shoulders. One of the bulldozers had moved under them to shave the side of the embankment they were parked on. If he had moved his feet a few inches out, the old man could have dangled them over the edge.

"If you don't watch him," Mary Fortune shouted above the noise of the machine, "he'll cut off some of your dirt!"

"Yonder's the stob," the old man yelled. "He hasn't gone beyond the stob."

"Not YET he hasn't," she roared.

The bulldozer passed beneath them and went on to the far side. "Well you watch," he said. "Keep your eyes open and if he knocks that stob, I'll stop him. The Pittses are the kind that would let a cow pasture or a mule lot or a row of beans interfere with progress," he continued. "The people like you and me with heads on their shoulders know you can't stop the marcher time for a cow. . . ."

"He's shaking the stob on the other side!" she screamed and before he could stop her, she had jumped down from the hood and was running along the edge of the embankment, her little yellow dress billowing out behind.

"Don't run so near the edge," he yelled but she had already reached the stob and was squatting down by it to see how much it had been shaken. She leaned over the embankment and shook her fist at the man on the bulldozer. He waved at her and went on about his business. More sense in her little finger than all the rest of that tribe in their heads put together, the old man said to himself, and watched with pride as she started back to him.

She had a head of thick, very fine, sand-colored hair—the exact kind he had had when he had had any—that grew straight and was cut just above her eyes and down the sides of her cheeks to the tips of her ears so that if formed a kind of door opening onto the central part of her face. Her glasses were silver-rimmed like his and she even walked the way he did, stomach forward, with a careful abrupt gait, something between a rock and a shuffle. She was walking so close to the edge of the embankment that the outside of her right foot was flush with it.

"I said don't walk so close to the edge," he called; "you fall off there and you won't live to see the day this place gets built up." He was always very careful to see that she avoided dangers. He would not allow her to sit in snakey places or put her hands on bushes that might hide hornets.

She didn't move an inch. She had a habit of his of not hearing what she didn't want to hear and since this was a little trick he had taught her himself, he had to admire the way she practiced it. He foresaw that in her own old age it would serve her well. She reached the car and climbed back onto the hood without a word and put her feet back on his shoulders where she had had them before, as if he were no more than a part of the automobile. Her attention returned to the far bulldozer.

"Remember what you won't get if you don't mind," her grandfather remarked.

He was a strict disciplinarian but he had never whipped her. There were some children, like the first six Pittses, whom he thought should be whipped once a week on principle, but there were other ways to control intelligent children and he had never laid a rough hand on Mary Fortune. Furthermore, he had never allowed her mother or her brothers and sisters so much as to slap her. The elder Pitts was a different matter.

He was a man of a nasty temper and of ugly unreasonable resentments. Time and again, Mr. Fortune's heart had pounded to see him rise slowly from his place at the table—not the head, Mr. Fortune sat there, but from his place at the side—and abruptly, for no reason, with no explanation, jerk his head at Mary Fortune and say, "Come with me," and leave the room, unfastening his belt as he went. A look that was completely foreign to the child's face would appear on it. The old man could not define the look but it infuriated him. It was a look that was part terror and part respect and part something else, something very like cooperation. This look would appear on her face and she would get up and follow Pitts out. They would get in his truck and drive down the road out of earshot, where he would beat her.

Mr. Fortune knew for a fact that he beat her because he had followed them in his car and had seen it happen. He had watched from behind a boulder about a hundred feet away while the child clung to a pine tree and Pitts, as methodically as if he were whacking a bush with a sling blade, beat her around the ankles with his belt. All she had done was jump up and down as if she were standing on a hot stove and make a whimpering noise like a dog that was being peppered. Pitts had kept at it for about three minutes and then he had turned, without a word, and got back in his truck and left her there, and she had slid down under the tree and taken both feet in her hands and rocked back and forth. The old man had crept forward to catch her. Her face was contorted into a puzzle of small red lumps and her nose and eyes were running. He sprang on her and sputtered, "Why didn't you hit him back? Where's your spirit? Do you think I'd a let him beat me?"

She had jumped up and started backing away from him with her jaw stuck out. "Nobody beat me," she said.

"Didn't I see it with my own eyes?" he exploded.

"Nobody is here and nobody beat me," she said. "Nobody's ever beat me in my life and if anybody did, I'd kill him. You can see for yourself nobody is here."

"Do you call me a liar or a blindman!" he shouted. "I saw him with my own two eyes and you never did a thing but let him do it, you never did a thing but hang onto that tree and dance up and down a little and blubber and if it had been me, I'd a swung my fist in his face and . . ."

"Nobody was here and nobody beat me and if anybody did I'd kill him!" she yelled and then turned and dashed off through the woods.

"And I'm a Poland china pig and black is white!" he had roared after her and he had sat down on a small rock under the tree, disgusted and furious. This was Pitts's revenge on him. It was as if it were *he* that Pitts was driving down the road to beat and it was as if *he* were the one submitting to it. He had thought at first that he could stop him by saying that if he beat her, he would put them off the place but when he had tried that, Pitts had said, "Put me off and you put her off too. Go right ahead. She's mine to whip and I'll whip her every day of the year if it suits me."

Any time he could make Pitts feel his hand he was determined to do it and at present he had a little scheme up his sleeve that was going to be a considerable blow to Pitts. He was thinking of it with relish when he told Mary Fortune to remember what she wouldn't get if she didn't mind, and he added, without waiting for an answer, that he might be selling another lot soon and that if he did, he might give her a bonus but not if she gave him any sass. He had frequent little verbal tilts with her but this was a sport like putting a mirror up in front of a rooster and watching him fight his reflection.

"I don't want no bonus," Mary Fortune said.

"I ain't ever seen you refuse one."

"You ain't ever seen me ask for one neither," she said.

"How much have you laid by?" he asked.

"Noner yer bidnis," she said and stamped his shoulders with her feet. "Don't be buttin into my bidnis."

"I bet you got it sewed up in your mattress," he said, "just like an old nigger woman. You ought to put it in the bank. I'm going to start you an account just as soon as I complete this deal. Won't anybody be able to check on it but me and you."

The bulldozer moved under them again and drowned out the rest of what he wanted to say. He waited and when the noise had passed, he could hold it in no longer. "I'm going to sell the lot right in front of the house for a gas station." he said. "Then we won't have to go down the road to get the car filled up, just step out the front door.

The Fortune house was set back about two hundred feet from the road and it was this two hundred feet that he intended to sell. It was the part that his daughter airily called "the lawn" though it was nothing but a field of weeds.

"You mean," Mary Fortune said after a minute, "the lawn?"

"Yes mam!" he said. "I mean the lawn," and he slapped his knee.

She did not say anything and he turned and looked up at her. There in the little rectangular opening of hair was his face looking back at him, but it was a reflection not of his present expression but of the darker one that indicated his displeasure. "That's where we play," she muttered.

"Well there's plenty of other places you can play," he said, irked by this lack of enthusiasm.

"We won't be able to see the woods across the road," she said.

The old man stared at her. "The woods across the road?" he repeated.

"We won't be able to see the view," she said.

"The view?" he repeated.

"The woods," she said; "we won't be able to see the woods from the porch."

"The woods from the porch?" he repeated.

Then she said, "My daddy grazes his calves on that lot."

The old man's wrath was delayed an instant by shock. Then it exploded in a roar. He jumped up and turned and slammed his fist on the hood of the car. "He can graze them somewheres else!"

"You fall off that embankment and you'll wish you hadn't," she said.

He moved from in front of the car around to the side, keeping his eye on her all the time. "Do you think I care where he grazes his calves! Do you think I'll let a calf interfere with my bidnis? Do you think I give a damn hoot where that fool grazes his calves?"

She sat, her red face darker than her hair, exactly reflecting his expression now. "He who calls his brother a fool is subject to hell fire," she said.

"Jedge not," he shouted, "lest ye be not jedged!" The tinge of his face was a shade more purple than hers. "You!" he said. "You let him beat you any time he wants to and don't do a thing but blubber a little and jump up and down!"

"He nor nobody else has ever touched me," she said, measuring off each word in a deadly flat tone. "Nobody's ever put a hand on me and if anybody did, I'd kill him."

"And black is white," the old man piped, "and night is day!"

The bulldozer passed below them. With their faces about a foot apart, each held the same expression until the noise had receded. Then the old man said, "Walk home by yourself. I refuse to ride a Jezebel!"

"And I refuse to ride with the Whore of Babylon," she said and slid off the other side of the car and started off through the pasture.

"A whore is a woman!" he roared. "That's how much you know!" But she did not deign to turn around and answer him back, and he watched the small robust figure stalk across the yellow-dotted field toward the woods, his pride in her, as if it couldn't help itself, returned like the gentle little tide on the new lake—all except that part of it that had to do with her refusal to stand up to Pitts; that pulled back like an undertow. If he could have taught her to stand up to Pitts the way she stood up to him, she would have been a perfect child, as fearless and sturdy-minded as anyone could want; but it was her one failure of character. It was the one point on which she did not resemble him. He turned and looked away over the lake to the woods across it and told himself that in five years, instead of woods, there would be houses and stores and parking places, and that the credit for it could go largely to him.

He meant to teach the child spirit by example and since he had definitely made up his mind, he announced that noon at the dinner table that he was negotiating with a man named Tilman to sell the lot in front of the house for a gas station.

His daughter, sitting with her worn-out air at the foot of the table, let out a moan as if a dull knife were being turned slowly in her chest. "You mean the lawn!" she moaned and fell back in her chair and repeated in an almost inaudible voice, "He means the lawn."

The other six Pitts children began to bawl and pipe, "Where we play!" "Don't let him do that, Pa!" "We won't be able to see the road!" and similar idiocies. Mary Fortune did not say anything. She had a mulish reserved look as if she were planning some business of her own. Pitts had stopped eating and was staring in front of him. His plate was full but his fists sat motionless like two dark quartz stones on either side of it. His eyes began to move from child to child around the table as if he were hunting for one particular one of them. Finally they stopped on Mary Fortune sitting next to her grandfather. "You done this to us," he muttered.

"I didn't," she said but there was no assurance in her voice. It was only a quaver, the voice of a frightened child.

Pitts got up and said, "Come with me," and turned and walked out, loosening his belt as he went, and to the old man's complete despair, she slid away from the table and followed him, almost ran after him, out the door and into the truck behind him, and they drove off.

This cowardice affected Mr. Fortune as if it were his own. It made him physically sick. "He beats an innocent child," he said to his daughter, who was apparently still prostrate at the end of the table, "and not one of you lifts a hand to stop him."

"You ain't lifted yours neither," one of the boys said in an undertone and there was a general mutter from that chorus of frogs.

"I'm an old man with a heart condition," he said. "I can't stop an ox."

"She put you up to it," his daughter murmured in a languid listless tone, her head rolling back and forth on the rim of her chair. "She puts you up to everything."

"No child never put me up to nothing!" he yelled. "You're no kind of a mother! You're a disgrace! That child is an angel! A saint!" he shouted in a voice so high that it broke and he had to scurry out of the room.

The rest of the afternoon he had to lie on his bed. His heart, whenever he knew the child had been beaten, felt as if it were slightly too large for the space that was supposed to hold it. But now he was more determined than ever to see the filling station go up in front of the house, and if it gave Pitts a stroke, so much the better. If it gave him a stroke and paralyzed him, he would be served right and he would never be able to beat her again.

Mary Fortune was never angry with him for long, or seriously, and though he did not see her the rest of that day, when he woke up the next morning, she was sitting astride his chest ordering him to make haste so that they would not miss the concrete mixer.

The workmen were laying the foundation for the fishing club when they arrived and the concrete mixer was already in operation. It was about the size and color of a circus elephant; they stood and watched it churn for a half-hour or so. At eleven-thirty, the old man had an appointment with Tilman to discuss his transaction and they had to leave. He did not tell Mary Fortune where they were going but only that he had to see a man.

Tilman operated a combination country store, filling station, scrap-metal dump, used-car lot and dance hall five miles down the highway that connected with the dirt road that passed in front of the Fortune place. Since the dirt road would soon be paved, he wanted a good location on it for another such enterprise. He was an up-and-coming man—the kind, Mr. Fortune thought, who was never just in line with progress but always a little ahead of it so that he could be there to meet it when it arrived. Signs up and down the highway announced that Tilman's was only five miles away, only four, only three, only two, only one; then "Watch out for Tilman's, Around this bend!" and finally, "Here it is, Friends, Tilman's!" in dazzling red letters.

Tilman's was bordered on either side by a field of old used-car bodies, a kind of ward for incurable automobiles. He also sold outdoor ornaments, such as stone cranes and chickens, urns, jardinieres, whirligigs, and farther back from the road, so as not to depress his dance-hall customers, a line of tombstones and monuments. Most of his businesses went on out-of-doors, so that his store building itself had not involved excessive expense. It was a one-room wooden structure onto which he had added, behind, a long tin hall equipped for dancing. This was divided into two sections, Colored and White, each with its private nickelodeon. He had a barbecue pit and sold barbecued sandwiches and soft drinks.

As they drove up under the shed of Tilman's place, the old man glanced at the child sitting with her feet drawn up on the seat and her chin resting on her knees. He didn't know if she would remember that it was Tilman he was going to sell the lot to or not.

"What you going in here for?" she asked suddenly, with a sniffing look as if she scented an enemy.

"Noner yer bidnis," he said. "You just sit in the car and when I come out, I'll bring you something."

"Don'tcher bring me nothing," she said darkly, "because I won't be here."

"Haw!" he said. "Now you're here, it's nothing for you to do but wait," and he got out and without paying her any further attention, he entered the dark store where Tilman was waiting for him.

When he came out in half an hour, she was not in the car. Hiding, he decided. He started walking around the store to see if she was in the back. He looked in the doors of the two sections of the dance hall and walked on around by the tombstones. Then his eye roved over the field of sinking automobiles and he realized that she could be in or behind any one of two hundred of them. He came back out in front of the store. A Negro boy, drinking a purple drink, was sitting on the ground with his back against the sweating ice cooler.

"Where did that little girl go to, boy?" he asked.

"I ain't seen nair little girl," the boy said.

The old man irritably fished in his pocket and handed him a nickel and said, "A pretty little girl in a yeller cotton dress."

"If you speakin about a stout chile look lak you," the boy said, "she gone off in a truck with a white man."

"What kind of a truck, what kind of a white man?" he yelled.

"It were a green pick-up truck," the boy said smacking his lips, "and a white man she call 'daddy.' They gone thataway some time ago."

The old man, trembling, got in his car and started home. His feelings raced back and forth between fury and mortification. She had never left him before and certainly never for Pitts. Pitts had ordered her to get in the truck and she was afraid not to. But when he reached this conclusion he was more furious than ever. What was the matter with her that she couldn't stand up to Pitts? Why was there this one flaw in her character when he had trained her so well in everything else? It was an ugly mystery.

When he reached the house and climbed the front steps, there she was sitting in the swing, looking glum-faced in front of her across the field he was going to sell. Her eyes were puffy and pink-rimmed but he didn't see any red marks on her legs. He sat down in the swing beside her. He meant to make his voice severe but instead it came out crushed, as if it belonged to a suitor trying to reinstate himself.

"What did you leave me for? You ain't ever left me before," he said.

"Because I wanted to," she said, looking straight ahead.

"You never wanted to," he said. "He made you."

"I toljer I was just going and I went," she said in a slow emphatic voice, not looking at him, "and now you can go on and lemme alone." There was something very final, in the sound of this, a tone that had not come up before in their disputes. She stared across the lot where there was nothing but a profusion of pink and yellow and purple weeds, and on across the red road, to the sullen line of black pine woods fringed on top with green. Behind that line was a narrow gray-blue line of more distant woods and beyond that nothing but the sky, entirely blank except for one or two threadbare clouds. She looked into this scene as if it were a person that she preferred to him.

"It's my lot, ain't it?" he asked. "Why are you so up-in-the-air about me selling my own lot?"

"Because it's the lawn," she said. Her nose and eyes began to run horribly but she held her face rigid and licked the water off as soon as it was in reach of her tongue. "We won't be able to see across the road," she said.

The old man looked across the road to assure himself again that there was nothing over there to see. "I never have seen you act in such a way before," he said in an incredulous voice. There's not a thing over there but the woods."

"We won't be able to see 'um," she said, "and that's the *lawn* and my daddy grazes his calves on it."

At that the old man stood up. "You act more like a Pitts than a Fortune," he said. He had never made such an ugly remark to her before and he was sorry the instant he had said it. It hurt him more than it did her. He turned and went in the house and upstairs to his room.

Several times during the afternoon, he got up from his bed and looked out the window across the "lawn" to the line of woods she said they wouldn't be able to see any more. Every time he saw the same thing: woods—not a mountain, not a waterfall, not any kind of planted bush or flower, just woods. The sunlight was woven through them at that particular time of the afternoon so that every thin pine trunk stood out in all its nakedness. A pine trunk is a pine trunk, he said to himself, and anybody that wants to see one don't have to go far in this neighborhood. Every time he got up and looked out, he was reconvinced of his wisdom in selling the lot. The dissatisfaction it caused Pitts would be permanent, but he could make it up to Mary Fortune by buying her something. With grown people, a road led either to heaven or hell, but with children there were always stops along the way where their attention could be turned with a trifle.

The third time he got up to look at the woods, it was almost six o'clock and the gaunt trunks appeared to be raised in a pool of red light that gushed from the almost hidden sun setting behind them. The old man stared for some time, as if for a prolonged instant he were caught up out of the rattle of everything that led to the future and were held there in the midst of an uncomfortable mystery that he had not apprehended before. He saw it, in his hallucination, as if someone were wounded behind the woods and the trees were bathed in blood. After a few minutes this unpleasant vision was broken by the presence of Pitts's pick-up truck grinding to a halt below the window. He returned to his bed and shut his eyes and against the closed lids hellish red trunks rose up in a black wood.

At the supper table nobody addressed a word to him, including Mary Fortune. He ate quickly and returned again to his room and spent the evening pointing out to himself the advantages for the future of having an establishment like Tilman's so near. They would not have to go any distance for gas. Anytime they needed a loaf of bread, all they would have to do would be step out their front door into Tilman's back door. They could sell milk to Tilman. Tilman was a likable fellow. Tilman would draw other business. The road would soon be paved. Travelers from all over the country would stop at Tilman's. If his daughter thought she was better than Tilman, it would be well to take her down a little. All men were created free and equal. When this phrase sounded in his head, his patriotic sense triumphed and he realized that it was his duty to sell the lot, that he must insure the future. He looked out the window at the moon shining over the woods across the road and listened for a while to the hum of crickets and treefrogs, and beneath their racket, he could hear the throb of the future town of Fortune.

He went to bed certain that just as usual, he would wake up in the morning lookng into a little red mirror framed in a door of fine hair. She would have forgotten all about the sale and after breakfast they would drive into town and get the legal papers from the courthouse. On the way back he would stop at Tilman's and close the deal.

When he opened his eyes in the morning, he opened them on the empty ceiling. He pulled himself up and looked around the room but she was not there. He hung over the edge of the bed and looked beneath it but she was not there either. He got up and dressed and went outside. She was sitting in the swing on the front porch, exactly the way she had been yesterday, looking across the lawn into the woods. The old man was very much irritated. Every morning since she had been able to climb, he had waked up to find her either on his bed or underneath it. It was apparent that this morning she preferred the sight of the woods. He decided to ignore her behavior for the present and then bring it up later when she was over her pique. He sat down in the swing beside her but she continued to look at the woods. "I thought you and me'd go into town and have a look at the boats in the new boat store," he said.

She didn't turn her head but she asked suspiciously, in a loud voice, "What else are you going for?"

"Nothing else," he said.

After a pause she said, "If that's all, I'll go," but she did not bother to look at him.

"Well put on your shoes," he said. "I ain't going to the city with a barefoot woman." She did not bother to laugh at this joke.

The weather was as indifferent as her disposition. The sky did not look as if were going to rain or as if it were not going to rain. It was an unpleasant gray and the sun had not troubled to come out. All the way into town, she sat looking at her feet, which stuck out in front of her, encased in heavy brown school shoes. The old man had often sneaked up on her and found her alone in conversation with her feet and he thought she was speaking with them silently now. Every now and then her lips moved but she said nothing to him and let all his remarks pass as if she had not heard them. He decided it was going to cost him considerable to buy her good humor again and that he had better do it with a boat, since he wanted one too. She had been talking boats ever since the water backed up onto his place. They went first to the boat store. "Show us the yachts for po' folks!" he shouted jovially to the clerk as they entered.

"They're all for po' folks!" the clerk said. "You'll be po' when you finish buying one!" He was a stout youth in a yellow shirt and blue pants and he had a ready wit. They exchanged several clever remarks in rapid-fire succession. Mr. Fortune looked at Mary Fortune to see if her face had brightened. She stood staring absently over the side of an outboard motor boat at the opposite wall.

"Ain't the lady innerested in boats?" the clerk asked.

She turned and wandered back out onto the sidewalk and got in the car again. The old man looked after her with amazement. He could not believe that a child of her intelligence could be acting this way over the mere sale of a field. "I think she must be coming down with something," he said. "We'll come back again," and he returned to the car.

"Let's go get us an ice-cream cone," he suggested, looking at her with concern.

"I don't want no ice-cream cone," she said.

His actual destination was the courthouse but he did not want to make this apparent. "How'd you like to visit the ten-cent store while I tend to a little bidnis of mine?" he asked. "You can buy yourself something with a quarter I brought along."

"I ain't got nothing to do in no ten-cent store," she said. "I don't want no quarter of yours."

If a boat was of no interest, he should not have thought a quarter would be and reproved himself for that stupidity. "Well what's the matter, sister?" he asked kindly. "Don't you feel good?"

She turned and looked him straight in the face and said with a slow concentrated ferocity, "It's the lawn. My daddy grazes his calves there. We won't be able to see the woods any more."

The old man had held his fury in as long as he could. "He beats you!" he shouted. "And you worry about where he's going to graze his calves!"

"Nobody's ever beat me in my life," she said, "and if anybody did, I'd kill him."

A man seventy-nine years of age cannot let himself be run over by a child of nine. His face set in a look that was just as determined as hers. "Are you a Fortune," he said, "or are you a Pitts? Make up your mind."

Her voice was loud and positive and belligerent. "I'm Mary—Fortune—Pitts," she said.

"Well I," he shouted, "am PURE Fortune!"

There was nothing she could say to this and she showed it. For an instant she looked completely defeated, and the old man saw with a disturbing clearness that this was the Pitts look. What he saw was the Pitts look, pure and simple, and he felt personally stained by it, as if it had been found on his own face. He turned in disgust and backed the car out and drove straight to the courthouse.

The courthouse was a red and white blaze-faced building set in the center of a square from which most of the grass had been worn off. He parked in front of it and said, "Stay here," in an imperious tone and got out and slammed the car door.

It took him a half-hour to get the deed and have the sale

paper drawn up and when he returned to the car, she was sitting on the back seat in the corner. The expression on that part of her face that he could see was foreboding and withdrawn. The sky had darkened also and there was a hot sluggish tide in the air, the kind felt when a tornado is possible.

"We better get on before we get caught in a storm," he said and added emphatically, "because I got one more place to stop at on the way home," but he might have been chauffeuring a small dead body for all the answer he got.

On the way to Tilman's he reviewed once more the many just reasons that were leading him to his present action and he could not locate a flaw in any of them. He decided that while this attitude of hers would not be permanent, he was permanently disappointed in her and that when she came around she would have to apologize; and that there would be no boat. He was coming to realize slowly that his trouble with her had always been that he had not shown enough firmness. He had been too generous. He was so occupied with these thoughts that he did not notice the signs that said how many miles to Tilman's until the last one exploded joyfully in his face: "Here it is, Friends, TILMAN'S!" He pulled in under the shed.

He got out without so much as looking at Mary Fortune and entered the dark store where Tilman, leaning on the counter in front of a triple shelf of canned goods, was waiting for him.

Tilman was a man of quick action and few words. He sat habitually with his arms folded on the counter and his insignificant head weaving snake-fashion above them. He had a triangular-shaped face with the point at the bottom and the top of his skull was covered with a cap of freckles. His eyes were green and very narrow and his tongue was always exposed in his partly opened mouth. He had his checkbook handy and they got down to business at once. It did not take him long to look at the deed and sign the bill of sale. Then Mr. Fortune signed it and they grasped hands over the counter.

Mr. Fortune's sense of relief as he grasped Tilman's hand was extreme. What was done, he felt, was done and there could be no more argument, with her or with himself. He felt that he had acted on principle and that the future was assured.

Just as their hands loosened, an instant's change came over Tilman's face and he disappeared completely under the counter as if he had been snatched by the feet from below. A

bottle crashed against the line of tinned goods behind where
he had been. The old man whirled around. Mary Fortune
was in the door, red-faced and wild-looking, with another
bottle lifted to hurl. As he ducked, it broke behind him on
the counter and she grabbed another from the crate. He
sprang at her but she tore to the other side of the store,
screaming something unintelligible and throwing everything
within her reach. The old man pounced again and this time
he caught her by the tail of her dress and pulled her backward out of the store. Then he got a better grip and lifted
her, wheezing and whimpering but suddenly limp in his arms,
the few feet to the car. He managed to get the door open and
dump her inside. Then he ran around to the other side and
got in himself and drove away as fast as he could.

His heart felt as if it were the size of the car and was racing forward, carrying him to some inevitable destination faster than he had ever been carried before. For the first five
minutes he did not think but only sped forward as if he were
being driven inside his own fury. Gradually the power of
thought returned to him. Mary Fortune, rolled into a ball in
the corner of the seat, was snuffling and heaving.

He had never seen a child behave in such a way in his life.
Neither his own children nor anyone else's had ever displayed
such temper in his presence, and he had never for an instant
imagined that the child he had trained himself, the child who
had been his constant companion for nine years, would embarrass him like this. The child he had never lifted a hand to!

Then he saw, with the sudden vision that sometimes comes
with delayed recognition, that that had been his mistake.

She respected Pitts because, even with no just cause, he
beat her; and if he—with his just cause—did not beat her
now, he would have nobody to blame but himself if she
turned out a hellion. He saw that the time had come, that he
could no longer avoid whipping her, and as he turned off the
highway onto the dirt road leading to home, he told himself
that when he finished with her, she would never throw another bottle again.

He raced along the clay road until he came to the line
where his own property began and then he turned off onto a
side path, just wide enough for the automobile and bounced
for a half a mile through the woods. He stopped the car at
the exact spot where he had seen Pitts take his belt to her. It
was a place where the road widened so that two cars could
pass or one could turn around, an ugly red bald spot surrounded by long thin pines that appeared to be gathered there to

witness anything that would take place in such a clearing. A few stones protruded from the clay.

"Get out," he said and reached across her and opened the door.

She got out without looking at him or asking what they were going to do and he got out on his side and came around the front of the car.

"Now I'm going to whip you!" he said and his voice was extra loud and hollow and had a vibrating quality that appeared to be taken up and passed through the tops of the pines. He did not want to get caught in a downpour while he was whipping her and he said, "Hurry up and get ready against that tree," and began to take off his belt.

What he had in mind to do appeared to come very slowly as if it had to penetrate a fog in her head. She did not move but gradually her confused expression began to clear. Where a few seconds before her face had been red and distorted and unorganized, it drained now of every vague line until nothing was left on it but positiveness, a look that went slowly past determination and reached certainty. "Nobody has ever beat me," she said, "and if anybody tries it, I'll kill him."

"I don't want no sass," he said and started toward her. His knees felt very unsteady, as if they might turn either backward or forward.

She moved exactly one step back and, keeping her eye on him steadily, removed her glasses and dropped them behind a small rock near the tree he had told her to get ready against. "Take off your glasses," she said.

"Don't give me orders!" he said in a high voice and slapped awkwardly at her ankles with his belt.

She was on him so quickly that he could not have recalled which blow he felt first, whether the weight of her whole solid body or the jabs of her feet or the pummeling of her fist on his chest. He flailed the belt in the air, not knowing where to hit but trying to get her off him until he could decide where to get a grip on her.

"Leggo!" he shouted. "Leggo I tell you!" But she seemed to be everywhere, coming at him from all directions at once. It was as if he were being attacked not by one child but by a pack of small demons all with stout brown school shoes and small rocklike fists. His glasses flew to the side.

"I toljer to take them off," she growled without pausing.

He caught his knee and danced on one foot and a rain of blows fell on his stomach. He felt five claws in the flesh of his upper arm where she was hanging from while her feet mechanically battered his knees and her free fist pounded him again and again in the chest. Then with horror he saw her face rise up in front of his, teeth exposed, and he roared like a bull as she bit the side of his jaw. He seemed to see his own face coming to bite him from several sides at once but he could not attend to it for he was being kicked indiscriminately, in the stomach and then in the crotch. Suddenly he threw himself on the ground and began to roll like a man on fire. She was on top of him at once, rolling with him and still kicking, and now with both fists free to batter his chest.

"I'm an old man!" he piped. "Leave me alone!" But she did not stop. She began a fresh assault on his jaw.

"Stop stop!" he wheezed. "I'm your grandfather!"

She paused, her face exactly on top of his. Pale identical eye looked into pale identical eye. "Have you had enough?" she asked.

The old man loked up into his own image. It was triumphant and hostile. "You been whipped," it said, "by me," and then it added, bearing down on each word, "and I'm PURE Pitts."

In the pause she loosened her grip and he got hold of her throat. With a sudden surge of strength, he managed to roll over and reverse their positions so that he was looking down into the face that was his own but had dared to call itself Pitts. With his hands still tight around her neck, he lifted her head and brought it down once hard against the rock that happened to be under it. Then he brought it down twice more. Then looking into the face in which the eyes, slowly rolling back, appeared to pay him not the slightest attention, he said, "There's not an ounce of Pitts in me."

He continued to stare at his conquered image until he perceived that though it was absolutely silent, there was no look of remorse on it. The eyes had rolled back down and were set in a fixed glare that did not take him in. "This ought to teach you a good lesson," he said in a voice that was edged with doubt.

He managed painfully to get up on his unsteady kicked legs and to take two steps, but the enlargement of his heart which had begun in the car was still going on. He turned his head and looked behind him for a long time at the little motionless figure with its head on the rock.

Then he fell on his back and looked up helplessly along the bare trunks into the tops of the pines and his heart expanded once more with a convulsive motion. It expanded so fast that the old man felt as if he were being pulled after it through the woods, felt as if he were running as fast as he could with the ugly pines toward the lake. He perceived that there would be a little opening there, a little place where he could escape and leave the woods behind him. He could see it in the distance already, a little opening where the white sky was reflected in the water. It grew as he ran toward it until suddenly the whole lake opened up before him, riding majestically in little corrugated folds toward his feet. He realized suddenly that he could not swim and that he had not bought the boat. On both sides of him he saw that the gaunt trees had thickened into mysterious dark files that were marching across the water and away into the distance. He looked around desperately for someone to help him but the place was deserted except for one huge yellow monster which sat to the side, as stationary as he was, gorging itself on clay.

The Enduring Chill

Asbury's train stopped so that he would get off exactly where his mother was standing waiting to meet him. Her thin spectacled face below him was bright with a wide smile that disappeared as she caught sight of him bracing himself behind the conductor. The smile vanished so suddenly, the shocked look that replaced it was so complete, that he realized for the first time that he must look as ill as he was. The sky was a chill gray and a startling white-gold sun, like some strange potentate from the east, was rising beyond the black woods that surrounded Timberboro. It cast a strange light over the single block of one-story brick and wooden shacks. Asbury felt that he was about to witness a majestic transformation, that the flat of roofs might at any moment turn into the mounting turrets of some exotic temple for a god he didn't know. The illusion lasted only a moment before his attention was drawn back to his mother.

She had given a little cry; she looked aghast. He was pleased that she should see death in his face at once. His mother, at the age of sixty, was going to be introduced to reality and he supposed that if the experience didn't kill her, it would assist her in the process of growing up. He stepped down and greeted her.

"You don't look very well," she said and gave him a long clinical stare.

"I don't feel like talking," he said at once. "I've had a bad trip."

Mrs. Fox observed that his left eye was bloodshot. He was puffy and pale and his hair had receded tragically for a boy of twenty-five. The thin reddish wedge of it left on top bore down in a point that seemed to lengthen his nose and give him an irritable expression that matched his tone of voice when he spoke to her. "It must have been cold up there," she said. "Why don't you take off your coat? It's not cold down here."

"You don't have to tell me what the temperature is!" he said in a high voice. "I'm old enough to know when I want to take my coat off!" The train glided silently away behind him,

327

leaving a view of the twin blocks of dilapidated stores. He gazed after the aluminum speck disappearing into the woods. It seemed to him that his last connection with a larger world was vanishing forever. Then he turned and faced his mother grimly, irked that he had allowed himself, even for an instant, to see an imaginary temple in this collapsing country junction. He had become entirely accustomed to the thought of death, but he had not become accustomed to the thought of death *here*.

He had felt the end coming on for nearly four months. Alone in his freezing flat, huddled under his two blankets and his overcoat and with three thicknesses of the New York *Times* between, he had had a chill one night, followed by a violent sweat that left the sheets soaking and removed all doubt from his mind about his true condition. Before this there had been a gradual slackening of his energy and vague inconsistent aches and headaches. He had been absent so many days from his part-time job in the bookstore that he had lost it. Since then he had been living, or just barely so, on his savings and these, diminishing day by day, had been all he had between him and home. Now there was nothing. He was here.

"Where's the car?" he muttered.

"It's over yonder," his mother said. "And your sister is asleep in the back because I don't like to come out this early by myself. There's no need to wake her up."

"No," he said, "let sleeping dogs lie," and he picked up his two bulging suitcases and started across the road with them.

They were too heavy for him and by the time he reached the car, his mother saw that he was exhausted. He had never come home with two suitcases before. Ever since he had first gone away to college, he had come back every time with nothing but the necessities for a two-week stay and with a wooden resigned expression that said he was prepared to endure the visit for exactly fourteen days. "You've brought more than usual," she observed, but he did not answer.

He opened the car door and hoisted the two bags in beside his sister's upturned feet, giving first the feet—in Girl Scout shoes—and then the rest of her a revolted look of recognition. She was packed into a black suit and had a white rag around her head with metal curlers sticking out from under the edges. Her eyes were closed and her mouth was open. He and she had the same features except that hers were bigger. She was eight years older than he was and was principal of the county elementary school. He shut the door softly so she wouldn't wake up and then went around and got in the front seat and closed his eyes. His mother backed the car into the road and in a few minutes he felt it swerve into the highway. Then he opened his eyes. The road stretched between two open fields of yellow bitterweed.

"Do you think Timberboro has improved?" his mother asked. This was her standard question, meant to be taken literally.

"It's still there, isn't it?" he said in an ugly voice.

"Two of the stores have new fronts," she said. Then with a sudden ferocity, she said, "You did well to come home where you can get a good doctor! I'll take you to Doctor Block this afternoon."

"I am not," he said, trying to keep his voice from shaking, "going to Doctor Block. This afternoon or ever. Don't you think if I'd wanted to go to a doctor I'd have gone up there where they have some good ones? Don't you know they have better doctors in New York?"

"He would take a personal interest in you," she said. "None of those doctors up there would take a personal interest in you."

"I don't want him taking a personal interest in me." Then after a minute, staring out across a blurred purple-looking field, he said, "What's wrong with me is way beyond Block," and his voice trailed off into a frayed sound, almost a sob.

He could not, as his friend Goetz had recommended, prepare to see it all as illusion, either what had gone before or the few weeks that were left to him. Goetz was certain that death was nothing at all. Goetz, whose whole face had always been purple-splotched with a million indignations, had returned from six months in Japan as dirty as ever but as bland as the Buddha himself. Goetz took the news of Asbury's approaching end with a calm indifference. Quoting something or other he said, "Although the Bodhisattva leads an infinite number of creatures into nirvana, in reality there are neither any Bodhisattvas to do the leading nor any creatures to be led." However, out of some feeling for his welfare, Goetz had put forth $4.50 to take him to a lecture on Vedanta. It had been a waste of his money. While Goetz had listened enthralled to the dark little man on the platform, Asbury's bored gaze had roved among the audience. It had passed over the heads of several girls in saris, past a Japanese youth, a blue-black man with a fez, and several girls who looked like secretaries. Finally, at the end of the row, it had rested on a lean spectacled figure in black, a priest. The priest's expression was a polite but strictly reserved interest. Asbury identified his own feelings immediately in the taciturn superior expression. When the lecture was over a few students met in Goetz's flat, the priest among them, but here he was equally reserved. He listened with a marked politeness to the discussion of Asbury's approaching death, but he said little. A girl in a sari remarked that self-fulfillment was out of the question since it meant salvation and the word was meaningless. "Salvation," quoted Goetz, "is the destruction of a simple prejudice, and no one is saved."

"And what do you say to that?" Asbury asked the priest and returned his reserved smile over the heads of the others. The borders of this smile seemed to touch on some icy clarity.

"There is," the priest said, "a real probability of the New Man, assisted, of course," he added brittlely, "by the Third Person of the Trinity."

"Ridiculous!" the girl in the sari said, but the priest only brushed her with his smile, which was slightly amused now.

When he got up to leave, he silently handed Asbury a small card on which he had written his name, Ignatius Vogle, S.J., and an address. Perhaps, Asbury thought now, he should have used it for the priest appealed to him as a man of the world, someone who would have understood the unique tragedy of his death, a death whose meaning had been far beyond the twittering group around them. And how much more beyond Block. "What's wrong with me," he repeated, "is way beyond Block."

His mother knew at once what he meant: he meant he was going to have a nervous breakdown. She did not say a word. She did not say that this was precisely what she could have told him would happen. When people think they are smart—even when they are smart—there is nothing anybody else can say to make them see things straight, and with Asbury, the trouble was that in addition to being smart, he had an artistic temperament. She did not know where he had got it from because his father, who was a lawyer and businessman and farmer and politician all rolled into one, had certainly had his feet on the ground; and she had certainly always had hers on it. She had managed after he died to get the two of them through college and beyond; but she had observed that the more education they got, the less they could do. Their father had gone to a one-room schoolhouse through the eighth grade and he could do anything.

She could have told Asbury what would help him. She could have said, "If you would get out in the sunshine, or if you would work for a month in the dairy, you'd be a different person!" but she knew exactly how that suggestion would be received. He would be a nuisance in the dairy but she would let him work in there if he wanted to. She had let him work in there last year when he had come home and was writing the play. He had been writing a play about Negroes (why anybody would want to write a play about Negroes was beyond her) and he had said he wanted to work in the dairy with them and find out what their interests were. Their interests were in doing as little as they could get by with, as she could have told him if anybody could have told him anything. The Negroes had put up with him and he had learned to put the milkers on and once he had washed all the cans and she thought that once he had mixed feed. Then a cow had kicked him and he had not gone back to the barn again. She knew that if he would get in there now, or get out and fix fences, or do any kind of work—real work, not writing—that he might avoid this nervous breakdown. "Whatever happened to that play you were writing about the Negroes?" she asked.

"I am not writing plays," he said. "And get this through your head: I am not working in any dairy. I am not getting out in the sunshine. I'm ill. I have fever and chills and I'm dizzy and all I want you to do is leave me alone."

"Then if you are really ill, you should see Doctor Block."

"And I am not seeing Block," he finished and ground himself down in the seat and stared intensely in front of him.

She turned into their driveway, a red road that ran for a quarter of a mile through the two front pastures. The dry cows were on one side and the milk herd on the other. She slowed the car and then stopped altogether, her attention caught by a cow with a bad quarter. "They haven't been attending to her," she said. "Look at that bag!"

Asbury turned his head abruptly in the opposite direction, but there a small, walleyed Guernsey was watching him steadily as if she sensed some bond between them. "Good God!" he cried in an agonized voice, "can't we go on? It's six o'clock in the morning!"

"Yes yes," his mother said and started the car quickly.

"What's that cry of deadly pain?" his sister drawled from the back seat. "Oh, it's you," she said. "Well well, we have the artist with us again. How utterly utterly." She had a decidedly nasal voice.

He didn't answer her or turn his head. He had learned that much. Never answer her.

"Mary George!" his mother said sharply. "Asbury is sick. Leave him alone."

"What's wrong with him?" Mary George asked.

"There's the house!" his mother said as if they were all

blind but her. It rose on the crest of the hill—a white two-story farmhouse with a wide porch and pleasant columns. She always approached it with a feeling of pride and she had said more than once to Asbury, "You have a home here that half those people up there would give their eyeteeth for!"

She had been once to the terrible place he lived in New York. They had gone up five flights of dark stone steps, past open garbage cans on every landing, to arrive finally at two damp rooms and a closet with a toilet in it. "You wouldn't live like this at home," she had muttered.

"No!" he'd said with an ecstatic look, "it wouldn't be possible!"

She supposed the truth was that she simply didn't understand how it felt to be sensitive or how peculiar you were when you were an artist. His sister said he was not an artist and that he had no talent and that that was the trouble with him; but Mary George was not a happy girl herself. Asbury said she posed as an intellectual but that her I.Q. couldn't be over seventy-five, that all she was really interested in was getting a man but that no sensible man would finish a first look at her. She had tried to tell him that Mary George could be very attractive when she put her mind to it and he had said that that much strain on her mind would break her down. If she were in any way attractive, he had said, she wouldn't now be principal of a county elementary school, and Mary George had said that if Asbury had had any talent, he would by now have published something. What had he ever published, she wanted to know, and for that matter, what had he ever written?

Mrs. Fox had pointed out that he was only twenty-five years old and Mary George had said that the age most people published something at was twenty-one, which made him exactly four years overdue. Mrs. Fox was not up on things like that but she suggested that he might be writing a very *long* book. Very long book, her eye, Mary George said, he would do well if he came up with so much as a poem. Mrs. Fox hoped it wasn't going to be just a poem.

She pulled the car into the side drive and a scattering of guineas exploded into the air and sailed screaming around the house. "Home again, home again jiggity jig!" she said.

"Oh God," Asbury groaned.

"The artist arrives at the gas chamber," Mary George said in her nasal voice.

He leaned on the door and got out, and forgetting his bags he moved toward the front of the house as if he were in a daze. His sister got out and stood by the car door, squinting at his bent unsteady figure. As she watched him go up the front steps, her mouth fell slack in her astonished face. "Why," she said, "there *is* something the matter with him. He looks a hundred years old."

"Didn't I tell you so?" her mother hissed. "Now you keep your mouth shut and let him alone."

He went into the house, pausing in the hall only long enough to see his pale broken face glare at him for an instant from the pier mirror. Holding onto the banister, he pulled himself up the steep stairs, across the landing and then up the shorter second flight and into his room, a large open airy room with a faded blue rug and white curtains freshly put up for his arrival. He looked at nothing, but fell face down on his own bed. It was a narrow antique bed with a high ornamental headboard on which was carved a garlanded basket overflowing with wooden fruit.

While he was still in New York, he had written a letter to his mother which filled two notebooks. He did not mean it to be read until after his death. It was such a letter as Kafka had addressed to his father. Asbury's father had died twenty years ago and Asbury considered this a great blessing. The old man, he felt sure, had been one of the courthouse gang, a rural worthy with a dirty finger in every pie and he knew he would not have been able to stomach him. He had read some of his correspondence and had been appalled by its stupidity.

He knew, of course, that his mother would not understand the letter at once. Her literal mind would require some time to discover the significance of it, but he thought she would be able to see that he forgave her for all she had done to him. For that matter, he supposed that she would realize what she had done to him only through the letter. He didn't think she was conscious of it at all. Her self-satisfaction itself was barely conscious, but because of the letter, she might experience a painful realization and this would be the only thing of value he had to leave her.

If reading it would be painful to her, writing it had sometimes been unbearable to him—for in order to face her, he had had to face himself. "I came here to escape the slave's atmosphere of home," he had written, "to find freedom, to liberate my imagination, to take it like a hawk from its cage and set it 'whirling off into the widening gyre' (Yeats) and what did I find? It was incapable of flight. It was some bird you had domesticated, sitting huffy in its pen, refusing to come out!" The next words were underscored twice. "I have no imagination. I have no talent. I can't create. I have nothing but the desire for these things. Why didn't you kill that too? Woman, why did you pinion me?"

Writing this, he had reached the pit of despair and he thought that reading it, she would at least begin to sense his tragedy and her part in it. It was not that she had ever forced her way on him. That had never been necessary. Her way had simply been the air he breathed and when at last he had found other air, he couldn't survive in it. He felt that even if she didn't understand at once, the letter would leave her with an enduring chill and perhaps in time lead her to see herself as she was.

He had destroyed everything else he had ever written—his two lifeless novels, his half-dozen stationary plays, his prosy poems, his sketchy short stories—and kept only the two note-books that contained the letter. They were in the black suitcase that his sister, huffing and blowing, was now dragging up the second flight of stairs. His mother was carrying the smaller bag and came on ahead. He turned over as she entered the room.

"I'll open this and get out your things," she said, "and you can go right to bed and in a few minutes I'll bring your breakfast."

He sat up and said in a fretful voice, "I don't want any breakfast and I can open my own suitcase. Leave that alone."

His sister arrived in the door, her face full of curiosity, and let the black bag fall with a thud over the doorsill. Then she began to push it across the room with her foot until she was close enough to get a good look at him. "If I looked as bad as you do," she said, "I'd go to the hospital."

Her mother cut her eyes sharply at her and she left. Then Mrs. Fox closed the door and came to the bed and sat down on it beside him. "Now this time I want you to make a long visit and rest," she said.

"This visit," he said, "will be permanent."

"Wonderful!" she cried. "You can have a little studio in your room and in the mornings you can write plays and in the afternoons you can help in the dairy!"

He turned a white wooden face to her. "Close the blinds and let me sleep," he said.

When she was gone, he lay for some time staring at the water stains on the gray walls. Descending from the top molding, long icicle shapes had been etched by leaks and, directly over his bed on the ceiling, another leak had made a fierce bird with spread wings. It had an icicle crosswise in its beak and there were smaller icicles depending from its wings and tail. It had been there since his childhood and had always irritated him and sometimes ha... ten had the illusion that it was ... descend mysteriously and set the icicl... his eyes and thought: I won't have t... more days. And presently he went to sleep...

When he woke up in the afternoon, there w... mouthed face hanging over him and from two ... ar ears on either side of it the black tubes of Block's ... cope extended down to his exposed chest. The doctor, s...ing he was awake, made a face like a Chinaman, rolled his eyes almost out of his head and cried, "Say AHHHH!"

Block was irresistible to children. For miles around they vomited and went into fevers to have a visit from him. Mrs. Fox was standing behind him, smiling radiantly. "Here's Doctor Block!" she said as if she had captured this angel on the rooftop and brought him in for her little boy.

"Get him out of here," Asbury muttered. He looked at the asinine face from what seemed the bottom of a black hole.

The doctor peered closer, wiggling his ears. Block was bald and had a round face as senseless as a baby's. Nothing about him indicated intelligence except two cold clinical nickel-colored eyes that hung with a motionless curiosity over whatever he looked at. "You sho do look bad, Azzberry," he murmured. He took the stethoscope off and dropped it in his bag. "I don't know when I've seen anybody your age look as sorry as you do. What you been doing to yourself?"

There was a continuous thud in the back of Asbury's head as if his heart had got trapped in it and was fighting to get out. "I didn't send for you," he said.

Block put his hand on the glaring face and pulled the eyelid down and peered into it. "You must have been on the bum up there," he said. He began to press his hand in the small of Asbury's back. "I went up there once myself," he said, "and saw exactly how little they had and came straight on back home. Open your mouth."

Asbury opened it automatically and the drill-like gaze swung over it and bore down. He snapped it shut and in a wheezing breathless voice he said, "If I'd wanted a doctor, I'd have stayed up there where I could have got a good one!"

"Asbury!" his mother said.

"How long you been having the so' throat?" Block asked.

"She sent for you!" Asbury said. "She can answer the questions."

"Asbury!" his mother said.

Block leaned over his bag and pulled out a rubber tube.

...ed Asbury's sleeve up and tied the tube around his ...per arm. Then he took out a syringe and prepared to find the vein, humming a hymn as he pressed the needle in. Asbury lay with a rigid outraged stare while the privacy of his blood was invaded by this idiot. "Slowly Lord but sure," Block sang in a murmuring voice, "Oh slowly Lord but sure." When the syringe was full, he withdrew the needle. "Blood don't lie," he said. He poured it in a bottle and stopped it up and put the bottle in his bag. "Azzberry," he started, "how long . . ."

Asbury sat up and thrust his thudding head forward and said, "I didn't send for you. I'm not answering any questions. You're not my doctor. What's wrong with me is way beyond you."

"Most things are beyond me," Block said. "I ain't found anything yet that I thoroughly understood," and he sighed and got up. His eyes seemed to glitter at Asbury as if from a great distance.

"He wouldn't act so ugly," Mrs. Fox explained, "if he weren't really sick. And *I* want you to come back every day until you get him well."

Asbury's eyes were a fierce glaring violet. "What's wrong with me is way beyond you," he repeated and lay back down and closed his eyes until Block and his mother were gone.

In the next few days, though he grew rapidly worse, his mind functioned with a terrible clarity. On the point of death, he found himself existing in a state of illumination that was totally out of keeping with the kind of talk he had to listen to from his mother. This was largely about cows with names like Daisy and Bessie Button and their intimate functions—their mastitis and their screwworms and their abortions. His mother insisted that in the middle of the day he get out and sit on the porch and "enjoy the view" and as resistance was too much of a struggle, he dragged himself out and sat there in a rigid slouch, his feet wrapped in an afghan and his hands gripped on the chair arms as if he were about to spring forward into the glaring china blue sky. The lawn extended for a quarter of an acre down to a barbed-wire fence that divided it from the front pasture. In the middle of the day the dry cows rested there under a line of sweetgum trees. On the other side of the road were two hills with a pond between and his mother could sit on the porch and watch the herd walk across the dam to the hill on the other side. The whole scene was rimmed by a wall of trees which, at the time of day he was forced to sit there, was a washed-out blue that reminded him sadly of the Negroes' faded overalls.

He listened irritably while his mother detailed the faults of the help. "Those two are not stupid," she said. "They know how to look out for themselves."

"They need to," he muttered, but there was no use to argue with her. Last year he had been writing a play about the Negro and he had wanted to be around them for a while to see how they really felt about their condition, but the two who worked for her had lost all their initiative over the years. They didn't talk. The one called Morgan was light brown, part Indian; the other, older one, Randall, was very black and fat. When they said anything to him, it was as if they were speaking to an invisible body located to the right or left of where he actually was, and after two days working side by side with them, he felt he had not established rapport. He decided to try something bolder than talk and one afternoon as he was standing near Randall, watching him adjust a milker, he had quietly taken out his cigarettes and lit one. The Negro had stopped what he was doing and watched him. He waited until Asbury had taken two draws and then he said, "She don't 'low no smoking in here."

The other one approached and stood there, grinning.

"I know it," Asbury said and after a deliberate pause, he shook the package and held it out, first to Randall, who took one, and then to Morgan, who took one. He had then lit the cigarettes for them himself and the three of them stood there smoking. There were no sounds but the steady click of the two milking machines and the occasional slap of a cow's tail against her side. It was one of those moments of communion when the difference between black and white is absorbed into nothing.

The next day two cans of milk had been returned from the creamery because it had absorbed the odor of tobacco. He took the blame and told his mother that it was he and not the Negroes who had been smoking. "If you were doing it, they were doing it," she had said. "Don't you think I know those two?" She was incapable of thinking them innocent; but the experience had so exhilarated him that he had been determined to repeat it in some other way.

The next afternoon when he and Randall were in the milk house pouring the fresh milk into the cans, he had picked up the jelly glass the Negroes drank out of and, inspired, had poured himself a glassful of the warm milk and drained it down. Randall had stopped pouring and had remained, half-bent, over the can, watching him. "She don't 'low that," he said. "That *the* thing she don't 'low."

Asbury poured out another glassful and handed it to him.

"She don't 'low it," he repeated.

"Listen," Asbury said hoarsely, "the world is changing. There's no reason I shouldn't drink after you or you after me!"

"She don't 'low noner us to drink noner this here milk," Randall said.

Asbury continued to hold the glass out to him. "You took the cigarette," he said. "Take the milk. It's not going to hurt my mother to lose two or three glasses of milk a day. We've got to think free if we want to live free!"

The other one had come up and was standing in the door.

"Don't want noner that milk," Randall said.

Asbury swung around and held the glass out to Morgan. "Here boy, have a drink of this," he said.

Morgan stared at him; then his face took on a decided look of cunning. "I ain't seen you drink none of it yourself," he said.

Asbury despised milk. The first warm glassful had turned his stomach. He drank half of what he was holding and handed the rest to the Negro, who took it and gazed down inside the glass as if it contained some great mystery; then he set it on the floor by the cooler.

"Don't you like milk?" Asbury asked.

"I likes it but I ain't drinking noner that."

"Why?"

"She don't 'low it," Morgan said.

"My God!" Asbury exploded, "she she she!" He had tried the same thing the next day and the next and the next but he could not get them to drink the milk. A few afternoons later when he was standing outside the milk house about to go in, he heard Morgan ask, "Howcome you let him drink all that milk every day?"

"What he do is him," Randall said. "What I do is me."

"Howcome he talks so ugly about his ma?"

"She ain't whup him enough when he was little," Randall said.

The insufferableness of life at home had overcome him and he had returned to New York two days early. So far as he was concerned he had died there, and the question now was how long he could stand to linger here. He could have hastened his end but suicide would not have been a victory. Death was coming to him legitimately, as a justification, as a gift from life. That was his greatest triumph. Then too, to the fine minds of the neighborhood, a suicide son would indicate a mother who had been a failure, and while this was the case, he felt that it was a public embarrassment he could spare her. What she would learn from the letter would be a private revelation. He had sealed the notebooks in a manila envelope and had written on it: "To be opened only after the death of Asbury Porter Fox." He had put the envelope in the desk drawer in his room and locked it and the key was in his pajama pocket until he could decide on a place to leave it.

When they sat on the porch in the morning, his mother felt that some of the time she should talk about subjects that were of interest to him. The third morning she started in on his writing. "When you get well," she said, "I think it would be nice if you wrote a book about down here. We need another good book like *Gone With the Wind*."

He could feel the muscles of his stomach begin to tighten.

"Put the war in it," she advised. "That always makes a long book."

He put his head back gently as if he were afraid it would crack. After a moment he said, "I am not going to write any book."

"Well," she said, "if you don't feel like writing a book, you could just write poems. They're nice." She realized that what he needed was someone intellectual to talk to, but Mary George was the only intellectual she knew and he would not talk to her. She had thought of Mr. Bush, the retired Methodist minister, but she had not brought this up. Now she decided to hazard it. "I think I'll ask Dr. Bush to come to see you," she said, raising Mr. Bush's rank. "You'd enjoy him. He collects rare coins."

She was not prepared for the reaction she got. He began to shake all over and give loud spasmodic laughs. He seemed about to choke. After a minute he subsided into a cough. "If you think I need spiritual aid to die," he said, "you're quite mistaken. And certainly not from that ass Bush. My God!"

"I didn't mean that at all," she said. "He has coins dating from the time of Cleopatra."

"Well if you ask him here, I'll tell him to go to hell," he said. "Bush! That beats all!"

"I'm glad something amuses you," she said acidly.

For a time they sat there in silence. Then his mother looked up. He was sitting forward again and smiling at her. His face was brightening more and more as if he had just had an idea that was brilliant. She stared at him. "I'll tell you who I want to come," he said. For the first time since he had come home, his expression was pleasant; though there was also, she thought, a kind of crafty look about him.

"Who do you want to come?" she asked suspiciously.

"I want a priest," he announced.

"A priest?" his mother said in an uncomprehending voice.

"Preferably a Jesuit," he said, brightening more and more. "Yes, by all means a Jesuit. They have them in the city. You can call up and get me one."

"What is the matter with you?" his mother asked.

"Most of them are very well-educated," he said, "but Jesuits are foolproof. A Jesuit would be able to discuss something besides the weather." Already, remembering Ignatius Vogle, S.J., he could picture the priest. This one would be a trifle more worldly perhaps, a trifle more cynical. Protected by their ancient institution, priests could afford to be cynical, to play both ends against the middle. He would talk to a man of culture before he died—even in this desert! Furthermore, nothing would irritate his mother so much. He could not understand why he had not thought of this sooner.

"You're not a member of that church," Mrs. Fox said shortly. "It's twenty miles away. They wouldn't send one." She hoped that this would end the matter.

He sat back absorbed in the idea, determined to force her to make the call since she always did what he wanted if he kept at her. "I'm dying," he said, "and I haven't asked you to do but one thing and you refuse me that."

"You are NOT dying."

"When you realize it," he said, "it'll be too late."

There was another unpleasant silence. Presently his mother said, "Nowadays doctors don't *let* young people die. They give them some of these new medicines." She began shaking her foot with a nerve-rattling assurance. "People just don't die like they used to," she said.

"Mother," he said, "you ought to be prepared. I think even Block knows and hasn't told you yet." Block, after the first visit, had come in grimly every time, without his jokes and funny faces, and had taken his blood in silence, his nickel-colored eyes unfriendly. He was, by definition, the enemy of death and he looked now as if he knew he was battling the real thing. He had said he wouldn't prescribe until he knew what was wrong and Asbury had laughed in his face. "Mother," he said, "I AM going to die," and he tried to make each word like a hammer blow on top of her head.

She paled slightly but she did not blink. "Do you think for

one minute," she said angrily, "that I intend to sit here and let you die?" Her eyes were as hard as two old mountain ranges seen in the distance. He felt the first distinct stroke of doubt.

"Do you?" she asked fiercely.

"I don't think you have anything to do with it," he said in a shaken voice.

"Humph," she said and got up and left the porch as if she could not stand to be around such stupidity an instant longer.

Forgetting the Jesuit, he went rapidly over his symptoms: his fever had increased, interspersed by chills; he barely had the energy to drag himself out on the porch; food was abhorrent to him; and Block had not been able to give her the least satisfaction. Even as he sat there, he felt the beginning of a new chill, as if death were already playfully rattling his bones. He pulled the afghan off his feet and put it around his shoulders and made his way unsteadily up the stairs to bed.

He continued to grow worse. In the next few days he became so much weaker and badgered her so constantly about the Jesuit that finally in desperation she decided to humor his foolishness. She made the call, explaining in a chilly voice that her son was ill, perhaps a little out of his head, and wished to speak to a priest. While she made the call, Asbury hung over the banisters, barefooted, with the afghan around him, and listened. When she hung up he called down to know when the priest was coming.

"Tomorrow sometime," his mother said irritably.

He could tell by the fact that she made the call that her assurance was beginning to shatter. Whenever she let Block in or out, there was much whispering in the downstairs hall. That evening, he heard her and Mary George talking in low voices in the parlor. He thought he heard his name and he got up and tiptoed into the hall and down the first three steps until he could hear the voices distinctly.

"I had to call that priest," his mother was saying. "I'm afraid this is serious. I thought it was just a nervous breakdown but now I think it's something real. Doctor Block thinks it's something real too and whatever it is is worse because he's so run-down."

"Grow up, Mamma," Mary George said, "I've told you and I tell you again: what's wrong with him is purely psychosomatic." There was nothing she was not an expert on.

"No," his mother said, "it's a real disease. The doctor says so." He thought he detected a crack in her voice.

"Block is an idiot," Mary George said. "You've got to face

the facts: Asbury can't write so he gets sick. He's going to be an invalid instead of an artist. Do you know what he needs?"

"No," his mother said.

"Two or three shock treatments," Mary George said. "Get that artist business out of his head once and for all."

His mother gave a little cry and he grasped the banister.

"Mark my words," his sister continued, "all he's going to be around here for the next fifty years is a decoration."

He went back to bed. In a sense she was right. He had failed his god, Art, but he had been a faithful servant and Art was sending him Death. He had seen this from the first with a kind of mystical clarity. He went to sleep thinking of the peaceful spot in the family burying ground where he would soon lie, and after a while he saw that his body was being borne slowly toward it while his mother and Mary George watched without interest from their chairs on the porch. As the bier was carried across the dam, they could look up and see the procession reflected upside down in the pond. A lean dark figure in a Roman collar followed it. He had a mysteriously saturnine face in which there was a subtle blend of asceticism and corruption. Asbury was laid in a shallow grave on the hillside and the indistinct mourners, after standing in silence for a while, spread out over the darkening green. The Jesuit retired to a spot beneath a dead tree to smoke and meditate. The moon came up and Asbury was aware of a presence bending over him and a gentle warmth on his cold face. He knew that this was Art come to wake him and sat up and opened his eyes. Across the hill all the lights were on in his mother's house. The black pond was speckled with little nickel-colored stars. The Jesuit had disappeared. All around him the cows were spread out grazing in the moonlight and one large white one, violently spotted, was softly licking his head as if it were a block of salt. He awoke with a shudder and discovered that his bed was soaking from a night sweat and as he sat shivering in the dark, he realized that the end was not many days distant. He gazed down into the crater of death and fell back dizzy on his pillow.

The next day his mother noted something almost ethereal about his ravaged face. He looked like one of those dying children who must have Christmas early. He sat up in the bed and directed the rearrangement of several chairs and had her remove a picture of a maiden chained to a rock for he knew it would make the Jesuit smile. He had the comfortable rocker taken away and when he finished, the room with its severe wall stains had a certain cell-like quality. He felt it would be attractive to the visitor.

All morning he waited, looking irritably up at the ceiling where the bird with the icicle in its beak seemed poised and waiting too; but the priest did not arrive until late in the afternoon. As soon as his mother opened the door, a loud unintelligible voice began to boom in the downstairs hall. Asbury's heart beat wildly. In a second there was a heavy creaking on the stairs. Then almost at once his mother, her expression constrained, came in followed by a massive old man who plowed straight across the room, picked up a chair by the side of the bed and put it under himself.

"I'm Fahther Finn—from Purrgatory," he said in a hearty voice. He had a large red face, a stiff brush of gray hair and was blind in one eye, but the good eye, blue and clear, was focussed sharply on Asbury. There was a grease spot on his vest. "So you want to talk to a priest?" he said. "Very wise. None of us knows the hour Our Blessed Lord may call us." Then he cocked his good eye up at Asbury's mother and said, "Thank you, you may leave us now."

Mrs. Fox stiffened and did not budge.

"I'd like to talk to Father Finn alone," Asbury said, feeling suddenly that here he had an ally, although he had not expected a priest like this one. His mother gave him a disgusted look and left the room. He knew she would go no farther than just outside the door.

"It's so nice to have you come," Asbury said. "This place is incredibly dreary. There's no one here an intelligent person can talk to. I wonder what you think of Joyce, Father?"

The priest lifted his chair and pushed closer. "You'll have to shout," he said. "Blind in one eye and deaf in one ear."

"What do you think of Joyce?" Asbury said louder.

"Joyce? Joyce who?" asked the priest.

"James Joyce," Asbury said and laughed.

The priest brushed his huge hand in the air as if he were bothered by gnats. "I haven't met him," he said. "Now. Do you say your morning and night prayers?"

Asbury appeared confused. "Joyce was a great writer," he murmured, forgetting to shout.

"You don't eh?" said the priest. "Well you will never learn to be good unless you pray regularly. You cannot love Jesus unless you speak to Him."

"The myth of the dying god has always fascinated me," Asbury shouted, but the priest did not appear to catch it.

"Do you have trouble with purity?" he demanded, and as

Asbury paled, he went on without waiting for an answer. "We all do but you must pray to the Holy Ghost for it. Mind, heart and body. Nothing is overcome without prayer. Pray with your family. Do you pray with your family?"

"God forbid," Asbury murmured. "My mother doesn't have time to pray and my sister is an atheist," he shouted.

"A shame!" said the priest. "Then you must pray for them."

"The artist prays by creating," Asbury ventured.

"Not enough!" snapped the priest. "If you do not pray daily, you are neglecting your immortal soul. Do you know your catechism?"

"Certainly not," Asbury muttered.

"Who made you?" the priest asked in a martial tone.

"Different people believe different things about that," Asbury said.

"God made you," the priest said shortly. "Who is God?"

"God is an idea created by man," Asbury said, feeling that he was getting into stride, that two could play at this.

"God is a spirit infinitely perfect," the priest said. "You are a very ignorant boy. Why did God make you?"

"God didn't. . . ."

"God made you to know Him, to love Him, to serve Him in this world and to be happy with Him in the next!" the old priest said in a battering voice. "If you don't apply yourself to the catechism how do you expect to know how to save your immortal soul?"

Asbury saw he had made a mistake and that it was time to get rid of the old fool. "Listen," he said, "I'm not a Roman."

"A poor excuse for not saying your prayers!" the old man snorted.

Asbury slumped slightly in the bed. "I'm dying," he shouted.

"But you're not dead yet!" said the priest, "and how do you expect to meet God face to face when you've never spoken to Him? How do you expect to get what you don't ask for? God does not send the Holy Ghost to those who don't ask for Him. Ask Him to send the Holy Ghost."

"The Holy Ghost?" Asbury said.

"Are you so ignorant you've never heard of the Holy Ghost?" the priest asked.

"Certainly I've heard of the Holy Ghost" Asbury said furiously, "and the Holy Ghost is the last thing I'm looking for!"

"And He may be the last thing you get," the priest said, his one fierce eye inflamed. "Do you want your soul to suffer eternal damnation? Do you want to be deprived of God for all eternity? Do you want to suffer the most terrible pain, greater than fire, the pain of loss? Do you want to suffer the pain of loss for all eternity?"

Asbury moved his arms and legs helplessly as if he were pinned to the bed by the terrible eye.

"How can the Holy Ghost fill your soul when it's full of trash?" the priest roared. "The Holy Ghost will not come until you see yourself as you are—a lazy ignorant conceited youth!" he said, pounding his fist on the little bedside table.

Mrs. Fox burst in. "Enough of this!" she cried. "How dare you talk that way to a poor sick boy? You're upsetting him. You'll have to go."

"The poor lad doesn't even know his catechism," the priest said, rising. "I should think you would have taught him to say his daily prayers. You have neglected your duty as his mother." He turned back to the bed and said affably, "I'll give you my blessing and after this you must say your daily prayers without fail," whereupon he put his hand on Asbury's head and rumbled something in Latin. "Call me any time," he said, "and we can have another little chat," and then he followed Mrs. Fox's rigid back out. The last thing Asbury heard him say was, "He's a good lad at heart but very ignorant."

When his mother had got rid of the priest she came rapidly up the steps again to say that she had told him so, but when she saw him, pale and drawn and ravaged, sitting up in his bed, staring in front of him with large childish shocked eyes, she did not have the heart and went rapidly out again.

The next morning he was so weak that she made up her mind he must go to the hospital. "I'm not going to any hospital," he kept repeating, turning his thudding head from side to side as if he wanted to work it loose from his body. "I'm not going to any hospital as long as I'm conscious." He was thinking bitterly that once he lost consciousness, she could drag him off to the hospital and fill him full of blood and prolong his misery for days. He was convinced that the end was approaching, that it would be today, and he was tormented now thinking of his useless life. He felt as if he were a shell that had to be filled with something but he did not know what. He began to take note of everything in the room as if for the last time—the ridiculous antique furniture, the pattern in the rug, the silly picture his mother had replaced. He even looked at the fierce bird with the icicle in its beak and felt that it was there for some purpose that he could not divine.

There was something he was searching for, something that he felt he must have, some last significant culminating experience that he must make for himself before he died—make for himself out of his own intelligence. He had always relied on himself and had never been a sniveler after the ineffable.

Once when Mary George was thirteen and he was five, she had lured him with the promise of an unnamed present into a large tent full of people and had dragged him backwards up to the front where a man in a blue suit and red and white tie was standing. "Here," she said in a loud voice. "I'm already saved but you can save him. He's a real stinker and too big for his britches." He had broken her grip and shot out of there like a small cur and later when he had asked for his present, she had said, "You would have got Salvation if you had waited for it but since you acted the way you did, you get nothing!"

As the day wore on, he grew more and more frantic for fear he would die without making some last meaningful experience for himself. His mother sat anxiously by the side of the bed. She had called Block twice and could not get him. He thought even now she had not realized that he was going to die, much less that the end was only hours off.

The light in the room was beginning to have an odd quality, almost as if it were taking on presence. In a darkened form it entered and seemed to wait. Outside it appeared to move no farther than the edge of the faded treeline, which he could see a few inches over the sill of his window. Suddenly he thought of that experience of communion that he had had in the dairy with the Negroes when they had smoked together, and at once he began to tremble with excitement. They would smoke together one last time.

After a moment, turning his head on the pillow, he said, "Mother, I want to tell the Negroes good-bye."

His mother paled. For an instant her face seemed about to fly apart. Then the line of her mouth hardened; her brows drew together. "Good-bye?" she said in a flat voice. "Where are you going?"

For a few seconds he only looked at her. Then he said, "I think you know. Get them. I don't have long."

"This is absurd," she muttered but she got up and hurried out. He heard her try to reach Block again before she went outside. He thought her clinging to Block at a time like this was touching and pathetic. He waited, preparing himself for the encounter as a religious man might prepare himself for the last sacrament. Presently he heard their steps on the stair.

"Here's Randall and Morgan," his mother said, ushering them in. "They've come to tell you hello."

The two of them came in grinning and shuffled to the side of the bed. They stood there, Randall in front and Morgan behind. "You sho do look well," Randall said. "You looks very well."

"You looks well," the other one said. "Yessuh, you looks fine."

"I ain't ever seen you looking so well before," Randall said.

"Yes, doesn't he look well?" his mother said. "I think he looks just fine."

"Yessuh," Randall said, "I speck you ain't even sick."

"Mother," Asbury said in a forced voice. "I'd like to talk to them alone."

His mother stiffened; then she marched out. She walked across the hall and into the room on the other side and sat down. Through the open doors he could see her begin to rock in little short jerks. The two Negroes looked as if their last protection had dropped away.

Asbury's head was so heavy he could not think what he had been going to do. "I'm dying," he said.

Both their grins became gelid. "You looks fine," Randall said.

"I'm going to die," Asbury repeated. Then with relief he remembered that they were going to smoke together. He reached for the package on the table and held it out to Randall, forgetting to shake out the cigarettes.

The Negro took the package and put it in his pocket. "I thank you," he said. "I certainly do prechate it."

Asbury stared as if he had forgotten again. After a second he became aware that the other Negro's face had turned infinitely sad; then he realized that it was not sad but sullen. He fumbled in the drawer of the table and pulled out an unopened package and thrust it at Morgan.

"I thanks you, Mist Asbury," Morgan said, brightening. "You certly does look well."

"I'm about to die," Asbury said irritably.

"You looks fine," Randall said.

"You be up and around in a few days," Morgan predicted. Neither of them seemed to find a suitable place to rest his gaze. Asbury looked wildly across the hall where his mother had her rocker turned so that her back faced him. It was apparent she had no intention of getting rid of them for him.

"I speck you might have a little cold," Randall said after a time.

"I takes a little turpentine and sugar when I has a cold," Morgan said.

"Shut your mouth," Randall said, turning on him.

"Shut your own mouth," Morgan said. "I know what I takes."

"He don't take what you take," Randall growled.

"Mother!" Asbury called in a shaking voice.

His mother stood up. "Mister Asbury has had company long enough now," she called. "You all can come back tomorrow."

"We be going," Randall said. "You sho do look well."

"You sho does," Morgan said.

They filed out agreeing with each other how well he looked but Asbury's vision became blurred before they reached the hall. For an instant he saw his mother's form as if it were a shadow in the door and then it disappeared after them down the stairs. He heard her call Block again but he heard it without interest. His head was spinning. He knew now there would be no significant experience before he died. There was nothing more to do but give her the key to the drawer where the letter was, and wait for the end.

He sank into a heavy sleep from which he awoke about five o'clock to see her white face, very small, as the end of a well of darkness. He took the key out of his pajama pocket and handed it to her and mumbled that there was a letter in the desk to be opened when he was gone, but she did not seem to understand. She put the key down on the bedside table and left it there and he returned to his dream in which two large boulders were circling each other inside his head.

He awoke a little after six to hear Block's car stop below in the driveway. The sound was like a summons, bringing him rapidly and with a clear head out of his sleep. He had a sudden terrible foreboding that the fate awaiting him was going to be more shattering than any he could have reckoned on. He lay absolutely motionless, as still as an animal the instant before an earthquake.

Block and his mother talked as they came up the stairs but he did not distinguish their words. The doctor came in making faces; his mother was smiling. "Guess what you've got, Sugarpie!" she cried. Her voice broke in on him with the force of a gunshot.

"Found theter ol' bug, did ol' Block," Block said, sinking down into the chair by the bed. He raised his hands over his head in the gesture of a victorious prize fighter and let them collapse in his lap as if the effort had exhausted him. Then he removed a red bandanna handkerchief that he carried to be funny with and wiped his face thoroughly, having a different expression on it every time it appeared from behind the rag.

"I think you're just as smart as you can be!" Mrs. Fox said. "Ashbury," she said, "you have undulant fever. It'll keep coming back but it won't kill you!" Her smile was as bright and intense as a lightbulb without a shade. "I'm so relieved," she said.

Asbury sat up slowly, his face expressionless; then he fell back down again.

B!ock leaned over him and smiled. "You ain't going to die," he said, with deep satisfaction.

Nothing about Asbury stirred except his eyes. They did not appear to move on the surface but somewhere in their blurred depths there was an almost imperceptible motion as if something were struggling feebly. Block's gaze seemed to reach down like a steel pin and hold whatever it was until the life was out of it. "Undulant fever ain't so bad, Azzberry," he murmured. "It's the same as Bang's in a cow."

The boy gave a low moan and then was quiet.

"He must have drunk some unpasteurized milk up there," his mother said softly and then the two of them tiptoed out as if they thought he were about to go to sleep.

When the sound of their footsteps had faded on the stairs, Asbury sat up again. He turned his head, almost surreptitiously, to the side where the key he had given his mother was lying on the bedside table. His hand shot out and closed over it and returned it to his pocket. He glanced across the room into the small oval-framed dresser mirror. The eyes that stared back at him were the same that had returned his gaze every day from that mirror but it seemed to him that they were paler. They looked shocked clean as if they had been prepared for some awful vision about to come down on him. He shuddered and turned his head quickly the other way and stared out the window. A blinding red-gold sun moved serenely from under a purple cloud. Below it the treeline was black against the crimson sky. It formed a brittle wall, standing as if it were the frail defense he had set up in his mind to protect him from what was coming. The boy fell back on his pillow and stared at the ceiling. His limbs that had been racked for so many weeks by fever and chill were numb now. The old life in him was exhausted. He awaited the coming of new. It was then that he felt the beginning of a chill, a chill so peculiar, so light, that it was like a warm ripple across a deeper sea of cold. His breath came short. The fierce bird which through the years of his childhood and the days of his illness had been poised over his head, waiting mysteriously, appeared all at once to be in motion. Asbury blanched and the last film of illusion was torn as if by a whirlwind from his eyes. He saw that for the rest of his days, frail, racked, but enduring, he would live in the face of a purifying terror. A feeble cry, a last impossible protest escaped him. But the Holy Ghost, emblazoned in ice instead of fire, continued, implacable, to descend.

The Comforts of Home

Thomas withdrew to the side of the window and with his head between the wall and the curtain he looked down on the driveway where the car had stopped. His mother and the little slut were getting out of it. His mother emerged slowly, stolid and awkward, and then the little slut's long slightly bowed legs slid out, the dress pulled above the knees. With a shriek of laughter she ran to meet the dog, who bounded, overjoyed, shaking with pleasure, to welcome her. Rage gathered throughout Thomas's large frame with a silent ominous intensity, like a mob assembling.

It was now up to him to pack a suitcase, go to the hotel, and stay there until the house should be cleared.

He did not know where a suitcase was, he disliked to pack, he needed his books, his typewriter was not portable, he was used to an electric blanket, he could not bear to eat in restaurants. His mother, with her daredevil charity, was about to wreck the peace of the house.

The back door slammed and the girl's laugh shot up from the kitchen, through the back hall, up the stairwell and into his room, making for him like a bolt of electricity. He jumped to the side and stood glaring about him. His words of the morning had been unequivocal: "If you bring that girl back into this house, I leave. You can choose—her or me."

She had made her choice. An intense pain gripped his throat. It was the first time in his thirty-five years . . . He felt a sudden burning moisture behind his eyes. Then he steadied himself, overcome by rage. On the contrary: she had not made any choice. She was counting on his attachment to his electric blanket. She would have to be shown.

The girl's laughter rang upward a second time and Thomas winced. He saw again her look of the night before. She had invaded his room. He had waked to find his door open and her in it. There was enough light from the hall to make her visible as she turned toward him. The face was like a comedienne's in a musical comedy—a pointed chin, wide apple cheeks and feline empty eyes. He had sprung out of his bed and snatched a straight chair and then he had backed her out the door, holding the chair in front of him like an animal trainer driving out a dangerous cat. He had driven her silently down the hall, pausing when he reached it to beat on his mother's door. The girl, with a gasp, turned and fled into the guest room.

In a moment his mother had opened her door and peered out apprehensively. Her face, greasy with whatever she put on it at night, was framed in pink rubber curlers. She looked down the hall where the girl had disappeared. Thomas stood before her, the chair still lifted in front of him as if he were about to quell another beast. "She tried to get in my room," he hissed, pushing in. "I woke up and she was trying to get in my room." He closed the door behind him and his voice rose in outrage. "I won't put up with this! I won't put up with it another day!"

His mother, backed by him to her bed, sat down on the edge of it. She had a heavy body on which sat a thin, mysteriously gaunt and incongruous head.

"I'm telling you for the last time," Thomas said, "I won't put up with this another day." There was an observable tendency in all of her actions. This was, with the best intentions in the world, to make a mockery of virtue, to pursue it with such a mindless intensity that everyone involved was made a fool of and virtue itself became ridiculous. "Not another day," he repeated.

His mother shook her head emphatically, her eyes still on the door.

Thomas put the chair on the floor in front of her and sat down on it. He leaned forward as if he were about to explain something to a defective child.

"That's just another way she's unfortunate," his mother said. "So awful, so awful. She told me the name of it but I forget what it is but it's something she can't help. Something she was born with. Thomas," she said and put her hand to her jaw, "suppose it were you?"

Exasperation blocked his windpipe. "Can't I make you see," he croaked, "that if she can't help herself you can't help her?"

His mother's eyes, intimate but untouchable, were the blue of great distances after sunset. "Nimpermaniac," she murmured.

"Nymphomaniac," he said fiercely. "She doesn't need to supply you with any fancy names. She's a moral moron. That's all you need to know. Born without the moral faculty—like somebody else would be born without a kidney or a leg. Do you understand?"

"I keep thinking it might be you," she said, her hand still on her jaw. "If it were you, how do you think I'd feel if nobody took you in? What if you were a nimpermaniac and not a brilliant smart person and you did what you couldn't help and . . ."

Thomas felt a deep unbearable loathing for himself as if he were turning slowly into the girl.

"What did she have on?" she asked abruptly, her eyes narrowing.

"Nothing!" he roared. "Now will you get her out of here!"

"How can I turn her out in the cold?" she said. "This morning she was threatening to kill herself again."

"Send her back to jail," Thomas said.

"I would not send *you* back to jail, Thomas," she said.

He got up and snatched the chair and fled the room while he was still able to control himself.

Thomas loved his mother. He loved her because it was his nature to do so, but there were times when he could not endure her love for him. There were times when it became nothing but pure idiot mystery and he sensed about him forces, invisible currents entirely out of his control. She proceeded always from the tritest of considerations—it was the *nice thing to do*—into the most foolhardy engagements with the devil, whom, of course, she never recognized.

The devil for Thomas was only a manner of speaking, but it was a manner appropriate to the situations his mother got into. Had she been in any degree intellectual, he could have proved to her from early Christian history that no excess of virtue is justified, that a moderation of good produces likewise a moderation in evil, that if Antony of Egypt had stayed at home and attended to his sister, no devils would have plagued him.

Thomas was not cynical and so far from being opposed to virtue, he saw it as the principle of order and the only thing that makes life bearable. His own life was made bearable by the fruits of his mother's saner virtues—by the well-regulated house she kept and the excellent meals she served. But when virtue got out of hand with her, as now, a sense of devils grew upon him, and these were not mental quirks in himself or the old lady, they were denizens with personalities, present though not visible, who might any moment be expected to shriek or rattle a pot.

The girl had landed in the county jail a month ago on a bad check charge and his mother had seen her picture in the paper. At the breakfast table she had gazed at it for a long time and then had passed it over the coffee pot to him.

"Imagine," she said, "only nineteen years old and in that filthy jail. And she doesn't look like a bad girl."

Thomas glanced at the picture. It showed the face of a shrewd ragamuffin. He observed that the average age for criminality was steadily lowering.

"She looks like a wholesome girl," his mother said.

"Wholesome people don't pass bad checks," Thomas said.

"You don't know what you'd do in a pinch."

"I wouldn't pass a bad check," Thomas said.

"I think," his mother said, "I'll take her a little box of candy."

If then and there he had put his foot down, nothing else would have happened. His father, had he been living, would have put his foot down at that point. Taking a box of candy was her favorite nice thing to do. When anyone within her social station moved to town, she called and took a box of candy; when any of her friends' children had babies or won a scholarship, she called and took a box of candy; when an old person broke his hip, she was at his bedside with a box of candy. He had been amused at the idea of her taking a box of candy to the jail.

He stood now in his room with the girl's laugh rocketing away in his head and cursed his amusement.

When his mother returned from the visit to the jail, she had burst into his study without knocking and had collapsed full-length on his couch, lifting her small swollen feet up on the arm of it. After a moment, she recovered herself enough to sit up and put a newspaper under them. Then she fell back again. "We don't know how the other half lives," she said.

Thomas knew that though her conversation moved from cliché to cliché there were real experiences behind them. He was less sorry for the girl's being in jail than for his mother having to see her there. He would have spared her all unpleasant sights. "Well," he said and put away his journal, "you had better forget it now. The girl has ample reason to be in jail."

"You can't imagine what all she's been through," she said, sitting up again, "listen." The poor girl, Star, had been brought up by a stepmother with three children of her own, one an almost grown boy who had taken advantage of her in such dreadful ways that she had been forced to run away and find her real mother. Once found, her real mother had sent her to various boarding schools to get rid of her. At each of these she had been forced to run away by the presence of perverts and sadists so monstrous that their acts defied description. Thomas could tell that his mother had not been spared the details that she was sparing him. Now and again when she spoke vaguely, her voice shook and he could tell that she was remembering some horror that had been put to her graphically. He had hoped that in a few days the memory of all this would wear off, but it did not. The next day she returned to the jail with Kleenex and cold-cream and a few days later, she announced that she had consulted a lawyer.

It was at these times that Thomas truly mourned the death of his father though he had not been able to endure him in life. The old man would have had none of this foolishness. Untouched by useless compassion, he would (behind her back) have pulled the necessary strings with his crony, the sheriff, and the girl would have been packed off to the state penitentiary to serve her time. He had always been engaged in some enraged action until one morning when (with an angry glance at his wife as if she alone were responsible) he had dropped dead at the breakfast table. Thomas had inherited his father's reason without his ruthlessness and his mother's love of good without her tendency to pursue it. His plan for all practical action was to wait and see what developed.

The lawyer found that the story of the repeated atrocities was for the most part untrue, but when he explained to her that the girl was a psychopathic personality, not insane enough for the asylum, not criminal enough for the jail, not stable enough for society, Thomas's mother was more deeply affected than ever. The girl readily admitted that her story was untrue on account of her being a congenital liar; she lied, she said, because she was insecure. She had passed through the hands of several psychiatrists who had put the finishing touches to her education. She knew there was no hope for her. In the presence of such an affliction as this, his mother seemed bowed down by some painful mystery that nothing would make endurable but a redoubling of effort. To his annoyance, she appeared to look on *him* with compassion, as if her hazy charity no longer made distinctions.

A few days later she burst in and said that the lawyer had got the girl paroled—to her.

Thomas rose from his Morris chair, dropping the review he had been reading. His large bland face contracted in anticipated pain. "You are not," he said, "going to bring that girl here!"

"No, no," she said, "calm yourself, Thomas." She had managed with difficulty to get the girl a job in a pet shop in town and a place to board with a crotchety old lady of her acquaintance. People were not kind. They did not put themselves in the place of someone like Star who had everything against her.

Thomas sat down again and retrieved his review. He seemed just to have escaped some danger which he did not care to make clear to himself. "Nobody can tell you anything," he said, "but in a few days that girl will have left town, having got what she could out of you. You'll never hear from her again."

Two nights later he came home and opened the parlor door and was speared by a shrill depthless laugh. His mother and the girl sat close to the fireplace where the gas logs were lit. The girl gave the immediate impression of being physically crooked. Her hair was cut like a dog's or an elf's and she was dressed in the latest fashion. She was training on him a long familiar sparkling stare that turned after a second into an intimate grin.

"Thomas!" his mother said, her voice firm with the injunction not to bolt, "this is Star you've heard so much about. Star is going to have supper with us."

The girl called herself Star Drake. The lawyer had found that her real name was Sarah Ham.

Thomas neither moved nor spoke but hung in the door in what seemed a savage perplexity. Finally he said, "How do you do, Sarah," in a tone of such loathing that he was shocked at the sound of it. He reddened, feeling it beneath him to show contempt for any creature so pathetic. He advanced into the room, determined at least on a decent politeness and sat down heavily in a straight chair.

"Thomas writes history," his mother said with a threatening look at him. "He's president of the local Historical Society this year."

The girl leaned forward and gave Thomas an even more pointed attention. "Fabulous!" she said in a throaty voice.

"Right now Thomas is writing about the first settlers in this county," his mother said.

"Fabulous!" the girl repeated.

Thomas by an effort of will managed to look as if he were alone in the room.

"Say, you know who he looks like?" Star asked, her head on one side, taking him in at any angle.

"Oh some one very distinguished!" his mother said archly.

"This cop I saw in the movie I went to last night," Star said.

"Star," his mother said, "I think you ought to be careful

about the kind of movies you go to. I think you ought to see only the best ones. I don't think crime stories would be good for you."

"Oh this was a crime-does-not-pay," Star said, "and I swear this cop looked exactly like him. They were always putting something over on the guy. He would look like he couldn't stand it a minute longer or he would blow up. He was a riot. And not bad looking," she added with an appreciative leer at Thomas.

"Star," his mother said, "I think it would be grand if you developed a taste for music."

Thomas sighed. His mother rattled on and the girl, paying no attention to her, let her eyes play over him. The quality of her look was such that it might have been her hands, resting now on his knees, now on his neck. Her eyes had a mocking glitter and he knew that she was well aware he could not stand the sight of her. He needed nothing to tell him he was in the presence of the very stuff of corruption, but blameless corruption because there was no responsible faculty behind it. He was looking at the most unendurable form of innocence. Absently he asked himself what the attitude of God was to this, meaning if possible to adopt it.

His mother's behavior throughout the meal was so idiotic that he could barely stand to look at her and since he could less stand to look at Sarah Ham, he fixed on the sideboard across the room a continuous gaze of disapproval and disgust. Every remark of the girl's his mother met as if it deserved serious attention. She advanced several plans for the wholesome use of Star's spare time. Sarah Ham paid no more attention to this advice than if it came from a parrot. Once when Thomas inadvertently looked in her direction, she winked. As soon as he had swallowed the last spoonful of dessert, he rose and muttered, "I have to go, I have a meeting."

"Thomas," his mother said, "I want you to take Star home on your way. I don't want her riding in taxis by herself at night."

For a moment Thomas remained furiously silent. Then he turned and left the room. Presently he came back with a look of obscure determination on his face. The girl was ready, meekly waiting at the parlor door. She cast up at him a great look of admiration and confidence. Thomas did not offer his arm but she took it anyway and moved out of the house and down the steps, attached to what might have been a miraculously moving monument.

"Be good!" his mother called.

Sarah Ham snickered and poked him in the ribs.

While getting his coat he had decided that this would be his opportunity to tell the girl that unless she ceased to be a parasite on his mother, he would see to it, personally, that she was returned to jail. He would let her know that he understood what she was up to, that he was not an innocent and that there were certain things he would not put up with. At his desk, pen in hand, none was more articulate than Thomas. As soon as he found himself shut into the car with Sarah Ham, terror seized his tongue.

She curled her feet up under her and said, "Alone at last," and giggled.

Thomas swerved the car away from the house and drove fast toward the gate. Once on the highway, he shot forward as if he were being pursued.

"Jesus!" Sarah Ham said, swinging her feet off the seat, "where's the fire?"

Thomas did not answer. In a few seconds he could feel her edging closer. She stretched, eased nearer, and finally hung her hand limply on his shoulder. "Tomsee doesn't like me," she said, "but I think he's fabulously cute."

Thomas covered the three and half miles into town in a little over four minutes. The light at the first intersection was red but he ignored it. The old woman lived three blocks beyond. When the car screeched to a halt at the place, he jumped out and ran around to the girl's door and opened it. She did not move from the car and Thomas was obliged to wait. After a moment one leg emerged, then her small white crooked face appeared and stared up at him. There was something about the look of it that suggested blindness but it was the blindness of those who don't know that they cannot see. Thomas was curiously sickened. The empty eyes moved over him. "Nobody likes me," she said in a sullen tone. "What if you were me and I couldn't stand to ride you three miles?"

"My mother likes you," he muttered.

"Her!" the girl said. "She's just about seventy-five years behind the times!"

Breathlessly Thomas said, "If I find you bothering her again, I'll have you put back in jail." There was a dull force behind his voice though it came out barely above a whisper.

"You and who else?" she said and drew back in the car as if now she did not intend to get out at all. Thomas reached into it, blindly grasped the front of her coat, pulled her out by it and released her. Then he lunged back to the car and sped off. The other door was still hanging open and her laugh, bodiless but real, bounded up the street as if it were about to jump in the open side of the car and ride away with him. He reached over and slammed the door and then drove toward home, too angry to attend his meeting. He intended to make his mother well-aware of his displeasure. He intended to leave no doubt in her mind. The voice of his father rasped in his head.

Numbskull, the old man said, put your foot down now. Show her who's boss before she shows you.

But when Thomas reached home, his mother, wisely, had gone to bed.

The next morning he appeared at the breakfast table, his brow lowered and the thrust of his jaw indicating that he was in a dangerous humor. When he intended to be determined, Thomas began like a bull that, before charging, backs with his head lowered and paws the ground. "All right now listen," he began, yanking out his chair and sitting down, "I have something to say to you about that girl and I don't intend to say it but once." He drew breath. "She nothing but a little slut. She makes fun of you behind your back. She means to get everything she can out of you and you are nothing to her."

His mother looked as if she too had spent a restless night. She did not dress in the morning but wore her bathrobe and a grey turban around her head, which gave her face a disconcerting omniscient look. He might have been breakfasting with a sibyl.

"You'll have to use canned cream this morning," she said, pouring his coffee. "I forgot the other."

"All right, did you hear me?" Thomas growled.

"I'm not deaf," his mother said and put the top back on the trivet. "I know I'm nothing but an old bag of wind to her."

"Then why do you persist in this foolhardy . . ."

"Thomas," she said, and put her hand to the side of her face, "it might be . . ."

"It is not me!" Thomas said, grasping the table leg at his knee.

She continued to hold her face, shaking her head slightly. "Think of all you have," she began. "All the comforts of home. And morals, Thomas. No bad inclinations, nothing bad you were born with."

Thomas began to breathe like some one who feels the on-set of asthma. "You are not logical," he said in a limp voice. "*He* would have put his foot down."

The old lady stiffened. "You," she said, "are not like him."

Thomas opened his mouth silently.

"However," his mother said, in a tone of such subtle accusation that she might have been taking back the compliment, "I won't invite her back again since you're so dead set against her."

"I am not set against her," Thomas said. "I am set against your making a fool of yourself."

As soon as he left the table and closed the door of his study on himself, his father took up a squatting position in his mind. The old man had had the countryman's ability to converse squatting, though he was no countryman but had been born and brought up in the city and only moved to the smaller place later to exploit his talents. With steady skill he had made them think him one of them. In the midst of a conversation on the courthouse lawn, he would squat and his two or three companions would squat with him with no break in the surface of the talk. By gesture he had lived his lie; he had never deigned to tell one.

Let her run over you, he said. You ain't like me. Not enough to be a man.

Thomas began vigorously to read and presently the image faded. The girl had caused a disturbance in the depths of his being, somewhere out of the reach of his power of analysis. He felt as if he had seen a tornado pass a hundred yards away and had an intimation that it would turn again and head directly for him. He did not get his mind firmly on his work until mid-morning.

Two nights later, his mother and he were sitting in the den after their supper, each reading a section of the evening paper, when the telephone began to ring with the brassy intensity of a fire alarm. Thomas reached for it. As soon as the receiver was in his hand, a shrill female voice screamed into the room, "Come get this girl! Come get her! Drunk! Drunk in my parlor and I won't have it! Lost her job and come back here drunk! I won't have it!"

His mother leapt up and snatched the receiver.

The ghost of Thomas's father rose before him. Call the sheriff, the old man prompted. "Call the sheriff," Thomas said in a loud voice. "Call the sheriff to go there and pick her up."

"We'll be right there," his mother was saying. "We'll come and get her right away. Tell her to get her things together."

"She ain't in no condition to get nothing together," the

voice screamed. "You shouldn't have put something like her off on me! My house is respectable!"

"Tell her to call the sheriff," Thomas shouted.

His mother put the receiver down and looked at him. "I wouldn't turn a dog over to that man," she said.

Thomas sat in the chair with his arms folded and looked fixedly at the wall.

"Think of the poor girl, Thomas," his mother said, "with nothing. Nothing. And we have everything."

When they arrived, Sarah Ham was slumped spraddle-legged against the banister on the boarding house frontsteps. Her tam was down on her forehead where the old woman had slammed it and her clothes were bulging out of her suitcase where the old woman had thrown them in. She was carrying on a drunken conversation with herself in a low personal tone. A streak of lipstick ran up one side of her face. She allowed herself to be guided by his mother to the car and put in the back seat without seeming to know who the rescuer was. "Nothing to talk to all day but a pack of goddamned parakeets," she said in a furious whisper.

Thomas, who had not got out of the car at all, or looked at her after the first revolted glance, said, "I'm telling you, once and for all, the place to take her is the jail."

His mother, sitting on the back seat, holding the girl's hand, did not answer.

"All right, take her to the hotel," he said.

"I cannot take a drunk girl to a hotel, Thomas," she said. "You know that."

"Then take her to a hospital."

"She doesn't need a jail or a hotel or a hospital," his mother said, "she needs a home."

"She does not need mine," Thomas said.

"Only for tonight, Thomas," the old lady sighed. "Only for tonight."

Since then eight days had passed. The little slut was established in the guest room. Every day his mother set out to find her a job and a place to board, and failed, for the old woman had broadcast a warning. Thomas kept to his room or the den. His home was to him home, workshop, church, as personal as the shell of a turtle and as necessary. He could not believe that it could be violated in this way. His flushed face had a constant look of stunned outrage.

As soon as the girl was up in the morning, her voice throbbed out in a blues song that would rise and waver, then plunge low with insinuations of passion about to be satisfied and Thomas, at his desk, would lunge up and begin frantically stuffing his ears with Kleenex. Each time he started from one room to another, one floor to another, she would be certain to appear. Each time he was half way up or down the stairs, she would either meet him and pass, cringing coyly, or go up or down behind him, breathing small tragic spearmint-flavored sighs. She appeared to adore Thomas's repugnance to her and to draw it out of him every chance she got as if it added delectably to her martyrdom.

The old man—small, wasp-like, in his yellowed panama hat, his seersucker suit, his pink carefully-soiled shirt, his small string tie—appeared to have taken up his station in Thomas's mind and from there, usually squatting, he shot out the same rasping suggestion every time the boy paused from his forced studies. Put your foot down. Go to see the sheriff.

The sheriff was another edition of Thomas's father except that he wore a checkered shirt and a Texas type hat and was ten years younger. He was as easily dishonest, and he had genuinely admired the old man. Thomas, like his mother, would have gone far out of his way to avoid his glassy pale blue gaze. He kept hoping for another solution, for a miracle.

With Sarah Ham in the house, meals were unbearable.

"Tomsee doesn't like me," she said the third or fourth night at the supper table and cast her pouting gaze across at the large rigid figure of Thomas, whose face was set with the look of a man trapped by insufferable odors. "He doesn't want me here. Nobody wants me anywhere."

"Thomas's name is Thomas," his mother interrupted. "Not Tomsee."

"I made Tomsee up," she said. "I think it's cute. He hates me."

"Thomas does not hate you," his mother said. "We are not the kind of people who hate," she added, as if this were an imperfection that had been bred out of them generations ago.

"Oh, I know when I'm not wanted," Sarah Ham continued. "They didn't even want me in jail. If I killed myself I wonder would God want me?"

"Try it and see," Thomas muttered.

The girl screamed with laughter. Then she stopped abruptly, her face puckered and she began to shake. "The best thing to do," she said, her teeth clattering, "is to kill myself. Then I'll be out of everybody's way. I'll go to hell and be out of God's way. And even the devil won't want me. He'll kick me out of hell, not even in hell . . ." she wailed.

Thomas rose, picked up his plate and knife and fork and

carried them to the den to finish his supper. After that, he had not eaten another meal at the table but had had his mother serve him at his desk. At these meals, the old man was intensely present to him. He appeared to be tipping backwards in his chair, his thumbs beneath his galluses, while he said such things as, She never ran me away from my own table.

A few nights later, Sarah Ham slashed her wrists with a paring knife and had hysterics. From the den where he was closeted after supper, Thomas heard a shriek, then a series of screams, then his mother's scurrying footsteps through the house. He did not move. His first instant of hope that the girl had cut her throat faded as he realized she could not have done it and continue to scream the way she was doing. He returned to his journal and presently the screams subsided. In a moment his mother burst in with his coat and hat. "We have to take her to the hospital," she said. "She tried to do away with herself. I have a tourniquet on her arm. Oh Lord, Thomas," she said, "imagine being so low you'd do a thing like that!"

Thomas rose woodenly and put on his hat and coat. "We will take her to the hospital," he said, "and we will leave her there."

"And drive her to despair again?" the old lady cried. "Thomas!"

Standing in the center of his room now, realizing that he had reached the point where action was inevitable, that he must pack, that he must leave, that he must go, Thomas remained immovable.

His fury was directed not at the little slut but at his mother. Even though the doctor had found that she had barely damaged herself and had raised the girl's wrath by laughing at the tourniquet and putting only a streak of iodine on the cut, his mother could not get over the incident. Some new weight of sorrow seemed to have been thrown across her shoulders, and not only Thomas, but Sarah Ham was infuriated by this, for it appeared to be a general sorrow that would have found another object no matter what good fortune came to either of them. The experience of Sarah Ham had plunged the old lady into mourning for the world.

The morning after the attempted suicide, she had gone through the house and collected all the knives and scissors and locked them in a drawer. She emptied a bottle of rat poison down the toilet and took up the roach tablets from the kitchen floor. Then she came to Thomas's study and said in a whisper, "Where is that gun of his? I want you to lock it up."

"The gun is in my drawer," Thomas roared, "and I will not lock it up. If she shoots herself, so much the better!"

"Thomas," his mother said, "she'll hear you!"

"Let her hear me!" Thomas yelled. "Don't you know she has no intention of killing herself? Don't you know her kind never kill themselves? Don't you . . ."

His mother slipped out the door and closed it to silence him and Sarah Ham's laugh, quite close in the hall, came rattling into his room. "Tomsee'll find out. I'll kill myself and then he'll be sorry he wasn't nice to me. I'll use his own lil gun, his own lil ol' pearl-handled revol-lervuh!" she shouted and let out a loud tormented-sounding laugh in imitation of a movie monster.

Thomas ground his teeth. He pulled out his desk drawer and felt for the pistol. It was an inheritance from the old man, whose opinion it had been that every house should contain a loaded gun. He had discharged two bullets one night into the side of a prowler, but Thomas had never shot anything. He had no fear that the girl would use the gun on herself and he closed the drawer. Her kind clung tenaciously to life and were able to wrest some histrionic advantage from every moment.

Several ideas for getting rid of her had entered his head but each of these had been suggestions whose moral tone indicated that they had come from a mind akin to his father's, and Thomas had rejected them. He could not get the girl locked up again until she did something illegal. The old man would have been able with no qualms at all to get her drunk and send her out on the highway in his car, meanwhile notifying the highway patrol of her presence on the road, but Thomas considered this below his moral stature. Suggestions continued to come to him, each more outrageous than the last.

He had not the vaguest hope that the girl would get the gun and shoot herself, but that afternoon when he looked in the drawer, the gun was gone. His study locked from the inside, not the out. He cared nothing about the gun, but the thought of Sarah Ham's hands sliding among his papers infuriated him. Now even his study was contaminated. The only place left untouched by her was his bedroom.

That night she entered it.

In the morning at breakfast, he did not eat and did not sit down. He stood beside his chair and delivered his ultimatum while his mother sipped her coffee as if she were both alone in the room and in great pain. "I have stood this," he said, "for as long as I am able. Since I see plainly that you care nothing about me, about my peace or comfort or working conditions, I am about to take the only step open to me. I will give you one more day. If you bring the girl back into this house this afternoon, I leave. You can choose—her or me." He had more to say but at that point his voice cracked and he left.

At ten o'clock his mother and Sarah Ham left the house.

At four he heard the car wheels on the gravel and rushed to the window. As the car stopped, the dog stood up, alert, shaking.

He seemed unable to take the first step that would set him walking to the closet in the hall to look for the suitcase. He was like a man handed a knife and told to operate on himself if he wished to live. His huge hands clenched helplessly. His expression was a turmoil of indecision and outrage. His pale blue eyes seemed to sweat in his broiling face. He closed them for a moment and on the back of his lids his father's image leered at him. Idiot! the old man hissed, idiot! The criminal slut stole your gun! See the sheriff! See the sheriff!

It was a moment before Thomas opened his eyes. He seemed newly stunned. He stood where he was for at least three minutes, then he turned slowly like a large vessel reversing its direction and faced the door. He stood there a moment longer, then he left, his face set to see the ordeal through.

He did not know where he would find the sheriff. The man made his own rules and kept his own hours. Thomas stopped first at the jail where his office was, but he was not in it. He went to the courthouse and was told by a clerk that the sheriff had gone to the barber-shop across the street. "Yonder's the deppity," the clerk said and pointed out the window to the large figure of a man in a checkered shirt, who was leaning against the side of a police car, looking into space.

"It has to be the sheriff," Thomas said and left for the barber-shop. As little as he wanted anything to do with the sheriff, he realized that the man was at least intelligent and not simply a mound of sweating flesh.

The barber said the sheriff had just left. Thomas started back to the courthouse and as he stepped on to the sidewalk from the street, he saw a lean, slightly stooped figure gesticulating angrily at the deputy.

Thomas approached with an aggressiveness brought on by nervous agitation. He stopped abruptly three feet away and said in an over-loud voice, "Can I have a word with you?" without adding the sheriff's name, which was Farebrother.

Farebrother turned his sharp creased face just enough to take Thomas in, and the deputy did likewise, but neither spoke. The sheriff removed a very small piece of cigaret from his lip and dropped it at his feet. "I told you what to do," he said to the deputy. Then he moved off with a slight nod that indicated Thomas could follow him if he wanted to see him. The deputy slunk around the front of the police car and got inside.

Farebrother, with Thomas following, headed across the courthouse square and stopped beneath a tree that shaded a quarter of the front lawn. He waited, leaning slightly forward, and lit another cigaret.

Thomas began to blurt out his business. As he had not had time to prepare his words, he was barely coherent. By repeating the same thing over several times, he managed at length to get out what he wanted to say. When he finished, the sheriff was still leaning slightly forward, at an angle to him, his eyes on nothing in particular. He remained that way without speaking.

Thomas began again, slower and in a lamer voice, and Farebrother let him continue for some time before he said, creased, all-knowing, quarter smile.
"We had her oncet." He then allowed himself a slow,
"I had nothing to do with that," Thomas said. "That was my mother."

Farebrother squatted.

"She was trying to help the girl," Thomas said. "She didn't know she couldn't be helped."

"Bit off more than she could chew, I reckon," the voice below him mused.

"She has nothing to do with this," Thomas said. "She doesn't know I'm here. The girl is dangerous with that gun."

"*He*," the sheriff said, "never let anything grow under his feet. Particularly nothing a woman planted."

"She might kill somebody with that gun," Thomas said weakly, looking down at the round top of the Texas type hat.

There was a long time of silence.

"Where's she got it?" Farebrother asked.

"I don't know. She sleeps in the guest room. It must be in there, in her suitcase probably," Thomas said.

Farebrother lapsed into silence again.

"You could come search the guest room," Thomas said in a strained voice. "I can go home and leave the latch off the front door and you can come in quietly and go upstairs and search her room."

Farebrother turned his head so that his eyes looked boldly at Thomas's knees. "You seem to know how it ought to be done," he said. "Want to swap jobs?"

Thomas said nothing because he could not think of anything to say, but he waited doggedly. Farebrother removed the cigaret butt from his lips and dropped it on the grass. Beyond him on the courthouse porch a group of loiterers who had been leaning at the left of the door moved over to the right where a patch of sunlight had settled. From one of the upper windows a crumpled piece of paper blew out and drifted down.

"I'll come along about six," Farebrother said. "Leave the latch off the door and keep out of my way—yourself and them two women too."

Thomas let out a rasping sound of relief meant to be "Thanks," and struck off across the grass like some one released. The phrase, "Them two women," stuck like a burr in his brain—the subtlety of the insult to his mother hurting him more than any of Farebrother's references to his own incompetence. As he got into his car, his face suddenly flushed. Had he delivered his mother over to the sheriff—to be a butt for the man's tongue? Was he betraying her to get rid of the little slut? He saw at once that this was not the case. He was doing what he was doing for her own good, to rid her of a parasite that would ruin their peace. He started his car and drove quickly home but once he had turned in the driveway, he decided it would be better to park some distance from the house and go quietly in by the back door. He parked on the grass and on the grass walked in a circle toward the rear of the house. The sky was lined with mustard-colored streaks. The dog was asleep on the back doormat. At the approach of his master's step, he opened one yellow eye, took him in, and closed it again.

Thomas let himself into the kitchen. It was empty and the house was quiet enough for him to be aware of the loud ticking of the kitchen clock. It was a quarter to six. He tiptoed hurriedly through the hall to the front door and took the latch off it. Then he stood for a moment listening. From behind the closed parlor door, he heard his mother snoring softly and presumed that she had gone to sleep while reading. On the other side of the hall, not three feet from his study, the little slut's black coat and red pocketbook were slung on a chair. He heard water running upstairs and decided she was taking a bath.

He went into his study and sat down at his desk to wait, noting with distaste that every few moments a tremor ran through him. He sat for a minute or two doing nothing. Then he picked up a pen and began to draw squares on the back of an envelope that lay before him. He looked at his watch. It was eleven minutes to six. After a moment he idly drew the center drawer of the desk out over his lap. For a moment he stared at the gun without recognition. Then he gave a yelp and leaped up. She had put it back!

Idiot! his father hissed, idiot! Go plant it in her pocketbook. Don't just stand there. Go plant it in her pocketbook!

Thomas stood staring at the drawer.

Moron! the old man fumed. Quick while there's time! Go plant it in her pocketbook.

Thomas did not move.

Imbecile! his father cried.

Thomas picked up the gun.

Make haste, the old man ordered.

Thomas started forward, holding the gun away from him. He opened the door and looked at the chair. The black coat and red pocketbook were lying on it almost within reach.

Hurry up, you fool, his father said.

From behind the parlor door the almost inaudible snores of his mother rose and fell. They seemed to mark an order of time that had nothing to do with the instants left to Thomas. There was no other sound.

Quick, you imbecile, before she wakes up, the old man said.

The snores stopped and Thomas heard the sofa springs groan. He grabbed the red pocketbook. It had a skin-like feel to his touch and as it opened, he caught an unmistakable odor of the girl. Wincing, he thrust in the gun and then drew back. His face burned an ugly dull red.

"What is Tomsee putting in my purse?" she called and her pleased laugh bounced down the staircase. Thomas whirled.

She was at the top of the stair, coming down in the manner of a fashion model, one bare leg and then the other thrusting out the front of her kimono in a definite rhythm. "Tomsee is being naughty," she said in a throaty voice. She reached the bottom and cast a possessive leer at Thomas whose face was now more grey than red. She reached out, pulled the bag open with her finger and peered at the gun.

His mother opened the parlor door and looked out.

"Tomsee put his pistol in my bag!" the girl shrieked.

"Ridiculous," his mother said, yawning. "What would Thomas want to put his pistol in your bag for?"

Thomas stood slightly hunched, his hands hanging helplessly at the wrists as if he had just pulled them up out of a pool of blood.

"I don't know what for," the girl said, "but he sure did it," and she proceeded to walk around Thomas, her hands on her hips, her neck thrust forward and her intimate grin fixed on him fiercely. All at once her expression seemed to open as the purse had opened when Thomas touched it. She stood with her head cocked on one side in an attitude of disbelief. "Oh boy," she said slowly, "is he a case."

At that instant Thomas damned not only the girl but the entire order of the universe that made her possible.

"Thomas wouldn't put a gun in your bag," his mother said. "Thomas is a gentleman."

The girl made a chortling noise. "You can see it in there," she said and pointed to the open purse.

You *found* it in her bag, you dimwit! the old man hissed.

"I found it in her bag!" Thomas shouted. "The dirty criminal slut stole my gun!"

His mother gasped at the sound of the other presence in his voice. The old lady's sibyl-like face turned pale.

"Found it my eye!" Sarah Ham shrieked and started for the pocketbook, but Thomas, as if his arm were guided by his father, caught it first and snatched the gun. The girl in a frenzy lunged at Thomas's throat and would actually have caught him around the neck had not his mother thrown herself forward to protect her.

Fire! the old man yelled.

Thomas fired. The blast was like a sound meant to bring an end to evil in the world. Thomas heard it as a sound that would shatter the laughter of sluts until all shrieks were stilled and nothing was left to disturb the peace of perfect order.

The echo died away in waves. Before the last one had faded, Farebrother opened the door and put his head inside the hall. His nose wrinkled. His expression for some few seconds was that of a man unwilling to admit surprise. His eyes were clear as glass, reflecting the scene. The old lady lay on the floor between the girl and Thomas.

The sheriff's brain worked instantly like a calculating machine. He saw the facts as if they were already in print: the fellow had intended all along to kill his mother and pin it on the girl. But Farebrother had been too quick for him.

They were not yet aware of his head in the door. As he scrutinized the scene, further insights were flashed to him. Over her body, the killer and the slut were about to collapse into each other's arms. The sheriff knew a nasty bit when he saw it. He was accustomed to enter upon scenes that were not as bad as he had hoped to find them, but this one met his expectations.

The Lame
Shall Enter First

Sheppard sat on a stool at the bar that divided the kitchen in half, eating his cereal out of the individual pasteboard box it came in. He ate mechanically, his eyes on the child, who was wandering from cabinet to cabinet in the panelled kitchen, collecting the ingredients for his breakfast. He was a stocky blond boy of ten. Sheppard kept his intense blue eyes fixed on him. The boy's future was written in his face. He would be a banker. No, worse. He would operate a small loan company. All he wanted for the child was that he be good and unselfish and neither seemed likely. Sheppard was a young man whose hair was already white. It stood up like a narrow brush halo over his pink sensitive face.

The boy approached the bar with the jar of peanut butter under his arm, a plate with a quarter of a small chocolate cake on it in one hand and the ketchup bottle in the other. He did not appear to notice his father. He climbed up on the stool and began to spread peanut butter on the cake. He had very large round ears that leaned away from his head and seemed to pull his eyes slightly too far apart. His shirt was green but so faded that the cowboy charging across the front of it was only a shadow.

"Norton," Sheppard said, "I saw Rufus Johnson yesterday. Do you know what he was doing?"

The child looked at him with a kind of half attention, his eyes forward but not yet engaged. They were a paler blue than his father's as if they might have faded like the shirt; one of them listed, almost imperceptibly, toward the outer rim.

"He was in an alley," Sheppard said, "and he had his hand in a garbage can. He was trying to get something to eat out of it." He paused to let this soak in. "He was hungry," he finished, and tried to pierce the child's conscience with his gaze.

The boy picked up the piece of chocolate cake and began to gnaw it from one corner.

"Norton," Sheppard said, "do you have any idea what it means to share?"

A flicker of attention. "Some of it's yours," Norton said.

"Some of it's *his*," Sheppard said heavily. It was hopeless. Almost any fault would have been preferable to selfishness— a violent temper, even a tendency to lie.

The child turned the bottle of ketchup upside-down and began thumping ketchup onto the cake.

Sheppard's look of pain increased. "You are ten and Rufus Johnson is fourteen," he said. "Yet I'm sure your shirts would fit Rufus." Rufus Johnson was a boy he had been trying to help at the reformatory for the past year. He had been released two months ago. "When he was in the reformatory, he looked pretty good, but when I saw him yesterday, he was skin and bones. He hasn't been eating cake with peanut butter on it for breakfast."

The child paused. "It's stale," he said. "That's why I have to put stuff on it."

Sheppard turned his face to the window at the end of the bar. The side lawn, green and even, sloped fifty feet or so down to a small suburban wood. When his wife was living, they had often eaten outside, even breakfast, on the grass. He had never noticed then that the child was selfish. "Listen to me," he said, turning back to him, "look at me and listen."

The boy looked at him. At least his eyes were forward.

"I gave Rufus a key to this house when he left the reformatory—to show my confidence in him and so he would have a place he could come to and feel welcome any time. He didn't use it, but I think he'll use it now because he's seen me and he's hungry. And if he doesn't use it, I'm going out and find him and bring him here. I can't see a child eating out of garbage cans."

The boy frowned. It was dawning upon him that something of his was threatened.

Sheppard's mouth stretched in disgust. "Rufus's father died before he was born," he said. "His mother is in the state penitentiary. He was raised by his grandfather in a shack without water or electricity and the old man beat him every day. How would you like to belong to a family like that?"

"I don't know," the child said lamely.

"Well, you might think about it sometime," Sheppard said.

Sheppard was City Recreational Director. On Saturdays he worked at the reformatory as a counselor, receiving nothing for it but the satisfaction of knowing he was helping boys no one else cared about. Johnson was the most intelligent boy he had worked with and the most deprived.

Norton turned what was left of the cake over as if he no longer wanted it.

"You started that, now finish it," Sheppard said.

"Maybe he won't come," the child said and his eyes brightened slightly.

"Think of everything you have that he doesn't!" Sheppard said. "Suppose you had to root in garbage cans for food? Suppose you had a huge swollen foot and one side of you dropped lower than the other when you walked?"

The boy looked blank, obviously unable to imagine such a thing.

"You have a healthy body," Sheppard said, "a good home. You've never been taught anything but the truth. Your daddy gives you everything you need and want. You don't have a grandfather who beats you. And your mother is not in the state penitentiary."

The child pushed his plate away. Sheppard groaned aloud.

A knot of flesh appeared below the boy's suddenly distorted mouth. His face became a mass of lumps with slits for eyes. "If she was in the penitentiary," he began in a kind of racking bellow, "I could go to seeeeee her." Tears rolled down his face and the ketchup dribbled on his chin. He looked as if he had been hit in the mouth. He abandoned himself and howled.

Sheppard sat helpless and miserable, like a man lashed by some elemental force of nature. This was not a normal grief. It was all part of his selfishness. She had been dead for over a year and a child's grief should not last so long. "You're going on eleven years old," he said reproachfully.

The child began an agonizing high-pitched heaving noise.

"If you stop thinking about yourself and think what you can do for somebody else," Sheppard said, "then you'll stop missing your mother."

The boy was silent but his shoulders continued to shake. Then his face collapsed and he began to howl again.

"Don't you think I'm lonely without her too?" Sheppard said. "Don't you think I miss her at all? I do, but I'm not sitting around moping. I'm busy helping other people. When do you see me just sitting around thinking about my troubles?"

The boy slumped as if he were exhausted but fresh tears streaked his face.

"What are you going to do today?" Sheppard asked, to get his mind on something else.

The child ran his arm across his eyes. "Sell seeds," he mumbled.

Always selling something. He had four quart jars full of nickels and dimes he had saved and he took them out of his closet every few days and counted them. "What are you selling seeds for?"

"To win a prize."

"What's the prize?"

"A thousand dollars."

"And what would you do if you had a thousand dollars?"

"Keep it," the child said and wiped his nose on his shoulder.

"I feel sure you would," Sheppard said. "Listen," he said and lowered his voice to an almost pleading tone, "suppose by some chance you did win a thousand dollars. Wouldn't you like to spend it on children less fortunate than yourself? Wouldn't you like to give some swings and trapezes to the orphanage? Wouldn't you like to buy poor Rufus Johnson a new shoe?"

The boy began to back away from the bar. Then suddenly he leaned forward and hung with his mouth open over his plate. Sheppard groaned again. Everything came up, the cake, the peanut butter, the ketchup—a limp sweet batter. He hung over it gagging, more came, and he waited with his mouth open over the plate as if he expected his heart to come up next.

"It's all right," Sheppard said, "it's all right. You couldn't help it. Wipe your mouth and go lie down."

The child hung there a moment longer. Then he raised his face and looked blindly at his father.

"Go on," Sheppard said. "Go on and lie down."

The boy pulled up the end of his t-shirt and smeared his mouth with it. Then he climbed down off the stool and wandered out of the kitchen.

Sheppard sat there staring at the puddle of half-digested food. The sour odor reached him and he drew back. His gorge rose. He got up and carried the plate to the sink and turned the water on it and watched grimly as the mess ran down the drain. Johnson's sad thin hand rooted in garbage cans for food while his own child, selfish, unresponsive, greedy, had so much that he threw it up. He cut off the faucet with a thrust of his fist. Johnson had a capacity for real response and had been deprived of everything from birth; Norton was average or below and had had every advantage.

He went back to the bar to finish his breakfast. The cereal was soggy in the cardboard box but he paid no attention to what he was eating. Johnson was worth any amount of effort because he had the potential. He had seen it from the time the boy had limped in for his first interview.

Sheppard's office at the reformatory was a narrow closet with one window and a small table and two chairs in it. He had never been inside a confessional but he thought it must be the same kind of operation he had here, except that he explained, he did not absolve. His credentials were less dubious than a priest's; he had been trained for what he was doing.

When Johnson came in for his first interview, he had been reading over the boy's record—senseless destruction, windows smashed, city trash boxes set afire, tires slashed—the kind of thing he found where boys had been transplanted abruptly from the country to the city as this one had. He came to Johnson's I. Q. score. It was 140. He raised his eyes eagerly.

The boy sat slumped on the edge of his chair, his arms hanging between his thighs. The light from the window fell on his face. His eyes, steel-colored and very still, were trained narrowly forward. His thin dark hair hung in a flat forelock across the side of his forehead, not carelessly like a boy's, but fiercely like an old man's. A kind of fanatic intelligence was palpable in his face.

Sheppard smiled to diminish the distance between them.

The boy's expression did not soften. He leaned back in his chair and lifted a monstrous club foot to his knee. The foot was in a heavy black battered shoe with a sole four or five inches thick. The leather parted from it in one place and the end of an empty sock protruded like a grey tongue from a severed head. The case was clear to Sheppard instantly. His mischief was compensation for the foot.

"Well Rufus," he said, "I see by the record here that you don't have but a year to serve. What do you plan to do when you get out?"

"I don't make no plans," the boy said. His eyes shifted indifferently to something outside the window behind Sheppard in the far distance.

"Maybe you ought to," Sheppard said and smiled.

Johnson continued to gaze beyond him.

"I want to see you make the most of your intelligence," Sheppard said. "What's important to you? Let's talk about what's important to *you*." His eyes dropped involuntarily to the foot.

"Study it and git your fill," the boy drawled.

Sheppard reddened. The black deformed mass swelled before his eyes. He ignored the remark and the leer the boy was giving him. "Rufus," he said, "you've got into a lot of senseless trouble but I think when you understand why you do these things, you'll be less inclined to do them." He smiled. They had so few friends, saw so few pleasant faces, that half his effectiveness came from nothing more than smiling at them. "There are a lot of things about yourself that I think I can explain to you," he said.

Johnson looked at him stonily. "I ain't asked for no explanation," he said. "I already know why I do what I do."

"Well good!" Sheppard said. "Suppose you tell me what's made you do the things you've done?"

A black sheen appeared in the boy's eyes. "Satan," he said. "He has me in his power."

Sheppard looked at him steadily. There was no indication on the boy's face that he had said this to be funny. The line of his thin mouth was set with pride. Sheppard's eyes hardened. He felt a momentary dull despair as if he were faced with some elemental warping of nature that had happened too long ago to be corrected now. This boy's questions about life had been answered by signs nailed on pine trees: DOES SATAN HAVE YOU IN HIS POWER? REPENT OR BURN IN HELL. JESUS SAVES. He would know the Bible with or without reading it. His despair gave way to outrage. "Rubbish!" he snorted. "We're living in the space age! You're too smart to give me an answer like that."

Johnson's mouth twisted slightly. His look was contemptuous but amused. There was a glint of challenge in his eyes.

Sheppard scrutinized his face. Where there was intelligence anything was possible. He smiled again, a smile that was like an invitation to the boy to come into a school room with all its windows thrown open to the light. "Rufus," he said, "I'm going to arrange for you to have a conference with me once a week. Maybe there's an explanation for your explanation. Maybe I can explain your devil to you."

After that he had talked to Johnson every Saturday for the rest of the year. He talked at random, the kind of talk the boy would never have heard before. He talked a little above him to give him something to reach for. He roamed from simple psychology and the dodges of the human mind to astronomy and the space capsules that were whirling around the earth faster than the speed of sound and would soon encircle the stars. Instinctively he concentrated on the stars. He wanted to give the boy something to reach for besides his neighbor's goods. He wanted to stretch his horizons. He wanted him to *see* the universe, to see that the darkest parts of it could be penetrated. He would have given anything to be able to put a telescope in Johnson's hands.

Johnson said little and what he did say, for the sake of his pride, was in dissent or senseless contradiction, with the club-foot raised always to his knee like a weapon ready for use, but Sheppard was not deceived. He watched his eyes and every week he saw something in them crumble. From the boy's face, hard but shocked, braced against the light that was ravaging him, he could see that he was hitting dead center.

Johnson was free now to live out of garbage cans and rediscover his old ignorance. The injustice of it was infuriating. He had been sent back to the grandfather; the old man's imbecility could only be imagined. Perhaps the boy had by now run away from him. The idea of getting custody of Johnson had occurred to Sheppard before, but the fact of the grandfather had stood in the way. Nothing excited him so much as thinking what he could do for such a boy. First he would have him fitted for a new orthopedic shoe. His back was thrown out of line every time he took a step. Then he would encourage him in some particular intellectual interest. He thought of the telescope. He could buy a second-hand one and they could set it up in the attic window. He sat for almost ten minutes thinking what he could do if he had Johnson here with him. What was wasted on Norton would cause Johnson to flourish. Yesterday when he had seen him with his hand in the garbage can, he had waved and started forward. Johnson had seen him, paused a split-second, then vanished with the swiftness of a rat, but not before Sheppard had seen his expression change. Something had kindled in the boy's eyes, he was sure of it, some memory of the lost light.

He got up and threw the cereal box in the garbage. Before he left the house, he looked into Norton's room to be sure he was not still sick. The child was sitting cross-legged on his bed. He had emptied the quart jars of change into one large pile in front of him, and was sorting it out by nickels and dimes and quarters.

That afternoon Norton was alone in the house, squatting on the floor of his room arranging packages of flower seeds in rows around himself. Rain slashed against the window panes and rattled in the gutters. The room had grown dark but every few minutes it was lit by silent lightning and the seed packages showed up gaily on the floor. He squatted motionless like a large pale frog in the midst of this potential garden. All at once his eyes became alert. Without warning the rain had stopped. The silence was heavy as if the downpour had been hushed by violence. He remained motionless, only his eyes turning.

Into the silence came the distinct click of a key turning in the front door lock. The sound was a very deliberate one. It drew attention to itself and held it as if it were controlled more by a mind than by a hand. The child leapt up and got into the closet.

The footsteps began to move in the hall. They were deliberate and irregular, a light and then a heavy one, then a silence as if the visitor had paused to listen himself or to examine something. In a minute the kitchen door screeked. The footsteps crossed the kitchen to the refrigerator. The closet wall and the kitchen wall were the same. Norton stood with his ear pressed against it. The refrigerator door opened. There was a prolonged silence.

He took off his shoes and then tiptoed out of the closet and stepped over the seed packages. In the middle of the room, he stopped and remained where he was, rigid. A thin bonyfaced boy in a wet black suit stood in his door, blocking his escape. His hair was flattened to his skull by the rain. He stood there like an irate drenched crow. His look went through the child like a pin and paralyzed him. Then his eyes began to move over everything in the room—the unmade bed, the dirty curtains on the one large window, a photograph of a wide-faced young woman that stood up in the clutter on top of the dresser.

The child's tongue suddenly went wild. "He's been expecting you, he's going to give you a new shoe because you have to eat out of garbage cans!" he said in a kind of mouse-like shriek.

"I eat out of garbage cans," the boy said slowly with a beady stare, "because I like to eat out of garbage cans. See?"

The child nodded.

"And I got ways of getting my own shoe. See?"

The child nodded, mesmerized.

The boy limped in and sat down on the bed. He arranged a pillow behind him and stretched his short leg out so that the big black shoe rested conspicuously on a fold of the sheet.

Norton's gaze settled on it and remained immobile. The sole was as thick as a brick.

Johnson wiggled it slightly and smiled. "If I kick somebody *once* with this," he said, "it learns them not to mess with me."

The child nodded.

"Go in the kitchen," Johnson said, "and make me a sandwich with some of that rye bread and ham and bring me a glass of milk."

Norton went off like a mechanical toy, pushed in the right direction. He made a large greasy sandwich with ham hanging out the sides of it and poured out a glass of milk. Then he returned to the room with the glass of milk in one hand and the sandwich in the other.

Johnson was leaning back regally against the pillow. "Thanks, waiter," he said and took the sandwich.

Norton stood by the side of the bed, holding the glass.

The boy tore into the sandwich and ate steadily until he finished it. Then he took the glass of milk. He held it with both hands like a child and when he lowered it for breath, there was a rim of milk around his mouth. He handed Norton the empty glass. "Go get me one of them oranges in there, waiter," he said hoarsely.

Norton went to the kitchen and returned with the orange. Johnson peeled it with his fingers and let the peeling drop in the bed. He ate it slowly, spitting the seeds out in front of him. When he finished, he wiped his hands on the sheet and gave Norton a long appraising stare. He appeared to have been softened by the service. "You're his kid all right," he said. "You got the same stupid face."

The child stood there stolidly as if he had not heard.

"He don't know his left hand from his right," Johnson said with a hoarse pleasure in his voice.

The child cast his eyes a little to the side of the boy's face and looked fixedly at the wall.

"Yaketty yaketty yak," Johnson said, "and never says a thing."

The child's upper lip lifted slightly but he didn't say anything.

"Gas," Johnson said. "Gas."

The child's face began to have a wary look of belligerence. He backed away slightly as if he were prepared to retreat instantly. "He's good," he mumbled. "He helps people."

"Good!" Johnson said savagely. He thrust his head forward. "Listen here," he hissed, "I don't care if he's good or not. He ain't *right!*"

Norton looked stunned.

The screen door in the kitchen banged and some one entered. Johnson sat forward instantly. "Is that him?" he said.

"It's the cook," Norton said. "She comes in the afternoon."

Johnson got up and limped into the hall and stood in the kitchen door and Norton followed him.

The colored girl was at the closet taking off a bright red raincoat. She was a tall light-yellow girl with a mouth like a large rose that had darkened and wilted. Her hair was dressed in tiers on top of her head and leaned to the side like the Tower of Pisa.

Johnson made a noise through his teeth. "Well look at Aunt Jemima," he said.

The girl paused and trained an insolent gaze on them. They might have been dust on the floor.

"Come on," Johnson said, "let's see what all you got besides a nigger." He opened the first door to his right in the hall and looked into a pink-tiled bathroom. "A pink can!" he murmured.

He turned a comical face to the child. "Does he sit on that?"

"It's for company," Norton said, "but he sits on it sometimes."

"He ought to empty his head in it," Johnson said.

The door was open to the next room. It was the room Sheppard had slept in since his wife died. An ascetic-looking iron bed stood on the bare floor. A heap of Little League baseball uniforms was piled in one corner. Papers were scattered over a large roll-top desk and held down in various places by his pipes. Johnson stood looking into the room silently. He wrinkled his nose. "Guess who?" he said.

The door to the next room was closed but Johnson opened it and thrust his head into the semi-darkness within. The shades were down and the air was close with a faint scent of perfume in it. There was a wide antique bed and a mammoth dresser whose mirror glinted in the half light. Johnson snapped the light switch by the door and crossed the room to the mirror and peered into it. A silver comb and brush lay on the linen runner. He picked up the comb and began to run it through his hair. He combed it straight down on his forehead. Then he swept it to the side, Hitler fashion.

"Leave her comb alone!" the child said. He stood in the door, pale and breathing heavily as if he were watching sacrilege in a holy place.

Johnson put the comb down and picked up the brush and gave his hair a swipe with it.

"She's dead," the child said.

"I ain't afraid of dead people's things," Johnson said. He opened the top drawer and slid his hand in.

"Take your big fat dirty hands off my mother's clothes!" the child said in a high suffocated voice.

"Keep your shirt on, sweetheart," Johnson murmured. He pulled up a wrinkled red polka dot blouse and dropped it back. Then he pulled out a green silk kerchief and whirled it over his head and let it float to the floor. His hand continued to plow deep into the drawer. After a moment it came up gripping a faded corset with four dangling metal supporters. "Thisyer must be her saddle," he observed.

He lifted it gingerly and shook it. Then he fastened it

around his waist and jumped up and down, making the metal supporters dance. He began to snap his fingers and turn his hips from side to side. "Gonter rock, rattle and roll," he sang. "Gonter rock, rattle and roll. Can't please that woman, to save my doggone soul." He began to move around, stamping the good foot down and slinging the heavy one to the side. He danced out the door, past the stricken child and down the hall toward the kitchen.

A half hour later Sheppard came home. He dropped his raincoat on a chair in the hall and came as far as the parlor door and stopped. His face was suddenly transformed. It shone with pleasure. Johnson sat, a dark figure, in a high-backed pink upholstered chair. The wall behind him was lined with books from floor to ceiling. He was reading one. Sheppard's eyes narrowed. It was a volume of the Encyclopaedia Britannica. He was so engrossed in it that he did not look up. Sheppard held his breath. This was the perfect setting for the boy. He had to keep him here. He had to manage it somehow.

"Rufus!" he said, "it's good to see you boy!" and he bounded forward with his arm outstretched.

Johnson looked up, his face blank. "Oh hello," he said. He ignored the hand as long as he was able but when Sheppard did not withdraw it, he grudgingly shook it.

Sheppard was prepared for this kind of reaction. It was part of Johnson's make-up never to show enthusiasm.

"How are things?" he said. "How's your grandfather treating you?" He sat down on the edge of the sofa.

"He dropped dead," the boy said indifferently.

"You don't mean it!" Sheppard cried. He got up and sat down on the coffee table nearer the boy.

"Naw," Johnson said, "he ain't dropped dead. I wisht he had."

"Well where is he?" Sheppard muttered.

"He's gone with a remnant to the hills," Johnson said. "Him and some others. They're going to bury some Bibles in a cave and take two of different kinds of animals and all like that. Like Noah. Only this time it's going to be fire, not flood."

Sheppard's mouth stretched wryly. "I see," he said. Then he said, "In other words the old fool has abandoned you?"

"He ain't no fool," the boy said in an indignant tone.

"Has he abandoned you or not?" Sheppard asked impatiently.

The boy shrugged.

"Where's your probation officer?"

"I ain't supposed to keep up with him," Johnson said. "He's supposed to keep up with me."

Sheppard laughed. "Wait a minute," he said. He got up and went into the hall and got his raincoat off the chair and took it to the hall closet to hang it up. He had to give himself time to think, to decide how he could ask the boy so that he would stay. He couldn't force him to stay. It would have to be voluntary. Johnson pretended not to like him. That was only to uphold his pride, but he would have to ask him in such a way that his pride could still be upheld. He opened the closet door and took out a hanger. An old grey winter coat of his wife's still hung there. He pushed it aside but it didn't move. He pulled it open roughly and winced as if he had seen the larva inside a cocoon. Norton stood in it, his face swollen and pale, with a drugged look of misery on it. Sheppard stared at him. Suddenly he was confronted with a possibility. "Get out of there," he said. He caught him by the shoulder and propelled him firmly into the parlor and over to the pink chair where Johnson was sitting with the encyclopedia in his lap. He was going to risk everything in one blow.

"Rufus," he said, "I've got a problem. I need your help."

Johnson looked up suspiciously.

"Listen," Sheppard said, "we need another boy in the house." There was a genuine desperation in his voice. "Norton here has never had to divide anything in his life. He doesn't know what it means to share. And I need somebody to teach him. How about helping me out? Stay here for a while with us, Rufus. I need your help." The excitement in his voice made it thin.

The child suddenly came to life. His face swelled with fury. "He went in her room and used her comb!" he screamed, yanking Sheppard's arm. "He put on her corset and danced with Leola, he . . ."

"Stop this!" Sheppard said sharply. "Is tattling all you're capable of? I'm not asking you for a report on Rufus's conduct. I'm asking you to make him welcome here. Do you understand?

"You see how it is?" he asked, turning to Johnson.

Norton kicked the leg of the pink chair viciously, just missing Johnson's swollen foot. Sheppard yanked him back.

"He said you weren't nothing but gas!" the child shrieked.

A sly look of pleasure crossed Johnson's face.

Sheppard was not put back. These insults were part of the

boy's defensive mechanism. "What about it, Rufus?" he said. "Will you stay with us for a while?"

Johnson looked straight in front of him and said nothing. He smiled slightly and appeared to gaze upon some vision of the future that pleased him.

"I don't care," he said and turned a page of the encyclopedia. "I can stand anywhere."

"Wonderful." Sheppard said. "Wonderful."

"He said," the child said in a throaty whisper, "you didn't know your left hand from your right."

There was a silence.

Johnson wet his finger and turned another page of the encyclopedia.

"I have something to say to both of you," Sheppard said in a voice without inflection. His eyes moved from one to the other of them and he spoke slowly as if what he was saying he would say only once and it behooved them to listen. "If it made any difference to me what Rufus thinks of me," he said, "then I wouldn't be asking him here. Rufus is going to help me out and I'm going to help him out and we're both going to help you out. I'd simply be selfish if I let what Rufus thinks of me interfere with what I can do for Rufus. If I can help a person, all I want is to do it. I'm above and beyond simple pettiness."

Neither of them made a sound. Norton stared at the chair cushion. Johnson peered closer at some fine print in the encyclopedia. Sheppard was looking at the tops of their heads. He smiled. After all, he had won. The boy was staying. He reached out and ruffled Norton's hair and slapped Johnson on the shoulder. "Now you fellows sit here and get acquainted," he said gaily and started toward the door. "I'm going to see what Leola left us for supper."

When he was gone, Johnson raised his head and looked at Norton. The child looked back at him bleakly. "God, kid," Johnson said in a cracked voice, "how do you stand it?" His face was stiff with outrage. "He thinks he's Jesus Christ!"

II

Sheppard's attic was a large unfinished room with exposed beams and no electric light. They had set the telescope up on a tripod in one of the dormer windows. It pointed now toward the dark sky where a sliver of moon, as fragile as an egg shell, had just emerged from behind a cloud with a brilliant silver edge. Inside, a kerosene lantern set on a trunk cast their shadows upward and tangled them, wavering slightly, in the joists overhead. Sheppard was sitting on a packing box, looking through the telescope, and Johnson was at his elbow, waiting to get at it. Sheppard had bought it for fifteen dollars two days before at a pawn shop.

"Quit hoggin it," Johnson said.

Sheppard got up and Johnson slid onto the box and put his eye to the instrument.

Sheppard sat down on a straight chair a few feet away. His face was flushed with pleasure. This much of his dream was a reality. Within a week he had made it possible for this boy's vision to pass through a slender channel to the stars. He looked at Johnson's bent back with complete satisfaction. The boy had on one of Norton's plaid shirts and some new khaki trousers he had bought him. The shoe would be ready next week. He had taken him to the brace shop the day after he came and had him fitted for a new shoe. Johnson was as touchy about the foot as if it were a sacred object. His face had been glum while the clerk, a young man with a bright pink bald head, measured the foot with his profane hands. The shoe was going to make the greatest difference in the boy's attitude. Even a child with normal feet was in love with the world after he had got a new pair of shoes. When Norton got a new pair, he walked around for days with his eyes on his feet.

Sheppard glanced across the room at the child. He was sitting on the floor against a trunk, trussed up in a rope he had found and wound around his legs from his ankles to his knees. He appeared so far away that Sheppard might have been looking at him through the wrong end of the telescope. He had had to whip him only once since Johnson had been with them—the first night when Norton had realized that Johnson was going to sleep in his mother's bed. He did not believe in whipping children, particularly in anger. In this case, he had done both and with good results. He had had no more trouble with Norton.

The child hadn't shown any positive generosity toward Johnson but what he couldn't help, he appeared to be resigned to. In the mornings Sheppard sent the two of them to the Y swimming pool, gave them money to get their lunch at the cafeteria and instructed them to meet him in the park in the afternoon to watch his Little League baseball practice. Every afternoon they had arrived at the park, shambling, silent, their faces closed each on his own thoughts as if neither were aware of the other's existence. At least he could be thankful there were no fights.

Norton showed no interest in the telescope. "Don't you

want to get up and look through the telescope, Norton?" he said. It irritated him that the child showed no intellectual curiosity whatsoever. "Rufus is going to be way ahead of you."

Norton leaned forward absently and looked at Johnson's back.

Johnson turned around from the instrument. His face had begun to fill out again. The look of outrage had retreated from his hollow cheeks and was shored up now in the caves of his eyes, like a fugitive from Sheppard's kindness. "Don't waste your valuable time, kid," he said. "You seen the moon once, you seen it."

Sheppard was amused by these sudden turns of perversity. The boy resisted whatever he suspected was meant for his improvement and contrived when he was vitally interested in something to leave the impression he was bored. Sheppard was not deceived. Secretly Johnson was learning what he wanted him to learn—that his benefactor was impervious to insult and that there were no cracks in his armor of kindness and patience where a successful shaft could be driven. "Some day you may go to the moon," he said. "In ten years men will probably be making round trips there on schedule. Why you boys may be spacemen. Astronauts!"

"Astro-nuts," Johnson said.

"Nuts or nauts," Sheppard said, "it's perfectly possible that you, Rufus Johnson, will go to the moon."

Something in the depths of Johnson's eyes stirred. All day his humor had been glum. "I ain't going to the moon and get there alive," he said, "and when I die I'm going to hell."

"It's at least possible to get to the moon," Sheppard said dryly. The best way to handle this kind of thing was with gentle ridicule. "We can see it. We know it's there. Nobody has given any reliable evidence there's a hell."

"The Bible has give the evidence," Johnson said darkly, "and if you die and go there you burn forever."

The child leaned forward.

"Whoever says it ain't a hell," Johnson said, "is contradicting Jesus. The dead are judged and the wicked are damned. They weep and gnash their teeth while they burn," he continued, "and it's everlasting darkness."

The child's mouth opened. His eyes appeared to grow hollow.

"Satan runs it," Johnson said.

Norton lurched up and took a hobbled step toward Sheppard. "Is she there?" he said in a loud voice. "Is she there burning up?" He kicked the rope off his feet. "Is she on fire?"

"Oh my God," Sheppard muttered. "No no," he said, "of course she isn't. Rufus is mistaken. Your mother isn't anywhere. She's not unhappy. She just isn't." His lot would have been easier if when his wife died he had told Norton she had gone to heaven and that some day he would see her again, but he could not allow himself to bring him up on a lie.

Norton's face began to twist. A knot formed in his chin.

"Listen," Sheppard said quickly and pulled the child to him, "your mother's spirit lives on in other people and it'll live on in you if you're good and generous like she was."

The child's pale eyes hardened in disbelief.

Sheppard's pity turned to revulsion. The boy would rather she be in hell than nowhere. "Do you understand?" he said. "She doesn't exist." He put his hand on the child's shoulder. "That's all I have to give you," he said in a softer, exasperated tone, "the truth."

Instead of howling, the boy wrenched himself away and caught Johnson by the sleeve. "Is she there, Rufus?" he said. "Is she there, burning up?"

Johnson's eyes glittered. "Well," he said, "she is if she was evil. Was she a whore?"

"Your mother was not a whore," Sheppard said sharply. He had the sensation of driving a car without brakes. "Now let's have no more of this foolishness. We were talking about the moon."

"Did she believe in Jesus?" Johnson asked.

Norton looked blank. After a second he said, "Yes," as if he saw that this was necessary. "She did," he said. "All the time."

"She did not," Sheppard muttered.

"She did all the time," Norton said. "I heard her say she did all the time."

"She's saved," Johnson said.

The child still looked puzzled. "Where?" he said. "Where is she at?"

"On high," Johnson said.

"Where's that?" Norton gasped.

"It's in the sky somewhere," Johnson said, "but you got to be dead to get there. You can't go in no space ship." There was a narrow gleam in his eyes now like a beam holding steady on its target.

"Man's going to the moon," Sheppard said grimly, "is very much like the first fish crawling out of the water onto land billions and billions of years ago. He didn't have an earth suit. He had to grow his adjustments inside. He developed lungs."

"When I'm dead will I go to hell or where she is?" Norton asked.

"Right now you'd go where she is," Johnson said, "but if you live long enough, you'll go to hell."

Sheppard rose abruptly and picked up the lantern. "Close the window, Rufus," he said. "It's time we went to bed."

On the way down the attic stairs he heard Johnson say in a loud whisper behind him, "I'll tell you all about it tomorrow, kid, when Himself has cleared out."

The next day when the boys came to the ball park, he watched them as they came from behind the bleachers and around the edge of the field. Johnson's hand was on Norton's shoulder, his head bent toward the younger boy's ear, and on the child's face there was a look of complete confidence, of dawning light. Sheppard's grimace hardened. This would be Johnson's way of trying to annoy him. But he would not be annoyed. Norton was not bright enough to be damaged much. He gazed at the child's dull absorbed little face. Why try to make him superior? Heaven and hell were for the mediocre, and he was that if he was anything.

The two boys came into the bleachers and sat down about ten feet away, facing him, but neither gave him any sign of recognition. He cast a glance behind him where the Little Leaguers were spread out in the field. Then he started for the bleachers. The hiss of Johnson's voice stopped as he approached.

"What have you fellows been doing today?" he asked genially.

"He's been telling me . . ." Norton started.

Johnson pushed the child in the ribs with his elbow. "We ain't been doing nothing," he said. His face appeared to be covered with a blank glaze but through it a look of complicity was blazoned forth insolently.

Sheppard felt his face grow warm, but he said nothing. A child in a Little League uniform had followed him and was nudging him in the back of the leg with a bat. He turned and put his arm around the boy's neck and went with him back to the game.

That night when he went to the attic to join the boys at the telescope, he found Norton there alone. He was sitting on the packing box, hunched over, looking intently through the instrument. Johnson was not there.

"Where's Rufus?" Sheppard asked.

"I said where's Rufus?" he said louder.

"Gone somewhere," the child said without turning around.

"Gone where?" Sheppard asked.

"He just said he was going somewhere. He said he was fed up looking at stars."

"I see," Sheppard said glumly. He turned and went back down the stairs. He searched the house without finding Johnson. Then he went to the living room and sat down. Yesterday he had been convinced of his success with the boy. Today he faced the possibility that he was failing with him. He had been over-lenient, too concerned to have Johnson like him. He felt a twinge of guilt. What difference did it make if Johnson liked him or not? What was that to him? When the boy came in, they would have a few things understood. As long as you stay here there'll be no going out at night by yourself, do you understand?

I don't have to stay here. It ain't nothing to me staying here.

Oh my God, he thought. He could not bring it to that. He would have to be firm but not make an issue of it. He picked up the evening paper. Kindness and patience were always called for but he had not been firm enough. He sat holding the paper but not reading it. The boy would not respect him unless he showed firmness. The doorbell rang and he went to answer it. He opened it and stepped back, with a pained disappointed face.

A large dour policeman stood on the stoop, holding Johnson by the elbow. At the curb a patrolcar waited. Johnson looked very white. His jaw was thrust forward as if to keep from trembling.

"We brought him here first because he raised such a fit," the policeman said, "but now that you've seen him, we're going to take him to the station and ask him a few questions."

"What happened?" Sheppard muttered.

"A house around the corner from here," the policeman said. "A real smash job, dishes broken all over the floor, furniture turned upside-down . . ."

"I didn't have a thing to do with it!" Johnson said. "I was walking along minding my own bidnis when this cop came up and grabbed me."

Sheppard looked at the boy grimly. He made no effort to soften his expression.

Johnson flushed. "I was just walking along," he muttered, but with no conviction in his voice.

"Come on, bud," the policeman said.

"You ain't going to let him take me, are you?" Johnson said. "You believe me, don't you?" There was an appeal in his voice that Sheppard had not heard there before.

This was crucial. The boy would have to learn that he could not be protected when he was guilty. "You'll have to go with him, Rufus," he said.

"You're going to let him take me and I tell you I ain't done a thing?" Johnson said shrilly.

Sheppard's face became harder as his sense of injury grew. The boy had failed him even before he had had a chance to give him the shoe. They were to have got it tomorrow. All his regret turned suddenly on the shoe; his irritation at the sight of Johnson doubled.

"You made out like you had all this confidence in me," the boy mumbled.

"I did have," Sheppard said. His face was wooden.

Johnson turned away with the policeman but before he moved, a gleam of pure hatred flashed toward Sheppard from the pits of his eyes.

Sheppard stood in the door and watched them get into the patrolcar and drive away. He summoned his compassion. He would go to the station tomorrow and see what he could do about getting him out of trouble. The night in jail would not hurt him and the experience would teach him that he could not treat with impunity someone who had shown him nothing but kindness. Then they would go get the shoe and perhaps after a night in jail it would mean even more to the boy.

The next morning at eight o'clock the police sergeant called and told him he could come pick Johnson up. "We booked a nigger on that charge," he said. "Your boy didn't have nothing to do with it."

Sheppard was at the station in ten minutes, his face hot with shame. Johnson sat slouched on a bench in a drab outer office, reading a police magazine. There was no else in the room. Sheppard sat down beside him and put his hand tentatively on his shoulder.

The boy glanced up—his lip curled—and back to the magazine.

Sheppard felt physically sick. The ugliness of what he had done bore in upon him with a sudden dull intensity. He had failed him at just the point where he might have turned him once and for all in the right direction. "Rufus," he said, "I apologize. I was wrong and you were right. I misjudged you."

The boy continued to read.

"I'm sorry."

The boy wet his finger and turned a page.

Sheppard braced himself. "I was a fool, Rufus," he said.

Johnson's mouth slid slightly to the side. He shrugged without raising his head from the magazine.

"Will you forget it, this time?" Sheppard said. "It won't happen again."

The boy looked up. His eyes were bright and unfriendly. "I'll forget it," he said, "but you better remember it." He got up and stalked toward the door. In the middle of the room, he turned and jerked his arm at Sheppard and Sheppard jumped up and followed him as if the boy had yanked an invisible leash.

"Your shoe," he said eagerly, "today is the day to get your shoe!" Thank God for the shoe!

But when they went to the brace shop, they found that the shoe had been made two sizes too small and a new one would not be ready for another ten days. Johnson's temper improved at once. The clerk had obviously made a mistake in the measurements but the boy insisted the foot had grown. He left the shop with a pleased expression, as if, in expanding, the foot had acted on some inspiration of its own. Sheppard's face was haggard.

After this he redoubled his efforts. Since Johnson had lost interest in the telescope, he bought a microscope and a box of prepared slides. If he couldn't impress the boy with immensity, he would try the infinitesimal. For two nights Johnson appeared absorbed in the new instrument, then he abruptly lost interest in it, but he seemed content to sit in the living room in the evening and read the encyclopedia. He devoured the encyclopedia as he devoured his dinner, steadily and without dint to his appetite. Each subject appeared to enter his head, be ravaged, and thrown out. Nothing pleased Sheppard more than to see the boy slouched on the sofa, his mouth shut, reading. After they had spent two or three evenings like this, he began to recover his vision. His confidence returned. He knew that some day he would be proud of Johnson.

On Thursday night Sheppard attended a city council meeting. He dropped the boys off at a movie on his way and picked them up on his way back. When they reached home, an automobile with a single red eye above its windshield was waiting in front of the house. Sheppard's lights as he turned into the driveway illuminated two dour faces in the car.

"The cops!" Johnson said. "Some nigger has broke in somewhere and they've come for me again."

"We'll see about that," Sheppard muttered. He stopped the car in the driveway and switched off the lights. "You boys go in the house and go to bed," he said. "I'll handle this."

He got out and strode toward the squad car. He thrust his head in the window. The two policemen were looking at him with silent knowledgeable faces. "A house on the corner of Shelton and Mills," the one in the driver's seat said. "It looks like a train run through it."

"He was in the picture show down town," Sheppard said. "My boy was with him. He had nothing to do with the other one and he had nothing to do with this one. I'll be responsible."

"If I was you," the one nearest him said, "I wouldn't be responsible for any little bastard like him."

"I said I'd be responsible," Sheppard repeated coldly. "You people made a mistake the last time. Don't make another."

The policemen looked at each other. "It ain't our funeral," the one in the driver's seat said, and turned the key in the ignition.

Sheppard went in the house and sat down in the living room in the dark. He did not suspect Johnson and he did not want the boy to think he did. If Johnson thought he suspected him again, he would lose everything. But he wanted to know if his alibi was airtight. He thought of going to Norton's room and asking him if Johnson had left the movie. But that would be worse. Johnson would know what he was doing and would be incensed. He decided to ask Johnson himself. He would be direct. He went over in his mind what he was going to say and then he got up and went to the boy's door.

It was open as if he had been expected but Johnson was in bed. Just enough light came in from the hall for Sheppard to see his shape under the sheet. He came in and stood at the foot of the bed. "They've gone," he said. "I told them you had nothing to do with it and that I'd be responsible."

There was a muttered "Yeah," from the pillow.

Sheppard hesitated. "Rufus," he said, "you didn't leave the movie for anything at all, did you?"

"You make out like you got all this confidence in me!" a sudden outraged voice cried, "and you ain't got any! You don't trust me no more now than you did then!" The voice, disembodied, seemed to come more surely from the depths of Johnson than when his face was visible. It was a cry of reproach, edged slightly with contempt.

"I do have confidence in you," Sheppard said intensely. "I have every confidence in you. I believe in you and I trust you completely."

"You got your eye on me all the time," the voice said sullenly. "When you get through asking me a bunch of questions, you're going across the hall and ask Norton a bunch of them."

"I have no intention of asking Norton anything and never did," Sheppard said gently. "And I don't suspect you at all. You could hardly have got from the picture show down town and out here to break in a house and back to the picture show in the time you had."

"That's why you believe me!" the boy cried, "—because you think I couldn't have done it."

"No, no!" Sheppard said. "I believe you because I believe you've got the brains and the guts not to get in trouble again. I believe you know yourself well enough now to know that you don't have to do such things. I believe that you can make anything of yourself that you set your mind to."

Johnson sat up. A faint light shone on his forehead but the rest of his face was invisible. "And I could have broke in there if I'd wanted to in the time I had," he said.

"But I know you didn't," Sheppard said. "There's not the least trace of doubt in my mind."

There was a silence. Johnson lay back down. Then the voice, low and hoarse, as if it were being forced out with difficulty, said, "You don't want to steal and smash up things when you've got everything you want already."

Sheppard caught his breath. The boy was thanking him! He was thanking him! There was gratitude in his voice. There was appreciation. He stood there, smiling foolishly in the dark, trying to hold the moment in suspension. Involuntarily he took a step toward the pillow and stretched out his hand and touched Johnson's forehead. It was cold and dry like rusty iron.

"I understand. Good night, son," he said and turned quickly and left the room. He closed the door behind him and stood there, overcome with emotion.

Across the hall Norton's door was open. The child lay on the bed on his side, looking into the light from the hall.

After this, the road with Johnson would be smooth.

Norton sat up and beckoned to him.

He saw the child but after the first instant, he did not let his eyes focus directly on him. He could not go in and talk to Norton without breaking Johnson's trust. He hesitated, but remained where he was a moment as if he saw nothing. Tomorrow was the day they were to go back for the shoe. It would be a climax to the good feeling between them. He turned quickly and went back into his own room.

The child sat for some time looking at the spot where his

father had stood. Finally his gaze became aimless and he lay back down.

The next day Johnson was glum and silent as if he were ashamed that he had revealed himself. His eyes had a hooded look. He seemed to have retired within himself and there to be going through some crisis of determination. Sheppard could not get to the brace shop quickly enough. He left Norton at home because he did not want his attention divided. He wanted to be free to observe Johnson's reaction minutely. The boy did not seem pleased or even interested in the prospect of the shoe, but when it became an actuality, certainly then he would be moved.

The brace shop was a small concrete warehouse lined and stacked with the equipment of affliction. Wheel chairs and walkers covered most of the floor. The walls were hung with every kind of crutch and brace. Artificial limbs were stacked on the shelves, legs and arms and hands, claws and hooks, straps and human harnesses and unidentifiable instruments for unnamed deformities. In a small clearing in the middle of the room there was a row of yellow plastic-cushioned chairs and a shoe fitting stool. Johnson slouched down in one of the chairs and set his foot up on the stool and sat with his eyes on it moodily. What was roughly the toe had broken open again and he had patched it with a piece of canvas; another place he had patched with what appeared to be the tongue of the original shoe. The two sides were laced with twine.

There was an excited flush on Sheppard's face; his heart was beating unnaturally fast.

The clerk appeared from the back of the shop with the new shoe under his arm. "Got her right this time!" he said. He straddled the shoe-fitting stool and held the shoe up, smiling as if he had produced it by magic.

It was a black slick shapeless object, shining hideously. It looked like a blunt weapon, highly polished.

Johnson gazed at it darkly.

"With this shoe," the clerk said, "you won't know you're walking. You'll think you're riding!" He bent his bright pink bald head and began gingerly to unlace the twine. He removed the old shoe as if he were skinning an animal still half alive. His expression was strained. The unsheathed mass of foot in the dirty sock made Sheppard feel queasy. He turned his eyes away until the new shoe was on. The clerk laced it up rapidly. "Now stand up and walk around," he said, "and see if that ain't power glide." He winked at Sheppard. "In that shoe," he said, "he won't know he don't have a normal foot."

Sheppard's face was bright with pleasure.

Johnson stood up and walked a few yards away. He walked stiffly with almost no dip in his short stride. He stood for a moment, rigid, with his back to them.

"Wonderful!" Sheppard said. "Wonderful." It was as if he had given the boy a new spine.

Johnson turned around. His mouth was set in a thin icy line. He came back to the seat and removed the shoe. He put his foot in the old one and began lacing it up.

"You want to take it home and see if it suits you first?" the clerk murmured.

"No," Johnson said. "I ain't going to wear it at all."

"What's wrong with it?" Sheppard said, his voice rising.

"I don't need no new shoe," Johnson said. "And when I do, I got ways of getting my own." His face was stony but there was a glint of triumph in his eyes.

"Boy," the clerk said, "is your trouble in your foot or in your head?"

"Go soak your skull," Johnson said. "Your brains are on fire."

The clerk rose glumly but with dignity and asked Sheppard what he wanted done with the shoe, which he dangled dispiritedly by the lace.

Sheppard's face was a dark angry red. He was staring straight in front of him at a leather corset with an artificial arm attached.

The clerk asked him again.

"Wrap it up," Sheppard muttered. He turned his eyes to Johnson. "He's not mature enough for it yet," he said. "I had thought he was less of a child."

The boy leered. "You been wrong before," he said.

That night they sat in the living room and read as usual. Sheppard kept himself glumly entrenched behind the Sunday New York *Times*. He wanted to recover his good humor, but every time he thought of the rejected shoe, he felt a new charge of irritation. He did not trust himself even to look at Johnson. He realized that the boy had refused the shoe because he was insecure. Johnson had been frightened by his own gratitude. He didn't know what to make of the new self he was becoming conscious of. He understood that something he had been was threatened and he was facing himself and his possibilities for the first time. He was questioning his identity. Grudgingly, Sheppard felt a slight return of sympathy for the boy. In a few minutes, he lowered his paper and looked at him.

Johnson was sitting on the sofa, gazing over the top of the encyclopedia. His expression was trancelike. He might have been listening to something far away. Sheppard watched him intently but the boy continued to listen, and did not turn his head. The poor kid is lost, Sheppard thought. Here he had sat all evening, sullenly reading the paper, and had not said a word to break the tension. "Rufus," he said.

Johnson continued to sit, stock-still, listening.

"Rufus," Sheppard said in a slow hypnotic voice, "you can be anything in the world you want to be. You can be a scientist or an architect or an engineer or whatever you set your mind to, and whatever you set your mind to be, you can be the best of its kind." He imagined his voice penetrating to the boy in the black caverns of his psyche. Johnson leaned forward but his eyes did not turn. On the street a car door closed. There was a silence. Then a sudden blast from the door bell.

Sheppard jumped up and went to the door and opened it. The same policeman who had come before stood there. The patrolcar waited at the curb.

"Lemme see that boy," he said.

Sheppard scowled and stood aside. "He's been here all evening," he said. "I can vouch for it."

The policeman walked into the living room. Johnson appeared engrossed in his book. After a second he looked up with an annoyed expression, like a great man interrupted at his work.

"What was that you were looking at in that kitchen window over on Winter Avenue about a half hour ago, bud?" the policeman asked.

"Stop persecuting this boy!" Sheppard said. "I'll vouch for the fact that he was here. I was here with him."

"You heard him," Johnson said. "I been here all the time."

"It ain't everybody makes tracks like you," the policeman said and eyed the clubfoot.

"They couldn't be his tracks," Sheppard growled, infuriated. "He's been here all the time. You're wasting your own time and you're wasting ours." He felt the *ours* seal his solidarity with the boy. "I'm sick of this," he said. "You people are too damn lazy to go out and find whoever is doing these things. You come here automatically."

The policeman ignored this and continued looking through Johnson. His eyes were small and alert in his fleshy face. Finally he turned toward the door. "We'll get him sooner or later," he said, "with his head in a window and his tail out."

Sheppard followed him to the door and slammed it behind

him. His spirits were soaring. This was exactly what he had needed. He returned with an expectant face.

Johnson had put the book down and was sitting there, looking at him slyly. "Thanks," he said.

Sheppard stopped. The boy's expression was predatory. He was openly leering.

"You ain't such a bad liar yourself," he said.

"Liar?" Sheppard murmured. Could the boy have left and come back? He felt himself sicken. Then a rush of anger sent him forward. "Did you leave?" he said furiously. "I didn't see you leave."

The boy only smiled.

"You went up in the attic to see Norton," Sheppard said.

"Naw," Johnson said, "that kid is crazy. He don't want to do nothing but look through that stinking telescope."

"I don't want to hear about Norton," Sheppard said harshly. "Where were you?"

"I was sitting on that pink can by my ownself," Johnson said. "There wasn't no witnesses."

Sheppard took out his handkerchief and wiped his forehead. He managed to smile.

Johnson rolled his eyes. "You don't believe in me," he said. His voice was cracked the way it had been in the dark room two nights before. "You make out like you got all this confidence in me but you ain't got any. When things get hot you'll fade like the rest of them." The crack became exaggerated, comic. The mockery in it was blatant. "You don't believe in me. You ain't got no confidence," he wailed. "And you ain't any smarter than that cop. All that about tracks—that was a trap. There wasn't any tracks. That whole place is concreted in the back and my feet were dry."

Sheppard slowly put the handkerchief back in his pocket. He dropped down on the sofa and gazed at the rug beneath his feet. The boy's clubfoot was set within the circle of his vision. The pieced-together shoe appeared to grin at him with Johnson's own face. He caught hold of the edge of the sofa cushion and his knuckles turned white. A chill of hatred shook him. He hated the shoe, hated the foot, hated the boy. His face paled. Hatred choked him. He was aghast at himself.

He caught the boy's shoulder and gripped it fiercely as if to keep himself from falling. "Listen," he said, "you looked in that window to embarrass me. That was all you wanted—to shake my resolve to help you, but my resolve isn't shaken. I'm stronger than you are. I'm stronger than you are and I'm going to save you. The good will triumph."

"Not when it ain't true," the boy said. "Not when it ain't right."

"My resolve isn't shaken," Sheppard repeated. "I'm going to save you."

Johnson's look became sly again. "You ain't going to save me," he said. "You're going to tell me to leave this house. I did those other two jobs too—the first one as well as the one I done when I was supposed to be in the picture show."

"I'm not going to tell you to leave," Sheppard said. His voice was toneless, mechanical. "I'm going to save you."

Johnson thrust his head forward. "Save yourself," he hissed. "Nobody can save me but Jesus."

Sheppard laughed curtly. "You don't deceive me," he said. "I flushed that out of your head in the reformatory. I saved you from that, at least."

The muscles in Johnson's face stiffened. A look of such repulsion hardened on his face that Sheppard drew back. The boy's eyes were like distorting mirrors in which he saw himself made hideous and grotesque. "I'll show you," Johnson whispered. He rose abruptly and started headlong for the door as if he could not get out of Sheppard's sight quick enough, but it was the door to the back hall he went through, not the front door. Sheppard turned on the sofa and looked behind him where the boy had disappeared. He heard the door to his room slam. He was not leaving. The intensity had gone out of Sheppard's eyes. They looked flat and lifeless as if the shock of the boy's revelation were only now reaching the center of his consciousness. "If he would only leave," he murmured. "If he would only leave now of his own accord."

The next morning Johnson appeared at the breakfast table in the grandfather's suit he had come in. Sheppard pretended not to notice but one look told him what he already knew, that he was trapped, that there could be nothing now but a battle of nerves and that Johnson would win it. He wished he had never laid eyes on the boy. The failure of his compassion numbed him. He got out of the house as soon as he could and all day he dreaded to go home in the evening. He had a faint hope that the boy might be gone when he returned. The grandfather's suit might have meant he was leaving. The hope grew in the afternoon. When he came home and opened the front door, his heart was pounding.

He stopped in the hall and looked silently into the living room. His expectant expression faded. His face seemed suddenly as old as his white hair. The two boys were sitting close together on the sofa, reading the same book. Norton's cheek rested against the sleeve of Johnson's black suit. Johnson's finger moved under the lines they were reading. The elder brother and the younger. Sheppard looked woodenly at this scene for almost a minute. Then he walked into the room and took off his coat and dropped it on a chair. Neither boy noticed him. He went on to the kitchen.

Leola left the supper on the stove every afternoon before she left and he put it on the table. His head ached and his nerves were taut. He sat down on the kitchen stool and remained there, sunk in his depression. He wondered if he could infuriate Johnson enough to make him leave of his own accord. Last night what had enraged him was the Jesus business. It might enrage Johnson, but it depressed him. Why not simply tell the boy to go? Admit defeat. The thought of facing Johnson again sickened him. The boy looked at him as if he were the guilty one, as if he were a moral leper. He knew without conceit that he was a good man, that he had nothing to reproach himself with. His feelings about Johnson now were involuntary. He would like to feel compassion for him. He would like to be able to help him. He longed for the time when there would be no one but himself and Norton in the house, when the child's simple selfishness would be all he had to contend with, and his own loneliness.

He got up and took three serving dishes off the shelf and took them to the stove. Absently he began pouring the butterbeans and the hash into the dishes. When the food was on the table, he called them in.

They brought the book with them. Norton pushed his place setting around to the same side of the table as Johnson's and moved his chair next to Johnson's chair. They sat down and put the book between them. It was a black book with red edges.

"What's that you're reading?" Sheppard asked, sitting down.

"The Holy Bible," Johnson said.

God give me strength, Sheppard said under his breath.

"We lifted it from a ten cent store," Johnson said.

"We?" Sheppard muttered. He turned and glared at Norton. The child's face was bright and there was an excited sheen to his eyes. The change that had come over the boy struck him for the first time. He looked alert. He had on a blue plaid shirt and his eyes were a brighter blue than he had ever seen them before. There was a strange new life in him, the sign of new and more rugged vices. "So now you steal?" he said, glowering. "You haven't learned to be generous but you have learned to steal."

"No he ain't," Johnson said. "I was the one lifted it. He only watched. He can't sully himself. It don't make any difference about me. I'm going to hell anyway."

Sheppard held his tongue.

"Unless," Johnson said, "I repent."

"Repent, Rufus," Norton said in a pleading voice. "Repent, hear? You don't want to go to hell."

"Stop talking this nonsense," Sheppard said, looking sharply at the child.

"If I do repent, I'll be a preacher," Johnson said. "If you're going to do it, it's no sense in doing it half way."

"What are you going to be, Norton," Sheppard asked in a brittle voice, "a preacher too?"

There was a glitter of wild pleasure in the child's eyes. "A space man!" he shouted.

"Wonderful," Sheppard said bitterly.

"Those space ships ain't going to do you any good unless you believe in Jesus," Johnson said. He wet his finger and began to leaf through the pages of the Bible. "I'll read you where it says so," he said.

Sheppard leaned forward and said in a low furious voice, "Put that Bible up, Rufus, and eat your dinner."

Johnson continued searching for the passage.

"Put that Bible up!" Sheppard shouted.

The boy stopped and looked up. His expression was startled but pleased.

"That book is something for you to hide behind," Sheppard said. "It's for cowards, people who are afraid to stand on their own feet and figure things out for themselves."

Johnson's eyes snapped. He backed his chair a little way from the table. "Satan has you in his power," he said. "Not only me. You too."

Sheppard reached across the table to grab the book but Johnson snatched it and put it in his lap.

Sheppard laughed. "You don't believe in that book and you know you don't believe in it!"

"I believe it!" Johnson said. "You don't know what I believe and what I don't."

Sheppard shook his head. "You don't believe it. You're too intelligent."

"I ain't too intelligent," the boy muttered. "You don't know nothing about me. Even if I didn't believe it, it would still be true."

"You don't believe it!" Sheppard said. His face was a taunt.

"I believe it!" Johnson said breathlessly. "I'll show you I believe it!" He opened the book in his lap and tore out a page of it and thrust it into his mouth. He fixed his eyes on Sheppard. His jaws worked furiously and the paper crackled as he chewed it.

"Stop this," Sheppard said in a dry, burnt-out voice. "Stop it."

The boy raised the Bible and tore out a page with his teeth and began grinding it in his mouth, his eyes burning.

Sheppard reached across the table and knocked the book out of his hand. "Leave the table," he said coldly.

Johnson swallowed what was in his mouth. His eyes widened as if a vision of splendor were opening up before him. "I've eaten it!" he breathed. "I've eaten it like Ezekiel and it was honey to my mouth!"

"Leave this table," Sheppard said. His hands were clenched beside his plate.

"I've eaten it!" the boy cried. Wonder transformed his face. "I've eaten it like Ezekiel and I don't want none of your food after it nor no more ever."

"Go then," Sheppard said softly. "Go. Go."

The boy rose and picked up the Bible and started toward the hall with it. At the door he paused, a small black figure on the threshold of some dark apocalypse. "The devil has you in his power," he said in a jubilant voice and disappeared.

After supper Sheppard sat in the living room alone. Johnson had left the house but he could not believe that the boy had simply gone. The first feeling of release had passed. He felt dull and cold as at the onset of an illness and dread had settled in him like a fog. Just to leave would be too anti-climactic an end for Johnson's taste; he would return and try to prove something. He might come back a week later and set fire to the place. Nothing seemed too outrageous now.

He picked up the paper and tried to read. In a moment he threw it down and got up and went into the hall and listened. He might be hiding in the attic. He went to the attic door and opened it.

The lantern was lit, casting a dim light on the stairs. He didn't hear anything. "Norton," he called, "are you up there?" There was no answer. He mounted the narrow stairs to see.

Amid the strange vine-like shadows cast by the lantern, Norton sat with his eye to the telescope. "Norton," Sheppard said, "do you know where Rufus went?"

The child's back was to him. He was sitting hunched, intent, his large ears directly above his shoulders. Suddenly he waved his hand and crouched closer to the telescope as if he could not get near enough to what he saw.

"Norton!" Sheppard said in a loud voice.

The child didn't move.

"Norton!" Sheppard shouted.

Norton started. He turned around. There was an unnatural brightness about his eyes. After a moment he seemed to see that it was Sheppard. "I've found her!" he said breathlessly.

"Found who?" Sheppard said.

"Mamma!"

Sheppard steadied himself in the door way. The jungle of shadows around the child thickened.

"Come and look!" he cried. He wiped his sweaty face on the tail of his plaid shirt and then put his eye back to the telescope. His back became fixed in a rigid intensity. All at once he waved again.

"Norton," Sheppard said, "you don't see anything in the telescope but star clusters. Now you've had enough of that for one night. You'd better go to bed. Do you know where Rufus is?"

"She's there!" he cried, not turning around from the telescope. "She waved at me!"

"I want you in bed in fifteen minutes," Sheppard said. After a moment he said, "Do you hear me, Norton?"

The child began to wave frantically.

"I mean what I say," Sheppard said. "I'm going to call in fifteen minutes and see if you're in bed."

He went down the steps again and returned to the parlor. He went to the front door and cast a cursory glance out. The sky was crowded with the stars he had been fool enough to think Johnson could reach. Somewhere in the small wood behind the house, a bull frog sounded a low hollow note. He went back to his chair and sat a few minutes. He decided to go to bed. He put his hands on the arms of the chair and leaned forward and heard, like the first shrill note of a disaster warning, the siren of a police car, moving slowly into the neighborhood and nearer until it subsided with a moan outside the house.

He felt a cold weight on his shoulders as if an icy cloak had been thrown about him. He went to the door and opened it.

Two policemen were coming up the walk with a dark snarling Johnson between them, handcuffed to each. A reporter jogged alongside and another policeman waited in the patrol-car.

"Here's your boy," the dourest of the policemen said. "Didn't I tell you we'd get him?"

Johnson jerked his arm down savagely. "I was waitin for you!" he said. "You wouldn't have got me if I hadn't of wanted to get caught. It was my idea." He was addressing the policemen but leering at Sheppard.

Sheppard looked at him coldly.

"Why did you want to get caught?" the reporter asked, running around to get beside Johnson. "Why did you deliberately want to get caught?"

The question and the sight of Sheppard seemed to throw the boy into a fury. "To show up that big tin Jesus!" he hissed and kicked his leg out at Sheppard. "He thinks he's God. I'd rather be in the reformatory than in his house, I'd rather be in the pen! The Devil has him in his power. He don't know his left hand from his right, he don't have as much sense as his crazy kid!" He paused and then swept on to his fantastic conclusion. "He made suggestions to me!"

Sheppard's face blanched. He caught hold of the door facing.

"Suggestions?" the reporter said eagerly, "what kind of suggestions?"

"Immor'l suggestions!" Johnson said. "What kind of suggestions do you think? But I ain't having none of it, I'm a Christian, I'm . . ."

Sheppard's face was tight with pain. "He knows that's not true," he said in a shaken voice. "He knows he's lying. I did everything I knew how for him. I did more for him than I did for my own child. I hoped to save him and I failed, but it was an honorable failure. I have nothing to reproach myself with. I made no suggestions to him."

"Do you remember the suggestions?" the reporter asked. "Can you tell us exactly what he said?"

"He's a dirty atheist," Johnson said. "He said there wasn't no hell."

"Well, they seen each other now," one of the policemen said with a knowing sigh. "Let's us go."

"Wait," Sheppard said. He came down one step and fixed his eyes on Johnson's eyes in a last desperate effort to save himself. "Tell the truth, Rufus," he said. "You don't want to perpetrate this lie. You're not evil, you're mortally confused. You don't have to make up for that foot, you don't have to . . ."

Johnson hurled himself forward. "Listen at him!" he screamed. "I lie and steal because I'm good at it! My foot don't have a thing to do with it! The lame shall enter first!

The halt'll be gathered together. When I get ready to be saved, Jesus'll save me, not that lying stinking atheist, not that . . ."

"That'll be enough out of you," the policeman said and yanked him back. "We just wanted you to see we got him," he said to Sheppard, and the two of them turned around and dragged Johnson away, half turned and screaming back at Sheppard.

"The lame'll carry off the prey!" he screeched, but his voice was muffled inside the car. The reporter scrambled into the front seat with the driver and slammed the door and the siren wailed into the darkness.

Sheppard remained there, bent slightly like a man who has been shot but continues to stand. After a minute he turned and went back in the house and sat down in the chair he had left. He closed his eyes on a picture of Johnson in a circle of reporters at the police station, elaborating his lies. "I have nothing to reproach myself with," he murmured. His every action had been selfless, his one aim had been to save Johnson for some decent kind of service, he had not spared himself, he had sacrificed his reputation, he had done more for Johnson than he had done for his own child. Foulness hung about him like an odor in the air, so close that it seemed to come from his own breath. "I have nothing to reproach myself with," he repeated. His voice sounded dry and harsh. "I did more for him than I did for my own child." He was swept with a sudden panic. He heard the boy's jubilant voice. Satan has you in his power.

"I have nothing to reproach myself with," he began again. "I did more for him than I did for my own child." He heard his voice as if it were the voice of his accuser. He repeated the sentence silently.

Slowly his face drained of color. It became almost grey beneath the white halo of his hair. The sentence echoed in his mind, each syllable like a dull blow. His mouth twisted and he closed his eyes against the revelation. Norton's face rose before him, empty, forlorn, his left eye listing almost imperceptibly toward the outer rim as if it could not bear a full view of grief. His heart constricted with a repulsion for himself so clear and intense that he gasped for breath. He had stuffed his own emptiness with good works like a glutton. He had ignored his own child to feed his vision of himself. He saw the clear-eyed Devil, the sounder of hearts, leering at him from the eyes of Johnson. His image of himself shrivelled until everything was black before him. He sat there paralyzed, aghast.

He saw Norton at the telescope, all back and ears, saw his arm shoot up and wave frantically. A rush of agonizing love for the child rushed over him like a transfusion of life. The little boy's face appeared to him transformed; the image of his salvation; all light. He groaned with joy. He would make everything up to him. He would never let him suffer again. He would be mother and father. He jumped up and ran to his room, to kiss him, to tell him that he loved him, that he would never fail him again.

The light was on in Norton's room but the bed was empty. He turned and dashed up the attic stairs and at the top reeled back like a man on the edge of a pit. The tripod had fallen and the telescope lay on the floor. A few feet over it, the child hung in the jungle of shadows, just below the beam from which he had launched his flight into space.

Revelation

The doctor's waiting room, which was very small, was almost full when the Turpins entered and Mrs. Turpin, who was very large, made it look even smaller by her presence. She stood looming at the head of the magazine table set in the center of it, a living demonstration that the room was inadequate and ridiculous. Her little bright black eyes took in all the patients as she sized up the seating situation. There was one vacant chair and a place on the sofa occupied by a blond child in a dirty blue romper who should have been told to move over and make room for the lady. He was five or six, but Mrs. Turpin saw at once that no one was going to tell him to move over. He was slumped down in the seat, his arms idle at his sides and his eyes idle in his head; his nose ran unchecked.

Mrs. Turpin put a firm hand on Claud's shoulder and said in a voice that included anyone who wanted to listen, "Claud, you sit in that chair there," and gave him a push down into the vacant one. Claud was florid and bald and sturdy, somewhat shorter than Mrs. Turpin, but he sat down as if he were accustomed to doing what she told him to.

Mrs. Turpin remained standing. The only man in the room besides Claud was a lean stringy old fellow with a rusty hand spread out on each knee, whose eyes were closed as if he were asleep or dead or pretending to be so as not to get up and offer her his seat. Her gaze settled agreeably on a well-dressed grey-haired lady whose eyes met hers and whose expression said: if that child belonged to me, he would have some manners and move over—there's plenty of room there for you and him too.

Claud looked up with a sigh and made as if to rise.

"Sit down," Mrs. Turpin said. "You know you're not supposed to stand on that leg. He has an ulcer on his leg," she explained.

Claud lifted his foot onto the magazine table and rolled his trouser leg up to reveal a purple swelling on a plump marble-white calf.

"My!" the pleasant lady said. "How did you do that?"

"A cow kicked him," Mrs. Turpin said.

"Goodness!" said the lady.

Claud rolled his trouser leg down.

"Maybe the little boy would move over," the lady suggested, but the child did not stir.

"Somebody will be leaving in a minute," Mrs. Turpin said. She could not understand why a doctor—with as much money as they made charging five dollars a day to just stick their head in the hospital door and look at you—couldn't afford a decent-sized waiting room. This one was hardly bigger than a garage. The table was cluttered with limp-looking magazines and at one end of it there was a big green glass ash tray full of cigaret butts and cotton wads with little blood spots on them. If she had had anything to do with the running of the place, that would have been emptied every so often. There were no chairs against the wall at the head of the room. It had a rectangular-shaped panel in it that permitted a view of the office where the nurse came and went and the secretary listened to the radio. A plastic fern in a gold pot sat in the opening and trailed its fronds down almost to the floor. The radio was softly playing gospel music.

Just then the inner door opened and a nurse with the highest stack of yellow hair Mrs. Turpin had ever seen put her face in the crack and called for the next patient. The woman sitting beside Claud grasped the two arms of her chair and hoisted herself up; she pulled her dress free from her legs and lumbered through the door where the nurse had disappeared.

Mrs. Turpin eased into the vacant chair, which held her tight as a corset. "I wish I could reduce," she said, and rolled her eyes and gave a comic sigh.

"Oh, *you* aren't fat," the stylish lady said.

"Ooooo I am too," Mrs. Turpin said. "Claud he eats all he wants to and never weighs over one hundred and seventy-five pounds, but me I just look at something good to eat and I gain some weight," and her stomach and shoulders shook with laughter. "You can eat all you want to, can't you, Claud?" she asked, turning to him.

Claud only grinned.

"Well, as long as you have such a good disposition," the stylish lady said, "I don't think it makes a bit of difference what size you are. You just can't beat a good disposition."

Next to her was a fat girl of eighteen or nineteen, scowling into a thick blue book which Mrs. Turpin saw was entitled *Human Development*. The girl raised her head and directed her scowl at Mrs. Turpin as if she did not like her looks. She

appeared annoyed that anyone should speak while she tried
to read. The poor girl's face was blue with acne and Mrs.
Turpin thought how pitiful it was to have a face like that at
that age. She gave the girl a friendly smile but the girl only
scowled the harder. Mrs. Turpin herself was fat but she had
always had good skin, and, though she was forty-seven years
old, there was not a wrinkle in her face except around her
eyes from laughing too much.

Next to the ugly girl was the child, still in exactly the same
position, and next to him was a thin leathery old woman in a
cotton print dress. She and Claud had three sacks of chicken
feed in their pump house that was in the same print. She had
seen from the first that the child belonged with the old
woman. She could tell by the way they sat—kind of vacant
and white-trashy, as if they would sit there until Doomsday if
nobody called and told them to get up. And at right angles
but next to the well-dressed pleasant lady was a lank-faced
woman who was certainly the child's mother. She had on a
yellow sweat shirt and wine-colored slacks, both gritty-looking,
and the rims of her lips were stained with snuff. Her dirty
yellow hair was tied behind with a little piece of red paper
ribbon. Worse than niggers any day, Mrs. Turpin thought.

The gospel hymn playing was, "When I looked up and He
looked down," and Mrs. Turpin, who knew it, supplied the
last line mentally, "And wona these days I know I'll we-eara
crown."

Without appearing to, Mrs. Turpin always noticed people's
feet. The well-dressed lady had on red and grey suede shoes
to match her dress. Mrs. Turpin had on her good black
patent leather pumps. The ugly girl had on Girl Scout shoes
and heavy socks. The old woman had on tennis shoes and the
white-trashy mother had on what appeared to be bedroom
slippers, black straw with gold braid threaded through
them—exactly what you would have expected her to have on.

Sometimes at night when she couldn't go to sleep, Mrs.
Turpin would occupy herself with the question of who she
would have chosen to be if she couldn't have been herself. If
Jesus had said to her before he made her, "There's only two
places available for you. You can either be a nigger or
white-trash," what would she have said? "Please, Jesus,
please," she would have said, "just let me wait until there's
another place available," and he would have said, "No, you
have to go right now and I have only those two places so
make up your mind." She would have wiggled and squirmed
and begged and pleaded but it would have been no use and
finally she would have said, "All right, make me a nigger

then—but that don't mean a trashy one." And he would have made her a neat clean respectable Negro woman, herself but black.

Next to the child's mother was a red-headed youngish woman, reading one of the magazines and working a piece of chewing gum, hell for leather, as Claud would say. Mrs. Turpin could not see the woman's feet. She was not white-trash, just common. Sometimes Mrs. Turpin occupied herself at night naming the classes of people. On the bottom of the heap were most colored people, not the kind she would have been if she had been one, but most of them; then next to them—not above, just away from—were the white-trash; then above them were the home-owners, and above them the home-and-land owners, to which she and Claud belonged. Above she and Claud were people with a lot of money and much bigger houses and much more land. But here the complexity of it would begin to bear in on her, for some of the people with a lot of money were common and ought to be below she and Claud and some of the people who had good blood had lost their money and had to rent and then there were colored people who owned their homes and land as well. There was a colored dentist in town who had two red Lincolns and a swimming pool and a farm with registered white-faced cattle on it. Usually by the time she had fallen asleep all the classes of people were moiling and roiling around in her head, and she would dream they were all crammed in together in a box car, being ridden off to be put in a gas oven.

"That's a beautiful clock," she said and nodded to her right. It was a big wall clock, the face encased in a brass sunburst.

"Yes, it's very pretty," the stylish lady said agreeably. "And right on the dot too," she added, glancing at her watch.

The ugly girl beside her cast an eye upward at the clock, smirked, then looked directly at Mrs. Turpin and smirked again. Then she returned her eyes to her book. She was obviously the lady's daughter because, although they didn't look anything alike as to disposition, they both had the same shape of face and the same blue eyes. On the lady they sparkled pleasantly but in the girl's seared face they appeared alternately to smolder and to blaze.

What if Jesus had said, "All right, you can be white-trash or a nigger or ugly"!

Mrs. Turpin felt an awful pity for the girl, though she thought it was one thing to be ugly and another to act ugly.

The woman with the snuff-stained lips turned around in

her chair and looked up at the clock. Then she turned back and appeared to look a little to the side of Mrs. Turpin. There was a cast in one of her eyes. "You want to know wher you can get you one of themther clocks?" she asked in a loud voice.

"No, I already have a nice clock," Mrs. Turpin said. Once somebody like her got a leg in the conversation, she would be all over it.

"You can get you one with green stamps," the woman said. "That's most likely wher he got hisn. Save you up enough, you can get you most anythang. I got me some joo'ry."

Ought to have got you a wash rag and some soap, Mrs. Turpin thought.

"I get contour sheets with mine," the pleasant lady said.

The daughter slammed her book shut. She looked straight in front of her, directly through Mrs. Turpin and on through the yellow curtain and the plate glass window which made the wall behind her. The girl's eyes seemed lit all of a sudden with a peculiar light, an unnatural light like night road signs give. Mrs. Turpin turned her head to see if there was anything going on outside that she should see, but she could not see anything. Figures passing cast only a pale shadow through the curtain. There was no reason the girl should single her out for her ugly looks.

"Miss Finley," the nurse said, cracking the door. The gum-chewing woman got up and passed in front of her and Claud and went into the office. She had on red high-heeled shoes.

Directly across the table, the ugly girl's eyes were fixed on Mrs. Turpin as if she had some very special reason for disliking her.

"This is wonderful weather, isn't it?" the girl's mother said.

"It's good weather for cotton if you can get the niggers to pick it," Mrs. Turpin said, "but niggers don't want to pick cotton any more. You can't get the white folks to pick it and now you can't get the niggers—because they got to be right up there with the white folks."

"They gonna *try* anyways," the white-trash woman said, leaning forward.

"Do you have one of those cotton-picking machines?" the pleasant lady asked.

"No," Mrs. Turpin said, "they leave half the cotton in the field. We don't have much cotton anyway. If you want to make it farming now, you have to have a little of everything. We got a couple of acres of cotton and a few hogs and chickens and just enough white-face that Claud can look after them himself."

"One thang I don't want," the white-trash woman said, wiping her mouth with the back of her hand. "Hogs. Nasty stinking things, a-gruntin and a-rootin all over the place."

Mrs. Turpin gave her the merest edge of her attention. "Our hogs are not dirty and they don't stink," she said. "They're cleaner than some children I've seen. Their feet never touch the ground. We have a pig-parlor—that's where you raise them on concrete," she explained to the pleasant lady, "and Claud scoots them down with the hose every afternoon and washes off the floor." Cleaner by far than that child right there, she thought. Poor nasty little thing. He had not moved except to put the thumb of his dirty hand into his mouth.

The woman turned her face away from Mrs. Turpin. "I know I wouldn't scoot down no hog with no hose," she said to the wall.

You wouldn't have no hog to scoot down, Mrs. Turpin said to herself.

"A-gruntin and a-rootin and a-groanin," the woman muttered.

"We got a little of everything," Mrs. Turpin said to the pleasant lady. "It's no use in having more than you can handle yourself with help like it is. We found enough niggers to pick our cotton this year but Claud he has to go after them and take them home again in the evening. They can't walk that half a mile. No they can't. I tell you," she said and laughed merrily, "I sure am tired of buttering up niggers, but you got to love em if you want em to work for you. When they come in the morning, I run out and I say, 'Hi yawl this morning?' and when Claud drives them off to the field I just wave to beat the band and they just wave back." And she waved her hand rapidly to illustrate.

"Like you read out of the same book," the lady said, showing she understood perfectly.

"Child, yes," Mrs. Turpin said. "And when they come in from the field, I run out with a bucket of icewater. That's the way it's going to be from now on," she said. "You may as well face it."

"One thang I know," the white-trash woman said. "Two thangs I ain't going to do: love no niggers or scoot down no hog with no hose." And she let out a bark of contempt.

The look that Mrs. Turpin and the pleasant lady exchanged indicated they both understood that you had to *have* certain things before you could *know* certain things. But every time Mrs. Turpin exchanged a look with the lady, she was aware that the ugly girl's peculiar eyes were still on her, and she had trouble bringing her attention back to the conversation.

"When you got something," she said, "you got to look after it." And when you ain't got a thing but breath and britches, she added to herself, you can afford to come to town every morning and just sit on the Court House coping and spit.

A grotesque revolving shadow passed across the curtain behind her and was thrown palely on the opposite wall. Then a bicycle clattered down against the outside of the building. The door opened and a colored boy glided in with a tray from the drug store. It had two large red and white paper cups on it with tops on them. He was a tall, very black boy in discolored white pants and a green nylon shirt. He was chewing gum slowly, as if to music. He set the tray down in the office opening next to the fern and stuck his head through to look for the secretary. She was not in there. He rested his arms on the ledge and waited, his narrow bottom stuck out, swaying slowly to the left and right. He raised a hand over his head and scratched the base of his skull.

"You see that button there, boy?" Mrs. Turpin said. "You can punch that and she'll come. She's probably in the back somewhere."

"Is thas right?" the boy said agreeably, as if he had never seen the button before. He leaned to the right and put his finger on it. "She sometime out," he said and twisted around to face his audience, his elbows behind him on the counter. The nurse appeared and he twisted back again. She handed him a dollar and he rooted in his pocket and made the change and counted it out to her. She gave him fifteen cents for a tip and he went out with the empty tray. The heavy door swung to slowly and closed at length with the sound of suction. For a moment no one spoke.

"They ought to send all them niggers back to Africa," the white-trash woman said. "That's wher they come from in the first place."

"Oh, I couldn't do without my good colored friends," the pleasant lady said.

"There's a heap of things worse than a nigger," Mrs. Turpin agreed. "It's all kinds of them just like it's all kinds of us."

"Yes, and it takes all kinds to make the world go round," the lady said in her musical voice.

As she said it, the raw-complexioned girl snapped her teeth together. Her lower lip turned downwards and inside out, re-

vealing the pale pink inside of her mouth. After a second it
rolled back up. It was the ugliest face Mrs. Turpin had ever
seen anyone make and for a moment she was certain that the
girl had made it at her. She was looking at her as if she had
known and disliked her all her life—all of Mrs. Turpin's life,
it seemed too, not just all the girl's life. Why, girl, I don't
even know you, Mrs. Turpin said silently.

She forced her attention back to the discussion. "It
wouldn't be practical to send them back to Africa," she said.
"They wouldn't want to go. They got it too good here."

"Wouldn't be what they wanted—if I had anythang to do
with it," the woman said.

"It wouldn't be a way in the world you could get all the
niggers back over there," Mrs. Turpin said. "They'd be hiding
out and lying down and turning sick on you and wailing and
hollering and raring and pitching. It wouldn't be a way in the
world to get them over there."

"They got over here," the trashy woman said. "Get back
like they got over."

"It wasn't so many of them then," Mrs. Turpin explained.

The woman looked at Mrs. Turpin as if here was an idiot
indeed but Mrs. Turpin was not bothered by the look, considering where it came from.

"Nooo," she said, "they're going to stay here where they
can go to New York and marry white folks and improve
their color. That's what they all want to do, every one of
them, improve their color."

"You know what comes of that, don't you?" Claud asked.

"No, Claud, what?" Mrs. Turpin said.

Claud's eyes twinkled. "White-faced niggers," he said with
never a smile.

Everybody in the office laughed except the white-trash and
the ugly girl. The girl gripped the book in her lap with white
fingers. The trashy woman looked around her from face to
face as if she thought they were all idiots. The old woman in
the feed sack dress continued to gaze expressionless across
the floor at the high-top shoes of the man opposite her, the
one who had been pretending to be asleep when the Turpins
came in. He was laughing heartily, his hands still spread out
on his knees. The child had fallen to the side and was lying
now almost face down in the old woman's lap.

While they recovered from their laughter, the nasal chorus
on the radio kept the room from silence.

> *"You go to blank blank*
> *And I'll go to mine*

> *But we'll all blank along*
> *To-geth-ther,*
> *And all along the blank*
> *We'll hep eachother out*
> *Smile-ling in any kind of*
> *Weath-ther!"*

Mrs. Turpin didn't catch every word but she caught enough to agree with the spirit of the song and it turned her thoughts sober. To help anybody out that needed it was her philosophy of life. She never spared herself when she found somebody in need, whether they were white or black, trash or decent. And of all she had to be thankful for, she was most thankful that this was so. If Jesus had said, "You can be high society and have all the money you want and be thin and svelte-like, but you can't be a good woman with it," she would have had to say, "Well don't make me that then. Make me a good woman and it don't matter what else, how fat or how ugly or how poor!" Her heart rose. He had not made her a nigger or white-trash or ugly! He had made her herself and given her a little of everything. Jesus, thank you! she said. Thank you thank you thank you! Whenever she counted her blessings she felt as buoyant as if she weighed one hundred and twenty-five pounds instead of one hundred and eighty.

"What's wrong with your little boy?" the pleasant lady asked the white-trashy woman.

"He has a ulcer," the woman said proudly. "He ain't give me a minute's peace since he was born. Him and her are just alike," she said, nodding at the old woman, who was running her leathery fingers through the child's pale hair. "Look like I can't get nothing down them two but Co' Cola and candy."

That's all you try to get down em, Mrs. Turpin said to herself. Too lazy to light the fire. There was nothing you could tell her about people like them that she didn't know already. And it was not just that they didn't have anything. Because if you gave them everything, in two weeks it would all be broken or filthy or they would have chopped it up for lightwood. She knew all this from her own experience. Help them you must, but help them you couldn't.

All at once the ugly girl turned her lips inside out again. Her eyes were fixed like two drills on Mrs. Turpin. This time there was no mistaking that there was something urgent behind them.

Girl, Mrs. Turpin exclaimed silently, I haven't done a thing to you! The girl might be confusing her with somebody else.

There was no need to sit by and let herself be intimidated. "You must be in college," she said boldly, looking directly at the girl. "I see you reading a book there."

The girl continued to stare and pointedly did not answer.

Her mother blushed at this rudeness. "The lady asked you a question, Mary Grace," she said under her breath.

"I have ears," Mary Grace said.

The poor mother blushed again. "Mary Grace goes to Wellesley College," she explained. She twisted one of the buttons on her dress. "In Massachusetts," she added with a grimace. "And in the summer she just keeps right on studying. Just reads all the time, a real book worm. She's done real well at Wellesley; she's taking English and Math and History and Psychology and Social Studies," she rattled on, "and I think it's too much. I think she ought to get out and have fun."

The girl looked as if she would like to hurl them all through the plate glass window.

"Way up north," Mrs. Turpin murmured and thought, well, it hasn't done much for her manners.

"I'd almost rather have him sick," the white-trash woman said, wrenching the attention back to herself. "He's so mean when he ain't. Look like some children just take natural to meanness. It's some gets bad when they get sick but he was the opposite. Took sick and turned good. He don't give me no trouble now. It's me waitin to see the doctor," she said.

If I was going to send anybody back to Africa, Mrs. Turpin thought, it would be your kind, woman. "Yes, indeed," she said aloud, but looking up at the ceiling, "it's a heap of things worse than a nigger." And dirtier than a hog, she added to herself.

"I think people with bad dispositions are more to be pitied than anyone on earth," the pleasant lady said in a voice that was decidedly thin.

"I thank the Lord he has blessed me with a good one," Mrs. Turpin said. "The day has never dawned that I couldn't find something to laugh at."

"Not since she married me anyways," Claud said with a comical straight face.

Everybody laughed except the girl and the white-trash.

Mrs. Turpin's stomach shook. "He's such a caution," she said, "that I can't help but laugh at him."

The girl made a loud ugly noise through her teeth.

Her mother's mouth grew thin and tight. "I think the worst thing in the world," she said, "is an ungrateful person. To have everything and not appreciate it. I know a girl," she said, "who has parents who would give her anything, a little brother who loves her dearly, who is getting a good education, who wears the best clothes, but who can never say a kind word to anyone, who never smiles, who just criticizes and complains all day long."

"Is she too old to paddle?" Claud asked.

The girl's face was almost purple.

"Yes," the lady said, "I'm afraid there's nothing to do but leave her to her folly. Some day she'll wake up and it'll be too late."

"It never hurt anyone to smile," Mrs. Turpin said. "It just makes you feel better all over."

"Of course," the lady said sadly, "but there are just some people you can't tell anything to. They can't take criticism."

"If it's one thing I am," Mrs. Turpin said with feeling, "it's grateful. When I think who all I could have been besides myself and what all I got, a little of everything, and a good disposition besides, I just feel like shouting, 'Thank you, Jesus, for making everything the way it is!' It could have been different!" For one thing, somebody else could have got Claud. At the thought of this, she was flooded with gratitude and a terrible pang of joy ran through her. "Oh thank you, Jesus, Jesus, thank you!" she cried aloud.

The book struck her directly over her left eye. It struck almost at the same instant that she realized the girl was about to hurl it. Before she could utter a sound, the raw face came crashing across the table toward her, howling. The girl's fingers sank like clamps into the soft flesh of her neck. She heard the mother cry out and Claud shout, "Whoa!" There was an instant when she was certain that she was about to be in an earthquake.

All at once her vision narrowed and she saw everything as if it were happening in a small room far away, or as if she were looking at it through the wrong end of a telescope. Claud's face crumpled and fell out of sight. The nurse ran in, then out, then in again. Then the gangling figure of the doctor rushed out of the inner door. Magazines flew this way and that as the table turned over. The girl fell with a thud and Mrs. Turpin's vision suddenly reversed itself and she saw everything large instead of small. The eyes of the white-trashy woman were staring hugely at the floor. There the girl, held down on one side by the nurse and on the other by her mother, was wrenching and turning in their grasp. The doctor was kneeling astride her, trying to hold her arm down. He managed after a second to sink a long needle into it.

Mrs. Turpin felt entirely hollow except for her heart which

swung from side to side as if it were agitated in a great empty drum of flesh.

"Somebody that's not busy call for the ambulance," the doctor said in the off-hand voice young doctors adopt for terrible occasions.

Mrs. Turpin could not have moved a finger. The old man who had been sitting next to her skipped nimbly into the office and made the call, for the secretary still seemed to be gone.

"Claud!" Mrs. Turpin called.

He was not in his chair. She knew she must jump up and find him but she felt like some one trying to catch a train in a dream, when everything moves in slow motion and the faster you try to run the slower you go.

"Here I am," a suffocated voice, very unlike Claud's, said.

He was doubled up in the corner on the floor, pale as paper, holding his leg. She wanted to get up and go to him but she could not move. Instead, her gaze was drawn slowly downward to the churning face on the floor, which she could see over the doctor's shoulder.

The girl's eyes stopped rolling and focused on her. They seemed a much lighter blue than before, as if a door that had been tightly closed behind them was now open to admit light and air.

Mrs. Turpin's head cleared and her power of motion returned. She leaned forward until she was looking directly into the fierce brilliant eyes. There was no doubt in her mind that the girl did know her, knew her in some intense and personal way, beyond time and place and condition. "What you got to say to me?" she asked hoarsely and held her breath, waiting, as for a revelation.

The girl raised her head. Her gaze locked with Mrs. Turpin's. "Go back to hell where you came from, you old wart hog," she whispered. Her voice was low but clear. Her eyes burned for a moment as if she saw with pleasure that her message had struck its target.

Mrs. Turpin sank back in her chair.

After a moment the girl's eyes closed and she turned her head wearily to the side.

The doctor rose and handed the nurse the empty syringe. He leaned over and put both hands for a moment on the mother's shoulders, which were shaking. She was sitting on the floor, her lips pressed together, holding Mary Grace's hand in her lap. The girl's fingers were gripped like a baby's around her thumb. "Go on to the hospital," he said. "I'll call and make the arrangements."

"Now let's see that neck," he said in a jovial voice to Mrs. Turpin. He began to inspect her neck with his first two fingers. Two little moon-shaped lines like pink fish bones were indented over her windpipe. There was the beginning of an angry red swelling above her eye. His fingers passed over this also.

"Lea' me be," she said thickly and shook him off. "See about Claud. She kicked him."

"I'll see about him in a minute," he said and felt her pulse. He was a thin grey-haired man, given to pleasantries. "Go home and have yourself a vacation the rest of the day," he said and patted her on the shoulder.

Quit your pattin me, Mrs. Turpin growled to herself.

"And put an ice pack over that eye," he said. Then he went and squatted down beside Claud and looked at his leg. After a moment he pulled him up and Claud limped after him into the office.

Until the ambulance came, the only sounds in the room were the tremulous moans of the girl's mother, who continued to sit on the floor. The white-trash woman did not take her eyes off the girl. Mrs. Turpin looked straight ahead at nothing. Presently the ambulance drew up, a long dark shadow, behind the curtain. The attendants came in and set the stretcher down beside the girl and lifted her expertly onto it and carried her out. The nurse helped the mother gather up her things. The shadow of the ambulance moved silently away and the nurse came back in the office.

"That ther girl is going to be a lunatic, ain't she?" the white-trash woman asked the nurse, but the nurse kept on to the back and never answered her.

"Yes, she's going to be a lunatic," the white-trash woman said to the rest of them.

"Po' critter," the old woman murmured. The child's face was still in her lap. His eyes looked idly out over her knees. He had not moved during the disturbance except to draw one leg up under him.

"I thank Gawd," the white-trash woman said fervently, "I ain't a lunatic."

Claud came limping out and the Turpins went home.

As their pick-up truck turned into their own dirt road and made the crest of the hill, Mrs. Turpin gripped the window ledge and looked out suspiciously. The land sloped gracefully down through a field dotted with lavender weeds and at the start of the rise their small yellow frame house, with its little flower beds spread out around it like a fancy apron, sat primly in its accustomed place between two giant hickory trees. She would not have been startled to see a burnt wound between two blackened chimneys.

Neither of them felt like eating so they put on their house clothes and lowered the shade in the bedroom and lay down, Claud with his leg on a pillow and herself with a damp washcloth over her eye. The instant she was flat on her back, the image of a razor-backed hog with warts on its face and horns coming out behind its ears snorted into her head. She moaned, a low quiet moan.

"I am not," she said tearfully, "a wart hog. From hell." But the denial had no force. The girl's eyes and her words, even the tone of her voice, low but clear, directed only to her, brooked no repudiation. She had been singled out for the message, though there was trash in the room to whom it might justly have been applied. The full force of this fact struck her only now. There was a woman there who was neglecting her own child but she had been overlooked. The message had been given to Ruby Turpin, a respectable, hardworking, church-going woman. The tears dried. Her eyes began to burn instead with wrath.

She rose on her elbow and the washcloth fell into her hand. Claud was lying on his back, snoring. She wanted to tell him what the girl had said. At the same time, she did not wish to put the image of herself as a wart hog from hell into his mind.

"Hey, Claud," she muttered and pushed his shoulder.

Claud opened one pale baby blue eye.

She looked into it warily. He did not think about anything. He just went his way.

"Wha, whasit?" he said and closed the eye again.

"Nothing," she said. "Does your leg pain you?"

"Hurts like hell," Claud said.

"It'll quit terreckly," she said and lay back down. In a moment Claud was snoring again. For the rest of the afternoon they lay there. Claud slept. She scowled at the ceiling. Occasionally she raised her fist and made a small stabbing motion over her chest as if she was defending her innocence to invisible guests who were like the comforters of Job, reasonable-seeming but wrong.

About five-thirty Claud stirred. "Got to go after those niggers," he sighed, not moving.

She was looking straight up as if there were unintelligible handwriting on the ceiling. The protuberance over her eye had turned a greenish-blue. "Listen here," she said.

"What?"

"Kiss me."

Claud leaned over and kissed her loudly on the mouth. He pinched her side and their hands interlocked. Her expression of ferocious concentration did not change. Claud got up, groaning and growling, and limped off. She continued to study the ceiling.

She did not get up until she heard the pick-up truck coming back with the Negroes. Then she rose and thrust her feet in her brown oxfords, which she did not bother to lace, and stumped out onto the back porch and got her red plastic bucket. She emptied a tray of ice cubes into it and filled it half full of water and went out into the back yard. Every afternoon after Claud brought the hands in, one of the boys helped him put out hay and the rest waited in the back of the truck until he was ready to take them home. The truck was parked in the shade under one of the hickory trees.

"Hi yawl this evening?" Mrs. Turpin asked grimly, appearing with the bucket and the dipper. There were three women and a boy in the truck.

"Us doin nicely," the oldest woman said. "Hi you doin?" and her gaze stuck immediately on the dark lump on Mrs. Turpin's forehead. "You done fell down, ain't you?" she asked in a solicitous voice. The old woman was dark and almost toothless. She had on an old felt hat of Claud's set back on her head. The other two women were younger and lighter and they both had new bright green sun hats. One of them had hers on her head; the other had taken hers off and the boy was grinning beneath it.

Mrs. Turpin set the bucket down on the floor of the truck. "Yawl hep yourselves," she said. She looked around to make sure Claud had gone. "No. I didn't fall down," she said, folding her arms. "It was something worse than that."

"Ain't nothing bad happen to you!" the old woman said. She said it as if they all knew that Mrs. Turpin was protected in some special way by Divine Providence. "You just had you a little fall."

"We were in town at the doctor's office for where the cow kicked Mr. Turpin," Mrs. Turpin said in a flat tone that indicated they could leave off their foolishness. "And there was this girl there. A big fat girl with her face all broke out. I could look at that girl and tell she was peculiar but I couldn't tell how. And me and her mama were just talking and going along and all of a sudden WHAM! She throws this big book she was reading at me and . . ."

"Naw!" the old woman cried out.

"And then she jumps over the table and commences to choke me."

"Naw!" they all exclaimed, "naw!"

"Hi come she do that?" the old woman asked. "What ail her?"

Mrs. Turpin only glared in front of her.

"Somethin ail her," the old woman said.

"They carried her off in an ambulance," Mrs. Turpin continued, "but before she went she was rolling on the floor and they were trying to hold her down to give her a shot and she said something to me." She paused. "You know what she said to me?"

"What she say?" they asked.

"She said," Mrs. Turpin began, and stopped, her face very dark and heavy. The sun was getting whiter and whiter, blanching the sky overhead so that the leaves of the hickory tree were black in the face of it. She could not bring forth the words. "Something real ugly," she muttered.

"She sho shouldn't said nothin ugly to you," the old woman said. "You so sweet. You the sweetest lady I know."

"She pretty too," the one with the hat on said.

"And stout," the other one said. "I never knowed no sweeter white lady."

"That's the truth befo' Jesus," the old woman said. "Amen! You des as sweet and pretty as you can be."

Mrs. Turpin knew just exactly how much Negro flattery was worth and it added to her rage. "She said," she began again and finished this time with a fierce rush of breath, "that I was an old wart hog from hell."

There was an astounded silence.

"Where she at?" the youngest woman cried in a piercing voice.

"Lemme see her. I'll kill her!"

"I'll kill her with you!" the other one cried.

"She b'long in the sylum," the old woman said emphatically. "You the sweetest white lady I know."

"She pretty too," the other two said. "Stout as she can be and sweet. Jesus satisfied with her!"

"Deed he is," the old woman declared.

Idiots! Mrs. Turpin growled to herself. You could never say anything intelligent to a nigger. You could talk at them but not with them. "Yawl ain't drunk your water," she said shortly. "Leave the bucket in the truck when you're finished with it. I got more to do than just stand around and pass the time of day," and she moved off and into the house.

She stood for a moment in the middle of the kitchen. The dark protuberance over her eye looked like a miniature tornado cloud which might any moment sweep across the horizon of her brow. Her lower lip protruded dangerously. She squared her massive shoulders. Then she marched into the front of the house and out the side door and started down the road to the pig parlor. She had the look of a woman going single-handed, weaponless, into battle.

The sun was a deep yellow now like a harvest moon and was riding westward very fast over the far tree line as if it meant to reach the hogs before she did. The road was rutted and she kicked several good-sized stones out of her path as she strode along. The pig parlor was on a little knoll at the end of a lane that ran off from the side of the barn. It was a square of concrete as large as a small room, with a board fence about four feet high around it. The concrete floor sloped slightly so that the hog wash could drain off into a trench where it was carried to the field for fertilizer. Claud was standing on the outside, on the edge of the concrete, hanging onto the top board, hosing down the floor inside. The hose was connected to the faucet of a water trough nearby.

Mrs. Turpin climbed up beside him and glowered down at the hogs inside. There were seven long-snouted bristly shoats in it—tan with liver-colored spots—and an old sow a few weeks off from farrowing. She was lying on her side grunting. The shoats were running around shaking themselves like idiot children, their little slit pig eyes searching the floor for anything left. She had read that pigs were the most intelligent animal. She doubted it. They were supposed to be smarter than dogs. There had even been a pig astronaut. He had performed his assignment perfectly but died of a heart attack afterwards because they left him in his electric suit, sitting upright throughout his examination when naturally a hog should be on all fours.

A-gruntin and a-rootin and a-groanin.

"Gimme that hose," she said, yanking it away from Claud. "Go on and carry them niggers home and then get off that leg."

"You look like you might have swallowed a mad dog," Claud observed, but he got down and limped off. He paid no attention to her humors.

Until he was out of earshot, Mrs. Turpin stood on the side of the pen, holding the hose and pointing the stream of water at the hind quarters of any shoat that looked as if it might try to lie down. When he had had time to get over the hill, she turned her head slightly and her wrathful eyes scanned the path. He was nowhere in sight. She turned back again and seemed to gather herself up. Her shoulders rose and she drew in her breath.

"What do you send me a message like that for?" she said in a low fierce voice, barely above a whisper but with the force of a shout in its concentrated fury. "How am I a hog and me both? How am I saved and from hell too?" Her free fist was knotted and with the other she gripped the hose, blindly pointing the stream of water in and out of the eye of the old sow whose outraged squeal she did not hear.

The pig parlor commanded a view of the back pasture where their twenty beef cows were gathered around the haybales Claud and the boy had put out. The freshly cut pasture sloped down to the highway. Across it was their cotton field and beyond that a dark green dusty wood which they owned as well. The sun was behind the wood, very red, looking over the paling of trees like a farmer inspecting his own hogs.

"Why me?" she rumbled. "It's no trash around here, black or white, that I haven't given to. And break my back to the bone every day working. And do for the church."

She appeared to be the right size woman to command the arena before her. "How am I a hog?" she demanded. "Exactly how am I like them?" and she jabbed the stream of water at the shoats. "There was plenty of trash there. It didn't have to be me.

"If you like trash better, go get yourself some trash then," she railed. "You could have made me trash. Or a nigger. If trash is what you wanted why didn't you make me trash?" She shook her fist with the hose in it and a watery snake appeared momentarily in the air. "I could quit working and take it easy and be filthy," she growled. "Lounge about the sidewalks all day drinking root beer. Dip snuff and spit in every puddle and have it all over my face. I could be nasty.

"Or you could have made me a nigger. It's too late for me to be a nigger," she said with deep sarcasm, "but I could act like one. Lay down in the middle of the road and stop traffic. Roll on the ground."

In the deepening light everything was taking on a mysterious hue. The pasture was growing a peculiar glassy green and the streak of highway had turned lavender. She braced herself for a final assault and this time her voice rolled out over the pasture. "Go on," she yelled, "call me a hog! Call me a hog again. From hell. Call me a wart hog from hell. Put that bottom rail on top. There'll still be a top and bottom!"

A garbled echo returned to her.

A final surge of fury shook her and she roared, "Who do you think you are?"

The color of everything, field and crimson sky, burned for a moment with a transparent intensity. The question carried over the pasture and across the highway and the cotton field and returned to her clearly like an answer from beyond the wood.

She opened her mouth but no sound came out of it.

A tiny truck, Claud's, appeared on the highway, heading rapidly out of sight. Its gears scraped thinly. It looked like a child's toy. At any moment a bigger truck might smash into it and scatter Claud's and the niggers' brains all over the road.

Mrs. Turpin stood there, her gaze fixed on the highway, all her muscles rigid, until in five or six minutes the truck reappeared, returning. She waited until it had had time to turn into their own road. Then like a monumental statue coming to life, she bent her head slowly and gazed, as if through the very heart of mystery, down into the pig parlor at the hogs. They had settled all in one corner around the old sow who was grunting softly. A red glow suffused them. They appeared to pant with a secret life.

Until the sun slipped finally behind the tree line, Mrs. Turpin remained there with her gaze bent to them as if she were absorbing some abysmal life-giving knowledge. At last she lifted her head. There was only a purple streak in the sky, cutting through a field of crimson and leading, like an extension of the highway, into the descending dusk. She raised her hands from the side of the pen in a gesture hieratic and profound. A visionary light settled in her eyes. She saw the streak as a vast swinging bridge extending upward from the earth through a field of living fire. Upon it a vast horde of souls were rumbling toward heaven. There were whole companies of white-trash, clean for the first time in their lives, and bands of black niggers in white robes, and battalions of freaks and lunatics shouting and clapping and leaping like frogs. And bringing up the end of the procession was a tribe of people whom she recognized at once as those who, like herself and Claud, had always had a little of everything and the God-given wit to use it right. She leaned forward to observe them closer. They were marching behind the others with great dignity, accountable as they had always been for good order and common sense and respectable behavior. They alone were on key. Yet she could see by their shocked and altered faces that even their virtues were being burned away. She lowered her hands and gripped the rail of the hog pen, her eyes small but fixed unblinkingly on what lay ahead. In a moment the vision faded but she remained where she was, immobile.

At length she got down and turned off the faucet and made her slow way on the darkening path to the house. In the woods around her the invisible cricket choruses had struck up, but what she heard were the voices of the souls climbing upward into the starry field and shouting hallelujah.

Parker's Back

Parker's wife was sitting on the front porch floor, snapping beans. Parker was sitting on the step, some distance away, watching her sullenly. She was plain, plain. The skin on her face was thin and drawn as tight as the skin on an onion and her eyes were grey and sharp like the points of two icepicks. Parker understood why he had married her—he couldn't have got her any other way—but he couldn't understand why he stayed with her now. She was pregnant and pregnant women were not his favorite kind. Nevertheless, he stayed as if she had him conjured. He was puzzled and ashamed of himself.

The house they rented sat alone save for a single tall pecan tree on a high embankment overlooking a highway. At intervals a car would shoot past below and his wife's eyes would swerve suspiciously after the sound of it and then come back to rest on the newspaper full of beans in her lap. One of the things she did not approve of was automobiles. In addition to her other bad qualities, she was forever sniffing up sin. She did not smoke or dip, drink whiskey, use bad language or paint her face, and God knew some paint would have improved it, Parker thought. Her being against color, it was the more remarkable she had married him. Sometimes he supposed that she had married him because she meant to save him. At other times he had a suspicion that she actually liked everything she said she didn't. He could account for her one way or another; it was himself he could not understand.

She turned her head in his direction and said, "It's no reason you can't work for a man. It don't have to be a woman."

"Aw shut your mouth for a change," Parker muttered.

If he had been certain she was jealous of the woman he worked for he would have been pleased but more likely she was concerned with the sin that would result if he and the woman took a liking to each other. He had told her that the woman was a hefty young blonde; in fact she was nearly seventy years old and too dried up to have an interest in anything except getting as much work out of him as she could. Not that an old woman didn't sometimes get an interest in a young man, particularly if he was as attractive as Parker felt he was, but this old woman looked at him the same way she looked at her old tractor—as if she had to put up with it because it was all she had. The tractor had broken down the second day Parker was on it and she had set him at once to cutting bushes, saying out of the side of her mouth to the nigger, "Everything he touches, he breaks." She also asked him to wear his shirt when he worked; Parker had removed it even though the day was not sultry; he put it back on reluctantly.

This ugly woman Parker married was his first wife. He had had other women but he had planned never to get himself tied up legally. He had first seen her one morning when his truck broke down on the highway. He had managed to pull it off the road into a neatly swept yard on which sat a peeling two-room house. He got out and opened the hood of the truck and began to study the motor. Parker had an extra sense that told him when there was a woman nearby watching him. After he had leaned over the motor a few minutes, his neck began to prickle. He cast his eye over the empty yard and porch of the house. A woman he could not see was either nearby beyond a clump of honeysuckle or in the house, watching him out the window.

Suddenly Parker began to jump up and down and fling his hand about as if he had mashed it in the machinery. He doubled over and held his hand close to his chest. "God dammit!" he hollered, "Jesus Christ in hell! Jesus God Almighty damn! God dammit to hell!" he went on, flinging out the same few oaths over and over as loud as he could.

Without warning a terrible bristly claw slammed the side of his face and he fell backwards on the hood of the truck. "You don't talk no filth here!" a voice close to him shrilled.

Parker's vision was so blurred that for an instant he thought he had been attacked by some creature from above, a giant hawk-eyed angel wielding a hoary weapon. As his sight cleared, he saw before him a tall raw-boned girl with a broom.

"I hurt my hand," he said. "I HURT my hand." He was so incensed that he forgot that he hadn't hurt his hand. "My hand may be broke," he growled although his voice was still unsteady.

"Lemme see it," the girl demanded.

Parker stuck out his hand and she came closer and looked at it. There was no mark on the palm and she took the hand and turned it over. Her own hand was dry and hot and rough and Parker felt himself jolted back to life by her touch. He looked more closely at her. I don't want nothing to do with this one, he thought.

The girl's sharp eyes peered at the back of the stubby reddish hand she held. There emblazoned in red and blue was a tattooed eagle perched on a cannon. Parker's sleeve was rolled to the elbow. Above the eagle a serpent was coiled about a shield and in the spaces between the eagle and the serpent there were hearts, some with arrows through them. Above the serpent there was a spread hand of cards. Every space on the skin of Parker's arm, from wrist to elbow, was covered in some loud design. The girl gazed at this with an almost stupefied smile of shock, as if she had accidentally grasped a poisonous snake; she dropped the hand.

"I got most of my other ones in foreign parts," Parker said. "These here I mostly got in the United States. I got my first one when I was only fifteen year old."

"Don't tell me," the girl said, "I don't like it. I ain't got any use for it."

"You ought to see the ones you can't see," Parker said and winked.

Two circles of red appeared like apples on the girl's cheeks and softened her appearance. Parker was intrigued. He did not for a minute think that she didn't like the tattoos. He had never yet met a woman who was not attracted to them.

Parker was fourteen when he saw a man in a fair, tattooed from head to foot. Except for his loins which were girded with a panther hide, the man's skin was patterned in what seemed from Parker's distance—he was near the back of the tent, standing on a bench—a single intricate design of brilliant color. The man, who was small and sturdy, moved about on the platform, flexing his muscles so that the arabesque of men and beasts and flowers on his skin appeared to have a subtle motion of its own. Parker was filled with emotion, lifted up as some people are when the flag passes. He was a boy whose mouth habitually hung open. He was heavy and earnest, as ordinary as a loaf of bread. When the show was over, he had remained standing on the bench, staring where the tattooed man had been, until the tent was almost empty.

Parker had never before felt the least motion of wonder in himself. Until he saw the man at the fair, it did not enter his head that there was anything out of the ordinary about the fact that he existed. Even then it did not enter his head, but a peculiar unease settled in him. It was as if a blind boy had been turned so gently in a different direction that he did not know his destination had been changed.

He had his first tattoo some time after—the eagle perched on the cannon. It was done by a local artist. It hurt very little, just enough to make it appear to Parker to be worth doing. This was peculiar too for before he had thought that only what did not hurt was worth doing. The next year he quit school because he was sixteen and could. He went to the trade school for a while, then he quit the trade school and worked for six months in a garage. The only reason he worked at all was to pay for more tattoos. His mother worked in a laundry and could support him, but she would not pay for any tattoo except his name on a heart, which he had put on, grumbling. However, her name was Betty Jean and nobody had to know it was his mother. He found out that the tattoos were attractive to the kind of girls he liked but who had never liked him before. He began to drink beer and get in fights. His mother wept over what was becoming of him. One night she dragged him off to a revival with her, not telling him where they were going. When he saw the big lighted church, he jerked out of her grasp and ran. The next day he lied about his age and joined the navy.

Parker was large for the tight sailor's pants but the silly white cap, sitting low on his forehead, made his face by contrast look thoughtful and almost intense. After a month or two in the navy, his mouth ceased to hang open. His features hardened into the features of a man. He stayed in the navy five years and seemed a natural part of the grey mechanical ship, except for his eyes, which were the same pale slate-color as the ocean and reflected the immense spaces around him as if they were a microcosm of the mysterious sea. In port Parker wandered about comparing the run-down places he was in to Birmingham, Alabama. Everywhere he went he picked up more tattoos.

He had stopped having lifeless ones like anchors and crossed rifles. He had a tiger and a panther on each shoulder, a cobra coiled about a torch on his chest, hawks on his thighs, Elizabeth II and Philip over where his stomach and liver were respectively. He did not care much what the subject was so long as it was colorful; on his abdomen he had a few obscenities but only because that seemed the proper place for them. Parker would be satisfied with each tattoo about a month, then something about it that had attracted him would wear off. Whenever a decent-sized mirror was available, he would get in front of it and study his overall look. The effect was not of one intricate arabesque of colors but of something haphazard and botched. A huge dissatisfaction would come over him and he would go off and find another tattooist and have another space filled up. The front of Parker was almost completely covered but there were no tattoos on his back. He had no desire for one anywhere he could not readily see it himself. As the space on the front of him for tattoos decreased, his dissatisfaction grew and became general.

After one of his furloughs, he didn't go back to the navy but remained away without official leave, drunk, in a rooming house in a city he did not know. His dissatisfaction, from being chronic and latent, had suddenly become acute and raged in him. It was as if the panther and the lion and the serpents and the eagles and the hawks had penetrated his skin and lived inside him in a raging warfare. The navy caught up with him, put him in the brig for nine months and then gave him a dishonorable discharge.

After that Parker decided that country air was the only kind fit to breathe. He rented the shack on the embankment and bought the old truck and took various jobs which he kept as long as it suited him. At the time he met his future wife, he was buying apples by the bushel and selling them for the same price by the pound to isolated homesteaders on back country roads.

"All that there," the woman said, pointing to his arm, "is no better than what a fool Indian would do. It's a heap of vanity." She seemed to have found the word she wanted. "Vanity of vanities," she said.

Well what the hell do I care what she thinks of it? Parker asked himself, but he was plainly bewildered. "I reckon you like one of these better than another anyway," he said, dallying until he thought of something that would impress her. He thrust the arm back at her. "Which you like best?"

"None of them," she said, "but the chicken is not as bad as the rest."

"What chicken?" Parker almost yelled.

She pointed to the eagle.

"That's an eagle," Parker said. "What fool would waste their time having a chicken put on themselves?"

"What fool would have any of it?" the girl said and turned away. She went slowly back to the house and left him there to get going. Parker remained for almost five minutes, looking agape at the dark door she had entered.

The next day he returned with a bushel of apples. He was not one to be outdone by anything that looked like her. He liked women with meat on them, so you didn't feel their muscles, much less their old bones. When he arrived, she was sitting on the top step and the yard was full of children, all as thin and poor as herself; Parker remembered it was Saturday.

He hated to be making up to a woman when there were children around, but it was fortunate he had brought the bushel of apples off the truck. As the children approached him to see what he carried, he gave each child an apple and told it to get lost; in that way he cleared out the whole crowd.

The girl did nothing to acknowledge his presence. He might have been a stray pig or goat that had wandered into the yard and she too tired to take up the broom and send it off. He set the bushel of apples down next to her on the step. He sat down on a lower step.

"Hep yourself," he said, nodding at the basket; then he lapsed into silence.

She took an apple quickly as if the basket might disappear if she didn't make haste. Hungry people made Parker nervous. He had always had plenty to eat himself. He grew very uncomfortable. He reasoned he had nothing to say so why should he say it? He could not think now why he had come or why he didn't go before he wasted another bushel of apples on the crowd of children. He supposed they were her brothers and sisters.

She chewed the apple slowly but with a kind of relish of concentration, bent slightly but looking out ahead. The view from the porch stretched off across a long incline studded with iron weed and across the highway to a vast vista of hills and one small mountain. Long views depressed Parker. You look out into space like that and you begin to feel as if someone were after you, the navy or the government or religion.

"Who them children belong to, you?" he said at length.

"I ain't married yet," she said. "They belong to momma." She said it as if it were only a matter of time before she would be married.

Who in God's name would marry her? Parker thought.

A large barefooted woman with a wide gap-toothed face appeared in the door behind Parker. She had apparently been there for several minutes.

"Good evening," Parker said.

The woman crossed the porch and picked up what was left of the bushel of apples. "We thank you," she said and returned with it into the house.

"That your old woman?" Parker muttered.

The girl nodded. Parker knew a lot of sharp things he could have said like "You got my sympathy," but he was gloomily silent. He just sat there, looking at the view. He thought he must be coming down with something.

"If I pick up some peaches tomorrow I'll bring you some," he said.

"I'll be much obliged to you," the girl said.

Parker had no intention of taking any basket of peaches back there but the next day he found himself doing it. He and the girl had almost nothing to say to each other. One thing he did say was, "I ain't got any tattoo on my back."

"What you got on it?" the girl said.

"My shirt," Parker said. "Haw."

"Haw, haw," the girl said politely.

Parker thought he was losing his mind. He could not believe for a minute that he was attracted to a woman like this. She showed not the least interest in anything but what he brought until he appeared the third time with two cantaloupes. "What's your name?" she asked.

"O. E. Parker," he said.

"What does the O.E. stand for?"

"You can just call me O.E.," Parker said. "Or Parker. Don't nobody call me by my name."

"What's it stand for?" she persisted.

"Never mind," Parker said. "What's yours?"

"I'll tell you when you tell me what them letters are the short of," she said. There was just a hint of flirtatiousness in her tone and it went rapidly to Parker's head. He had never revealed the name to any man or woman, only to the files of the navy and the government, and it was on his baptismal record which he got at the age of a month; his mother was a Methodist. When the name leaked out of the navy files, Parker narrowly missed killing the man who used it.

"You'll go blab it around," he said.

"I'll swear I'll never tell nobody," she said. "On God's holy word I swear it."

Parker sat for a few minutes in silence. Then he reached for the girl's neck, drew her ear close to his mouth and revealed the name in a low voice.

"Obadiah," she whispered. Her face slowly brightened as if the name came as a sign to her. "Obadiah," she said.

The name still stank in Parker's estimation.

"Obadiah Elihue," she said in a reverent voice.

"If you call me that aloud, I'll bust your head open," Parker said. "What's yours?"

"Sarah Ruth Cates," she said.

"Glad to meet you, Sarah Ruth," Parker said.

Sarah Ruth's father was a Straight Gospel preacher but he was away, spreading it in Florida. Her mother did not seem to mind his attention to the girl so long as he brought a basket of something with him when he came. As for Sarah Ruth herself, it was plain to Parker after he had visited three times that she was crazy about him. She liked him even though she insisted that pictures on the skin were vanity of vanities and even after hearing him curse, and even after she had asked him if he was saved and he had replied that he didn't see it was anything in particular to save him from. After that, inspired, Parker had said, "I'd be saved enough if you was to kiss me."

She scowled. "That ain't being saved," she said.

Not long after that she agreed to take a ride in his truck. Parker parked it on a deserted road and suggested to her that they lie down together in the back of it.

"Not until after we're married," she said—just like that.

"Oh that ain't necessary," Parker said and as he reached for her, she thrust him away with such force that the door of the truck came off and he found himself flat on his back on the ground. He made up his mind then and there to have nothing further to do with her.

They were married in the County Ordinary's office because Sarah Ruth thought churches were idolatrous. Parker had no opinion about that one way or the other. The Ordinary's office was lined with cardboard file boxes and record books with dusty yellow slips of paper hanging on out of them. The Ordinary was an old woman with red hair who had held office for forty years and looked as dusty as her books. She married them from behind the iron-grill of a stand-up desk and when she finished, she said with a flourish, "Three dollars and fifty cents and till death do you part!" and yanked some forms out of a machine.

Marriage did not change Sarah Ruth a jot and it made Parker gloomier than ever. Every morning he decided he had had enough and would not return that night; every night he returned. Whenever Parker couldn't stand the way he felt, he would have another tattoo, but the only surface left on him now was his back. To see a tattoo on his own back he would have to get two mirrors and stand between them in just the correct position and this seemed to Parker a good way to make an idiot of himself. Sarah Ruth who, if she had had better sense, could have enjoyed a tattoo on his back, would not even look at the ones he had elsewhere. When he attempted to point out especial details of them, she would shut her eyes tight and turn her back as well. Except in total darkness, she preferred Parker dressed and with his sleeves rolled down.

"At the judgement seat of God, Jesus is going to say to you, 'What you been doing all your life besides have pictures drawn all over you?' " she said.

"You don't fool me none," Parker said, "you're just afraid that hefty girl I work for'll like me so much she'll say, 'Come on, Mr. Parker, let's you and me . . .' "

"You're tempting sin," she said, "and at the judgement seat of God you'll have to answer for that too. You ought to go back to selling the fruits of the earth."

Parker did nothing much when he was at home but listen to what the judgement seat of God would be like for him if he didn't change his ways. When he could, he broke in with tales of the hefty girl he worked for. " 'Mr. Parker,' " he said she said, 'I hired you for your brains.' " (She had added, "So why don't you use them?")

"And you should have seen her face the first time she saw me without my shirt," he said. " 'Mr. Parker,' she said, 'you're a walking panner-rammer!' " This had, in fact, been her remark but it had been delivered out of one side of her mouth.

Dissatisfaction began to grow so great in Parker that there was no containing it outside of a tattoo. It had to be his back. There was no help for it. A dim half-formed inspiration began to work in his mind. He visualized having a tattoo put there that Sarah Ruth would not be able to resist—a religious subject. He thought of an open book with HOLY BIBLE tattooed under it and an actual verse printed on the page. This seemed just the thing for a while; then he began to hear her say, "Ain't I already got a real Bible? What you think I want to read the same verse over and over for when I can read it all?" He needed something better even than the Bible! He thought about it so much that he began to lose sleep. He was already losing flesh—Sarah Ruth just threw food in the pot and let it boil. Not knowing for certain why he continued to stay with a woman who was both ugly and pregnant and no cook made him generally nervous and irritable, and he developed a little tic in the side of his face.

Once or twice he found himself turning around abruptly as if someone were trailing him. He had had a granddaddy who had ended in the state mental hospital, although not until he was seventy-five, but as urgent as it might be for him to get a tattoo, it was just as urgent that he get exactly the right one to bring Sarah Ruth to heel. As he continued to worry over it, his eyes took on a hollow preoccupied expression. The old woman he worked for told him that if he couldn't keep his mind on what he was doing, she knew where she could find a fourteen-year-old colored boy who could. Parker was too preoccupied even to be offended. At any time previous, he would have left her then and there, saying drily, "Well, you go ahead on and get him then."

Two or three mornings later he was baling hay with the old woman's sorry baler and her broken down tractor in a large field, cleared save for one enormous old tree standing in the middle of it. The old woman was the kind who would not cut down a large old tree because it was a large old tree. She had pointed it out to Parker as if he didn't have eyes and told him to be careful not to hit it as the machine picked up hay near it. Parker began at the outside of the field and made circles inward toward it. He had to get off the tractor every now and then and untangle the baling cord or kick a rock out of the way. The old woman had told him to carry the rocks to the edge of the field, which he did when she was there watching. When he thought he could make it, he ran over them. As he circled the field his mind was on a suitable design for his back. The sun, the size of a gold ball, began to switch regularly from in front to behind him, but he appeared to see it both places as if he had eyes in the back of his head. All at once he saw the tree reaching out to grasp him. A ferocious thud propelled him into the air, and he heard himself yelling in an unbelievably loud voice, "GOD ABOVE!"

He landed on his back while the tractor crashed upside-down into the tree and burst into flame. The first thing Parker saw were his shoes, quickly being eaten by the fire; one was caught under the tractor, the other was some distance away, burning by itself. He was not in them. He could feel the hot breath of the burning tree on his face. He scrambled backwards, still sitting, his eyes cavernous, and if he had known how to cross himself he would have done it.

His truck was on a dirt road at the edge of the field. He moved toward it, still sitting, still backwards, but faster and faster; halfway to it he got up and began a kind of forward-bent run from which he collapsed on his knees twice. His legs felt like two old rusted rain gutters. He reached the truck finally and took off in it, zigzagging up the road. He drove past his house on the embankment and straight for the city, fifty miles distant.

Parker did not allow himself to think on the way to the city. He only knew that there had been a great change in his life, a leap forward into a worse unknown, and that there was nothing he could do about it. It was for all intents accomplished.

The artist had two large cluttered rooms over a chiropodist's office on a back street. Parker, still barefooted, burst silently in on him at a little after three in the afternoon. The artist, who was about Parker's own age—twenty-eight—but thin and bald, was behind a small drawing table, tracing a design in green ink. He looked up with an annoyed glance and did not seem to recognize Parker in the hollow-eyed creature before him.

"Let me see the book you got with all the pictures of God in it," Parker said breathlessly. "The religious one."

The artist continued to look at him with his intellectual, superior stare. "I don't put tattoos on drunks," he said.

"You know me!" Parker cried indignantly. "I'm O. E. Parker! You done work for me before and I always paid!"

The artist looked at him another moment as if he were not altogether sure. "You've fallen off some," he said. "You must have been in jail."

"Married," Parker said.

"Oh," said the artist. With the aid of mirrors the artist had tattooed on the top of his head a miniature owl, perfect in every detail. It was about the size of a half-dollar and served him as a show piece. There were cheaper artists in town but Parker had never wanted anything but the best. The artist went over to a cabinet at the back of the room and began to look over some art books. "Who are you interested in?" he said, "saints, angels, Christs or what?"

"God," Parker said.

"Father, Son or Spirit?"

"Just God," Parker said impatiently. "Christ. I don't care. Just so it's God."

The artist returned with a book. He moved some papers off another table and put the book down on it and told Parker to sit down and see what he liked. "The up-t-date ones are in the back," he said.

Parker sat down with the book and wet his thumb. He began to go through it, beginning at the back where the up-to-date pictures were. Some of them he recognized—The Good Shepherd, Forbid Them Not, The Smiling Jesus, Jesus the Physician's Friend, but he kept turning rapidly backwards and the pictures became less and less reassuring. One showed a gaunt green dead face streaked with blood. One was yellow with sagging purple eyes. Parker's heart began to beat faster and faster until it appeared to be roaring inside him like a great generator. He flipped the pages quickly, feeling that when he reached the one ordained, a sign would come. He continued to flip through until he had almost reached the front of the book. On one of the pages a pair of eyes glanced at him swiftly. Parker sped on, then stopped. His heart too appeared to cut off; there was absolute silence. It said as plainly as if silence were a language itself, GO BACK.

Parker returned to the picture—the haloed head of a flat stern Byzantine Christ with all-demanding eyes. He sat there trembling; his heart began slowly to beat again as if it were being brought to life by a subtle power.

"You found what you want?" the artist asked.

Parker's throat was too dry to speak. He got up and thrust the book at the artist, opened at the picture.

"That'll cost you plenty," the artist said. "You don't want all those little blocks though, just the outline and some better features."

"Just like it is," Parker said, "just like it is or nothing."

"It's your funeral," the artist said, "but I don't do that kind of work for nothing."

"How much?" Parker asked.

"It'll take maybe two days work."

"How much?" Parker said.

"On time or cash?" the artist asked. Parker's other jobs had been on time, but he had paid.

"Ten down and ten for every day it takes," the artist said.

Parker drew ten dollar bills out of his wallet; he had three left in.

"You come back in the morning," the artist said, putting the money in his own pocket. "First I'll have to trace that out of the book."

"No no!" Parker said. "Trace it now or gimme my money back," and his eyes blared as if he were ready for a fight.

The artist agreed. Any one stupid enough to want a Christ on his back, he reasoned, would be just as likely as not to change his mind the next minute, but once the work was begun he could hardly do so.

While he worked on the tracing, he told Parker to go wash his back at the sink with the special soap he used there. Parker did it and returned to pace back and forth across the room, nervously flexing his shoulders. He wanted to go look at the picture again but at the same time he did not want to. The artist got up finally and had Parker lie down on the table. He swabbed his back with ethyl chloride and then began to outline the head on it with his iodine pencil. Another hour passed before he took up his electric instrument. Parker felt no particular pain. In Japan he had had a tattoo of the Buddha done on his upper arm with ivory needles; in Burma, a little brown root of a man had made a peacock on each of his knees using thin pointed sticks, two feet long; amateurs had worked on him with pins and soot. Parker was usually so relaxed and easy under the hand of the artist that he often went to sleep, but this time he remained awake, every muscle taut.

At midnight the artist said he was ready to quit. He propped one mirror, four feet square, on a table by the wall and took a smaller mirror off the lavatory wall and put it in Parker's hands. Parker stood with his back to the one on the table and moved the other until he saw a flashing burst of color reflected from his back. It was almost completely covered with little red and blue and ivory and saffron squares; from them he made out the lineaments of the face—a mouth, the beginning of heavy brows, a straight nose, but the face was empty; the eyes had not yet been put in. The impression for the moment was almost as if the artist had tricked him and done the Physician's Friend.

"It don't have eyes," Parker cried out.

"That'll come," the artist said, "in due time. We have another day to go on it yet."

Parker spent the night on a cot at the Haven of Light Christian Mission. He found these the best places to stay in the city because they were free and included a meal of sorts. He got the last available cot and because he was still barefooted, he accepted a pair of second-hand shoes which, in his confusion, he put on to go to bed; he was still shocked from all that had happened to him. All night he lay awake in the long dormitory of cots with lumpy figures on them. The only light was from a phosphorescent cross glowing at the end of the room. The tree reached out to grasp him again, then burst into flame; the shoe burned quietly by itself; the eyes in the book said to him distinctly GO BACK and at the same time did not utter a sound. He wished that he were not in this city, not in this Haven of Light Mission, not in a bed by himself. He longed miserably for Sarah Ruth. Her sharp tongue and icepick eyes were the only comfort he could bring to mind. He decided he was losing it. Her eyes appeared soft and dilatory compared with the eyes in the book, for even though he could not summon up the exact look of those eyes, he could still feel their penetration. He felt as though, under their gaze, he was as transparent as the wing of a fly.

The tattooist had told him not to come until ten in the morning, but when he arrived at that hour, Parker was sitting in the dark hallway on the floor, waiting for him. He had decided upon getting up that, once the tattoo was on him, he would not look at it, that all his sensations of the day and night before were those of a crazy man and that he would return to doing things according to his own sound judgement.

The artist began where he left off. "One thing I want to know," he said presently as he worked over Parker's back, "why do you want this on you? Have you gone and got religion? Are you saved?" he asked in a mocking voice.

Parker's throat felt salty and dry. "Naw," he said. "I ain't got no use for none of that. A man can't save his self from whatever it is he don't deserve none of my sympathy." These words seemed to leave his mouth like wraiths and to evaporate at once as if he had never uttered them.

"Then why . . ."

"I married this woman that's saved," Parker said. "I never should have done it. I ought to leave her. She's done gone and got pregnant."

"That's too bad," the artist said. "Then it's her making you have this tattoo."

"Naw," Parker said, "she don't know nothing about it. It's a surprise for her."

"You think she'll like it and lay off you a while?"

"She can't hep herself," Parker said. "She can't say she don't like the looks of God." He decided he had told the artist enough of his business. Artists were all right in their place but he didn't like them poking their noses into the affairs of regular people. "I didn't get no sleep last night," he said. "I think I'll get some now."

That closed the mouth of the artist but it did not bring him any sleep. He lay there imagining how Sarah Ruth would be struck speechless by the face on his back and every now and then this would be interrupted by a vision of the tree of fire and his empty shoe burning beneath it.

The artist worked steadily until nearly four o'clock, not stopping to have lunch, hardly pausing with the electric instrument except to wipe the dripping dye off Parker's back as he went along. Finally he finished. "You can get up and look at it now," he said.

Parker sat up but he remained on the edge of the table.

The artist was pleased with his work and wanted Parker to look at it at once. Instead Parker continued to sit on the edge of the table, bent forward slightly but with a vacant look. "What ails you?" the artist said. "Go look at it."

"Ain't nothing ail me," Parker said in a sudden belligerent voice. "That tattoo ain't going nowhere. It'll be there when I get there." He reached for his shirt and began gingerly to put it on.

The artist took him roughly by the arm and propelled him between the two mirrors. "Now *look*," he said, angry at having his work ignored.

Parker looked, turned white and moved away. The eyes in the reflected face continued to look at him—still, straight, all-demanding, enclosed in silence.

"It was your idea, remember," the artist said. "I would have advised something else."

Parker said nothing. He put on his shirt and went out the door while the artist shouted, "I'll expect all of my money!"

Parker headed toward a package shop on the corner. He bought a pint of whiskey and took it into a nearby alley and drank it all in five minutes. Then he moved on to a pool hall nearby which he frequented when he came to the city. It was a well-lighted barn-like place with a bar up one side and gambling machines on the other and pool tables in the back. As soon as Parker entered, a large man in a red and black checkered shirt hailed him by slapping him on the back and yelling, "Yeyyyyyy boy! O. E. Parker!"

Parker was not yet ready to be struck on the back. "Lay off," he said, "I got a fresh tattoo there."

"What you got this time?" the man asked and then yelled to a few at the machines. "O.E.'s got him another tattoo."

"Nothing special this time," Parker said and slunk over to a machine that was not being used.

"Come on," the big man said, "let's have a look at O.E.'s tattoo," and while Parker squirmed in their hands, they pulled up his shirt. Parker felt all the hands drop away instantly and his shirt fell again like a veil over the face. There was a silence in the pool room which seemed to Parker to grow from the circle around him until it extended to the foundations under the building and upward through the beams in the roof.

Finally some one said, "Christ!" Then they all broke into noise at once. Parker turned around, an uncertain grin on his face.

"Leave it to O.E.!" the man in the checkered shirt said. "That boy's a real card!"

"Maybe he's gone and got religion," some one yelled.

"Not on your life," Parker said.

"O.E.'s got religion and is witnessing for Jesus, ain't you, O.E.?" a little man with a piece of cigar in his mouth said wryly. "An o-riginal way to do it if I ever saw one."

"Leave it to Parker to think of a new one!" the fat man said.

"Yyeeeeeeyyyyyyy boy!" someone yelled and they all began to whistle and curse in compliment until Parker said, "Aaa shut up."

"What'd you do it for?" somebody asked.

"For laughs," Parker said. "What's it to you?"

"Why ain't you laughing then?" somebody yelled. Parker lunged into the midst of them and like a whirlwind on a summer's day there began a fight that raged amid overturned tables and swinging fists until two of them grabbed him and ran to the door with him and threw him out. Then a calm descended on the pool hall as nerve shattering as if the long barn-like room were the ship from which Jonah had been cast into the sea.

Parker sat for a long time on the ground in the alley behind the pool hall, examining his soul. He saw it as a spider web of facts and lies that was not at all important to him but which appeared to be necessary in spite of his opinion. The eyes that were now forever on his back were eyes to be obeyed. He was as certain of it as he had ever been of anything. Throughout his life, grumbling and sometimes cursing, often afraid, once in rapture, Parker had obeyed whatever instinct of this kind had come to him—in rapture when his spirit had lifted at the sight of the tattooed man at the fair, afraid when he had joined the navy, grumbling when he had married Sarah Ruth.

The thought of her brought him slowly to his feet. She would know what to do. She would clear up the rest of it, and she would at least be pleased. It seemed to him that, all along, that was what he wanted, to please her. His truck was still parked in front of the building where the artist had his place, but it was not far away. He got in it and drove out of the city and into the country night. His head was almost clear of liquor and he observed that his dissatisfaction was gone, but he felt not quite like himself. It was as if he were himself but a stranger to himself, driving into a new country though everything he saw was familiar to him, even at night.

He arrived finally at the house on the embankment, pulled the truck under the pecan tree and got out. He made as much noise as possible to assert that he was still in charge here, that his leaving her for a night without word meant nothing except it was the way he did things. He slammed the car door, stamped up the two steps and across the porch and rattled the door knob. It did not respond to his touch. "Sarah Ruth!" he yelled, "let me in."

There was no lock on the door and she had evidently placed the back of a chair against the knob. He began to beat on the door and rattle the knob at the same time.

He heard the bed springs screak and bent down and put his head to the keyhole, but it was stopped up with paper.

"Let me in!" he hollered, bamming on the door again. "What you got me locked out for?"

A sharp voice close to the door said, "Who's there?"

"Me," Parker said, "O.E."

He waited a moment.

"Me," he said impatiently, "O.E."

Still no sound from inside.

He tried once more. "O.E.," he said, bamming the door two or three more times. "O. E. Parker. You know me."

There was a silence. Then the voice said slowly, "I don't know no O.E."

"Quit fooling," Parker pleaded. "You ain't got any business doing me this way. It's me, old O.E., I'm back. You ain't afraid of me."

"Who's there?" the same unfeeling voice said.

Parker turned his head as if he expected someone behind him to give him the answer. The sky had lightened slightly and there were two or three streaks of yellow floating above the horizon. Then as he stood there, a tree of light burst over the skyline.

Parker fell back against the door as if he had been pinned there by a lance.

"Who's there?" the voice from inside said and there was a quality about it now that seemed final. The knob rattled and the voice said peremptorily, "Who's there, I ast you?"

Parker bent down and put his mouth near the stuffed keyhole. "Obadiah," he whispered and all at once he felt the light pouring through him, turning his spider web soul into a perfect arabesque of colors, a garden of trees and birds and beasts.

"Obadiah Elihue!" he whispered.

The door opened and he stumbled in. Sarah Ruth loomed there, hands on her hips. She began at once, "That was no hetfy blonde woman you was working for and you'll have to pay her every penny on her tractor you busted up. She don't keep insurance on it. She came here and her and me had us a long talk and I . . ."

Trembling, Parker set about lighting the kerosene lamp.

"What's the matter with you, wasting that keresene this near daylight?" she demanded. "I ain't got to look at you."

A yellow glow enveloped them. Parker put the match down and began to unbutton his shirt.

"And you ain't going to have none of me this near morning," she said.

"Shut your mouth," he said quietly. "Look at this and then

I don't want to hear no more out of you." He removed the shirt and turned his back to her.

"Another picture," Sarah Ruth growled. "I might have known you was off after putting some more trash on yourself."

Parker's knees went hollow under him. He wheeled around and cried, "Look at it! Don't just say that! *Look* at it!"

"I done looked," she said.

"Don't you know who it is?" he said in anguish.

"No, who is it?" Sarah Ruth said. "It ain't anybody I know."

"It's him," Parker said.

"Him who?"

"God!" Parker cried.

"God? God don't look like that!"

"What do you know how he looks?" Parker moaned. "You ain't seen him."

"He don't *look*," Sarah Ruth said. "He's a spirit. No man shall see his face."

"Aw listen," Parker groaned, "this is just a picture of him."

"Idolatry!" Sarah Ruth screamed. "Idolatry! Enflaming yourself with idols under every green tree! I can put up with lies and vanity but I don't want no idolator in this house!" and she grabbed up the broom and began to thrash him across the shoulders with it.

Parker was too stunned to resist. He sat there and let her beat him until she had nearly knocked him senseless and large welts had formed on the face of the tattooed Christ. Then he staggered up and made for the door.

She stamped the broom two or three times on the floor and went to the window and shook it out to get the taint of him off it. Still gripping it, she looked toward the pecan tree and her eyes hardened still more. There he was—who called himself Obadiah Elihue—leaning against the tree, crying like a baby.

Judgement Day

Tanner was conserving all his strength for the trip home. He meant to walk as far as he could get and trust to the Almighty to get him the rest of the way. That morning and the morning before, he had allowed his daughter to dress him and had conserved that much more energy. Now he sat in the chair by the window—his blue shirt buttoned at the collar, his coat on the back of the chair, and his hat on his head—waiting for her to leave. He couldn't escape until she got out of the way. The window looked out on a brick wall and down into an alley full of New York air, the kind fit for cats and garbage. A few snow flakes drifted past the window but they were too thin and scattered for his failing vision.

The daughter was in the kitchen washing dishes. She dawdled over everything, talking to herself. When he had first come, he had answered her, but that had not been wanted. She glowered at him as if, old fool that he was, he should still have had sense enough not to answer a woman talking to herself. She questioned herself in one voice and answered herself in another. With the energy he had conserved yesterday letting her dress him, he had written a note and pinned it in his pocket. IF FOUND DEAD SHIP EXPRESS COLLECT TO COLEMAN PARRUM, CORINTH, GEORGIA. Under this he had continued: COLEMAN SELL MY BELONGINGS AND PAY THE FREIGHT ON ME & THE UNDERTAKER. ANYTHING LEFT OVER YOU CAN KEEP. YOURS TRULY T. C. TANNER. P.S. STAY WHERE YOU ARE. DON'T LET THEM TALK YOU INTO COMING UP HERE. IT'S NO KIND OF PLACE. It had taken him the better part of thirty minutes to write the paper; the script was wavery but decipherable with patience. He controlled one hand by holding the other on top of it. By the time he had got it written, she was back in the apartment from getting her groceries.

Today he was ready. All he had to do was push one foot in front of the other until he got to the door and down the steps. Once down the steps, he would get out of the neighborhood. Once out of it, he would hail a taxi cab and go to the freight yards. Some bum would help him onto a car. Once he got in the freight car, he would lie down and rest. During the night the train would start South, and the next day or the morning after, dead or alive, he would be home. Dead or alive. It was being there that mattered; the dead or alive did not.

If he had had good sense he would have gone the day after he arrived; better sense and he would not have arrived. He had not got desperate until two days ago when he had heard his daughter and son-in-law taking leave of each other after breakfast. They were standing in the front door, she seeing him off for a three-day trip. He drove a long distance moving van. She must have handed him his leather headgear. "You ought to get you a hat," she said, "a real one."

"And sit all day in it," the son-in-law said, "like him in there. Yah! All he does is sit all day with that hat on. Sits all day with that damn black hat on his head. Inside!"

"Well you don't even have you a hat," she said. "Nothing but that leather cap with flaps. People that are somebody wear hats. Other kinds wear those leather caps like you got on."

"People that are somebody!" he cried. "People that are somebody! That kills me! That really kills me!" The son-in-law had a stupid muscular face and a yankee voice to go with it.

"My daddy is here to stay," his daughter said. "He ain't going to last long. He was somebody when he was somebody. He never worked for nobody in his life but himself and had people—other people—working for him."

"Yah? Niggers is what he had working for him," the son-in-law said. "That's all. I've worked a nigger or two myself."

"Those were just nawthun niggers you worked," she said, her voice suddenly going lower so that Tanner had to lean forward to catch the words. "It takes brains to work a real nigger. You got to know how to handle them."

"Yah so I don't have brains," the son-in-law said.

One of the sudden, very occasional, feelings of warmth for the daughter came over Tanner. Every now and then she said something that might make you think she had a little sense stored away somewhere for safe keeping.

"You got them," she said. "You don't always use them."

"He has a stroke when he sees a nigger in the building," the son-in-law said, "and she tells me . . ."

"Shut up talking so loud," she said. "That's not why he had the stroke."

There was a silence. "Where you going to bury him?" the son-in-law asked, taking a different tack.

"Bury who?"

"Him in there."

"Right here in New York," she said. "Where do you think? We got a lot. I'm not taking that trip down there again with nobody."

"Yah. Well I just wanted to make sure," he said.

When she returned to the room, Tanner had both hands gripped on the chair arms. His eyes were trained on her like the eyes of an angry corpse. "You promised you'd bury me there," he said. "Your promise ain't any good. Your promise ain't any good. Your promise ain't any good." His voice was so dry it was barely audible. He began to shake, his hands, his head, his feet. "Bury me here and burn in hell!" he cried and fell back into his chair.

The daughter shuddered to attention. "You ain't dead yet!" She threw out a ponderous sigh. "You got a long time to be worrying about that." She turned and began to pick up parts of the newspaper scattered on the floor. She had grey hair that hung to her shoulders and a round face, beginning to wear. "I do every last living thing for you," she muttered, "and this is the way you carry on." She stuck the papers under her arm and said, "And don't throw hell at me. I don't believe in it. That's a lot of hardshell Baptist hooey." Then she went into the kitchen.

He kept his mouth stretched taut, his top plate gripped between his tongue and the roof of his mouth. Still the tears flooded down his cheeks; he wiped each one furtively on his shoulder.

Her voice rose from the kitchen. "As bad as having a child. He wanted to come and now he's here, he don't like it."

He had not wanted to come.

"Pretended he didn't but I could tell. I said if you don't want to come I can't make you. If you don't want to live like decent people there's nothing I can do about it."

"As for me," her higher voice said, "when I die that ain't the time I'm going to start getting choosey. They can lay me in the nearest spot. When I pass from this world I'll be considerate of them that stay in it. I won't be thinking of just myself."

"Certainly not," the other voice said, "You never been that selfish. You're the kind that looks out for other people."

"Well I try," she said, "I try."

He laid his head on the back of the chair for a moment and the hat tilted down over his eyes. He had raised three boys and her. The three boys were gone, two in the war and one to the devil and there was nobody left who felt a duty toward him but her, married and childless, in New York City like Mrs. Big and ready when she came back and found him living the way he was to take him back with her. She had put her face in the door of the shack and had stared, expressionless, for a second. Then all at once she had screamed and jumped back.

"What's that on the floor?"

"Coleman," he said.

The old Negro was curled up on a pallet asleep at the foot of Tanner's bed, a stinking skin full of bones, arranged in what seemed vaguely human form. When Coleman was young, he had looked like a bear; now that he was old he looked like a monkey. With Tanner it was the opposite; when he was young he had looked like a monkey but when he got old, he looked like a bear.

The daughter stepped back onto the porch. There were the bottoms of two cane chairs tilted against the clapboard but she declined to take a seat. She stepped out about ten feet from the house as if it took that much space to clear the odor. Then she had spoken her piece.

"If you don't have any pride I have and I know my duty and I was raised to do it. My mother raised me to do it if you didn't. She was from plain people but not the kind that likes to settle in with niggers."

At that point the old Negro roused up and slid out the door, a doubled-up shadow which Tanner just caught sight of gliding away.

She had shamed him. He shouted so they both could hear. "Who do you think cooks? Who do you think cuts my firewood and empties my slops? He's paroled to me. That nogood scoundrel has been on my hands for thirty years. He ain't a bad nigger."

She was unimpressed. "Whose shack is this anyway?" she had asked. "Yours or his?"

"Him and me built it," he said. "You go on back up there. I wouldn't come with you for no million dollars or no sack of salt."

"It looks like him and you built it. Whose land is it on?"

"Some people that live in Florida," he said evasively. He had known then that it was land up for sale but he thought it was too sorry for anyone to buy. That same afternoon he had found out different. He had found out in time to go back with her. If he had found out a day later, he might still be there, squatting on the doctor's land.

When he saw the brown porpoise-shaped figure striding across the field that afternoon, he had known at once what had happened; no one had to tell him. If that nigger had owned the whole world except for one runty rutted pea-field and he acquired it, he would walk across it that way, beating the weeds aside, his thick neck swelled, his stomach a throne for his gold watch and chain. Doctor Foley. He was only part black. The rest was Indian and white.

He was everything to the niggers—druggist and undertaker and general counsel and real estate man and sometimes he got the evil eye off them and sometimes he put it on. Be prepared, he said to himself, watching him approach, to take something off him, nigger though he be. Be prepared, because you ain't got a thing to hold up to him but the skin you come in, and that's no more use to you now than what a snake would shed. You don't have a chance with the government against you.

He was sitting on the porch in the piece of straight chair tilted against the shack. "Good eyening, Foley," he said and nodded as the doctor came up and stopped short at the edge of the clearing, as if he had only just that minute seen him though it was plain he had sighted him as he crossed the field.

"I be out here to look at my property," the doctor said. "Good evening." His voice was quick and high.

Ain't been your property long, he said to himself. "I seen you coming," he said.

"I acquired this here recently," the doctor said and proceeded without looking at him again to walk around to one side of the shack. In a moment he came back and stopped in front of him. Then he stepped boldly to the door of the shack and put his head in. Coleman was in there that time too, asleep. He looked for a moment and then turned aside. "I know that nigger," he said. "Coleman Parrum— how long does it take him to sleep off that stump liquor you all make?"

Tanner took hold of the knobs on the chair bottom and held them hard. "This shack ain't in your property. Only on it, by my mistake," he said.

The doctor removed his cigar momentarily from his mouth. "It ain't my mis-take," he said and smiled.

He had only sat there, looking ahead.

"It don't pay to make this kind of mis-take," the doctor said.

"I never found nothing that paid yet," he muttered.

"Everything pays," the Negro said, "if you knows how to make it," and he remained there smiling, looking the squatter up and down. Then he turned and went around the other side of the shack. There was a silence. He was looking for the still.

Then would have been the time to kill him. There was a gun inside the shack and he could have done it as easy as not, but, from childhood, he had been weakened for that kind of violence by the fear of hell. He had never killed one, he had always handled them with his wits and with luck. He was known to have a way with niggers. There was an art to handling them. The secret of handling a nigger was to show him his brains didn't have a chance against yours; then he would jump on your back and know he had a good thing there for life. He had had Coleman on his back for thirty years.

Tanner had first seen Coleman when he was working six of them at a saw mill in the middle of a pine forest fifteen miles from nowhere. They were as sorry a crew as he had worked, the kind that on Monday they didn't show up. What was in the air had reached them. They thought there was a new Lincoln elected who was going to abolish work. He managed them with a very sharp penknife. He had had something wrong with his kidney then that made his hands shake and he had taken to whittling to force that waste motion out of sight. He did not intend them to see that his hands shook of their own accord and he did not intend to see it himself or to countenance it. The knife had moved constantly, violently, in his quaking hands and here and there small crude figures— that he never looked at again and could not have said what they were if he had—dropped to the ground. The Negroes picked them up and took them home; there was not much time between them and darkest Africa. The knife glittered constantly in his hands. More than once he had stopped short and said in an off-hand voice to some half-reclining, head-averted Negro, "Nigger, this knife is in my hand now but if you don't quit wasting my time and money, it'll be in your gut shortly." And the Negro would begin to rise—slowly, but he would be in the act—before the sentence was completed.

A large black loose-jointed Negro, twice his own size, had begun hanging around the edge of the saw mill, watching the others work and when he was not watching, sleeping, in full view of them, sprawled like a gigantic bear on his back. "Who is that?" he had asked. "If he wants to work, tell him to come here. If he don't, tell him to go. No idlers are going to hang around here."

None of them knew who he was. They knew he didn't want to work. They knew nothing else, not where he had come from, nor why, though he was probably brother to one, cousin to all of them. He had ignored him for a day; against the six of them he was one yellow-faced scrawny white man with shaky hands. He was willing to wait for trouble, but not forever. The next day the stranger came again. After the six Tanner worked had seen the idler there for half the morning, they quit and began to eat, a full thirty minutes before noon. He had not risked ordering them up. He had gone to the source of the trouble.

The stranger was leaning against a tree on the edge of the clearing, watching with half-closed eyes. The insolence on his face barely covered the wariness behind it. His look said, this ain't much of a white man so why he come on so big, what he fixing to do?

He had meant to say, "Nigger, this knife is in my hand now but if you ain't out of my sight . . ." but as he drew closer he changed his mind. The Negro's eyes were small and bloodshot. Tanner supposed there was a knife on him somewhere that he would as soon use as not. His own penknife moved, directed solely by some intruding intelligence that worked in his hands. He had no idea what he was carving, but when he reached the Negro, he had already made two holes the size of half dollars in the piece of bark.

The Negro's gaze fell on his hands and was held. His jaw slackened. His eyes did not move from the knife tearing recklessly around the bark. He watched as if he saw an invisible power working on the wood.

He looked himself then and, astonished, saw the connected rims of a pair of spectacles.

He held them away from him and looked through the holes past a pile of shavings and on into the woods to the edge of the pen where they kept their mules.

"You can't see so good, can you, boy?" he said and began scraping the ground with his foot to turn up a piece of wire. He picked up a small piece of haywire; in a minute he found another, shorter piece and picked that up. He began to attach these to the bark. He was in no hurry now that he knew what he was doing. When the spectacles were finished, he handed them to the Negro. "Put these on," he said. "I hate to see anybody can't see good."

There was an instant when the Negro might have done one thing or another, might have taken the glasses and crushed them in his hand or grabbed the knife and turned it on him. He saw the exact instant in the muddy liquor-swollen eyes when the pleasure of having a knife in this white man's gut was balanced against something else, he could not tell what.

The Negro reached for the glasses. He attached the bows carefully behind his ears and looked forth. He peered this way and that with exaggerated solemnity. And then he looked directly at Tanner and grinned, or grimaced, Tanner could not tell which, but he had an instant's sensation of seeing before him a negative image of himself, as if clownishness and captivity had been their common lot. The vision failed him before he could decipher it.

"Preacher," he said, "what you hanging around here for?" He picked up another piece of bark and began, without looking at it, to carve again. "This ain't Sunday."

"This here ain't Sunday?" the Negro said.

"This is Friday," he said. "That's the way it is with you preachers—drunk all week so you don't know when Sunday is. What you see through those glasses?"

"See a man."

"What kind of a man?"

"See the man make theseyer glasses."

"Is he white or black?"

"He white!" the Negro said as if only at that moment was his vision sufficiently improved to detect it. "Yessuh, he white!" he said.

"Well, you treat him like he was white," Tanner said. "What's your name?"

"Name Coleman," the Negro said.

And he had not got rid of Coleman since. You make a monkey out of one of them and he jumps on your back and stays there for life, but let one make a monkey out of you and all you can do is kill him or disappear. And he was not going to hell for killing a nigger. Behind the shack he heard the doctor kick over a bucket. He sat and waited.

In a moment the doctor appeared again, beating his way around the other side of the house, whacking at scattered clumps of Johnson grass with his cane. He stopped in the middle of the yard, about where that morning the daughter had delivered her ultimatum.

"You don't belong here," he began. "I could have you prosecuted."

Tanner remained there, dumb, staring across the field.

"Where's your still?" the doctor asked.

"If it's a still around here, it don't belong to me," he said and shut his mouth tight.

The Negro laughed softly. "Down on your luck, ain't you?" he murmured. "Didn't you used to own a little piece of land over acrost the river and lost it?"

He had continued to study the woods ahead.

"If you want to run the still for me, that's one thing," the doctor said. "If you don't, you might as well had be packing up."

"I don't have to work for you," he said. "The government ain't got around yet to forcing the white folks to work for the colored."

The doctor polished the stone in his ring with the ball of his thumb. "I don't like the governmint no bettern you," he said. "Where you going instead? You going to the city and get you a soot of rooms at the Biltmo' Hotel?"

Tanner said nothing.

"The day coming," the doctor said, "when the white folks IS going to be working for the colored and you mights well to git ahead of the crowd."

"That day ain't coming for me," Tanner said shortly.

"Done come for you," the doctor said. "Ain't come for the rest of them."

Tanner's gaze drove on past the farthest blue edge of the treeline into the pale empty afternoon sky. "I got a daughter in the north," he said. "I don't have to work for you."

The doctor took his watch from his watch pocket and looked at it and put it back. He gazed for a moment at the back of his hands. He appeared to have measured and to know secretly the time it would take everything to change finally upsidedown. "She don't want no old daddy like you," he said. "Maybe she say she do, but that ain't likely. Even if you rich," he said, "they don't want you. They got they own ideas. The black ones they rares and they pitches. I made mine," he said, "and I ain't done none of that." He looked again at Tanner. "I be back here next week," he said, "and if you still here, I know you going to work for me." He remained there a moment, rocking on his heels, waiting for some answer. Finally he turned and started beating his way back through the overgrown path.

Tanner had continued to look across the field as if his spirit had been sucked out of him into the woods and nothing was left on the chair but a shell. If he had known it was a question of this—sitting here looking out of this window all day in this no-place, or just running a still for a nigger, he would have run the still for the nigger. He would have been a nigger's white nigger any day. Behind him he heard the daughter come in from the kitchen. His heart accelerated but after a second he heard her plump herself down on the sofa. She was not yet ready to go. He did not turn and look at her.

She sat there silently a few moments. Then she began. "The trouble with you is," she said, "you sit in front of that window all the time where there's nothing to look out at. You need some inspiration and an out-let. If you would let me pull your chair around to look at the TV, you would quit thinking about morbid stuff, death and hell and judgement. My Lord."

"The Judgement is coming," he muttered. "The sheep'll be separated from the goats. Them that kept their promises from them that didn't. Them that did the best they could with what they had from them that didn't. Them that honored their father and their mother from them that cursed them. Them that . . ."

She heaved a mammoth sigh that all but drowned him out. "What's the use in me wasting my good breath?" she asked. She rose and went back in the kitchen and began knocking things about.

She was so high and mighty! At home he had been living in a shack but there was at least air around it. He could put his feet on the ground. Here she didn't even live in a house. She lived in a pigeon-hutch of a building, with all stripes of foreigner, all of them twisted in the tongue. It was no place for a sane man. The first morning here she had taken him sightseeing and he had seen in fifteen minutes exactly how it was. He had not been out of the apartment since. He never wanted to set foot again on the underground railroad or the steps that moved under you while you stood still or any elevator to the thirty-fourth floor. When he was safely back in the apartment again, he had imagined going over it with Coleman. He had to turn his head every few seconds to make sure Coleman was behind him. Keep to the inside or these people'll knock you down, keep right behind me or you'll get left, keep your hat on, you damn idiot, he had said, and Coleman had come on with his bent running shamble, panting and muttering, What we doing here? Where you get this fool idea coming here?

I come to show you it was no kind of place. Now you know you were well off where you were.

I knowed it before, Coleman said. Was you didn't know it.

When he had been here a week, he had got a postcard from Coleman that had been written for him by Hooten at the railroad station. It was written in green ink and said, "This is Coleman—X—howyou boss." Under it Hooten had written from himself, "Quit frequenting all those nitespots and come on home, you scoundrel, yours truly, W. P.

Hooten." He had sent Coleman a card in...
Hooten, that said, "This place is alrite if you...
truly, W. T. Tanner." Since the daughter had to...
card, he had not put on it that he was returning as s...
his pension check came. He had not intended to tell her o...
to leave her a note. When the check came, he would hire
himself a taxi to the bus station and be on his way. And it
would have made her as happy as it made him. She had
found his company dour and her duty irksome. If he had
sneaked out, she would have had the pleasure of having tried
to do it and to top that off, the pleasure of his ingratitude.

As for him, he would have returned to squat on the doctor's land and to take his orders from a nigger who chewed
ten-cent cigars. And to think less about it than formerly. Instead he had been done in by a nigger actor, or one who
called himself an actor. He didn't believe the nigger was any
actor.

There were two apartments on each floor of the building.
He had been with the daughter three weeks when the people
in the next hutch moved out. He had stood in the hall and
watched the moving-out and the next day he had watched a
moving-in. The hall was narrow and dark and he stood in the
corner out of the way, offering only a suggestion every now
and then to the movers that would have made their work
easier for them if they had paid any attention. The furniture
was new and cheap so he decided the people moving in might
be a newly married couple and he would just wait around until they came and wish them well. After a while a large Negro in a light blue suit came lunging up the stairs, carrying
two canvas suitcases, his head lowered against the strain. Behind him stepped a young tan-skinned woman with bright
copper-colored hair. The Negro dropped the suitcases with a
thud in front of the door of the next apartment.

"Be careful, Sweetie," the woman said. "My make-up is in
there."

It broke upon him then just what was happening.

The Negro was grinning. He took a swipe at one of her
hips.

"Quit it," she said, "there's an old guy watching."

They both turned and looked at him.

"Had-do," he said and nodded. Then he turned quickly
into his own door.

His daughter was in the kitchen. "Who you think's rented
that apartment over there?" he asked, his face alight.

She looked at him suspiciously. "Who?" she muttered.

"A nigger!" he said in a gleeful voice. "A South Alabama nigger if I ever saw one. And got him this high-yeller, high-stepping woman with red hair and they two are going to live next door to you!" He slapped his knee. "Yes siree!" he said. "Damn if they ain't!" It was the first time since coming up here that he had had occasion to laugh.

Her face squared up instantly. "All right now you listen to me," she said. "You keep away from them. Don't you go over there trying to get friendly with him. They ain't the same around here and I don't want any trouble with niggers, you hear me? If you have to live next to them, just you mind your business and they'll mind theirs. That's the way people were meant to get along in this world. Everybody can get along if they just mind their business. Live and let live." She began to wrinkle her nose like a rabbit, a stupid way she had. "Up here everybody minds their own business and everybody gets along. That's all you have to do."

"I was getting along with niggers before you were born," he said. He went back out into the hall and waited. He was willing to bet the nigger would like to talk to someone who understood him. Twice while he waited, he forgot and in his excitement, spit his tobacco juice against the baseboard. In about twenty minutes, the door of the apartment opened again and the Negro came out. He had put on a tie and a pair of horn-rimmed spectacles and Tanner noticed for the first time that he had a small almost invisible goatee. A real swell. He came on without appearing to see there was anyone else in the hall.

"Haddy, John," Tanner said and nodded, but the Negro brushed past without hearing and went rattling rapidly down the stairs.

Could be deaf and dumb, Tanner thought. He went back into the apartment and sat down but each time he heard a noise in the hall, he got up and went to the door and stuck his head out to see if it might be the Negro. Once in the middle of the afternoon, he caught the Negro's eye just as he was rounding the bend of the stairs again but before he could get out a word, the man was in his own apartment and had slammed the door. He had never known one to move that fast unless the police were after him.

He was standing in the hall early the next morning when the woman came out of her door alone, walking on high gold-painted heels. He wished to bid her good morning or simply to nod but instinct told him to beware. She didn't look like any kind of woman, black or white, he had ever seen before and he remained pressed against the wall, frightened more than anything else, and feigning invisibility.

The woman gave him a flat stare, then turned her head away and stepped wide of him as if she were skirting an open garbage can. He held his breath until she was out of sight. Then he waited patiently for the man.

The Negro came out about eight o'clock.

This time Tanner advanced squarely in his path. "Good morning, Preacher," he said. It had been his experience that if a Negro tended to be sullen, this title usually cleared up his expression.

The Negro stopped abruptly.

"I see you move in," Tanner said. "I ain't been up here long myself. It ain't much of a place if you ask me. I reckon you wish you were back in South Alabama."

The Negro did not take a step or answer. His eyes began to move. They moved from the top of the black hat, down to the collarless blue shirt, neatly buttoned at the neck, down the faded galluses to the grey trousers and the high-top shoes and up again, very slowly, while some unfathomable dead-cold rage seemed to stiffen and shrink him.

"I thought you might know somewhere around here we could find us a pond, Preacher," Tanner said in a voice growing thinner but still with considerable hope in it.

A seething noise came out of the Negro before he spoke. "I'm not from South Alabama," he said in a breathless wheezing voice. "I'm from New York City. And I'm not no preacher! I'm an actor."

Tanner chortled. "It's a little actor in most preachers, ain't it?" he said and winked. "I reckon you just preach on the side."

"I don't preach!" the Negro cried and rushed past him as if a swarm of bees had suddenly come down on him out of nowhere. He dashed down the stairs and was gone.

Tanner stood there for some time before he went back in the apartment. The rest of the day he sat in his chair and debated whether he would have one more try at making friends with him. Every time he heard a noise on the stairs he went to the door and looked out, but the Negro did not return until late in the afternoon. Tanner was standing in the hall waiting for him when he reached the top of the stairs. "Good evening, preacher," he said, forgetting that the Negro called himself an actor.

The Negro stopped and gripped the banister rail. A tremor racked him from his head to his crotch. Then he began to come forward slowly. When he was close enough he lunged and grasped Tanner by both shoulders. "I don't take no crap," he whispered, "off no wool-hat red-neck son-of-a-bitch peckerwood old bastard like you." He caught his breath. And then his voice came out in the sound of an exasperation so profound that it rocked on the verge of a laugh. It was high and piercing and weak. "And I'm not no preacher! I'm not even no Christian. I don't believe that crap. There ain't no Jesus and there ain't no God."

The old man felt his heart inside him hard and tough as an oak knot. "And you ain't black," he said. "And I ain't white!"

The Negro slammed him against the wall. He yanked the black hat down over his eyes. Then he grabbed his shirt front and shoved him backwards to his open door and knocked him through it. From the kitchen the daughter saw him blindly hit the edge of the inside hall door and fall reeling into the living-room.

For days his tongue appeared to be frozen in his mouth. When it unthawed it was twice its normal size and he could not make her understand him. What he wanted to know was if the government check had come because he meant to buy a bus ticket with it and go home. After a few days, he made her understand. "It came," she said, "and it'll just pay the first two weeks' doctor-bill and please tell me how you're going home when you can't talk or walk or think straight and you got one eye crossed yet? Just please tell me that?"

It had come to him then slowly just what his present situation was. At least he would have to make her understand that he must be sent home to be buried. They could have him shipped back in a refrigerated car so that he would keep for the trip. He didn't want any undertaker up here messing with him. Let them get him off at once and he would come in on the early morning train and they could wire Hooten to get Coleman and Coleman would do the rest; she would not even have to go herself. After a lot of argument, he wrung the promise from her. She would ship him back.

After that he slept peacefully and improved a little. In his dreams he could feel the cold early morning air of home coming in through the cracks of the pine box. He could see Coleman waiting, red-eyed, on the station platform and Hooten standing there with his green eyeshade and black alpaca sleeves. If the old fool had stayed at home where he belonged, Hooten would be thinking, he wouldn't be arriving on the 6:03 in no box. Coleman had turned the borrowed mule and cart so that they could slide the box off the platform onto the open end of the wagon. Everything was ready and the two of them, shut-mouthed, inched the loaded coffin toward the wagon. From inside he began to scratch on the wood. They let go as if it had caught fire.

They stood looking at each other, then at the box.

"That him," Coleman said. "He in there his self."

"Naw," Hooten said, "must be a rat got in there with him."

"That him. This here one of his tricks."

"If it's a rat he might as well stay."

"That him. Git a crowbar."

Hooten went grumbling off and got the crowbar and came back and began to pry open the lid. Even before he had the upper end pried open, Coleman was jumping up and down, wheezing and panting from excitement. Tanner gave a thrust upward with both hands and sprang up in the box. "Judgement Day! Judgement Day!" he cried. "Don't you two fools know it's Judgement Day?"

Now he knew exactly what her promises were worth. He would do as well to trust to the note pinned in his coat and to any stranger who found him dead in the street or in the boxcar or wherever. There was nothing to be looked for from her except that she would do things her way. She came out of the kitchen again, holding her hat and coat and rubber boots.

"Now listen," she said, "I have to go to the store. Don't you try to get up and walk around while I'm gone. You've been to the bathroom and you shouldn't have to go again. I don't want to find you on the floor when I get back."

You won't find me atall when you get back, he said to himself. This was the last time he would see her flat dumb face. He felt guilty. She had been good to him and he had been nothing but a nuisance to her.

"Do you want you a glass of milk before I go?" she asked.

"No," he said. Then he drew breath and said, "You got a nice place here. It's a nice part of the country. I'm sorry if I've give you a lot of trouble getting sick. It was my fault trying to be friendly with that nigger." And I'm a damned liar besides, he said to himself to kill the outrageous taste such a statement made in his mouth.

For a moment she stared as if he were losing his mind. Then she seemed to think better of it. "Now don't saying something pleasant like that once in a while make you feel better?" she asked and sat down on the sofa.

His knees itched to unbend. Git on, git on, he fumed silently. Make haste and go.

"It's great to have you here," she said. "I wouldn't have you any other place. My own daddy." She gave him a big smile and hoisted her right leg up and began to pull on her boot. "I wouldn't wish a dog out on a day like this," she said, "but I got to go. You can sit here and hope I don't slip and break my neck." She stamped the booted foot on the floor and then began to tackle the other one.

He turned his eyes to the window. The snow was beginning to stick and freeze to the outside pane. When he looked at her again, she was standing there like a big doll stuffed into its hat and coat. She drew on a pair of green knitted gloves. "Okay," she said, "I'm gone. You sure you don't want anything?"

"No," he said, "go ahead on."

"Well so long then," she said.

He raised the hat enough to reveal a bald palely speckled head. The hall door closed behind her. He began to tremble with excitement. He reached behind him and drew the coat into his lap. When he got it on, he waited until he had stopped panting, then he gripped the arms of the chair and pulled himself up. His body felt like a great heavy bell whose clapper swung from side to side but made no noise. Once up, he remained standing a moment, swaying until he got his balance. A sensation of terror and defeat swept over him. He would never make it. He would never get there dead or alive. He pushed one foot forward and did not fall and his confidence returned. "The Lord is my shepherd," he muttered, "I shall not want." He began moving toward the sofa where he would have support. He reached it. He was on his way.

By the time he got to the door, she would be down the four flights of steps and out of the building. He got past the sofa and crept along by the wall, keeping his hand on it for support. Nobody was going to bury him here. He was as confident as if the woods of home lay at the bottom of the stairs. He reached the front door of the apartment and opened it and peered into the hall. This was the first time he had looked into it since the actor had knocked him down. It was dank-smelling and empty. The thin piece of linoleum stretched its moldy length to the door of the other apartment, which was closed. "Nigger actor," he said.

The head of the stairs was ten or twelve feet from where he stood and he bent his attention to getting there without creeping around the long way with a hand on the wall. He held his arms a little way out from his sides and pushed forward directly. He was half way there when all at once his legs disappeared, or felt as if they had. He looked down, bewildered, for they were still there. He fell forward and grasped the banister post with both hands. Hanging there, he gazed for what seemed the longest time he had ever looked at anything down the steep unlighted steps; then he closed his eyes and pitched forward. He landed upsidedown in the middle of the flight.

He felt presently the tilt of the box as they took it off the train and got it on the baggage wagon. He made no noise yet. The train jarred and slid away. In a moment the baggage wagon was rumbling under him, carrying him back to the station side. He heard footsteps rattling closer and closer to him and he supposed that a crowd was gathering. Wait until they see this, he thought.

"That him," Coleman said, "one of his tricks."

"It's a damn rat in there," Hooten said.

"It's him. Git the crowbar."

In a moment a shaft of greenish light fell on him. He pushed through it and cried in a weak voice, "Judgement Day! Judgement Day! You idiots didn't know it was Judgement Day, did you?

"Coleman?" he murmured.

The Negro bending over him had a large surly mouth and sullen eyes.

"Ain't any coal man, either," he said. This must be the wrong station, Tanner thought. Those fools put me off too soon. Who is this nigger? It ain't even daylight here.

At the Negro's side was another face, a woman's—pale, topped with a pile of copper-glinting hair and twisted as if she had just stepped in a pile of dung.

"Oh," Tanner said, "it's you."

The actor leaned closer and grasped him by the front of his shirt. "Judgement day," he said in a mocking voice. "Ain't no judgement day, old man. Cept this. Maybe this here judgement day for you."

Tanner tried to catch hold of a banister-spoke to raise himself but his hand grasped air. The two faces, the black one and the pale one, appeared to be wavering. By an effort of will be kept them focussed before him while he lifted his hand, as light as a breath, and said in his jauntiest voice, "Hep me up, Preacher. I'm on my way home!"

His daughter found him when she came in from the grocery store. His hat had been pulled down over his face and his head and arms thrust between the spokes of the banister; his feet dangled over the stairwell like those of a man in the stocks. She tugged at him frantically and then flew for the police. They cut him out with a saw and said he had been dead about an hour.

She buried him in New York City, but after she had done it she could not sleep at night. Night after night she turned and tossed and very definite lines began to appear in her face, so she had him dug up and shipped the body to Corinth. Now she rests well at night and her good looks have mostly returned.

SELECTED BIBLIOGRAPHY

Works by FLANNERY O'CONNOR

Wise Blood 1952   Novel
A Good Man Is Hard to Find 1955   Stories
The Violent Bear It Away 1960   Novel
Everything That Rises Must Converge 1965   Stories
Mystery and Manners: Occasional Prose 1969
The Complete Stories   1971
The Habit of Being Letters of Flannery O'Connor   1979

Selected Biography and Criticism

Asals, Frederick. *Flannery O'Connor: The Imagination of Extremity*. Athens, Ga.: University of Georgia Press, 1982.

Dowell, R. "The Moment of Grace in the Fiction of Flannery O'Connor." *College English*, VII (December 1965), 235–39.

Eggenschwiler, David. *The Christian Humanism of Flannery O'Connor*. Lexington: University of Kentucky Press, 1971.

Esprit, VIII (Winter 1964). Flannery O'Connor memorial issue.

Feeley, Sister Kathleen. *Flannery O'Connor: The Voice of the Peacock*. New Brunswick: Rutgers University Press, 1972.

Friedman, Melvin J., and Lewis A. Larson, eds. *The Added Dimension: The Art and Mind of Flannery O'Connor*. New York: Fordham University Press, 1966; rev. and exp. 1977.

Hawkes, John. "Flannery O'Connor's Devil." *Sewanee Review*, LXX (Summer 1962), 395–407.

Martin, Carter W. *The True Country: Themes in the Fiction of Flannery O'Connor*. Nashville: Vanderbilt University Press, 1968.

McFarland, Dorothy Tuck. *Flannery O'Connor*. Modern Literature Monographs. New York: Frederick Ungar, 1976.

Orvell, Miles. *Invisible Parade: The Fiction of Flannery O'Connor*. Philadelphia: Temple University Press, 1972.

Tate, J.O. and Heinz-Karl Westarp. *Flannery O'Connor Bulletin*, 1980–1982, Georgia College, Milledgeville, Georgia 31061.

Walters, Dorothy. *Flannery O'Connor*. TUSAS No. 216. New York: Twayne, 1973.

American SIGNET CLASSICS

(0451)

☐ **THE CELESTIAL RAILROAD And Other Stories by Nathaniel Hawthorne.**
Afterword by R. P. Blackmur. (517849—$2.95)

☐ **THE MARBLE FAUN by Nathaniel Hawthorne.** Afterword by Murray Krieger.
(517717—$2.95)

☐ **THE SCARLET LETTER by Nathaniel Hawthorne.** Foreword by Leo Marx
(516524—$1.50)

☐ **THE BLITHEDALE ROMANCE by Nathaniel Hawthorne.** Introduction by
Alfred Kazin. (514882—$1.95)

☐ **THE HOUSE OF THE SEVEN GABLES by Nathaniel Hawthorne.** Afterword
by Edward C. Sampson. (512626—$1.50)

☐ **THE FALL OF THE HOUSE OF USHER AND OTHER TALES by Edgar Allan
Poe.** Afterword by R. P. Blackmur. (516591—$2.75)

☐ **CALL OF THE WILD AND SELECTED STORIES by Jack London.** Foreword
by Franklin Walker. (513835—$1.75)

☐ **THE SEA WOLF AND SELECTED STORIES by Jack London.** Afterword
by Franklin Walker. (515528—$1.50)

☐ **MOBY DICK by Herman Melville.** Afterword by Denham Sutcliffe.
(515382—$1.95)

☐ **BILLY BUDD AND OTHER TALES by Herman Melville.** Afterword by
Willard Thorp. (517148—$1.95)

☐ **THE CONFIDENCE MAN by Herman Melville.** Afterword by R. W. B. Lewis
(516982—$3.50)

☐ **PIERRE or THE AMBIGUITIES by Herman Melville.** Afterword by Lawrence
Thompson. (518969—$4.95)

☐ **TYPEE by Herman Melville.** Afterword by Harrison Hayford.
(518543—$3.50)

☐ **WHITE JACKET by Herman Melville.** Introduction by Alfred Kazin.
(517326—$3.95)

☐ **MUTINY ON THE BOUNTY by Herman Melville.** (518799—$2.95)

*Prices slightly higher in Canada